THE SECRET LIFE OF CAROLYN RUSSELL

GAIL ALDWIN

All best wishes,
Gail Aldwin

BLOODHOUND
— BOOKS —

Print ISBN: 978-1-5040-8671-4

For Angela
and those heady teenage years

RIDDLE OF THE MISSING TEENAGER

BY STEPHANIE BRETT

West Country Post, 27 June 1979

The search for 16-year-old Carolyn Russell continues one week after she left school following a CSE examination. A conscientious pupil keen to gain good qualifications, Carolyn was last seen swinging her school bag as she walked along Greensleeves Road in the county town of Belmont. Suspicion she has run away from home has been ruled out and her disappearance has no links to other cases of missing children. Additional police have been drafted into the area although they face a dead end to their investigation. No new leads have been found in spite of an alert for a yellow Ford Cortina seen near the school at the time of Carolyn's disappearance. Mrs Russell hopes her daughter will be found alive and well but she is distraught by speculation to the contrary.

1

2014

I t was well past five o'clock when Stephanie prepared to leave the office. Glancing through the window, a great belly of cloud suggested a downpour was likely. She opened her desk drawer expecting to see her foldable umbrella tucked beside the desk tidy which always contained a ready-sharpened HB pencil. Not in its correct place, Stephanie wondered where the hell it was. From the corner of her eye, she saw Doug approaching. He probably wanted to share one of his larger-than-life stories and she really wasn't in the mood.

'Can I have a word?' he asked.

'I was about to go home.'

'It's important.' Doug frowned. 'Let's go to my office.'

Shit. 'Right this minute?'

Doug didn't answer, just turned and Stephanie was obliged to follow.

They walked between rows of abandoned hot desks. Conscientious colleagues cleared their workspaces while others left the detritus of a birthday celebration: screwed-up napkins, cake crumbs and a shrivelled pink balloon. Stephanie remembered the days of greasy fingerprints on a shared keyboard. Honestly, there should be some rules about office hygiene. That was before the restructure at the *West Country Post*. Now, she had a permanent base in a quiet corner and the title of Features Editor.

Doug took his place behind the desk and Stephanie sat opposite.

'What's all this about?' she asked.

Doug tapped the Manila folder in front of him. 'I expect you know what's coming.'

'Expect what?' Stephanie undid a button on her cardigan as heat surged. Of all the times to have a hot flush.

'You must have heard the rumours.'

'Rumours?' Her fingernail snagged on the buttonhole stitching. Oh for an emery board (also stored in her desk tidy). She was tempted to bite the jagged edge of nail to prevent it catching on anything else but she stopped herself.

'Are you all right, Stephanie?'

'Absolutely.' She crossed one ten-denier, pale-crystal leg over the other.

'This business needs knocking into shape and economies have to be made,' said Doug.

'Don't worry. I'm not going to stockpile the office stationery to take home.'

Doug didn't crack a smile. 'Jokes aside.'

Bloody hell. She flapped her collar in an attempt to cool down. The Meno-Ease sage tablets she'd been taking for the last month were having little or no effect.

'There are to be redundancies.'

'I see.' She glanced at Doug and his look of consternation made her realise she should say more. 'If it's the only way forward.'

'I'm glad you feel like that. I've been dreading this moment.'

'My shoulders are broad, Doug. You know I can take on extra responsibilities.'

'You don't understand.' Doug's expression was strangely contorted. This made Stephanie focus. His cheeks were rosy and probably complemented her own shade of too much heat.

'What's wrong?' she asked.

'I'm afraid it's your job that's being cut. I'm very sorry.'

As the news sank in, Stephanie sagged. Doug droned on about payments and notice periods and new beginnings, but nothing registered.

'I thought we were…' She was going to say *friends*. Christ, how had it come to this? She'd been at the *Post* for so long. 'What about the big project?'

'Change of plan.' Doug sighed. 'You know how it is.'

Returning to her desk, Stephanie saw the umbrella hanging by its cord from the coat stand. There it was! She gripped it, thinking somehow the folded spokes could steady her. Loyalty to the *Post* meant nothing. She flung the umbrella at her chair and when metal hit metal there was a loud dong. Fortunately, no one saw her little act of rebellion, or the tears streaming down her face.

Back at home, Stephanie scanned the kitchen counters and was satisfied with the gleaming surfaces but the tumbler she'd left upright on the draining board spoiled the effect. She rinsed the glass and returned it to the shelf. All was better. Well really, nothing was better. Before she knew it, the weight of rejection blurred her vision. She sat, letting her head rest on the table and she ran her fingers along the joint where the extension turned it into a six-seater. It had been a nonsense buy. Why on earth did she need a large dining table when hardly anyone visited? The jolt of reality made her sob.

Early evening and already in her pyjamas, Stephanie skipped dinner and instead drank chilled Pinot. The alcohol was reassuringly anaesthetic. As she checked the level in the bottle, it was a shock to see half already gone. She screwed the lid into place and enjoyed the tinny sound that broke the silence.

Planning what she would wear the next morning, Stephanie decided on her mandarin jacket with the silky trim that matched her henna-rinsed hair. A careful choice was necessary. She needed every bit of help to get through the days and weeks until her notice period ended. She sighed at the thought and memories drifted. Decades earlier she'd nearly lost her job as a trainee for inaccurate reporting on the disappearance of Carolyn Russell. Although she'd avoided a disciplinary by having her work scrutinised, the humiliation had been hard to bear. Eventually, she earned the respect of colleagues and was able to establish her career. Yet the whole fiasco of Carolyn's disappearance and Stephanie's fumbled attempts to tell the story still weighed on her conscience.

The next two weeks dragged but by taking leave and time in lieu, Stephanie finished at the *Post* before the end of March. Her speedy departure also meant she could slip away without the embarrassment of a leaving do. Sitting at the kitchen table, she skimmed the jobs page of *The Guardian* on her mobile. She dreaded the prospect of compiling a CV. She didn't have enough employment history to fill an A4 page. Okay, she'd swapped sides for eight years when she'd worked for a communications team in the city and then returned to the *Post*. Life in the big smoke had never suited and although the change had set her career back, it was the right decision. Stephanie squashed the memories and inadvertently jerked her arm. This sent her new phone skidding off the table and across the floor. Collecting it, she was relieved the screen hadn't cracked. She'd invested some of her redundancy money in the purchase and it was hard not to obsess about her shrinking bank balance with the mortgage to pay.

Draining the coffee in her mug, Stephanie decided to tackle the contents of the spare bedroom of her terraced home. She referred to the space as her study, but in times of financial need it was an unnecessary luxury. Of course, if she was offered some freelance work that would be different. Only drumming up a few pitches was bound to end in rejection and she simply wasn't ready, not for that. A tear seeped from her eye. Taking the tissue tucked into her sleeve, Stephanie wiped away the evidence of her emotional state. Never in her life had she been so pathetic. One way of coping was to get on with stuff except the thought of letting her spare room made her grimace. Sharing with a stranger wasn't going to be easy. Even her ex's weekend stays had sometimes been a challenge.

Kneeling on the sable bedroom carpet, she noticed it had frayed due to the wheels on her swivel chair. Trying to forget the damage, she became convinced a strategically placed bed would cover the bald patches. From the lower shelf of the bookcase, she removed a box file that contained cuttings from her early days as a trainee journalist. She'd been so proud of her byline but reading about carnivals and new appointments to the local council made her heart sink. It wasn't hard disposing of the pages. As she took a second file from the shelf, she noticed a shoebox wedged between her desk and the wall. Its label showed a picture of the bargain-priced, too-small denim ankle boots she'd bought in a sale. How many years ago was it? She'd dashed into town during the sixth-form college lunch break and had bought them because Janine egged her on. Not long after, Stephanie's circle of friends disintegrated when Janine and the others went to university. They regrouped each year during the summer holidays but in 1979 everything changed because of Carolyn.

Stephanie pressed her back against the wall and stretched her legs, trying to dislodge a feeling of heaviness she experienced whenever she remembered events from that year. It was no good, she needed to get on. Taking a breath, she eased the lid off the box and peered inside. It was a relief to find bundles of postcards held together by rubber bands. It was her mother's collection and something she couldn't part with, yet she couldn't sort through either. She didn't want to arouse the sense of loneliness only an adult orphan would recognise. Christ. Stephanie returned to the box files and continued looking through the pieces she'd written for the *Post*. She wanted to get rid of anything which connected her to the rag. If she came across clippings about Carolyn Russell, perhaps she should hang on to them. The unsolved case was forever at the back of her mind.

Ah, there was one! Stephanie examined the column with its small photo of Carolyn. It must have been a school shot judging from her shirt and tie. There was something enigmatic about Carolyn's smile but Stephanie couldn't put her finger on it. She read the words she'd laboured over following Carolyn's disappearance. Stephanie cringed. Why on earth had she used the term 'dead end' in relation to the investigation? Was it a prophecy of what actually happened, that Carolyn was dead? Everybody at the *Post* had their own theory and she'd stuck to hers. Carolyn had been abducted – she was sure of it. The clipping described details of the hunt for a yellow Ford Cortina parked near the school on the day Carolyn disappeared. Stephanie pressed the report into a folder. There may come a day when she might need it.

2

2014

Stephanie's shopping list:

Bananas, washing up liquid, rubber gloves, bin liners. New job.

Friday came and Stephanie was ready for her monthly meet-up with Doug. He'd sent a text checking she was going for their 'drinks after work'. Although she wanted to take issue about his insensitivity, she realised it was just Doug being Doug. Arriving a little late, she pushed through the crowd at the bar and found Doug in the usual place. The small round table appeared child-sized beside Doug's long legs. She pulled out the stool covered in blood-red velour. His pint was already half finished but there was a gin and tonic lined up for her.

'Cheers.' Doug raised his glass.

Stephanie upended the mixer into the tumbler. It was her

habit to sip alcoholic beverages, but this time she gulped a mouthful. Realising Doug was still sitting there with his glass raised, she lifted hers to chink. 'Sorry. Too forgetful.'

'Or desperate for a drink?'

'You could say that. I've been having a sort out.'

'Dangerous activity. You never know what you might unearth.'

'Very true,' said Stephanie.

'Go on... what did you find?'

Doug gave a sly smile and tilted his head. His hair had gone through the salt-and-pepper stage and he could now be thought of as a silver fox. Only Stephanie wouldn't utter those words and inflate his ego. He'd been a catch back in the day before he'd married and he continued to welcome flattery. On no account would he get that from Stephanie. So why the tilting head? One of his mannerisms.

'As if I'd tell you.'

Doug must've thought he was doing Stephanie a favour by avoiding mention of the *Post*. Of course, she was bursting to know what was happening, yet couldn't bring herself to ask. Instead, Doug droned on about home decorating. Eventually, she could stand it no longer.

'What's the gossip?'

'Nothing much to tell from the office, but Miss Treacle Tart's going to take on a new assistant.'

'Don't call her that.'

'Why not? You rate her baking as much as the rest of us. Praise the day she started her business in Belmont.'

Angel Cakes had become the regular lunch venue for anyone with spare cash at the *Post*. Formerly a tobacconist shop, Beth was the talented baker who put the café at the top of TripAdvisor reviews. Stephanie adored the fig-and-apricot flapjacks for their lovely aniseed crunch. This hadn't stopped her from trying other delights including the chocolate truffle balls laced with chilli. Beth was about as exotic as her range of cakes. As the manager of a successful shop, Beth had to be of a certain age even if her smooth golden-brown skin belied the years. She was a new businesswoman in town and an asset to the community. Her enthusiasm for tempting treats was also a joy.

'Angel Cakes is one of the reasons I've decided Belmont isn't such a bad place to live,' said Stephanie.

'It's taken an entire lifetime to reach that conclusion?'

'There's no job tying me down, I need to be sure I actually want to stay. I like my house, but there's not much chance of alternative employment.'

'You could take a diversion. How about podcasting? You've got a voice that's easy on the ear and you're good at winkling out stories. There's huge potential in–'

Stephanie showed Doug her palm to halt the talk. Clearly, she had the investigative skills to develop a podcast, only she didn't want Doug taking credit for a new direction in her career. Besides, she couldn't stand hearing him bang on about the future of streaming and his contacts already in the field. Stuck in the rhythms and routines of the newspaper, she didn't want a change. This meant her career options were limited to say the least. 'I've a contingency plan to stay financially afloat.'

'Doing what?'

'I'm going to rent out my spare bedroom.'

'Funny you should say that. Miss Treacle...' Stephanie was about to scold when Doug corrected himself, 'I mean Beth.'

'Yes?'

'She's looking for a place as she's sold her flat to invest in the business. You can't get a better housemate than someone who bakes.'

Absolutely, thought Stephanie. 'I'll give her a ring.'

GAIL ALDWIN

Weather over the weekend was atrocious and Stephanie, huddled in a throw on the sofa, relocated the laptop from the floor and balanced it on her knees. A little distraction on social media was needed. Of course, she preferred Friends Reunited in its peak, but once it started slipping, she deserted the site in favour of Facebook. Scrolling the pages, she quickly became fed up with reading about mother-of-the-bride responsibilities and who was soon to be a granny for the first time. As for Stephanie's Facebook profile, she'd have to update her details and remove the *West Country Post* as her workplace. One tap on the delete option and it was done. She wished there was something new to add. This was her life now – a career in shreds. She needed to get a grip. Facebook was the last place she should be spending time when feeling like this: inadequate. She continued to scroll in spite of her better judgement and as the photos flashed in front of her, Stephanie considered the merits of getting in touch with some of the old gang. They couldn't have all morphed into happy families. Take Janine, for example, how had life gone for her? Not very smoothly, Stephanie suspected. A tide of regret washed over her. By emphasising the connection she'd had with Janine, the older sister of the missing Carolyn, Stephanie had persuaded colleagues at the *Post* to let her try reporting on Carolyn's case. A sliver of guilt caused Stephanie to tense up. It wasn't entirely her fault things had gone off-kilter. She'd been far too inexperienced. The whole episode had happened years ago and maybe now was the time to get in touch with Janine and make up for the past. If she was using her old name, Janine would be easy to track down on Facebook. A nagging curiosity spurred her to action. After a few minutes, Janine's face beamed from a profile picture and there remained a sense of the young Janine in the contours of her middle-aged look. From what Stephanie could gather, they were in the same boat. Single. Janine had a job at least, employed by a boarding school next to a large country house. She'd stayed reasonably local, too. The urge to get in touch was almost overpowering but it palled due to the legacy of Carolyn's disappearance.

3

APRIL 1979

The tring-tring of the telephone echoed through the house and into my bedroom. Racing down the stairs two at a time, I crash-landed in the hall.

'There's no need to hurtle about the place, Carolyn.'

Ignoring Mum, I grabbed my chance and sat at the telephone table regularly reserved for her derrière. With the receiver pressed to my ear, I listened to the pips. It had to be my sister. Janine's usual fumbling with coins meant it couldn't be anyone else. I caught my breath then chanted our number – hopefully putting Mum off the scent. It might give me a few minutes of chat before she realised her firstborn was on the line. I wanted to cling on as long as possible before Mum played her *I'm-in-charge* card and hoicked the receiver away. It really wasn't fair when Mum hogged the phone.

'Hiya, Carolyn.' Janine's voice was chirpy.

'It's you!' I acted surprised.

'How are things?' she asked.

'Much the same. Loads of revision.' I had to lie as Mum looked on, her ears flapping. In a whisper, I shared the real news. 'I've got my eye on a silky green top in Chelsea Girl.'

'Let's plan on a day in town soon.'

Janine had been dripping money ever since she got her student grant.

'Perhaps the Easter bunny will bring me a pound or two.' There wasn't any harm in hinting. Janine agreed my pocket money was miserly. I turned to see Mum's eyebrows springing halfway up her forehead. Her disapproval was obvious.

'I've been eating baked beans every day so we can have a bit of a spend,' said Janine.

'Super-duper.' Oh no, why use such a daft expression?

'Don't get too excited. I've got to pay for my coach fare home yet. And there's another thing – I'll be back next Thursday not at the weekend as planned. Sorry.'

I held my breath, not knowing what to say. The silence between us bit.

Janine sighed. 'It's a shame but it can't be helped. Research at the Bodleian comes first.'

I literally couldn't believe it. 'I want to see you.'

'I know…'

I let the receiver drop into my lap and Janine's voice became a squeak. The next minute, Mum was beside me, her eyes full of concern. The question was, concern for who, me or Janine? It took less than a second to find out. Taking the phone, Mum waved her arm and made me move out of the way. I slunk off without another word. In the kitchen, disappointment had me drooping. Perhaps a strong cup of tea would give me a boost. My fingers shook as I removed the lid and my wrist ached as I filled the kettle. Why was I such a weakling? The pilot light on the cooker never worked for me. Anyone else pressed it and two clicks later the hissing gas burst into a yellowy blue flame. I searched for matches and shook the box. The rattle reminded me of Dad and how he liked to set the fire. I was only little back then but I could almost feel the warmth he brought. We were an ordinary family once. According to Mum, it was best not to dwell.

A ching sounded as Mum returned the receiver to the cradle and then the trundle of the dial turning followed. Janine must have run out of coins and Mum was calling her back. Why wasn't she bothered about Janine not coming home? I thought there'd be at least a raised voice if not a full-scale row. Holding a mug in each hand, I offered Mum the one plastered in college badges. It was her favourite, bought at a gift shop in Oxford the last time we visited. The trip hadn't been a huge success. Mum objected to the continental quilt at the B&B but couldn't bring herself to tell the landlady. The woman was far too common.

'Thank you.' Mum took the mug, then balanced it on her knee. She sat there nodding as the bubble of Janine's voice came down the line. Those two were in the thick of it as usual. I turned around and left them alone, not wanting to show I actually cared.

Back in my room, I pushed the piles of books to the side of my desk. The little chair creaked and I thought it might collapse but Mum said she couldn't afford a new one. It was typical. Janine got everything she wanted and I was left without. Leaning on my elbows, I let the disappointment swirl. My sister was the favourite but that didn't stop me from wanting to see her. I glanced at my maths text book. It was doing the splits, the pages hunched, the hard cover coming away at the spine. The largest and heaviest book to be lugged from school to home and back again, I resented its weight and pages full of questions and sums that baffled. Why couldn't my brain cope with numbers?

The thought of maths filled me with loathing for Mr Forsyth. Him and his grey coil of hair dangling. I couldn't hate him any more if I tried. Mum told me about the way he went on at parents' evening, saying I was *feigning difficulties* and that I could succeed *if only I put my mind to it*. He said I was from *intelligent stock* which Mum took as a compliment even though it made me sound like a horse. I formed a fist and slammed it into my other open palm and enjoyed the thwack. What would it be like to bash his face? I imagined his pudgy cheeks flattened under my punch. Bop! Shaking out my hands, I waggled my fingers then stretched them into stars. Could wishing on a star make things real? Not with my luck. I was never going to do well in the maths exam and everyone knew it.

4

2014

The search for Carolyn Russell continues by Stephanie Brett
West Country Post, 10 July 1979

16-year-old Carolyn's disappearance has perplexed members of the close-knit community in Belmont. The teenager was last seen leaving Greensleeves Comprehensive on Friday 20 June. School staff and pupils have been questioned. Hopes were raised following a sighting at Waterloo Station and police are following this development. Her widowed mother thinks it unlikely Carolyn would have gone off with a stranger, but abduction has not been ruled out.

After Janine had accepted Stephanie's friend request, there was no point in hesitating. Stephanie composed and sent a message. From the speed of Janine's reply, it indicated she was keen to catch up. They both remained non-committal but as the questions and replies came, it felt like they were on track to reforming an acquaintance, if not a friendship. There were areas of shared experience: both living in the West Country, both single (even though Janine was recently divorced) and both, well, interested in each other. Following further exchanges, Stephanie built up enough rapport to suggest meeting for a coffee. They settled on Saturday afternoon because Janine worked full time at a boys' school over the other side of the county and she taught classes in the morning.

Leaving the house, Stephanie noticed her next-door neighbour cleaning her windowsills. Dressed in her trusty pinny and wearing a dab of fuchsia lipstick, Mrs Walker was from a generation who took much pride in the presentation of her home.

'You're busy,' said Stephanie.

'It's a pity the window cleaner doesn't bother with anything beyond the panes of glass,' she said. 'Back in my day when they went up a ladder, you could be sure they'd give the paintwork a going over too.'

'Whoops, I didn't notice he'd been. I'll have to check through the junk mail for his slip.'

'Don't keep him waiting long, dear. You know these local businesses need prompt payment.'

Stephanie smiled at the ticking-off. 'Will do.'

With Mrs Walker being chatty, Stephanie decided it would be a good time to break her news properly. She took a breath. 'I'm planning to let out my spare room.'

'Whatever for?'

'I've been made redundant from the *Post* and I need a bit of help paying the mortgage.'

Mrs Walker took a step closer and rubbed Stephanie's arm. 'Oh, you poor thing. You've been at the *Post* for ages. I can't believe they'd let you go.'

'It's not so bad.' Stephanie realised any more of Mrs Walker's sympathy would leave her a blubbing mess. She repositioned her handbag by strapping it across her shoulder. 'New chapter and all.'

'Just remember, Stephanie, it's their loss not yours.'

'Quite.' Now the information was out, Stephanie wanted a hasty getaway. 'I'm off for the afternoon.'

'Well, you enjoy yourself,' said Mrs Walker.

Stephanie allowed plenty of time to arrive at the meeting with Janine. Trains ran twice an hour and she knew Warren town centre was a fair walk from the station. With twenty minutes to spare, Stephanie took a detour around the streets. When she reached the church, she sat on a bench and appraised the squat grey building. The origins were Norman, but the addition of a porch and a tower made it appear quirky. The little tea shop was the same – leaded windows yet a strangely modern oak front door.

At the entrance, Stephanie was directed to a table in the bay. As she sat, the grandfather clock in the corner chimed. According to Stephanie's watch it was five minutes fast. Janine could still arrive at the designated time of half past two although she was never known for her punctuality in sixth-form college. She and Janine had been in the same year at school and had studied science together, but they didn't become close until A-levels. Noticing a flutter of nerves in her stomach, Stephanie scolded herself for being ridiculous again. By watching people on the street, Stephanie remained calm. There were pensioners pulling shopping trolleys and parents chivvying young children along. When there was still no sign of Janine, she studied the menu.

Reference to cake was limited to a line which advised viewing the freshly baked items on display. Stephanie's gaze drifted to the glass domes on the counter. She could spot a Victoria sponge from a distance of twenty feet – the dusting of icing sugar and the jam and buttercream stripes around the girth were a giveaway. From the frosted icing on another, Stephanie guessed it was a carrot cake. Further scrutiny was abandoned as the bell above the door tinkled. Stephanie shoved the menu back into the holder and returned it to the centre of the embroidered cloth.

Casually, she swung her head to glance at the woman standing on the doormat. She recognised Janine on meeting her brown eyes. As a teenager, she thought those eyes were more suited to a cow, yet as an adult she admired the singularity of her appearance. Beckoning Janine over, Stephanie tuned into her footsteps as she approached. She wondered if a hug was appropriate and decided a handshake was too formal. Instead, she gave a broad smile and Janine grinned back.

'I'd recognise you anywhere,' said Stephanie.

'You too,' said Janine.

They studied each other a little longer. It was funny how old friends remained the same in spite of the changes age brought. Gone were the curls Janine had worn in bunches. Back in the day, Stephanie had joked the hairstyle was designed to cover a pair of big ears. Now there was no trace remaining of her chestnut locks. Instead, Janine wore an impish crop with a claret rinse and a blue leather biker's jacket completed the look. Casually slinging her jacket over the back of the chair, Janine sat. Stephanie was positively envious of her style and wished she'd worn something more impressive than cords and a polo jumper.

'I haven't been here before. Have you?' asked Janine.

'It was ages ago. Now they've smartened the place up.'

'It's years since we've seen each other,' said Janine.

'Too long.'

They exchanged smiles. Stephanie held out a menu but Janine shook her head. 'An Earl Grey will do for me.'

'Make that two,' Stephanie told the waitress who had appeared. Her mind had been set on a slice of sponge except she couldn't wolf down a whole plateful if Janine was abstaining. She tried not to show her disappointment.

'Don't let me stop you,' said Janine. 'I've had a cooked lunch. School dinners are considered a perk of the job.'

'Best not,' said Stephanie. Yet all the time she was thinking about the purchase of a takeaway cake that could be eaten at the picnic table she'd spotted by the church.

When the tea arrived, Stephanie was disconcerted by the waitress banging a postbox-red pot and milk jug on the table. These were accompanied by spotted cups and striped saucers. Before the sugar bowl landed (it was lurid) Stephanie shook her head. Thankfully, Janine didn't take sugar either and the waitress replaced it on her tray. Although unsettled by the clashing crockery, Stephanie poured the tea.

'Don't you just love the shabby chic look?' asked Janine.

Trying to make the best of the situation, Stephanie gave an upbeat reply. 'It's a new lease of life for cups and saucers that haven't been chipped or smashed over the years.'

'I'm still cack-handed when it comes to anything dainty. Do you remember all the test tubes I destroyed?'

The incident which left Janine surrounded by shattered glass was written up in the history of Greensleeves School. Stephanie had been one of the girls who formed a circle around Janine to giggle and gasp. 'Minor explosion, wasn't it?'

'A most *unfortunate incident*, the teacher called it,' said Janine.

'Oh yes. We were made to stand outside the science block until the fire brigade gave the all clear while you were cosied up to the headteacher. I've never been so cold in my life. An old lab coat is nowhere near warm enough during a winter freeze.'

'Cosied up, I think not. It was an interrogation.'

Janine rolled her eyes and Stephanie could hold the laughter no longer. They chuckled as if they were still schoolgirls, their shoulders going up and down like ventriloquists' dummies. Once they'd become composed, silence returned. Janine fiddled with her teaspoon, letting the chinking disrupt the quiet. 'Why did you want to meet, Stephanie?'

'Stuff has happened and I've found myself thinking about the past.'

'What stuff?'

Christ, Stephanie wasn't ready to admit the truth but she couldn't think of anything else to say. 'My glorious career as a journalist is finished.'

'Surely not.'

'Redundancy couldn't have come at a worse time.'

'That explains why I haven't seen your byline lately. I'm sorry to hear it. Get to our age and we become dispensable. It's happening to me as well. I'm being manoeuvred out of my job by the senior leadership team. They've asked me to teach media studies due to the low uptake in Spanish. It's ridiculous. The responsibility should fall within the English department, not modern foreign languages. I'm expected to get up to speed with everything including bloody podcasts. I've never even listened to one.'

'Strange you should say that, my old boss suggested I make a podcast.'

'Rather you than me... although I understand they're catching on.'

'I listen to a series in the middle of the night and it helps send me back to sleep,' said Stephanie.

'Not exactly a recommendation. But I get your drift about disturbed nights. The bloody menopause, eh?'

Their eyes met for a moment of shared understanding.

'Perhaps you *should* make one,' said Janine. 'How about investigating Carolyn's disappearance? You couldn't do worse than the police.'

Maybe Doug's idea wasn't completely off the wall. It might even do some good. She'd earned her stripes making recordings when she'd worked at the communications firm. 'There's a thought. A podcast could revisit Carolyn's disappearance from a community angle – show how the story impacted at the time she went missing – and how the legacy of loss continues. Who knows what fresh leads I might dig out. And it could make up for my over-zealous reporting back in the day.' This was as close as

Stephanie could get to admitting she'd actually complicated things.

'Woah,' said Janine. 'Don't get too eager. You'd have to convince my mother about the idea first.'

Surprised at her enthusiasm for the project, Stephanie took a chance and ploughed on. 'If I got the balance right from recorded interviews, it would give a real sense of Carolyn. How it's been for your family and what is revealed by sieving through the rumour and gossip.'

Stephanie waited for a response while Janine took a sip of tea. 'Get anywhere, and you'll have to pass on a few tips to my students.'

'You wouldn't mind me developing the idea? I need something to get my teeth into.'

'You are talking about my sister.'

'Sorry, I didn't mean to offend.'

'You're better placed than most to take up the story.'

'Exactly, it's about understanding the context of Carolyn going missing from a West Country town. It seems we all share a sense of responsibility for her disappearance. Or at least, that's the way I feel. Obviously, I didn't know Carolyn well, but I met her at your house and I saw her around school.'

'Yes.'

Stephanie judged it wasn't right to admit the suspicion that had got her into so much trouble. Instead, she stuck to familiar territory, the old chestnut about the girl and the tutor. 'What did you think when Graham Simmons became a suspect?'

'Carolyn mentioned Sim once or twice. For all I knew she was going on about Simon and Garfunkel. Most of the time she talked a lot of nonsense. It was a shock to realise he was the one giving Carolyn help with maths. I'd been living away from home and I'd switched off from Belmont. I was wrapped up in Oxford life and Spanish studies – I didn't want to think about anything else. Coming from a West Country comprehensive was my dirty little secret in college.'

'I can imagine.'

'When I first heard Carolyn had gone off, that was how Mum put it, I thought *good for her*. Maybe she'd grown up a bit and was becoming independent. Each time I went home, Carolyn was clingy and I resented it. To make matters worse, she and Mum didn't get along too well. After I'd left, the spotlight turned onto Carolyn and she found it hard being the sole focus of Mum's attention. Later, it became clear Carolyn wasn't going to rush back and I started to realise how far I'd grown away from her, abandoned her even.'

'You can't blame yourself.'

'Can't I?' Janine twiddled the lacy hem of the tablecloth.

'You had a lot going on. It was the rest of us in Belmont who should've been more aware. I remember Carolyn's disappearance being announced in the office and how some people raised knowing eyebrows. Then, rumours about Graham Simmons spread.'

'Do you really think he was involved?' asked Janine.

'If suspicion had fallen on teachers in the PE department, I would've understood. Southy and Gove were cleared early on, but you can never forget them.'

'Those two. Southy in his tight yellow shorts,' said Janine.

'And Gove flashing a hairy chest through his string-vest top.'

'We shouldn't joke about it,' said Janine. 'One thing's for sure, they'd never get away with it these days.'

'There are a lot of unanswered questions and Carolyn's disappearance is begging to be looked at again. So many possibilities that haven't been properly investigated.'

'I suppose you know about Carolyn's secret life. It wasn't until she'd gone that Mum discovered the lies.'

Stephanie's ears pricked up; what could she be referring to? Of course, now wasn't the time to admit a lack of knowledge. 'I do think a podcast is a good idea. It gives people the chance to open up in a different way to a police investigation. I could track down her old friends, talk to residents. It would be a new challenge.'

'You'll have a job finding Carolyn's friends. Her best mate was French and returned home with her family before the final year at school. After that, Carolyn was on her own a lot and the other pupils weren't proper friends.'

'She's been gone such a long time now,' said Stephanie.

'Thirty-five years. It's hard to believe.' Janine sighed, pushed her chair back, and scanned the room.

'The ladies' loo is in the corner,' said Stephanie.

As Janine walked away, Stephanie rehearsed silent lines in her head. She absolutely needed Janine on board if she was going to make any headway with this idea. The suggestion that Carolyn had a secret life was more than just interesting.

On returning to the table, Janine lifted her jacket from the back of the chair. Oh shit! Surely she wasn't leaving already. Stephanie played it cool. 'That's such a fabulous outfit.'

Janine wrinkled her nose as she slipped an arm into the sleeve. 'You mean *this*?'

'Yes.' The word came out louder than Stephanie expected and she laughed.

Janine smiled. 'If we can joke about stuff, it's a good sign.'

'What about the podcast? Give me the nod and I can get the whole thing moving.'

'I'll think about it. And as I said, you'd need to get Mum's agreement. All these years and you would've thought I'd be reconciled to losing Carolyn.' Janine dropped a few coins on the table in payment for the tea.

'There's no need,' said Stephanie, but her words were left hanging as Janine gave a smile and walked out of the shop.

5

APRIL 1979

It was Maundy Thursday and eight o'clock in the evening by the time Janine arrived. I might have renamed it Maddening Thursday for all the waiting. If she'd left it any longer, chances were Janine might've been stuck at Victoria coach station for the night. Anyone would think she didn't want to come back. Mum contained her excitement about the return of her best child by attaching herself to the carpet sweeper. Thank God she didn't get the vacuum out again – I'd had enough of her going into overdrive the previous weekend. Janine's homecoming was an excuse for a full-scale spring clean and I was ejected from my room while Mum made out with the extension nozzle to remove dust lurking on the picture rails. Now she was off again, sweeping the entire house. When she got to Janine's room, she began shoving furniture about and the blast from my transistor couldn't drown out the huffing and puffing that accompanied whatever Mum was doing in there. Finally, the sound of her footsteps along the landing meant the coast was clear, and I could check what she'd been up to.

The creak of Janine's door could've given me away, and I stayed frozen, my fingers wrapped around the handle as I waited for a telling-off from Mum. It never came. Phew! In the all-quiet, I tucked my head into Janine's room. What a transformation! Her collection of pottery owls were arranged in a neat group on the dressing table and a new bedspread complete with a tasteful quilted top was draped over the single mattress. Janine had complained the old candlewick cover was moulting, but I thought it was a joke. There was me, still stuck with a tufted turquoise number. I hated the colour. My bedspread was a legacy from Mum's heyday of liking all shades bright and beautiful. It didn't match anything in my room. Janine only came home once in a blue moon yet she got special treatment. I should have expected no less – favouritism ruled in our house.

A flurry of high-pitched greetings marked Janine's arrival. Following the bedspread revelation, I decided not to rush downstairs as I usually did. They could miss me if they wanted. Stretching my hearing, I clung to every word they said and my heart strained as I tried not to move. I knew Janine would come to find me, eventually. A tap on my door signalled her presence and I turned my head all surprised, hoping to feel my hair swing around my shoulders in a wind-blown Farrah Fawcett-Majors way. Janine approached to see what I was reading and I closed the cover of *Valley of the Dolls*. She must have recognised the well-thumbed copy I'd nicked from her bookshelf but she didn't say anything. Instead, she slung her arm around my shoulders and closed in for a cuddle. I caught a whiff of flowery scent before breaking free.

'Why are you hiding up here?' she asked.

I pushed my feet into the Snoopy slippers she'd given me. 'I didn't want to get in the way and ruin your special welcome. Mum's been counting the days. I might've combusted and she'd never have noticed.'

'Don't be daft,' said Janine. 'I couldn't get away earlier.'

I made one of my slippers growl at the other.

Janine laughed. 'You're mad as ever.'

'It was you that turned me into a Snoopy fan.' We'd hunted high and low for the slippers and the little knotted wire ring that were my sixteenth birthday gift. It had been fun going into town and we'd even had a hamburger for lunch. Whenever I got lonely, I liked to retrace our steps. The last time I went to the market I bought a matching Snoopy nightie. I loved the wonky Snoopy expression beneath the 'smile' sign. Taking it from the chest of drawers, I held the nightie against me. 'What do you think?'

'Love it.'

At least that got her attention. 'I spent the money you gave me on it.'

'Bargain.' Janine sat on my bed and looked around the room. 'Anything else?'

'Nah.' I flopped next to her and Janine toppled against me. I gave her a nudge and she elbowed me back. I flicked her thigh. She poked me in the ribs. The next minute, we were into a proper wrestling match. It was the sort of thing that had Mum tearing up the stairs and sending us into separate rooms when we were younger. Now we just did it for fun. A couple of swift moves and Janine had me pinned down.

'Say pretty please and I'll let you go.' She tightened her grip around my wrists.

I wasn't going to surrender that easily. Her hair was dangling into my mouth so I spat out the ends.

'Yuk!' she said.

I kneed Janine and escaped.

'I'll need to wash my hair and get rid of your germs.' Janine was smiling, she didn't really mean it.

'Best of luck. The only shampoo Mum buys is medicated.'

'Don't you have anything better?'

'A secret stash of Clairol sachets,' I boasted.

'Herbal Essence?'

'Of course!' My face was beaming because I realised what was coming. She took a *Charlie's Angels* pose, her fingers pointing at me like a revolver. 'Hand them over.'

It wasn't fun dragging myself out of bed on Good Friday for a nine o'clock breakfast but the promise of toasted hot-cross buns was reason to make an effort. I spread butter thickly and watched it melt into the currant-spotted halves. Folding a soggy piece, I lifted it to my mouth. As I bit, an avalanche of yellow sprayed onto my plate and droplets landed on the cloth.

'I might've guessed.' Mum sprang to her feet and dabbed the table linen using the corner of her apron. 'Trust you, Carolyn. You're such a clumsy clot.'

'I'll get a sponge.' Janine rushed into the kitchen and I heard the tap running in the hope of warm water.

'It's a tiny spot,' I said.

Janine arrived wielding a washing-up cloth that dripped its own pattern of bubbles.

'You should've given it a squeeze,' said Mum.

Back into the kitchen went Janine and by the time she returned, Mum had slid newspaper under the cloth to protect the wood and I needed a magnifying glass to see the speck. With my plate held under my chin, I ate the rest of the bun. By then, it was far from an Easter treat but at least Mum had calmed down.

'I inherited this tablecloth from Aunt Jean,' said Mum. 'I still have some pieces wrapped in tissue upstairs. I thought they might do for your bottom drawer, Janine.'

'Oh, please,' said Janine. 'Nobody has a *bottom drawer* these days. Marriage is the last thing on my mind.'

'Give it time.' Mum then turned her attention to me. 'What about you, Carolyn? Have you got your eye on anyone at school?'

Normally, she only wanted to know about lessons. For a

minute, I imagined telling Mum to mind her own beeswax, but I didn't have the nerve. 'Not likely.'

'You're much better off concentrating on exams,' said Mum. 'You need all the help you can get.'

'Don't rub it in. Everyone knows I'm a complete waste of space at maths.'

'I'm not surprised you find it difficult,' said Janine. 'Mathematics is the hardest subject.'

'Take a look at Carolyn's exercise book and you'll understand what Mr Forsyth's up against,' said Mum.

Whose side was she on? I covered my ears to show I wasn't listening but I heard.

'Can't you give her a hand, Janine? After all, you're the clever one.'

'What does that make me?' I blurted.

Mum smiled. 'The pretty one.'

Me and Janine shared a look. I didn't exactly know what she was thinking but then Mum started humming and neither of us could stand it. Janine rolled her light-brown eyes and the colour reminded me of toffee bonbons. In truth, sweets weighed into a paper bag weren't my thing any longer. My tastes were becoming sophisticated.

'In my day, we had to sit matriculation,' said Mum. 'I had to pass every single exam or get no certificate at all.'

I'd heard it before. Her great qualification gained her what exactly? A secretarial job at a driving school. 'Bully for you.'

If looks could kill, I would've been dead on the floor. 'That's enough, young lady.'

'I was thinking, Mum, perhaps you should get Carolyn some extra maths lessons to help.'

The last thing I wanted was MORE maths. Besides, I didn't want to be the laughing stock of the whole school. Poor little swot. 'No way!'

'It's something to bear in mind,' said Mum. 'You shouldn't dismiss suggestions out of hand, Carolyn.'

I nudged Janine and said under my breath, 'Don't give her ideas.'

'It's only a thought,' she whispered back.

Bank holidays were boring and I couldn't wait until Saturday for the promised shopping trip with Janine. Disappointment struck again when Janine confessed she didn't have enough money to buy me the silky green top from Chelsea Girl. I got into a bad mood because going into town wasn't worth it with no spending money. To cheer me up, Janine showed me how to apply smoky golden eye shadow from a sweet little compact. Mum wasn't impressed when she saw me dolled up. As it was Janine's idea, I knew there wouldn't be trouble.

The high point on Sunday was breaking into our Easter eggs. The polka dot mugs were topped by an egg (mine wrapped in purple foil, Janine's in orange) and covered in cellophane. Janine had it in mind to take the whole thing back to Oxford, but after I'd scoffed my chocolate, I stared at hers. One knock turned the chocolate into shards and we finished the lot between us.

We did go into town on Tuesday to wave Janine off. I couldn't believe she was leaving. There'd hardly been time to do anything. And I wasn't in a hurry to forgive her for spending hours and hours with her old schoolmates. I thought she was coming back to see me. I'd told her how badly Mum got on my nerves the last time she was home and things hadn't changed. Janine seemed to understand, then she stuck up for Mum saying it wasn't easy for her either. Her words came as another sign that she and Mum were together and I was the odd one out.

Janine read the coach timetable wrongly, so we had time to kill. It was strange for her to make a mistake. We went into the

Wimpy bar even though Mum hated the place. She wouldn't eat anything but ordered a cup of tea. When it arrived, she complained there was a tea ring inside the white Pyrex and I was so embarrassed I nearly didn't eat my hamburger. In the end, hunger got the better of me and I polished it off. Me and Janine fought over the last few chips and Mum called us scavengers. We had to laugh. Mum paid the bill using luncheon vouchers and we walked to where the bus was parked. We watched Janine find a seat and waited until the coach pulled away. I waved goodbye until my hand nearly fell off. The bus turned at the roundabout and disappeared. I tucked my arm through Mum's and we walked along each in our own thoughts. I guessed Mum would miss Janine although she'd be back in the summer. It wasn't such a big deal and besides, Mum had me for company. Just as I was enjoying the feeling of being close to her for once, Mum broke away. There I was abandoned on the street corner while she searched in her bag for a handkerchief. Fancy getting tearful because Janine was off. Obviously, I didn't count at all. After a good blow, Mum wanted to link arms again, but I was having none of it. Mum couldn't expect me to play second fiddle to Janine my entire life.

6

2014

Stephanie's to-do list:

Attach lock to toilet door

While Stephanie waited for Janine to confirm about the podcast, her plan for letting the spare bedroom took shape. Following an exchange of texts, Beth arrived an hour later to see the room. She stood on the doorstep wearing a sailor top and flap collar. The thought of scrubbing decks flashed into Stephanie's mind (probably because she'd mopped earlier).

'Come in!' Stephanie swung the door open.

Instead of walking in, Beth twisted around to activate the remote lock on the van emblazoned with the Angel Cakes logo: an iced gateau made airborne thanks to a pair of feathered wings. Stephanie shuddered at how Mrs Walker might react. The rear end of Beth's van jutted into the area Mrs Walker saw as her personal parking space. As Stephanie didn't have a car, and had no intention of taking a driving test after years of surviving without wheels, the spot outside her place was usually occupied by the family who lived opposite and owned two vehicles. If Beth rented the room, things were going to change and not just for Stephanie.

Beth straightened and presented the plate she'd been hiding behind her back. 'Ta-dah!'

There were six cannoli dusted in icing sugar and arranged in a star formation. Stephanie had first encountered the sweet treat when an Italian food market came to town during a bank holiday a few years back. Not that Stephanie was an expert on cannoli, but she had been first in the queue. Beth's baking was bound to be different thanks to the flavours she included from her Asian heritage.

'How lovely.' Stephanie accepted the offering as Beth entered the hallway. Standing side by side, Stephanie couldn't resist taking another look at the crisp pastry and flashes of orange zest in the filling. She imagined the joy of crunching into one. It would only take a moment to pop the kettle on for strong black coffee to accompany.

'I hope you like cannoli,' said Beth.

'You're a mind-reader,' said Stephanie. 'They're one of my favourites.'

Beth smiled. Her nude lipstick complemented her complexion.

'Let's go into the kitchen.' Stephanie set the plate on the table and looked around the surfaces that gleamed thanks to her dash about the house using antibacterial spray and a microfibre cloth. 'Would you like coffee now or after the tour?'

'I'd love to see the room.'

Shit. Stephanie was conscious not to lick her lips. It was becoming increasingly difficult to concentrate with the cannoli tempting her. 'I'll put on the kettle before we set off.'

A viewing should've taken five minutes but answering Beth's questions, it went on forever. When Beth produced a retractable tape measure, Stephanie decided to leave her measuring up the spare room and returned to the kitchen. While she waited for Beth to join her, Stephanie prepared the cafetière and removed the cling film cover from the plate of cannoli. Sitting at the table, Stephanie tapped her fingernails on the composite wooden surface. A couple of minutes later Beth burst through the doorway. Finally, Stephanie could pour the coffee.

'Help yourself to milk and sugar,' she said.

Beth sat and then added milk to the flowered mug which made it full to the brim. Fortunately, she gripped the handle and sipped without a spill.

'It's a great room, great location,' said Beth. 'What's not to like?'

'Splendid.' Stephanie wondered if it would be impolite to reach for a cannoli right then. She clasped her hands. 'How about the rent? I believe it's the going rate.'

'No probs. I'll transfer the money if you give me your bank details.'

'Let's not worry about that now,' said Stephanie. 'Shall we try your baking instead?'

Beth moved in later that week and during one of the drop-offs, where Stephanie assisted in carrying a double duvet, Mrs Walker approached holding a bunch of lilac stems, some of the early blooms from her back garden. The froth of tiny white flowers bobbed with each step Mrs Walker took.

'I can smell the scent from here.' Stephanie peered from above the swathe of bedding.

'Thought you might like a few flowers to welcome your new lodger.'

'We call it house sharing these days.' Beth returned the box she'd been holding to the back of her van and took the bunch. 'They're lovely.'

'So that's your van, is it?'

'Yes, I'm Beth.'

She extended her hand and Mrs Walker grasped her fingers then released them rather quickly. 'You can call me Mrs Walker.'

'Everyone is friends with Mrs Walker.' Stephanie stiffened. She knew her neighbour of old but hoped she wouldn't say anything inappropriate.

Beth pressed her nose to the flowers. 'They're divine.'

'I don't suppose you get many perfumed blooms where you're from.'

Beth and Stephanie exchanged a look.

'You'd be surprised how well things grow in Watford,' said Beth.

'That far away?' said Mrs Walker. 'Almost a different country.'

'Hardly.' Stephanie laughed.

It was best to brush off the comment even though Mrs Walker continued to wear a perplexed expression.

'Seriously, where are you really from?'

'Let's save that for another time,' said Stephanie. 'My hands are going to fall off if I don't find somewhere to put this duvet.'

'And I better get these in water,' said Beth.

They escaped into the house with Beth dropping the flowers onto the kitchen table until the rest of the unloading had been completed. Regrouping downstairs, Stephanie searched for a vase, and found a large one in the hall cupboard. She filled it with water and placed the stems to make a display.

'Take no notice of Mrs Walker,' said Stephanie. 'She really does have a good heart. You have to remember she was born and bred in Belmont, so she's a bit inexperienced.'

'I'll take your word for it.'

By the next day Beth was ready to stay over. She'd labelled the final boxes with the names of different destinations including *kitchen* and *lounge.* Alarmed, Stephanie thought Beth's possessions would be confined to the bedroom. It was a big enough space and had plenty of storage. Offering accommodation to a chef, Stephanie should have known. She watched as Beth unpacked a block of professional knives that she positioned on the worktop.

Gone is the time of minimalism, thought Stephanie. 'I normally like the kitchen surfaces to be clear.'

'These don't take up much space and you can use them whenever you like. Please be careful, the blades are extra sharp.'

Disconcerted by the suggestion her utensils were less than satisfactory, Stephanie checked in a drawer. Arranged in military alignment were her tools and gadgets. She picked out a pair of bamboo tongs, and demonstrated their pincer action. 'These are ideal for removing bread from the toaster.' With that, she swiftly returned the tongs to the drawer.

'That's kind,' said Beth. 'I do like to cook up a storm.'

'I guessed as much,' Stephanie mumbled.

'Baking is my thing but you can't live on cakes alone. How about a curry for dinner tonight? I'll use a special recipe handed down through my family.'

The offer was not to be refused. 'Cakes and curry, quite a combination.'

'That's me all over. A proper mixed bag.'

Wondering what that was supposed to mean, Stephanie asked, 'How so?'

'My grandparents are from India but my family actually lived in Uganda.'

There was much about Beth that Stephanie didn't know. 'Weren't Asians expelled from there?'

'That was before I was born. I'm an NHS baby.'

'Don't tell me – you arrived at Watford General Hospital.'

'You got it in one.' Beth smiled.

The house became a different entity with another person in it. Beth breathed life into the brickwork. Stephanie enjoyed the companionship, like before she and Ben had split. Sounds of pottering in the kitchen were comforting, although with Ben there had been the added bonus of tea in bed. Beth did her best not to intrude on the patterns of Stephanie's daily life. The bathroom was always free for Stephanie to use, and she praised the day she'd had the foresight to buy a house with a separate loo. There were times Stephanie's sleep was broken, whether she was too hot or needed a wee. Likewise, she heard Beth's feet padding across the landing on occasions. An agreement about no flushing until morning was observed. This made the first appointment in Stephanie's busy schedule an engagement with the toilet brush and a squirt of bleach.

Beth usually arrived back from work around six o'clock. The revving engine became an alarm of sorts, bringing Stephanie to the window. Several attempts at parallel parking would eventually result in tyres pressed tight against the kerb, making it another spectacle when Beth left in the morning. Watching her park became a pleasurable distraction until Beth noticed her and asked why Stephanie was staring out. She used the excuse of checking on the hydrangea in the front garden to see if it displayed any tightly knotted buds. She was confident there would be flowers in the summer. It was news to Beth that the petals changed colour due to acidity in the soil and Stephanie expected the usual spray of pink would turn blue in the future.

On the occasion of a particularly intense day, Stephanie looked forward to Beth's return. Starting on the podcast project required an injection of energy and enthusiasm. Even though she still hadn't received the go-ahead from Janine, there was no harm in beginning the research. She'd identified a podcast (developed in North America) which provided a model for her own brand of investigation. There were still a couple of hours until Beth would bounce through the doorway, and Stephanie wanted something to show for her efforts. Thoughts about Carolyn Russell bubbled at the back of her mind so Stephanie turned to her laptop and typed material for an introduction.

The year was 1979, the winter of discontent continued with substantial industrial action and bad weather conditions. A general election in May saw Mrs Thatcher elected Tory prime minister. The hunt for the Yorkshire Ripper focused on hoax recorded messages and failed to prevent a twelfth murder. Entertainment highlights on television included John Cleese's performance in Fawlty Towers *and during the summer, Blondie hits belted over the airwaves. But what was sixteen-year-old Carolyn Russell doing? Was she diligently studying in her bedroom for end of school exams or was there more going on? Carolyn Russell has never been heard from since June 1979 when she walked out of her maths examination and was never seen again. Although the case is well known locally, it didn't receive the national attention that might have solved the mystery decades ago. This is Stephanie Brett, formerly a journalist at the* West Country Post, *now investigating a cold case that has never left the hearts and minds of Belmont residents.*

Satisfied she had at least a few words down, Stephanie saved the document in a folder on her desktop named *Podcast Development*. It would have to do until she came up with a proper title for the work. Absorbed in what she'd been doing, Stephanie only realised Beth was on the doorstep by the jangling keys and the clunk and turn of the lock which let her in.

'I'm back!'

Stephanie wasn't used to the sound of yelling in her house and didn't want to encourage the practice. She closed the laptop and placed it on the coffee table. By the time she got to the kitchen, Beth was wrestling with a bottle of Prosecco.

'Want a glass?' she asked.

Christ, if Beth didn't keep control of the cork, it might cause some damage. 'Shall I help you?'

Beth handed over the bottle which Stephanie noted was suitably chilled. She removed what remained of the foil covering and turned the tab six times to release the wire. Using her thumb to secure the cork, she rotated the bottle slowly until a hiss confirmed it was open.

'I like to send the cork off with a big bang,' said Beth.

She was nothing if not effervescent.

'What are we celebrating?' Stephanie took the first flute from the glazed cupboard, tilted it to forty-five degrees and poured.

'A week in my new home requires a celebration.'

Just a week? It was more like ten days. Stephanie gave a glass to Beth and raised her own. After the chink, she took a sip. It was amazing how bubbly wine lifted her mood. 'I've something to celebrate as well. I've finally put a few words on the page… I've made a start on the podcast about Carolyn Russell.'

Beth looked stumped for anything to say.

'You remember Carolyn Russell, don't you?'

'No.' Beth shook her head making her dark locks flick around her face and then they fell back into place. She was so pretty with her rich brown eyes.

'It was back in the seventies. A schoolgirl went missing and was never seen again.'

'Oh that,' said Beth. 'It happened before I was born.'

Now it was Stephanie stumbling on her words. 'How old are you, exactly?'

'Thirty-four,' said Beth. 'Born at the start of the eighties.'

'And too young to know much about my missing girl.'

'Sorry, I can't help.'

They sipped their drinks while Stephanie pondered the relative youth of her housemate. Thank God it wasn't a squirming sort of silence. Finally, she came up with a line. 'It'll make the story fascinating for you.'

'True.' Beth turned the bottle to study the label. 'I picked this up at the corner shop. I'm surprised they stock such a classy brand. Shall I find us an appetiser?'

Without waiting for an answer, Beth opened the cupboard

where Stephanie stored an unused tea set.

'Good luck in there.' Stephanie took another sip while Beth searched. As she was taking a long time, Stephanie leaned forward to have a look in the cupboard she rarely visited. The cups and saucers were pushed to the back and stacked in front were a plethora of containers covered in jolly fabric tops secured with raffia ties. This was evidence of Beth getting her feet well under the table *and* into the cupboards.

'Where did they come from?' asked Stephanie.

'The Greek stall at the market.'

It was years since Stephanie had bothered going there. 'The last time I went it was full of cheap clothes and chipped crockery.'

'Really?' Beth picked out a slender jar. 'Belmont's getting cool.'

Stephanie stifled a laugh; the one thing you couldn't call Belmont was cool.

'You should check it out.' Beth drained liquid from the jar and then placed the contents on a dish. There lay an arrangement of green berries on stalks.

'Maybe I should.' Curiosity about the appetiser had got to Stephanie. There was nothing to stop her from visiting the market now she wasn't keeping office hours. Perhaps she should become reacquainted with the town she'd lived in most of her life.

Beth reached for a stalk, let the berry dangle between her fingers and offered the plate to Stephanie. Copying Beth's lead, Stephanie was reminded of holding a cherry, although this green oval was clearly savoury and from the way Beth nipped it between her teeth, there was no stone.

'Don't you just love capers?' said Beth.

Stephanie took a bite and considered. 'They're rather like an olive.'

'You could say,' Beth agreed. 'With more texture.'

'Absolutely,' said Stephanie.

The evening with Beth was turning into quite an education.

7

The Easter holidays dragged without Janine. Even though I could hardly believe it, I was glad when school started again. The day also marked a breakthrough in my powers of persuasion with Mum. My very last term and she finally agreed to let me take a packed lunch instead of having awful school dinners. How I hated the clicking ice-cream scoop as a dollop of lumpy mashed potato landed on my plate. No more of that crap for me, but I had to search the kitchen for something to eat. I went for a cheese sandwich using the ready-sliced split-tin loaf. As I had a sweet tooth, I needed something sugary to follow. A pot of strawberry yoghurt and a Golden Delicious apple would see me through the day.

At the school gate, there was a line of girls ahead of me. The boys were sent to the other entrance where Forsyth inspected their uniforms. Thank God I didn't have to face him. It was Miss Grant checking us and I knew she'd be soft. I was in her form and it had to count for something. Heading for the back of the queue, I saw Patricia who grabbed my arm and said, 'Squeeze in here.'

I didn't have much choice and stumbled into the gap. Tutting came from the girl behind as I accidentally (on purpose) trod on her patent leather toe. She squealed until Patricia turned and gave one of her *stuff that in your cakehole* stares. That made her shut up. Then, Patricia unrolled the waistband of her skirt and lengthened the hem to around her knees. She was a short-arse and had to put up with wearing hand-me-downs from her cousin. Lucky for me, I had a skirt that fitted although it didn't when Mum first bought it. According to her, there was a need for *growing room* in every purchase. Two years later and the hem was way above regulation length. I had expanded around the middle as well which meant leaving the button at the waist undone or risk being cut in two. Mum had decided the expense of another skirt wasn't worth the bother as I'd never get the wear out of it. A prefect studied her clipboard while Miss Grant eyed me up and down then waved me through. I was pleased she let me off but Patricia was caught wearing navy mascara. Walking into the school grounds alone, I wished it wasn't the case.

At the path to the new block, I saw Patricia with a wad of cotton wool in her hand. Her eyes were raw where she'd had to scrub the make-up off. Listening to her moaning, I ignored the school bell. We hadn't seen each other for a whole fortnight and I wasn't ready to dash away. We loitered at the turning where she went for registration in the art room and I headed for the old building. It was called old, even though that part of the school was built in the 1930s so not exactly ancient. The one good thing about being in 5G was that we were in the home economics room and the ovens were fired up ready for cooking practice during first period. It was the only warm place in the entire school and the extra heat was welcome during cold spells. It wasn't so good during the hot summer months though.

We said goodbye and as I made my way over with my tote bag banging against my hip, I spotted Forsyth again. I swear he lugged a pile of exercise books under his arm as a drama prop. No one in their right mind believed he spent hours marking. Weirdly, he was talking to somebody I hadn't seen before. A new face in school. He definitely wasn't a student teacher – it was too late in the year for one of them to turn up. I couldn't help but stop and stare. The bloke was young and dishy. His dark-blond hair was feather cut and although his jacket was corduroy, he looked trendy.

Rushing into my form room, I arrived as Miss Grant was closing the register. She'd made a speedy return from gate duty and she realised I should've been on time. I managed to pull a pathetic expression and she took pity on me. After tapping her pen against the desk, she marked me in. Phew, detention avoided! I hurried over to the table where my group were hanging out but they turned away as I approached. For some reason, I wasn't flavour of the month. Sticking my head into my locker, I rummaged around. I had nothing to say to them either. Perhaps they'd turned against me because I'd chummed up with Patricia. Anyway, they were a load of snobs. Just because they were certain to get good grades didn't mean we no-hopers were on the rubbish heap. Maths was my downfall but I wasn't completely useless. I'd actually come top of the class in the history and geography mocks except Mum didn't think the subjects were important. She actually had the bright idea I should learn typing and shorthand at Pitman's instead of going to sixth form. That way being awful at maths wouldn't stop me from getting a job in a cushy office. Then I remembered, I'd have to do bookkeeping as part of the course and suddenly I was wracked with guilt. I should've spent more time working on the maths practice questions over the holidays.

2014

MEMORANDUM

To: Stephanie Brett, trainee
From: Stuart Finch, Newsdesk
Date: 12 July 1979
Re: Carolyn Russell
While your enthusiasm for covering this case is laudable, please ensure that you do not allow personal theories to influence reporting. You must let the police decide the significance of the yellow Cortina and the potential for abduction. Come to my office and we'll discuss your responsibilities.
Yours, SF

The kitchen cupboard doors banging announced Beth's breakfast routine. Stephanie turned her pillow and slumped against the cool linen then she slid a leg onto the unslept side of the bed where the sheets were fresh. Another night disrupted by toilet visits and soaring heat. How long was this going to last? She remembered being outraged at forty-six when the peri phase started. Convinced she was far too busy for any of that middle-aged nonsense, it had taken a good few months to acknowledge her thermostat was broken and the chance of becoming a mother was slipping away. Although having a child had never been at the top of Stephanie's list, she was concerned about the indignity of aging.

Stirring from under the covers, Stephanie's limbs were heavy. A regular routine with a nine o'clock start at the office, would have given her cause to be sprightly. Now she was following a self-organised timetable, there were limits to her motivation. Stephanie reached for her mug and took a sip from the brew she'd made in the early hours. Cold camomile tea didn't taste too bad, she discovered. Honestly, she'd tried drifting off but sleep had become elusive. Awake in the middle of the night, she wondered what other menopausal women were doing. At least listening to a podcast she'd downloaded provided a distraction during some of the most uncomfortable hours. The investigation traced an unsolved case in America where a random search of a gravestone website provided the missing clue. Stephanie wondered what would be the key to finding Carolyn.

After a shower, she dressed in comfortable bootleg trousers and a cotton-knit top. With her hair spruced into shape thanks to her trusty straighteners, there was only the need for a dusting of make-up. While working at the *Post*, she occasionally visited a nail bar where she chatted to a Vietnamese assistant from Hoi An. This was a destination for travellers who wished to purchase quality tailored clothes. Stephanie had thought about a holiday but without regular income, plans were abandoned. It was irritating to have the time but not the funds for a journey. Back when she attended team meetings at the *Post*, Stephanie had enjoyed using her polished nails to drum a tune onto the boardroom table when the discussions became tedious. Doug had taken her aside one day to suggest it wasn't appropriate behaviour although that didn't stop her in the days leading up to redundancy. It was a small victory to disrupt the agenda.

Beth had long gone by the time Stephanie settled to work. With her laptop on the kitchen table, she sat staring at the blank screen. Janine's last phone call had confirmed the family's support and even if Mrs Russell wasn't ready to be interviewed, it was enough for Stephanie to feel confident about proceeding. Her first task was to track down DI Spencer who had once been in charge of the case. She knew him from the early days of Carolyn's disappearance but heard he'd retired and moved along the coast. Thanks to an online directory, a few phone calls later, she was sure the last name on her list had to be him.

Stephanie listened to the thrum of the ringtone. A minute passed and she wondered why a voicemail hadn't clicked in. Maybe DI Spencer wasn't into gadgets. She moved over to the worktop just as the urge for coffee became another priority. Yet she continued to hold the line for three more rings. On the point of giving up, a breathy voice answered *hello*. Shit. Now she would have to talk to him when she was really more interested in a cup of coffee. Stephanie introduced herself with one hand attached to the mobile while with the other, she pressed the switch on the kettle. Flipping the lid off the coffee jar wasn't easy, especially as she simultaneously gave an overview of the podcast. Bill Spencer interjected using an occasional 'I see' and by the time she'd returned to the table with black coffee and pen within reach, he was into a diatribe against press coverage of Carolyn's case. Her early involvement (cut short by her supervisor) allowed Stephanie to feel suitably guilty. As his protestations rolled, this time it was Stephanie who interjected using the occasional 'I see.' Letting him get his frustrations out was the best thing to do and when he'd calmed down, Stephanie was in a position to pose a question or two.

It turned out Bill Spencer was able to overlook Stephanie's earlier relationship with the *Post*. He didn't remember her as a trainee at the time, and over the years, she must've learnt not to be pushed around by those at the top. Yes, he was willing to become involved in the podcast. It was a newfangled trend and even if it did mean hearing his dulcet tones over the airwaves, it might help. He'd always carried feelings of responsibility for the case. Because of cuts and changes to the force, there wasn't a safe pair of hands to keep the inquiry going after he retired. Jesus Christ, he couldn't believe there'd been so little progress since the day Carolyn went missing. Of course, he'd done his bit but the girl had dropped down the list of priorities. Now was the time to take a closer look and he was there for Stephanie.

'I assume the Russell family are behind you. Their support is essential if you're to get anywhere,' he said.

'I've met Carolyn's sister to discuss the podcast.'

'Good,' he said. 'Can you send Mrs Russell my regards?'

'Okay.' Stephanie wasn't entirely sure she'd extend the greeting.

With that, DI Spencer was off again. It had been the only unsolved case in his entire career and to tell the truth, he'd been thinking of writing a book about his life to give his grandkids. Something for them to read when they were old enough. He'd penned a few thousand words and he'd had positive feedback from the writing group at the Scout hut even if one woman was particularly fierce. She said if he didn't read, what qualified him to write? Bloody cheek. He had too much reading to do with gardening books and now cookery ones since his wife had thrown in the towel and he was responsible for preparing meals at least twice a week. Did Stephanie like coq au vin? It was his speciality, although he understood from chefs on TV that wasn't the right word anymore. It was now a signature dish. Enough of his rambling. What did Stephanie want to know?

'I'd like to make recordings of you talking about Carolyn Russell's disappearance. Your inside knowledge would be especially valuable. I expect you'll be able to share some interesting observations.'

'The whole thing was a complete conundrum. The maths teacher was our prime suspect but after checking his alibi, we were left without leads. I can't help thinking there's lots to uncover. You do know Carolyn took extra lessons from him? Absolute shenanigans.'

Stephanie was aware of the rumours. 'Where exactly was he when Carolyn went missing?'

'On his way to a job interview.'

'He must have been one of the last people to see Carolyn. Didn't he invigilate during her maths examination?'

'Yes. And straight after he caught a lift to Bristol. His onward journey was by public transport. According to him, he needed to get a job or he'd have no employment.'

'But why leave Greensleeves? He'd only started there in the summer term.'

'Now you're asking. Something to do with his colleagues. They didn't take to him from what I remember.'

'Seems rather odd,' she said.

'A lot of things don't add up.'

'I always wondered about the yellow car.' Stephanie couldn't resist alluding to her theory of abduction even though she'd been slapped down for suggesting it back in the day at the *Post*. 'It was an odd place to park. There's nothing at that end of Greensleeves Road besides the school entrance.'

'There was a trading estate a bit further along and a garage once upon a time. You wouldn't believe the hours we spent trying to track down the vehicle. Strange as it might seem there were more than a few yellow Cortinas. Hundreds of them, in fact.'

'Did you actually find it?'

'Not me personally. The search led to an interview that got us precisely nowhere. Rotten bit of luck.'

Stephanie's heart sank. She made a mental note to press the point with Bill on a future occasion. It wasn't the time to focus on failings, not when she wanted his help. In the silence, she worried he was about to end the conversation. Then another thought rushed into her head. She'd been puzzling over what Janine had said about Carolyn's lack of real friends. Stephanie thought about Carolyn palling up with the French girl. There weren't many kids from anywhere but Belmont back then, so the girl must've been something of a novelty. 'What about the French girl in her class? Did you learn much about Carolyn from her?'

'It rings a bell. I'll have a look in my notebook. Now if you'll excuse me, I have a rice pudding that needs attention before it boils over.'

9

APRIL 1979

I escaped from the house before Mum's usual blast about the importance of breakfast. The first meal of the day and something substantial was required. I understood the need for a balanced diet, we did learn something at school, but why a round of toast and marmalade should be praised was beyond me. As I was in a rush, I picked a few flakes straight from the cereal box. It saved washing up and the need for milk. Genius.

Patricia waited for me by the footbridge over the railway line. From a distance I could see her eating crisps. By the time I got there, she'd emptied the Golden Wonder packet into her mouth and caught the broken bits. If she thought I wanted any, she was wrong. I hated the taste of Bovril. After she'd finished crunching, she blew into the bag and clapped it, making a loud bang. A couple of first-years jumped out of their skins and then walked in a wide circle around us. This left plenty of room to stare them out. None of them would dare mess with Patricia. She laughed as they shuffled by and I barged against her to show we were together.

I didn't talk much on the way to school because some of Patricia's friends from the estate joined us. They were spreading gossip: who'd been snogging, who'd been chucked and who'd been caught up the duff. I was suspicious of everyone because of what happened to a girl in our year. One day, she didn't turn up for school and the next minute, she was pushing a pram around town. (Okay, not literally a minute.) She got her name on the list for a council flat pretty quick although I didn't envy her soaking nappies and mopping up sick.

Tuesday morning and first off it was double English. That meant I was in the room next to the library. I couldn't be sure which lesson Patricia had. We met again outside the science block at break. Rumour had it that sitting on the concrete steps would result in piles except we didn't take any notice.

'Bollocks,' said Patricia. 'As if I care.'

'I think we would mind if it actually happened.' I shifted position to make sure a bit of skirt actually covered my bum. 'Chances are we'll be okay.'

'Too right.' Patricia took an Afro comb from her bag and teased it through the perm she'd done at home using her gran's matchstick curlers and perming paper. Her auburn frizz contrasted with my silky locks, cut to look like Joanna Lumley's Purdy in *The New Avengers*. The only trouble was my hair grew quickly and the style had lost its shape. The chance of regaining the look from another wet cut at the salon was like the prospect of a third series of the TV programme, doubtful. As for the blondish colour, it turned darker each day after a hair wash. Not even dry shampoo could revive it... and I couldn't forget about my greasy skin either. The last school photo showed shiny patches on my forehead and cheeks. It was the end to any self-respect I possessed.

'Look at them.' Patricia pointed to the first-years chasing around the playground.

'So juvenile.'

'I was never like that.'

'Me neither.' Now wasn't the time to admit I played those games when Floria was my best friend.

'D'you reckon we'll have Forsyth again?' asked Patricia.

The idea sent me into a fit of depression. It must have shown all over my face because Patricia spluttered into hysterics. While I was pleased she thought me funny, Forsyth for maths was a disaster. 'I can't stand him.'

'You and me both.'

'Mrs Hoskins must've had her baby by now.' A pang of loss threaded my heart. She hadn't been the greatest teacher in the world but at least she wasn't snide.

'You always sucked up to her. *I just love your brooch, Mrs Hoskins.*' Patricia mimicked my voice.

'Well, it was nice.' I knew about cameo brooches because my dad had given one to my mum on their wedding anniversary. It happened only months before he died and Mum always referred to it as his parting gift.

'No wonder you haven't got friends,' she said.

I was dumbstruck by her disloyalty and my face became so hot I must've shone like a Belisha beacon. I grabbed my bag but before I had a chance to storm off, she hooked her arm through mine and dragged me back.

'Except me, of course.' Patricia's smile made her cheeks bulge.

Her words were a peace offering I had to accept. 'As if I haven't got enough to worry about with Forsyth.'

'You get off lightly.' She gave me a nudge and I realised we were friends again. 'He doesn't pick on quiet girls.'

What was she on about? More than once I'd had him barking a so-called *explanation* at me. It wasn't funny when his spit flew everywhere. Too many germs! And I couldn't bear his pointing finger right in my face.

'You're better at maths,' I said. 'He's got it in for dimwits like me.'

The bell rang and interrupted us. It was the signal to make for the next lesson and we dragged ourselves to the first-floor landing where Forsyth fumbled with the key to the classroom. I crossed my fingers behind my back and hoped we wouldn't have him for much longer. There had to be a replacement for Mrs Hoskins soon. Finally, the door swung open and we filed in. As he knew none of us by name, he demanded *you boy* open the window, and *that girl* give out the books. He wasted no time in talking about our *sloppy attitude* and the need to *smarten up our act*. All the time a strand of hair dangled over his forehead and bobbed in front of his eyes.

Everyone was organised with their books and pencils when there was a knock at the door. It was a school rule that should an adult enter the room, we were expected to stand as if a member of the royal family had arrived. The scraping of chair legs against the floor was the sound of our rebellion. It was bloody ridiculous. I kept my eyes down, not wanting to draw attention to myself. I didn't even take a sneaky look to check who was coming in but then Patricia dug me in the ribs. There was Forsyth, clapping the back of someone who could've been our new teacher. This was confirmed when Forsyth introduced the dishy bloke I'd seen the day before as Mr Simmons. Funny thing was, he looked even tastier than at first sight. He was slim and I thought him stylish with the crisp creases in his trousers. I clenched my fingers, trying to get a grip, while my knees quaked. Mr Simmons greeted us using a cheery *good morning*. While the others in my row scuffled and droned back a reply, I returned his gaze. I got the distinct impression he was smiling straight at me. This teacher was special. I held my head high and my hair flicked around my shoulders. Forsyth waved his arms, indicating for us to sit. Patricia yanked me down. My timing was off and I was the last person to land on a chair.

Forsyth explained about the work we needed to complete. After he'd gone, Mr Simmons said he'd be our teacher for the rest of term. Thank God! A sigh of relief from the back of the class worked its way forwards. To start the lesson, Mr Simmons shot off some quick-fire sums and we scribbled the answers down. My paper was messy but I managed to keep up. The questions were coming so fast, I didn't have time for a sneaky look at Patricia's page to check what she'd written. At the end of the test, Mr Simmons made us swap books with the next person and Patricia marked mine. As the answers came, I knew I'd be ticking all of her sums. Working down the page, I remembered some of my answers were the same as hers! Excitement galloped through my veins. When I got my book back, there were a few big ticks on my page. Disbelief and amazement made me smile.

'Put your hand up if you've got more than five questions right.'

Six bloody ticks. I shot my arm into the air and waved it around to make sure he saw.

'Brilliant,' said Mr Simmons. 'That's the whole class with over half the calculations answered correctly.'

Twenty minutes later, I was in a daze. Surprisingly, I did know a bit about maths. While everyone was packing away, I couldn't help but stare at Mr Simmons. He was such a hunk. Even when Patricia clicked her fingers in front of my face, I didn't want to be brought back to my senses. There was something mesmerising about him.

10

2014

Entry from Stephanie Brett's 2014 notebook:

What made Carolyn vulnerable/susceptible? Could include:
isolation --- naivety --- mental health --- family tensions --- family history --- inexperience --- social skills --- overconfidence --- sense of infallibility

Frank Forsyth, deputy head at Greensleeves School had been easy to find and strangely enthusiastic about an interview, although Stephanie wasn't looking forward to the prospect. As she walked to his front door, she noticed the precision planting of marigolds in the borders. One or two pansy heads remained but they had flopped, seemingly overwhelmed by the blast of orange. It was rather like that at school, the academic students paraded in assemblies where the getting-on-with-it were overlooked. If any of the boys dared to show a feminine side, they were promptly rebuked by Mr Forsyth whose castigation frequently ended using a sneering utterance of the word *pansy*. She'd never liked him, and Stephanie sensed the same stiffening of her spine she had experienced whenever around the over-inflated deputy. Glad to think she never actually quaked, Stephanie dismissed the memories and focused her mind. It was likely he had developed an increased range of prejudices as those growing older often did. Take Mrs Walker as an example of this. For the interview, Stephanie's questions would need to tap into Mr Forsyth's core values and unearth the vitriol beneath. What if he vented during the interview? She would suppress her instinct to reprimand and capture the flow on tape.

Scanning the duck-egg-blue front door, Stephanie couldn't see a bell or a knocker. Visitors were clearly expected to make their presence known by other means. She rapped her knuckles on the obscured glass panel and wished she hadn't exerted quite so much pressure as the sound reverberated. While she waited, she admired the troughs of purple petunias beside the porch wall, their heads basking in the morning sun.

When Mr Forsyth (she couldn't bring herself to call him Frank) agreed to be interviewed, she had initially balked at the idea of a nine o'clock meeting but an early bus journey through the lanes and down to the coast had been refreshing. She liked riding the X32 and it was recommended to tourists as one of the most scenic public transport routes in the country. It went some way along the coast giving wonderful glimpses of golden cliffs and swathes of beaches which were currently deserted yet would fill up as the holiday season arrived.

The door swung open and Stephanie was surprised to see the shrunken figure of Mr Forsyth. His head was outsized and still covered with a crop of curly hair now turned white. A collar peeked above the neckline of his faded jumper. On his sleeve, a ladder travelled from elbow to wrist and was reminiscent of a surgical scar. She assumed he hadn't noticed this when dressing.

Looking down, she saw tweed slippers under his chocolate-brown trousers. He no longer sported the buffed suede loafers or polished Oxfords that clumped along corridors in warning of his approach.

'Greetings.' The single word was gruffly spoken. Mr Forsyth cleared his throat then stretched out a rough and mottled hand. They shook while Stephanie wittered about the beautiful morning. When she finally ran out of suitable adjectives there was a momentary silence before he spoke again.

'There is a bell.' Mr Forsyth pointed to the luminated rectangle mounted on the door jamb and pressed it for good measure. It chirped a welcome far friendlier than his. How on earth had she missed it?

'Now I see it.' Stephanie laughed.

'I thought you journalists were supposed to have enquiring minds.'

'We do.'

Stephanie was directed to the lounge where an armchair was positioned like a throne and on a small table only an arm's length away appeared the necessaries. (The TV remote, a copy of the *Radio Times*, strips of blister-packed pills and a water glass covered in fingerprints.) Mr Forsyth offered to make drinks and recommended Stephanie used his absence to set up her recording equipment. He swept a few *West Country Now* magazines from the coffee table and gestured towards a dining chair she could sit on.

Sounds of clanking crockery emanated from the kitchen while Stephanie organised the microphone and laptop. Scanning the questions she'd written in her notebook, Stephanie prepared for an onslaught. She imagined Mr Forsyth was keen on being interviewed for the sole purpose of distancing himself from any wrongdoing. They both knew male teachers at Greensleeves were at liberty to spread prejudices and predilections. He was a member of that club while she had been a passive observer.

Again, she sensed a creeping tension rooted in the days when she was confused by the teacher-led bullying considered to be humour and watched flirting excused as friendliness.

He arrived carrying a tea tray in unsteady hands. Two mugs slid about the surface. Stephanie collected both and put the one with black coffee beside her laptop while setting his builder's tea on the table next to his chair. Mr Forsyth tucked the tray out of sight then sat and pulled a handle on the recliner to raise his legs. It was distracting, watching him in a laid-back position, as if he were a patient in a dentist's chair.

'You've done all right for yourself at the *Post*,' said Mr Forsyth. 'There are a few Greensleeves students who've stayed local and enjoyed success. It's strange I haven't seen your name in the paper lately.'

Stephanie wasn't entirely upfront when she'd called to make the appointment and now this gave Mr Forsyth the upper hand. The superiority of his position as deputy head was going to overshadow the entire interview unless she did something about it. Before she had time to practise a line or two in her mind, Mr Forsyth reached over and inspected the microphone. He blew into the head, as he had done at the start of every school assembly. The dull whistle of his breath sounded.

'For recording purposes, it's better to have the microphone close but not too close.' She repositioned the stand.

'A number of former students are in the paper for reasons the school would rather not boast about. I could always sniff out a dud.'

'You could predict which students would turn out bad?' She tied the trailing wires using a clip.

'You get a nose for that kind of thing.'

Stephanie glanced over and gave Mr Forsyth a broad smile. It was intended to put him at ease and had the effect of steadying her too. 'What did you look for?'

Mr Forsyth stared again at the microphone. 'Why are you

bothering with one of them? I thought traditionally trained journalists used shorthand.'

Stephanie bristled. She'd interviewed so many of his type. Council members were often the worst. Yet something about her earlier relationship with this man made the situation unwieldy. His attitude, no different from her teenage years, rankled.

'I've actually left the *Post*. I'm conducting this interview for a podcast. I'll record our discussion and then liaise with others to produce a series of quality programmes looking into Carolyn Russell's disappearance.'

'Oh yes, you explained on the phone. I have no trouble speaking on the subject. I rather pride myself as an orator.'

'I remember those regular Friday assemblies.' A bit of buttering up did no harm although Stephanie cringed as the reprimands he bellowed came to mind.

'These days my specialist subject involves gardening tips for members of the Rotary Club.'

Was this an attempt at humour? Stephanie gave an obliging smile. 'Everything's set. We can start the interview now.'

'Let's get on with it.'

Stephanie activated the equipment and gave a brief introduction. During the bus ride, she'd rehearsed by intermittently posing silent questions to her own reflection in the mud-splattered window. As a reporter, she'd been good at holding eye contact and making notes simultaneously. Now she needed to keep the talk going and extract possible clues.

'What do you remember about Carolyn Russell?'

'She only came to my attention after she went missing. There was a lot of talk in the staffroom. Speculation about why Carolyn had gone off the rails. I didn't have much involvement with her. As deputy head, my priority was management of the school. Or rather, enabling a stream of headteachers who came and went to make sensible decisions. Mrs Mould was in charge at the time. Now *she* was a difficult woman. One of the down-from-London lot who couldn't get her head around the fact that schooling is different in a rural area.'

Rumour had it that Mr Forsyth applied for the headship each time a vacancy arose. Somehow, he never managed to get his hands on the top job.

'She was appointed the year I left school. I didn't get to know her.'

'As soon as Mrs Mould arrived, she was out of her depth. Wouldn't admit it, of course. She suffered from migraines – I ask you! They'd put her out of action for days at a time. Weeks, even.' Mr Forsyth gave a knowing smile and adopted a conspiratorial tone. 'No one called it stress in those days.'

Stephanie coughed. A deliberate strategy to distance herself from his views.

'You wore many hats, Mr Forsyth. What were your priorities during that summer?'

'When it became apparent Mrs Mould wasn't up to the job, I knew additional responsibilities were coming my way. I was head of maths as well as deputy, so you can imagine how busy I was. Finding someone to take a little of the teaching workload off my shoulders and provide cover elsewhere wasn't easy, but then Graham Simmons turned up. He'd gone travelling after he finished his teaching qualification and I assume came back once his money ran out. To be honest, I didn't care. I was relieved we had a decent candidate who would free me up to steer an otherwise sinking ship. Little did I know what he was actually like until later.'

'To be clear, which classes did Graham Simmons teach?'

'Let me think. He took over a few of the top sets in the lower school. I didn't want to risk the success of my exam pupils, but with a part-time teacher going on maternity leave, he had to take over the CSE maths group that Carolyn was in. Organising a timetable for a new teacher is like sewing a patchwork quilt. There were lots of different youngsters to consider. Simmons saw it as good experience and was willing to run with whatever I threw at him.'

'Only one examination class?'

'We avoided changing teachers for fourth- and fifth-year pupils. That woman's pregnancy threw a spanner in the works. You would have thought with contraception readily available she might have timed things better. At the end of the day, the results of the CSE class were the least of our concerns.'

Stephanie felt her eyes widening but managed to keep her mouth shut. Her expression didn't prevent Mr Forsyth from continuing. 'Those students were bound for the local factory although I believe Carolyn could have made more of herself. She didn't present as a rule-breaking student so I never had cause to log her behaviour or discipline her. Looking back, it was very strange. There was an intelligent streak in her family with her sister being academic. Perhaps as the younger sibling, Carolyn was short-changed. To tell you the truth, I think she was wilful. I mean, if you've got skills across the curriculum, there's no reason why she couldn't have succeeded in mathematics.'

'There are such things as specific learning difficulties,' Stephanie suggested.

'Not back then. I expect Carolyn would have made a very good secretary.'

'Why do you say that?'

'Because her mother was one.'

'Okay.' Stephanie needed to get him back on track. 'I understand your contact with Carolyn was limited. Can you tell me how other staff members reacted when she went missing?'

'There was talk about her being... how can I put this nicely? I remember someone calling her a little minx. Don't ask me who. It could have been one of the pupils, for all I know. When I heard you were coming, I decided to name all the head boys in reverse order from my last year in post. That was 1999. I could do it without too much bother, my memory is completely intact. But trying to place Carolyn is not easy. I expect she was an unremarkable type of girl.'

'Why was she called a minx?'

'I can't be doing with the specifics.'

Stephanie sensed her irritation rising and then a bloom of heat pricked her cheeks. She was in for a full-scale flush and used the notepad to fan her face. Careful that the motion could not be picked up in the recording, she framed another question. Before she had time to pose it, Mr Forsyth was off again.

'Robert Shuttle was head boy in 1979. He got sucked into the questions about Carolyn's disappearance. When the term ended, the incident wasn't an issue any longer.'

'You mean Carolyn wasn't your problem?'

Mr Forsyth frowned.

Stephanie fired another question. 'Who was head girl?'

'It was Robert who had knowledge about the pupils. During that difficult period of the school's history, he was invaluable. He could gauge situations... and he fed back to us at meetings in the staffroom. Such a very personable young man and so eloquent. You could sense his underlying empathy for the girl. As you can imagine, the police were quickly involved and we, as a school, did everything expected.'

'Tell me a bit more about Mr Simmons and his relationships with pupils.'

'After I got wind of his approach, I began to doubt his suitability. The modus operandi of the maths department involved teaching to the top. If you can extend the learning of the brightest, others will follow. Simmons ignored this advice and was magnanimous with the stragglers. What was the point in that? All it did was gain him popularity with those who were about to drop out of education. In my opinion it was pointless but he wouldn't have it. He even argued in a departmental meeting. I shall never forget it – the arrogance of the man. In the end, I simply gave him a wide berth and encouraged him to keep his opinions to himself.'

'When people suggested Mr Simmons was involved in Carolyn's disappearance, what did you think?'

'A part of me thought it served him right. I mean, who on earth would want to offer extra lessons to pupils who couldn't be bothered to learn in school? It was quite ridiculous. Would you believe he hadn't mentioned it in our maths meetings? Some of the other staff knew and when the police asked questions, they reported the fact he was a private tutor to Carolyn. It opened a can of worms.'

'How so?'

'There had to be a big inquiry into all after-school activities. Completely unnecessary. It particularly affected the PE department and warnings about teacher conduct were issued.'

I'll bet, thought Stephanie, *Southy and Gove finally disciplined*. And although she was pleased at the admission, she needed to stay focused.

'Can you tell me anything else about Graham Simmons?'

'Not really. I didn't know him well and his employment ended by the summer holidays. He went on to work elsewhere. I gave him a reference in spite of everything. It wouldn't do to thwart a young man's career.'

Mr Forsyth adjusted his chair and stood. He downed the last of his drink and held out his other hand, indicating for Stephanie to pass hers over.

'It's about time I was getting on,' said Mr Forsyth.

She gathered the interview was over and packed away the microphone. 'Thank you for your time.'

'Robert Shuttle might be able to fill you in with other details. As far as I know, he's remained local. I'm not sure where Simmons is now. But that's your job, isn't it? Tracking people down.'

11

APRIL 1979

I did a double take when I saw Mr Simmons coming out of the corner shop. Not any old corner shop, but the one at the end of my road. I dashed out of the way because I didn't want him to see me with my mousy hair gone lanky. I felt foolish ducking into the launderette especially when the manageress gave me the staring-eye treatment. She usually chucked out school kids who went in there for shelter – the ones who caught the bus into town. As I was dressed in a pair of flares and a checked top, she didn't realise I went to Greensleeves too. (For once in my life, I'd actually changed out of my uniform before heading to the shop.) Thank God she never asked why I was pressed between the end dryer and the window but this was the best place for looking out. He stood near the kerb where sunlight caught the golden threads in his gorgeous hair.

Never before had I thought of a teacher as good-looking. I wasn't like the other girls who got hot and bothered over Southy. In my opinion, all swimming sessions in the outdoor pool were awful. Thank God I wasn't taught by him. I couldn't bear the thought of one of Southy's inspections. It was bad enough having bee stings for boobs without him checking me over. I hated swimming. My Speedo went see-through when wet and it was impossible to cover all my bits and pieces using my arms. As exams approached, 5G's swimming lessons ended and I enjoyed a sense of sheer relief.

Mr Simmons took a packet of cigarettes from his pocket. From the flash of gold, I think they were Bensons. Classy. Cupping his hand around a match, he lit up and took a long drag. I loved the way he held the cigarette between his thumb and first finger, how he exhaled smoke in a long line. I fixed my eyes on his lips – they seemed permanently turned into a smile. I noticed his shirt collar was undone and a few curls from his chest showed against the cream cotton. A spark of electricity sent my fingers tingling but this wasn't a static shock. Mr Simmons was doing it for me and I'd keep him to myself. The others could go crazy over that creep Southy.

Rumours about the goings-on at after-school synchronised swimming started when pop music blasted from the open-air pool. Screened by a fence, if boys took a sneaky look through the holes where wooden knots had been poked away, they were told to clear off by Mr Gove, who acted as Southy's back-up. It was by accident I got the full picture. My lie about being on failed to convince my teacher and I had to join the last swimming session. I was still in the changing rooms just as *his girls* trouped in. I'd had a terrible time in the pool and I needed to recover. Avoiding the communal showers, I waited until the one single cubicle became free. There, I doused myself in fresh water to get rid of the chlorine stink and then grabbed my towel exactly as the Sync Club arrived. There wasn't a regulation costume in sight. Instead, they wore bikinis and halter necks. The talk was about where Southy placed his hands and how he sent them swooning.

They never noticed me hiding behind the shower curtain in my next to nothing. After they'd gone, I dressed, and had a look through the open doorway where a few of the bikini-clad girls pranced around the pool while others were making waves in the water. Southy was in the thick of it, mucking about and splashing with the rest of them. Only when he blew his whistle did he act like a proper teacher. The team watched in awe as he flexed his muscles and sprung out of the water to sit on the edge. Droplets glistened on his tanned skin. Swinging his head, he flicked hair away from his eyes and gave instructions to the stupid girls. Another blast on the whistle, and they were organised in pairs, ready to try out a new routine. Sliding back into the pool, Southy encouraged one of them to climb onto his shoulders – she didn't take much persuading – and all for the sake of showing a lift. It was horrible to see Southy's head scrunched between her thighs. The ghastly smile on his face made me sick.

Shaken back into the moment by a washing machine switching to a spin cycle, I sensed the manageress lurking. She fed coins into a slot and activated one of the dryers. There was a whine as the drum turned and a tinny clink as buttons and clasps collided. I had to get out. But how to leave the shop without Mr Simmons seeing me look my worst? The heat in the launderette and the pressure of not knowing what to do made me panic. Right then, an orange Maxi pulled up. At first, I didn't realise the driver actually knew Mr Simmons. Peering over, I recognised the baby-blue coat of the lady at the steering wheel, her hair swept into a tortoiseshell comb and the brick-coloured lipstick. It was Miss Grant. What on earth was she doing there? Then he opened the door and sat beside her in the passenger seat. It couldn't be true! Not Mr Simmons and Miss Grant going out.

12

Text from Stephanie to Beth

ok, c u l8r.

Although Stephanie had replied positively to Beth's text, it was a surprise to be banished from the kitchen. This was a consequence of letting her spare room to a chef. Beth explained that cooking regular recipes at work was fine but it wasn't any use for cake experimentation. What would the customers think if plagued by a whiff of something disastrous? Angel Cakes would be no more.

Settled in the lounge, Stephanie played back the interview with Frank Forsyth. The sound quality was okay and she thought a few phrases were great. *Little minx*, she'd have to include that. Talk about blaming the victim. Stephanie checked her watch. Early evening might be a good time to catch Janine. She needed to share an update now Mrs Russell was behind the project. The ringing was answered by an energetic hello.

'Have you got a minute to talk, Janine? It's Stephanie.'

'I'm just back from a run around the fields. Can you hang on? I need to get a glass of water.'

In Janine's absence, Stephanie prioritised developments in her mind.

'Fire away,' said Janine.

'I interviewed Mr Forsyth earlier. He was exactly the same, even if the tweed jacket had been replaced by a moth-eaten jumper.'

'Standards have fallen,' said Janine. 'I remember him bleating to the press: Carolyn was such a careful, cheerful, confident student, or words to that effect. He didn't know her at all.'

'He tried to be the voice of authority during the interview. I got some useful background material on the staff and a mention for the head boy. He couldn't be bothered to recall the name of the head girl, but then she never had much of a role.'

'Girls were always down the pecking order at Greensleeves. Things must've changed by now.'

'We're living in a different time although I'm not sure Mr Forsyth has caught up.' Stephanie refocused on the podcast. 'I need your thoughts to build up a bank of material. Have you got any time to meet? Or we can do a telephone recording if that's easier.'

'How about we go for it right now? I don't want to start overthinking.'

'Spontaneous responses always come across well. Give me a moment and I'll get the equipment ready.'

The talk ping-ponged and Stephanie didn't feel she was getting any fresh information. She knew the chronology of events as it had been the first big story she'd experienced at the *Post*. While planning the project, she'd gone through online reports to check for updates but there were few new details. The clipped conversation with Janine continued until finally they got onto the question of Carolyn's friendships. First there was quiet and the recording simply captured Janine's breathing. A little later, she spoke.

'After Carolyn's best friend went back to live in France, she was left hanging out with someone called Patricia. The girl came round to our house once and that was enough. I can't help feeling guilty when I think of Carolyn as lonely. It all makes sense now. Why she was so needy whenever I went back. I couldn't stand being home for long. Oxford gave me freedom – anonymity even – at least at the start. I lapped up the opportunity to be this new sort of me. And as my circle of friends grew, going home became an obligation rather than something I wanted to do. I used any excuse, from practising my language skills with native Spanish speakers to doing research. Mum didn't ask many questions and I'd reached the conclusion Belmont had nothing to offer... or at least that's how I felt then. I didn't admit as much to Carolyn. She would've seen it as a rejection of her as well as everything else. It wasn't...' Janine caught her breath. Just as Stephanie was about to ask another question, she continued. 'Getting Carolyn to see things a different way never worked. She was often moody and it became a little joke between me and Mum. She would storm off at the silliest thing. Her bedroom door slammed shut and there wasn't any way of coaxing her out. We made the best of it. Left her alone until she was in a better frame of mind or starving hungry and wanting food. Sometimes, I could jolly her along but it was hard work.'

'It sounds like Carolyn cut herself off.'

'You could say that. We laughed about her mood swings... we never took Carolyn's behaviour too seriously. It was something we thought she'd grow out of. You'll get a better idea of how Carolyn was in the weeks before her disappearance from Mum. She's happy to talk to you. I'll text the number of her care home. It's best you ring before visiting.'

'How is your mum?'

'Frail, but still very with it.'

'I'm looking forward to seeing her. Thanks. I've one more...'
Before Stephanie could finish the sentence, there was an
almighty crash, loud enough to vibrate through the front room.

'What's going on?' asked Janine.

'Shit! I think a car's reversed into the back of the house. I'd
better go. Thanks, Janine.'

In the kitchen, Beth stood holding a massive pot and stared at
the table extension that had dislodged and crashed onto the floor
along with two saucepan lids and a metal mixing bowl. It took a
second for Stephanie to register what had happened. Somehow
Beth had managed to break the table.

'I caught this before jam splattered all over the place.' Beth
tilted the pot to show the red gooey contents.

'That's one good thing.' Stephanie observed the state of her
kitchen. Every surface was cluttered with packets, all the pans
were off the rack, a haze of flour hung in the air. 'Help me pick
things up.'

Beth returned the pan to the hob. 'I'm sorry about this. I'll
sweep up the splinters.' Next minute, Beth was on her hands and
knees using the dustpan and brush. Stephanie watched for a
minute, then collected the scattered cutlery. Once that was done,
Stephanie sat, glad to have sturdy chair legs beneath her.

'I might've guessed,' said Beth. 'Those cast-iron pans are really
heavy.'

'The table's never been right.'

'I'll get you a new one.'

'Let's not worry about it now,' said Stephanie. 'Although I do
think using this place as an industrial kitchen isn't such a good
idea.'

Before Beth had a chance to reply, there was another almighty
thundering, this time someone banging on the front door.

'I'll go.' Stephanie darted along the passageway. Through the glazed panel she recognised the outline of Mrs Walker with her petite figure and trademark bouffant hairstyle. Stephanie opened the door just as her neighbour was ready to knock again. Mrs Walker tucked her hand away. 'I'm glad you're okay, Stephanie. I thought for a moment the kitchen cupboards had collapsed on top of you.'

'Nothing quite so dramatic. We've had a mishap with the table.'

'I brought my screwdriver in case anything needs tightening.' Mrs Walker removed a long-reach tool from her pocket and wielded it. Before Stephanie had a chance to respond, Mrs Walker brushed past her.

'Do come in and have a look.' Stephanie spoke to the door as she closed it. By the time she reached the kitchen, Mrs Walker was eyeballing Beth who was crouched on the floor.

'It was a silly accident.' Beth spoke rapidly, like she was on the defensive.

'I can see that,' said Mrs Walker.

As Beth stood, Stephanie positioned herself between the two of them. She had to do something to break up the tension in the room. 'Seriously, Mrs Walker. We'll clear up and then everything will be back to normal.'

'If you say so,' said Mrs Walker.

Stephanie wanted to mediate an understanding between Mrs Walker's digs and Beth's responses. There really wasn't any need to have a battleground in her kitchen or on either side of the dividing wall.

'We're both fine, aren't we, Beth?'

'Absolutely,' said Beth.

Mrs Walker sniffed.

'Shall I walk you to the door, Mrs Walker?'

'Don't worry, I'll see myself out.'

They listened to her footsteps along the corridor and as soon as the door latch clicked, Stephanie and Beth burst out laughing.

'Was she in the emergency services before retirement?' asked Beth.

'Nothing so grand.'

'Honestly, Stephanie, I'll make this up to you. Let me clear away and then I'll cook supper. Herby fish and rice do you? I've got some fillets in the freezer and a cupboard full of ingredients.'

'Now you're talking. Only *do not* introduce a rice cooker into this kitchen. I can hardly see the surfaces for all your gadgets.'

'Rice makers are not my thing.' Beth pulled a puzzled expression. 'Pilau takes special handling.'

'Okay.' Perhaps it was just Chinese people who went in for them. To divert attention from what could have been an insensitive remark, Stephanie peered at the rough edge where the table extension had once stuck out. She could smooth the surface using sandpaper and no one would be the wiser. It had never been a very reliable extension but the rest of the table was sound. 'There's no need to go to the expense of a replacement.'

'Are you sure?' asked Beth.

'Positive.'

The kitchen catastrophe made an excellent anecdote to share with Doug at Friday night drinks. He was on the road to inebriation when she arrived: quiet, nodding and smiling. Stephanie chattered away and the interjections from Doug made it clear she wasn't talking to herself. He even came up with a suggestion for someone to offer professional help with the podcast and she noted the name. When it came to discussing how to get the podcast aired, he became impassioned. Who would have guessed the old hospital radio becoming a community station called Belair was so inspiring? In truth, the idea was already on Stephanie's radar but surely someone could've chosen a better name. While Doug went off to the gents, Stephanie found that day's issue of the *Post* on a windowsill and searched for Belair on the entertainment page. Scheduling included a range of programmes from music and local reports to weather and travel. An hour-long feature called *County Magazine* profiled important events, local initiatives and people in the news. Carolyn's story might very well find a home during that slot.

Doug returned and finishing his pint, it looked like he was ready to leave.

'Do you know anyone at Belair?' she asked.

'Try Dr Shuttle.'

'Shuttle? Robert Shuttle?'

'That's him. He works in paediatrics and followed his interest in radio to become a trustee.'

'He has done well for himself.'

Doug pulled a quizzical expression. 'You know him?'

'He was the head boy at Greensleeves the year Carolyn went missing.'

Doug smiled. 'Cracking. I'll let him know you'll be in touch.'

13

APRIL 1979

The little desk in my room was purchased for the eleven-year-old me. I'd been crying buckets because I didn't want to leave Poplar Road Primary and it was meant to help me feel better about going to Greensleeves. The comprehensive was massive and frightening. All the kids from my school were split into different classes and I was on my own. I'd loved being in the top class at Poplar Road where it was safe and cosy and I wanted to stay there forever. Neither Mum nor Janine could convince me I'd make new friends and enjoy new subjects at so-called 'big school'. I was right and it didn't work out fine. That first half term I hung around with Janine at break. She was sympathetic at the beginning and some of her mates called me *sweet* but they soon got bored. Janine had too many important mock exams to worry about me. A bit later Floria arrived. I twigged her the time she came into school with her mum and dad. They were shown around by a secretary and looked into our art class. This was the one subject where I could relax. The tables were grouped rather than in rows, and after a little chat from the teacher at the start of the lesson, we collected our materials. We were experimenting with shade, trying out the softness of the different B pencils. As usual, I was the last to choose something for drawing. My still life involved a halved pear but others had grabbed a chunk of cabbage which was much more intricate. Anyway, we were told to get on with our work although I couldn't ignore the visitors gawking through the glass panel on the door. Their faces were pressed together and it made me feel like a caged animal. A minute or two later, the girl turned away and the rest followed. When they'd gone, the talk started. *What did that girl want? Who did she think she was?*

Only a week later on the Monday, Floria joined my class. She stood next to our form teacher and we spied the girl who said her name using a French flourish. Some boys at the back laughed at her accent and she shrank, peering out with big, scared eyes. As there was a spare place next to me, she sat and unpacked her satchel, not knowing we'd be moving to a different classroom when registration was over. I helped her return the bits and pieces to her bag and for a whole day she clung to me like a limpet. I loved every minute of being needed and it didn't take long for Floria to make her mark. We were best friends by the end of the week.

With my knees pressed under the desk, I stared out of the window. It was a good excuse for not actually getting on with my homework. There wasn't much to see except a handkerchief of garden grass and beside it a flower-bed where next-door's cat liked to piss. The washing line split the space in two and the trees at the end were a screen that stopped me nosing into the gardens on the next street. It wasn't much of a place. Holidaymakers headed straight for the coast, two stops away on the train.

Patricia had her sights on better things. Her family had booked a fortnight in Benidorm for when the exams were over. She'd already bought a new bikini and a bottle of Ambre Solaire, and she kept going on about her fear of flying. It was Patricia's way of getting one over me. I wish I'd had the chance to travel by plane instead of the car trip to Floria's house in France. The visit had been last summer yet it seemed a lifetime ago. I was happy to go abroad although it didn't ease the pain of Floria not coming back. Catching *Wish You Were Here* on telly was the nearest I got to another holiday. I'd tried persuading Mum to watch it with me but she couldn't stand that smug-faced Judith Chalmers. I'd had a plan if only she'd gone along with it. I'd use the moment to suggest me and Janine and Mum take a holiday in Italy. As Mum refused to watch the programme, I blurted the idea while we ate dinner. She burst into fits of laughter. I don't know what she found funny. We all deserved a little sun after the cold winter, but I wasn't able to convince her.

Opening my exercise book, I found the page where Mr Simmons had written to me. My fingers traced the words *super stuff, Carolyn.* This was evidence of the connection between us. Even Patricia had to admit it meant more than a star and a few ticks. For once, I was keen to sit in the front row, and I'd hang on to Mr Simmons' every word. He had the knack of explaining in a way I could understand. Thank God Forsyth's teaching was a thing of the past and although I had a soft spot for Mrs Hoskins, even I got fed up with the way she kept repeating herself. Each time the same words came out of her mouth only a little louder. The pity of it was, the higher the volume, the less likely anybody was willing to listen. Not me, of course, I was the little swot who kept trying to get the answers right. Take addition and carrying ten – what was that supposed to mean? I knew the rule, I'd heard it often enough, but why? All it took from Mr Simmons was a drawing with two columns on the blackboard, one for the units another for the tens. Bingo! I could see there wasn't enough space for two digits in one box. It was obvious really. Why had it been a mystery to me for so long? Mum would have called it *letting the penny drop.* In my case, it was a whole fifty pence of learning.

I couldn't keep my mind on maths all the time. That would've been expecting too much especially when I had *feelings* for Mr Simmons. The rest could go crazy over Southy and Gove. Mr

Simmons was mine and I was determined to keep it that way. I put the sighting of Miss Grant giving him a lift to the back of my mind, there was more important stuff to do including fending off the twins who were making moves. They thought it funny to drape themselves over his desk, trying and failing to look like Greek goddesses in their manky Greensleeves uniforms. I'd found out a bit about them from my mum who went to their house one time. She'd scoffed at the fact their kitchen wasn't modernised and still contained a bath. I happened to let word slip that the twins didn't wash and probably had scabies. After that, everyone gave them a wide berth and they stopped making a play for Mr Simmons.

Rumour had it, Mr Simmons' Christian name was Graham. Apparently, Forsyth had bellowed a greeting using it. (That man never talked in a normal voice.) I didn't much like the name Graham and besides, he was becoming my very own Sim. Once I'd seen off the twins, I had to keep Miss Grant's greasy fingers away. While ideas rippled through my mind, my face tingled and then my cheeks burnt. When I set my heart on something, or in this case someone, nothing was going to stop me.

14

2014

Megan Hart 11:26
Re: Podcast
To: Stephanie Brett
Hi Stephanie
Thanks for your email. I'd be delighted to
offer support for your podcast on the
disappearance of Carolyn Russell. Your instinct
to capture the views of residents is spot on.
Let's make a date to meet up and bring Doug
along. I'm sure his input will be useful.
All the best, Megan

Taking a mug of tea into the front room, Stephanie watched the sun make stripes on the carpet. Had it gone lunchtime already? Usually a gnawing hunger alerted her to regular mealtimes but she'd been so focused on research, she hadn't noticed. How strange it was to be working in isolation and enjoying the process. Rolling her shoulders released the tension that accumulated from her sedentary existence. It really was time she took some exercise and had a taste of the weather.

With an apple in her handbag, Stephanie stepped outside. It was pleasant to feel the sun warming her bones. She'd taken the precaution of changing into comfortable sandals and with her sunglasses perched on her nose, she was ready for a walk across town. This was another aspect of her research into Carolyn's homelife. The family had lived in a house amongst a cluster of streets behind the railway station. Although Stephanie travelled by train regularly, she'd never had friends living over that side of Belmont and even in her school days, she'd simply hung around with other kids from the estate. In a town of only thirty thousand people, it was strange that pockets of the community remained less familiar than others.

Stephanie walked using a steady pace. She wasn't one to dawdle and besides she needed to burn off a few calories. Beth's curries were delicious but soaked in ghee. It was a shock to realise how much went into the pan. An equivalent might involve eating a whole half pound of butter straight from the dish. And then there was always a cake for dessert. It was an odd meal, curry and cake, but a smidgeon of chocolate brownie finished off the dinner surprisingly well.

The neighbourhood Carolyn had lived in was known as The Grid thanks to the criss-cross of parallel streets comprising Victorian terraces. Most of the houses had modest front gardens that may once have boasted a flower-bed but were now mainly paved. Stephanie walked a few blocks noting the roads were named with a royal connection. Coronation Path led to Queen's Road which was joined by Prince of Wales Road. Stephanie had covered quite some ground before she arrived at the far end of King's Street to find Carolyn's old house. It was situated opposite the entrance to Crossways and Stephanie realised from an interest in feng shui, that the house wasn't well positioned for balance or harmony.

While the building was another turn-of-the-century home, it had an oddly naked feel. The appearance had changed from the house she'd visited for tea with Janine and her family. New occupants had left their mark with sandy-coloured plaster now covering the ground floor. Protruding at the front was a covered porch and the two front doors of the pair standing side by side. As a distinctly different building on the street, Stephanie wondered if this gave the owners a sense of superiority. The current residents had plantation blinds covering the front windows. Even using a fixed stare, it was impossible to see between the slats. Many things must have happened within those walls, but only Carolyn's disappearance had left its mark on the community. Stephanie imagined the family who lived there now. There were enough bedrooms for children and the roof showed a tell-tale Velux which was evidence of extra accommodation and possibly an en-suite bathroom. The neighbouring house flaunted solar panels attached to the south-facing elevation. Stephanie always thought the additions were equivalent to flashing a healthy bank balance at the world.

Beside Carolyn's house was an old fence that sparked memories. Paint chipped from the corrugated iron and mossy patches showed it had been there ages, although currently it separated the terraced housing from the gated community of new-build detached properties on the other side. In her mind's eye, she saw the wasteland before any houses existed. It had been the stomping ground for older pupils at Greensleeves. There, she and others had congregated after the exams during her last weeks at school.

In Belmont, the current school-leaving tradition meant every shirt became the page of an autograph book where scribbled messages and stick figures celebrated the end of an era. To desecrate school uniform would have been frowned upon by parents in Stephanie's day. Hand-me-downs were always needed by younger children or donations to the school second-hand uniform shop required. Instead, school leavers took to dumping exercise books in the brook but with her future uncertain, Stephanie hadn't joined the ceremonial disposal. She always thought she might need them again. As for Carolyn, four years later and the choices couldn't have been much different. What plans did Carolyn have?

Whoever lived on King's Street now, cars dotting both sides of the road indicated that only some residents were home. Parking restrictions flashed on signs regularly positioned along the pavement which prevented commuters from taking advantage of free on-street parking. They were exiled to roads further afield. Turning her head, Stephanie checked along Crossways and King's Street. Nobody was about on that sunny afternoon. She took the apple from her bag and bit into the green skin. As she crunched, she was reminded of the time she'd been told off by a neighbour for eating outside. She remembered shrugging, thinking *it's just an apple* but apparently the behaviour was evidence of *being common*. Unaware of the meaning, Stephanie wore an ashamed expression for all of five seconds and once the neighbour turned away, she carried on munching.

At home, her mother used a special fruit knife with a pearly handle. It was kept in a leather sheath to protect the blade. Stephanie wondered what had happened to it. During the house clearance, it must've got lost. She'd been too devastated by her mother's early passing from cervical cancer to focus on the small things although she kept the memories safe. How her mother was skilled at peeling an apple and keeping the skin twirled into a spiral. It was then the denuded fruit was cut into quarters and the core removed. Dear old Mum. For years, Stephanie thought her mum actually preferred eating skin to the apple. Little did she know how tight their finances were.

Continuing to the main road, Stephanie dithered on the street corner. There she was approached by an old woman wearing flaky face powder. 'Do you need some help, my dear?'

Stephanie smiled. 'I'm having a mooch about.'

'On holiday, are you?' The woman leaned on her walking stick. 'The roads round here used to get really clogged during the school breaks. Thank goodness for the bypass.'

Tell me about it, thought Stephanie. 'I live on the other side of town and came to reacquaint myself with this neighbourhood. Have you lived here long?'

'My husband bought our house in 1961. It cost a fortune back then. Fifteen hundred pounds, would you believe?'

'Prices have changed.'

'I wanted a modern house but he insisted older properties were better value so that's what we bought. There was a scullery and an outhouse at the beginning. My husband was clever with his hands and over the years we got all the mod cons, including an upstairs bathroom. Stan passed away ten years ago but I'm still going strong.'

'You certainly are,' said Stephanie. 'There must've been lots of changes over the years. I'm wondering, do you remember Carolyn Russell? She lived on King's Street and went missing in the seventies?'

The woman sighed. 'She was an attractive young lady. Goodness knows what happened. And to think of her poor mother.'

'You knew the family?'

'I was on chatting terms with Mrs Russell. Her girls were always polite.'

'That's interesting. I'm working on a project about Carolyn. Can I talk to you some more?'

'Well, my dear.' The woman looked down at her white Velcro-strapped sandals and pop socks. 'As long as I can sit down. Why don't you come round to my house tomorrow? I've nothing planned then.'

Beryl Smith lived at 26 Crossways. As Stephanie entered, a breeze whipped up the long hall and slammed the front door shut. Mrs Smith tutted and directed Stephanie further inside. Before turning into the front room, Stephanie glanced through the kitchen and into the garden. Herbaceous borders showed beside a neatly trimmed lawn and a path to the gate. A high fence acted as a screen providing a perfect sunspot. Regretting she hadn't been offered the chance to go into the garden, Stephanie was directed to sit in an armchair but avoided leaning against the antimacassar, clean as it was.

Tea was served in china cups and Stephanie carefully consumed a chocolate digestive, leaving only a crumb or two speckled on the plate. When everything was returned to the trolley, Mrs Smith settled in her chair and Stephanie unpacked the recording equipment. Mrs Smith stared at the microphone.

'The last time I heard my own voice was on a cassette player. It didn't sound like me at all.'

'The new technology is much more effective,' said Stephanie.

Mrs Smith continued to look perturbed.

'Once we get started, you'll forget all about being recorded.'

'I suppose you're right, my dear. What exactly do you want me to say?'

'Tell me what it was like living here around the time Carolyn disappeared.'

'Do you mean before or after she went?'

'Let's start with before.'

15

APRIL 1979

I got home from school to find a letter from Janine. It was addressed to Mum and according to her it was illegal to open other people's mail. Giving the envelope a squeeze, I thought it might release a secret. Some hopes! Janine didn't write to me much these days, not unless there was something she wanted me to do, like go out and buy Mum a special gift for Mother's Day. The money she'd sent was enough for a Marks and Sparks square scarf and the coins left over I kept for myself. It wasn't fair that I got a pittance for pocket money. There were lots of things that a girl needed and Mum and Janine should've known.

In my bedroom, I found the little compact of golden eye shadow Janine had left behind. Tough luck if she wanted it back. Taking the foam brush, I posed in front of the mirror and my eyelids flickered as I applied the powder. Two or three times I returned the brush to the compact for a good amount of colour. According to Patricia, mascara was needed to lengthen eyelashes and no amount of eye make-up was complete without this. Pity for me, the mascara I'd nicked from Mum's room was past its best and was probably the reason Mum hadn't kicked up a fuss about it going missing. She simply opened a new one she'd bought and I was left trying to add drops of water to the dried-up clogs for the chance of experimenting with a new look. Of course, I couldn't go anywhere dolled up – Mum would've had a fit – not to mention the secret of the purloined mascara would be out. No, this was an activity that took place in the privacy of my room.

Last month, Patricia plucked her eyebrows into thin lines and I wanted to do the same. Mum's tweezers lived in the medicine cabinet alongside her razor. I couldn't get the hang of them, but the razor was useful for getting rid of underarm hair. Janine left me a stock of sanitary pads so I didn't have the embarrassment of asking Mum. She used Tampax and I thought I'd try them sometime. I had my own spray-on deodorant that I kept in my bedroom. Mum made it clear she didn't approve when she was poking around with a duster and she sniffed out the aerosol. Really, it wasn't any of her business.

Patricia told me she had a load of lipstick testers because her mum was an Avon lady. She said she was going to bring them into school but hadn't bothered yet. It was okay for Patricia, she made extra pocket money delivering Avon orders. I told Mum and she said working for Avon wasn't terribly respectable: knocking on people's doors and selling stuff made the job no better than a travelling salesman. I had to stick up for my friend so I said it was more like being a milkman and everybody thanked them for their daily pint. Plus, generous mothers also paid for bottles of Corona lemonade to be delivered as part of their order. I wasn't lucky because Mum didn't agree. Then my mother came out with a classic. She said she couldn't see me as an Avon lady or a lady milkman. I suppose she had a point.

I went into the bathroom for a proper look at my stunning eyes – this was where Janine got ready for a night out. I batted my lashes and this confirmed I could compete with her any day. But for now, I filled the sink and washed the lot off. A wodge of toilet paper removed the last traces and I was back to being boring old Carolyn. I never did understand why my parents lumbered me with such a stupid name. Some of Janine's friends called her Jan, and I wished my name could be made fashionable. There I was, stuck with three syllables that didn't exactly roll off the tongue.

Going downstairs, I gave Janine's letter another stare. She'd written the address in purple biro and I wished I was allowed to use the same at school. Instead, I had a cartridge pen. Although it was an improvement on lugging a bottle of ink around in my bag, it wasn't much better. Teachers at Greensleeves were trapped in Victorian times. Would Belmont ever get with it? I turned Janine's envelope over and noticed the embossed stamp said Basildon Bond. Quality stationery no less. I suspected Mum would be impressed even if it didn't do anything for me. My life was much better back in the day when me and Janine spent evenings in her room listening to Radio Luxembourg. It was never the same if I tuned in on my own.

There was still an hour before Mum came home. That left plenty of time for a snoop around her room. I wasn't being nosy, just interested. Rather than poking about her drawers, I was drawn to the large sash window at the front of the house. When I pressed my face against the glass, I enjoyed the coolness on my cheek. By crossing my eyes, I watched my breath make clouds on the pane. When I got bored with messing about, I looked to the left and could see above the fence and into the wasteland. I'd legged it over there once or twice, and I never forgot the time Patricia got stranded on the wrong side and had to walk the long way round to the gate. I laughed my head off but when we eventually met again, she had the hump. Patricia told me to put a sock in it and said she couldn't understand what was so funny. (She never got my sense of humour.) In the end, I had to say sorry because I didn't want to annoy Patricia. She was the only one at school who spent any time with me. I did a whole load of sucking up and then she said I was forgiven.

Turning the other way, there was a view up to the main street where I could see a single-decker bus bumbling into town. The road opposite our house was empty. No one of much importance lived on Crossways. As I was about to go and watch *Magpie* on TV, I noticed a bloke walking along the pavement. I couldn't help being a curtain twitcher and as he got further into my line of vision, I nearly fell right over from shock. There was Sim! He stopped in front of the house on Crossways where the alley ran beside it. The next thing I saw was his arm going up to the lock. The door swung open and he went in. Literally, the real him. Living near my road. That did it, I definitely had some news for Patricia in the morning.

16

2014

Bank statement, Ms Stephanie Brett
Arranged overdraft: £750

Beth arrived home carrying a presentation box of cakes. The star-spangled yellow-printed cardboard held the promise of something special. She abandoned it on the kitchen table where Stephanie worked and then nipped upstairs to use the loo. Stephanie peered through the clear plastic sheet. An array of cupcakes with fancy swirls of pink and chocolate frosting nestled in their silver cases. Stephanie could almost taste the glistening sugary tops but she knew these were unlikely to be for the two of them to share. Whenever Beth brought back after-dinner treats they usually came in a brown paper sandwich bag.

Drumming on the staircase announced Beth's return and she hummed as she looked through the unopened letters she'd brought home from the café. Taking a knife from the drawer, she split the envelopes and then fell silent as she read the first.

'Is everything okay?'

'The business rates for Angel Cakes are shockingly high.'

Shit, Stephanie hoped Beth wasn't having money worries too. The last thing she wanted was for Beth to go off and find cheaper accommodation elsewhere. Stephanie had only just got used to having her around. Beth worked her way through the other letters and there were no further comments.

'Can I take it all's well?' asked Stephanie.

'My new assistant's working out. She has this knack of being able to read the room, like she instinctively knows when customers are ready for the bill or when they want to order something else.'

The change of subject obviously meant things weren't too bad in the financial department. Stephanie only wished the same was true for her. Releasing a sigh, she rid herself of further thoughts about money and her mind reset to the cupcakes positioned beside her. 'Who are these for?'

'A prepaid customer didn't collect them so I thought they'd do for Mrs Walker.'

'Oh!' This was a surprise, a peace offering, perhaps.

'We're never going to be besties but we might as well try and get along.'

'Good idea.' Stephanie was relieved at the gesture. It was difficult to navigate a path between the two of them.

'When I parked the van yesterday, I saw her walking to the shop using a stick.'

'That's strange. She's usually steady on her feet.'

'Perhaps she's had a fall,' said Beth.

'I'm surprised she didn't say anything.' Stephanie noted a feeling of concern. Whenever there were health issues, Mrs Walker often confided in Stephanie. She was pleased to return the favour following the many good turns Mrs Walker had done.

'We can drop the cupcakes round together if you want to check on her,' said Beth.

'Better still, let's invite her here.' It would be one way to address the tension between Beth and Mrs Walker. Stephanie didn't like to think that neighbourly relationships had deteriorated. 'She's probably had her dinner. Perhaps a cupcake could be a dessert.'

Beth's frown showed her dislike of the idea.

'Come on, Beth, she's an old woman with outdated attitudes but she's not all bad.'

Five minutes later and with Beth left to arrange the best tea set, Stephanie accompanied Mrs Walker back to their place. Beth had been right about Mrs Walker's need to use a stick. She'd been diagnosed with cellulitis in her left leg which was painful but she was a trooper and wanted a change of scene. Once Mrs Walker was settled at the kitchen table, Beth poured the tea, rather too hurriedly in Stephanie's opinion.

'Mrs Walker went to the doctor for antibiotics,' said Stephanie.

'Yes, I finally managed to get an appointment this morning.'

'It's rotten when you're ill.' Beth opened the cake box and showed the contents. 'I thought one of these might make you feel better.'

'How kind,' said Mrs Walker. 'What are they?'

'The pink ones are raspberry cupcakes and the others are chocolate.'

'They're so big,' said Mrs Walker. 'But anything raspberry is very tempting.'

'I think you'll find these are standard size.' Beth put a raspberry cake on a plate and handed it over.

Stephanie wished the two of them would get along. Oh well, at least there was cake. 'I'll have the same.'

Beth passed around some napkins and the three peeled away the paper casing. While Beth and Stephanie lifted theirs for a bite, Mrs Walker stared at her plate. Stephanie proceeded to take a mouthful regardless. She couldn't stand holding a delicious cake and resist enjoying the flavour. She loved the hint of vanilla in the sponge and the soaring sweetness of the topping. Honestly, she was a sucker for cake any time of day or night. When Stephanie returned to her senses, she realised Mrs Walker's cupcake was untouched. 'Is something wrong?'

'It looks too beautiful to eat,' said Mrs Walker. 'The icing sits so neatly on top.'

Beth had a smear of frosting on her top lip which she wiped away with her napkin. 'It's easy to do with a piping bag.'

'I used to have a gadget for buttercream, but my cakes never came out nearly so good.'

Mrs Walker turned the plate in a circle and examined the cupcake from every angle. Beth's expression showed exasperation and Stephanie wondered if there was more to Mrs Walker's delay in eating. 'Would you like a cake fork, Mrs Walker?'

'I don't want to be a bother.'

'It's no trouble,' said Stephanie. 'There's one in a canteen where the china lives.'

'I'll get it.' Beth poked through the cupboards and then presented the required item.

'I've never had much of a sweet tooth.' Mrs Walker deconstructed the cupcake, scraping away much of the frosting and gouging the sponge underneath. 'This looks lovely and light.'

'Glad to hear it.' Beth angled her face away from Mrs Walker and gave an eye-roll.

Things weren't going according to plan but Stephanie was determined to make the best of it. Fortunately, Beth managed to join the conversation until seventeen minutes later when Mrs Walker announced it was time to go home. A palpable sense of relief settled and Stephanie offered to return with Mrs Walker to make sure she got back safely. The chat as they walked comprised of complaints about the NHS. Stephanie was glad Mrs Walker hadn't let rip within earshot of Beth, especially her disgust at the foreign locum who kept calling her Daphne when she hadn't given permission for use of her Christian name. Mrs Walker would have words when her regular doctor was back at the practice. Also, she couldn't understand what the locum was doing in Belmont when he was probably needed in his own country. Didn't Stephanie agree? Clearly, there was an argument about robbing developing countries of their homegrown talent by overseas recruitment. Where was the locum actually from? Spain, it turned out. Oh dear, Stephanie didn't have the will to explain that free movement of labour was an entitlement in the EU.

17

APRIL 1979

Janine's letter had apparently persuaded Mum to be a bit more lenient with me. (I never got to read the actual words but I was pleased at the result.) It meant Mum agreed Patricia could come round after school on condition we did maths revision. Revision my foot. Me and Patricia had a plan to find out more about Mr Simmons. Her chin literally hit the floor as I shared the news about our maths teacher living near me. I swore her to secrecy because I didn't want others to know.

Mum said we could have pizzas as a treat for our tea. She'd bought a frozen pack from Sainsbury's. There was one each for me and Patricia. I would've preferred cooking Vesta chow mein but even after countless cookery lessons, Mum wasn't willing to let me loose with a pan of hot fat. It was a pity. Watching the crispy noodles frizzle into the shape of question marks was as much fun as eating them. Instead, we would shove pizzas into the oven once our mission was over.

We had to be there and ready before Sim arrived home. I knew he sometimes took a lift from Miss Grant. At first, I'd been suspicious about the two of them. I mean, he was single and quite a catch. When Miss Grant came into school flashing a diamond solitaire, I nearly died thinking she was engaged to my Sim. If a heart can crumble, it was what happened to mine although it only lasted a minute until a wave of hatred surged. Literally. I had to control an impulse to slap her. The way she acted! Waggling her finger to make the ring sparkle in the light. I never could bear a show-off. Obviously, everyone in our form noticed and one of the cheeky boys whistled. It was then she made an official announcement about being engaged. I gagged as voices around me swirled. A mingle of congratulations and speculation over who the lucky man was. Miss Grant called above the ruckus and announced she was to marry a member of the police force and we wouldn't be getting rid of her too soon, the wedding was planned for the following year. Relief swelled but it took five minutes for my heart to stop banging and the blood bolting through my veins to ease. I disguised what was happening by hanging my head and I let my hair cover my face. Calmness brought with it the realisation I didn't just have feelings for Sim. I was in love.

In my bedroom, me and Patricia planned our encounter. It had to be casual, like we were walking down the road and bumping into Mr Simmons was a sheer accident. We needed perfect timing, as if fate had brought us together.

'The problem might be Blasted Mrs Smith,' I said.

'Who's she?'

'The nosy neighbour living opposite.' Mum had fallen out with her years ago and that's how she got the nickname. Blasted Mrs Smith couldn't keep her trap shut when it came to gossiping. She especially liked to talk about *our misfortune*, as Mum put it.

'We've all got nosy neighbours.'

Phew, thank God Patricia didn't want to know more. It would be all too easy for her to wheedle out the truth behind the gossip. I squinted to block out the blur of memory.

'You'll get stuck with that chinky face if the wind changes.'

I turned my expression into a smile.

Dressing in my denim jeans, I decided my daisy-embroidered top would go well with them. Patricia said it wasn't fair for me to get all dressed up because she only had her school uniform. To make her feel better, I put my school skirt back on and lent her one of my T-shirts. It was fun wearing the same sort of clothes. At last I thought of her as a good friend although not a best friend. Not yet. She couldn't replace Floria in a hurry.

After we'd finished dressing, Patricia tried the seat at my desk and looked over the pens and pencils in a holder flashing glitter on the rim.

She fingered the pot. 'Very posh.'

'It isn't,' I said. 'Can't you see it's an old tin can? Baked beans, I think. My sister made it.'

'I remember her, back when we first went to Greensleeves. You used to go off and spend break with the fourth-years. I was dead jealous.'

'I didn't have any friends in my class.'

'Now you're on your own again because Floria's left.'

'Don't rub it in. I feel like such a reject.'

'Why don't you chum up with the other big brainers in 5G?'

I didn't like to admit I was never included. No one wanted me to elbow into their group. 'We're not all clever.'

'No, but you're all big-heads.'

Did she think I was a big-head too? It was best to keep quiet. Patricia smiled from under her frizzy mop of hair. Then, she picked up the hand mirror I kept on the window ledge and stared at her reflection. 'I forgot to bring my make-up bag. You could've tried some of my Avon testers.'

'How about using my golden eye shadow?' I regretted the offer immediately. I didn't want Patricia ruining it.

'Give us a look.'

'Only if you're careful.' I loved the little compact. Turning to the drawer where my precious things were hidden, I searched amongst my nighties and underwear.

'Bloody hell!' Patricia was behind me. Before I could slam the drawer shut, she hooked the strap of my clean bra over her little finger and was swinging it around like a striptease dancer. I scrambled to catch it. She hooted with laughter and turned it faster. Eventually I caught the end and a tug of war began.

'Stop!' I didn't want my bra stretching out of shape.

Patricia dropped her hand. 'Don't be such a cry-baby.'

I examined the strap. Even before Patricia grabbed it, the elastic threads had begun to ping and another few had broken thanks to her little joke.

'You'll have to get a new one when your boobs develop.'

'Fat chance.' I was lumbered with a size 32A chest for the rest of my life.

'There's time.'

Although I hated the way Patricia had taken the piss out of my bra, at least she'd admired the eye shadow. Out we went, both with the glint of gold on our eyelids. We did our best catwalk moves as we walked along his side of the street. I checked for Blasted Mrs Smith gawking but thank God there wasn't any sign of her. Of course, we didn't have a clue whether Sim was on his way home or even if he'd made it back before us. Once we were beside his house, we couldn't see inside because the curtains were drawn.

'Shall we have a look round the back?' Patricia pointed to where the track joined the pavement. 'Does the alley go all the way?'

'And onto the wasteland.'

The garden fence was six foot high and stopped us peering over but through the trellis I could see the roof of a shed and a tree. At the very end there was a back gate and I dared Patricia to try the handle. She flicked the thumb latch up and down but the gate was bolted. At the sound of a window opening, we glanced up and saw his neighbour shaking a mat in the fresh air.

'Scarper!' shouted Patricia.

We ran to the road and leaned against the brick wall at the front of his house until we got our breath.

'Do you think he's inside?' I asked.

'For all we know he could be in there having a bath.'

The thought of Sim naked on the other side of the wall launched me into hysterics.

'Get a grip.' Patricia slapped me on the back and I almost fell over. I wanted to return the thump but the thought of a full-scale fight put me off. I stood there staring at his front door. All of a sudden it juddered and I realised it was about to open. At least we had a moment's warning. Me and Patricia ducked behind a parked car. Although I recognised Sim's voice, I couldn't make out who he was speaking to. The talk bumbled on about arrangements for another meeting. Oh no! Who was he seeing?

'I'm going to take a look,' whispered Patricia.

Grabbing her arm, I held Patricia back. I didn't want her showing us up. Sim was bound to see her, and as soon as the thought entered my head, Patricia collapsed against me. She panted her head off and nearly made me tumble over. The next thing we heard was the door slamming. We were in a state of silence until one of us dared move. Patricia stood up first, looked both ways and declared the coast was clear. That was when I joined her and spotted the boy in grammar-school uniform heading for the main street.

'That boy's just left his house,' I said. 'What do you think's going on?'

Patricia stood on tiptoes to catch a glimpse of him. 'There's only one way to find out.'

18

2014

Note stuffed through Stephanie's letterbox:

DEAR STEPHANIE,
PLEASE ASK YOUR FRIEND BETH TO STOP PARKING HER VAN IN
FRONT OF MY BAY WINDOW. THAT THING IS BIG ENOUGH TO BLOCK
OUT LIGHT AND AS FOR THE LOGO. I DON'T BLAME HER OF COURSE.
SHE'S NOT FROM AROUND HERE SO SHE DOESN'T KNOW THE
ETIQUETTE.
THANK YOU,
MRS WALKER

Stephanie recognised Robert Shuttle the moment he walked into the pub. Her recent research had unearthed footage of him from years back on a regional TV programme and his face hadn't changed much from the sixteen-year-old. He'd stood shoulder to shoulder with Frank Forsyth while the deputy spluttered about Carolyn's disappearance. Robert had also been in the reconstruction – amongst a mêlée of fifth-year students in front of the school. It created an impression of Carolyn's isolation as she walked out of the gates and headed along Greensleeves Lane to who knew where.

Robert approached the bar and Stephanie waved to catch his attention. He smiled and strolled over to the table she'd taken in the corner. He was much broader in the chest than the schoolboy Robert, and when he offered his hand, his grip was firm.

Stephanie declined a second glass of Pinot but while Robert was at the bar, she took intermittent glances at him. On her pad, she used shorthand to jot her first impressions: tall, confident, floppy hair. Looking down, she noted his taste in two-tone boat shoes.

Robert returned carrying a pint of ale and nodded his head towards the garden. 'Shall we sit outside?'

'If you like.' Stephanie gathered her things and followed him through the double doors. A burst of honeysuckle scented the air and she realised it was a good idea. The late sun gave a peachy glaze to the pretty garden, where clumps of cornflowers attracted bees. Wooden furniture was organised in sociable groups on a paved patio and they took seats near the lawn. Stephanie laid her drink and notebook on the table. She enjoyed the sensation of her silky jade shirtdress sliding over her bare legs. While she waited for Robert to get comfortable, Stephanie admired her slingback sandals on their first outing. If it hadn't been for Beth encouraging her to shop online, Stephanie would never have indulged in such a purchase and blown her budget. She hoped the shiny buckles did as Beth suggested and made her ankles appear slender.

'You really do mean business,' said Robert.

Stephanie became stiff while she wondered what the hell he meant. It was then he gestured towards her pad and she understood. Lowering her shoulders, she began to relax. 'Thank you for helping with the podcast.'

'My pleasure' he said. 'And it's great to see you again.'

Again? Stephanie didn't think they'd met before. 'You were a first year when I was at Greensleeves.'

'You were a prefect.'

'No.' There was an unwritten rule that only students who had prospects were given responsibilities and Stephanie didn't qualify as a girl from the estate. Then she realised he was referring to her job serving staff lunches on a rota. She got to push an unwieldy trolley of plates mounted with stainless-steel covers to keep the food warm. 'I helped occasionally… and my role never had any official standing.'

'So, I did bump into you.'

'Did you?'

'We collided the day I was hurtling down the main corridor. A food cover went spinning along like a hubcap but I managed to rescue it before the thing bashed into Mr Forsyth's door.'

'And all was well?' Stephanie had no recollection of the event and she wondered if he was teasing.

'Yeah.' He took a swig of beer and Stephanie watched his Adam's apple slide as he swallowed.

'It sounds like the sort of thing that might happen.' She was so out of touch. Could he possibly be flirting? Of course not! Robert was only being friendly. 'I'll take a few notes now and do a recording another time. How does that sound?'

'Fine,' he said.

Before she got down to the serious questions, she wanted to know Robert better. It turned out he had unexpectedly failed the eleven-plus and found it difficult to settle into Greensleeves especially as his older grammar-school brothers took the piss and his mum sighed in disappointment whenever they referred to him using the nickname Hen's Boy (as in short for compreHENsive). Stephanie warmed to Robert and his openness. She wondered, did his poor primary report give him the boot up the backside required to become a medical doctor? Actually, it did. Stephanie was charmed. Robert was easy to talk to, had a sense of humour and seemed a totally agreeable person to spend time with. But hold on a minute. Stephanie checked herself. There was work to be done. It was time she gave proper attention to the questions she'd prepared and Robert's replies. Although he was in the same year as Carolyn, he hadn't known her before she went missing. The truth was, his O-level options were in the sciences and she was the arty type.

'She would have known your name. Head boy and all,' said Stephanie.

'Honestly, I didn't have much to do with girls. Call me a late developer.' Robert smiled and around his bovine eyes, the lines crinkled. 'Besides, if a girl had a problem, she'd talk to Sandra Abbotts.'

Stephanie frowned. The name didn't ring a bell.

'Head girl,' he said.

'Oh yes. Your understudy, I believe.' Stephanie scribbled the name.

'You're not wrong.' He took another swallow from his pint. 'There was nothing I could do about the way she got treated. No matter how Sandra tried to make a mark, she always struggled. There was a long history of treating head girls less favourably at Greensleeves.'

'Not only head girls,' said Stephanie. 'Any girl.'

'Are you giving me a hard time?'

'I could get furious,' said Stephanie. 'I hated the way they pretended to give equal status, you know – head boy and head girl – then completely undermined the girl's role.'

'It was the culture of the school,' said Robert. 'I'm not sure it was any different at the grammar school. Maybe worse.'

'How could it be worse? At Greensleeves, girls with potential were overlooked and those without it, simply ridiculed.'

'Okay.' Robert showed his palms as if in surrender. 'There was inequality, but I didn't know what to do about it. Besides, I was probably too full of myself.'

'Your honesty's refreshing.'

'There's a lot I have to regret about those days. Chauvinism was rife amongst the male teachers and it filtered down to us students. You must have been aware.'

'Of course. It would've been easy to end up a shop girl destined for early marriage. I praise the day I made it to sixth form where at least the expectations were a little higher. After I got the trainee offer from the *Post*, there was no looking back.'

'You were well out of it.' Robert studied his fingers and the neatly clipped nails. 'Girls in the bottom sets didn't stand a chance. Back then it was usual to turn a blind eye.'

'Exactly!' Stephanie had her pencil poised. 'From your point of view, what was really happening?'

'I'm not saying every teacher, just some of them.'

'Come on, Robert.'

'You remember the two PE teachers, Gove and Southy?'

'How could I forget! Talk about smarm.'

'There's an accurate description,' said Robert.

'I was always relieved their names never ended up on my timetable. I know half the girls in school had a crush on them, but really. They were absolutely awful.'

'Yeah, you could always tell who was the latest teacher's pet.'

'The one getting her shoulders massaged – obviously for therapeutic reasons,' said Stephanie.

'Usually because she'd fallen over and hurt her knee.'

Stephanie laughed. 'They were so transparent.'

'You know, Stephanie, they didn't only prey on girls in lessons.'

'Hang on a minute, what are you saying?'

'I saw them in action at the pub.'

'When was this?'

'Back in the fifth year.'

'What! You? An underage drinker.'

'Weren't we all?'

'Tut-tut, head boy.'

'Half a shandy at best and strictly after cricket matches. My dad was captain of the village team and it was tradition to invite the opposition for a pint. Usually, we grabbed one of the picnic benches in the garden and congregated around there. One time it was raining, and the team were stuck in a corner of the pub on a Saturday night. The bowler, he was my dad's mate, asked me to get some fags from the vending machine. Said it would be easy for a skinny rake like me to push through the crowds. Biddable as ever, that's what I did. It was on my way back, I spotted them. Gove and Southy leering over these two girls. When I think about it now, it's shocking what they got up to.'

'Shit, I should get this on tape.'

'I'll go over it again for the recording.'

A thrill zipped through her bones – they were really going to meet again. Honestly, she was being ridiculous about him. She pressed her pencil to her notepad and tried to concentrate.

'If you give me the information now, I can work up some questions for the interview.'

'No problem... and I haven't got to the interesting bit yet.'

'Go on.' She smiled.

'The two girls were in my year. I knew them from catching the school bus but we never really talked. They were with Gove and Southy, each snuggled up to a teacher. And there was another man. He was sitting on a stool at the end of the table. I had to push past him to get to the gents.'

'Another teacher?'

'Yes. I mean he wasn't doing much. Southy was slobbering over the blonde girl and the other one had her head resting on Gove's shoulder. I could see his hand halfway up her skirt. I think she was too far gone to notice. It looked like they'd been drinking cider from the empty glasses lined up on the table.'

'Bloody hell. They'd be in loads of trouble if they tried that today.'

'I saw them and froze. Gove recognised me straight away. He lifted his glass and said "Cheers".'

'Good grief,' said Stephanie.

'I wasn't sure what to do, so I did nothing. From what I could tell, most of the teachers already knew about their behaviour. That sort of thing was tolerated. According to Mr Forsyth, any girl turned sixteen could carry on like a little slut. His words not mine.'

'Hmm, stands to reason. What about the other man?'

'It was Graham Simmons. I wasn't sure at the time – he had his back to me – but the more I think about it, the more certain I am. Gove and Southy must've been inducting him into their club of misbehaviour.'

'This is dynamite, Robert. It adds substance to the rumours of Simmons' involvement in Carolyn's disappearance.'

'I thought you'd be interested.'

'Did you tell the police?'

'No. At the time, I didn't think it was important.'

Robert drove Stephanie home in his soft-top Mini. She was surprised a man of Robert's height could sit upright in such a tiny car. The vehicle was something of a Tardis. He offered to put the roof down and they sped around the lanes, wind blowing Stephanie's hair so wildly, she couldn't resist laughing.

'I had a Mini Traveller as my first car,' he said. 'It sprung leaks and mushrooms grew on the wooden trim.'

'Carolyn's mum worked at the driving school. Did you take lessons there?'

'No, my dad taught me. We spent hours on the old airstrip with Dad trying not to show his bad driving habits and me trying not to notice. Then, I inherited the car from an ancient aunt who had the keys taken off her before she went into a home. It did nothing for my image. These days I'm rather pleased to have a Mini.'

Robert turned and gave Stephanie a crooked smile. She loved

the way his words were accompanied by expressions. It made the conversation lively and spontaneous. As she sat in the passenger seat, she was flooded by a sensation of ease. There was something very personable about Robert Shuttle.

When they drove into Stephanie's road, Beth was getting out of her little van parked outside the front door. At least that would stop Mrs Walker from moaning. Stephanie didn't want to receive another letter of complaint. Further along, Robert spotted a space and demonstrating his skill at parallel parking, he performed a neat manoeuvre. Stephanie unclipped her seat belt while her mind raced. What was she supposed to do now? It hadn't been a date but she wanted to invite him in for coffee. Or would that be presumptuous? The next thing she knew, Beth tapped at the window.

Stephanie was relieved at the interruption. 'Beth rents my spare room,' she explained. 'Would you like to meet her?'

The three of them stood together as the sun sank behind the church at the end of the road. While Beth and Robert chatted, Stephanie imagined the silhouette of the spire stirring the clouds into raspberry sorbet. It was rather mesmerising, but she couldn't waste time observing the sky with Beth and Robert getting on rather too well. Concentrating on their conversation, she noticed Beth showing off an antique cake slice she'd bought in the market. There was nothing to worry about.

'It was only a quid,' said Beth. 'I'll give it a plunge in silver dip and have it sparkling.'

'You've an eye for a bargain,' said Robert.

Hang on a minute, thought Stephanie.

'I'll take it into the café. I'm thinking of adding a proper afternoon tea to the menu.'

'There's nothing I like more than a cucumber sandwich,' said Robert.

'Enough of that.' Stephanie was determined to stop the chat

getting too friendly. 'Your TV programme's on in a minute, isn't it, Beth?'

Beth glanced at her watch. 'Yeah. I'd better get inside. It was nice to meet you, Robert.'

'I need to get going too.' Stephanie wanted to remove herself from the situation as quickly as possible. She should've realised Robert charmed everyone. While Beth pulled out her key to open the front door, Stephanie gave him a tight smile. 'I'll be in touch about the recording, Robert.'

'Fine,' he said. 'I'm happy to help.'

'Great.' She whizzed up the path and was inside before there was a chance to say goodbye. What a fool she'd been.

19

APRIL 1979

I was starving by the time I got home from school. The one thing I wanted to eat was a Club biscuit. It was my fourth day of dieting but trying to lose weight wasn't easy. Ripping the silver foil, I stuffed the end into my mouth. The sweetness of the orangey milk chocolate and the crunch of biscuit lasted only a few chews. Before I knew it, I'd gobbled the whole bar. I had to stash the wrapper in the dustbin outside or risk Mum seeing it and giving me the Spanish Inquisition over my eating habits. It was my ambition to be shapely for Sim but I hadn't bargained on hunger pains. Would nothing relieve them? The empty belly syndrome was worse than a period, and because it was self-inflicted, the ache was definitely stronger.

The whole horrible business with Patricia had put me off my lunch, and the Ryvitas I'd prepared before school got tipped into the bin along with my low-fat yoghurt. I took a couple of munches from my apple before I bit my lip. That was the last straw. Bloody Patricia. I could've chewed her up and spat her out. I mean, why did she break a promise? She obviously didn't care and that left me seething. Patricia said she'd keep the news to herself and there she was blabbing about Mr Simmons to a whole group of girls gathered around her like a giant rubber ring. I could've decked the lot of them. It was precisely none of their business where he lived. As for Patricia. Well. Anger surged like hot lava through my veins – I might've been destined for a heart attack. It would serve every one of them right if I keeled over and died. The disloyalty of it all.

Dragging myself to bed, I needed a lie down. It wasn't laziness – I did actually feel ill. I stared at the ceiling rose and tried to calm my heart. I suppose it wasn't actually Patricia's fault if she really didn't understand the measure of my feelings for Sim. Some stupid girls had infatuations, like the ones who drooled over Southy and Gove. My love for Sim was pure. As I closed my eyes, I used an imaginary paintbrush to create a watercolour image of his face. Long straight lashes framing those hazel eyes, lips that were bowed and soft. At last, I became calm but no sooner had my world been filled with the light that was Sim, than the front door slammed. Mum was home from work. Now the real task of the day was here. I was on a mission.

Going downstairs in my slippers, I didn't want my clodhopper school shoes announcing my approach. It would be better to catch Mum off-guard, while she was busy doing stuff. An eyeball-to-eyeball discussion might not give the desired result. Determination to get my way made me stiff and turning my neck almost produced a creak. I went into the kitchen and saw Mum's bright beaded shopping bag on the worktop. The tins she'd already unpacked were lined up on the surface. When she turned back from placing what looked like a packet of cheese in the refrigerator, she glanced over.

'Hiya.' I used my best sing-song voice.

'What are you doing lurking there?'

In true fashion, this was Mum's standard greeting. 'I'm not lurking – just wondered if you need a hand unpacking.'

'It's nearly done.'

Great timing! I reached over to the tins and recognised one

was the right shape for pineapple rings and the other halved apricots. I twirled the rest to read the labels. There was a mixture of baked beans and spaghetti hoops. Neither were my favourite for weekend lunches but Mum enjoyed anything on toast. Quick and easy was her motto.

'Would you like a cup of tea?' I asked.

'Now you're talking.' Mum tucked the tins into the corner cupboard and raised the roll-up top of the bread bin. 'I don't know what to do with this loaf now you've started eating Ryvita.'

'Sorry for the inconvenience.' I filled the kettle and set it onto the stove. Pressing the knob, I hoped that for once the pilot light would work, but the tick, tick, ticking went on for ages and no flame appeared. Mum grabbed the candle lighter from its hook and shoved it in my direction. 'Use this.'

Once the kettle was on, I turned to Mum. From her frown, I reckoned she'd had a bad day. It might not be the best time to share my plan. But the situation was urgent and swallowing the words I'd practised seemed worse than actually saying them.

'Muuum.' The extended vowel was such a giveaway. 'What I mean is, Mum.'

'Something on your mind, Carolyn?'

'Do you remember what Janine said about getting extra help for maths?'

'Yes.' Mum gave a snort. 'I seem to recall she was shot down in flames.'

'Well, I've given it a bit of thought and actually, it's a good idea.'

'That's all very well, Carolyn. But have you thought of the expense?'

Aha, now my preparation would come in handy. 'I have.'

Mum folded her arms making her cleavage show above her V-neck blouse. It wasn't fair that Janine inherited Mum's body shape leaving me with next to nothing. I fixed my mind and concentrated.

'Remember how you've promised to buy me driving lessons after I turn seventeen?' It had been my ambition to pass the test first time but now I had other priorities.

'What's that got to do with anything?'

'I thought you could pay for some extra maths instead. It honestly doesn't cost that much.' It was worth the sacrifice to get close to Mr Simmons.

'How would you know?'

I wasn't about to admit what had happened. It was all Patricia's doing anyway. We followed the grammar-school boy to the bus stop and pretended we were waiting in the queue. As there was no one around, Patricia pounced on him (not literally on top of him) but she fired questions and got closer and closer until he was backed up against the shelter. That's when the truth came out. He was having maths tutoring each week from Mr Simmons. Apparently, there'd been a small advert in the *Post* and his mum had arranged everything. It was okay for some. And only a fiver for a whole hour with Mr Simmons. Bargain.

'One of the grammar-school boys was telling his friend about it. Says his work's come on a treat. I'd just need enough help to get that grade-one CSE. And it doesn't cost any more than a driving lesson.'

'You forget, Carolyn. As an employee of the firm, I receive a discount. Besides, I won't hear of you giving up your ambition to drive my car.'

The revelation was like a punch to the stomach. My idea had been scuppered. I was about to begin pleading when the telephone rang. Mum read the time on the clock.

'It's gone six. That must be Janine.'

She rushed to the telephone table and I was left dangling.

20

2014

Ridgeway Care Home brochure:
Have your caring needs met in homely
surroundings.

It was going to take an hour to reach Mrs Russell owing to a
massive detour around the Winterborne hills. Although
Stephanie kept a paperback in her bag for long journeys, she
frequently preferred looking out the bus window. She never tired
of seeing fields aglow in shimmering yellow rapeseed and trees
on the ridges, puffed with leaves like candyfloss on a stick.
Sinking down into the valleys, there were sheep, recently
sheared, showing their ribs and gathered in the shade. When her
mobile vibrated, she plucked the phone from her pocket and read
the contact number. Frank Forsyth was calling. What did he
want? She answered using her telephone voice. 'Good morning,
Stephanie Brett speaking.'

'Ah. It is you, Stephanie. This is Frank Forsyth.'

As if she didn't know. 'How can I help?'

'It's rather a case of what I can do for you.'

Irritated by his reply, Stephanie shook her head but knew better than to alienate a potential source of information. 'I'm all ears.'

'I've kept my office diaries from every year I spent in education. I always insisted on leather-bound. I don't have much cause to read them these days even though they do make an impressive display on my bookshelf. Except, you got me thinking, and I'm always willing to take up a challenge.'

Stephanie had no idea what he was going on about. 'Have you found something?'

'I'm not totally sure it's of any use, my dear.'

Stephanie cringed. Why didn't he get on with it? 'I'd love to know what you've discovered.'

'You remember Graham Simmons left the school's employment at the end of the year and I provided a reference? I don't have a copy of the letter but there's a note in my diary. If he took up the post, you might want to check with St Agnes, a school in the west of Ireland. Galway, I believe.'

Stephanie jotted a note.

'Also, I have the name of the head girl from 1979.'

Before he could say more, Stephanie blurted, 'Sandra Abbott.'

There was a silence then Mr Forsyth spoke again. 'Sandra *Abbotts*, I think you'll find.'

As if the extra 's' made much difference. 'Of course, you're right. Abbotts.'

'To be fair, she's less important. It's Graham Simmons you need to go after. I always had a feeling about him. He thought he understood our pupils better than established members of staff. Little upstart. I had words with him on several occasions. His manner was far too casual. How do they say it? He wanted to *get down with the kids*. That's it! I feared if he didn't change his approach his career would be ruined.'

'Thanks for the information. I'll be in touch if I need anything else.' Stephanie hung up. She couldn't wait to get off the phone, she didn't want to hear any more. Wait a minute. Could it be Mr Forsyth was behind the rumours relating to Graham Simmons? It would be one way of deflecting attention from his own incompetence.

When Stephanie arrived at the care home, an assistant pointed out Mrs Russell. She sat in a winged chair in the day room. Sunshine from the open patio doors flooded the lounge and a fresh breeze slinked inside. As she approached, Stephanie admired Mrs Russell's painted nails. They weren't talons but blunt-ended rubies. Warned by Janine that her mother was a little frail, Stephanie put on her most nurturing voice to say hello. Her introduction was cut short by the assistant who appeared again, this time pushing a tea trolley.

'I thought you'd like a cuppa, Mrs Russell,' she said in an extra-loud voice. 'One for you and one for your visitor?'

'Yes, thank you,' said Mrs Russell.

After bustling with teacups and saucers, the assistant finally left. Mrs Russell's frown smoothed as soon as she'd gone. 'That young lady is a fusspot and no mistake. The one good thing she does is make a reasonable brew.'

'I see you've got the measure of the staff.' Stephanie smiled. 'How long have you lived here?'

'Too long,' said Mrs Russell. 'I'd be pleased to pop off anytime now.'

'Surely not.'

'It's an ambition to have the words *died in her sleep* written on my death certificate. Honestly, I may be immobile but my heart's too strong to let me simply fade away.'

In spite of her years of experience at interviewing, Stephanie didn't quite know how to respond. Death was a touchy subject. She tried to think of something else to say but judged she couldn't launch into questions about Carolyn yet. Before she had an idea, Mrs Russell continued. 'I shouldn't be maudlin, especially with you, Stephanie. It was years ago your poor mother came to such an untimely end. Cancer, wasn't it?'

'Cervical and too advanced to treat.' Thirty years back and that period of Stephanie's life remained a haze of emotion and loss. The *Post* had been a good employer then. Extended compassionate leave was offered after the funeral and it enabled Stephanie to clear the house. Then, she shared a flat with a girl from the classified section. If it hadn't been for her job providing distraction from grief, it would've been far more difficult to get her life back on track. 'It was a long time ago.'

'Such a shame for you,' said Mrs Russell. 'Do you ever see your father?'

'No.' Finding information about him was impossible. Mum had regarded Stephanie's questions as an interrogation. It had been best to steer clear of the subject.

'Not an easy situation but you've made a success of things. And now Janine tells me you're going to find out what happened to Carolyn.'

Stephanie embraced the change of subject. 'I'll try to.'

'You're sure to make a better job of it than the police. I've completely lost confidence in them. I haven't heard from DI Spencer in years. He could've retired for all I know.'

Stephanie decided against saying she'd been in touch with him. She wanted to win Mrs Russell's trust not give the impression she'd gone ahead regardless. 'From what I can tell, he's drawing his pension and living along the coast.'

'Typical.'

According to Mrs Russell, talking about her missing daughter to people in the care home was unimaginable. Not many residents had their wits about them and as for the staff, they'd blanked out her personal history. No one was interested. Care workers were happy to go on and on about anyone who'd died, but the missing lacked clarity and only caused gossip. Mrs Russell couldn't abide it.

'I'm pleased you came, Stephanie. There's nobody better to share the facts about my own daughter than me.' Mrs Russell took a handkerchief from her sleeve and rubbed her nose. 'You do need to explain a thing or two first. What exactly is the programme you're making?'

'It's called a podcast. I'll record some interviews and develop a series of episodes. It'll be aired on the local radio station and available to download.' Thank God Belair had turned up trumps and agreed to the plan. 'The format includes a trailer and a series of episodes, probably six, lasting thirty minutes each. My aim is to shed light on what happened to Carolyn.'

'In that case, you may ask anything you wish,' said Mrs Russell. 'It's important to get to the truth. I'd rather know than remain in the dark. Janine's gone through the steps to have Carolyn declared dead but it isn't the confirmation I want.'

In the discussion that followed, Mrs Russell gave a commitment to sharing what her younger daughter was really like. She relished the idea of talking directly to listeners. Her previous encounters with the media had involved police appeals, and what good had they done? No good at all. This was an excellent opportunity. Stephanie had been to the same school as Carolyn, so she was better placed to ask questions than other journalists. Mrs Russell was glad Stephanie had made something of her life. She remembered her as a girl from the estate who had manners. It was quite unusual in Mrs Russell's experience. Most teenagers she knew had piled into the driving-school office showing very little respect. In her mind's eye she could see them now, lounging on the office furniture. It sent her half mad. What was wrong with sitting up straight for goodness' sake? At this point, Stephanie adjusted her position to make sure her shoulders were pinned back. Mrs Russell continued by saying there really wasn't any point in getting het up about the business she'd worked at for years. No one else did. She and Stephanie's mum had one thing in common. Keeping the wolf from the door as head of the household. Of course, Stephanie's mum had been unmarried and Mrs Russell was widowed.

'I didn't choose to take on the responsibilities.' Mrs Russell sighed. 'Sometimes life throws difficulties in the way. I assume you know what happened to my husband.'

Stephanie hesitated; she didn't want to admit she'd listened to some colourful rumours although it was common knowledge at school that Janine's dad had died. If only she'd thought to look up what had actually happened in a coroner's report. 'He passed away years ago, didn't he?'

'It was suicide.' Mrs Russell used a matter-of-fact voice. 'I thought I'd never get over the shock of it, finding him there. But as time's gone on, my feelings have mellowed and I realise he must've been desperate.'

'I'm sorry,' said Stephanie.

'The secret of his death remained with me for years but I intended to tell the girls once they were both adults. I protected them as best I could. They were with me when we came home and I found him. Janine was closing the garden gate and Carolyn was halfway up the path but as soon as I got a glimpse, I went into autopilot, shut the front door and made some excuse to visit a neighbour. She helped out enormously and I was able to keep the circumstances from them. But you don't want the details, do you?'

'Not if you're uncomfortable.'

'Comfort, now there's a thing. It's a case of least said soonest mended as far as I'm concerned.'

'I understand.'

'Now, where were we?'

Mrs Russell redirected the conversation back to safer ground. What was Stephanie's driving like these days? No points for speeding, she hoped. But Stephanie couldn't get Mrs Russell's admission out of her mind. A parent's suicide would have all sorts of implications for the family. She glimpsed Mrs Russell's face, expectant for an answer, and did her best to keep the conversation going while her mind raced with ideas. 'I've never actually taken a driving test.'

'Dear me! How on earth do you get around?'

Could Carolyn have guessed about her father's suicide? It might account for her interest in an older man like Simmons. Stephanie forced her mind back to the moment and formulated an answer. 'It's a well-kept secret that the network of buses and trains is better than people realise.'

'That's a surprise,' said Mrs Russell. 'But how did you manage at work?'

Stephanie paused as she reflected on her own fatherless upbringing, and what it would've meant for Carolyn with her dad's early death. Perhaps it was the cause of Carolyn's vulnerability. Maybe she was targeted, perpetrators can always spot those who are easy to pick off. 'Err, I usually managed to get a lift from one of my colleagues. The photographers were handy like that.'

'Of course.' Mrs Russell stared out of the window. A little robin which hopped from step to branch had become the source of Mrs Russell's interest. Stephanie buttoned her jacket as a way to indicate her imminent departure. She had a lot of thinking to do. Mrs Russell turned back to Stephanie and smiled. There were a few more sentences exchanged and everything was agreed. Stephanie would book a return visit and log it into the care home's calendar. For a moment, Mrs Russell looked withered. Was it due to admitting the suicide or finally being able to tell Carolyn's story?

'In my head I realise Carolyn's dead, but in my heart, I hope she's alive. Although if that were the case, why has she never been in touch?'

'That's a good question,' said Stephanie.

'I might be an old woman riddled with arthritis but I never

wanted to come here. I expected to live out my days in the family home. That way, if Carolyn ever returned, I'd be there.'

Poor Mrs Russell, forced into a care home. Stephanie scoured her brain to think of an upbeat way of leaving. 'I'll bring my recording equipment next time.'

'Remind me when you're coming again.'

'I'll book in for this time next week.'

'On the morning I have my nails painted?'

Stephanie glanced over to the care assistant who hovered by the desk. She called back, 'That's right, Mrs Russell.'

Mrs Russell grimaced, then she brightened. 'I'll remember.' She examined her polished nails. 'Two treats in one day. If you can call it that.'

21

MAY 1979

Thank God for Janine. She backed up my idea to get extra maths lessons and now in the pocket of my tote bag was a note for Mr Simmons. There it was in writing, Mum asking if Sim would be my tutor. The money hadn't been a hurdle after Janine got a word in. She convinced Mum to look on the expense as an investment in my future. I couldn't agree more but maths wasn't my priority. I'd do anything to grab a chance of being close to Sim. And if Patricia managed to keep her big trap shut, I'd be the only one at Greensleeves to have his undivided attention.

The first challenge was passing the note to Sim without making it obvious. On Wednesdays, I didn't meet Patricia by the footbridge because she and her mum delivered Avon orders. This was my opportunity. I planned to arrive at school before the bell. Usually, I checked Sim's house to monitor his comings and goings but with Mum around, I couldn't always get into her room for a proper look. My guess was he'd caught a lift at the corner from Miss Grant. A flash of envy ripped through me at the thought of them sitting in her car. I kept the green-eyed dragon under control. She was taken and he was mine.

I decided to chance it and wait for him outside the staffroom. Trying to look inconspicuous, I buried my head in my bag and scrambled about as if I'd lost something important. A first-class piece of homework for example. That would need reporting to Mr Simmons. It was just my luck when he finally appeared, there was Forsyth next to him. Standing two paces from the deputy nearly did my brain in. All I could manage was following at a distance. As they parted and Forsyth headed for the new block, I rushed over to Sim. Fortunately, he didn't have the shock of his life seeing me there, panting.

'You've got a few minutes until registration,' he said.

I was almost overcome by the fact I was standing right in front of him. Not knowing how to answer, I pressed the note into his hand. He opened the page and read. 'You'd like some tutoring, Carolyn?'

'Yes.' My tiny voice trembled.

'I'd be delighted.'

I had to prepare for my first session with Sim. Not that I was bothered about the maths but I needed something flattering to wear. Rummaging through my wardrobe, I discarded the duff dresses with lacy trim and focused on my trendy outfits. The flared jeans were an obvious choice and I could match them with the red pumps and a skin-tight T-shirt. I wouldn't be seen dead going round to his house in my uniform. I didn't want to be like that boy from the grammar school. He turned up after a day in class and acted like tutoring was the same as school. It was going to be different for me. I had to underline the fact that I was... how shall I put it? Special! Patricia called me a one-off – it wasn't exactly a compliment. She could hardly believe that as a toff (she gave the name to everyone in 5G) I was thick at maths. It was the let-down of my life but with strangely positive benefits now Sim was around. I didn't need praise from my French teacher anymore. I couldn't care less about my accent and that I was sure to get an A in the oral. If speaking another language ever became useful, I'd have Floria to thank for it. Taking the ring made from knotted wires which lived on my dressing table, I pressed it onto the third finger of my left hand. It was too big and slipped around. One day, I would have a proper ring that fitted.

The faded poppy-print T-shirt matched well with the blue denims. Nice and casual. In preparation for the big day, I tried on the jeans and threaded a belt through the loops. I breathed in and secured the buckle at the last notch. I admired my waist in the mirror. At least one thing about my body was worth flaunting. Over my head went the T-shirt, but having matchstick arms wasn't a good look. I swapped it for a long-sleeved crew top. The pity of it was, I didn't possess a single V-neck in my entire wardrobe. I checked my appearance. An untold force schemed against me with my barely visible boobs. I swore if it wasn't for my bra, anyone would think I was a boy. Then, that got me thinking about underwear. I would definitely need to spruce up things in the knicker and bra department if I was ever going to feel like a real woman.

22

2014

Angel Cakes dish of the day:
ROLEX AND SALAD

'I wish she could've stayed longer.' Stephanie watched Megan Hart leave Angel Cakes in her smart suit. It had been a productive meeting and she was glad Doug had tagged along.

'She's a busy woman,' he said.

Stephanie frowned. Was he having a dig? 'We can't all be employed.'

'You mark my words, Stephanie, everything will go well with your podcast. Once you get your teeth into something, you're like a terrier.'

She didn't enjoy being compared to a dog but Doug was oblivious to any offence and it wasn't worth taking issue. 'What do you think of the title *Extra Lessons*?'

'It picks up on questionable things happening at Greensleeves and it's ambiguous enough to attract interest.'

'I wasn't sure at first but Megan persuaded me. She said

hooking into the gossip about Simmons was a great way to secure an audience. And I suppose the title could relate to life lessons. The things we need to learn from past experiences. Anyway, I can't wait to see how Megan works up the early interviews and pieces them together with the scripted sections I've developed. The discussion around sound-mixing was fascinating. It's really quite exciting.'

'You're in a safe pair of hands thanks to Megan,' said Doug.

'Assuming she's right about streaming, who knows where this might lead.'

'You've got a perfect way of reaching an audience through Belair. Radio regulars will tune into the programme and you'll get more listeners thanks to the download facility. It's a great launchpad.'

Trust Doug to put a dampener on her enthusiasm for being an international crime podcaster. 'Why can't *Extra Lessons* reach listeners in Outer Mongolia?'

'All in good time. When the trailer's ready, I'll do a piece for the *Post*. It's a regional audience you want to target first. World domination can wait for another day.'

'Ha bloody ha.' Stephanie pondered the prospect of appearing in the *Post*. 'It'll make a change to be the subject of a story rather than slogging behind the scenes.'

'Don't be hard on the old place.'

'Okay.' There was no point in holding grudges. 'Make sure you send that new photographer round to do a headshot. Kel, isn't it?'

'That would be an unnecessary expense when I can use your old staff photo.' Doug gave a sneaky smile.

'Don't try it,' said Stephanie. 'I know you lot are a pack of cheapskates.'

Doug smirked. 'As if.'

Stephanie drained the last of her coffee. They'd only ordered drinks, because Megan had to get to another meeting, but now

Stephanie's stomach grumbled. As she reached for the menu, Stephanie scanned the café, noting most of the tables were taken. She hadn't wanted to meet there during a busy lunchtime and risk bumping into former colleagues but Doug insisted on a venue close to his office. At least he'd reserved an inconspicuous table at the back. Before leaving the newspaper, she'd visited Angel Cakes often and had intended to continue doing so, but somehow the sense of rejection that accompanied redundancy had forced her to keep a low profile. Was she even missed at the *Post*? Doug twiddled his thumbs.

'Best I was off,' he finally announced.

'You haven't eaten anything.'

'I'll grab a sandwich to eat back at base.'

Doug waved his hand hoping to catch the attention of a waiter but Beth clocked him from behind the counter and walked over. A neat little chef's hat was angled on her head and her skin glistened with heat from the kitchen.

'What can I get you, Doug?'

'Chicken mayo sandwich and banana cake to take away, please.'

'That's an interesting combination,' said Stephanie.

'Want to try a rolex for a change?'

Doug looked dumbfounded. 'What are you on about?'

'Thought that would get you!' Beth said. 'It's an omelette pinwheeled into a chapati.'

'I'll give one a try,' said Doug. 'But why on earth name it after a watch?'

'It's called that in Uganda. Street food from my family's home country.'

'I didn't know you were from the land of Idi Amin,' said Doug.

'He's not the only person of note in Uganda,' said Beth.

'The expulsion of Asians happened in the early seventies.' Stephanie had been reading about it. 'Only a few families settled in the West Country but the news took more column inches in the *Post* than Carolyn's disappearance ever did.'

'It was a national event.' Doug was on the defensive, as if he couldn't stand his precious newspaper being criticised.

'We moved here when I started primary school. Ours was the only Asian family for miles around. The kids down our street called us darkies.'

Doug and Stephanie exchanged a look. Stephanie certainly didn't know how to respond then Doug stepped in. 'It can't have been all bad.'

Beth shrugged.

Once Doug had left, Stephanie abandoned the idea of ordering lunch and went straight for another long black coffee and a brownie. The chilli heat sang through the dark-chocolate mix and it was difficult to read her notebook with her taste buds tingling. She pushed her papers aside to enjoy the thrum of music that spilled from speakers placed around the café. Beth's singing mingled with the recorded voices, which gave the place a homely feel. As the midday rush subsided, the clearing up and sorting out progressed. The arrival of afternoon tea customers would be next and then the music changed to classical. Beth was clever at creating a lovely ambience at Angel Cakes and Stephanie thought she had a formula to make the café a huge success. Some evenings, Beth pored over the accounts and shared her dream of opening another shop. Stephanie envied Beth's youth and energy, but she could make a success of things as well. Redundancy from the *Post* didn't have to mean the end of her career.

Turning to her notebook again, Stephanie studied her jottings about *Extra Lessons*. She ran her finger down the column where she'd listed the calls she'd made to Graham Simmons. Nearly every day since tracking down his landline she'd rung without an answer. In spite of the various messages she'd left, he never returned her call. Could she draw any conclusion from his unavailability? Not really. He wasn't the only one who hadn't responded to her queries. Maybe he was too busy or simply didn't care. But Graham Simmons had a vested interest in clearing his name. During her last message, she'd suggested that by staying silent and not joining the podcast, he gave gossips the perfect excuse to keep the rumour mill turning.

The café beginning to fill again was the signal for Stephanie to leave. Besides, she had an appointment at Greensleeves and enough time to make the walk over a pleasant option. With the bill settled and goodbyes made, she followed the route taken by so many schoolchildren over the years. Those living in the outlying villages caught a school bus, and the vehicles were renowned for causing many a jam on the country lanes. Swinging her handbag over her shoulder, Stephanie became in tune with the pavements and paths. The feeling of retracing a journey surprised her. It had been a long time since she'd reported on events at the school and even longer since she'd actually attended. She hadn't thought much about it when Patricia suggested meeting there. It was her place of work and she could nip out during a break. Why on earth would anyone who went to Greensleeves actually want to work in the school? It was a conundrum to Stephanie but the focus of the interview would revolve around Carolyn: what she was like in class and how she behaved around Graham Simmons.

23

MAY 1979

S tood on his doorstep, my heart banged so hard I thought it might escape from my chest. I imagined a cartoon heart with little legs working nineteen to the dozen. I saw it bounce over car bonnets and leap for joy at its new-found freedom. Ha ha ha! By the time Sim opened the door, I stifled the giggles. I don't think he noticed my near hysterics or at least he didn't say anything. The ends of his lips twitched into a smile and lines rippled across his forehead.

'Hello!' The word blasted out and I immediately regretted speaking first. I should have waited. According to the problem page in *Jackie*, being forward was a right turn-off for some blokes.

'Good afternoon, Carolyn.'

I didn't have a clue what to say next but I was sure he didn't mind. He simply stretched out his arm as a way of welcoming me. For a moment, I imagined us wrapped in a cuddle and I couldn't stop smiling.

'Come in,' he said.

As I entered the gloomy hallway, a ray of sun shot through the fanlight and I was on a stage, ready to take a bow.

'Let's go through here.' He pointed to the back room. 'I've set up everything on the table.'

I stared at the modern furniture including a sleek sideboard with shiny golden knobs and fitted cabinets flanking the chimney breast. One showed books on the shelves, the other had drawers and a glazed cupboard containing cut glass. I had to squeeze around the square table to reach the place where he'd left some paper, a twelve-inch ruler and a pencil. Setting my bag on the empty chair between us, I gawped out of the window as I passed. The garden was covered in crazy paving including broken slabs of grey, pink and yellow. Relief drifted over me as I realised Sim's house wasn't a replica of my own. Here was a place I could relax and be myself. This was where I was meant to be.

'Can I get you some water before we begin?'

His voice was slinky and I used the long vowels I'd practised in my reply.

'If you liiike.'

When I turned, he was gone but I could hear him drawing water in the kitchen. He came back carrying a single tumbler and disappointment made me fold over. I'd hoped to be chinking glasses with him. Maybe he was saving that for later. As he pulled out his chair, he flashed the flat of his palm. I wondered how the lines lay on his milky skin and whether I'd be able to read his future.

'Let's get on with these questions. You can write your answers on the worksheet.' He tapped the page in front of me.

How could I possibly concentrate on sums when Sim was only an arm's reach away? I took a sip of water to compose myself and watched as he studied the textbook. I couldn't help staring at the parting of his hair. It ran in a sharp, straight line through his feathery locks. I picked up the pencil just as he looked over.

'Come along, Carolyn.' He gave an encouraging smile. 'Anyone would think you weren't keen on maths.'

Not knowing how to reply, I kept quiet and slid my bag onto the floor. There was another difference. Our table had a central pedestal unlike Sim's. His was set upon four square legs. I considered them to be... manly.

'Well, let's not bother with the starter.' He whipped the paper away. 'We've some weeks before the exams so it would be a good idea to think about the questions you find most difficult.'

Oh God. He really was about to begin. I dived into my bag and brought out my pencil case. It was one I'd been given at Christmas and I'd saved it for a special occasion. There was silver glitter on one side and an elastic fabric back. Gripping the zip, the teeth hummed as I opened it and admired a set of multicoloured biros found in a pack Mum had squirreled away. I'd gone all out to impress.

'How confident are you with multiplication tables?'

'Not too bad,' I lied.

'Have a go at some of these.' He turned the textbook my way and I saw three lots of calculations in one question. I was completely undone and didn't know how to admit it. His eyes rested on me while I dithered.

'Don't worry,' he said.

The words soothed.

'A lot of pupils find the nine times table difficult but I've a special trick. Show me your hands.'

Although I didn't like being compared to *other pupils*, I rested my fingers on the edge of the table.

'Copy me to start.' He bent a little finger and I made the one on my left hand do the same.

I was his reflection.

'There are nine fingers stretched out and one finger bent. This stands for one times nine. Do you see?'

I nodded. Sim folded his arms.

'Keep your hands on the table and change the bent finger to the second one.'

I had to do this on my own. My fingers didn't want to stay in place but I made them by pressing my weight down.

'That's the way,' he said. 'Fingers to the left of the bent one stand for tens. You've got one ten and the other straight fingers are units. How many have you got altogether?'

I counted. One ten and eight units. 'Eighteen.'

'With your second finger bent, it means two times nine equals eighteen.'

Getting the hang of this, I changed my bent finger to the third one.

He said, 'Three times nine equals…'

I worked out the answer. 'Twenty-seven.'

'Correct!' he said.

I had to smile. And so it went on. Sim chanted the words and I called back the answer. I'd never experienced the nine times table as fun before. It was amazing. I wanted to do it over again but when I looked down at my hands, I saw my chewed nails. I never bit them in public, only under the covers at night. The habit helped me get to sleep. Turning my fingers into fists prevented him from seeing my shame.

'Let's do it another way,' he said.

Wondering what he meant, I looked over. This time, his hands were stretched on the table. I admired his long slim fingers and the knots of skin on the knuckles of his manicured hands. Gorgeous.

'Right,' he said. 'You ask the questions; I'll show you the answers on my fingers and then we'll say it together.'

We'll say it together.

Sim moved his fingers into position, and I took my chance by reaching over and tapping the bent one. Like magic, the answer flew from my lips. By the time we reached ten times nine, I let my touch linger on his pinky. The closeness of the moment held me in a trance.

'You'll have to remember the pattern of the eleven times table and memorise twelve times nine to complete the set. How about you write out the nine times table on this piece of paper to make sure it's set in your mind?'

I was obedient and didn't grumble. As the sums spread across the page, it gave me time to think. A wife had to love, honour and obey. Doing as Sim wanted was good practice.

24

Greensleeves Comprehensive Website, Parent & Teacher Association Page:
Would you like to join our school PTA? There's always a cup of coffee on hand and one of Mrs Deacon's famous flapjacks. Do get in touch by emailing pdeacon@greensleeves.net.

P atricia Deacon was free to talk during a break from her duties as a teaching assistant at Greensleeves School. Although an odd place to meet, it gave Stephanie a chance to glimpse the school as it was now. Approaching the entrance, she recognised the manicured lawn that no one was allowed to walk on and from the corner of her eye, she saw a woman hunched at the end of a new extension, out of sight from the main windows. She guessed this was Patricia. Walking towards her, she noticed Patricia take the last drag on a cigarette. Dropping the butt on the ground, she rolled a foot over then collected the dead end and slipped it into a small tin taken from her pocket. She gave a smile and showed Stephanie to a bench at the edge of the staff car park where sensible hatchbacks with metallic paint were parked in orderly lines. A smell of grease emanated from an open door to the kitchens. For a moment, Stephanie wondered what was on the menu but decided Greensleeves didn't offer turkey twizzlers. She scotched the idea of unhealthy school meals as she unpacked her equipment and then caught a glance of Patricia's quizzical expression.

'Don't worry about the mic,' said Stephanie. 'It's a way of collecting your memories. And I might be able to use snippets on the podcast, if that's okay.'

'It's about time somebody took Carolyn's disappearance seriously. All these years and the police have been bloody useless.'

'Let's see what we can do about it. This podcast might shed light on something they've overlooked. From what I understand, you knew Carolyn in school. How did that come about?'

'We sat together in maths during the last year. I never really had much to do with her before she got sent down to our set... she was from a different league but completely hopeless at numbers. I think that's one of the reasons we chummed up. It made me feel better not to be at the bottom of the pile.'

'What did other students think of her?'

'She wasn't exactly popular because of the way she sucked up to teachers. Women mostly, and then she had eyes for Mr Simmons. She never fitted in with our lot and she didn't have friends in her tutor group either. I used to watch her trailing behind them. Shame really. Nowadays she'd be included in a friendship scheme to build her social connections.'

'I'm getting a picture of her being very much alone. Do you think she tried to curry favour with teachers because no one else was interested?'

'It's possible. When her best friend went back to France, she didn't have anybody and I felt sorry for her. Being in the bottom set for maths didn't do much for our self-esteem.'

'Tell me about the lessons.'

'Carolyn was rubbish at maths so she kept her head down and copied my answers. Mrs Hoskins, the teacher we had at the beginning of the year, fell for her act. She was only too happy to mark Carolyn's calculations correct. Because Carolyn was such a polite girl, I don't think she ever suspected there were problems. Looking back, I'm sure she suffered from dyscalculia. In the seventies, special needs in maths was often undiagnosed. After Mrs Hoskins went on maternity leave, Forsyth took over. Everyone hated him, even Carolyn. We spent the whole time dodging his spit as he bellowed at the class. Mr Simmons was a different kind of teacher altogether.'

'How did Carolyn behave around him?'

'At first she was introverted and got his attention that way. It was later she marked her territory. Whenever he praised other girls, you'd see her muscle in. He was a bit too *hands on* for my liking. There were twin girls in our class who had hair down to their waists. I noticed him twirling strands of the blonde one's curls around his fingers. Carolyn saw and she shot over. She couldn't compete on the long-hair front but she nuzzled up to him. He laughed and put his arm around her shoulder, guiding Carolyn back to her place. I don't know what she saw in him really. He was hardly fashionable in his corduroy jacket and Crimplene trousers. Young chap turning forty if you asked me. But she couldn't get enough of him and called him Sim when she thought no one was listening. Poor bloke, fresh out of college and stuck with us lot. One thing's for sure, he didn't take the exams too seriously and that's how he got us to learn. Forsyth and the others thought we were thick and I was determined to prove them right by failing every exam. Stupid really. I spent years making up for lost time to get where I am today. Carolyn was a revelation. She didn't act posh like the other kids in the O-level class and she had ambition.'

'Can you say more about that?'

'It wasn't only what went on in class. The private lessons she took from Mr Simmons gave her an edge. We were very impressed she'd go round to his house.'

'It was common knowledge she saw Graham Simmons outside school?'

'Her mum paid for the privilege. I can't say I was jealous, just amazed. My mum and dad wouldn't dream of paying someone to teach me but Carolyn got her way.'

'What do you think was really going on between Graham Simmons and Carolyn?'

'You might call it grooming these days. To be honest, I'm not sure. Carolyn knew her own mind. She was always... determined. It's easy to finger him.'

'Do you think they had a relationship?'

'Look, most girls in my crowd lost their virginity long before it was legal. That's the trouble with being a bus ride from the beach. You get comfy on the sand and one thing leads to another. I don't know about Carolyn though. Whenever I asked what was going on, she wouldn't say. Maybe she was sworn to secrecy. On the other hand, if Carolyn made up her mind to do something, I've no doubt she would. Perhaps she realised there wasn't a future for her in Belmont. She wouldn't be the first.'

'You think she got up and left?'

'She was sixteen and all grown up, at least in her mind.' Patricia checked her watch. 'I'm sorry, I've got to go. The bell's going to ring any minute. Oh, there it is.'

The trill didn't sound too loudly from where they were but Patricia was ready to move. She watched a group of boys with their shirt tails hanging out as they ambled to the next lesson. 'They might look like yobs, but they're good lads. Only a few weeks to go until the school holidays.'

Stephanie rushed to pose another question. 'Is there anything else you can shed light on to help me understand Carolyn better?'

'You know she had a job?'

'That's news to me.'

'I told the police after she'd gone. It was in a shop, one after-school shift and half day on Saturdays. Carolyn liked to play her cards close to her chest.'

Getting to her feet, Patricia indicated the interview was over. Desperate for further information, Stephanie asked, 'Which shop?'

'The Mini Market in town. A right dump.'

25

MAY 1979

That morning, an airmail envelope was hanging by a corner from the letterbox. I pulled the stripey edge and listened to the flap twang back into place. I guessed Floria had written. She was the only person we knew who lived abroad. If Janine had made penfriends from her Spanish studies they'd contact her in Oxford, not here. In Mum's opinion, Janine's course was miles more important than anything I did. She even promised to buy Janine a Linguaphone set to help her succeed. I knew this was an attempt to lure my sister home. Although it didn't work, I was still narked she'd made the offer. Anyone would think my French exam didn't count.

Floria's handwriting was tidy with its loops and capitals. You could tell she was foreign simply from the way she wrote. Clean and neat. It was so rare to hear from her. The last time was a little *bonne année* greeting, as if to make up for the Christmas card that never arrived. I tore it to shreds before Mum noticed. I didn't want her thinking I cared that Floria wasn't around.

I walked into the kitchen and took a vegetable knife from the drawer. Using it to slice open the envelope in one swift move, I enjoyed the splitting sound. The airmail paper was flimsy as tissue and Floria's handwriting stood out, black against pale blue. The letter began with regards from her parents of all things. I wondered if they'd been peeping over her shoulder as she wrote the first line. It was the sort of thing her father might've done but her mum was soft as dough. She was a nice lady and encouraged me to try a few lines in French. Last summer at their house in Dijon had been one to remember. I cringed as I thought about the first morning. The journey had been long and Floria slept in. I could hear her breathing from the other side of the bedroom where they'd put a blow-up mattress for me. I crept downstairs as I needed a drink of water. Madame found me in the kitchen and offered to make hot chocolate. Breakfast was already laid on the table. I'd never actually seen a croissant before, let alone tasted one. Cakes at breakfast nearly had my eyes popping out of my head. We had to wait as French families always eat together. Madame was kind. She didn't stare at my nylon nightie and she let me sit at the kitchen table. After only a minute or two, she offered me a bowl of milky liquid. I liked hot chocolate as much as the next person, but in a bowl? Being a guest, I used my manners to spoon the hot chocolate exactly as we ate soup at home. It was hard trying to drink the chocolate. I struggled on until Madame realised what I was doing. She didn't laugh or tell me off, just took another bowl from the shelf, filled it with a little hot milk and drank straight from the rim. So that was what I was meant to do. Duh! How embarrassing!

Because of the hot chocolate mistake, I couldn't help but like Madame even though I never got on very well with Monsieur. I blamed him for taking Floria away. Waves of sadness cast a shadow because Floria wasn't coming back to Greensleeves. She would finish her schooling in France. The reason had something to do with her father's job. As an engineer, he had to move about. I don't think he ever realised the devastation this caused me, probably because it didn't bother Floria.

I expected to read about the new friends Floria had made and how well she was doing. The letter said no such thing. Excitement made my fingers twitch as I reached the end of the page. Floria was going to spend the month of June in London at a language school to keep her English fluent and wouldn't it be great to meet for a weekend? We could go to Regent's Park and have a picnic, or see a show. What an opportunity! My head throbbed with ideas, but how on earth would I get Mum to agree? I imagined her reaction: two young girls in a big city – not on your life. It was all right for Floria, her parents trusted her. The same couldn't be said of Mum. I remembered the fuss she made when Janine went to Oxford, the countless lectures on how to avoid being hoodwinked. I wasn't sure I could blast my way through the concerns Mum was bound to raise. There was only one thing to do: keep it secret.

26

West Country Post, holiday TV guide, 2014

As usual during the summer there is a dearth of good telly but you can always rely on the old favourites. Amongst them is a repeat of the *Come Dine with Me* series from the West Country in 2006. Unmissable.

T he afternoon was gobbled up with phone calls and note-taking. Stephanie was surprised as she glanced at the time and realised she had to make a start on the compote for the dessert chilling in the fridge. Preparing the cheesecake had been the first task of the day. It was one of her faithful recipes that always turned out right. She didn't want to risk failure when cooking for a chef and invited guests. Beth had the idea for a *Come Dine with Me* evening but the format wasn't followed exactly. Stephanie invited Doug, and Beth said she'd cook the main course. The element of surprise was Beth's mystery guest.

Doug wore a jumper even though it was warm enough to sit

in the garden with only shirtsleeves. It had crossed Stephanie's mind to invite Margaret but Doug insisted she'd get bored. She didn't like newspaper talk although there was unlikely to be much of it. No. Doug had a social life of his own while Margaret preferred to watch the soaps. It was the way their marriage worked according to Doug. He brought a bottle of Prosecco *for the ladies* which made Stephanie cringe. Beth was delighted to pop the cork now she'd learnt how to do it properly. Sticking to beer, Doug raised his glass in celebration of the summer. Beth sipped from a flute with a twisted stem, an oddment from her collection and Stephanie had to let go of her preference for all things matching. It took a little getting used to, but she was ever the pragmatist.

Beth sat on the edge of the picnic bench, poised to answer the door on hearing the bell. She was in a funny mood: a bit agitated, a bit excited about the arrival of her guest. Her behaviour surprised Stephanie, as Beth had said he was simply someone to make up the numbers. The idea of a man in Beth's life was intriguing. Watching Beth in her state of anticipation, reminded Stephanie of those feelings, best kept as part of her personal history. The thorny subject of Beth inviting a date to stay overnight had yet to be addressed. It was early days and Stephanie was amused Beth fancied anyone. She'd always assumed Beth was too busy with the business. It would be interesting to see the type of person Beth went for. She'd been terribly secretive. Stephanie also noticed she was dressed in a strapless salmon jumpsuit and looking very pretty. Stephanie could've carried off such an outfit at her age except the days of wearing anything without easy fastenings were long gone. She didn't want clothing becoming hazardous on a quick nip to the loo. Accidents were more than possible.

Just then Mrs Walker's face appeared above the fence like a jack-in-the-box. Caught unawares, Stephanie was startled and pressed her hand against her heart.

'Don't mind me, I'm watering my tomato plants.' Mrs Walker pulled a happy smile. 'You've picked a good evening for a party.'

Stephanie wondered whether this was a hint to join them. She tried to deflect the idea. 'We've invited a couple of friends. Doug was my boss at the *Post*.'

'Evening.' He doffed an imaginary cap.

'I don't remember your face in the paper.'

Stephanie couldn't help but smirk. Doug's staff photo had been taken years before and he'd avoided having it updated until the picture was almost unrecognisable.

'I work behind the scenes,' he said.

'Well, you've got a lot to answer for.'

Doug pulled a quizzical expression.

'Don't give me any of your excuses.' Mrs Walker's cheeks bloomed pink as she spoke with an anger Stephanie rarely heard. In fact, the last time had been a year before when Mrs Walker had told off some kids who'd been playing football in the back alley and she'd got a mouthful for bothering. Undeterred, Mrs Walker had reported the incident to the school and it hadn't happened again.

'What have I done?' Doug's voice was all innocence.

'You can tell me this much. Why on earth did you let Stephanie go? She worked at the *Post* for years and from what I can tell, she did an excellent job.'

'That's true.'

Their conversation was riveting and Stephanie enjoyed watching Doug squirm under Mrs Walker's beady eyes.

'Speak up,' she said.

'It was a management decision.'

'And what are you, if not part of the management?'

'You've got me there.'

Stephanie took pity on him. 'It's okay, Mrs Walker, Doug's on my side.'

'I'm not so sure. Yours was a perfectly good job, Stephanie, and he had no right to take it away.'

'Actually, it's Doug who's helping me with the podcast.'

'I'm not sure about moving in that direction either,' she said. 'It doesn't sound like a very professional role.'

'It's a great investment of Stephanie's skills,' said Doug. 'She's in at the beginning and there's going to be a bright future for new media.'

'I suppose you'd know more about it than me,' grumbled Mrs Walker. 'I'd best be getting on and leave you alone. It's well past my supper time anyhow. I've got some cold meat and potatoes waiting. I'll see you soon.' She stepped back from the fence and disappeared.

'Goodbye, Mrs Walker.' The sing-song voice Stephanie used was in celebration of her departure. It was no good Mrs Walker getting wound up about Stephanie's career suddenly being cut short although it was touching she cared.

'Didn't think I was coming round here to get my head bitten off,' said Doug.

'You should hear what she says to me.' Beth laughed.

'She's not racist, just unaware,' said Stephanie. 'A lifetime of living in the West Country hasn't prepared her for modern, multicultural Britain.'

Beth shook her hair and her curls fell around her shoulders. 'You're sticking up for her again.'

'Maybe the Equality Act will set everyone straight.' Stephanie didn't really believe the words coming out of her mouth but felt she had to say something.

'I remember Tony Benn talking about racism and old people at the Tolpuddle Festival a few years back,' said Doug.

'What did he say?' asked Beth.

'The older generation should be forgiven for their attitudes. They grew up in a time when it was normal to think of anyone black as other.'

Beth rolled her eyes. 'Lesser.'

In Stephanie's mind, the conversation wasn't taking them anywhere. 'It's a pity Tony Benn has gone. He died in March. Good old Tony.'

Finally, the doorbell sounded and Beth seemed relieved. She leapt up. In her absence, Stephanie stretched her hearing, trying to make out what was being said in the bubbles of conversation that drifted through the back door ahead of Beth and her man. This heightened Stephanie's sense of excitement but Doug was oblivious. 'You and Beth seem to be hitting it off.'

Brought back to the moment, Stephanie replied: 'Strange, isn't it? I never thought I'd be sharing my house, but Beth is great. We have our ups and downs, yet on the whole, it's fine. The rent is keeping me afloat while I work on the podcast. It's a fascinating project.'

It was all right for Doug oozing confidence when he had a full-time job and pension contributions. Stephanie had to hold her nerve and keep going. As she came to this resolve, Beth appeared.

'Ta-dah!' Her arms were stretched in an extravagant gesture and Robert stood there wearing a silly smile.

Stephanie mouthed the words *did you know* at Doug. He shrugged and turned to Robert, reaching out a hand ready to shake. 'Good to see you.'

It was Robert's turn to now approach Stephanie. She was so surprised at his arrival, she didn't know how to greet him. In the end, she pushed her hand out but he was already looming towards her. She turned her cheek in time to salvage the situation and his kiss landed appropriately. What the hell was Beth up to? There she stood with a daft smile on her face, holding the stem of her glass between painted nails. To say she looked smug was an understatement. Now it was Stephanie's turn to dither and a rush of rising heat was uninvited. Shit! What was Beth playing at? She must've known Robert was more

Stephanie's sort of man than would ever suit a younger woman. It was outrageous. After all the carefully laid hints that she was interested in him, now she felt totally rebuffed. And to have it happen in her own home. Anger pulsed through Stephanie. She would have it out with Beth.

'There are some crisps in the cupboard,' said Stephanie in her calmest voice. 'Can you help me find them, Beth?'

'Sure.'

Even as she agreed, Beth seemed oblivious to the insult and tilted her head to one side. What kind of gesture was that? Stephanie fumed.

Stephanie beckoned Beth into the hallway, hoping if she lowered her voice, it wouldn't be overheard by the men who remained in the garden.

'What's going on?' Stephanie hissed.

Beth jolted, confusion on her face. 'I thought you'd be pleased.'

'Pleased? To find you with Robert?'

Beth laughed and placed her hand on Stephanie's shoulder, but she pulled away.

'You've got it wrong, Stephanie.'

'Explain.'

'I invited Robert as company for you. It's about time! You do like him, don't you?'

'What's that got to do with it?'

'I thought you'd enjoy an evening with Robert and I wanted to make it casual. You know. A chance for you to hit it off without the pressure of calling it a blind date. I guessed you'd never go for one of them anyway.'

Absolutely, thought Stephanie. But even if the evening did result in disaster, at least she'd completed the recorded interview with Robert. The tension in Stephanie's neck eased. 'It mustn't interfere with the professional relationship he and I have developed.'

'Of course it won't,' said Beth.

The heat swirling around Stephanie's body subsided. 'I do have a podcast to make and get online.'

'You've got it planned, haven't you? I thought it was only a question of another few interviews.'

Although she was pleased Beth thought everything was in the bag, Stephanie knew differently. Carolyn's form tutor had remembered the best friend's name, Floria Pavel, and now she was on the hunt to find her. Honestly, a broken friendship was exactly the sort of lead the police should have followed up. As for Carolyn working at the Mini Market, she had more enquiries to make. Beth had no idea of what Stephanie was up against. 'It's not that simple.'

'Well, you deserve an evening off. Relax. I'm going to have a fine old time winding up Doug.'

'You may find *cranking* a more appropriate verb.'

After a moment's silence, Beth burst into laughter. Stephanie hadn't realised she was being funny. The tension between them eased and the evening could begin.

The main course was plated in the kitchen and Beth brought out servings to the picnic table. It was one of Stephanie's favourites, tray-baked salmon on a bed of roasted vegetables including slivers of fennel. Adjusting his place on the bench, Robert's thigh brushed against her own. Was it deliberate? One thing was for sure, he ate with impeccable manners. No jabs in her side with his elbow. She could see Doug doing precisely that to Beth, but she was ready to dig him back. Beth was able to bring out the playfulness in everyone.

Stephanie's dessert was admired for its ruby-bright sauce which covered the crusted top of cheesecake, then dripped down the sides. One of Beth's knives ensured a clean cut and it took only a little time for the bowls to be scraped clean. If Stephanie put her mind to it, she could excel in the kitchen. They went inside when the evening became cool. Stephanie watched Beth walk over to her laptop. She said she wanted to know what

Robert's recorded voice sounded like. Could she listen in? Robert was too embarrassed to hear his own voice and Stephanie respected his choice. Instead, she found a section of recording from Janine, where she reflected on Carolyn. It was sure to find a place in the podcast:

Although I enjoyed my student life, it didn't stop me worrying about Carolyn. The older she got, the more needy she became. Me and Mum put our heads together to try and work out ways to help. Whenever we came up with an idea, Carolyn dismissed it. She said she had friends and didn't need us. As evidence, she invited Patricia round. My mother squirmed as Patricia went on about her life on the estate. How her dad did the pools and her mum wore curlers. I know it sounds ridiculous, but back then my mother regarded herself as middle class and couldn't abide the idea of Carolyn mixing. She so wanted the talk to stop that she started humming to prevent further revelations from Patricia. I remember when she told me about it I went rigid, trying to hold myself together and not laugh out loud. I felt for them both: Mum longing for Carolyn to have nice friends... and Carolyn, grasping at the only friendship on offer.

According to Beth, the excerpt was cool and even Doug seemed impressed. Their responses confirmed what Stephanie already knew, a successful podcast meant exposing the emotional impact of the story from both a historical and a current perspective. As the chatter continued, she realised there were echoes between Carolyn's isolation and her own situation. When had she last enjoyed entertaining at home? Certainly not in the last couple of years. Maybe that was it. Perhaps she should forget about Robert being a potential date and enjoy having friends for a change.

27

The tea was strong and milky just how I liked it. I'd made a pot because Mum would be home any minute. She approved of loose tea and didn't think those pickers in Ceylon would give teabags the time of day. Mum assumed this from the adverts during those rare occasions she'd watch ITV (the commercial channel wasn't a patch on BBC). Musing as I made a whirlpool by stirring sugar into my mug, I wondered if the shrivelled leaves were really freshly plucked by women wearing bright saris and nose-clip jewellery. I glanced at my reflection in the kitchen window and imagined what it would be like to wear a chain dangling from ear to nose. Freaky! That didn't stop me from craving the day I could get my ears pierced. I'd need to get the money and my nerves together first. I scratched the nobble on my arm left by the BCG inoculation. Seeing the needle had almost made me faint. When I told Patricia about it, she thought I was a big joke. She reckoned I'd do anything to gain a bit of sympathy. Even from a nurse.

Taking the drink up to my room, I was in the habit of counting every step to reach the landing. Drat! There were some things I never grew out of. Sat at my desk, I blew over the tea and took a sip. It was another one of my tea-drinking traditions I'd never been able to break. One day, I'd get away from Belmont and find a new way of being. A life where I'd be comfortable in my own skin, thanks to a special person at my side. As there wasn't a lot of time before my first maths exam, I'd increased to having two extra lessons a week. Lucky me! Two glorious hours alone with Sim like we were going steady. From the very first time I'd seen him, Sim meant something special. It was because of the little things. The way he held his head, strands of hair framing his narrow face. His eyes and those long straight lashes. Oo-er, I couldn't help going weak at the knees. Yet this was simply on the surface when my love was deep and definitely real. I sensed he knew about the tingle in the pit of my stomach and my pounding heart – because it was the same for him.

Startled by the front door slamming, I heard Mum's footsteps thunder along the hallway. Whether she was carrying shopping in slippery carrier bags or had her handbag slung over her shoulder, Mum's steps were always deliberate. Sometimes, she laughed at herself for being heavy-footed, particularly if the glass in the tiny chandelier above the dining table chinked. How Mum loved that light fitting and as part of her yearly spring cleaning, she washed the individual glass droplets in soapy water. With the promise of extra pocket money, I'd been persuaded to help and I didn't mind too much. That was ages ago when I wanted to hang around at home. Now I didn't need her approval because there was Sim.

Sounds of Mum bumbling in the kitchen sent me on a mission to spend time with her. She leaned against the cooker, her hands clasped around a teacup. It was her habit to do this in winter when the oven was warm. Mum was a creature of habit and she stood there even if the oven was off.

'How was your day?' she asked.

At least Mum had changed the question from *how was school?* I didn't like being defined by attendance at Greensleeves. I was sixteen and grown up. No one could stop me from smoking or having sex or joining the army if I wanted to.

'It was fine,' I said. 'And yours?'

'Oh, you know. Same as ever.'

Obviously, she wasn't in the mood to share one of her stories from the office. Even I had to admit they were sometimes funny.

'Dinner at half past six?' she continued. 'I'll put a couple of lamb chops in the oven. Jacket potato okay for you? We'll have frozen peas and beans. I can't be bothered preparing veg this evening.'

I nodded even though I wasn't keen on a square meal. It would cause an argument if I suggested something less calorific.

'What on earth...?' Mum stared out the window.

On the washing line was the underwear I'd carefully selected when I got home from school. I knew the recently bought silky bra would pass muster so I chose the cotton items for special treatment: the bra with broderie anglaise trim, the lacy-edged briefs. They'd been bought by Mum after I'd protested about wearing a vest and regulation navy knickers to school. The pity of it was, those first purchases of womanly underwear still fitted. It was all I owned and I had to make the best of the situation. My liaison with Sim meant I needed appropriately alluring undergarments.

Confusion spread across Mum's face as she turned to me and then peered out the window again. My bra which I'd carefully pegged to the line, flapped in the breeze and spread fat purple splashes. The knickers attached by the side seams had less room for movement and simply dropped their colour to form purple puddles on the grass.

'Have you been raking through Janine's things?' asked Mum.

'No.' I pressed my chin to my collarbones and looked up. 'It's my underwear.'

'I didn't mean the undies, I meant the dye.'

'The bottle was lying there on Janine's chest of drawers. It's not as if she needs it.' The pair of pillowcases she'd tie-dyed were back with her in Oxford.

'That doesn't give you the right...' One of Mum's eyebrows turned to the shape of a steeple.

I played my trump card. 'No one likes waste.'

'That's beside the point.'

'You can't stop me from growing into a woman.'

'That's true,' said Mum. 'But purple underwear?'

28

2014

Transcript of a telephone message left on Graham Simmons' voicemail, August 2014:

Hello again, this is Stephanie Brett. I'm sorry to bother you but it's really important we talk. The podcast I'm making about Carolyn Russell's disappearance needs your input. I know it might be a difficult subject but you hold some key information. Please get in touch.

After a morning stuck at the kitchen table, it was time to move around. Nipping to the loo, Stephanie then went into the bathroom to wash her hands and noticed her dishevelled appearance in the mirror. Her hair needed sorting and using the brush, she dislodged a tangle. As she cleared the loose strands from the bristles, she was relieved enough hair remained attached to her scalp. Barefoot back down the stairs, she listened for the familiar creak of the fourth step and then anticipated the cool tiled hallway and the whine of the hinge on the stripped wooden door as she returned to the kitchen. She'd lived in this house long enough to know its idiosyncrasies. Stephanie was pleased Beth had made a concerted effort the previous evening to follow her tidy up and put away routine. It meant she could work without distractions. The kitchen remained the way she liked it, gleaming.

Stephanie checked her list of things to do. It was good seeing items crossed through yet she recognised many were easy to accomplish. Now she was more confident in proceeding, she'd get to the heart of the project. Shaking her head, Stephanie corrected herself. It wasn't only confidence she'd summoned but a real commitment to uncovering Carolyn's story. Accounts from Janine and Mrs Russell provided a tangible sense of a young person trying to find her way through the social and academic hurdles of comprehensive education. Carolyn's emotional vulnerability came through too.

On her laptop, all things related to the podcast were stored in a new folder titled *Extra Lessons.* Inside were other folders and Stephanie's nimble fingers located the podcast recordings. Looking for a specific date, it was simple to locate the interview with Beryl Smith of 26 Crossways. In her mind's eye, Stephanie pictured Mrs Smith and her agile eyebrows, which she pinched together to share feelings of confusion and irritation. She was quite a character. Using the slider, Stephanie skipped over the first few minutes of the recording, where Mrs Smith muttered about injustice and Mrs Russell's poor family. Stephanie wanted to remind herself of what she'd said about Graham Simmons:

That young man lived at number twenty-one. Turn around and you can see the house through the net curtains. It's painted white, heaven knows what's wrong with the colour of bricks, but some people must have a liking for it. The last owner was a DIY enthusiast hence the so-called improvements.

.   .   .

In her mind's eye she saw Mrs Smith wagging her finger, and then the story continued.

I've got a reliable memory for people. I can tell you he kept himself to himself because round here we're all families. I never did understand why a single chap would want to live in a three-bedroomed house. He told me, he was hoping a couple of friends would move in. Rent on that place must have set him back a pretty penny. He was always respectably dressed, so maybe he came from money. In those days, house sharing wasn't the fad it is today. Taking lodgers was much more usual.

Stephanie suppressed a smile, thinking of Beth as her lodger.

I wouldn't want to live on that side of the road. The houses are overlooked by the new builds on the gated development. Some don't have access from the garden and they have to drag those huge wheelie bins through the house. Can you imagine? And I don't mind telling you, they're a hazard left on the pavement.

Not another account of wheelie-bin wars. Stephanie had her fill during her time at the *Post* when she reported on nuisance and antisocial behaviour.

In the early days it was different. I would've given an arm and a leg for the view from number twenty-one. There was nothing but countryside out the back and you could walk straight into the fields. By the seventies, of course, the council let the land turn to scrub and it became a wasteland where youths gathered.

. . .

Oh yes, Stephanie remembered scaling the fence and walking that way to meet her friends by the brook. It was there they played games of truth or dare that involved her first kiss.

You've heard the rumours, haven't you? I don't normally pay much attention, but if that young man was intent on murder, he could easily have disposed of a body. She must have been light as a feather. Perhaps she's there in some shallow grave. It doesn't bear thinking about.

Stephanie had heard the talk, but really? If a body had been buried, it would've been found after construction started on the new development. The idea was far-fetched to say the least.

Not that I'm casting aspersions – he seemed like a nice chap to me. He said good morning whenever I was out the front and he was leaving for work. I think he was quite the dedicated teacher because he helped students by giving them after-school lessons. They paid for the privilege but there weren't many teachers who went the extra mile. He called them his tutees. I'd never heard the word before. It meant he helped them with revision for exams. Carolyn used to go round once or twice a week. I was surprised her mother could afford it. The sacrifices that woman made for her daughters. How horrible, the way things turned out. And to have a second tragedy in the family, it really is too much.

Stephanie paused the recording. She remembered what was coming next and took a breath before continuing to listen.

I suppose you've heard what happened to Mr Russell. Lord knows why he took his life but he must've had reasons. Just an ordinary day and then Mrs Russell found him hanging. Or to get the story right, he'd been hanging until one of the spindles broke. Not a pretty sight. Those poor girls.

When Stephanie looked up the facts, the details were confirmed in the coroner's report. Following such a tragedy, Carolyn had grown into a troubled teenager. The experience was bound to make her vulnerable, possibly to Graham Simmons, and if not him, there were other predatory men about. Of course, she'd tried time and again to get hold of Simmons. It was disappointing that even the recorded voicemail was computer generated. She would've liked to hear him speak, get a sense of the man. At least there'd been a glimpse of him from a newspaper article where he'd won first prize in a charity raffle. She'd stumbled upon the image in which he stood squarely with the hamper of goodies in his arms. It was hard to imagine he sent a young girl's heart racing. Stephanie thought on. She really couldn't believe a young teacher would bump off one of his pupils. But Graham Simmons' reluctance to give his side of the story was reason for suspicion. She needed to find out whether anyone had actually gone in person to ask questions about Simmons' job interview. From what she could tell, there'd been one call and then that whole line of inquiry was closed. Come to think of it, had anyone actually checked the plans for the new development?

Stephanie pushed the laptop aside. It was one task trying to get to the bottom of suspicions over Simmons, it was quite another making progress in other areas. She glanced at her watch. It had been by dogged determination that she'd finally found Floria Pavel's phone number. She was glad to make use of the French evening classes she'd taken a few years ago – the only previous benefit had been an introduction to Ben – although that particular aspect was best forgotten. She enjoyed her ability to converse and followed Mrs Russell's information that the Pavel family were based in Dijon. When this came to nothing, a few phone calls to a relative in Bordeaux finally turned up a number in Montargis, a town situated about one hundred kilometres from Paris. The call confirmed Floria lived there but Stephanie was advised to phone later in the day and catch her after work. As it was half past five, and the time in France an hour ahead, maybe she should try again.

Stephanie listened to the curious tone that bleeped rather than rang. Her heart quickened as a woman answered with a recited line. Stephanie responded in French and then reverted to English. It would be her best way of getting to the finer details.

'Am I speaking to Floria Pavel?'

'Yes. What do you want?'

'I'm investigating the disappearance of Carolyn Russell in 1979. I believe you were friends with her at Greensleeves School.'

'That is correct.'

'From what I gather, you were very close. I'm wondering if you can shed any light on what happened?'

'I was not there at the time.'

'But you knew her better than most. You were in the same class for four years.'

'We were just silly girls.'

If only Stephanie could get Floria to say a bit more. 'I understand you were best friends. Surely you shared some secrets.'

'We may have. I cannot recall.'

For Christ's sake, Stephanie needed a crumb of information to work on. 'What did you like doing together?'

'The usual things: going to the park, going into town.'

Perhaps a leading question would draw something different. 'How did you feel about the teachers at Greensleeves? Were there any you particularly liked or disliked?'

'I returned to France and finished my education. I didn't have contact with Carolyn. No letters, no telephone calls, nothing.'

'How did you feel about that?'

'Me and Carolyn had our own lives. Of course, I was sad she went missing but it wasn't my concern. We were not in touch.'

'In that case, I'm sorry to have troubled you.'

'Okay.'

The bleep sounding in Stephanie's ear couldn't have been clearer. She crossed the name Floria Pavel off her list of contacts. Another lead over. Now, she could look forward to tracking down maps of the new development. She'd foil the theory of a burial in the wasteland if it killed her.

29

MAY 1979

The culottes had been a Christmas present. It was a family habit to wear new clothes as a celebration of the day. I'd been impressed at my mother's choice (although I suspected Janine had something to do with it). A fashionable separate for once and oh-so practical according to Mum. If I ever worked in an office, I'd know the advantage of trousers that looked like a skirt, especially when clambering over filing cabinets in the basement, or standing on steps to reach high shelves. Really, I didn't need reminding of such things. It was usual to have boys lurking on the stairs at school and sniggering if they managed a glimpse of thigh or knickers. If my skirt flapped, I'd hold the hem whenever boys were up to their tricks. Some girls actually flaunted themselves but I'd never give one of *those* boys the time of day. My sights were set on a little more sophistication. I would never put it past Southy or Gove to try such a thing. I imagined them loitering near the escalators at Randalls Department Store. One flight up to ladies' wear and a few men were always gathered. Strategically placed or what?

Thanks to the bit of weight I'd lost, the waistband was loose. It was only because I'd resewn the side button further along that the culottes didn't fall right off. I tucked the silky long-sleeved blouse inside and hoped the outfit wouldn't appear bulky. A sack of potatoes tied in the middle wasn't a good look. I spent what seemed like hours trying to get the collar to sit tidily. With several clasps undone it might give a glimpse of cleavage if I twisted my arms and leaned forward at the same time. I'd rehearsed the manoeuvre until I'd perfected the art. One last look in the rainbow-rimmed mirror and I checked the splash of golden eye shadow, then I puckered my lips to show off the sparkling gloss. Ready as I'd ever be, I left the house.

Using extra-long strides, I enjoyed the feel of material fluttering around my legs. Bottle green wasn't the nicest shade for a summer's day, but I could hardly turn up at Sim's wearing jeans yet again. I was in the mood to surprise him and anticipated his reaction on first sight of me. From close observation in class, I recognised his repertoire of expressions. It might be eyebrows raised in surprise, flat lips to demonstrate understanding, a flash of teeth in a broad smile. I didn't need to guess as I'd be in front of him and under his gaze in a few paces. In my bag was the homework I'd sweated over, the page I'd kissed leaving barely discernible lip prints and the invisible hearts I'd traced.

Sim opened the door before I had a chance to grip the knocker. Usually, I liked the sound that ricocheted around, but with him already there, I didn't have a chance to prepare for a big entrance. Adjusting my pose, I put my weight on my right hip which made my curves more obvious.

'Hello, Carolyn,' he said. 'There's no need to stand on ceremony.'

Ceremonial, was I? I didn't know how to take the compliment. Not wanting to get flustered, I simply said *thank you* and tried to stop the blushes burning.

'Let's go straight in.' Sim tilted his head to indicate I should walk in front of him into the dining room. I couldn't help lingering. His hair was freshly combed and the feathered ends laid neatly around his face. One day, I might persuade him to get an ear pierced. David Essex sported one gold loop and had a certain appeal. Who knows – maybe we could have it done together. I'd love going into a unisex salon with him. He'd be there to support me if I fainted from the pain.

'Chop-chop.' He pointed towards the back room.

I didn't want to budge. It was delicious, the two of us just standing there. In the end, Sim brushed past me and I knew what it was like to feel his arm against mine. Taking my time, I followed. Before sitting, I smoothed the fabric of my culottes over my hips.

'There really is no need to dress for the occasion,' said Sim. 'Other tutees arrive in school uniform.'

He had noticed my outfit and was clearly impressed. No one else dressed for him. 'It's my pleasure.'

'Don't go to the trouble of changing, was all I meant.' Sim coughed into a curled fist; he had such perfect manners. 'How did you get on with the homework from Tuesday?'

I turned to the bag that I'd left on the chair between us. Here was my opportunity. It was awkward to unbuckle when my arms were fully extended. Showing the inside of my wrist was *de rigueur*, or at least it had been in days gone by. There wasn't any harm in trying out the moves I'd practised. Sim pushed the chair closer towards me and the legs scraped against the floor. The noise rattled me and I started faffing. Sim sighed and slumped back. He wore a short-sleeved shirt and with my bionic vision, I could see through his vest and detected dark hairs on his chest. My pulse raced but Sim was calm. He sat there twiddling a pen. I loved to watch the way he turned it between his fingers. Anyone would be impressed by the half-moons on his nails. Hiding my own, I tried not to show the bitten ends.

'Let's be having you, Carolyn.'

He couldn't wait for me. The dilly-dallying was paying off, creating a sense of anticipation. Eventually, the flap on my bag fell open and the corner of the homework sheet poked out. It took only a second for him to whip it away and he read the calculations I'd laboured over.

I watched his fingers as they followed the lines of my working out, he touched the spaces where my lips had lain.

'Well done.' These were the words he uttered and I clung to them for my life's worth. Sim turned to the textbook and pointed at the next set of calculations. I couldn't help but feel deflated although I wasn't going to show it. The knowledge that his eyes had traced every mark I'd made on the page was enough to give me encouragement. He had consumed every bit of me that I'd poured onto the paper.

30

2014

Belair website, excerpt from the news page:
At Belair, we're proud to be at the forefront
of new developments. As part of our speech-
based, magazine-style programmes we're
introducing a true crime podcast by journalist
Stephanie Brett, formerly with the *West
Country Post*. Think back to 1979 and the
teenage Carolyn Russell who went missing from
Belmont. Now's your chance to find out what
really happened.

S tephanie put the handset down after talking to Megan. She'd
agreed the slightly sinister soundtrack was ideal for the
trailer and the selected snippets of talk which included Mrs
Russell's fury about police incompetence, Patricia's scepticism
over rumours, Janine's sadness. It was a good balance. With
Doug's piece included in the weekend section of the *Post* and the
trailer on the radio station's schedule, Stephanie became quietly

confident there would be an audience for the first show. In the meantime, there was plenty to do.

Scanning her list of potential interviewees, Stephanie realised getting hold of Simmons was virtually impossible, yet it didn't stop her trying. As she listened to the ringtone, Stephanie prepared to deliver an interested but not urgent message. Instead of hearing the voicemail click into action, the line went dead. How strange. She hadn't expected that. Tapping the numbers again, she knew the sequence by heart, this brought another failed connection. Could this be the clue that Simmons was around? Had he listened to each and every message but didn't want to hear more? Or perhaps his commitment to silence was waning. Stephanie would mull it over and come to a decision about moving forward.

Next, she turned to the interview with Janine. Megan reported she'd made the recording cleaner and edited out some of Stephanie's questions and interjections. This was necessary to get an uninterrupted flow of talk. (The Q&A strategy could be reserved for later in the podcast to heighten tension.)

Me and Mum talk about Carolyn to keep the memories alive. Every birthday there's a cake and when it comes to Christmas, we lay a place for her at the table. No presents but there's a cracker to pull, if miraculously she walked in. Thinking about Carolyn is like sinking into mud – the weight of missing her. It's easy to rationalise there was nothing I could've done. In my heart there's always an ache.

I wish I'd spent more time at home that year but the gulf between us had grown. I was the brainy one and she was pretty; I was chatty and she was quiet; I had friends and she had... Patricia. At least she had someone. When I came home, I tried to make up for not being around. I gave her bits of jewellery and her sixteenth birthday involved a trip into town. I didn't do enough.

In the beginning, the police suspected Carolyn had run away. They didn't take it seriously although Mum kept on at them to extend the search. She was worried sick but she believed Carolyn was sensible. According to Mum, she wouldn't do anything to jeopardise the promise of driving lessons as soon as she turned seventeen. Driving lessons, really. Mum even offered to put her on the car insurance. It was Carolyn's ambition to pass first time because I failed my driving test twice. Her chance to beat me.

I can't be sure what Mum thought after a sighting of Carolyn at Waterloo Station. We wanted to believe it, but Carolyn didn't even like London. You should've heard the way she moaned about her one and only school trip there. Filthy place, she said. Half of me held tight to the idea she'd be on the next train back. As time wore on, it was never going to happen. And what you're left with after so many years is a longing that's hard to describe. All the should-have-been occasions that never got celebrated. It would be the same if she'd died, but the not knowing and the guilt makes me feel... I don't know... worthless? Like I haven't earned the right to enjoy my life.

Tapping the keyboard to stop the player, Stephanie noticed her shoulders had tightened while listening to Janine's raw emotions. She rolled them a couple of times to release the tension. Even though she'd written about heart-breaking reports of car crashes and accidents, Janine's experiences had the power to churn Stephanie's sense of her own well-being. She liked the way Megan had spliced together the segments, making the whole effect powerful. The thrill of a new achievement was addictive and Stephanie was becoming more confident the podcast would lead to potential paid employment. It had to. Returning to the opening, Stephanie listened again to the scene setting she'd become proud of.

. . .

Welcome to Extra Lessons, *a podcast investigation into the disappearance of sixteen-year-old Carolyn Russell. It was the day of her maths examination during the summer of 1979 when she threw down her pen and walked out of the school hall at Greensleeves Comprehensive in Belmont, our rural West Country town. Her paper was incomplete like the story of what happened to her next. This episode comes from me, Stephanie Brett, also a former pupil of the school but that summer I was working as a trainee journalist. Carolyn's disappearance was the biggest story covered by the local press and its lack of a resolution remains a puzzle. Now it's time to set the record straight and dig deep to find out what really happened.*

Today I share an interview with Carolyn's mother, Mrs Vera Russell who at seventy-nine hasn't seen or heard from her youngest daughter in over thirty-five years. Mrs Russell sits in the lounge of the care home dwarfed by the armchair. Her nails are painted and she wears matching lipstick. With her hair set into neat curls, Mrs Russell is a woman of quiet determination. You'll note from her voice, she's physically frail but nothing is going to stop her from contributing to this podcast. She's been waiting years to air her experiences. Will her words uncover some new information to shed light on what happened to Carolyn that sunny day in 1979? Over to Mrs Russell.

I was relieved when Carolyn went to school in the morning. We'd had a disagreement about money in the housekeeping tin. It was a bit short and she exploded, saying I blamed her for everything that went wrong. I put it down to nerves. Maths had never been her strong suit but the extra lessons from Mr Simmons gave her a boost. Or at least, that's what I thought at the time. Lord knows what was really going on. Carolyn was never one to talk freely. She did feel the pressure to get a good result otherwise her place in the sixth-form college would be threatened. Oh, how she struggled with numbers, poor girl. It was days later that the gossip machine started. At the beginning, I had complete faith in Graham Simmons, that his intentions were honourable. Over time there have been many questions. I only hope he'll talk to you.

Carolyn was under a cloud because Janine went to Oxford. She missed her big sister. It's a shame she took after me rather than her father who was the mathematician in the family. He was too clever really and it all ended in tragedy when he took his own life. And with losing Carolyn, it... it's rather a lot to bear. Excuse me. (Mrs Russell cleared her throat.) I've never thought for a moment that Carolyn would consider suicide despite the police saying it runs in families.

Once Janine went to Oxford, there was no one to dilute the relationship between me and Carolyn. She was an intense girl and things got even worse after her best friend went back to France. I wanted Carolyn and Floria to keep in touch, become penfriends at least. I even encouraged her to phone France, although goodness knows how much that would've cost. I tried to be supportive but she could be so... difficult. I really didn't know what to do. It was a relief when she went out on Saturdays – I thought it was a positive sign. Little did I know she had a job and that's what's confusing. Why did she keep her work a secret? She might have known I'd be proud of her for taking the initiative. Back in the seventies, you could be on the bottom rung and make your way up. A career in retail might've been the right thing. I never did understand her need for secrecy. It came as quite a shock when the police told me about it. At first, I blamed others for the deception. Later I realised it had more to do with our relationship. We were never close like Janine and me.

Stephanie reflected on the recording and was pleased she'd been able to elicit such a comprehensive overview. Why on earth had she never thought of doing this before? Just as she sat there with a self-satisfied smile on her face, a knock at the front door interrupted her musing. It was the usual pattern of three taps and a bang that was Mrs Walker's trademark. Always ready to give her neighbour the time of day, Stephanie didn't mind breaking off from her work. When she pulled the door open, there was Mrs Walker proffering a jam jar.

'What's this?' Stephanie asked.

'I thought Beth would like it.'

Stephanie studied the pretty handmade label which read *green tomato chutney 2013* with the contents showing sludge-coloured chunks and tomato seeds. It didn't look altogether appetising and with Beth's sweet tooth, she probably would've preferred jam. 'You'd like me to give this to Beth?'

'I can't keep track of her movements, but I guessed you'd be home. Did you know chutney originates in India? I thought it would make a proper gift for her. I didn't bring anything earlier because I lacked inspiration. After reading about an Indian cookery programme in the *Radio Times*, I came up with the answer. Beth was so kind making those cupcakes. I've been trying to think of a way to repay the compliment.'

Stephanie didn't have the heart to burst Mrs Walker's bubble when she looked so pleased with herself. 'I'm sure she'll find a use for it.'

'I remembered there was a spare jar in the larder from the batch I made last autumn. It will have matured beautifully by now. Goes lovely with a bit of cold meat.'

'I'll be sure to pass it on.'

'Thank you, dear. And do give her my regards. It's good to have two young women as neighbours.'

Well, this was a turnaround. Mrs Walker had obviously put her misgivings about Beth to one side. Progress, absolutely. Although Beth would hoot with laughter at the gift, she'd have to agree it was a friendly gesture. Stephanie chuckled about the irony of Mrs Walker's timing. There she'd been listening to the complicated female relationships in the Russell household only to realise the three-way dynamic of her own situation. Stephanie would do anything to keep the peace between Beth and Mrs Walker. Did anyone take a similar role in the Russell home?

31

Patricia hadn't waited for me at the footbridge. I tried to catch up with her but I didn't want to be seen running. Anyone might think I was keen about getting into school. Breathless by the time I reached her, I clung on to the metal railings by the gate. I picked at a chip of shiny black paint which revealed the charcoal undercoat.

'What's with you?' asked Patricia.

I let a beaming smile stretch across my face and she sent me a sneer in return. I knew what this meant – she was fed up hearing titbits about Sim and wanted the whole story. I couldn't risk telling her everything. I wasn't sure how she'd react and I didn't want details of our relationship blasted around school by Patricia's big fat gob. It was enough that my love for Sim was reciprocated.

'I get the message,' I said.

'At last! I can't be bothered with your love life when I've got problems of my own.'

This sounded interesting. 'What's going on?'

'It's nothing to do with a boy, if that's what you're thinking.'

'Oh.' The smile on my face must have dropped as I caught Patricia acting like a mirror to copy my expression.

'I can read you like a book,' she said.

'I thought you only gave the time of day to magazines.' My attempt at a joke.

Patricia rolled her eyes. 'You've so much to learn.'

'Now who's being enigmatic?' I'd learnt the word in my English Lit class and immediately regretted using it.

'Stop showing off,' she said. 'Remember I've the upper hand in one particular subject.'

Once upon a time, her remark would've been the undoing of me but in the last few weeks, being thick at maths had proved a distinct advantage. An advantage in the love stakes. 'There's no need to rub it in.'

'I bet you'd like Mr Simmons to rub it in.'

'There's a thought.'

I'd watched an episode on TV where Hazell (the dishy actor in the newish series of the same name) had been lying on a massage table wrapped in a white towel. Gentle hands were seen rubbing his shoulders. When the masseuse left the room, a villain entered and thumped him. I squirmed at the sight of his hairy backside. I was fascinated too. The trouble about watching Hazell at home, was having Mum there. Totally embarrassing.

Just then the bell rang – the dinging lasted at least a minute – as if we were all deaf and couldn't actually hear the command. At school, they treated us like idiots. I stepped away from Patricia but she caught my arm.

'I'll see you in maths,' she said.

She stated the obvious. 'Yeah.'

'Meet me after school as well.'

Although I never liked the way Patricia bossed me about, I was interested. My hour with Sim had been postponed until the end of the week. It meant Friday night drinks (even if it was a glass of water) and I couldn't wait. It also meant I had nothing to

32

2014

Equality Report, Belmont (2012)

Although the Equality Act legally protects
individuals from discrimination in the
workplace and society, it is widely understood
that black and ethnic minority people are more
likely to suffer hate crimes in rural areas
than in urban towns.

'It would happen on my one day off.' Beth's usually smooth forehead creased as she pushed her mobile into her pocket.

'What's up?' Stephanie poured coffee into a mug and passed it over.

Beth's hand trembled as she sipped. 'Trouble is, it's personal.'

'How so?'

Leaning against the edge of the kitchen worktop, Beth steadied herself.

'You better sit down.' Stephanie pulled out a chair. She always liked to have them neatly tucked under the table. 'There you go.'

Sinking onto the seat, Beth blinked back tears. This really must be serious. Stephanie patted Beth's shoulder for want of knowing what else to do. Then she saw the kitchen roll and ripped off a sheet. 'Need a tissue?'

Beth scrunched the paper then dabbed her eyes to avoid ruining her make-up. What the hell had happened?

'I've got to check on the café.' Beth dug inside her bag to find the keys. 'I'm sure it's not going to be as bad as...'

'What's happened?'

'I can't say. It's too upsetting.'

'I'll come with you.' Stephanie placed her hand on top of Beth's.

'If you must.'

On Sundays it was possible to drive along the street that was normally pedestrianised. As they approached Angel Cakes, Stephanie saw some black spray on the windows but only when Beth parked could she read the words: *paki go home*. A sense of pity and outrage pinned Stephanie to the passenger seat. This was outrageous and Beth wasn't even from Pakistan. Stephanie turned to look at Beth who wrestled her seat belt in a hurry to get out. A security guard approached.

'Was it you who phoned?' asked Beth.

'Yep. Sorry to bring you bad news. I guess you can sort it from here.'

Beth stared at the window, her face frozen in a look of resignation. 'There's no point in wasting time. I need to get the worst scrubbed off today.'

'You should inform the police. It's criminal damage,' said the security guard.

'What are they going to do about it?'

'Good question,' he said.

'Don't worry about that now.' Stephanie rolled up her sleeves. 'Let's make a start.'

'Take a photo first,' said the security guard. 'You might change your mind about reporting it.'

'I'll do it.' Stephanie whipped out her phone, glad she had invested her redundancy money in one with a quality camera. She took several shots while Beth unlocked the shop.

A few minutes later Beth returned outside, rubber gloves already donned. She was carrying a box of cleaning equipment. 'You don't have to stay, Stephanie. I can manage. There's no point in spoiling your clothes.'

'These old jeans?' said Stephanie. 'A few rips and a splattering of paint, they might end up looking fashionable.'

Beth smiled as she handed over a spare pair of gloves. 'It shouldn't take too long. Thanks for helping.'

The way to clean graffiti from glass was relatively simple. Beth demonstrated by spraying on special cleaning fluid then scrubbing off the paint using a scouring brush. Stephanie applied fresh water and used a clean cloth to remove the residue. They were a good team. Beth had to stand on a chair at one point. Whoever had done the damage must've been tall. Stephanie assumed it was a group of youths. There wasn't much for young people to do in Belmont during the school holidays but that was no excuse. After a while of wiping down, Stephanie offered to swap jobs, only Beth wanted to carry on scraping. She could vent her fury in the process.

In truth, Beth didn't seem that angry but adopted a resigned acceptance. This made Stephanie livid on her behalf. Who the bloody hell would pick on Beth? She didn't ask for trouble. It was pure ignorance. As she sloshed water and wiped up, her anger mingled with heat from the furnace of her stomach.

'I've got to take a break,' said Stephanie.

'Shall I make us a coffee?'

'A cold drink would be better.'

'Help yourself from the fridge.' Beth smiled and gave an encouraging nod.

'Do you want one?'

'Not for me. I'll carry on until I've got the place cleaned up.'

It was strange being inside Angel Cakes without the lights on. Beth invested in daylight quality bulbs and they made the space comfortable. At that moment, the place was a shell of stalagmites bursting from the floor where chairs were upturned on the tabletops. Beth had done brilliantly setting up the café. Finally, there was the chance to buy a proper panini using real mozzarella. When Stephanie had been going out with Ben, he'd been sniffy about cafés where they were served with cheddar. Some of Ben's snobbishness had obviously caught. That was probably one good reason for their parting. Stephanie let the memories slip, found a bottle of water, and returned outside.

Beth was leaning against the bonnet of her van, staring up at the café windows. Most of the black spray paint had gone.

'It just takes a minute or two with a can,' she said.

'Incomprehensible, isn't it?'

'Not really.'

Unsure she was following the conversation correctly, Stephanie frowned.

'Don't look so confused,' said Beth. 'You must be aware of racism in rural communities.'

'I've read the reports…'

'But this is the first time you've had any experience of it?' said Beth. 'Indirectly.'

'Yes.'

'Welcome to my world,' said Beth.

'You mean it's happened before?'

Beth laughed. 'I'll tell you about it when I'm not pissed off with the whole thing.' She took Stephanie's cleaning cloth from the bucket and squeezed out excess water. 'Let's finish the job. The quicker the graffiti's gone, the less likely there'll be a repeat. That's the theory. After it's scrubbed off, the scumbags can't come back and admire their handiwork.'

33

MAY 1979

Bully for Patricia working in such a hole! We waited outside the Mini Market while Patricia plucked up the courage to go in. She rabbited on about the manager, Mr Rogers, and how he knew her mum and dad from nights out at The Legion. My mum frowned upon *that particular establishment*. It all started because two members legged it the wrong way down King's Street and ended up balancing on our front fence. Around midnight, Mum actually went and told them to stop singing. I could hardly believe it. I dived under my covers to hide my embarrassment. Only when Mum came back and bolted the door, was I able to relax. My mother had the ability to make me cringe without even trying. I hoped the people weren't from near our street and that they wouldn't hold it against me.

Between the Mini Market and the neighbouring shop was an alleyway where a cool wind whipped along. Patricia shivered. She should've worn her jumper like I'd said but she was having none of it. Shielded from the wind by ducking in front of me, Patricia tickled my neck using her icicle fingers. I shoved her away. For once, I was in the know and she was... cold. It served her right. Killing time, I shuffled my feet from side to side and then checked my watch. There were still three minutes to go.

'That much longer?' said Patricia.

'You might as well go in now and make a good impression by arriving early.'

'Not yet.' Patricia rubbed her arms. Her bright-pink bra straps showed through the cotton school shirt.

'You'll warm up after you get inside.'

'I don't want to go in on my own.'

'It'll be fine.'

'You promised to come with me. Don't let me down.'

One look at Patricia's pleading face and I agreed. 'Okay. Two minutes.'

I chased a five-pence piece around the pocket of my school blazer. It was change from an errand Mum had sent me on. The coin never made it back into her ball-clip purse. When there was a lot to buy, Mum raided the housekeeping tin for a crisp note and then she checked the money I brought back. On days she only wanted a packet of custard creams or half a pound of butter, she never missed the coppers. It was like payment for a job well done and I usually spent the money on penny sweets. Fruit Salads were my favourite chews and Black Jacks were a close second. A bit of liquorice never did any harm. But my tastes were changing and if I had the money, I'd go for a Fry's Chocolate Cream. I could last for hours on two pieces without needing to eat another thing. Or Turkish Delight. Some days I was a dark chocolate girl and others I was milk.

'It's time to go in,' I announced.

'You first.' Patricia pushed me.

I resisted. 'Age before beauty.'

She tutted. Patricia was a few weeks older and never let me forget it. After a bit of huffing and puffing, Patricia marched inside. I followed like a timid lamb.

A layer of cigarette smoke hung like clouds in the valley. The man behind the counter stubbed out the end on a jam jar lid as Patricia approached. To make myself inconspicuous, I studied the birthday cards stuffed into a rotating rack. The contraption wobbled as I turned it and for a moment, I thought the whole thing would topple over. Good job I grabbed it in time, but I wasn't sure it stopped me from being seen. I could hear Patricia's nervous voice, asking if the man was Mr Rogers. Of course, he was. After a bit of chat, Mr Rogers dragged the plastic strips covering a doorway to one side. Patricia slipped under his arm and disappeared. What was I supposed to do? Thank God she returned only seconds later. I nearly laughed my head off when I saw what she was wearing. It was a brown tabard that made her look like a dinner lady. (I bet she was glad she didn't have to wear her hair scooped into a net cap.) Controlling my giggles, I had to admit she took the biscuit with the collar of her school shirt covered by the high neck and silky ribbon.

I didn't know if Mr Rogers heard my laughter or if it was the rack shaking as I clung on to it for dear life. I soon realised he was looking in my direction. He'd definitely twigged I'd been standing there all along.

'You may as well come out, young lady,' he said.

I hesitated for a moment, but his voice was so loud there wasn't any way I could pretend I hadn't heard. Taking a sideways step, I was caught by his staring eyes. To be honest, I didn't quite know what to make of him. He looked like he was ready for retirement with a big bald patch on the top of his head. This reminded me of Mum's favourite pudding (or *dessert* as she called it) otherwise known as peach melba. I had a chuckle.

'One of Patricia's friends, are you?'

Embarrassment made me clam up. Supposing he'd read my mind? Patricia gave me the evil eye but I still couldn't find any words. Gripping the hem of my skirt, I yanked it tight against my legs.

'Cat got your tongue?' he continued.

Now I needed to say something. 'We're in the same maths class.'

Mr Rogers tapped the side of his nose using the cap on his biro and Patricia was frowning like I'd put my foot in it. I looked down and realised with my skirt clamped between my fingers, I was showing even more leg than usual. Dropping the hem, I smoothed the crinkles.

'Nice set of pins,' said Mr Rogers. 'Are you after a job as well?'

Confusion darted around my head. I'd never thought of working while at school. When Janine had joined the sixth form, she'd got a Saturday job in Marks and Spencer. With my future looking desperate, I didn't think there was much chance. 'Is there a vacancy?'

'There is for you,' he said. 'Two and a half hours this afternoon, do you? Come up trumps and I'll give you a regular slot each Wednesday. Can't have you working on early closing Thursday, so I'll give you Saturday morning too.'

I smiled. It was the surprise of my life to be offered work.

As soon as I'd donned an identical tabard to Patricia, Mr Rogers laughed and said we looked like a right pair of Laurel and Hardys. I felt a bit sorry for Patricia. She always referred to her chubbiness as puppy fat, but Mr Rogers must've thought otherwise. We had different duties. I was assigned to tidy the magazine rack while Patricia checked ice creams in the chest freezer. Poor Patricia, she got even colder sorting out the fruit Mivvis from the choc ices. Mr Rogers returned to his place behind the till and lit another Embassy. I got busy taking down magazines from the display and gave them a dust. He barked instructions at me and I did exactly as he said, lining up the spines to show a bit of each front cover. I used a stool to reach up high and every time a customer came into the shop, the wind blew straight up my skirt. It was awkward balancing the duster and the magazines as well as trying to stop my skirt flapping. I managed it somehow.

Customers liked to chat with Mr Rogers and I got used to hearing mumbled voices while I concentrated on the work. I had the distinct impression the talk was smutty. When I dusted the magazines from the top shelf, the lewd remarks made sense. I'd never seen models close up showing such enormous boobs *and* in colour. (Boys at school flashed the occasional page three of the newspaper, but I never took any notice.) Balanced on the stool, I tuned into the talk.

'Crikey Moses, schoolgirl knickers,' said one bloke.

'Feast your eyes on that bit of totty,' came the reply. It was only then I realised they were talking about me. That did it, I turned to see who was there. One glance and I liked the admiration, even if they were workmen. They didn't look too bad in their overalls, each with a gold loop threaded through their left earlobe. I towered above them, a princess on a pedestal. In all the years I'd watched *The Generation Game*, it seemed at that moment totally appropriate to twirl like Anthea Redfern. I wasn't as elegant, but teetered around in a circle. The shorter one did a wolf-whistle and I gave him a smile.

34

2014

West Country Post

Letters to the editor are welcome on any subject, but priority is given to those which address topics of local interest. Concise letters are more likely to be published.

I t really did turn into a version of *Come Dine with Me* when Robert invited Beth and Stephanie round and Doug tagged along. He was making his own way there but Beth drove Stephanie in her Angel Cakes van. They left plenty of time knowing there were likely to be delays if caught behind a caravan. On this occasion the traffic was backed up on the lanes thanks to a tractor. When they got into the village, Stephanie read the directions sent by Robert on her mobile and then Beth pulled up beside a hedge that ran the length of a property. Stephanie had never been to the end of Evershot Lane before. She'd always turned around once she'd got to the biscuit factory (where she sometimes bought a job lot for colleagues at the *Post*). She never actually indulged herself – Stephanie was always a serious cake person.

'He wasn't wrong.' Stephanie slipped her mobile into her bag. 'It does look like a caterpillar.'

'Caterpillar?'

'See the way the hedge goes up and down,' said Stephanie.

'Oh yes.' But Beth appeared fascinated by the cottage behind the gate.

Stephanie gazed at the building too, noting the golden colour of the new thatch and the dressing around the gable windows which gave eyebrows to the glass panes.

'Robert's home has got a mind of its own,' said Stephanie. 'See the way it frowns at us.'

'What are you talking about? First it's caterpillars and now faces.' Beth shook her head and tightened the wrap around her shoulders. 'Let's get inside. It's funny how the evenings get chilly after the first weeks of August.'

Doug held a flute containing fizz and Robert distributed further glasses showing bluish bubbles. One sip and Stephanie was delighted to find Prosecco with a hint of lavender.

'What's on the menu?' Beth wasn't backwards in coming forwards.

'I want to let the food speak for itself,' said Robert. 'You'll have to wait and see.'

Beth pulled a disappointed expression but Robert wasn't drawn. He turned to Stephanie. 'How are things going with the podcast?'

'Haven't you seen the letter in the *Post*?' Beth interrupted.

'No,' said Robert. 'I don't take a daily paper.'

'You don't know what you're missing,' said Doug.

'Grab the laptop, Stephanie.' Beth pointed to the study nook in the corner. 'You can read it out loud.'

'Is that all right?' asked Stephanie.

'Of course,' said Robert. 'The log-on password is Belmont.'

'Very original.' Doug gave a teasing smile.

Settled at the desk, Stephanie found the page that displayed the letters section. Clearing her throat to announce the start, she put on her best BBC voice and read: *'Sirs, renewed media interest in the disappearance of Carolyn Russell has been brought to my attention. While I feel for family and friends who are looking for answers, I would like to reiterate that rumour and suspicion around my involvement is misplaced. I cooperated fully with police as part of the early enquiries and there is no evidence against me. I live a quiet and purposeful life and would like this to remain so. Graham Simmons.'*

'Now there's a surprise,' said Robert. 'Simmons coming forward at last.'

'Short and sweet,' said Doug.

'Not everyone agrees.' Stephanie noticed the number of comments on the page had increased to over one hundred. 'Readers are reacting in none too positive ways. Listen to this: *your silence says more than your pathetic plea. Get back here and come clean. It's the only way you'll ever find peace.* Here's another, *we all know you did it, creep.* There's reams and reams of people who believe he's guilty. I didn't realise the level of vitriol.'

'Come on, Stephanie,' said Doug. 'You've lived around here long enough to know mud sticks.'

'I don't think he's to blame,' she said. 'He may have been an idiot for chumming up with Southy and Gove and perhaps he imitated some of their tricks but it doesn't add up.'

'My scoop didn't convince you?' said Robert.

'It was great material for the podcast but he had an alibi. Simmons is entirely correct to say there's no evidence against him. Ooh, hang on a minute, here's a supporter: *Mr Simmons taught me at Greensleeves and nothing unseemly ever happened. Why can't you leave the man alone? says Elizabeth Fletcher.'*

'I bet she's popular,' said Doug.

'I see what you mean. Mr and Mrs Anonymous have got it in for her too.'

'Come on, guys, let's take a break,' said Beth. 'I'm getting depressed.'

In the wood-panelled dining room, Robert brought in the food ready plated. Stephanie was surprised to be presented with a whole bird, even if it was diminutive. She recognised it as poussin, although she'd never eaten one before. When Robert joined the party with servings for Doug and himself, the four stared at their plates.

'You're not obliged to eat the lot.' Robert flapped his napkin and laid it on his lap.

The others did likewise and Stephanie worried for a moment Doug was going to tuck his into his collar.

'It's mainly bones anyway.' Doug was the first to lift his cutlery and skilfully filleted a sliver of meat.

Robert picked up his knife and fork. 'I can't get Simmons out of my mind.'

Beth groaned.

'It's a fascinating story,' said Stephanie. 'You know there was only ever one sighting of Carolyn and that was at Waterloo Station. It's odd no one else came forward.'

'When a person wants to disappear, they're not going to leave any tracks,' said Doug. 'Although I doubt a sixteen-year-old would have the nous.'

'I'm pursuing a lead that suggests one of the customers at the old Mini Market in town might have been involved. The shop's closed and the manager's dead but I just need a lucky break. I'm convinced the police didn't investigate properly.'

'That lot were known for their incompetence,' said Doug.

'You're telling me,' said Stephanie. 'I'm not even sure the

reconstruction of her last movements was well handled.'

'I was involved in the filming around school,' said Robert. 'I couldn't make head nor tail of what was going on.'

'Come on, guys, can we stop the work talk?' said Beth. 'I've had enough of hearing about dud leads and all the crap that went on at Greensleeves.'

'You're too young to remember any of this?' asked Doug.

'The school had moved on by the time I enrolled. There was a zero-tolerance policy on sexism and racism.'

'Things were different for you,' said Robert.

'Not really. It sent everything underground. Students who'd been vocal found other ways to make it clear I didn't belong. I'd be bumped by backpacks as I walked along the corridors. One teacher apologised for the lack of procedures in reporting negative body language. The euphemism! Did you experience anything similar at the *Post*, Stephanie? Journalism seems such a tough profession for a woman.'

'You could say.' Stephanie glanced at Doug to see whether he wanted to chip in but he was too busy dissecting his dinner. 'I'm well out of it. There aren't many prospects for someone like me at the *Post*.'

'Steady on,' Doug cued into the conversation. 'You were my right-hand woman and doing pretty well. If it hadn't been for the cuts…'

'They were an excuse to push me out. On reflection, I think some colleagues felt threatened by my length of service and experience. Don't you agree, Doug?'

'I honestly couldn't say.' Doug kept his head down. 'Although I do believe you're on to a winner with *Extra Lessons*. I can't think who first suggested the podcasting idea.'

'Okay, Doug. Praise goes to you.' Stephanie wasn't about to say it was really Janine who'd spurred her on. She let him have a moment in the sun and found herself doing something she wouldn't normally have dreamed of. She was actually puckering up to blow him a kiss. What the hell had come over her? The moment of panic and possible humiliation eased when Doug blithely caught the floating kiss and tucked it into his pocket.

'Why did you set up your own business, Beth?' asked Robert.

'I was sick of being overlooked for promotion at the hotel kitchen where I first worked. It doesn't bother me now. Those years as a pastry chef set me up. Angel Cakes is a thriving business, don't you know?'

'I'm full of admiration for your entrepreneurial skills,' said Robert.

Stephanie was a bit miffed he hadn't included her in the compliment. She'd shown initiative in setting up the podcast. Rather than make a fuss, Stephanie refocused her attention. 'Beth is more than a businesswoman. She's ready to tackle antisocial behaviour in the community. We got properly exhausted scraping graffiti off the windows at Angel Cakes.'

Robert gave a look of concern and Doug stopped munching for a second. The table became strangely quiet.

'The graffiti's gone,' said Beth. 'I'm completely over it.'

'But the message was racist,' said Stephanie.

'For every person who wants to see me off, there are plenty of others who are pleased I'm here. I wouldn't have such a strong customer base at Angel Cakes if everyone was like those thugs.'

'Indeed.' Doug raised another forkful. 'Ignoring stuff is what's kept me sane at the *Post*.'

Stephanie realised it had been a mistake to mention the incident. She wasn't happy about Doug's response but Beth had made it clear she wanted nothing else said. With a sense of discomfort, Stephanie pushed the food around her plate. The nest of little bones was rather off-putting. Stephanie rationalised that as she had no trouble eating chicken, this shouldn't be any different. Knives scraping the crockery were the only sounds to be heard until Robert put on a CD, or soothing music as he called it.

35

MAY 1979

It was lunchtime and crowds of first-year girls left the
building in their green-and-white gingham dresses making
for the playing field. At their age, I'd worn a dress too, but mine
had been jazzed up by Mum sewing rickrack around the neck
and on the bodice. I'd been proud of the dress that first summer
then the next year me and Floria wore short-sleeved shirts
tucked into our grey skirts like the rest. Even during the weeks
before leaving school we still had to wear a tie. For boys it wasn't
bad because they'd need to get used to it. Us girls were unlikely to
wear a tie again. Especially not a bottle green one with lime
stripes. Ghastly. That was the trouble with school, teachers
lacked imagination (except Mr Simmons, of course). He who was
perfect.

I followed Patricia to the far end of the field and she came to a
stop beside the white lines of the running track. The ground was
damp from an earlier shower so we laid our jumpers on the grass
to sit. A mower had recently cut the field to within an inch of its
life, and pins of yellowing ends laid about the place. A group of
girls had gone nearer to the fence but we didn't want to get close.
They were the sort who knotted their shirt ends into a bra top

and showed off their flat stomachs while they sunbathed. A few others were gathered under the shady branches of trees which reached over the diamond wires of the boundary fence.

The trudge to our spot was more than I'd bargained for. If I'd known Patricia wanted to walk the length of the field, I would've left my textbooks in my locker before heading over. Unlike the others, I didn't store my lunchbox there – I couldn't be sure when waves of hunger would strike. A pear for breakfast only kept the pangs away for a while but it was amazing how sustaining a Ryvita could be. It was my habit to have a couple of dry crispbreads ready to eat in case of emergency. As it was, I still had the Ryvita sandwich I'd made that morning with a sliver of cheese. I unwrapped the greaseproof paper to reveal what had become my regular lunch. It took two seconds to wolf it down.

'Is that all you're having?' Patricia was munching into her second half of a doorstop sandwich. I watched jam oozing between the crusts. How I longed for a bite, but I'd never slim down enough to be anything like Jerry Hall if I copied Patricia.

'I've lost ten pounds.'

'Bloody hell. Your savings have taken a hit.'

I sniffed. It wasn't worth trying to celebrate weight loss with Patricia.

'You'll turn into a stick insect if you're not careful.'

Ha bloody ha. I was doing this, going through near starvation, for Sim.

The huge sandwich wasn't enough for Patricia and I had the torment of listening to her slurp the full contents from a pineapple yoghurt pot. The action of spoon to mouth and back to pot was mesmerising. I had to take my mind off food and Sim was the ideal distraction. It was only one hour ago when he leaned over me, pen in hand ready to mark my work. I could sense his chin brushing my hair, his hand was so close to mine, I was tempted to stroke it.

'What are you daydreaming about this time?' Patricia interrupted my musing.

'Who not what.'

'Should've guessed.' Patricia ran her fingers over the grass cuttings and scooped up a pile. She selected one of the longest blades and peered at it, as if she were about to thread a needle. 'My gran says a gap-tooth look is attractive.'

'That's news to me.' I watched as Patricia tapped the end of the grass against her teeth then prised it between the two front ones.

'Get a load of this!' The grass stayed in place, stuck out from her lips at a right angle.

She looked daft and I couldn't help laughing.

'Why don't you give it a try?'

'Not me. I didn't spend months wearing braces for nothing.'

'I thought that was to do with sticking-out teeth.'

'It was to correct the damage caused by thumb-sucking when I was younger.'

'So, there's no harm.'

It was easier to give in than argue with Patricia. A bit of grass wouldn't do much harm. Taking a cutting, I tried feeding it between my teeth but there wasn't any room. I chucked the stem away while Patricia continued to show off her new-found skill. It seemed a bit juvenile to me. I took a swig of orange squash from my Tupperware beaker.

Having Patricia to myself at lunchtime was a change. Often, she wanted to hang about with her friends from the estate, but as our last lesson that morning had been maths, we traipsed the field together. I looked back towards the school buildings. There wasn't any sign of Patricia's gang. They were probably mucking around in the far playground. This was my chance to make the most of being with Patricia. The sound of cars chasing along the dual carriageway gave a sense of connection to the outside world and absorbed me for a minute.

'I know you want to be the teacher's pet,' said Patricia. 'It's not really working, is it?'

That just showed how much *she* knew. A vein in my forehead pulsed. The cheek of it. Although I wanted to put her straight, this wasn't the time for bragging. Eventually I came up with a reply. 'Mr Simmons isn't one for favourites.'

'Your mum's paying for extra lessons, shouldn't that buy you special attention in class?'

'He wouldn't make it obvious.'

'Wouldn't make it obvious,' Patricia copied.

I sensed outrage but put my feelings in check. Falling out with the one person I could call a friend at school wasn't the best idea. 'You're jealous.'

'No way,' said Patricia. 'He wears the same shoes as my dad. At least my dad polishes them.'

Patricia talked a load of nonsense. I didn't bother replying. Then, from the corner of my eye, I spotted a couple of fourth-years coming our way. What did they want? Using my hand to shade my eyes, I looked up and recognised Tracy Dickens.

'Lost your way?' asked Patricia.

'No,' said Tracy. 'I want a word with Carolyn.'

Patricia gave a sly smile. 'Be my guest.'

Tracy's friend stood beside her, as if egging her on with this so-called word.

'What's up?' I asked.

Tracy didn't speak. Her friend gave a nudge, sending Tracy a step closer. 'I've had an after-school lesson with Mr Simmons. You're not the only one – the only girl – I know what it's like.'

This wasn't what I wanted to hear. I turned to Patricia hoping she'd spout a suitable put-down. She shrugged and said, 'Nothing to do with me.'

Although annoyed, I couldn't quiz Patricia when I had to see Tracy off. 'Is that so?'

Tracy hesitated. 'I didn't like it much.'

'It's a matter of taste,' I said.

'Ha ha ha! *Matter of taste,*' Patricia repeated.

Whose side was she on? I'd had enough of her sense of humour for one day. 'Give it a rest.'

'Ooh, get you!' said Patricia.

The fourth-years looked at each other and Tracy took a deep breath.

'Spit it out,' I said.

'You want to watch yourself.'

'Says who?'

Just then a scream pierced the air. Everyone turned to where the sound came from. The group by the fence were picking up their stuff and staggering back towards school. One girl burst into tears and was comforted by arms around her shoulders. She may have got heatstroke for all I knew. Served her right for sunbathing. Except, it was more than that. The girls were straightening their clothes, unknotting their shirt ends. This was some sort of fall out.

'Hey, what's going on?' Patricia called.

The group of girls rushed by but a straggler answered, 'There's a flasher.'

My eyes spun back to where the bushes were jiggling on the other side of the fence. The outcry hadn't put him off. The man stood there with his trousers around his knees and his hand clasped in front of him. I could hardly take my eyes off the rhythmic movement. It was ugly and fascinating.

'Ignore him.' Patricia got to her feet as the two fourth-years took flight.

One last look.

'Filthy old git,' Patricia shouted over her shoulder as we walked towards the new block.

36

2014

NHS public health campaign poster:
CATCH IT, BIN IT, KILL IT

S tephanie answered the mobile using her best telephone voice. As soon as she'd got the words out, a tickle at the back of her throat resulted in a coughing fit. Getting up from her workspace at the kitchen table, she took a glass and gulped water. This was no way to impress. She returned the handset to her ear.

'When you've quite finished,' said a man.

Stephanie failed to recognise the person speaking.

'Can I help you?'

'Now you've stopped coughing.'

Sick of guessing who was on the line, she asked, 'Who is this?'

'It's important to be cautious,' he said. 'Your approach to answering the phone shows you're security conscious. It's Bill.'

Bill? The name didn't immediately register. It wasn't surprising as Stephanie had spent the morning wading through online research relating to other teenage disappearances nationally. So far, there had been no similarities to Carolyn's case. The phone call intruded into her thoughts and then the name clicked into place. 'Bill Spencer?'

'No good comes from repeating.'

What was he on about? 'Can you...'

'Never mind. The reason I'm calling is to let you know I've found the last known contact details for Floria Pavel.'

Stephanie sensed he was waiting for a word of surprise or appreciation. Silly old fool. Little did he know Stephanie's conversation with Floria had come to nothing. 'That's kind of you.'

'Although I really don't know why you're bothering when you could get a much fuller picture directly from me. I am available to appear on your podcast.'

Stephanie smothered a laugh. People like Bill Spencer did nothing to generate a sense of confidence in the police but it was worth getting him on tape. A few words from the man himself and listeners would make up their own mind.

'That's a good idea. Let's meet.'

'The sooner the better.'

'Absolutely.' Stephanie played along and checked her diary. 'Does tomorrow suit you?'

Why Bill Spencer chose a car park for their meeting was beyond Stephanie. It's not as if they were filming. She imagined him turning up incognito on the top of a high-rise block for a discussion between puffs on his cigarette, like in a seventies TV show. The Tesco car park on the outskirts of town had plenty of spaces even though an NHS van offering breast cancer screening took up a whole row of parking. Stephanie didn't look forward to the discomfort of having her breasts squashed between glass plates on her next mammogram due the following year. At least no lumps had been identified so far. Closing her mind to the thought of her mother's cervical cancer, Stephanie looked for Bill's car. The distinctive sienna Hyundai was easy to locate.

As she approached, he swung open the passenger door and she noticed the fleece cover on the chair. She took off her raincoat before sitting inside, knowing she'd be much too hot on a late summer day for a fluffy seat.

'You don't mind meeting here, do you?' he said.

For a moment, Stephanie imagined he was going to lock the car and spirit her away. Common sense prevailed. Bill Spencer didn't look like a well man with his pallid complexion and dark circles under his eyes.

'It's fine. Just give me a minute while I get the recording equipment out.'

Turning sideways in the passenger seat, Stephanie prepared for the interview. She liked to eyeball her interviewees and Bill Spencer was no exception. From his inside jacket pocket, Bill took a piece of lined paper and passed it to Stephanie as if it were a bribe.

'Floria's details,' he whispered.

'Oh yes.' Stephanie found herself whispering her reply. She glanced at the number and recognised the Dijon code. It may have been the last known contact but she had received updated information. She decided against mentioning the fact.

'Everything else is up here.' Bill tapped his temple.

'Thank you so much for agreeing to share your thoughts on Carolyn's case.' She checked the recording and placed the mic on the arm rest between them. 'This'll pick up your voice very well.'

'Glad to hear it. I've pressing things to say.'

'Please, go ahead.'

'Did you know Graham Simmons' house backed onto derelict land? Along an alley and he was straight there. Would've been easy for him to remove a body and bury it where no one would see.'

What was he on? The former DI Spencer making such a suggestion. Great stuff for the podcast, if not his reputation.

'Is there any proof?'

'Of course not, I'm simply telling you some of my random thoughts from the time.'

Random thoughts? Stephanie expected something more concrete. 'I've heard the gossip. If there'd been a body buried, it would've shown up when the new properties were built in the eighties. I've checked the plans.'

'Not necessarily. Some of those houses have big gardens. I bet the ground was simply levelled.'

Perhaps he was right. 'That's not something I can use unless you can substantiate it.'

'You remember back in 2002, the Soham murders of Holly and Jessica?'

'Yes.' He truly was going off-piste but the mention of their names brought to mind the two girls in their Manchester United shirts.

'The whole country had a theory.'

This was news to Stephanie. 'Really?'

'Believe me they did.'

'Okay.'

'It's the same with Carolyn. Most of us in the force thought Simmons had something to do with her disappearance, if not her murder. Unlike the Soham case, Simmons didn't crumble under questioning.'

Did Ian Huntley give up that easily? Stephanie wasn't convinced. 'And your point is?'

'We were unlucky. He had the alibi of a job interview but Simmons could still have got to Carolyn.'

She'd heard about the interview before but this last comment was more outrageous than ever. 'What? And then they returned to his house where he murdered her?'

'It may sound implausible but Simmons had a whiff of guilt about him.'

'There must have been other suspects.'

'Oh yes! But no one sticks in the mind like Simmons.'

'Well, it would be very helpful to shed a bit of light on the others.'

Bill rubbed his chin. 'One of the Mini Market customers came under scrutiny. You know Carolyn had a Saturday job, don't you?'

'Not only Saturdays.'

'Have it your own way,' muttered Bill.

Was he being difficult, or were Stephanie's questions clumsy? 'Can you tell me more about this person?'

'He worked as a mechanic at a garage and he used to pop in there for fags. There was easy parking outside.'

Bloody hell. 'Was he connected with the yellow car?'

'We checked him out.' Bill tossed his head. 'He did own a lemon Cortina. At the time of Carolyn's disappearance, the car was off the road and he was doing MOTs the whole day. Records show he dated and signed each certificate.'

Stephanie held her breath. There'd been so many cock-ups on this case. 'Do you have his name?'

Bill Spencer rubbed his chin. 'Rick something or other. Rick Salisbury, I think.'

'Is it worth referring to your notebooks, just to be sure?'

'That's not necessary,' said Bill Spencer. 'It's Simmons you need to go after.'

Stephanie was flabbergasted. Did the police overlook a lead because they were convinced of Simmons' guilt? She really couldn't put up with his speculation any longer.

At home again, Stephanie found a cup of camomile tea soothing. She'd stomped most of the way back trying to get Bill Spencer out of her mind. As if she didn't have enough to think about without him piling suspicion on Graham Simmons. The poor teacher had made some silly mistakes at Greensleeves but he was young, twenty-three was no great age. After Forsyth had become an enemy, things were unlikely to turn out well for him. If only Simmons would answer her calls. Of course, she understood his reluctance. Stephanie had tried her best to leave telephone messages including an upbeat view. She hoped each and every one of them might persuade Simmons that the podcast would provide the fair hearing he deserved. It had been over a week since she'd last tried to reach him and even his letter to the *Post* didn't deter her. Another call was worth the effort. She knew the number by heart and sat with her ear to the phone. When the ringtone stopped and a woman said *hello*, Stephanie nearly fell off her chair. Composing herself, she found a reply.

'Hello.' She smiled to make her voice cheerful. 'May I speak to Graham Simmons?'

'Who's calling?' The woman's voice was hesitant.

'I'm Stephanie Brett – I've been trying to reach Graham for such a long time.'

'I know,' said the woman. 'I'm his wife.'

Stephanie put her free hand on her chest to calm her thumping heart. 'It's really important I speak to Graham.' She used his first name again, as if it were an olive branch. 'The podcast I'm developing is Graham's chance to tell his side of the story.'

'There's no one he can trust.'

'Give me a try. I promise to let Graham have his say.'

'There isn't any point. Your town, your Bel...' Mrs Simmons' voice fluttered. 'I can't even say the name. They have never believed him.'

'I'll work with you. Together we can find a way to challenge the rumour and gossip.'

'No,' she said. 'You can't. We hoped the letter to the *Post* would appeal to their better nature. That they'd stop touting your podcast. We never expected them to print it. Now we're in a worse position than ever. I can't believe people who don't even know Graham would write such awful comments. We have children to protect.'

'Breaking your silence was a brave thing to do. There's one way to beat bullies – by standing up to them.'

'No,' she said. 'We can't expose ourselves to more of this.'

'I can understand your thinking but–'

'We are broken people. Please, leave us alone. *Please.*'

Before Stephanie had a chance to speak again the line went dead.

37

MAY 1979

At night I snuggled my pillow and imagined Sim lying beside me. My dreams were a flurry of images and sensations. His lips brushed mine and he wrapped his arms around my nakedness. As his kisses teased my nipples and he descended to my lower regions, I became stiff and expectant. Desire drove me half mad until my fingers pressed between my legs. With steady, rapid strokes, I found relief. There was nothing to be ashamed of, really there wasn't. All it took was a trip to the bathroom and by washing my hands, the briny smell of my misdeed was gone.

Returning to my room, I found the bed-sheet coiled into a skein of rope from the tossing and turning. How would it be if I used the sheet to scale from the window and into the freedom of the night? I could turn up at Sim's in nothing but my nightdress and I was sure he'd welcome me. But only if that bitch Tracy Dickens kept her paws off. I could throttle her and her stupid, *you want to watch yourself*. As if she knew something I didn't. The connection between me and Sim was undeniable yet I had to guard against idiotic girls throwing themselves at him. It wasn't easy for any man to remain faithful, especially when our union hadn't been consummated. We had to be patient and wait for the day to come.

Of course, the thought of Sim straying had crossed my mind but he'd never go for a girl like Tracy. Stupid cow. If Sim did find someone else, there'd be nothing for it. I'd have to tie the sheet around my neck and… I winced. Memories of my father flooded, darkening my outlook, making my limbs heavy. No, I'd never resort to that but if there wasn't a future with Sim, I'd have to do something dramatic. Stones in my pockets and a leap into cold quarry water perhaps. A dramatic ending. Mum would regret her rules and expectations once I was gone. As for Sim, he'd become a lonely bachelor pining for me. Unfurling the sheet to cover the bed, I pushed the morbid thoughts aside. I knew by the time I saw Sim at our next after-school session, I'd be feeling positive.

Beneath my short-sleeved top, I wore my now purple bra. The dyeing had been a success. A standard-issue bra transformed into a sexy undergarment. Sim was bound to be impressed. Swinging my hips (also clad in purple) helped to clear my mind as I focused on my one true love. At his front door, I rang the bell and practised smiling. Hours of standing in front of the mirrored medicine cupboard in the bathroom had perfected my technique. A little lowering of the top bow while bringing up the edges gave a smile that suggested pleasure at seeing him. The dab of lip gloss accentuated my look. I was ready for him.

Half hidden behind the door, he had to manoeuvre something in the hall that was blocking the way. Giving me room, he backed against the wall, yet I managed to brush his chest. He wore the smell of Lifebuoy soap and for a moment, I thought of him soaking in the bath, the ends of his hair spreading in the water, bubbles of lather running down his chest. Oh dear! I needed to get a grip.

'Sorry about the squash, and excuse the pram,' he said.

'A pram?' I ducked to look under the hood and saw a sleeping baby in a blue romper suit. I would have oohed at his tiny fingers but my mind buzzed in confusion. What on earth was going on? My forehead tightened into a frown.

'I'm minding the baby for a neighbour.'

Relief flooded over me. Of course, the baby wasn't his. I should've known to trust Sim. He read the time on his watch and I admired his sturdy wrist. Large and steady enough to sport a clunky metal strap.

'She should've been back by now,' he said.

Who the hell was *she*?

'Thankfully, the little lad's away with the fairies. His grandmother's had to pop out.'

Phew! His *grandmother*.

'The baby's no trouble while he's asleep. Let's go over the work we did in class today.'

I sat on my usual chair, not wanting to actually admit I hadn't been listening in the lesson. My mind had been busy planning our new life together. With the weather heating up and holidays approaching, I couldn't help thinking about it most of the time. Just the exams to get out of the way, then we'd be free. I imagined myself clad in a yet to be purchased bikini and Sim chasing me along a sandy beach. We would make a perfect couple.

'I noticed you and Patricia talking,' he said.

'Oh.' It was true. When I wasn't dreaming about Sim, I was whispering about him. Fortunately, by the end of the lesson we'd answered the questions on the board. Or at least Patricia had. 'We were doing stuff together.'

'Having someone to work things out with is fun, isn't it?'

He really didn't mind me discussing our plans with Patricia? I wasn't so sure. She might start blabbing. I gave him a smile because I didn't want him to worry.

'Come on.' Sim struck his knuckles on the table.

I admired the signet ring on his little finger. Very stylish. One day, I would have a gold band of my own.

'We can't afford to waste time,' he said.

I was shaken back to my senses. We had to at least look like we were doing some maths. Spilling the books and pens from my bag onto the table, a pencil rolled off on its own. I needed to stop it dropping onto the floor. I reached over and my head brushed against Sim's. Funny thing was, he got there first and as he returned the pencil to me, our fingers lingered.

'Right.' He rubbed his hands together like something exciting was going to happen. My heart danced a merry tune. Perhaps he wanted to warm his fingers before he touched me again. He must've known the very idea of his skin against mine sent my feelings wild.

'I'm ready.' My stupid lips quavered.

'We shall move on.'

I could've listened to him forever. In English vocab, the term *mellifluous* had been introduced and there wasn't a better adjective. Clinging on to his every word, I somehow absorbed the maths and was lulled by his talk. I couldn't love him any more if I tried. Whilst Sim was in full flow, the door-knocker drummed. It sent an echo through the house and shoved us off course.

'Sorry,' he said. 'I'll have to get that. It's probably my neighbour come for the baby.' He slipped a new page of maths questions in front of me. 'Have a read of these problems. We'll go through them when I'm back.'

With that, Sim slid off his chair and I watched him turn. (His shoulders were broad like Superman's.)

Talk at the door delayed Sim. It was a lady chatting about waiting at the doctor's surgery and then she went on about the huge queue at the chemist's shop. All of a sudden, I needed to stretch my legs. I had to navigate around the furniture and it wasn't easy moving about with Sim's chair stuck out. I managed to get by and went to the storage unit where books were displayed. They were mainly about sport but I wondered which novels he'd enjoy. Maybe we could read to each other at night. I ran my fingers over the wood, smooth as anything. Was Sim a good carpenter? Perhaps he could change plugs. These were the marks of a real handyman. As the chat continued, I tuned into what they were saying. Sim was busy complimenting the baby: how he slept soundly, how he was no trouble at all. Next, he explained about me. That I'd come for extra lessons and I was waiting for his help. The lady kept rambling on and I was beginning to resent her for taking the time when Sim and I should be alone together. Out of nowhere, I heard him say the word *gorgeous*. A thrill zipped through me from my toes upwards. It was as if I'd been caught in magic dust from Tinkerbell's wand. I was positive he'd said I was gorgeous. Sim was talking about me.

I dashed back to my place as I heard the front door close and Sim's footsteps approaching. He sat and scanned the page to find some calculation for me to try. He passed me another sheet and set the kitchen timer to ten minutes. How could he be so cruel? Expecting me to work following such a revelation. I was hot with delight at his compliment and I wanted to say I felt exactly the same way. But it was hard giving words to my feelings even though he'd said I was gorgeous first. He tapped the paper, as if he was embarrassed. I didn't need to speak. Sim and I could read each other's minds. And, when he didn't return my look, I knew he was acting like a gentleman. I appreciated his thoughtfulness.

After he'd marked the first sheet of questions – I hadn't quite finished them all in the given time although there was a line of red ticks – I became all hot again. It wasn't due to the success but a longing to tell him my feelings and hear his reply. Bottled-up emotions were nearly driving me mad. I needed to hang in there.

Another set of questions answered, and then a new need arose. I could hardly believe it. Trying to prevent my bladder from bursting, I jiggled around on my chair. That caught his attention and now he was staring directly at me. I had to say something.

'May I be excused?' I didn't want to sully the atmosphere but I couldn't wait for a reply. I wanted to get out yet I wasn't going to waste the moment of being close to him. My boobs brushed his shoulders as I squeezed behind his chair. Sim was a gentleman and wouldn't want me crushed. He pulled in his chair and gave me more room.

'The door's off the kitchen,' he said.

Running water from the cold tap, I drenched a wad of toilet paper and dabbed it over my face and neck. I needed to stop the glowing pink from spreading. This was the effect he had on me. Further thoughts of Sim and the shakes took hold. The trembling started with my knees and juddered up my body. I couldn't leave the bathroom – I wanted to impress Sim not end up a whimpering mess. Five minutes went by and then I heard Sim calling my name. Now I really had to get a grip. Taking a breath, I emptied my lungs in one long stream. Just as I was making my way back on unsteady feet, the knocker sounded again. Sim dashed in front of me then turned.

'Are you okay, Carolyn?' A frown creased his forehead. 'You were in there a long time.'

I hadn't meant him to worry. 'Just a little problem.'

He nodded as though he really understood.

When Sim opened the door, a grammar-school boy appeared on the step. Sim turned to face me. 'I'm so sorry, Carolyn. I haven't been able to give you my full attention today. How about you stay a little longer after our next session? I'll make it up to you. Here, take a few of these index cards. I think you'll like the colours.' He picked up a pile from the shelf and passed them to me. 'They're useful for revision notes. Right now, as you can see, I have another tutee.'

I fanned the cards and realised there was nothing for me to do other than pack up my things. My heart raced at the thought of our parting. How could he cut me off? Then I realised he had a plan. I'd accepted his gift and next time, it would be a special date.

38

2014

PASSENGER NOTICE
Do NOT speak to the bus driver without good
cause while the vehicle is in motion.

Reflecting on two recent conversations had sent Stephanie's mind into overdrive. Although she considered Bill Spencer to be slightly barking, there was no denying his power to cast a shadow over Graham Simmons. And talking to Simmons' poor wife had been pitiful. She needed a break and as a walk often cleared Stephanie's head, she put on a wide-brimmed hat and trainers. Stephanie made for the end of the street where a path led into a cul-de-sac of bungalows which offered sheltered accommodation for the over fifty-fives. Bloody hell, she wasn't far off reaching an age when she could get her name on the list for one. She scoffed at the very idea. No. There was plenty she wanted to achieve in the next few years and she certainly didn't want to end up living cheek by jowl to someone like the retired

DI Bill Spencer. That man had the power to irritate with his assertions. Perhaps this was his way to cover up incompetence or worse, police conspiracy. There was so much corruption in the 1970s, she wouldn't put it past him.

Through the alleyway she went. High panel fencing offered privacy to the gardens on either side and at the end lay the start of a shingle track. This led through fields where sheep grazed and towards the huge grassy hump of the Iron Age hill fort. The sheer scale of it was impressive. She revelled in the sense of following the same route as those who had lived in this very place centuries before. Yet, recent history remained at the forefront of her mind. It was hard not to sympathise with Simmons' wife. Trust the *Post* to take advantage and publish his letter. It was a cheap stunt that had cost the couple dearly. Getting into her stride, Stephanie enjoyed the sense of covering ground. She wasn't one to dawdle and making progress along the track towards her goal gave a feeling of satisfaction. If only it were as simple to get ahead on the podcast.

Bill Spencer's motivation in fingering Simmons continued to perplex. There can't have been any financial gain. Stephanie wondered about the networks in Belmont and whether there had been collusion amongst key members of staff at Greensleeves who had their own reasons for muddying the waters. She recounted her research. Graham Simmons was a newly qualified teacher who lived in a home usually occupied by a family. House sharing with friends was a possibility that never materialised. Imagine the responsibilities for a young man recently out of college. Taking up his post after the Easter holidays, it should've been an ideal time to get to grips with a new role. He was covering maternity leave so the job must have been temporary but may well have become permanent. How many women went back to work in the seventies if there was a baby to look after? As for tutoring, given his financial circumstances, it was an available option. Simmons was up against it at home, trying to make enough money for rent and he had problems at school, trying to convince the old guard a new way of working was possible. He had a lot on.

Stephanie clambered over a stile and began her ascent to join a track that led around the hill fort. Catching her breath for a moment, she studied the undulating ground beneath her. She remembered rolling sausage-like down the lower sections when she was young. Redirecting her gaze towards Belmont, she considered it a compact town with church spires and towers to boast on its skyline. When she'd circumnavigated the top, Stephanie was ready to go home. She was wearier than she'd expected to feel. There remained plenty of work waiting for her and rather than use up the last vestiges of energy, Stephanie ambled down the path and made it through a field that brought her to a bus stop on the edge of town. Glad the shelter contained a timetable and a seat, she realised it was five minutes until a cross-county bus would arrive. If she'd remembered to bring a bottle of water with her and a snack, she might not have needed to rely on public transport.

During the wait, Stephanie thought about Carolyn. An impressionable teenager, struggling at home and in school. Did she have any respite? Stephanie supposed this came in the form of Patricia. Her only friend even though they were terribly mismatched. As her mind wandered, Stephanie was suddenly aware of the parallels to her own situation. Beth was an unlikely companion, but that didn't mean she wasn't genuine. Stephanie quickly refocused on the subject of her podcast and mulled over the reasons behind Carolyn's tendency to deceitfulness. Perhaps that was going over the top, reading too much into the fact that Carolyn had obtained a shop job without her mother knowing. Yet, it did say something about the relationship between Mrs Russell and Carolyn.

As the bus pulled up at the stop, Stephanie reached into her pocket where her purse contained enough change for the fare.

She hopped onboard and stepped past a standing passenger to find the back of the bus half empty. Taking a place next to the window, Stephanie settled into the jolts and spurts of progress along the tree-lined residential roads. Closer to the centre of town, the bus stopped again and a black woman lumbered onboard with her shopping trolley. She slapped the right money onto the shelf where the driver issued tickets. Somehow the coins dropped to the floor. There was a kerfuffle as she collected the ones that had rolled out of reach. The man Stephanie had pushed past earlier continued to stand, his stomach flopping over his belt. Close enough to offer assistance, he didn't move a muscle but watched her grapple. By the time the woman was upright again, her hair had sprung free from the clips keeping it neat and her skin was glistening with sweat. The bus pulled away. She gripped a pole and clutched the shopping trolley in her other hand.

'You need the right money,' the man shouted.

Taken aback by the volume of his speech, the woman nodded. 'I know.'

'No change here.' Again, he shouted.

'I had the right money.'

'Must be different in your country.' His voice carried along the bus and Stephanie flushed with discomfort.

'This is my country,' she said. 'I live here.'

'Come off it, you don't belong.'

The woman rammed her trolley along the aisle. It was difficult for her to move, especially as his big feet were blocking the way. When she managed to get by, Stephanie raised her hand and waved. 'There's a seat next to me.'

Looking over, the woman smiled and continued along the aisle. Stephanie slid over to the window to make space and tucked her skirt around her. The woman sat and took a deep breath.

'Take no notice of him,' said Stephanie. 'He's a one-off.'

The woman raised her eyebrows. She didn't say anything. She didn't need to. And Stephanie was hot with embarrassment. Was this what Beth had to put up with all the time? Making excuses for the man's ignorance was the last thing she should've been doing.

39

MAY 1979

Saturday morning and I was ready to leave for work but I couldn't go without reading Floria's postcard again. Propped against the pencil pot on my desk, it had arrived yesterday. I'd managed to extract it from the pile of mail before Mum saw it. The picture showed a London bus, a beaming red double-decker. I'd travelled on one like that twice before when I'd been on a school trip to the Museum of London which included an overnight stay at a youth hostel close to Waterloo Station. Miss Grant had been there to supervise us girls and insisted on travelling by road. (After one Tube journey, she'd been sick with worry we'd end up on the line because of jostling on the platform.) I had to agree with her that the underground was filthy but the announcement to *mind the gap* was fun. At the hostel, I took the top bunk while the fat girl underneath grumbled. To my mind it was only sensible to have her ballast holding us down. She didn't see it my way but I managed to stop her complaining to Miss Grant.

Turning the postcard over, I read Floria's words and imagined her at the language school chatting away. Some of the boys at Greensleeves teased Floria about her accent, but she never cared.

She was pretty and had a lovely complexion, *olive skin* it was called. I didn't have a clue why. From spending time at Floria's place in France, I knew there were two types of olives, black and green. I always chose the black whenever a bowl was passed around while we sipped drinks known as aperitifs. Her brothers had small bottles of beer while me and Floria drank squash made from real lemons and sugar. It seemed to me the black olives were more sophisticated than the green. They were little bullets that tasted salty. It took a while to master the art of spitting out the stones without appearing horribly rude.

At mealtimes in Floria's house, I drank wine from a proper glass. It didn't matter that it had been watered down. The whole experience of clinking and sipping was joyous. So different from the stingy Christmas drinks at home. That was the one time alcohol was allowed. Mum made snowballs from lemonade and yolk-yellow advocaat. It was Janine's bright idea and Mum bought the bottle to make it happen. I never much cared for eggs but I didn't mind knocking back a snowball and eating the glacé cherry from the cocktail stick. I was never sure what Floria's family would've made of it. They didn't go in for fizzy drinks – apart from champagne – which they cracked open on my last night to wish me well.

In her neat French handwriting, Floria told me about her excellent London life. She'd been to Carnaby Street and had bought a flared flowered skirt. I was immediately envious. How come she got to do exciting stuff? I actually lived in the country and hadn't seen many of the sights. It simply wasn't fair. But maybe Floria's trip could be turned to my advantage. In her earlier letter she'd invited me to visit. Now she'd arrived, the time had come to make plans. And planning it would take. How on earth would I convince Mum to let me go? She didn't even want me to visit Janine in Oxford without her tagging along. Really! How old did she think I was? I had to pay full fare on the bus, that must count for something.

Checking my watch, there was a little time before I planned to leave for the Mini Market. It was a mistake to leave the postcard on display. Mum had a habit of poking around and I needed to keep so much away from her. Obviously, my relationship with Sim was under wraps. If Mum got a sniff, she'd put an end to my extra lessons. She couldn't bear to think of me as grown into a woman with *desires*. The very fact that Sim reciprocated was bound to send her into a frenzy. Never before had she approved of Janine's boyfriends or any man who had LONG HAIR. Not that Sim's was too long, just nicely cut around his jaw. I think Janine would've understood the passion me and Sim felt for each other, but as she was thick as thieves with Mum, I couldn't confide in her. It made sense to keep Floria's correspondence for my eyes only. Mum was never able to get her head around Floria's fancy French ways. For ages, she didn't understand why we were best friends. Once I told her Floria's dad worked as an engineer at the big plant, she began to think of our friendship positively.

The summer holiday with Floria had been something else. I hated her dad after he announced they were moving back to France but then I had to forgive him when I was invited to stay. I squeezed onto the back seat of the Renault alongside Floria. There was the ferry crossing and then a long journey by road. Her mum did all the driving because her dad and her brothers went ahead with the removal van.

Memories of that holiday gave me an idea. I dug out my treasure box and lifted the lid. It was my habit to count the money slipped between the tissue paper and the cardboard side. The blue ones were especially thrilling as I remembered my manoeuvres at the post office. It wasn't my fault the old boy in front of me couldn't keep hold of his savings. I watched as two notes drifted like feathers in the breeze and landed at my feet. It was instinct to cover them with my shoes. After he'd gone, I dropped the pen from the counter and scooped up my find.

Scotching the memory, I let my fingers trace the edges of my stash. I knew the notes were numbered and could be traced, so it stopped me from spending them. Instead, I enjoyed the sense of having money. The others I'd discovered in Mum's housekeeping tin. She never noticed they were gone so it was simply a case of relocation. I arranged the cash into a fan and then slotted the notes back into place.

Peeling back the tissue paper, I found the clay figures nestled. There was my long-necked Siamese cat and a cheeky Scottie dog. Beside them was my passport. Mum would only buy one that lasted a year, but turning the cardboard cover, I spotted the expiry date. There were still a couple of months left. A last look at Floria's postcard, and I memorised the address she'd squeezed into the corner with her phone number. Like a bookmark, I pressed the postcard into the folded pages of the passport. Plans leapt into my mind. One possibility was meeting up with Floria. Then, the most desired opportunity, a getaway abroad with Sim.

40

2014

Public Sign, Strawberry Field, Belmont:
Please keep off the GRASS

If Stephanie was going to thwart rumours about Graham Simmons, she needed to get back in touch with Patricia. She was the one person who'd raised the possibility of Carolyn going off on her own accord. Now with another nugget of information from Bill Spencer (in the form of a customer at the Mini Market called Rick Salisbury) she had to make the most of the lead. Stephanie didn't want a repeat performance of conversation stifled by proximity to the school when they met before the holidays, so she arranged to see Patricia early one morning at the start of the autumn term. There was a nip to the air but otherwise the day was calm. Only this time, Patricia arrived with her dog. It was too late to do anything about it as they entered the field. Somewhat overweight for a Labrador, Brucie had a handsome chocolate-brown coat. Taking a ball from her pocket,

Patricia threw it over arm and the dog lolloped through the crunchy brown leaves.

'He's an old boy now,' said Patricia. 'Vet calls him a senior.'

Stephanie was inexperienced with dogs yet she made positive noises. 'He looks in fine form to me.'

They followed a path which cut across the grass to a bench. Now it was time for Patricia to get out a dog-poo bag, collect the mess and drop it in a bin. Afterwards, they sat and Stephanie set up the recording equipment. Patricia flipped the top of her cigarette packet and counted how many remained. Please no! Stephanie pulled a frown. She didn't want puffing amongst the talk and as for the smell of smoke, she didn't want that either. Back into the pocket of Patricia's man-sized fleece they went. Stephanie was prepared for any twitchiness Patricia might display for want of nicotine. It took a minute to organise the recording equipment, and with Brucie settled at Patricia's feet, Stephanie was off.

[Stephanie] *Patricia, we've learnt about your friendship in class with Carolyn but you also knew her outside school. Can you tell us about the Mini Market where you both worked?*

[Patricia] *We did the Wednesday after-school session together. I've no idea what Carolyn got up to on Saturdays because she worked in the morning and I was on the afternoon rota. No one could deny the manager was a dirty old man and he egged her on, but Mr Rogers couldn't put a foot wrong in my mum's opinion, so I continued working there long after Carolyn had gone. None of the customers were interested in me if Carolyn was around. She was a proper little flirt and loved to be at the centre of things.*

[Stephanie] *I always got the impression Carolyn was quiet and shy. Was there really a different side to her when she was in the shop?*

[Patricia] *She craved attention so it wasn't altogether surprising she responded in the way she did. Her dad passed away years before and she didn't have uncles or brothers to act as role models. Mr Rogers showed her off like she was employed to titillate the customers. She responded by playing up to it. Perhaps she enjoyed having power over men. Sexual power.*

[Stephanie] *That gives me quite a different picture of Carolyn. Can you say more about the customers? Was there a Rick Salisbury amongst them?*

[Patricia] *I don't remember the name but that's not to say he didn't exist. When Carolyn talked about the different customers, she gave them nicknames. Her favourite was Mr Canary. I never saw him because he was a Saturday morning regular. According to Carolyn, he looked like a reincarnation of Marc Bolan with corkscrew curls and a sexy smile. She tried to teach me how to wink and click my tongue at the same time, just like he did. It was strange the things we found funny but even then, I had a feeling she was out of her depth.*

[Stephanie] *Why was he called Mr Canary?*

[Patricia] *Now you're asking. She may have felt he was eating out of her hand.*

[Stephanie] *Did the name have anything to do with a yellow Cortina? There was one seen outside the school on the day Carolyn disappeared.*

[Patricia] *You're right, there was. It's too easy forgetting things these days.*

Patricia flapped a hand in front of her glistening face and Stephanie sensed she might come over hot in sympathy. At least Stephanie's hot flushes didn't result in actual sweating.

[Stephanie] *I know what you mean, although your memory seems fine to me. In an earlier interview, you said Carolyn might've gone off on her own. Is that likely, given she was experiencing the power of her burgeoning sexuality?*

[Patricia] *That's one way of putting it. The girl was a complete enigma. One minute she was all over Simmons, the next it was non-stop talk about others who fancied her. Perhaps that was one of the reasons we stayed friendly. I never could nail exactly what drove her.*

[Stephanie] *It sounds like she was on a path to risk-taking.*

[Patricia] *You know what it was like back then, so many men taking advantage. She might've thought she had control but she was insecure. She definitely had a chip on her shoulder and never stopped going on about how her sister was the golden girl and she didn't measure up. I got the sense she felt abandoned by her family. It could've been enough for her to do something desperate.*

Patricia checked her mobile. 'It's time I was going. I need to get Brucie back and be ready for school. Sorry I can't stay longer but I think you've got the gist.'

Stephanie pulled one of her new business cards from her wallet and offered it to Patricia who glanced at the writing. '*Extra Lessons* is a good name for the podcast. It sums up what happened to Carolyn in more ways than one.'

'Listen out for the first episode – I'm sure you'll get a mention,' said Stephanie.

41

MAY 1979

I recognised Sheila Reynolds standing behind the till at the Mini Market. She was in the year above me at Greensleeves and I guessed she'd gone on to join sixth-form college. Her half smile indicated a sense of superiority that seeped from anyone a little bit older. I was at the bottom of the pecking order for sure.

'I'll find your tabard, Carolyn.' She ducked under the counter then pressed it into my hands. 'You don't want to get your *pretty* dress dirty, do you?'

Her voice confirmed she was being snide. At least on Saturdays I didn't have my school uniform on. The dress with its flouncy layers had been passed down from Janine. It boasted a Laura Ashley label and was much better than the navy top and trousers Sheila wore. I pulled the tabard over my head and secured the sides.

'I'm surprised *you've* been chosen as his special helper,' she said.

What was she on about? Before I had time to ask, Mr Rogers breezed into the shop. 'Good morning, ladies.'

I sang out *good morning* in reply. Sheila scowled. She must've gotten out of the wrong side of bed.

Me and Sheila were set to work packing shelves at the near end of the aisle where the tinned food was stacked. Standing at the till, Mr Rogers towered over us as we squatted to organise the lower shelves. I didn't like being told what to do by Sheila, but Mr Rogers nodded his approval while she talked me through stock rotation. This meant the tins already on the shelf had to be brought to the front and the new ones packed behind. Whenever the bell above the door rang, I glanced over. I was curious to see who shopped at the Mini Market. Mr Rogers operated the till. Ladies doing shopping bought biscuits and bread. Most of the blokes wore builders' overalls and wanted their morning fags and a newspaper.

'Stop staring,' hissed Sheila.

'Why should I?' I hissed back.

Mr Rogers' chat drifted and I managed to earwig some of his conversation. Talk referred to the topless model in the newspaper who had a great pair of knockers. It made me all hot and bothered.

'We need to organise the apricot halves.' Sheila stood up to stretch her arms.

I had to admit it was awkward, reaching to the back of the shelf and grabbing the tins that rolled away. With my knees jutting out and arms akimbo, I didn't mind the men who watched and offered encouragement. 'Go a bit further,' one of them said and I obliged by catching hold of the last tin. I waved it in the air triumphantly and he offered a handclap. It gave me one over Sheila.

'Stop playing up,' said Sheila.

What was she on about now? I couldn't help being friendly.

The next box contained pineapple rings and then I went on to sliced peaches. It wasn't so bad stacking the shelves higher up but still it meant a lot of bending. I only realised my dress was riding up after one of the customers said, 'Atta girl.' I smiled at the compliment.

'Get a grip,' said Sheila.

I'd stopped listening to her sniping by then. If it brought a smile, I didn't mind flashing a bit of leg.

Mr Rogers announced it was time for coffee at eleven o'clock. Sheila knew what to do and nipped into the back office to put the kettle on. That left me and Mr Rogers alone. He called me over to the till and asked if I was interested in having a go. I loved punching in numbers, making me feel I had some control over them. Then he told me I was getting carried away and I should return to packing. As I squeezed by, I noticed his hand on my back. The polite thing to do was turn and smile. Mr Rogers grinned, and I noticed his wonky yellow teeth. Not so nice. It was down to chain-smoking. When he lit up again, I really didn't think it a good idea but it wasn't my place to say anything. If Sim ever started smoking heavily, I'd use Mr Rogers as an example. I'd also remind Sim to brush his teeth with Colgate.

'One sugar and plenty of milk for me,' Mr Rogers shouted loud enough for Sheila to hear. The next minute she appeared carrying two mugs and offered us one each.

'I've done the same for you,' she said, then went to get a mug for herself. She sat on a stool beside the storeroom and with Mr Rogers at the till, I ended up between the two of them. He waved a packet of Bourbon biscuits at me and I got to take one before Sheila. It wasn't every day a boss would give biscuits to his newest recruit.

'Now you've finished your drink,' he said. 'Let's pop into the back room, I've got something for you.'

I didn't have a clue what was going on. As I followed him, Sheila rolled her eyes.

'Watch the till while we're gone,' he called to Sheila.

She didn't reply but I heard footsteps as she took her place behind the counter.

Mr Rogers came up close and I could feel his breath on my face. It made me stand straighter. I was almost as tall as him.

'Thought you might want your wages.' He dangled a small brown envelope in front of me. As soon as I reached for it, he snatched his hand away. So this was his little game. When I tried to grab it a second time, he dodged around and I had to laugh.

'Don't mind my teasing,' he said. 'Give me your hand.'

I opened my palm and he wrapped my fingers around the package. There were coins inside.

'Thank you,' I said.

'No,' he said. 'Thank you.'

Then, he reached into the pocket of his trousers and drew out another envelope. 'Do me a favour and give this to Sheila.'

With a smile, I left the room.

———

Mum sat at the table flapping the piece of paper I'd written on. It contained my carefully crafted excuse for not being at home that morning. I remembered the biro slipping over the lines as the idea took shape. The note was ready for her when she came down from a lie-in. What more did she want? While Mum continued with the silent treatment, I studied her outfit. She wore her Saturday casual clothes, a cotton skirt buttoned down the front and a cap-sleeved top which I knew she regretted buying (full sleeves were so much more flattering for those with flabby arms). At least I didn't have that problem, but it was something I might inherit. Mum twisted the paper between her fingers.

'You might've mentioned this last night. I really don't like being kept in the dark.'

Couldn't she read? The reason was there in black and white (or in this case, blue). Even from the doorway I could see the swirl of letters. I'd taken to a relaxed way with my penmanship. Before Sim, my words and numbers were neat and tidy. These days, it paid to be a bit free and easy. 'I didn't decide to go until the last minute.'

'You're telling me.' Mum folded the note in two, running her nail over to make the edge crisp.

I shifted my weight from the left hip to my right. Uncomfortable under Mum's glare, I twirled the ends of my hair.

'Where has this sudden interest in the youth club come from?'

Lies buzzed around my head. I had to think fast or the silence would give me away. 'A couple of girls from my tutor group meet there.' I was impressed, the line had a ring of truth.

'Who?'

'Deborah and Carol.' I could hardly believe it when *their* names popped out of my mouth. Deborah, who liked to be known as Debs and Carol, who lived in the big house, reported to have shag carpet fitted throughout.

'Well, as long as you're spending your time productively.'

'There was a discussion about the need for equal pay.' The clever ideas were coming one after another.

'Most women can work as well as any man,' said Mum. 'And you girls, of course.'

She always found a way to put me down. There wasn't any point in hanging about for insults. I turned to make for my bedroom. Mum would get the message of my anger with each stomp of my wedge-heeled sandals. Not even the striped carpet dulled the drumming.

42

2014

Continental Cookery
For the perfect spaghetti bolognese use an
all-purpose Italian sauce such as ragù.

S tephanie would have preferred listening to the very first
airing of *Extra Lessons* alone at home, but Beth was having
none of it. That morning, she'd barged into the bathroom while
Stephanie was giving her hair a henna rinse. It wasn't the best
place for a discussion. By the time Stephanie's hair was wrapped
in a towel and the vestiges of red-tainted water ran from the
sink, she'd agreed to join the others for a *Come Dine with Me* at
Doug's place. Beth was dying to meet the long-suffering
Margaret and although it was a little exposing listening to the
podcast together, Stephanie would get some immediate feedback.

The last time Stephanie had seen Margaret was at the annual
business awards when they'd sat next to each other for the three-
course meal and Doug thought he had a prize in the bag. Doug
didn't win yet he showed no sign of being put out. Waving his

consolation trophy in the air, Doug congratulated the winner in his usual affable way. It was later in the shared taxi home that Stephanie sensed Doug's disappointment and Margaret's confusion. At last, they had reached Stephanie's house and she couldn't wait to get out of the stifling atmosphere in the cab.

It was going to be different with Doug and Margaret hosting in their own home. Stephanie was in one of her smart-casual outfits: heavy linen trousers and a cotton jumper, while Beth had gone the whole hog in a layered dress and a loose cardigan. The change of season to autumn meant a change of wardrobe. Not that the summer had been brilliant with only a few hot days. As they drew up in front of Doug's townhouse, Stephanie noted the square of grass at the front was freshly cut. Doug was going all out to impress. He'd parked his car in the garage, leaving room for Beth to squeeze her van beside Robert's Mini on the drive. They stood at the front door by the *welcome* mat, and Beth reached for the knocker, belting it in a regular rhythm. As they waited, Beth studied her new kitten-heel shoes and announced they were very practical for driving.

The door opened and there stood Doug fanning his steamy red face. 'Who knew it could get this hot in a kitchen?'

'Welcome to my world.' Beth offered her cheek and Doug obliged with a kiss.

'And mine,' said Stephanie. 'Regarding the heat not the kitchen.'

Doug frowned – he didn't get it. Instead, he leaned forward, replicating the greeting he'd given Beth. Stephanie tried not to grimace.

'Go through to the lounge.' He waved in the general direction. 'Robert and Margaret are there. I'll join you in a bit when I've mastered the art of cooking on a hob.'

'Good for you.' Stephanie's mind whirred at the prospect.

As Beth and Stephanie entered, Margaret and Robert got to their feet. Relieved another round of kissing was out of the way,

Stephanie made for the armchair while the others settled on the sofa. Seconds later Margaret got up again, this time distributing glasses of dry or sweet sherry and moving tables so that everyone had a place to put drinks. Stephanie pushed aside the folded newspaper to make room for a little bowl of peanuts Margaret offered.

'He's been saving that for you.' Margaret nodded at the newspaper.

Stephanie did a double take. The crossword was half completed and she hated trying to finish them.

'On the other side,' said Margaret. 'Doug kept the article about your podcast. You might like to clip it.'

'Oh great.' Stephanie was long past the stage of wanting to clutter up her files with paper copies but she opened the page and then winced at the headline HOW TO FIND A MISSING GIRL. Reading it in print (she'd already seen it online when the trailer was first released) the words seemed even more inappropriate. At least the half-page spread included a decent photo of Carolyn and a shot of the community radio with its new equipment. Doug had been a big help in raising awareness about the podcast, even if it had resulted in Simmons' letter which had caused another load of complications. She noted Doug's byline and squashed a momentary feeling of resentment at how the *Post* had treated her.

'*Extra Lessons* is listed in the weekly entertainment guide.' Margaret pressed her to look at the most recent edition.

'Very good.' New opportunities were opening up thanks to Robert. Her relationship with him needed to remain on a platonic level rather than develop into a possible romance. The group friendship meant too much. Stephanie turned to Robert. 'I'm so grateful for your help. I'm not sure I'd have got the podcast aired if it wasn't for you.'

'My pleasure. The team at the station are very enthusiastic and they're excited to be one of the first to facilitate a podcast.

According to them, they're supporting a new way of listening. I expect *Extra Lessons* will attract a wide audience. Carolyn's disappearance has haunted this town.'

Stephanie wasn't sure haunted was the right word although the unsolved case certainly cast a shadow.

'I don't want to spoil our enjoyment of the first episode, but have you got any new leads?' asked Margaret.

This simple question, which Stephanie should've been able to answer without difficulty, undermined her confidence. For some reason, she'd found it difficult to follow up with Rick Salisbury. Oh, the irony. As soon as her theory of abduction had become more feasible, she wasn't able to push through. What the hell was happening? Stephanie rested the palm of her hand against her forehead.

'Are you okay, Stephanie?'

'It's nothing.' Her inactivity had been perplexing. She didn't have time to waste and couldn't admit it. Perhaps asking for help from Bill Spencer would be the best thing. The stupid idea caused her to smirk.

'Have you got a headache?'

Margaret's look of concern made Stephanie's feelings of desperation worsen. She had to pull herself together. Once the first episode was out in the world, she needed to get on and finalise the rest.

'Only nerves.' Stephanie consciously relaxed the tension in her shoulders. She could do this, she really could. 'And as for new leads, let's hope the podcast can winkle out some of those.'

Just then, Doug burst into the room, all arms, legs and flapping pinny. This made Stephanie hoot – he looked ridiculous!

'Steady on.' Doug picked up a spare glass of sherry and downed it. 'I might look a pretty sight but you haven't seen the dinner yet.'

With that, he turned on his heel and vanished.

'What is he cooking, Margaret?' Stephanie felt the need to prepare.

'I persuaded him to go basic. Even Doug can't spoil spaghetti bolognese. Although I'd better get along to stop him from ruining the décor.'

'How's he going to manage that?' asked Robert.

'Doug has an idiosyncratic method for ensuring pasta is perfectly cooked. It's not surprising I never usually let him near the oven. You're very honoured this evening. He told me I couldn't contribute to his *Come Dine with Me* extravaganza. Wouldn't let me do a thing.'

A little later, Margaret accompanied the guests through the kitchen towards the dining table in the conservatory. No dawdling was allowed. Margaret then went back to the kitchen. The three guests sat around an oval table covered in a pretty lace cloth. In the centre was a glass filled with breadsticks. Beth offered them around and while Stephanie shook her head, Robert took one. The sound of crunching emanated and Beth helped herself to a second.

'He really is going all out with the Italian theme,' said Beth. 'Are you sure you don't want one, Stephanie?'

As if on cue, Stephanie's stomach grumbled so loudly anyone would have thought she hadn't eaten for days. 'Perhaps I should.'

'Come on, let's tuck in,' said Robert. 'I have a feeling we might be waiting a while for the meal.'

'It better arrive before the podcast airs,' said Beth.

'We've plenty of time,' said Robert. '*Extra Lessons* is on at nine o'clock.'

Although she had concerns over her lack of progress with Salisbury, it was strange and exciting to think about her work reaching an audience. The podcast had existed in Stephanie's mind for so long, it was something of a relief to have it broadcast. The thought didn't stop Stephanie becoming flooded by nerves and she stuffed another breadstick into her mouth. In truth, the idea of Doug's dinner was enough to turn her stomach but nothing could go wrong nibbling a dry breadstick. She ate a third and let the crunching drown out the bickering between Margaret and Doug. When an almighty clang of dropped pots came from the kitchen, the voices quietened. Beth raised her eyebrows and Robert drummed his thumbs on the table edge.

'Do you think they need help?' asked Beth.

'It's best to stay put. I know the maestro doesn't like being interrupted,' said Stephanie.

'Was he like this at work?' whispered Robert.

'You always knew never to bother Doug if his office door was shut.'

As Stephanie's words came out, Margaret appeared at the glass door that separated the conservatory from the kitchen. She glanced over and smiled, then slid the door to close the gap between the hosts and their guests. Stephanie couldn't resist laughing and the others joined in.

With the breadsticks devoured, they waited. Robert drained the last drop of sherry and Beth checked for messages on her mobile. Stephanie stared at the place mats, wondering about the choice of Klimt's *The Kiss* as a suitable image for dressing a table.

A little later Doug appeared holding a vast serving dish and Margaret followed like a foot servant carrying crockery.

'Here we go.' The bowl steamed as he set it down.

'Pass these around.' Margaret offered Beth a plate. 'Mind, they're hot.'

'Warmed if you please.' Doug wielded a ladle ready to dole out pasta bows in some kind of sauce.

'What happened to the spaghetti?' asked Robert.

'Put it this way,' said Margaret. 'If I wanted a new piece of art to decorate the place, I'd have bought one.'

'Usually, it's a tried and trusted method,' said Doug. 'But burnt spaghetti chucked against a wall doesn't only stick to show it's ready to eat, it leaves a very interesting pattern.'

'Can I see?' Beth was half out of her seat ready to look.

'Sit and relax. I can give you a tour of the gallery later,' said Margaret.

The meal was surprisingly edible, thanks to Margaret heaping grated parmesan on top of each portion Doug served. Glasses were filled with Valpolicella, which Doug recommended as the ideal accompaniment to his meal. As the others were driving, there was an expectation for Stephanie to join Margaret and Doug in glugging some back. In the circumstances, she obliged.

When the plates were emptied (Beth had left a small portion unconsumed) Doug ferried dishes to the sink. It was while he was busy washing up that Margaret whispered his pudding was a write-off. In the course of her apologies, she had an idea and scuttled away to share this with Doug. Thrashing noises from the kitchen came and then Doug appeared holding a silver tray. Mounted on top was a block of ice cream with swirls of green and a dusting of chocolate.

'You can't beat a mint Viennetta for finishing a meal,' said Doug.

'Wow,' said Beth. 'That's normally a Christmas day treat in our family.'

Stephanie guessed the same was the case for Doug and Margaret judging by the hoo-ha that had somehow unearthed the offering.

'You managed to keep up the Italian theme,' Robert congratulated.

'Naturally,' said Doug.

Although the black coffee that was served didn't come from an espresso machine, it was served in tiny cups. There was even Disaronno. Stephanie loved the almond-flavour liqueur but neither she nor anyone else was in the mood.

'You've done us proud,' said Robert.

'Yes. Three cheers for Doug,' said Beth. The hip-hips were followed by slightly embarrassed hurrahs yet Doug was none the wiser. He was rosy-cheeked either from the joy of his first dinner party success, the stress of delivering it or copious glasses of wine.

'Of course, I have to thank Margaret for assisting in the discovery of my new cooking skills.'

'Here's to Margaret.' Stephanie raised her glass and the others copied.

'It's not me you should be celebrating but Stephanie,' said Margaret.

'Indeed.' Doug looked at his watch. 'Thirty minutes till lift-off.'

Stephanie could've done without the reminder, which did nothing for her nerves. By the time the podcast started, they were gathered on comfy chairs in the lounge.

'Long live *Extra Lessons* and all who sail in her,' Doug proposed.

'Shush,' said Margaret, as bars of introductory music for the first episode played.

43

JUNE 1979

Racing to the maths room, I was surprised there wasn't a class pouring out. Then I remembered, the fourth-years were on a school trip to an open-air production of *Romeo and Juliet*. I'd sat through it the previous year and ended up stripping off thanks to the heat. Dithering at the doorway, I couldn't decide whether I should enter. It was the rule to wait outside but for all I knew, Sim could be in there and alone. I needed to take a chance. Poking my head inside, I glanced at the teacher's desk. His place was empty.

'Excuse me, Carolyn.'

I swung back to see him. Gazing into his mellow eyes, I sensed his closeness. I lingered a moment then moved aside. His jacket brushed my arm and a zing chased through my bones. If I'd been a weakling, I might have fainted. As it was, I heard Patricia's footsteps thumping towards us. Any false move now and she'd accuse me of *making a show*. There was a time I thought she was on my side but ever since I'd started working at the Mini Market, things had turned nasty. I got to brew the tea for our break on the Wednesday shift, but it didn't mean I was better than her. She got back at me by saying my relationship with Sim was a fantasy. Little did she know. Come to think of it, Patricia wasn't much kinder at school. Pushing past, she made for our regular desk at the front. At least she hadn't abandoned our friendship altogether.

Patricia had her books and pencil case out. I watched others traipse into the classroom while I dithered. Was I mesmerised by my close encounter with Sim or the sunshine flooding the room? Good question. The windows were wide open in anticipation of another scorcher. A plan was forming. If I stayed put, I could volunteer to close the blinds. He looked at me and gave a nod. That was all I needed, I dropped the bag from my shoulder and began untangling the cords of the first venetian blind.

I wondered why they were called venetian. Who'd choose an exotic name for the purpose of blocking out the sun? Thinking about it, maybe Venice would make a great destination. I imagined strolling along the canals and walkways, my arm through his. As I fiddled with the blind, sunlight caught my eye and swatted my dreams. I needed to concentrate on the task in hand. Straightening the cords, I held them at a good angle to release the blind. A little tug was needed to zip the slats into place. Only that morning, I didn't have the knack. Maybe my daydreaming had forced a mistake. The blind failed to make a screen of horizontal lines, and instead produced a fan of twisted spokes. There I was, hanging on to the cords for dear life.

'Pull it back up,' shouted a boy from the back row.

I did my best but all I could hear were groans from my so-called classmates. Over walked Mr Simmons. He took the cords from my hands.

'Take your seat, Carolyn. I'll sort this.'

I didn't move, I couldn't. I stood there watching him miraculously correct the blinds and they slung into place. As he adjusted the strips to shade the room, I knew I had to act quickly or miss my chance.

'I'll get my things.' Dropping down to pick up my bag, I rose again and bumped his arm.

He acted startled and pulled away. I knew it was a little joke between us.

'Sorry,' I whispered.

Sim shook his head in a forgiving way.

'Stop messing about,' the boy at the back shouted.

'I'm impressed at your enthusiasm to begin work,' Sim replied in a teacherly voice.

Annoyance that my moment with Sim had been interrupted made me hot and weak. The boy's shouting chiselled a chip from my heart but blood still flowed through my veins. He couldn't take away the memory of Sim's smile.

Walking over to the space next to Patricia, I cherished the moment. Things were changing and it wasn't only the stirrings in my heart. I had a future. In my out-of-school life, I knew about the world of work, I was skilled in applying make-up and I'd learnt how to shimmy. These were important for my life with Sim. At school, he took the sting out of learning and I was able to tackle calculations. I was developing skills and in more ways than one.

Sim turned to the blackboard and Patricia whispered: 'Don't you realise what a bloody fool you're being? He might be a new teacher, but that doesn't mean he'll fall for your stupid tricks.' I wasn't going to listen to her bitching. I shuffled my chair along to make a space between us. Sim turned to see who was making the noise.

'Settle down, everyone.' His eyes skimmed over me and then he turned back to write another sum.

The rest of the day passed in a haze of humiliation and regret. All through break Patricia didn't stop going on about what a fucking idiot I'd been and why didn't I have more self-respect? It wasn't worth arguing and I was pleased the bell rang and we headed off in different directions. I avoided her for the rest of the day and when it came to going home, I was out through the gates before you could say Jack Robinson. Back in my bedroom, I had time to reflect. Okay, so perhaps my tangle with the venetian blind hadn't been such a brilliant idea, but I was desperate for an ounce of Sim. In my book desperate feelings equalled desperate measures and I had to do something or fade away completely. Now I was on home territory, I could think about things rationally. There wasn't any reason why I shouldn't flex my new-found muscles in grabbing attention. I had enough practice at doing this with customers at the shop and it might play a very necessary part in my plans for Sim.

At my desk, I twirled hair around my finger and looked out from under my fringe. Batting eyelids was a bit too obvious so I'd developed the knack of a coy little smile that always brought a response. When Rick dropped in to the Mini Market, he was good for a laugh. Only the other week, Mr Rogers used a stage whisper to suggest I could do worse than go out for a drink with Rick. I shrugged because he wasn't altogether my type and besides, I was spoken for. This didn't make any difference and I think it actually gave Rick ideas. I walked home after work and noticed the queue of cars at the junction. The yellow Cortina didn't register as Rick's until he revved it. I didn't want to draw attention to myself and kept my eyes down. When the traffic lights changed, Rick sailed by with Marc Bolan's 'Celebrate Summer' blasting through the open window. The repeated beat caught my attention and when he beeped, I gave Rick a wave... it was a reflex action.

Rick called into the shop again last Saturday and announced I was Miss Flipping Hot. I didn't know what to say but Mr Rogers hooted with laughter. Later, Mr Rogers suggested Rick was my fancy man. I played along. Picking up my pen, I wrote a few names on one of the index cards Sim had given me. I had to get back at Rick one way or another. I wrote Mr Lucky, Mr Breezy...

and then it hit me. I was up against the coalface in my quest for Sim —and Rick could be my practice thing in his canary-coloured car. A little bird to hone my skills on. That was it, he'd be my Mr Canary.

44

2014

E arly that morning, Stephanie was shocked by the post that popped to the top of the community Facebook page. Someone had added the comment *Good on ya, Rix* to an advert promoting reduced-price MOTs from months previously. Did the S of S & B Autos relate to Rick Salisbury? The shock of realising the possible connection made Stephanie jerk to attention. What was the chance? Filled with renewed energy and a commitment to find out, it became clear Stephanie's mojo was back. She had no idea where the garage was based, but after she'd checked an online map, Stephanie realised it was tucked away nearby. Standing on the pavement, she appraised the shop front. S & B Autos had two cars parked in bays to the side of the building and a glazed door showed the words *customer entrance*. She went in and a bleep sounded. From under the bonnet of a car parked in the main part of the building, a man looked out.

'Give us a minute,' he shouted and then ducked away again.

Stephanie moved further into the office and considered taking a seat. Pushed against the wall was a bench covered in bright-orange plastic that showed oily patches. No thank you, Stephanie didn't fancy getting her cords dirty. As for the chair by the desk, it was piled with paperwork. After a minute or two, Stephanie opened her backpack and pulled out a notebook and pencil. She might as well be prepared. Wondering who the man that had spoken to her actually was, Stephanie looked around the garage. The pitched roof was made from corrugated iron and the concrete floor was littered with tyres and pieces of equipment Stephanie didn't recognise. Feeling out of her depth, Stephanie questioned the wisdom of dropping by unannounced. She'd let curiosity bring her this far. The strange thing was, she so rarely checked the town's Facebook group, even if a notification flashed up, but with the mention of Rix and a garage, she couldn't let it go.

The sound of footsteps approaching made Stephanie turn. Dressed in overalls, he was a little shorter than Stephanie and walked with a swagger. She took an immediate dislike to the sneering smile he pulled. Could this be Carolyn's Mr Canary? He was hardly a catch by anyone's standards. Stephanie clocked the man's craggy features and the stringy hair tied into a ponytail. He took another step closer and reached for a rag to wipe his hands, smearing black marks rather than cleaning them.

'What can I do for you?' He threw the rag on the floor.

'I'm looking for Rick Salisbury.'

'Are you really?'

'Yes. I'd like a few minutes of his time.'

'Fire away.' Rick's eyes showed more pupil than coloured rim.

'It's about the disappearance of Carolyn Russell.'

'Don't know who you're talking about.'

'She was the sixteen-year-old who went missing from Belmont in 1979.'

'Fucking years ago.' Although his feet remained planted to the spot, his body swayed.

Was he high on something? Stephanie held her nerve and fixed her gaze. This little short arse wasn't going to intimidate her. 'But you remember her?'

'The police came sniffing round at the time. And a few journos. I bet you're one of them.' Salisbury picked up a heavy spanner. 'I had nothing to say then and the same's true today.'

'I won't need much…'

Salisbury cocked his head. 'Mind you don't trip on your way out.'

'I have a couple of questions.' Stephanie stood her ground.

Salisbury tutted. 'Why is it some people never take the hint?'

'I'm wondering how well you knew Carolyn. She had a job at the Mini Market on Saturdays before her disappearance. You shopped there, didn't you? There's a note about it.' Stephanie knew she was prattling but didn't stop. 'And she worked on Wednesday afternoons too.'

'What of it?'

'How well did you know her?'

'Now you're asking. Who didn't know her? She was game for anyone, that little tart.'

Stephanie was taken aback but tried not to show it. 'What makes you say that?'

'Look, I don't have to talk to you, I don't even know who you are.'

'My name's Stephanie Brett and I'm looking into Carolyn's disappearance. She's been missing over three decades and it's about time someone–'

Salisbury chucked the spanner into the air and caught the end. 'I've heard it all before. Poor little lamb.'

Stephanie gulped. 'It's just that I'm trying to–'

'I'll give you trying.' Salisbury took a step closer and puffed out his chest.

'Perhaps it's time I was going.' Stephanie rammed her notebook into her bag and made for the door.

'That's right,' he called after her. 'And don't come bothering me again.'

Back at home, first aid training from years previously had Stephanie adding a spoonful of sugar to the tea she'd made. The trouble was, most of the grains scattered due to her shaking hand. Knowing she couldn't bear to sit surrounded by mess, she took a cloth and wiped away the spill. She could do without the sugar. Taking the mug in both hands, she raised it to her lips for a sip. The tea was comforting and warm. How she'd even made it home was quite beyond her. Blindly rushing along the roads and alleys had brought her back in double-quick time. Thank God she could now sit in the security of her own kitchen. In one way, she was pleased Beth was out (she didn't want anyone to see her in a state) but a bit of support after the encounter with Salisbury would've been welcome. And reflecting on the talk that had taken place, it hadn't moved things forward. Or perhaps it had. Salisbury's threats and demeanour kept flashing into her mind. Although she hadn't been physically chased away, his words had done the job. If she'd been afraid, grown woman and all, how on earth had Carolyn felt?

45

JUNE 1979

S itting at my desk, I fanned the index cards from Sim and admired the lovely pastel colours. I tossed the yellow ones aside, needing no reminder of Mr Canary. Closing my eyelids, I blocked out the image of him leering towards me. Not for a moment had I imagined he'd try something on. Thank God I'd escaped in time. Squeezing my eyes tighter, I extinguished the memory and my heart settled to a regular beat. It was a relief he hadn't returned to the shop since. He was an utter waste of space compared to my one true love. Choosing a red biro from the pot, I gripped the end and prepared to write. Sim had suggested I used the cards for revision, yet I couldn't set my mind to maths when my heart was full of yearning for him. I needed to find new ways of telling Sim how much he meant.

The doodling began with a heart in the top-right corner of the pale-pink page. It wasn't big and bulging like the graffiti on the railway bridge. Some boys thought they were clever taking risks with their spray cans. I just didn't understand their stupidness and it wasn't evidence of real love. I could testify for love, but not them. Love seeped from every pore of me and was destined for Sim. As I made more hearts pattern the card, it was like a cascade of affection. When all the edges were covered in a border, I wondered what to write in the middle. At that moment, I wasn't inspired by lines of poetry. More out of interest than anything, I decided to try a new signature. I wrote my name all the time at school, but for a signature I'd use only my initial and adopt his surname as if we were married. *C. Simmons* had a nice ring to it and with its double M, my signature had a flourish. It was so much better than the double S and double L of my maiden name. One day me and Sim might marry, except it wasn't a priority. Being together was the main thing.

I was used to keeping a low profile on Sundays. It was Mum's day of rest and I usually found something to do. But peeling potatoes was never a favourite chore and we ended up having a row. I couldn't understand why she didn't accept my suggestion for once. In my book, jacket potatoes went fine with roast chicken although the idea sent Mum over the edge. She stormed off in a fit of tears and I was left confused. When the telephone rang, she didn't appear and that's how I got the news from Janine that it was Mum and Dad's twenty-fourth wedding anniversary. It made me feel guilty, but I wasn't going to apologise because I hadn't done anything wrong. In this country, everyone's allowed to express an opinion.

From the smell of roast dinner rising, it was clear Mum had got over our little disagreement, but I still wasn't leaving my room. She could eat the entire chicken herself and I really didn't care. When I finally went into the kitchen and saw her eyes were red-rimmed, the whole thing seemed silly. She opened her arms and we gave each other a cuddle. It was good we'd reached a truce. Then, the greens on the stove boiled over and she pulled away. I was left feeling like rubbish all over again. After lunch, I wanted to please her, so I did the washing up, and the drying and the putting away while Mum had her feet on the pouffe and dozed. I knew I should've been more sympathetic about news of their anniversary. She didn't usually celebrate. There wasn't actually much to be happy about. Their wedding anniversary also meant the anniversary of Dad's death was approaching. I braced myself as memories flooded. Managing to divert my thoughts to happier times, I remembered Dad playing with me and Janine in the garden. On hot summer days when we were in the paddling pool, he'd get out the hose to cool us down with a shower. My dad rolled up his shirtsleeves as soon as he got in from work and I liked to stroke his hairy arms. Later came the day that changed our lives forever. Mum collected me and Janine from school as usual, and I ran all the way along the road to get to our house first. While I waited for Mum and Janine to catch up, I squeezed my feet onto the swirls of the iron gate and made it wiggle about on its hinges. Mum told me to get off, but I didn't mind as I'd already had my fun. I always wanted to be first, so I raced up the path ahead of Mum. She squeezed next to me and slid the key into the lock. Behind, I heard the squeak of the gate and Janine fiddling with the latch. The next moment, Mum was turning me around and screaming and flopping over. It was too late. I'd already seen Dad sprawled on the stairs, his arms and knees jutting out, his glassy eyes staring.

Early on I believed what she'd told me, that there'd been a terrible accident and Dad had toppled and died. It was only later the truth came out when the kids at primary chanted words I didn't understand, 'Your dad's a crim, your dad's a crim.' One of the big girls explained how he'd hanged himself and that made Dad a criminal. Everyone knew the horrible details but Mum kept her secret. I couldn't bring myself to tell her the gossip – couldn't stand the thought of her crying. She'd had the bannisters replaced using fashionable horizontal planks as if nothing untoward had ever happened. I never told her I'd seen Dad lying there. The shock of it left me with a feeling of shame: that I'd looked when I shouldn't have seen. Was it all my fault?

According to Mum, it never helped to dwell on things. Switching off the memories, I returned my attention to the index card. I disguised my signature by doodling another row of hearts. Mum would never know about my secret love. It was a blessing really, saving her from a situation she'd never be able to cope with. As for Sim, I wouldn't let anything bad happen to him.

46

Stephanie's diary entry:

CALL MEGAN

U p half the night and Stephanie was limp as a dishcloth. She'd had crazy dreams and one that replayed in her head involved an oil stain she couldn't scrub off a white bath towel. Stephanie's disturbed sleep was obviously due to Salisbury. In all her years as a journalist, she'd never felt so exposed and vulnerable. Okay, she'd covered court proceedings where some violent criminals had been convicted, but she'd always been a safe distance away. As for pressure of work, she was feeling it. With the podcast launched, there was an end date in sight and material for the final two episodes was left deliberately loose. This allowed space for updates and new information to be included. Stephanie had confidence in Megan, even though this wasn't how she liked to operate. Having everything pinned down was much more her style.

Although her laptop was beside her bed, listening to a podcast wasn't the greatest idea. Another person's success now had the capacity to intimidate rather than inspire. Instead, she padded downstairs and made a cup of camomile tea. The shrivelled flowers bobbing inside the pyramid bag were a strange source of calmness. Into the cup went a spoonful of honey and after a couple more stirs, Stephanie held the rim to her lips and blew over the surface. The action reminded Stephanie of her mother. She was always in a hurry and needed to down her morning brew quickly. The memory brought a smile. Her mum had always been of the opinion that two heads were better than one.

It took no longer than a couple of minutes to compose an email to Megan. She didn't want to ring in the morning on the off-chance she would be free, but to set up a formal arrangement. Knowing Megan looked at her emails early, they were sure to find a time. That was the best she could do for the moment. Before closing the laptop, Stephanie glanced at the clock. If the camomile tea worked its soothing magic, she might get some shut-eye before the alarm sounded.

Stephanie had been at work a couple of hours when her mobile rang. Accepting the call she pulled a broad smile, mostly in relief. 'Thanks for getting in touch, Megan.'

'No problem,' said Megan. 'What's wrong?'

Direct as ever, Megan never wasted time on pleasantries.

'Uhm.'

'Spit it out.' There was a smile in Megan's voice. 'Any email sent in the early hours is cause for concern.'

'I'm such a giveaway.'

'You don't make a habit of it,' said Megan. 'Come on, spill.'

'I've got myself in a mess. You remember I was following up on a lead about Rick Salisbury?'

'He's the one from the shop, yes? Possibly behind an abduction.'

Megan's words sounded so black and white. Up until Stephanie had actually set eyes on Salisbury, he'd been a fantasy. A pet theory she'd developed as a trainee journalist and somehow the idea had stuck. 'I went to see him.'

'Was that wise? I mean, he could be dangerous.'

'I think he was!'

'Calm down,' said Megan. 'Tell me what happened.'

Stephanie managed to get the story out in spite of her embarrassment. It'd been foolish to turn up on spec and the meeting had left her jittery. It was good she'd chosen Megan to confide in – her voice was reassuring.

'Did you feel physically threatened?' she asked.

'Yes.'

'Well, there's no way you should go back on your own.'

'Absolutely.' Stephanie had no intention of returning. The few words he'd said didn't add up to much and he'd been very clear he wasn't going to say more.

'Have you reported it to the police?'

'Nothing actually happened. He just didn't like the questions I was asking.'

'Was there any indication he was involved in Carolyn's disappearance?'

'I didn't handle it well. I'm not sure I made much sense.' Stephanie wanted to add *you know how it is* even though she suspected Megan didn't have experience of being foggy-headed. Come to that, she'd probably never been frightened out of her wits either.

'Did you notice anything about him?'

'His pupils were dilated. I think he might've been high.'

'Never mind about that now,' the matter-of-fact Megan replied. 'What other leads can we build on? I was counting on something turning up to fill gaps in the last couple of episodes.'

Trust Megan to be on the case for new material but Stephanie followed her own train of thought. 'Perhaps that's what Salisbury had to hide, illicit drugs.'

'That's a whole different story, Stephanie. Let's have a think. There must be other things to feed into the podcast.'

'There's an interview with a customer from the Mini Market. It's repeated gossip. Her daughter said one of the young assistants gave a blow job to the manager in exchange for a packet of fags.'

'It sets the tone for the place.'

'The incident happened more recently. I think she said in the eighties.'

'It suggests grooming patterns over time,' said Megan. 'Perhaps we can work it in. Can you talk to the girl? Or I should say woman.'

'I've tried,' said Stephanie. 'No chance.'

'Okay. We still have time to come up with additional material. You've got your feelers out and I'll go over some of the cuts to see if we can work anything up. Don't worry, Stephanie. This is the beauty of podcasting. It's about drawing on leads as they become available.'

'To be honest, it's feeling unwieldy.'

'Because you're used to the print deadlines of a newspaper. Our approach is solid. It's usual to make last-minute changes. And besides, we can always record you talking about the meeting with Salisbury if nothing else materialises.'

'Of course!' Why hadn't Stephanie thought of it?

'Sounds like we're sorted,' said Megan. 'Let's speak again in a couple of days.'

47

JUNE 1979

Sim's frown took the form of a vertical slit that darted between his eyebrows. I wasn't distracted by the way he tore through the pile of booklets on the table, looking for a particular practice paper. My eyes continued to trace the lovely contours of his face.

'Found it.' He waved the page which stopped my musing.

'Where in the world would you choose to live?' I asked. 'I mean if you could go anywhere?'

Sim tilted his head. 'We should be getting on with some work, but if you really want to know...' He was such a tease, him and his gorgeous smile. 'Milan, New York, Paris.'

I nearly burst with joy. 'I've been to France! And I speak the language. I could show you around.'

'That's a generous offer, but we need mathematical knowledge to convert pounds into francs.'

We, he said, *we.*

'It can be complicated using exchange rates.'

I hadn't a clue what he was going on about, I was already thinking of us hand in hand walking along the Seine. 'How about we go to the Louvre and see the famous Mona Lisa?'

'Now you're talking.' He winked and I tried an enigmatic smile, same as in the famous portrait. 'In the meantime, there is the small matter of a CSE to sit. Have a look through this paper and we'll check your exam technique. Just a little extra practice and I'm confident you'll do well, Carolyn.'

A flicker of excitement caught whenever he said my name. Carolyn. I looked away, it was my chance to act coy.

The next few minutes were spent in a shared silence while I tried out thought transference. I planted a seed in his mind to see how it would flower. I imagined our hotel room in Paris. A huge double bed and French windows leading to a balcony with a view of the Eiffel Tower.

'Take this question,' he said. 'It's about doubling.'

'Is a double room twice the price of a single one?'

'What makes you think that?'

I stared into his hazel eyes and knew we were on the same wavelength. Savouring his question, I held the moment. I needed to think of some clever reply to keep the connection going. But I couldn't concentrate. A wasp had found its way into the room and buzzed around my head. If there was one thing I hated, it was wasps. Stung as a child, I wasn't about to let another get close. I shot out of my chair and shook my head, thinking the strands of flying hair would distract it. I was wrong. It actually caught in a tangle and the buzzing was terrifyingly near.

'Keep still,' Sim commanded.

I angled my face away from the wasp snagged in the nest of my hair. Fear of being stung sent me practically demented and I whimpered. Sim held my shoulder and examined the situation. Scared to death, I flung my arms around him in the hope he'd protect me from the horror. As my face pressed against his shirt, a button gouged my cheek yet the vibrations from the wasp continued.

'Stay where you are – I'll pick it out.'

I couldn't see what Sim was doing, but his closeness soothed and I tried to stop crying.

'Almost got it.'

He rubbed my back but my snuffles continued.

'There!' He drew away, holding the wasp by a wing. Then, he threw it on the floor and stamped on it.

Sheer relief took my breath. A damp patch made by my tears showed as a heart on his shirt. I had left my mark. The memory of our first embrace would stay with me forever.

Back in the dregs of home life, I sat opposite Mum at our dining room, so drab and without excitement. Our meal included potato which I'd pushed to the side of my plate using the excuse I'd gone off mash. Even Mum agreed it was rather too lumpy. The rest I had to eat, although I sliced away the rind of fat from the lamb chop and only ate the meat. Mum tutted, but I didn't care. As for the cabbage, I metaphorically held my nose and shovelled down the lot to stop Mum moaning. I would've given my right arm to be with Sim instead. Yet I couldn't complain. There were sacrifices to be made. I endured being with Mum and he put up with stupid kids. Sim was working for our future. The extra cash from tutoring would see us on our way.

'How are you finding drama?' Mum asked.

My eyes darted as I gathered my wits.

'At the youth club,' she continued.

Now, I had it. 'Oh, that.'

'Are you enjoying it?'

'Yes.' Little did she know I was actually a working woman earning money for an escape.

'What sort of things do you do?'

'This and that.' I didn't have time to give a full answer.

'Come on, Carolyn. I'm showing an interest.'

'Okay,' I huffed. 'Sometimes we read scripts and sometimes we make up our own plays.' Any story to keep her off the scent of the real drama in my life – a serious romance.

'I'm so pleased you're getting out and about,' said Mum.

And a plan to travel further than she could imagine was on the cards. Mum reached for the newspaper. Phew! The interrogation was over.

48

2014

TV Listing: *Luther*

Where a detective has more in common with the criminals he hunts.

Stephanie swung her hips in a happy dance around the kitchen. Pushing her mobile into her pocket, she celebrated Robert's news: listener numbers at Belair had reached several hundred for *Extra Lessons*. It was one of the few occasions this had happened. He loved the second episode where little hints and clues resonated. The podcast was bound to gain a following, which was great for the radio station and Stephanie. The feedback gave her a sense of lightness. Robert actually knew something about radio audiences which was far more than Doug. Really, she could've decked him after his back-handed compliment. *Fairly enjoyable.* At least Beth had been enthusiastic and she was determined to celebrate by having a girls' night in with dinner and an episode of *Luther.* Stephanie had missed out on the series the first time around and now she was catching up by watching the DVDs. Although Beth had seen every episode, she didn't mind sharing the pleasure again. Sparring between the obsessive DCI and his muse made the storyline addictive. Of course, the very fact that Luther was tall and handsome had nothing to do with it. But Beth's lusting over the actor had become infectious, and now Stephanie could appreciate the charms of this attractive black man. Stephanie paused for a moment. The adjective *black* (when related to skin colour) hadn't been used when she was at Greensleeves. The random thought caught Stephanie's attention. Back in the seventies, it was thought polite to call the only family from Africa living in the area *coloured*. The Adjoa boys had been popular amongst their classmates thanks to their football skills, but it didn't stop the name calling. At the time, Stephanie hadn't thought much of it. The word *wog* was excused as harmless, like the cute golliwogs on the marmalade jars. It was when the sneering started that she'd realised there was more going on. Embarrassed at the memory, Stephanie refocused on *Luther*. Who would win the battle of wits? She'd have to wait until Beth came home to find out. There would be dinner first. Beth had texted to say there were leftovers from the café. Although her bean casserole was a popular lunchtime special, she'd gone mad with the quantities. Stephanie guessed she'd over-catered on purpose as the freezer at home was emptying and neither of them were in the mood for cooking from scratch each evening.

Jangling keys and a clatter announced Beth's return. She bundled into the kitchen, a shoulder bag swinging and a cooking pot in hand. 'Just got to make some rice.'

'Calm down,' said Stephanie. 'There's no rush.'

Beth shoved the pan onto the hob and set about filling the kettle.

'I thought you'd like a glass of Prosecco rather than a cup of tea.'

'The water's for rice. You may not be starving but I am.'

'Why don't I cook the rice?'

Beth puffed a breath. 'Good idea. It's been a crazy day.'

'How so?'

'A customer tried to walk out without paying. I intercepted only to have the woman claim she was pregnant and going to give birth. In truth, I think she had a cushion stuffed up her jumper. I was ready to call 999 when she realised the game was up. She turned out her purse and paid the bill in coins. I ask you!'

'She won't be showing her face at Angel Cakes again.'

'Don't you believe it.'

Beth headed off to freshen up. From the kitchen it was possible to hear the drone of the shower and water splattering against tiles in the bathroom above. A little later, the noise stopped and Beth reappeared, this time dressed in jogging bottoms and a top. Stephanie offered a flute of Prosecco to Beth who flopped onto a kitchen chair. The timer sounded and Stephanie checked the rice. A puff of steam leaving the pan confirmed it was perfectly cooked. From a stir of the casserole, Stephanie could tell it was heating up nicely.

After they'd eaten, Beth carried the remains of the bottle into the lounge and refreshed their glasses. As the theme tune for *Luther* filled the room, they sat in their respective seats: Stephanie at the end of the sofa, Beth on the armchair. The episode of confrontation and cunning culminated in stalemate.

'Did you see that coming?' asked Beth.

'Bloody hell, poor Luther.'

'You'll never guess what he's going to do,' said Beth.

'I'll find out next time. And there are rumours of another series. Idris Elba has made the part his own.'

Beth plumped her cushion. In a moment of reflection, Stephanie was reminded of an interview with an angry black mother a few years earlier. The ferocity of the woman's argument even had Stephanie worried. At first, she'd thought it was a case of pushy parenting but it wasn't so. 'A while ago, I wrote a piece about a black family who were utterly aggrieved about the treatment of their teenage daughter. She'd auditioned for a lead part at the local drama club and had outshone everyone. The point was, the teacher in charge didn't think Belmont was ready for a black Miss Jean Brodie.'

Beth stopped reorganising the armchair and sank back into the seat. 'I bet she would've been brilliant. That's the trouble with living in Belmont, it's so far behind the times. Even now. I've got cousins in Birmingham and they can't believe the stories I tell. One time, I was in a queue for the cashpoint. I'd been scrolling on my mobile and didn't realise the person in front had moved on. The next thing I knew, this man was waving his arms about like he was crazy. I didn't know what was happening. Then, he used an extra loud voice: *it's ... your ... turn ... now.* It was so embarrassing. After that he went on about people not speaking English and it was an insult to the Queen. When I got my money, I told him in perfectly good English that he was an idiot and stomped off.'

'I didn't realise these incidents were a regular occurrence.'

'Oh come on, we live next to Mrs Walker.'

Stephanie had to acknowledge Beth had a point, but she didn't know how to respond. She wanted to say Mrs Walker was making an effort, yet she realised how pathetic that would sound.

'Don't look so put out,' said Beth. 'I know she's *trying.*'

Stephanie prickled with embarrassment. 'Are you cross with me for making excuses for her?'

'I understand it. I could even admit to understanding Mrs Walker. We've reached a truce thanks to her chutney.'

Even though it didn't look very appetising, Beth had taken a liking to the green tomato chutney and finished the jar. She'd even returned the empty container to Mrs Walker for another batch come the autumn preserving season.

Beth sighed. 'I know Mrs Walker's a product of her

upbringing but sometimes it's just relentless. Racism is always worse in mainly white areas.'

There was the nub of it. Stephanie had witnessed racism as a reporter for the *Post* but had never really understood the impact. It now occurred to her that by not drawing sufficient attention to the problem she was actually colluding with it. 'You know, I have a feeling it would be worth shining a light on your experiences.'

'Aha,' said Beth. 'An idea for your next podcast! I'll be your first interviewee.'

'That's not a bad plan.' It would be one way for Stephanie to make amends for her inaction in the past.

49

JUNE 1979

Everything changed when classes ended ready for exams to begin. The time off was just as boring as half term had been, but I still had one last session at Sim's house and then we'd be together. I so longed to be with him, my whole body ached for his embrace. I pondered again how he'd gripped me in his arms during our last session. The waiting to see him again felt like forever. At least when I'd been at school, there was respite from the yearning. A whole lesson with him gave a chance for our eyes to meet, for me to hear the low murmur of his voice. It was enough to ease the heaviness in my stomach. Alone at home, I roamed like the polar bear at London Zoo I'd seen on TV. The bear paced the enclosure, back and forth it went, tossing its head as a demonstration of longing for life beyond the confines. For me, I took a route from my bedroom to the kitchen for a cup of tea. Down and back, down and back. How I craved our new life.

In the kitchen, I didn't bother making a whole new pot but sloshed hot water over the dregs and poured. I was being lazy and with the house empty, there wasn't anyone to object. As I carried the mug to my room, an idea gnawed at my brain and I couldn't resist the urge of a little detour into Mum's bedroom.

Peering towards Sim's house, I found this was enough to settle my heart. Although I knew he was at school and joining other teachers for a break in the staffroom, I raised my cup to him.

'Cheers, Sim.' The words I spoke were like cherries on my tongue. Our life together would be sweet and juicy. Sim was my future. It was easy to be swept away by ideas of our life in France. I knew about warm evenings drinking wine on a terrace. I'd cycled alongside fields full of sunflowers, and I saw their heads nodding in agreement to our plan. The vision of us together, holding hands as we strolled to buy *pain* from the boulangerie was brought to a sudden end when I heard the milkman place two pints on the front step of the house next door. The silver tops glared at me. A sinking feeling made me realise there was revision to be done. Was that really what Sim wanted? I couldn't decide. Now that he'd agreed to going away, my efforts should be invested in making preparations. It was a much better use of my time.

I watched the milkman as he leaned over the dividing fence that separated our front path from the next. He reached for our empty bottle and pulled Mum's scrolled note that stuck from the neck: *no milk today*. Scrunching the paper into a ball, he chucked it into the gutter as he returned to the milk float.

My life lay with Sim. Plans had to be made but we didn't need to talk. That was a measure of our love. Thought transference allowed communication without words. I knew what he was thinking, and we were totally in tune. It wouldn't be long before we'd be off. Obviously, Sim was going to see me through the exam and then we'd be free from Greensleeves.

The history and geography papers were already completed and I was only in school on the days I had to sit exams. Whenever there, I searched to see if Sim was about. I had the knack of being able to hone in. Around the new block, I'd see his shadow pass. From behind a doorway, I heard his voice. Along the corridors, his footsteps were unmistakable. The thought of his presence sent feathers of delight tickling my skin and nestling around my neck. I valued Sim even if the staff at Greensleeves didn't recognise his potential. It was clear Sim had been pushed aside at school. Now that his teaching with our group was over, he was used as a dogsbody. Covering lessons wasn't a proper role for him. We'd find something better in France. It would be a fresh start. We'd be able to rely on each other.

Sim made a point of getting to see me during the first exam. Timing it perfectly, he walked beside the hall where the full-length glass windows gave me a view of him from head to foot. Sim was my lucky mascot. I couldn't help staring, consuming every drop of him as he went by. It was Forsyth who disturbed me, marching down the row of desks to stand next to me until Sim was out of sight. I didn't have a choice so returned my attention to the page. After that, Forsyth moved on, ignorant of the connection between me and Sim. None of the others sitting the paper noticed either because their heads were down and they were scribbling away.

I reckoned Sim had been sent to cover some of Forsyth's lessons. As deputy, he liked to big himself up and got to bellow the instructions about putting our full names on the front of the exam paper and adding our candidate number. He seemed to especially relish the moment of saying when we could turn the page. I hated the way he treated Sim like a poodle. The sooner we were out of there the better.

Sitting in my bedroom, I glanced out of the window and clocked how the summer was progressing. The lilies Mum had planted by the shed showed stems bending under the weight of the purple amulets that would burst open given time. How Mum loved her flowers. They offered distraction. The lilies particularly, traditionally used to comfort those in mourning. She would enjoy them when I was gone.

It was good having ideas for our travels, but I needed to square things with Sim. Putting plans on paper would be a mistake. Suppose someone found them – it wasn't worth the risk. At sixteen, I was too young to marry without parental consent. The ridiculous laws of this country meant we had to proceed carefully. I didn't care about a wedding; I wasn't one of those silly girls who dreamed of a fairy-tale marriage. My dad was never going to walk me down the aisle. Besides, living together was a proper thing. Common law would do for me and Sim.

In our final tutoring session, we had to make the most of the opportunity. It was lovely being around him, yet there wasn't time to waste. Sim's passion for my exam success was touching. I wanted to please him and annoy Forsyth. We used creative and clever ways to make our feelings clear. Now was the time to map our movements and make sure our elopement was successful.

I turned to the page containing my last piece of homework and read Sim's feedback for the umpteenth time. There, in his gorgeous writing, Sim had asked me to make up some maths problems for him to answer. He explained, if I was able to pose questions, I'd get a better handle on the steps needed to calculate them. He was a genius. We were to converse through the language of mathematics. Only Sim could decipher the underlying message. For anyone else, it would simply be questions cooked up for the sake of revision. I used the index cards to play around with ideas. Once I'd practised, the time had come to compose the plan on a few pages purloined from Mum's stationery pad.

One train leaves Belmont at three o'clock, another leaves at five. The journey takes three and a half hours. Two lovers go on separate trains, the youngest goes first. What time will they meet under the clock at Waterloo?

I did wonder if the word *lovers* was too much. Perhaps I should've written *couple* instead. It was more discreet but I couldn't make changes and spoil the presentation. The next question involved a calculation about the price of rooms in a hotel. How much money would a couple save if they shared a double rather than a twin? And the last problem related to the travelling distance to Paris. Perfect.

Folding the page in half, I wrote *Mr Simmons* on the envelope and added a few swirling lines beneath as a substitute for kisses. He would know exactly what I meant. With that, I was ready for my last session. It would be sad spending our final hour together, but there was a bright future ahead. All I had to do was make sure Sim understood the coded messages. He was sure to, he always checked the work I'd done.

50

2014

Science Today article:

Why you may not be able to trust your own
memories. Recent research has found...

Stephanie studied the Belair website. She recognised the copy
and images she'd provided but was interested in listeners'
comments. Robert had told her there'd been a huge surge in
feedback and the *Extra Lessons* page was updated. Although she'd
tried to counter the idea that Graham Simmons was involved, the
groundswell of opinion continued to finger him. Perhaps they
were right. As a trainee, she'd been so convinced she knew better
than others. Young self-righteousness became moderated over
time and maybe the podcast would finally do it for Stephanie.
Thoughts of Salisbury and the incident at the garage she
conveniently slipped to the back of her mind. Nothing but a
pragmatist, Stephanie categorised the experience as too hard to
handle. There was an occasional criticism about the quality of the

recording which she ignored. Telephone interviews had since been abandoned because meeting face to face had much better outcomes. Of course, she'd make an exception for Graham Simmons, only after the telephone call with his wife, that seemed unlikely. Besides, he lived in western Ireland, so making the journey without a meeting arranged would be a wild goose chase. She had enough to do at the moment. There were still a few more leads with links to the Mini Market.

During the week she planned to meet Doug at his office. It had been months since she'd been in the building but now with the start of a successful podcast series under her belt, she could face her old colleagues. According to Doug, Stephanie's appearance as a podcaster featured as an agenda item at the senior managers' meeting and they were keen to talk about a possible campaign putting pressure on the police to have another look at Carolyn's case. She anticipated a few grudging words from the big boss, but realised Doug would be delegated to make negotiations.

The opening episodes of *Extra Lessons* had provided the opportunity to introduce Carolyn and build listener empathy for the experiences of Mrs Russell and Janine. They were both articulate about what it was like to lose a close family member. One of the most memorable excerpts had been Janine describing packing up Carolyn's room. Stephanie scrolled to find the recording.

We spent years getting used to being without Carolyn although I thought about her every day: hoping she was okay but realising the worst had probably happened. Eventually, I persuaded Mum we should clear her room – years of avoiding the task wasn't healthy. The police had rifled through Carolyn's possessions early on. Knowing her things were soiled by their searching made it easier to put her stuff into black sacks. When I dropped the bags into the skip, I saw index cards covered in what must have been revision notes poking through a split in the plastic. I stood there thinking about the effort she made for exam success – and she might've got a grade one had she completed the papers. Then, two men in high-vis jackets lobbed a fraying sofa over the top. It was then I got yelled at for not using the paper recycling bins.

Irony made the excerpt powerful. Not that the refuse workers would've known the significance of finally disposing of Carolyn's possessions but when Beth heard about it, she'd been outraged. People should be sensitive to others and not blurt the first thing that came into their heads. Stephanie was surprised at Beth; she didn't usually criticise. Or maybe the whole scenario of Carolyn's disappearance was making its mark. If it could affect Beth, then the podcast had the power to influence change.

Filing had never been one of Stephanie's strengths, even though she'd purchased a large oak cupboard for the purpose which now sat in the lounge. There she kept her research for the podcast including clippings, maps and documents plus the bits and pieces she printed. The recordings were saved on her computer, her external hard drive and important documents were also on a memory stick. She was nothing if not a belt and braces type of person.

Looking at the pile of papers she'd referred to recently, she wished she'd introduced a better labelling system from the beginning. She found that tracking down notes was easily done by date order, so now her diary became an invaluable resource. Stephanie was proud of the way she'd examined home and community aspects of the case. It was Megan's genius idea to include Graham Simmons' voicemail message and one of her scripted replies in the latest recording. It gave a sense of his elusive presence and the stack of unanswered questions. *Why didn't he want to be involved in the podcast? What opportunities had tutoring afforded?* As much as she'd tried to offer alternative possible scenarios to those she interviewed, many were so convinced of Simmons' involvement, there was literally no budging their ideas. Stephanie believed Bill Spencer magnified the suspicion but the root of the rumour was connected to Forsyth. There was obviously some grudge between them. The rules about tutoring were blurred, yet it had been a risky path even if Simmons was perfectly innocent. You'd never find male teachers tutoring teenage girls alone in their own homes these days. To give a balanced view of Carolyn's disappearance, it was necessary to also consider alternatives. An examination of exploitation at the Mini Market was scheduled. She was sure this could be achieved without another encounter with Salisbury. Although if needs must. Perhaps it would be a better idea to skirt around the edges. Get some memories from customers about skewed happenings at the shop. Another challenge was locating the person who'd reported seeing Carolyn at Waterloo Station. If Carolyn had travelled to London, she must've had a plan. She was a long way from home for a sixteen-year-old but at her age, she was entitled to travel the country if she wished. According to police attitudes of the time, she would return home when she was ready. Well, they couldn't have got that more wrong.

While Stephanie assembled documents relating to the sighting, her mobile rang. Blast, she was beginning to get a handle on possible journeys from Waterloo. Tempted to let the call go to voicemail, she changed her mind at the final ring and barked hello.

'Is that Stephanie… Brett?' a woman asked.

'Yes. Sorry. This is Stephanie.'

'I got your number from the radio station. I'm calling about Carolyn Russell.'

Stephanie was beginning to wish she hadn't answered. There were loads of people dying to give their views about what had happened and leaving a comment on the website simply wasn't enough for some. Stephanie pulled a smile hoping to feign interest. 'How can I help?'

'It's awful that her mother and sister have no idea what happened. I can't stand it any longer and that's why I'm coming forward. Of course, I didn't think much about it at the time but these days we're much more aware.'

What was she talking about? 'Did you know Carolyn?'

'Not exactly. We weren't friends or anything.'

Another timewaster, Stephanie assumed. 'Is there something you'd like to share?'

'I went to Graham Simmons' house for a private lesson and never went back again.'

Stephanie's eyes skimmed over the files to locate her notepad. 'This could be very helpful information.'

'I hope so.'

'Why did you only go for one session?'

'That's the story,' said the woman.

51

JUNE 1979

There wasn't much room in my school bag – I had to be selective. The culottes Sim admired were rolled into a neat cylinder and packed. In went the purple bra, it would be the one I'd wear for special occasions. We were sure to dine on mussels and frites in a small café with a carafe of wine. The little compact of golden eye shadow took up no room at all. I could squeeze in a couple of tops including the cheesecloth shirt with angel sleeves and I'd better take a jumper, something for when the nights got cool. On second thoughts, during any walk with Sim, he would have his arm around my shoulders and I would bathe in his warmth.

The important documents went into the side pocket, which until that point had been used for last-minute notes and lists of things to do. Clearing out the rubbish, I slid my passport between the prongs of the zip, then stopped to open it and took a look at my photo. I almost didn't recognise the picture of the girl in the Woolworths booth. No one could mistake the change. I'd become a woman in the last few months and I wasn't going back. Lastly, I folded the fivers that had accumulated in my treasure box and pressed them into a plastic wallet that once held Janine's coach ticket. The wallet would be a reminder of her but in truth, would I miss my sister? Not much. She'd decided to spend the summer in Oxford. Mum relayed the fact after a recent phone conversation. Janine had a job in a small bookshop. According to Mum, it was employment that would definitely offer a good reference and shouldn't be turned down. The only thing for me to do was agree. Little did Mum know this had given me a final spurt of courage. I would find a new life and never look back. I ran my finger over the long neck of the Siamese cat figurine. I was tempted to slip it into my bag, but why bother? It belonged in my past.

As I walked to school, I didn't care that I'd slammed the door in Mum's face. It served her right for asking stupid questions. My bulging bag banged against my hip with every step but no one would guess what me and Sim had in mind. There would be no trail to follow, no finding us and dragging us back. This was a kind of freedom I had longed for in the days and weeks I'd sat at my little desk, wishing to be somewhere else. I was away from my mother's suffocating presence, and it made me feel light. Not even my tote bag could weigh me down.

After registration, I had a few spare minutes. I stowed my bag in a locker, took my exam things in my clear plastic pencil case and headed for the hall. The skirt of my uniform flapped against my thighs as I walked. This would be the very last time wearing it. I'd change in the ladies' lavatory at the train station and slip into an empty carriage unseen. No one would recognise me and I'd be agile in avoiding any contact. In the hustle and bustle at Waterloo, I'd be totally safe. I'd managed to squeeze Janine's floppy hat amongst my things. It had been a last-minute addition to my packing and would provide a disguise. Maybe even Sim would have trouble recognising me in my fancy gear and make-up. As I was catching the early train, I'd be there under the clock waiting for him. At first sight, I'd dash into his arms and feel his kiss on my lips. Putting the idea into check, I realised our reunion would have to be discreet. We couldn't make a show and risk being remembered. Anything to keep them off our tracks.

The silhouette of Forsyth in the entrance hall shook me back to my senses. He was the last person I wanted to see. Peering through the opened double doors, I scanned the rows of tables and checked the invigilators to see Sim amongst them. There he was, his feathered hair framing his face, the ends of his lips tweaked into a smile. I stiffened, trying to calm my heart as it ricocheted around my chest. *Be still*, I told myself, *be still*.

As a crowd gathered, Sim walked over. He had words of encouragement for the others in my class. I respected his need for fairness. It wasn't the time to be greedy – I would have him entirely to myself before long. Edging away from the group, I wondered if he would be drawn to me. I did need a little attention – a final word before the next chapter of our lives. Eventually, he came. 'Are you all set for the big day, Carolyn?'

'Yes, I'll be sticking to the plan.' A place on the three o'clock train was mine.

'Don't forget the approach we discussed to tackling problem questions.'

'When two of us are on the train, the cost of the fare doubles.' I was happy to disguise our arrangements and keep up the pretence.

'Oh yes!' He took the cue. 'And moving on to Paris, if the journey to the ferry port takes three hours and fifteen minutes...'

'And the ferry crossing is two hours, thirty minutes. How long will it take to get there?'

'You've got the measure of it, Carolyn.' Thank God for that!

A group pushed past us, keen to grab desks that were out of the sun. I took a step closer to Sim. I could risk a few words. 'I'll see you later.'

'Of course.' He nodded but his eyes looked beyond me and into the hall. I turned to see the rows filling up.

'I'd better go,' I said.

'Break a leg, Carolyn.' He gave me a wink. 'On second thoughts, perhaps not. We don't want you stumped for getting about with your leg in plaster.'

I smiled. Sim had a great sense of humour.

Forsyth was at the front of the hall, for once not bothering to take his place on the stage. That flop of hair and his scratchy red cheeks reminded me of a garden gnome. I had to smother my laughter but the joke caused me such distraction that I missed leaving the starting blocks and was behind in turning the page of the exam booklet. Not a good beginning, yet did it really matter? I could hardly concentrate on mathematics when the fizz of love turned my brain mushy. But Sim had programmed me to tackle the exam, and I skim-read the questions to make an informed decision about which to try first. To my absolute amazement, none of them were too difficult. I took my pick. Within minutes I was turning the page and attempting the next set. A sneaky glimpse around the hall and I was able to tell Patricia was doing fine. Good for her – there was no need to hold a grudge. And then I used a few seconds for a reviving look at Sim. There he stood at the front, flicking through the pages of the exam paper. He caught my eye for a moment, and a beaming smile covered his face. Excitement sent my heart trilling. It was only me who knew what his smile meant.

52

2014

West Country Post headline:

Belair to broadcast new information about the missing Carolyn
Russell

Stephanie nodded and smiled at her former colleagues who
sat at their hot desks. She could have been a bride walking
up the aisle: her chin lifted, her stride long and every pace was
testament to the magnanimity she felt towards the management
who had rejected her. They were hidden behind boardroom
doors but news of her visit would penetrate even the most hard-
faced amongst them. They would know she had made a success
of things, they might even regret sacrificing her role.

When she reached Doug's office, she noticed the room was
empty. Rather than linger outside, she entered and set her
shoulder bag on his desk. Inside was her laptop containing the
first edit of her interview with Tracy Dickens. If this wasn't
enough to fire up his campaign to reopen the investigation into

Carolyn's disappearance, nothing would. For Stephanie, the revelations Tracy brought were timely. It was her opportunity for ditching the Rick Salisbury inquiry altogether. Of course, she had to re-evaluate and admit her instincts about Graham Simmons were wrong. Bill Spencer had been on the right track and Forsyth for that matter. Yet it was Stephanie who had found a witness who exposed Simmons' involvement with young girls. A smug little smile crept onto her lips and lodged there. This was her triumph and she was going to enjoy it.

A few minutes later Doug appeared carrying a disposable cup in each hand. 'You beat me here!' He smiled and passed her a drink. One sip of the long black he had rushed to purchase from Angel Cakes made Stephanie smile. No vending machine muck for her.

'I'm so pleased you've come to me with this new development,' he said.

'I'm pretty pleased with it myself.'

Doug sat up straight in his chair. 'I can't wait to hear.'

With her laptop already set up, she pressed the play button. Settled in a chair, Stephanie listened to the countdown and was ready for her own voice.

Tracy Dickens keeps her dark hair shoulder length but the layering is different from the crop style she wore in the seventies. As for Carolyn, one of the few photos shows her in uniform with a big smile but startled eyes. Following the early episodes of this podcast there's been much interest in Carolyn's case and new people have come forward with information about Graham Simmons. Tracy Dickens is one of them. She went to Greensleeves Comprehensive with Carolyn and she can hold her silence no longer. Here's what Tracy has to say:

. . .

It was a bit like keeping up with the Joneses. Carolyn had extra lessons and my mum wasn't going to let Mrs Russell from the driving school have one over us. She persuaded me it was a good idea but I was never keen. Mr Simmons wasn't even my teacher and when I saw him about the place, I thought he looked weird in his camel-coloured corduroys. My mother was convinced it would do me good to have extra help and I ran out of excuses.

I turned up at his house a complete bag of nerves. Can you imagine? A schoolgirl on the doorstep of a teacher. I got inside and you should've seen the place. There was junk everywhere. I remember an old pram rammed in the hall, piled with blankets and rugs. I had to breathe in and squeeze past. When I got into the back room it wasn't much better. At least the table was set like we were going to do some work but nothing else seemed right. I sat in the chair he pointed to and he squeezed in beside me. He was too close for comfort and I went rigid.

I couldn't believe it when he got a pack of playing cards out and did a show-off shuffle. He said we could use the cards to practise maths but I didn't understand. Not even when he said we could do order of operations or some other thing. Sitting there with my arms crossed, I refused to take off my blazer. Then he tried coaxing me. He had a wheedling type of voice and eventually, I relented just to shut him up. That was a big mistake. Next thing, he used some stupid excuse to massage my shoulders. He talked about relieving tension and his hands were all over me. If he'd had his way, I would've been naked and sat there in a losing game of strip poker. I wasn't having any of it. Making an excuse, I grabbed my blazer and rushed to the toilet. Thank God it was downstairs and I managed to escape through the window and into an alley. I ran all the way home. On my doorstep, I calmed down and went in without drawing attention. Then, up in my room, I made myself presentable. It was a lucky escape.

By saying the extra lesson wasn't any different to classes in school, I got out of more sessions. It was too embarrassing to talk about what happened. I felt guilty anyway, as if it was my fault, and I didn't want Mum making a scene either. She decided Mrs Russell had been taken for a mug and that was an end to it. I avoided Mr Simmons in school and didn't answer when he tried to find out what had happened to me. I did warn Carolyn about him, but she wouldn't listen. When I think about it now, it's clear something unfortunate went on between them. These days you'd call it grooming, but if it happened back then, the girl was simply unlucky or stupid.

53

2014

The Lot, France

Autumn sun poured into the little suntrap beside the pool where I sat drinking my morning coffee. I'd had my choice of farmhouses in The Lot, my favourite part of France. The location was suitably distanced from the English expats in the Dordogne and however much I liked to chat in my mother tongue, I was really a local. Although I took a daily paper, I liked to browse the internet on my laptop, the latest of my playthings. It was a habit to check the happenings in Belmont. Such a shitty little town but it was impossible to be completely removed from the place of my birth. I burst out laughing at the headline in the *West Country Post*. I was in the news again, over thirty years since I'd packed my bags and left. Adding to my amusement, there was good old Stephanie Brett plying her wares in a podcast about my disappearance. Obviously, I downloaded the episodes and got up to speed with this new investigation. Funnily enough, the intriguing case of Carolyn Russell was providing something of a conundrum. Back then they'd misjudged her – little did they know the stuff I was made from.

I had to thank Floria for being there when Sim left me waiting at Waterloo Station. I'd invested everything in a future with him and couldn't believe he'd let me down. One phone call to Floria and she smuggled me into her hostel room where we shared her single bed. I was beside myself but she stroked my back and soothed me. It was a surprise when we kissed. Even though I'd dreamed of kissing Sim, Floria was a passable substitute. In the morning, our intimacy gave me renewed confidence but Floria was devastated. 'I don't want to be a lesbian,' she said. Silly cow. It was only one night. Telling her it was for us to know and others to find out, I enlisted her help to set up a new life. How she begged me never to reveal the truth about our liaison.

Floria's travel arrangements for the next day were booked and paid for. It was easy to purchase an additional ticket and we practised French conversation during the journey. As it was a hot day, Janine's big floppy hat provided shade and an appropriate disguise. Once in France, we returned to Floria's house near Dijon where I'd visited the previous summer. (Her family had relocated due to her father's work and the old place was empty.) Floria knew where a key was hidden. It took a few days to find work as an au pair for a handsome French widower, Francois Dubois. Everything fell into place and the secret me and Floria shared was sealed. I knew she'd never tell the authorities we'd been in contact, her shame was too deep.

Blackmail (what an ugly word) worked again when I was ready to divorce. Francois had been so keen to marry me, he engaged in a little shenanigan to secure the necessary papers after my passport expired. It cost him dearly in terms of our settlement but it was nothing less than I deserved. I'd been a waif-like bride who was the envy of his contemporaries and a suitable replacement to bring up his young daughters.

Listening to the podcast, I realised how totally disconnected I was from the girl in the story. I'd long since dropped the pretentious *Caro* to become Lyn and now with my French family name, there were no links between us. But Carolyn had become a legend in her hometown. A mysterious disappearance that hung over the place like a big black cloud. Or that was the impression I got. I nearly choked as I heard there was a campaign to reopen an inquiry into the case. On second thoughts, who wouldn't want to know exactly what happened to Carolyn Russell? It was such a well-executed vanishing. They may have thought Carolyn dim and not a patch on her older sister, but they didn't account for her determination, her ability to plan and deliver. She got the better of Janine and her Oxbridge education. On occasions, I did wonder if Janine and Mum *really* missed me. They made so many protestations but I wasn't convinced. I could perhaps admit to feeling a pang of remorse when I heard their voices on the podcast. Things would've been so different if they hadn't squeezed me out. Thinking about it rationally, they'd chosen each other over me and losing them was a sacrifice I was willing to make. Far too much time had gone by for me to show up. I'd be cast as the criminal for putting *them* through it. I preferred to leave things as they were, and besides, it was far simpler. I didn't have the energy to change what was in the past. And Floria had kept her promise. It wouldn't be fair to reveal the truth after years of sticking to the plan.

A newspaper report online gave me the biggest laugh: Graham Simmons was in the frame for my murder. To think Tracy Dickens had come forward. If Sim didn't want me, he'd never have fancied her. I put Tracy's account of grooming down to an overactive imagination. Boy oh boy was her timing good. Precisely when he was getting on with his career, suspicion raised its ugly head again. Sim was working at a school in the west of Ireland. Deputy headteacher, in fact. His position in life wasn't likely to last. Of course, I could've cleared everything up in an email or a phone call. I could so easily have explained the entire mystery and made Tracy Dickens look stupid in the process. But what was the point in spoiling my fun? I didn't want to make Sim's life easy. Why should I? He would have to cope with whatever came his way.

54

2014

After Tracy Dickens' revelations, other former students came forward with stories of grooming by male teachers at Greensleeves. The usual suspects in the PE department were in the frame. Many wanted to be interviewed but in asking a few questions, Stephanie was able to identify those who simply had an opinion to share. On her list to be urgently followed up was a resident of Crossways who'd lived on the street his entire life and gave a view about a possible burial spot under the new development. Before the housing boom of the 1980s, some of the neighbours cut turf to replace patches of lawn and in the war years whole swathes of land were used as allotments. Who would have guessed? Stephanie didn't think the idea that Carolyn was buried there held much weight but there were mumblings about needing to dig up a few gardens, just to check.

Stephanie glanced at her diary, no actual meetings were arranged for that afternoon and she'd wanted to get everything tied up before drinks with Doug. The second Friday of the month was a regular commitment. Stephanie absolutely had to avoid payday drinks on the last Friday seeing as she had yet to acquire an income, but things were going to change soon. The walk into town took twenty minutes but as there was a bus pulling up, she hopped on. She didn't want Doug to get there first. It was embarrassing to find him always paying for the first round and sitting at one of the small tables, pint of beer half drunk and a gin and tonic lined up for her with the ice melting. No, she would get there early and be waiting for him.

Stephanie found a chair with a proper back and sat with her legs stretched so she could admire her purple suede boots. With podcast production costs covered, and enough redundancy money to hold out for another few months, she deserved a little treat. The woollen-knit fabric on her crossover skirt draped and Robert had complimented her outfit when the Angels last met. The name had been given to the group by Beth (much to Doug's disdain and Robert's hilarity). They met if anyone had the enthusiasm to try out a new recipe, or lately there had been circular Sunday walks from a pub where they met outside town.

Doug arrived and dropped onto the chair opposite Stephanie.

'Here.' She passed the straight glass to him. 'Looks like you could do with this.'

'You're not wrong.' He took a swig. 'The team meeting went on and on. Fortunately, there was a positive outcome.'

'And?'

'The next step in the campaign is to lobby the MP for support. I have a feeling in my bones the police are ready to reopen the investigation.' Doug raised his glass. 'Thanks to you we'll find out what happened to Carolyn Russell.'

Stephanie clinked her glass against Doug's.

'And the final episode has yet to be aired,' said Stephanie. 'It would be good if we could get confirmation of reopening the case before the podcast ends. Icing on the cake.'

'An angel cake.'

Stephanie smiled. 'Beth's been a champion and Megan's a godsend. I'd never have managed without her podcasting skills. Thanks for sending her my way.'

'No problemo,' said Doug.

'You're in a cheery mood.'

'So I should be. A freelance opportunity is opening up. It'll take some of the burden off me and might suit you down to the ground, Stephanie.'

'Me?' she said. 'Back at the *Post*? I think not.'

'Don't be hasty. The pay's generous and you can pick your hours.' Doug nodded. 'The management have seen the error of their ways in giving you the push.'

'I should think so.' When to break the news? Now was as good a time as any. 'My pitch to the regional radio station has been accepted. I'm going to be working on a new six-part podcast for them and it's bound to reach a wider audience.'

'Bugger me,' said Doug. 'There's no stopping you.'

'Absolutely.' Stephanie pulled a self-satisfied smile.

'What's the big new idea?' Doug made an effort to sound casual.

'Very topical and close to home.'

'Jesus! You're not going to take issue with the *Post* are you?' Doug took a huge slug of beer.

'Funny you should say that, Doug.'

'Holy shit, I know you were put out by the redundancy, but they're offering you an olive branch.' Doug felt in his pocket for a handkerchief and dabbed his forehead.

Stephanie wondered how long she could keep him sweating.

'I tried to defend your job,' he said. 'Truly.'

It didn't matter either way. Stephanie had moved on but she teased Doug. 'Surely you realise it's time someone investigated the unfair power dynamic in an employer like the *Post*.'

'Is that person you?' Doug looked positively scared.

'No!'

He slumped back, relieved. 'I'm pleased to hear it.'

'I think you'll agree my new podcast is even more pressing. It's something I'd never taken seriously before.'

'What might that be?' Doug gave a clueless expression.

'The idea started with Beth. I'm going to investigate racism in rural areas.'

'Now that's something well worth putting under the microscope.'

'Cheers.' Stephanie raised her glass. 'I'm back on the job.'

THE END

ACKNOWLEDGEMENTS

A big thank you to beta readers Sue Borgersen, John Nixon and Andrew Wolfendon. Also thanks to writers who gave feedback along the way including members of the Vestas (Sue, Carol and Denise), Vivo Group (Sean, SJ, Ingrid, Barbara, Lesley and Val) and the online writing group Pens Around the World. I've enjoyed camaraderie and help from the Women Writers Network, and the Society of Women Writers & Journalists. Cheers to all the folk at Writers' Hour hosted by the London Writers' Salon who offer inspiration and encouragement each weekday morning at eight o'clock. For pointers on polishing the submission package, thanks go to Louise Jensen and Amy Durant. Also thanks to Joanna Barnard who helped finalise the manuscript.

It was following a Twitter pitch that my brilliant publisher Bloodhound Books picked up the story. Thank you to everyone in the team, especially Betsy Reavley and Tara Lyons for bringing this novel to readers. I'd also like to thank Abbie Rutherford for her meticulous editing. Lastly, thanks go to my patient and supportive family including David, Shirley, Jonny, Izzy and Will. And there's Truffle, too.

AUTHOR'S NOTE

I became hooked on true crime podcasts in early 2020. At the time, I was living in a remote town in the north-west of Uganda and volunteering with VSO at a nearby refugee settlement. The power supply was very erratic and cuts happened regularly. With no light to read by, I was often in bed and under my mosquito net by nightfall. My evening's entertainment involved listening to the podcasts I'd downloaded during daylight hours at a local hotel.

The many and varied podcasts I've listened to have acted as research in creating *The Secret Life of Carolyn Russell*, an entirely fictional text. Like streamed podcasts, I've included gems of detail, serendipitous findings and interviewing techniques which have added colour and texture to the story. The real-life motivation to commit crimes has caused me to reflect on what drives my characters. Podcasts detailing cases set in the seventies and eighties have helped me to reimagine the norms of the time and give voice to Carolyn Russell.

Please find below some of the true crime podcasts which have fascinated me:

Finding Cleo is hosted by the Canadian Broadcasting Corporation (CBC) with Connie Walker. She follows a search for a young Cree girl who was taken by child welfare workers in the 1970s as part of a programme of adoption into white families across North America.

Sweet Bobby is a podcast series from Tortoise which investigates a case of catfishing, where a person assumes a fake social media identity to lure a woman into an online relationship.

Fake Heiress from the BBC documents the highpoints and pitfalls of Anna Delvey's daring attempt to con New York society into believing she was about to inherit millions.

Paradise from the BBC gets to the truth of missing couple Peta and Chris who left home in 1978 to travel the world but came to an untimely end off the coast of Guatemala.

The Teacher's Pet is created by journalist Hedley Thomas of *The Australian* who investigates the case of a missing woman. Lynette Dawson vanished in 1982 from the home on Sydney's Northern Beaches that she shared with her husband Chris and two young daughters. In 2018, Chris Dawson was charged with Lynette's murder. Another series *The Teacher's Trial* reports on events at the trial and the sentencing of Chris Dawson.

ABOUT THE AUTHOR

Novelist, poet and scriptwriter, Gail Aldwin has been writing for over a decade. In 2018, she was awarded a PhD in creative writing and still laughs whenever she's called Doctor. Gail has appeared at Bridport Literary Festival, Stockholm Writers Festival and the Mani Lit Fest in Greece. She splits her time between a tiny flat in South West London and a home overlooking water meadows in Dorset.

Gail is active on social media and loves connecting with readers. Do get in touch.

Twitter: @gailaldwin
Facebook: @gailaldwinwriter
Instagram: @gailfaldwin
Blog: https://gailaldwin.com

JANINA RAMIREZ

THE PRIVATE LIVES OF THE SAINTS

POWER, PASSION AND POLITICS IN ANGLO-SAXON ENGLAND

WH
ALLEN

3 5 7 9 10 8 6 4 2

WH Allen, an imprint of Ebury Publishing,
20 Vauxhall Bridge Road,
London SW1V 2SA

WH Allen is part of the Penguin Random House group of companies
whose addresses can be found at global.penguinrandomhouse.com

Penguin
Random House
UK

First published by WH Allen in 2015
This edition first published by WH Allen in 2016

www.eburypublishing.co.uk

A CIP catalogue record for this book is available from the British Library

ISBN 9780753555613

Printed and bound in Great Britain by Clays Ltd, St Ives PLC

Penguin Random House is committed to a sustainable future
for our business, our readers and our planet. This book is made
from Forest Stewardship Council® certified paper.

MIX
Paper from
responsible sources
FSC
www.fsc.org   FSC® C018179

This work is dedicated to Dan, Kuba, Kama, Babi, Papa, and all those who love and inspire me. *Aere Perennius*.

ANGLO-SAXON BRITAIN
"THE HEPTARCHY."

English Miles

'All it takes to make a man a saint is grace. Anyone who doubts this knows neither what makes a saint nor a man.'

Blaise Pascal, *Pensées*, VII, 508

Contents

Introduction

Saints' names echo through the centuries. Today we may walk down St Gregory Street, past St Bede's Primary School, or find a church dedicated to St Cuthbert. The saints are in our peripheral vision, part of the subtext of the nation, but the actual people behind the names are shrouded in the mists of time. Inhabitants of a 'dark age', figures like Alfred the Great, Edward the Confessor or Bede the Venerable straddle the part of our collective memories that dissolves legend with historical fact, myth with real people. But the saints can provide a pin upon which to hang other evidence of a lost past. They are fascinating in their diversity, and can reveal a great deal about the times in which they lived and died. It is now their time for reassessment; time to reveal their private lives.

Growing up in a Polish/Irish Catholic household, I am well acquainted with the saints. Images of the traditional early saints, like Christopher, Catherine and Peter, jostled for supremacy next to Padre Pio and Pope John Paul II. Comforting faces peering out from frames, they provided the young me with a sense that an army of righteous, sacred souls were guiding me through life. These early interactions with the saints left a lasting impression. Although I now approach them as historical figures, rather than the focus of devotion, this experience allowed me to reconcile my own probing academic view on medieval saints with a more fundamental understanding of the spiritual potency these individuals can command.

However, my recent renewed fascination with the saints, and the Anglo-Saxon ones in particular, began while reading a tabloid newspaper. I have been passionate about the Anglo-Saxon period from the first moment I encountered the Old English 'Elegies' as an undergraduate student. One passage from *The Wanderer* in particular seemed to resonate down the centuries:

'Her bið feoh læne,	'Here money is fleeting,
her bið freond læne,	here friend is fleeting,
her bið mon læne,	here man is fleeting,
her bið mæg læne,	here kinsman is fleeting,
eal þis eorþan gesteal	all the foundation of this world
idel weorþeð!'	turns to waste!'
The Wanderer.[1]	

Old English texts like this offer timeless insights into the human condition, and yet they grew from the minds and imaginations of people with their own distinct views, attitudes, concerns and symbolic frameworks. It's the world of *Beowulf*, of mystical smiths crafting unimaginably beautiful jewellery, of wandering monks in the wilderness, of the clash and howl of hand-to-hand combat. It was a world that, to me, seemed both within my reach and at the same time impossible to grasp fully, as to understand it I had to learn more about the people themselves and the landscapes (both intellectual and real) that they inhabited.

However, as I flicked through newspaper pages, past models, actors, politicians and celebrities, I began to wonder what an Anglo-Saxon version of such a publication would look like. Whose faces would be staring out at me? Whose lives would readers be following? Who would be the pin-ups and heroes of the Anglo-Saxon period? Traditionally, we might think it would be kings, queens, nobles and warriors. But we are overlooking a far more prevalent and influential body of individuals, whose importance resonated across the social spectrum – the saints. Representatives of a powerful, all-pervading Church, their designation as extra-special Christians ensured their celebrity and reputation. It is their stories that have been passed down the centuries, and their names that are repeatedly tied to specific places and events.

To uncover the lives of Anglo-Saxon saints is to open a window onto a fascinating and rich period in our nation's history.

This close-up of the Sutton Hoo shoulder clasp shows two overlapping boars executed in gold and garnet cloisonné. The skill required to cut the garnets, secure them in the gold fittings with no adhesive, and include a minutely detailed chequerboard-impressed piece of gold leaf behind each gem is testament to the technical skills that Anglo-Saxon jewellers possessed.

Archaeological discoveries over the past century have rendered the term Dark Ages redundant. Far from 'nasty, brutish and short',[2] life in the Anglo-Saxon period could be vibrant and exciting. Anglo-Saxons didn't simply live in wooden huts, but in grand palace and monastic complexes like those at Yeavering and Winchester. They weren't primitive, uncivilised people, but were instead capable of technical wizardry that could produce stunning objects like the Sutton Hoo shoulder clasps and the Lindisfarne Gospels.

The evidence from this period is regrettably sparse. For every spectacular collection of metalwork discovered, like the Staffordshire Hoard, many hundreds have been lost. With literacy in the hands of a few, far fewer documents survive from this period than from those either side. But occasionally certain individuals, places and objects speak across the millennium. The saints are the best-documented individuals of their time, so opening up their stories should also shed light on the periods in which they lived.

This is not a 'warts and all' reveal about the seedy side of saints' lives. It is incredibly hard to find out almost anything truly private about them, since they were public people, with connections to the world of power and politics. Vellum was very expensive, and scribes would write the authorised and publically acceptable version of history, so any hints of scandal or personal insight are only ever subtly or accidentally expressed. But the idea of writing about the private side of saints' lives evolved from a desire to move outside the established canonical information that has been regurgitated over the centuries, to explore the real settings that the saints inhabited and the worlds of which they were a part.

This is an interdisciplinary study, which crosses the boundaries between archaeology, art history, history, literary studies, linguistics, theology and palaeography. And this book is also a journey across the landscapes of Britain and Ireland. Travelling over the terrain that these Anglo-Saxon individuals may have crossed can be a means of getting closer to them. Ancient echoes resonate particularly strongly in some locations. The artefacts, too, are of paramount importance. They were witnesses of the time, and reading their imagery and symbolism can be a way of hearing a true voice across the ages. But to understand the Anglo-Saxon saints, it is essential to begin by understanding the period in which they lived.

What is Anglo-Saxon England?

The Anglo-Saxon period, roughly AD 450 to 1066, is often described as a 'dark age': a time when the failing of the Roman Empire triggered a wave of barbarism that swept away the civilised society that preceded it. The original tribes of Angles, Saxons and Jutes came over from territories around the modern-day Netherlands, northern Germany and Denmark after the collapse of Roman military control in AD 410. Sources state that the bewildered Romano-British, who were being attacked on different borders by Picts and Scots, initially invited the Germanic soldiers over as mercenaries to help them defend themselves.[3]

The question of exactly how and why so many Angles, Saxons and Jutes came to England is one that divides scholars.[4] The two divergent approaches suggest they arrived either through aggressive conquest or via peaceful and gradual settlement. While there is some evidence for destruction and conflict, the *Adventus Saxonum* (coming of the Saxons) hasn't provided the archaeological record with the mass of graves and mutilated skeletons that the Viking incursions did. It seems expedient to think of the arrival of the Angles, Saxons and Jutes as beginning with military expeditions, which were followed by a more steady flow of settlers across the North Sea.

The Germanic homelands left behind by these settlers may have been subject to flooding and over-farming, so their movement across the North Sea could have been prompted by a search for more fertile land to cultivate. Yet they settled in great enough numbers to transform the linguistic, cultural and social framework of England. In a famous passage, the Venerable Bede gives a context for where these tribes came from:

> *Those who came over were of the three most powerful nations of Germany: Saxons, Angles, and Jutes. From the Jutes are descended the people of Kent, and of the Isle of Wight, and those also in the province of the West Saxons who are to this day called Jutes, seated opposite to the Isle of Wight. From the Saxons, that is, the country which is now called Old Saxony, came the East Saxons, the South Saxons, and the West Saxons. From the Angles, that is, the country which is called Anglia, and which is said, from that time, to remain desert to this day, between the provinces of the Jutes and the Saxons, are descended the East Angles, the Midland Angles, Mercians, all the race of the Northumbrians, that is, of those nations that dwell on the north side of the River Humber, and the other nations of the English.*[5]

This was mass immigration, and it was to transform the complexion of the British Isles permanently and profoundly.

There is a temptation to speak of the 'Anglo-Saxon kingdoms' as if they were all part of a unified whole. However, each kingdom had very rigid and defined ways of differentiating themselves from those on their borders. Archaeological finds suggest that different tribes wore their jewellery in recognisable arrangements to indicate their tribal affiliation.[6] Most textiles from the period have been lost, but it is probable that their dress was differentiated too.[7] A recent equivalent would be the clans of Scotland, each clearly distinct from the other through the colour and design of tartan displayed on their kilts. The hostilities between neighbouring tribes – who apparently on the surface were not so different – could be more violent than any aggression towards external threats. Yet there were also a number of factors that bound the Anglo-Saxon tribes together. They all spoke a similar Germanic tongue and followed the same polytheistic religion, and their social structure was based on tribal affiliation and loyalty to the lord of the hall.

Only a handful of writers recorded the Anglo-Saxon period, including Gildas, Bede and Adomnán. However, there are law codes, theological treaties and vernacular texts from the later part of the period to consolidate our knowledge. Alongside these, of course, there are the large numbers of saints' lives, known as hagiographical texts. These do not belong in a single genre, since they often range widely, focusing on topics such as warfare, sexuality, torture and politics, and they can be in Latin or in the vernacular. To read these texts requires a working knowledge of dead languages, and because of their often formulaic and theological subject matter, saints' lives are usually only studied by a small number of historians and literary scholars. Yet behind the symbols and metaphors lies a rich well of information about the Anglo-Saxon period that still has much to offer.

Although this book is about Anglo-Saxon England, it will be apparent from the off that this is a fluid and complex term. How do we define what Anglo-Saxon England is? It is essentially a racial term, and these are fraught with difficulty. The names 'English', 'British', 'Scottish', 'Irish', 'Welsh', 'Manx' and 'Cornish' are still divisive, and the roots of many of these lie in the period discussed in this book.[8] This was the time of the birth of nations, and these racial distinctions feed on a latent belief in the 'differences' between the separate parts of the United Kingdom. There is certainly a historical basis for these differences.

With the coming of the Angles, Saxons and Jutes from the Germanic homelands, the Celtic Britons seem to have moved their strongholds into areas to the west: Wales, Cornwall, the Isle of Man, western Scotland and Ireland. Connected through the early medieval period by ties of trade, marriage and political allegiance, these territories still preserve a native Celtic language, and although each is distinct and different from the other, they have their roots in an older vernacular tongue.[9] What is incredible, however, is that the language of modern-day England – that lingua franca English, which has absorbed elements from Latin, French, Scandinavian and others – has virtually no survivals from the earlier British Celtic tongue that was spoken in this region for centuries. There was, essentially, a linguistic cleansing. The many changes brought about by the *Adventus Saxonum* were most clearly evinced in language and religion. The Celtic fringes remained Christian – a religion that had arrived with the Romans – while Anglo-Saxon England was pagan.[10]

To fully understand the saints of Anglo-Saxon England, it is important to position this little kingdom within a wider geographical and ideological framework. What happened in England was, and remains, profoundly influenced by events, ideas and people outside of its ever-changing boundaries. As we now have a racially fluid, diverse mix of people living within the British Isles, so in the early medieval period there was constant interaction, intermarriage and integration between different groups. Studying the lives of saints undermines the idea of medieval life as local and parochial. They, more than most members of medieval society, moved locations, met with people from different lands and backgrounds, and established or settled in ecclesiastical sites or monasteries that were often geographically distant from their place of birth. The medieval world was not one of racial segregation and national pride, but rather one where individuals relocated to those places that were most politically or economically expedient.

This book will examine the saints that circled and entered Anglo-Saxon England, since their actions and personalities affected the complexion of sanctity within. The saints of Ireland, Wales and Scotland, as well as missionaries from Rome and the Continent, and the movement of individuals across the North Sea, are all of great significance. As a result, early medieval scholars have devised the term 'Insular' to talk of the British Isles – literally 'of the isles'.[11] It is most important, for example, when considering how and why the Anglo-Saxon pagans of England converted to Christianity, to examine the efforts of Patrick and the twelve apostles of Ireland. The work of Columba in particular, founding a monastery at Iona and encouraging missionary activity in the pagan north of the Anglo-Saxon kingdoms, would influence the early saints of England in many ways.

As Christianity came over from Ireland, it also edged its way into England from Rome with Augustine, via the Christian continent. The influence of the papacy, and the premise that Pope Gregory the Great's mission to the Anglo-Saxons in 597 AD 'saved' their pagan souls from damnation, would lead to a particularly esoteric form of Roman Christianity setting down roots in England. Although Anglo-Saxon Christians considered themselves at the edge of the world, the missionary fervour of the newly converted English would have wide-reaching effects throughout the medieval period. As Roman and Irish missionaries moved in, so Anglo-Saxons moved out, taking their ideas, art and culture across the known world.

The notion of geographically distinct countries in the early medieval period was problematised by the absence of maps and ways of defining and enforcing borders. Racial identity could be crafted, but one small scratch of the surface reveals that diversity was the norm. English kings married Franks, Welsh princesses married Irish rulers, and Danish conquerors tied themselves to the Crown through political and marital allegiances. This nation's history is one of racial complexity, and the saints are similarly diverse. The majority of saints covered in this work come from mixed lineage; they travelled and tied themselves to a pan-European notion of Christendom, rather than to a boundary-specific idea of nations. There are always the exceptions, but there are lessons on diversity and tolerance to be learnt from delving back into the Anglo-Saxon period.

End of an Era?

The Anglo-Saxon period is traditionally seen to end in 1066, with the Norman Conquest and its cataclysmic impact on all levels of society, art, architecture and the landscape. Technically, this is correct, since with the defeat of the nobleman proclaimed king, Harold Godwinson, a separate Anglo-Saxon identity became subsumed beneath a French-speaking elite. This would remain the case for many centuries, until ultimately the Hundred Years' War severed the bonds between the ruling classes of England and France. However, the end of Anglo-Saxon England in terms of Anglo-Saxon saints and an England that resembles our modern geographical boundaries began much earlier. The biggest threat to Anglo-Saxon identity came from across the North Sea, not far from where the original Germanic settlers heralded in the fifth century. The Vikings began to attack the British coast at the end of the eighth century, and they would never go away.

The efforts of Alfred the Great made sure that the total transformation of Anglo-Saxon England into a pagan Viking outpost was halted in the ninth century. Through his astute military leadership, he managed to secure a fragile relationship with the Scandinavian settlers in the north, paying vast amounts in Danegeld (a heavy tax upon the Anglo-Saxons, paid to Viking rulers) to stop their repeated attempts to take the whole of England. Alfred's successors, particularly charismatic and influential leaders like Edgar, maintained their uniqueness as Anglo-Saxon leaders in the face of Scandinavian rulers across the virtual borderline of the Danegeld. They halted the process for a few generations, but never removed the threat completely. There was a cultural and social evolution taking place, whereby Anglo-Saxons were absorbing Viking elements, as well as Viking DNA.

By 1016, Anglo-Saxon England was finally and convincingly absorbed by Scandinavia. England had a Danish king. Cnut is reduced in history to a few anecdotes, such as his fabled encounter with the sea.[12] But, as English history has traditionally been taught, it is an overlooked fact that the majority of Anglo-Saxon England was already Scandinavian in terms of taste, culture, intermarriage and economics by the tenth century. And this conquest was completed by Cnut, who was declared King of Denmark and of England. We all know William the Conqueror changed the face of England, but with Cnut the British Isles became as Scandinavian as it was English.

The events of 1066 were the culmination of over two centuries of Viking assaults. Harold Godwinson first fought the Danes at Stamford Bridge and held them back, so preventing a second wave of northern Viking conquest. He then succumbed to William of the Norsemen (the Normans) at the Battle of Hastings. One way or another, the Vikings succeeded, and even that most saintly of kings, Edward the Confessor, was brought up in Normandy under the watchful eye of Norman lords themselves only a few generations settled in the north of France, having a century or so earlier left their Scandinavian lands. In terms of Anglo-Saxon saints, the pagan Vikings did little to encourage their cults, apart from ensuring martyrdom for a few. With the arrival of the Normans, native Anglo-Saxon saints were sidelined, and Anglo-Saxon culture was subsumed beneath that of Normandy.

This book will take 1016, and the dramatic build-up to the overthrow of an independent Anglo-Saxon kingdom, as the climax of the Anglo-Saxon period. Yet as with all historical divisions used to define groups of people – be they terms like 'Anglo-Saxon' or 'Celtic' – or periods, such as 'late antiquity' or 'early medieval', there is no black and white. There are rarely historical moments when entire populations acknowledge that they have left behind one era or identity and emerged into another. Change can be sudden, as with the events of 1016 or 1066, but their effects can take generations to be realised.

Grace, Notoriety and the Saints

The quote on page vii, by the seventeenth-century mathematician and philosopher Blaise Pascal, provides a clear equation for defining sanctity: 'All it takes to make a saint is grace'. Grace = Saint. However, trying to understand this definition today is difficult. So many intellectual, religious and social changes have taken place over the past few centuries that it is now hard to give any clear-cut meaning to the words grace, saint or, indeed, man. What makes a saint, like what makes a man, presents an endless web of alternatives and possibilities.

The word 'saint' conjures up a variety of associations in our modern minds. Some might connect it with suffering, self-deprivation, charity, service to the weak and devotion to Christian values. Others might envisage miracles, martyrdom and heavenly attributes like stigmata, while others still might feel it is a word wrapped up in superstition, religious fanaticism and the power of the papacy. It is an emotive word, and one that has developed a different set of meanings in recent centuries. A saint is defined, according to the *Oxford English Dictionary*, as 'a person acknowledged as holy or virtuous and regarded in Christian faith as being in heaven after death'. Our modern notions of the word 'saint' are very different to those of the medieval period.

In the early years of the Church all Christians were referred to as 'saints'. For example, Paul begins his letter to the Ephesians:

Paul, an apostle of Jesus Christ, by the will of God, to all the saints who are at Ephesus and to the faithful in Christ Jesus.

Paul's Letter to the Ephesians, 1:1

There seems to have been little distinction between types of saints in the first centuries of Christianity. But during the years of persecution (through the third century and into the fourth), martyrs were held in particular esteem.[13] Christians would flock to their sites of burial to celebrate feast days, and commune with the remains of those who had died for their faith. As the cult of saints grew, the burial places and body parts of early martyrs became prized. But in AD 313 the Emperor Constantine the Great ended the persecution of Christians and promoted the faith across the Empire, so sanctity took on a different complexion. It was no longer easy to die a martyr's death, although some of the saints covered in this book managed it at the hands of Germanic or Viking pagans. Instead, saints were made.

Individuals could earn their status as 'saint' through performing miracles or selfless acts, and living an exemplary Christian life. But the rules were lax. The early Church recognised all manner of people, from hermits to popes, monks to soldiers and virgins to rulers as saints. When it comes to understanding the saints of the Anglo-Saxon period, these distinctions become all the more relevant, as at this stage in the history of the Church what constituted a saint could reach across a broad spectrum of characteristics. All that was needed to declare someone a saint was a consensus of the people, so anyone in the public eye could earn this title.

Far from being one-dimensional, pious figures – part of a faceless mass of the blessed – Anglo-Saxon saints were complex, socially significant individuals. Among those declared saints during the early medieval period, we encounter the full range of human achievements and failings. Every one is driven by those basic characteristics that bind humanity together across centuries: the desire for love, fame, adulation, power, wealth, legacy. Many Anglo-Saxon saints are especially pious, and do or say things that set them apart, making them worthy of particular attention both during their lifetime and beyond. But most are wrapped up in the politics and power of their time: players on a bloody and often morally questionable stage.

The lines between secular and sacred, the worldly and the otherworldly, are incredibly hard to define in the early medieval period. A king could be a saint, and a bishop could rule like a king. The idea that someone could be declared a saint simply due to popularity is something that is hard to grasp from our twenty-first century perspective. To us, the word saint presumes that the individual commemorated was particularly pious and holy. But sanctity in the early medieval period was equivalent to notoriety. And the treatment of their cult after death is also hard to fathom from our modern perspective. Why did cult centres arise and why did medieval people believe that the relics of saints had powers?

It might help to cite a modern equivalent. In 1997 Princess Diana died in a tragic car accident. She was a member of the royal family, mother to heirs to the throne, and of noble birth herself. She had lived her life in the glare of public attention, with both good and bad things written about her. She did many acts of kindness and magnanimity, but she also lived a very real life, complete with temptations and extravagances. She moved in circles alongside other important people, some of whom also performed good deeds, such as Mother Teresa and Nelson Mandela. Her unexpected death created a fascinating response around the world, as there was a mass outpouring of grief on an unprecedented scale. People travelled to her home to lay flowers, and there they wept for a woman they might not have known personally, but with whom they felt a connection. And after her death there followed a long and complicated process of blame, forgiveness and, eventually, an attempt to commemorate her. The Diana Memorial was envisaged as a point of convergence for modern-day pilgrims.

Go back ten centuries and Diana would most probably have been declared a saint. A cult certainly would have grown up around her. She would have been buried at the heart of a new ecclesiastical complex, her relics on display to offer the visitor the hope of divine intervention and miracles. That she hasn't been declared a saint can be explained by two factors: the rigour with which canonisations are treated in modern times has led to far fewer saints; and our notions of what constitutes a saint have changed as we have moved towards a more secular world, where the Christian Church in many countries has less control over worldly matters. Yet her example should highlight some of the problems that have arisen in terms of defining the word 'saint' within the medieval period. It encompasses notions of piety, virtuous living and generosity, but it is also wrapped up in celebrity, public profile and social status.

This book will look at men and women who were celebrated as saints during a time when the process of canonisation was not formalised. Now it is a laborious and complex process, with an entire branch of the Vatican – the Congregation for the Causes of the Saints – dedicated to working through reams of evidence and numerous claims. To be declared a saint, an individual has to have been dead for at least five years,[14] and be proved beyond scientific doubt to have performed miracles. This was not the case in the medieval period. Hundreds of people could be declared saints every decade, and they made up 'the blessed dead in heaven' (*OED*), of which there are many thousands.

In many ways, the saints discussed in this book, particularly those who were intimately bound up with the ruling powers of the time, share characteristics and narratives with other figures from their lifetime. But the fact that they had a role within the Church meant that their stories were recorded with the stylistic formulae and narrative flourishes that had originated with the first martyrs and, further back still, the Bible. One text which seems to have influenced Anglo-Saxon writers significantly was the *Life of St Martin* (the Bishop of Tours known as 'the hammer of the heretics', who died around AD 397), written by Sulpicius Severus. Another was the *Life of St Anthony,* the desert hermit who died in AD 373.[15] Echoes of these exemplary saintly texts resonate through the written lives of Anglo-Saxon saints, and it often appears that writers were using narratives and symbols that were recognisable of the genre, rather than rooted in reality. The saints could become characters in a broader fictional genre, and loosen ties with actual living individuals.

Why do Saints Matter?

In some cases the information written about a particular saint is fragmentary, a mere reference. But this has prevented their names from being lost among the millions of anonymous men and women who lived alongside them. This fact, combined with the faith of the Christian communities that kept their memory alive for centuries, ensures that they serve as identifiable individuals, intimately connected with the periods in which they lived. That they were considered 'sacred', and their bodies thought to be able to exert power by performing miracles and ensuring pilgrimage for long after their death, also made the preservation of their memory expedient. As Robert Bartlett says: 'of all the religions, Christianity is the one most concerned with dead bodies'.[16] This fascination with not just the saintly lives of the individuals covered by this book, but also with their physical remains, meant that, unlike the majority of secular figures, their legacy continued after their death in a very real sense.

The communities in which they had lived, and the people that would benefit from developing a focal point for worship after their death, could engineer cults. Official saints' lives were written, relics were made from the individual's body parts or possessions, and the sites connected with them were enlarged to accommodate the streams of pilgrims they hoped to entice with promises of miracles. Sanctity was big business, and relics would change hands for the sort of money today associated with a Picasso painting. Medieval pilgrims were the equivalent of modern-day tourists, bringing wealth and investment to the communities that housed the relics of saints.

Saints and their relics were important because they enhanced the prestige of local churches, monasteries and towns or provinces. And their significance was not lost on the political decision makers of early medieval England. Bodies could be moved and stories modified to ensure that a particular site (perhaps a struggling monastery or a church that had suffered a scandal) could be tied to a particular saint. There is a trend during the tenth century towards royal patrons nurturing those saints' cults that enhanced the special status of the royal line.[17] This was an exercise in PR and advertising, and the trappings of a saint's cult were meticulously designed to create new centres of power.

But saints were not just politically and economically important. They were the linchpin of belief for many Christians. Saints were understood to have gained a special communion with God, which entitled them to sit by Him at the Day of Judgement, and to intercede on behalf of other people with Him. Early medieval

Christians were fixated on the coming of the end of days, and missionaries and evangelists were racing against time to draw people to the 'true faith' to save their souls from eternal damnation. Saints played their part, both as missionaries themselves and as a conduit for Christians to help them reach salvation. They were spiritually elevated, and praying to a particular saint could ensure that a message would be received more effectively by God. Maximus of Turin wrote:

> The martyrs will keep guard over us, who live with our
> bodies, and they will take us into their care ... Here they
> prevent us from falling into sinful ways, there they will
> protect us from the horrors of hell.[18]

The divide between living and dead was less fixed then, and the saints acted as portals between the two. There are clearly links between the veneration of saints and the setting up of household deities in earlier societies. This fact was not lost on later Protestant reformers, who saw the cult of saints as a superstitious barrier to individual communion with the divine. They would cite biblical quotations like 'There is one God and one mediator between God and man, the man Christ Jesus' (1 Timothy 2:5) to undermine the roles of saints as mediators.[19] Yet the saints were passionately believed in by early Christians, not least because of their capacity to perform miracles, both during their lives and after death.

The supernatural nature of miracles is proclaimed throughout the Gospels, as Christ performs feats of magic by raising Lazarus from the dead and healing the blind, sick and infirm. Indeed, in very early wall paintings of Christ performing miracles he is shown with a wand, a symbol of his magical role as healer. That saints could perform miracles in imitation of Christ is one of the central themes in hagiographical texts. These miracles could take on many complexions; so Cuthbert gains the respect of ravens, while a clod of earth where Oswald's body was washed prevents a building from being completely consumed by fire. It was this belief in the efficiency of relics to continue performing miracles that enhanced the cult of saints.

There was a transcendental element to saintly relics, which was connected with the position of the saint in heaven. Individuals could possess their own relics, or seek to be buried near to the site of a saint, in the hope that, when God called all the faithful together at the Day of Judgement, their proximity to a part of a saint would bring them closer to Him. It is possible to see relics as a form of fast-track ticket to a privileged place in heaven. A saint's body would be brought back together in perfection after death, and if a wealthy Anglo-Saxon could die possessing a part of that saint, then they would be drawn towards him or her at the end of days.

Saints did matter profoundly in a spiritual sense to those who believed in them during the early medieval period, and they continue to matter to those who believe in them today. Christians across the world still report miraculous cures at the hands of holy people, as well as weeping statues and bleeding pictures. Saints, sanctity, relics and an unerring belief in the tenets of the Christian faith remain entrenched throughout the world. Saints lived in the real world, as this study will prove, but their role in the afterworld was equally, if not more, important to the Anglo-Saxons who believed in them, treasured them and venerated them.

Anglo-Saxon Saints: Fact and Fiction

This study will look at individual saints chronologically, and attempt to untangle historical fact from the web of myths and legends that have grown up around their names. There is a sense of a developing narrative among the saints. They move from the early martyrs, like St Alban, to the missionary fervour of St Augustine, and are replaced by theological scholarship in the time of Bede, before moving on to the intimate relationship secured between Church and State displayed between King Edgar and Athelwold. A similar development could be charted by focusing on the reigns of kings or royal houses. But I want to give insights into the world of Anglo-Saxon England by looking at a group of people who are arguably well known, but have secured their legacy through texts that often don't present reality.

The earliest saint covered by this book, Alban, was not an Anglo-Saxon, but his legacy was given muscle most significantly by later Anglo-Saxon rulers and churchmen. He was a martyr, prepared to die for his faith, and his story is recounted with an almost macabre celebration of suffering. Brigid, Patrick and Ninian similarly predate the Anglo-Saxon period, but their roles in developing the Celtic form of Christianity, which was to exert such an influence on the early Church in England, is of paramount importance. What's more, aspects of their cults, such as Brigid's association with a pagan goddess and Patrick's political game-playing, make them fascinating characters who encapsulate a great deal about the way conversion developed within the British Isles.

The importance of Gregory the Great and Columba centres on the early Roman and Irish missions to the pagan English. Columba, an exile and member of the powerful Uí Néill clan, set up the influential monastery of Iona, while the Roman mission made inroads to the south, particularly in Kent. While superficially very distinct characters, with Columba exemplifying the Irish tradition and Pope Gregory a sophisticated Roman with the most powerful job in Christendom, a strength of will and desire to evangelise ran through the veins of both men. With Cuthbert, the peace-weaver, the two approaches appear deliberately harmonised, and cult objects like the Lindisfarne Gospels exemplify attempts by the Anglo-Saxon Church to bring the two disparate approaches of the Irish and Roman parties closer together.

From the seventh century onwards, Anglo-Saxon saints would grow in power, influence and intellect. Hilda and Aethelthryth were female saints in a male-dominated world. Originally members of royal households, they gained autonomy by becoming abbesses of their own monastic communities. Their influence was so great that Hilda's site at Whitby was chosen as the location for the decisive Synod of Whitby. Here, the inimitable Saint Wilfrid had a platform to empower both himself and the papacy, securing the backing of the Northumbrian royal family and ensuring primacy of Roman practices over Irish ones.

With characters like Bede and Alcuin, the story shifts from one of conversion to one of consolidation. Bede was declared a Doctor of the Church, and remains the only British person to receive this title. His monastery of Wearmouth–Jarrow was at the heart of a publishing campaign that resulted in the oldest surviving single copy of the Bible, and a collection of bestselling works penned by Bede himself. Similarly, the Northumbrian monk Alcuin became one of the most sought-after minds of his time. He was headhunted by the Emperor Charlemagne to become a foremost force behind the Carolingian Renaissance.

Viking raids on monasteries from the eighth century onwards affected both Anglo-Saxon Church and State. Alfred the Great's efforts halted the complete conquest of England by Danes and propped up the failing Church. With royal backing the Anglo-Saxon Church would again become a force to be reckoned with. King Edgar realised the value of creating a close relationship with monks and clergy, and gave his support to the campaigns of Athelwold, Dunstan and Oswald. Leaders of the Benedictine Reform, which saw the variety of early monasteries honed into a more manageable and compliant form, they developed an intellectual and artistic campaign, led by an army of monks, which was to be the final flowerings of Anglo-Saxon saints. With Edward the Confessor, the narrative finally shifts away from Britain, towards the Continent, until ultimately Anglo-Saxon sanctity came to an abrupt end.

The lives of saints act as a lens through which broader social, historical, religious and artistic changes can be focused. They were the movers and shakers, the decision makers of their time. This is not intended as an exhaustive list of every Anglo-Saxon saint recorded, but rather a web of those individuals whose lives, locations and stories weave together to bring the time into focus. A favourite saint may well have been overlooked, but with the hundreds of men and women recognised as saints between the fourth and eleventh centuries, it's important to concentrate carefully on a few, rather than provide a cursory glimpse of many.

That said, in relation to their private lives there are some things that would have been common to all of them. In terms of the food they ate, the sort of clothes they wore and the buildings they lived in, there would be minor variations, yet there were many things they shared in common. The Anglo-Saxons ate a good deal of meat (pigs, goats, deer, sheep and cows), poultry (ducks, chicken and geese), fish (herring, eel, pike, salmon and roach) and shellfish (oysters, cockles and mussels), but fruit and vegetables formed the staple diet of most.[20] They did not have potatoes, tomatoes, bananas, lemons or other imported variants. Even native vegetables, like carrots, would have looked different – less orange, and rather small and purpled. They also ate wild garlic, onion, leeks and legumes. In terms of crops, wheat was cultivated for bread, barley was used for brewing beer and oats fed livestock.

The majority of Anglo-Saxons' hot dishes would have been stews or broths made in a cauldron over an open fire. Bread could be baked in a clay oven or over a griddle, with flour ground either by water mills or hand querns. They could have flavoured dishes with home-grown herbs like dill and thyme, or used some imported spices, like ginger, cinnamon and pepper. Drinks like cider and mead could be sweetened with honey, but beer was drunk most regularly. Some wine may have been consumed, but the skills to make it in the British Isles died out with the Romans.

Everything was used to good effect, so a sheep could provide wool while alive, and meat and skins when killed. Likewise, a cow would be used for milk, leather and beef, while bones and horns could be used for drinking vessels or for carved objects like buckles and pins. Even the blood would be collected and used to make a form of black pudding. The wealthier the person, the more meat they would eat, and some high-class banquets would run to many courses, featuring elaborately spiced and flavoured dishes. But the majority of the saints featured in this book would have lived on a more modest diet, dictated by the seasons and the landscape.

Anglo-Saxon buildings were predominantly timber, with wattle and daub walls and thatched roofs. They tended to be designed on a 2:1 ratio, so were rectangular. At the heart of these halls was the hearth, which provided heat, food and light. Smaller *grubenhaus* would often be found in settlements, with sunken floors and pitched timber and thatched sides. These seem to have been the site of industrial activities like weaving, pottery making and metalworking. Our saints would have slept on a wooden-framed bed if they were fortunate, with a mattress stuffed with wool, and blankets for warmth. Their clothing would have been woollen too, although some of the wealthier saints would have had silk trimmings, gold thread and jewels stitched into their garments.

The social structure was hierarchical; at the top were kings and their relatives; ealdormen or nobility below, who governed sections of land, imparted justice and organised taxes; thegns, who propped up the military aspects of Anglo-Saxon society; then the ceorls, freedmen, farmers and craftsmen who worked the land and managed the production of everything from leather shoes to high status jewellery. Life in an Anglo-Saxon settlement would have depended on the passage of time. As the sun moved over the homes it would determine where light would fall, and after dark the only illumination would be the central hearth and possibly candles. Existence depended on the elements, as a harsh wind or a passing frost could destroy a year's worth of crops or wipe out timber houses. The relationship between man and the natural environment was far closer than that of our modern way of life, and this is reflected in the lives of many of the saints. Not only did they straddle the earthly and the divine, but here on earth they had to exist in fine balance between a world created by man and one created by God.

Speaking Across Time: Why the Saints are Relevant Today

Saints and relics are shrouded in a world view that seems almost lost, and so it is tempting to perceive the miracles, piety and especial sanctity attributed to them as echoes of a latent ignorance endemic among the medieval populace. To do so is to misunderstand both ourselves and our predecessors. It presupposes an intellectual sophistication in the present day that far outreaches even the most intelligent of our ancestors. True, there have been developments, and knowledge is progressed by standing on the shoulders of giants that have gone before. But this attitude undermines the levels of intellectual rigour and virtuosity that could be reached within different historical periods. Every age produces great minds, and to dismiss those of the medieval period as simply superstitious and ignorant is to display an astonishing arrogance in our own time. We have not reached the zenith of knowledge, and more will come after us.

Our ideas of sanctity have changed over a millennium. As the cults of heroes, the divine right of kings and the role of geniuses have been eroded by modern developments in philosophy and politics, so the majority of people in Britain today have developed scepticism and disregard for both religious and social hierarchy. Salient historical moments like the French Revolution and the English Civil War, which led to devolved rights for the monarchy, have eroded attitudes of deference across the social spectrum. In terms of religion, the increasing atheism of the last century has led to the Christian faith being treated with disregard at best, and with loathing at worst. This is all part of an inevitable flux towards modernity, but these changes have a retrogressive effect in terms of our present-day attitudes towards the past.

Yet it is a central premise when studying the past to remember that humanity never changes beyond recognition, and regardless of the seeming differences between people past and present, basic human interests remain largely the same.

The past is not so different from our present. There are many things that bind us together across the ages. There were differences, but they would be no more startling than travelling to an unknown part of the world today. The fundamental human concerns remain the same. The desire for love, power, wealth, prestige, fame, security, children, a home ... these preoccupy the majority of people today. So do the more mundane issues like making clothes, preparing meals, educating children and looking after the sick or infirm.

The Anglo-Saxon saints are separated from us in time and ideology. Yet we would recognise their emotions, understand their concerns and relate to their challenges. So this book is primarily an attempt to remove the veil of mystique and fantasy that the historical past can hold, and make the saints people with whom we can identify today. Finding out what motivated them in life and what characteristics they displayed will inevitably be founded on conjecture, as it is impossible to know for sure what a person alive over a millennium ago was really like. The journey into their lifetime, however, can be illuminating and exciting. At times certain characters really do emerge from the ageing pages of vellum and speak to us across the centuries.

Chapter One
Alban: Dying for Faith

> 'The head of the most courageous martyr
> [St Alban] was struck off, and here he received
> the crown of life, which God has promised to
> those who love Him. But he who gave the wicked
> stroke, was not permitted to rejoice over the
> deceased; for his eyes dropped upon the ground
> together with the blessed martyr's head.'

Bede, *Ecclesiastical History of the English People.*[1]

Alban was a rebel, a non-conformist and a religious activist. He died for his faith; a faith whose founder also died for his beliefs by being crucified. Although not an Anglo-Saxon (he was Romano-British), he was England's first saint and martyr. Blood and bones lie at the heart of Alban's story, so the natural starting point for understanding this earliest of English saints is to visit the site of his tomb and remains. However, as with the majority of saints, Alban's body was destroyed during the Reformation. Now a reliquary containing a single shoulder blade is all that sits in the heart of the magnificent cathedral in the centre of the ancient city that still bears his name.

St Albans wears its history on its sleeve. Following brown heritage signs towards 'Roman Verulamium', the traveller winds past medieval gateways, the bishop's palace and historic watermills. Different-coloured stones and styles of architecture jostle next to one another, vying for supremacy and providing a visual narrative for the city's evolution over two millennia. The mismatched grey stones of the ruinous Roman wall clashes with the cracked wooden beams of Britain's oldest pub, Ye Olde Fighting Cocks, and the elegant cream Palladian façade of the Old Town Hall. This is a place of contrasts, and a place where the passage of time plays out before your eyes.

The undulating roads are disorientating, and the towers of the cathedral at the heart of the city dip in and out of view as visitors follow in the footsteps of Alban himself and thousands of later pilgrims, moving from the remains of the Roman town Verulamium in the south-west towards the later-sprawling ecclesiastical centre. There is a sense of dramatic climax for the modern-day tourist on approaching the grand west front of the cathedral, getting ever closer to the bones of the martyr. The Norman building, with its mismatched brickwork, square, crenellated central tower and rebuilt Gothic West End, emerges out of oak trees; it seems implanted on the landscape, and embraced by the city. Within the very heart of the cathedral St Alban's now empty tomb nestles behind the high altar, presented in Romanesque luxury within its own quiet sanctuary.

Being under twenty miles from London, St Albans is a desirable place to live. Indeed, its location has secured its continual importance. The Celtic Catuvellauni tribe had their major settlement just a mile to the west of the present-day city, and Roman Verulamium was second only to London and Cirencester in terms of size and importance. The Magna Carta was drafted here, and St Albans School is the only one in the English-speaking world to have educated a pope. Yet, while the name of the city is well known, the character behind the name, St Alban himself, remains frustratingly inaccessible.

What we do know is that the Alban who became England's earliest saint is remembered as a convert from Romano-British paganism to Christianity during a time of great change and unrest. He lived during the third to fourth centuries, when the Romans in Britain had absorbed Celtic culture beneath their mantle and seemed all-powerful. Yet this was a time when, spiritually, people were searching for alternatives to the stagnant imperial cult.[2] Across the Empire new religious groups emerged with mysterious rituals, like those focused on eastern deities such as Mithras, or the Egyptian goddess Isis. Among these mystery cults, a seemingly innocuous group emerged who celebrated the coming of the Messiah predicted by the Jewish faith, and focused on a poor man from Galilee named Jesus. Although their impact was minimal in the first century after their founder's death, Christians soon began to permeate society, particularly because they had to be literate in order to read their sacred texts, and their literacy made them valuable civil servants.

Yet their beliefs made them different. Because they were monotheistic and held to the commandment that they should worship no other gods, they were seen as dissenters. Across the

Roman Empire, Christians were persecuted and died for their faith.

Certain emperors were more vehement than others in pursuing and punishing Christians, the most infamous of which is Diocletian, who in AD 303 issued the 'Edict against the Christians'. This demanded that books and buildings were destroyed, and Christians were not allowed to gather together. There were attacks against the Emperor in response to the edict, and widespread executions followed. Diocletian's own butler, Peter Cubicularius, met a particularly grisly end, as he was stripped, strung up and had the flesh torn away from his bones. Then salt and vinegar were rubbed into his open wounds, before he was finally boiled alive.

Diocletian had good political reasons for punishing Christians: they were non-conformists. Other religious groups, particularly those with polytheistic elements like the cults of Isis or Mithras, were shown a greater degree of tolerance. The essential premise of worshipping the Emperor was upheld throughout the Empire, and as long as people were willing to recognise him and sacrifice to his image, their individual faiths were less worrisome. But at the very heart of Christianity and Judaism, in the Ten Commandments lies the refusal to sacrifice to false gods.

It is this rejection of divinities other than the one Christian God that led to the early martyrdoms, since this refusal to conform to the state and its official religion was subversive. Martyrs, however, chose to embrace a heroic death in the eyes of their followers, and the cults that grew up around them were similarly a form of dissension against the Empire. These hero-saints laid the foundations for future attitudes that bound sanctity to suffering, self-deprivation to divinity and fortitude to fortune. Alban was one such martyr-saint. By opposing the Roman authorities he was refusing to subscribe to the status quo. He died because he chose Christianity, but the stance he was taking was more than religious. He was standing up to an oppressive dictatorship, which had transformed Britain and subjected its native people. He was a political activist prepared to die for what he believed in.

Who was Alban?

Saint Alban was a Roman-Briton who was killed by Roman authorities for refusing to sacrifice to the Roman gods. According to the earliest sources, he lived and died in Verulamium, close to the cathedral in the town that still bears his name. His cult was not forgotten, despite the fact that the site of his martyrdom moved from Roman hands to those of pagan Anglo-Saxon for some two centuries. The memory of the place where he died and the major events leading to his death was transmitted down the centuries like an elaborate Chinese whisper. His is a story of conversion, fanatical dedication, persecution and martyrdom. His is the story of the earliest Christians in Britain, and an echo of the cults that emerged across Europe in the first flowerings of this new religion. To date he has been consistently put forward as a replacement for St George as patron saint of England.

The story of Alban states that he took in and gave shelter to a fugitive priest who was hiding from the authorities.[3] The priest stayed with him, and in this time Alban became enchanted by the new religion he preached. When he was finally discovered, Alban managed to deceive the authorities by switching his clothes with the priest's, and went with the soldiers in his place. This deception, and his declaration that he would not sacrifice to the old gods, but instead embrace the new Christian God, led to his martyrdom. This is the little of his life that has been repeated down the centuries.

According to this account, Alban must have been brave to give sanctuary to a Christian during a time of persecution, and open-minded – or possibly easily led – to be influenced by what was an outlawed religion. He was outspoken too – unafraid to stand up to the inquisition of the authority figures in his Roman town – and so bloody-minded that he refused to take the easier route of public sacrifice, instead choosing a painful death over life. He was a religious fanatic, dying for his faith as religious martyrs continue to do today. Alban could even be seen to represent the notion of jihād, 'striving or resisting in the name of God'.[4] It can be hard to fathom why people embrace martyrdom, but for Alban death was a release that allowed the promise of greater reward in the afterlife.

Saint Alban takes us back beyond the boundaries of the Anglo-Saxon period (traditionally beginning in the fifth century), to the earlier Roman, and even Celtic, roots of the country. While not an Anglo-Saxon saint, much of Alban's life and legacy were recorded and crafted by later Christian Anglo-Saxons, and what we know of Britain's protomartyr can help illuminate the cultural and religious climate that the early Anglo-Saxon settlers encountered when they settled in England. During his lifetime Christians were persecuted, but there was also a climate of religious change, evolution and syncretism.

Around the end of the third and beginning of the fourth centuries, the religious complexion of the Roman Empire was changing. This was seen clearly in art, where the imagery of different cults was drawn together in an attempt to find common ground, with the prevailing interest in salvation and life after death. This could explain why St Alban was persuaded by the Christian priest he gave refuge to that the saving message of Christianity was pertinent and worth dying for. He may have listened to the prayers of the renegade priest and found the ideas attractive. Alban can be seen as a rebel, defying the establishment, and a convert, entranced by a basic understanding of a faith he had only recently accepted. When we compare this with the lure of religious cults or the campaigns of ISIS today, the similarities are compelling.

On the Trail of Alban

The earliest saints were made of stern stuff, and so were the readers of their hagiographies. Some saints' lives make for unsettling reading, with detailed descriptions of the torture and suffering they endured. The Gothic tastes of later centuries, and the fascination with blood and horror that continues today, was just as strong in the Anglo-Saxon period, and saints' lives were the main conduit for these visceral narratives. The details surrounding St Alban's martyrdom are shrouded in mystery, but at the heart of his story lies a bloody and dramatic death, complete with his beheading and the executioner's eyes popping out as soon as he delivered the deadly blow. Despite these seemingly detailed observations, the majority of what we know about Alban the man is dressed up in hagiographical finery crafted many centuries after his death.

It is still uncertain which phase of Roman persecution he died under. While the notorious acts of Diocletian in AD 303 have been a popular theory, more recent research suggests that he may have died in an earlier wave, coordinated either by Decius, emperor from AD 249 to 51, or Valerian, AD 253 to 60.[5] It is a frustrating fact that, when studying early medieval texts and individuals, dating can prove almost impossible. Alban may have lived within a hundred-year time span – between the third and fourth centuries – which is as vague as saying Winston Churchill may have lived between the 1880s and the 1980s. So much can change in the course of a century, and while these incredibly broad chronological scales have to be accepted by scholars, it makes any accurate context for the saint's life difficult to establish.

The first surviving textual reference to Alban is in a text written around AD 396 by a bishop of Rouen called Victricius.[6] He had travelled to Britain to settle a dispute that had arisen between the bishops – an indication that Christianity was established enough by the end of the fourth century for bishops to be settled across the land. Victricius doesn't mention Alban by name, but does record that there was a native saint who 'told rivers to draw back', and this detail connects him with later versions of the story. However, the first named reference to him comes from a fifth-century text written about another saint, *The Life of St Germanus*. There are only passing references to Alban, since the majority of the text focuses on the work of the Gaulish bishop Germanus in refuting the Pelagian heresy that had been spreading through Britain around AD 429.

The author of this heresy, Pelagius, was most probably British, and he called for greater austerity in the Church, a stronger sense of free will, and argued against predestination as set out by St Augustine.[7] He was very popular in Britain, but his claims made him heretical in the eyes of the papacy. Throughout the wider

Christian world, Britain was starting to be connected with practices that were deemed unacceptable, and the Orthodox Church intervened directly. Germanus was sent to St Albans to combat the followers of Pelagius, and he conducted a successful diplomatic mission by preaching to the Britons and turning them away from Pelagius. There may even be the remains of a large open space in the fifth-century town where Germanus met with the Britons – archaeological evidence for a papal mission to direct the early British Christians away from the stain of heresy.

The Gaulish bishop found an opportunity to focus the British away from the heretical Pelagius and connect them instead with a far more acceptable rallying figure – the martyred saint, Alban. In a symbolic act, he opened Alban's shrine and placed alongside the martyr the relics of the apostles. This piece of propaganda would have presented a powerful message for British Christians to follow the orthodox route.[8] And what more orthodox a saint was there to follow than one who had died a traditional martyr's death at the hands of Roman pagans like Christ himself? While the account from Saint Germanus's *Life* does not reveal much about Alban, the important fact is that, by the fifth century, the saint was firmly linked with Verulamium, his cult was still active and he was seen as a fitting rallying point for the Church in England.

The British cleric Gildas also mentions Alban. He is a complex writer, and his sixth-century text *On the Ruin and Conquest of Britain* gives tantalising clues as to the state of the British Isles during a period of great social and cultural change. It is written as a sermon, and is full of dramatic language and hyperbole designed to give a 'fire and brimstone' account of the decline of Roman Britain, seen as the inevitable punishment for a weak and sinful people. While there are historical facts within the text, Gildas is primarily moralising, so his text has to be sieved through carefully, particularly when he is describing the life and death of a man who lived centuries earlier.

In terms of his account of St Alban, it is revealing in the first instance that he chose to include his martyrdom at all, since again it shows that the saint's story was preserved down the centuries; Alban clearly mattered to the British. However, Gildas makes some interesting assumptions about the events of Alban's death. For example, he describes how the saint separated the River Thames in a manner similar to that in which Moses opened up the Red Sea. Given that the river that runs through St Albans is a higher branch of the Thames known as the Ver, rather than the Thames proper, this casts some doubt on the accuracy of Gildas's account. The importance of this act of draining the Ver, however, would not have been lost on the Romano-British living in the town at the time of Alban. The river was believed to be sacred, and many finds have been discovered there, which suggests that Britons made offerings to it and valued it highly. Gildas's account of the saint manipulating the sacred river would have been a powerful sign of his sanctity in early medieval Britain.

The primary author on the majority of early Anglo-Saxon saints' lives is the Venerable Bede. This one writer is the all-pervading voice underlying all work on early medieval Britain, and this study is no exception. Without Bede's *Ecclesiastical History of the English People* we would be able to reconstruct only a fraction of the dates, names and events of significance from the so-called Dark Ages. We would be greatly impoverished without his accounts of Anglo-Saxon saints, too. Yet it does rather leave us at his mercy. What Bede includes, or doesn't include, in his texts has become canonical, and we depend on him for the foundations of many of our saints' lives, not least that of the first British martyr and recorded saint.

The fact that Bede wrote about Alban in the eighth century, while the saint himself was most probably martyred in the third or fourth, suggests his legend had been continually transmitted. He records that, having protected a rebel priest and been entranced by his promises and practices, Alban put himself forward for martyrdom in his place. The text describes the ultimate heroic act of a martyr. They must 'put on the armour of spiritual warfare'. Alban is following the example of St Paul, whose revelations on the road to Damascus had become the defining example of conversion from the Roman way to the Christian.

Interestingly, Alban is asked by the Roman official 'of what family or race are you?' This brings into sharp relief the redundancy of national boundaries and geographical concepts of countries that we hold to in our modern world. In the late antique and early medieval world there were no maps, and loyalties or allegiances were determined by whom you were related to, or whom you owned fealty to through social ties. National identities were not a priority, but kinship and bonds (religious, political, economic or social) were.

Bede's *A History of the English Church and People* helped develop a radical new conception of identity, which was partly intended as a national manifesto, to give a sense of Christian English identity in the eighth century. Alban's response to the Roman official's question in this context is entirely fitting. 'What does it concern you,' he said, 'of what stock I am? If you desire to hear the truth of my religion, be it known to you that I am now a Christian, and bound by Christian duties.' Whatever Alban's real response to the judge, which is no doubt lost to the sands of time, Bede's treatment of England's primary martyr reflects his significance as the major saint of the nation, and as a rallying point for a sense of Christian camaraderie rather than tribal individuality.

Alban: Resident of Verulamium

Bede records that Alban was an inhabitant of the Roman town of Verulamium, a strategically important place given its location along Watling Street and its links with the powerful British Catuvellauni tribe. There is strong archaeological proof for the location of the Romano-British town, which includes complex villa mosaics, and there is evidence of surviving Celtic practices alongside Roman innovations.[9] The earlier Celtic settlement was significant, as indicated by the destruction of Verulamium by Boudicca in the revolts of AD 61. Her tribe, the Iceni, led an angry retaliation against the Catuvellauni because of their willing subservience to their Roman overlords, and by razing the city to the ground she was able to break contact between Londinium and the Roman holdings along Watling Street. Verulamium was wealthy and self-sufficient, as indicated by the fact that it was able to quickly rebuild itself after Boudicca's fires

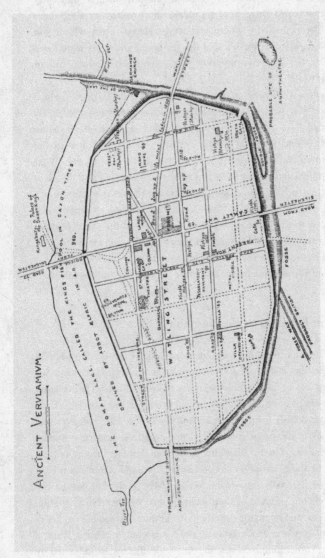

This plan of Roman Verulamium shows how it was arranged on a grid pattern, with the forum at the centre. Watling Street runs right through the centre of the town, and the River Ver bends around the northern half. Alban was martyred towards the north-east of the town, outside the walls, which is where the present-day cathedral stands.

and another later attack in AD 160. This Roman town held great significance; it was powerful, prosperous and a thriving centre where Roman urban development met with Celtic national identity.

This was where Bede says Alban lived and died. By the fourth century, Verulamium was the third-largest town in Britain after London and Cirencester, with a population of around 10,000. Having been damaged by fire twice, its timber buildings were mostly rebuilt in the third century in stone, and larger private dwellings were constructed. Alban would have walked down the grid-like street system, past stone façades and a combination of Roman and British households. Fragments of lavish wall paintings have been discovered at the site, which depict candelabra, garlands of flowers, pheasants and panthers.[10] A magnificent theatre dominated the town, and at its heart a thriving market centre, perhaps the most important in Roman Britain, flourished. The villas boasted fine mosaics, Italian marble and a piped water supply.

Information about Romano-British Verulamium can shed greater light on the life of St Alban. By combining the archaeological evidence with later textual evidence, some semblance of the life and times of the saint emerge. The town was wealthy, with monumental arches at the entrances to Watling Street and grand public spaces including a forum and a number of temples. The theatre complex at Verulamium was extensive, and could accommodate up to 7,000 spectators. It would have been used for plays and gladiatorial events, including trials against animals. The location of the temple right next to the theatre suggests it was also used for religious ceremonies.

The story of Alban states that he had a house in which he protected the hiding Christian priest, so it is tempting to speculate if his home resembled those discovered in the Roman town. Of those excavated, many were large and grand, with well-wrought mosaic floors and painted walls. There was an elite residential area to the south-east of the town, and one villa in particular (Building 2 in Insula XXVII) had twenty-two rooms and a colonnaded corridor wrapped around a courtyard. The town had a number of temples, which served the pagan Romano-British population. Yet, while there is little evidence for Christianity within Verulamium, and no definitive early church, there is an interesting fixation with issues of salvation and the afterlife evinced in some of the images discovered in the town, which may give a context for Alban's conversion.

The location of where Alban was martyred, and where his cult eventually grew up, relies partly on Bede's account and perhaps latent memories of the site. This is not far-fetched, since the sites of martyrs' deaths and burials had been preserved in the memories of Christians. The great basilical complex at St Peter's has, beneath its foundation stones, the remnants of the earlier cemetery outside the walls of the city of Rome, and evidence suggests that St Peter was killed and buried at that site.

Similarly, Alban was taken outside of the city towards the arena, perhaps for his death to act as a form of entertainment. Bede records: 'Being led to execution, he came to a river, which, with a most rapid course, ran between the wall of the town and the arena where he was to be executed.' Recent excavations have revealed a Roman cemetery beneath the south cloister of the current cathedral, so it seems likely that this is the location, outside of the city walls, where Alban was buried.[11] What's more, when Alban got to the site of his martyrdom, he called for refreshment and a spring miraculously appeared. There is a spring of water – now known as Holywell Hill – alongside the current cathedral.

The cathedral is on the other side of the River Ver to the Roman city, and sits on a slope outside the original Roman walls. Bede's description of the site of Alban's martyrdom bears many similarities with the area around St Albans Cathedral, which still holds the saint's tomb:[12]

> 'the reverend confessor, accompanied by the multitude,
> ascended a hill, about 500 paces from the place, adorned, or,
> rather clothed with all kinds of flowers, having its sides
> neither perpendicular, nor even craggy, but sloping down
> into a most beautiful plain, worthy from its lovely
> appearance to be the scene of a martyr's sufferings.'

Alban's Changing World

The original saints were seen as heroes. The men and women who were burnt on fires, run through with swords and consumed by wild beasts were celebrated for the example they set to other Christians; and on a more basic level, they were enjoyed for the entertainment their exciting stories provided. Their written lives emerged from the centuries of persecution endured by martyrs in the early years of the Christian Church. The rise in saints during the third century coincided with tumultuous times within the Roman Empire. The martyrdom of Alban suggests that the religious unrest on the Continent had spread to Britain, which had otherwise been a loyal and relatively peaceful part of the empire for some 200 years.

The power of Rome was imprinted upon Britain from AD 43, when the armies of Emperor Claudius successfully suppressed the native Celtic Britons and imposed imperial taxes upon the majority of what roughly constitutes modern-day England. There was some opposition, and uprisings like those of Boudicca and the Iceni in AD 61 presented a formidable challenge to the Roman armies. But, on the whole, many aspects of Roman life were absorbed by the native Celtic population, and they adapted to the pressures exerted upon them in terms of taxation and urban development.

The Celts were not a homogenous and unified race, but rather a set of distinct tribes with links across northern Europe and Asia. Before the arrival of the Romans, Britain was composed of many separate Celtic tribes, each of which fiercely defended their borders and had separate identities from one another. However, there were unifying features between the tribes, most obviously in their language, religion and art. They were the people of the Iron Age; they set up megalithic structures, lived predominantly in round houses and created fine jewellery and armour. Their art was that of metalworking, where circular motifs – including the whorl, spiral and triskele – created patterns that contrasted light and dark areas. Understanding the Celts is essential in terms of examining Anglo-Saxon England, since their presence is never fully eradicated. When the Angles, Saxons and Jutes arrived in England they lived alongside native Celts, Romanised by three centuries of occupation, but still distinct in terms of the language they spoke, the clothes they wore and the religious beliefs they held to.

The early Celts practised a religion focused on Druid priests and a pantheon of gods connected to the natural landscape. While there was regional variety, there was enough homogeneity to speak of 'Celtic polytheism' as a formalised religion.[13] There are certain gods and goddesses whose names appear on a pan-European level, suggesting that they were major deities within the Celtic religion. These include Lugus, who has an Irish equivalent Lugh, and in Welsh was known as Lleu. Another central figure is the goddess Brigantia, whose name means 'the one of high', and whose legacy continued down the ages in the figure of the saint Brigid.[14] However, it is difficult to know anything for certain of the religious practices of the Celts, since they left no written records. Roman and Greek sources state that the religious leaders were known as Druids, and that they performed human sacrifices. Archaeology provides tantalising glimpses of the spiritual world of the Celtic Britons, recorded in stone sculpture and found among early temples.

There is one place, however, where it is possible to witness the ways in which Celtic beliefs were melded with incoming Roman ones in a form of syncretism that illuminates both world views: the ruined remains at Bath. Here, a Roman town grew up on the site of a previously important Celtic settlement, centred on the natural springs, which were seen as divine. The compound name given to the site by the Romans was Aquae Sulis, and the central goddess worshipped at the temple was the otherwise unattested Sulis Minerva. This compound name suggests that the Roman goddess of the hearth, Minerva, was worshipped here alongside a Celtic equivalent. This form of syncretism is evidenced across the Roman Empire, where incoming troops encountered native deities and attempted to find an equivalent in their own pantheon. So, although we know little about the goddess Sulis, the assumption is that she may have been similar to Minerva in the minds of the incoming Romans.

The name Sulis is recorded in only one other instance, and is otherwise exclusively confined to the inscriptions found at Bath.

This shows that the Celtic pantheon of gods and goddesses could include those that were specific to one place, particularly to a sacred shrine, grove or spring, which is borne out in the artistic styles represented at Roman Bath. There seems to have been a conscious effort to appease the local people in terms of the temple complex. In the classical world, the central temple building (known as the *aedes*) was believed to be the home of the deity, where they would live in statue form during the day and be revived behind closed doors. This explains the grandeur with which temple architecture was treated. Vitruvius's *Ten Books on Architecture,* which travelled the length and breadth of the Empire with the Roman army and administrators, gives clear instructions on how a temple could be reproduced effectively in fora from Britain to Syria. The gods' homes must outstrip all human buildings in beauty and grandeur.

When the forum complex at Bath was built, it needed to house a temple, but because of the syncretic nature of the goddess worshipped there, the building had to serve two functions. Outside in the courtyard animal sacrifice would have taken place on the altars, and offerings made to the goddess. The interior, however, was reserved for the priests and those who were allowed privileged access – namely, Romans. The head of the cult statue of the goddess that would have been housed within has fortunately survived. It shows that the original statue was classical, with naturalistic proportions and an attempt at realism. This is the art of Rome, derived from Greece, which prized harmonious representations of the human body.

In contrast, on the exterior of the temple, in the pediment, is a gorgon's head. Unlike the Medusa type, this is male, appearing more similar to Green Man representations that have echoes from the Celtic past through medieval cathedrals and beyond. This face is more abstracted and visceral, with wide eyes and strands of beard and hair creating intricate patterns. It seems that the architects at work on this temple in Roman Britain may have sought an artistic syncretism to echo the name of the hybrid goddess – the interior boasting a classically inspired statue, with the exterior presenting a different face.

All that remains of the cult statue of Sulis Minerva is a very rare gilt-bronze head. The aquiline nose, delicate hair and proportioned features all indicate that this was a fine piece of classical sculpture. In contrast, the stone gorgon head from the exterior pediment of the temple is more abstracted, with incised sections of hair and wide, deeply drilled eyes.

The incoming Romans accepted many local cults, and brought a variety of their own religious practices with them. Along Hadrian's Wall (where as much as one tenth of the Roman army was stationed at one point), it is possible to see the extent of this diversity. Gods from the pagan pantheon, including the god of war, Mars, were venerated alongside other cults from the East, like Mithras. There is a large Mithraeum at Carrawburgh, which would have housed those military men dedicated to this elusive Eastern god, who shrouded their rituals in mystery. Another religious group was able to find a footing in Roman Britain under this climate of apparent tolerance: Christians. Indeed, a lead tablet from Aquae Sulis, written in reverse lettering, reflects the religious hybridity of third-century England:

> *Whether pagan or Christian, whether man or woman,*
> *whether boy or girl, whether slave or free, whoever has*
> *stolen from me, Annianus [son of] Matutina [?], six silver*
> *coins from my purse, you, Lady Goddess, are to exact*
> *[them] from him.*[15]

It is clear that Christianity had arrived in Britain via Roman settlers by the third century, and it was able to set down roots more openly than in core areas like Rome. The later stories that grew up around the site of Glastonbury, which say that Joseph of Arimathea first brought Christianity to Britain and set up a religious site there, are probably the stuff of legend. But Christianity was definitely prevalent among the Romano-British population by the fourth century. However, although Christianity may have been one of the new cults practised alongside others, it was still a problematic religion at that time and could not sit comfortably alongside pantheonic faiths like those of the native Britons. While parts of the country were booming, with lavish villas erected and investment in infrastructure and architecture, there was an undercurrent of violence and persecution directed towards Christians. It's onto this stage that St Alban steps.

What the evidence from Aquae Sulis emphasises is that, from the arrival of the Romans in the first century, mainland Britain was a complex place socially and religiously. While those in power were tied to a pan-European empire focused on Rome, the native people continued to revere their ancient gods while absorbing influences from abroad. This situation would be repeated when the Romans abandoned Britain, and those in power became pagan Anglo-Saxons. They too would absorb and assimilate elements of the native people they conquered. With Christianity, and the saints in particular, we can see the legacy of such earlier syncretism as aspects of the Romano-British past reappear. The ruins of Rome remained implanted on the landscape, and the Anglo-Saxons inherited this complex, diverse and cosmopolitan world.

Saint Alban in Context

The translation of Alban's relics into a custom-built church was overseen by the great Anglo-Saxon King Offa in AD 793, some sixty years after Bede completed his account of the saint's life. The event was full of symbolism and ceremony, as Offa was modelling his actions on those of worthy early Christian counterparts like Helena – the mother of Constantine – who 'discovered' the true cross and tomb of Christ in Jerusalem and had a huge church erected at the location. Offa, like Helena, claimed to have discovered the tomb of this important early martyr, and he was able to elevate his status by lavishing attention on the burial place of Alban. There's an interesting connection between Helena and Britain, since a legend recorded by the twelfth-century historian Geoffrey of Monmouth states that she was the daughter of 'Old King Cole' of Colchester. This may not be entirely farcical, since Constantine's father, Constantius Chlorus, was based in Britain for parts of his career; he died in York in AD 306, and could have met and married Helena there.

The man responsible for encouraging the spread of Christianity across the Roman Empire, Constantine, was declared emperor in York.[16] Although Constantine only converted openly to Christianity at the end of his life, he set in motion changes that would lead it to become the dominant religion of the West. The first was the

Edict of Milan in AD 313, which stopped the persecution of Christians. He then set about a building programme across the Empire, which saw the erection of huge basilical churches above the graves of saints and martyrs. The most famous is St Peter's in Rome, but in the decades after his death other basilical churches went up over the major cemeteries around Rome, including San Sebastiano, San Lorenzo and Sant'Agnese. These churches set the blueprint for public Christian buildings across Europe, and in later centuries would be emulated by Anglo-Saxon Christians like Wilfrid and Athelwold.

The effects of the state sanctions that liberated Christians from a position of persecution were felt in Britain, where there is some of the earliest evidence for open practising of Christianity. At the Roman town of Silchester, a possible candidate for the earliest custom-built church was discovered on the south-east corner of the forum. The building has a nave and transepts, and at the end where an altar may have been is a mosaic featuring an equal-armed cross. Some doubt has now been cast on whether this was a church, but elsewhere around Roman Britain there is more evidence for early church buildings.

The earliest surviving Christian liturgical objects have also been found in Roman Britain. The Water Newton treasure contains votive offerings which could have been nailed to the wall of a church, many bearing Constantine's banner of the Chi-Rho. A bowl with a Christian prayer inscribed on it was also found among the treasure, as well as a silver two-handled cantharus, which may have served as a chalice. The treasure has been dated to the fourth century, soon after Constantine issued his Edict of Milan. This suggests that Britain may already have had a community of Christians throughout the land, including individuals like Alban and the priest he defended, and that they began to express themselves more obviously through buildings and high-status objects very soon after persecution against them was halted.

One of the most intriguing pieces of evidence to survive and provide clues as to how Christians and Roman-Britons interacted with one another is the earliest identifiable depiction of Christ. The floor mosaic from Hinton St Mary, dated to around AD 350,

The Hinton St Mary Mosaic was discovered in Dorset in 1963, and is now displayed in the British Museum. It was part of a large floor mosaic within a villa complex. Christ is indicated by the letters Chi and Rho behind his head, and he is youthful and static.

provides a unique image of a male bust placed centrally in the composition and surrounded by other symbols and scenes.

The simple representation has been identified as Christ because behind his head are the Greek letters Chi and Rho: the first letters of the name Christos in Greek. He is clean-shaven, wears a tunic and has pomegranates either side of his head. These symbols would have recalled the story of Persephone's descent into hell, but they have been reinterpreted here as a sign of the resurrection. The fact that Christ appears on a floor mosaic, where his face could potentially have been walked over, indicates that this is an early and experimental example. In later mosaics, like the fourth-century image from Santa Pudenziana in Rome – where Christ is shown dressed in gold, with a bejewelled cross hovering above his head – he was raised up to appear on walls in an apse, seated in majesty and surrounded by the saints.

In contrast, the Christ depicted in the Hinton St Mary Mosaic is youthful, beardless, unadorned and in the traditional guise of a Roman citizen. There are other indicators in the surrounding images that this is a transitional representation – an attempt to give a new visual language to Christianity. For example, the religious syncretism prevalent throughout the Roman Empire in the fourth century is evinced by the abutting of Christ's portrait with one of Bellerophon riding Pegasus into battle with the Chimera. That this traditional classical scene can appear alongside an image of Christ may appear incongruous, but this blending of religious ideas was common in Roman Britain, and here a parallel is being drawn between the heroism of Bellerophon and Christ. He is not suffering pain through crucifixion, but instead is shown as a hero who defeated death and the devil.

Mosaics (now sadly lost, but recorded in some magnificent eighteenth-century lithographs) from Frampton show a similar combination of themes, in this case combining Bacchic/Orphic imagery with Christian/Gnostic. It has been suggested that this shows deliberate attempts in the decorative interiors of villas to create artistic schemes that would provoke discussion among the visitors and inhabitants regarding the evolution of religious ideas in the fourth century.[17] Other symbols that surround Bellerophon at Frampton include the head of the god of the sea, Neptune, and canthari, which are the vessels used to mix water and wine in preparation for entertainment. These images could carry Christian meanings, since the connection of Neptune with water may suggest the rite of baptism, while the vessels to hold wine could refer to the Eucharistic chalice. Both these symbols are repeated in mosaics from Verulamium: this location seems to have reflected a similar interest in the potential to find shared meaning with Christian and pagan myths and ideas.

The mosaics from Verulamium show that the world Alban inhabited was filled with religious experimentation. He was an early Christian convert, and around him, in the town in which he lived, others were also grappling with the intellectual drift away from the old gods. It is important to appreciate how Christianity came to Britain, how it was accepted alongside the Celtic religion and how individuals like Alban became rallying points later for the Anglo-Saxon Church, since all these elements have a bearing on the rest of this study. The Romano-British past, combined with the arrival of Christianity, formed the foundation of the Anglo-Saxon period, and Alban is pivotal in understanding this.

Not only was Alban Britain's first martyr, but within his life-time Christianity emerged, evolved and began to set down roots. His story helps to explain the origins of Christian belief and worship in the British Isles. In Alban we also see the power of words in how a saint is remembered. If Alban lived today he would be cast as a religious fanatic, someone opposing the status quo and seeking death as a martyred hero. Parallels with modern equivalents are there – so-called martyrs continue to die in hope of a better after-life, and their legacy becomes what they perceive as an act of bravery in an ongoing religious war. In sacrificing his life for his cause, Alban became a hero-martyr, and the Christians that have celebrated him down the ages should remember this, regardless of the hagiographic finery his story has been embroidered in by Bede and other Anglo-Saxon writers.

Yet alongside Alban's more orthodox story of martyrdom, cathedrals, bishops and relics, a different form of sanctity was to emerge within the British Isles. Though they weren't martyrs in the sense of dying for their faith, the early ascetics of the Celtic Church were willing to put their life in the hands of God as they travelled across hostile terrains to spread His message, and they would suffer a form of living death in the eremitical and physically punishing existence that emerged in early Celtic monasteries. A new type of saint was emerging, and they were the products of a new monastic world.

Chapter Two
Brigid: Rebirth of a Goddess

*'Capraria rears itself, a filthy isle full of men
who shun the light. Their name for
themselves is a Greek one, "Monks" (from
"monos"), because they wish to live alone.
They fear fortune's gifts, dreading its harm.
What silly fanaticism of a demented brain
cannot endure good things for fear of evil?'*

Rutilius, *A Voyage Home to Gaul.*

Brigid is a patron saint of Ireland, and is remembered as a nun, founder and abbess of the 'Church of the Oak' in Kildare. The character of Brigid blends an extreme form of early monasticism with pagan Celtic beliefs. Through her a goddess became a saint. Hers is the era of the ascetic monks and nuns, whose austere and harsh existence appeared fanatical to those who encountered it. For example, in the early fifth century a senior Roman official called Rutilius took a sea voyage up the west coast of Italy.[1] His route took him past the many small islands that scatter the Mediterranean near Corsica, and along the way he saw the island of Caprera, where monks had chosen a life of extreme seclusion and isolation. Their ascetic approach to Christian ideals repulsed Rutilius, but these early monks were following the example of the earlier desert fathers of northern Africa. Their goal was to withdraw from the temptations of the world in order to do battle with demons and protect humankind from their polluting influence.

A small shard of rock in the ocean, ten miles off the coast of County Cork in Ireland, presents a similar insight into early monastic ideals. Skellig Michael is notoriously difficult to access, even today in modern boats with powerful engines. But the earliest inhabitants of this inhospitable island were Irish Christians, and this location, complete with its beehive cells and monastic graveyard, opens a window onto the next stage of sanctity within Britain – the emergence of Celtic Christianity. Perhaps as early as the fifth century, Christians pursuing a rather fanatical form of seclusion set sail in open-topped *curachs* (boats made from wooden timbers with animal skin stretched over the sides) across the turbulent waves of the sea, in search of the most challenging and isolated sites where they could set up small colonies. These men were physically tough, could sail boats and land on oceanic outcrops, were hardened to the elements and extreme in their desire for physical suffering. They were prepared to exist outside of society and were willing to embrace death as part of their pursuit of a fundamental and ascetic form of monasticism.

The journey from the mainland to Skellig must have claimed many lives over the centuries, due to the immense swell of the waves against its sheer rocks. It is an unwelcoming and lonely crag of stone, emerging from the sea as the peak of a much greater sub-aquatic mountain. Seasickness on the journey over is somewhat inevitable, and actually landing on the island is difficult and entirely subject to weather conditions. If a boat can manage to beat the swell and pull into the crack in the rock on the east side of the island, the only access to the steep face of the mountain is a set of steps hewn out of the stone. Every journey involves a hazardous jump from the moving boat onto the slippery steps. There are three modern routes up to the monastic site at the top of the mountain. The most difficult, and the one most frequently used by the earliest monks, is now too steep and dangerous for tourists. However, even the least challenging of the routes is treacherous, curving dangerously near craggy edges and requiring great physical fitness to traverse the 600 feet to the monastery on the north peak.

The experience of travelling further upwards with each step on the mountainside is an awe-inspiring one, and the rare birds and plant life either side of the man-made path add to the feeling of being in an exceptional place. The approach to the monastic site is particularly impressive. Moving through a break in the stone wall, you are met suddenly by nine intact beehive cells, nestled together within an enclosure as if huddling from the elements; they are unexpected and almost otherworldly. The rigid, dark monastic cells, abutting one another and yet solidly differentiated from those either side, reinforce the central paradox at the heart of the monastic ideal: monks came together to be alone.

While we don't know the names of the earliest monks that lived on the island, the location evokes the new type of saint that was to become celebrated across the British Isles. The reach of the Celtic monk was great throughout the fifth to ninth centuries, and no book on Anglo-Saxon sanctity would be complete without a firm understanding of how Christianity evolved in Ireland, Wales and Scotland. Skellig Michael is an evocative, and yet not unique, form of early Irish monastic settlement, where developments in the Celtic Church appear most tangible.

Archaeological excavations have been conducted at Skellig Michael, particularly on the monastic burial ground.[2] The evidence is startling, as the skeletons reveal the levels of extreme hardship and asceticism endured by the monks on the island. The bones indicate years of injuries, including damage to the feet and back, brought about through labouring and transporting materials up the slopes of the craggy mountain. They seem to have survived on a diet of vegetables grown on the island and sea birds, which they could hunt, eating their eggs as well. They had small quantities of meat, which must have been brought in on *curachs* from the mainland. This suggests that items the monks couldn't get from the island could be imported, and that contact was maintained with communities on the shore.

More interesting still is that many of the skeletons belonged to people who died very young, with few living beyond the age of thirty. The eldest skeleton belonged to a man in his fifties, but there were the bones of children as young as eight, which suggests that even novices and oblates went to Skellig. On the whole, it is clear that the pursuit of an extreme ascetic way of life was a youthful one, designed to test the physical limitations of those who were either dedicated to the monastic founder by their families or who chose to follow this lifestyle. This was hard living, and part of the tough, visceral existence was mirrored in the secular world by the physical exertion of soldiers and those who worked the land. The earliest textual references to a monastic site on Skellig Michael date from the eighth century, although archaeological finds suggest earlier settlement that may date back centuries before writers committed the place to vellum.

At the south peak of the island is a more treacherous and inhospitable site, where a simple chapel and hermit's cell attest to the fact that sometimes even the small community 600 feet up the mountain to the north of the island was too comfortable for some of the monks.[3] The tiny oratory and hermit's cell on the tip of the south peak are almost impossible to access today, and climbing ropes are needed to survey it effectively. The monk living in this cell was emulating the example of hermits like Simeon Stylites (c. AD 390–459), who lived for decades on the top of a column fifty feet high. The monks sought ever-higher locations and more discomfort in order to separate themselves from humanity and gain greater access to an uninterrupted relationship with the divine. As military strategists know, the higher ground gives an advantage to those wishing to do battle with the enemy. In the case of monks, this enemy was the devil himself and his army of demons.

Early Monastic Ideals

To third-century Christians the desert was seen as the rightful abode for devils on earth, since it acted as the antithesis of Creation. Everything that was abundant and plentiful elsewhere – flora, fauna, food and shelter – was absent in the desert, and consequently where God is not, there will be demons. The early desert fathers went into battle with these evil forces in a form of supernatural warfare. This idea continues throughout the medieval period in the three estates. Peasants work the land to provide food; knights work to defend the people here on earth; monks work to defend people's souls for eternity.

The earliest recorded hermit and desert father was St Paul of Thebes. He retreated to the desert to escape the persecutions of Decius and Valerian in around AD 250. His life was recorded not long after by St Jerome, the Father of the Church and great translator of the Bible from Hebrew to Latin, around AD 375. By the time Jerome wrote his famous *Life of Saint Paul the First Hermit,* the desert was full of men and women seeking to follow Paul's example and escape from the temptations of the world.[4] Paul's life can be seen as a foundation text of sorts, providing a narrative and explanation for the explosion of monasticism that took place in the fourth century. Paul lived his long life (Jerome states he lived to 113) in a cave, with just the shade of a single palm tree, a spring of water and, from the age of forty-three onwards, half a loaf of bread brought to him by a raven.

Saint Paul was clearly a religious fanatic. He went to extraordinary physical extremes to escape from the world and dedicate his life and body to prayer and suffering in the example of Christ. Today, we might be concerned about his mental health, but during the time of the early martyrs he was celebrated. He sought to embrace a form of living death in order to be removed from the distractions of a comfortable existence, and so gain a greater sense of communion with God.

His story was preserved through the account of a fellow hermit monk, St Anthony, who had a dream about Paul and sought him out. In an interesting example of nature bending to the will of saints, on the day Paul was to die, Anthony went to him. The raven brought a whole loaf, instead of half, which they ceremonially broke between them in imitation of the Eucharist. This motif has become a central one within monasticism, found throughout English and Irish sculpture, such as on the famous Ruthwell Cross, where it symbolises the brotherly ideals at the heart of the monastic life.

Outside of the desert, however, there were still opportunities for devout men and women to follow a life of monastic asceticism and withdrawal. They had to make use of different types of landscape in the British Isles, but equally hostile and remote locations were found in which to retreat as hermits. The most popular were hilltops, valleys, marshes and islands. Saint Gwyddfarch chose the first, a hilltop, as his retreat near the modern-day village of Meifod, Wales. We know little about him, apart from the fact that he lived during the sixth century, but despite his hilltop looking lush and green in spring, it would have been a cold and uninviting wilderness in the winter for a hermit.

Valleys were also popular in Wales. The virgin saint Melangell chose a deserted valley near Llangynog, in Powys, to hide away as a hermit. She was reputedly a princess who chose to escape court in favour of a life of seclusion, and she managed to remain isolated for many years in the valley. However, one day the prince of the region came to the site and, after talking with her, granted her land on which to build a monastery. A church remains on this location, and the virgin saint's restored shrine lies within. It is believed to be the oldest Romanesque shrine in Britain.[5]

There are other echoes of the distant past in the existing church at Pennant Melangell, for it is enclosed within a ringed churchyard, which sits on top of an older Bronze Age burial site. It is surrounded by yew trees, which have a long symbolic history, particularly among the Celts, possibly because of their extended life (some yew trees are over 2,000 years old), or because of their toxicity. The life of St Melangell, however, emphasises that sanctity and monastic isolation were not simply the preserve of men in the fifth and sixth centuries – women could be influential spiritual leaders, retreat to the wilderness to do battle with demons and even establish their own monasteries.

Marshes and islands were more favoured by the saints of Ireland and England. Saint Guthlac sought hermetic isolation in the Fens, which covered nearly a million acres of marshland. Legends grew up around him. Supposedly, he was seen engaged in battle with horrific marsh creatures, giving physical manifestation to the otherwise cerebral battles monks were supposed to engage in. Saint Cuthbert, despite being Bishop of Lindisfarne, retreated to the smaller island of Inner Farne to seek separation from worldly concerns. The island is lashed on all sides by the sea, and in winter it is a cold, exposed and desolate place.

Both these men were members of Anglo-Saxon military society, and saw themselves as spiritual warriors, akin to the soldiers that propped up the social structure of their times. Yet they also had strong connections with the Celtic Church and its particular form of monasticism. Guthlac had been a monk at Repton, which was a Mercian monastery reputedly founded by the patron saint of Wales, David. Cuthbert had trained at Melrose, Scotland, which was a daughter-house of St Aidan's Celtic monastery at Lindisfarne. The eremitic ideals they clung to indicate that the legacy of the Celtic approach of monastic isolation and self-deprivation lasted for many centuries, despite the fact that it stood in opposition to the more orthodox monasticism prevalent on the Continent. Early Anglo-Saxon monasticism had its roots in Celtic practices.

The extreme ascetics of the time, capable of withstanding the harshest of conditions, were respected for being able to punish

The monastery on Skellig Michael was formed between the sixth and the eighth centuries. Six-hundred feet above sea level are a set of six beehive cells, two chapels and a cemetery. The cells are dry-built, meaning they are not held together with cement, and by radiating each of the layers out slightly the rain water will wash down the sides, rather than into the cells. They are amazingly intact after so many years of being assaulted by the elements.

their bodies more than most, in a way that top-tier athletes, climbers and explorers could appreciate today. These individuals would fascinate and inspire the people in their community through their suffering and apparent closeness to God.

Hermits became important members of many towns and villages, and their counsel was sought by the good and the great. Saint Guthlac gave refuge to Aethelbald, the future king of Mercia, and Melangell counselled a prince. The irony of hermit life for many was that, although they retreated from human company for spiritual isolation, this made them sought-after in terms of providing counsel and advice. So hermits and anchorites (an extreme form of enclosure which involved being physically sealed up in a cell for life) were often visited, and they retained influence in the worldly concerns they had sought to escape. This untapped Christian influence was something the papacy feared, since it positioned influential individuals outside of the remit of their control.

Man's World vs. the Natural World

In many ways, early monasticism put it in opposition with other aspects of the Church. From when it gained the support of Emperor Constantine, the Christian Church was structured around the administrative and ideological framework of the Roman Empire. In Roman paganism gods, goddesses and the divine imperial family were celebrated as being human in appearance and sensibility. In Christian thought the divine God and his son Jesus also appear in a human guise – the central idea underlying Christianity is that the unknowable divine took human form, and that God fashioned mankind in his own image.

This meant that both Roman and Christian beliefs placed a profound importance on the appearance of man, which was modelled on the divine. For example, images showing the creation of Adam and Eve represent God as a distinctly human and sympathetic figure. The treatment of the body in these scenes, whereby Adam and Eve mirror the gestures, attributes and appearance of God, enhances that central premise of Christianity. As such, humans and the places they made and inhabited, namely cities, were the focus of the Christian Church. The word 'civilisation' derives from the Latin for city and civilians, 'civitas', since it was within these constructed sites that man could escape from the brutality of the untamed wild to pursue more elevated, human-centric experiences.

When Christianity became the official religion of the Roman Empire in the fourth century, it inherited many of the trappings of the secular power force that had given it an international footing. From its origins in house churches and rebellious martyrs, the early Church developed into an intricately structured, hierarchical, coordinated institution. The administrative structure of the Church was taken over wholesale from the Roman imperial system, so every city had a patriarch or bishop, while the Pope himself retained the Roman title of 'pontiff' (chief bridge-builder). Both the Church and the Empire were international organisations, and just as the Emperor had to maintain control over his subjects from Hadrian's Wall to Syria, so the Pope had to maintain orthodoxy and order between cities the length and breadth of Europe and beyond.

In contrast, however, the polytheistic gods of the Celtic and Germanic people of northern Europe were partly human, but their forms could change. The Celtic gods were bound up with nature, and deities like Cernunnos were part human, part animal. On the third-century Gundestrup Cauldron – discovered in a peat bog near to the modern-day town of Aars, Denmark – the god has antlers and is surrounded by animals, including a snake that he holds up towards his face.[6] Similarly, Germanic gods like Odinn could shape-shift, transforming themselves from human to animal. While the Romans had a big impact on the Celtic world in England and along the borders of Wales and Scotland, their reach was not felt in Ireland, where the people continued to practise a form of Druidic worship with deities that had not been classicised into toga-wearing men and women. The significance of the Romans not reaching parts of the British Isles like Ireland and Scotland shouldn't be underestimated.

Ireland had not felt the impact of the roads, aqueducts and cities that the Roman Empire introduced elsewhere. As a result, it remained a society structured around tribal leaders and a landscape that was harsh to navigate, with pockets of habitation. Unlike mainland Europe, where an individual could use Roman roads to move between areas of civilisation – each similar to the other with its bath houses, churches and forums – the people of Ireland were conscious of the unpredictable nature of the woods, mountains, rivers and seas around them. To traverse the Irish landscape in any season, but particularly in the hostile winter months, could be life-threatening, and this may explain why a particularly hardy form of monasticism grew up in Ireland. Carvings on White Island, County Fermanagh, show a Celtic monk alongside other members of early medieval society, such as a warrior on the far right. The monk is characterised by the long cloak he wears to protect himself from the elements, the walking stick to help him navigate the landscape and the bell to call together people from the surrounding countryside to hear him speak of God and the Bible. Irish monks were hardy and able to travel long distances.

The carvings on the walls of the now ruined church at White Island, County Fermanagh, date to between AD 800 and 1000, yet they portray individuals who would have been recognisable in the fifth and sixth centuries. The missionary two in from the left carries a bell and staff, and the warrior two in from the right has a sword, shield and large penannular brooch.

In the eyes of Continental Christians, however, Ireland was barbaric and needed taming. The Roman troops had withdrawn from Britain in the early fifth century, by which time Roman-Britons were predominantly Christian. The faith of the Britons was acknowledged by those close to the papacy, including Prosper of Aquitaine. Writing in the AD 430s, he records how action had to be taken against the Pelagian heresy, but states clearly that the land of the Britons was populated with the true faith:

> He (Pope Celestine I) has been, however, no less energetic in freeing the British provinces from this same disease (the Pelagian heresy): he removed from that hiding-place in the Ocean certain enemies of grace who had occupied the land of their origins; also, having ordained a bishop for the Irish, while he labours to keep the Roman island catholic, he has also made the barbarian island Christian.[7]

The Christian faith seeped over from Roman Britain to Ireland in the fifth century, most notably through the work of St Patrick. But before focusing on the primary male patron saint of Ireland, there is another saint that most effectively highlights the way Christianity set down roots in Ireland and the other Celtic areas of Britain in its earliest years: our first female saint.

Brigid: Christian Saint or Celtic Goddess?

If it has been difficult to get a sense of the person behind the name with well-known saints like Alban, it is more complex still when we come to St Brigid. While extremely well known and widely venerated, Brigid is an almost intangible saint, who may not be connected with a living individual at all, but rather with a place and its pre-Christian cult goddess. To this day, school children weave reeds and straw into equal-armed crosses, known as Brigid's Cross. This symbol, like its namesake, connects Ireland back to Celtic Druidic roots.

Alongside Patrick, the character of St Brigid also raises interesting problems about the early Church in Ireland, the role of the first monastic settlements and the real figure behind the hagiography. She is remembered as the founder of a particularly powerful and influential monastery at Kildare. Here, women could embrace the harsh monastic ideals and mirror the extreme ascetic exploits of their male counterparts on distant isles like Skellig Michael. Yet Brigid is difficult to grasp, since she leaves none of her own writings, and some of the miracles later attributed to her appear entirely formulaic. She emulates Christ in turning water into beer, heals the sick and provides food for those in need.[8]

She is a female saint who does not suffer a martyr's death to single her out, so her *Life* reads as a set of formulas drawn from biblical examples.[9] However, there are some tantalising details in the texts written about her that give an insight into the political and religious landscape the saintly character of Brigid (real or invented) inhabited. Her part in the pre-Christian society of Druidic Ireland can be surmised through a number of suggestions.

Firstly, she is best known for founding a monastery for women at Kildare, which translates as 'the Church of Oak'. This suggests that it was established on a site that had connections to oak trees, which were sacred within the Druidic religion. In this respect, she emulated other early Christian monastic founders in Ireland. At Labbamolaga, in County Cork, a monastic community was established alongside a sacred Druidic stone circle, and the walls of the monastery enclosed the great standing stones within its precinct. Christian and pagan, church and Druidic megaliths were incorporated together.

In terms of the real Brigid, sources suggest that she may have lived between AD 450 and 520, since a number of individuals named in accounts of her life can be connected with people alive around this time. The earliest text mentioning her, however, was written by Broccan Cloen in the seventh century. She certainly appears from later texts to have been a hugely powerful and influential woman. She founded the nunnery at Kildare, along with other monasteries for both men and women. She also seems to have held considerable authority with regards to selecting the bishops of Kildare who would rule alongside her – a staggering responsibility for a woman. This relationship between the Bishop and the Abbess of Kildare continued through the centuries, with the female head of the monasteries bearing some episcopal authority.

The monastery at Kildare flourished under strong female leadership, and became a centre of learning and the arts. A later twelfth-century chronicler, Gerald of Wales, described a Gospel book he had seen at Kildare: 'You will make out intricacies, so delicate and so subtle, so full of knots and links, with colours so fresh and vivid, that you might say that all this were the work of an angel, and not of a man.'[10] This book has been associated with the famous Book of Kells, but it is possible that a similarly extraordinary manuscript was produced at St Brigid's flourishing art school in Kildare.

Accounts of Brigid's life reveal connections with the earlier animistic belief systems of Ireland, since many of her miracles involved manipulating nature. She had control over wild and domestic animals, and one of her most famous miracles involved hanging her cloak on a sunbeam. She even performed an act that has continued to trouble Christians down the ages by terminating the pregnancy of a young girl simply through placing her hands on her womb. The girl had supposedly strayed from the path of righteousness, but this action may imply that Brigid had qualities of the local wise woman, and could perform rites that would become highly questionable – and even associated with witchcraft – in later Christian history.

Women could hold important positions within Celtic society; they could be involved with health care and medicine. Within a religious framework they could be seers, and were included in sacred acts, particularly surrounding fertility. In the secular sphere, a Celtic woman could be a peace-weaver, able to secure marriages between tribes. And like Boudicca, they could even lead armies and fight. Women were equal to men in a number of ways, and this bothered the Romans, whose world was far more misogynistic. The Christian Church, too, was a homocentric institution where men held the majority of positions of authority.

For early medieval societies like that of fifth- to sixth-century Ireland, the sidelining of women was not something that could take place immediately, since there were long traditions of prizing female contributions to religion and state formation. The most attractive proposal for women in the face of the arrival of Christianity was to establish monastic communities with themselves at the head. Saint Brigid and her nunnery at Kildare may well be an early example of this sort of re-articulation of female influence.

Whether St Brigid existed as a single identifiable fifth-century woman has been debated. Recent work on her cult concludes that she was, in fact, not a real Christian saint at all, but the result of symbolic manipulation; a means of adapting a pre-Christian Druidic cult into a Christian context.[11] There appears to have been a powerful Druidic cult centre at Kildare, where the goddess Brigid was worshipped in her triple form. The separating of a deity into three was a common practice in Celtic religion, as evinced by the goddess in triplicate sculpture from Aquae Sulis. Brigid was also worshipped in triple form, with two sisters who both shared her name.

Traditionally, the three aspects of a goddess have been considered as mother, maiden and crone. This carving from Aquae Sulis shows the three women with their arms touching, signifying that they are three, yet one.

The goddess or goddesses had an exclusive female priesthood at Kildare and an ever-burning fire, which was tended to by nineteen priestesses, representing the nineteen-year cycle of the Celtic 'Great Year'. This tradition seems to have continued after the priestesses became nuns, for a group of young women kept an eternal flame alight to the saint. Indeed, it was seen to be such a haven for women that a much later Christian visitor to Kildare, Gerald of Wales, said that men could not approach the sacred flame. It was surrounded by a hedge, and any men that crossed this would be cursed to go insane. This influential religious hub at Kildare could have become redundant in the wake of Christianity, and its priestesses scattered. However, the establishment of a nunnery on the site of the Druidic temple, and the elevation of the pagan goddess Brigid to St Brigid, meant that this sacred place among the oak trees remained powerful and prosperous.

There are many examples of this sort of syncretism, whereby Christianity adapted itself in line with native cults in order to smooth the road of conversion. Indeed, we need look no further than the naming of Easter. Bede records how this most significant of Christian feasts was named after a pagan goddess:

> *Eosturmonath has a name which is now translated 'Paschal month', and which was once called after a goddess of theirs named Eostre, in whose honour feasts were celebrated in that month. Now they designate that Paschal season by her name, calling the joys of the new rite by the time-honoured name of the old observance.*[12]

In this extract from Bede's work *The Reckoning of Time,* he records how the other months of the year were also tied to pre-Christian festivals. 'Hrethmonath', the name for April, was related to another goddess, Hretha, and sacrifices were made to her in that month.

A similar translation of festivities from a pagan event to a Christian one centres on Brigid herself. Her feast day is 1 February, which was also the date on which the pagan festival Imbolc was celebrated. Imbolc was one of the four seasonal celebrations, designed to usher in spring. The festivities were focused on Brigid, the goddess of sacred wells, poetry, craftsmanship and the hearth. She was said to have invented 'keening', which is a combination of singing and crying, and which may continue in the mournful Irish ballads that have come down the centuries.

Her festival marked the start of the new season of life and fertility, and the fact that this pagan event was grafted onto the feast day of St Brigid is yet further evidence that her cult continued under a different guise. Furthermore, Brigid's Cross, which has long been associated with Imbolc and 1 February, has its roots far back beyond the arrival of Christianity. Despite the fact that later writers sought to make sense of this symbol by creating a story in which St Brigid crafts the cross out of reeds on the deathbed of a nobleman, the tradition of hanging them outside houses to ward off fire has no connection to Christian practices, and seems an echo of older pagan rituals. But there may be yet another layer of symbolism to Brigid.

Brigid or Brigantia?

The Irish goddess Brigid may be connected to the Celtic deity worshipped in Britain as Brigantia. She is most closely associated with Minerva, goddess of the hearth and harvest, and played an important role across Celtic tribes – for example, there was a tribe in Austria who also honoured the goddess. Offerings were made to the goddess Brigantia in wells, springs and rivers across Britain. Indeed, this special sacredness of water as a life-giving force to animals, plants and humans continued in the number of sacred springs and wells associated with saints, particularly in Celtic regions.[13]

There are fifteen wells across Ireland dedicated to St Brigid, suggesting that she in particular retained this connection with water. One near Buttevant in County Cork is regularly visited by people wishing to be healed. Crutches have been left at the site, to indicate that people could walk after being healed by the waters. Although we know little with certainty about Druidic religious practices because the Druids did not write down their traditions, the sacredness of water is a defining aspect. Finds dating from across the centuries are found in rivers or bogs, where they seem to have been ritualistically placed as a form of offering to a deity. That St Brigid maintained her links with sacred springs is another indicator that her Christian cult preserves much more ancient Celtic practices.

The tribe for which Brigantia was the most important goddess of the pantheon was named after her – the Brigantes – and their stronghold stretched across the north of England, close to the border with Scotland. Images of her in this area showed her as a divine ruler. For example, on the Birrens Altar from Dumfries and Galloway, she is shown with spear, crown and orb to reflect that she was protector of the tribe. She wears a gorgon's head around her neck, and combines the attributes of Minerva with Juno, queen of the gods. Around the helmet are depicted battlements, perhaps

This sculpture, made between AD 120 and 180, shows the goddess Brigantia, but was set up by a Roman. The inscription reads: 'Sacred to Brigantia: Amandus, the engineer, fulfilled the order by command.' It was found at the Roman fort of Birrens in Dumfriesshire, and testifies to the absorption of local cults by Roman soldiers along the northern frontiers.

indicating that she was a protective deity of a particular region. To all intents she has been Romanised. Only the inscription indicates that the image shows not Minerva, but Brigantia. Her image is also recalled in later ones of Britannia.

The leader of the Brigantes, a queen called Cartimandua, managed to maintain the security of her kingdom against Romans and competing tribes for many years through diplomacy and marriage. However, the Brigantes were finally destroyed by the coordinated military campaigns of the Roman twentieth legion around the year AD 80, with Agricola at its head. On the back of this defeat, a number of the Brigantes tribes-people left northern England and settled in southern Ireland. This included the remaining Druids.

In AD 60 the Romans had made a concerted effort to annihilate Druidism, since many of their leaders had questioned the authority of Rome in Britain. This culminated in an attack on the Isle of Anglesey, which had become a stronghold and sanctuary for British Druids. The site was levelled, and with this act, the long history of Druid practices in Celtic Britain was brought to a hasty end. However, the relocation of many Brigantes from their territories in northern England to southern Ireland would have included the Druidic leaders. Their powerbase was located close to the site where Brigid's monastery was established, near Kildare, and here a branch of the Irish ruling family Ui Brigte was to gain a secure footing.[14]

That the Druids had great influence over the kings is revealed by Dio Chrysostom:

> The Celts appointed those whom they call Druids, these also being devoted to the prophetic art and to wisdom in general. In all these cases the kings were not permitted to do or plan anything without the assistance of these wise men.[15]

In Ireland over the fifth century, as kings began to convert to Christianity, so their advisers had to find new footings within the establishments. Druids and Druidesses could continue to offer support and advice to the royal family, play a role in fertility rites and impart blessings, but only as heads of monasteries, and ultimately as saints. It seems likely in this context that the St Brigid we know from later hagiographical texts may in fact have been a Druidess who founded a monastery at the great oak where the goddess Brigid had been venerated. Stories connect her with healing, fertility and nature, and her reputation continued down the ages as a powerful and venerable woman, who wielded great influence within her world.

The acceptance of the basic premises underlying Christianity may not have been so difficult for the Druids, as many of their beliefs were founded on similar principles. At the heart of the Gospels lies a story of human sacrifice, since the Son of God – a wise teacher and preacher – gave up his life for the benefit of his community. However, he was an even finer sacrifice, since he was born again to wield power as Lord over heaven alongside his Father. There is a cyclical sense of regeneration and rebirth in the Gospel story that could be connected to the Druidic cycle of the year, where gods and goddesses are born, nourished, grow and decay across the seasons. Also, like many Druids, Jesus was a healer and a preacher, who imparted wisdom and spiritual guidance to his followers.

Celtic Christianity focused on the idea that God is present in all His creation – woods, animals, trees, plants – and used this as a means of adapting their pagan animistic beliefs. Springs, wells, woodlands and mountains could all maintain their spiritual potency through their part in God's creation, and often through their association with the miracles worked by saints. Druids used wands to perform magic, while Celtic saints used their staffs to perform miracles. Many of these have been preserved as relics, and later became the model for elaborate bishops' croziers. Even down to the seventeenth century, members of the community known as *Áes Dána* performed the role of earlier Druidic leaders, preserving traditions and genealogies through oral recitation. There is a long and unbroken legacy of these forms of pre-Christian rites, and although Christianity meant a re-articulation of spirituality in Celtic lands, the Druidic past was never fully eradicated. Early Irish saints like Brigid indicate how pagan and Christian could be combined, and how the fascination with nature and the landscape remained central through times of religious and social change.

Brigid is entirely fitting as one of the earliest and most important saints of Ireland, since in this one name the concept of gradual conversion from one religious world to another is preserved. Ireland didn't receive a single papally sanctioned mission in the way that the Anglo-Saxons did which allowed them to benefit from an orthodox approach to the new religion that could be rolled out across kingdoms. Instead, its conversion was slow, and fuelled by practical choices, such as maintaining social order and structure. Significantly, the natural landscape of Ireland and the long-held Celtic beliefs in the spiritual potency of the environment were preserved through early saints like Brigid. She is held, alongside Patrick and Columba, as a patron saint of Ireland. The individuals whom particular kingdoms chose to tie themselves to spiritually by electing patron saints can tell us much about their values and the way they wished to be perceived. Brigid encompassed echoes of a much-treasured ancient Druidic Celtic past. But those saints who would come to fly the flag for the nations of the British Isles would represent other equally valued attributes.

Chapter Three
Patrick: From Slave to Patron

'*The sorcerer then knelt before Saint George and begged him to make him a Christian. Seeing that his own sorcerer had converted to Christianity, the provost cut off his head. The provost had Saint George placed between two wheels mounted with swords, but the wheels broke, and Saint George remained unharmed. Then the provost had him thrown into a caldron filled with molten lead, but Saint George sat there comfortably, as if he were in a warm bath.*'

'The Legend of St George', from *The Golden Legend.*[1]

The choice of patron saint for England, St George, has long been a controversial one. In a recent poll many more people voted for St Alban to represent the spiritual life of the nation.[2] George wasn't a native of this country; in fact, he never set foot in Britain, and had no tangible connections with it whatsoever. George's roots lie in Palestine. That he existed is accepted, but the many fantastical legends associated with him, particularly his famed encounter with the dragon, were later elaborations. What can be known with some certainty about George is that he was born to a Greek Christian family around AD 280, and served as a soldier under Diocletian. When an edict was passed arresting all Christians that served in the Roman army in AD 303, George refused to concur with the Emperor's wishes by sacrificing to the pagan gods, and so suffered a brutal martyrdom. Accounts suggest that he was lacerated with a wheel of swords, before he was boiled alive and finally decapitated. George was a prominent and important early martyr. But why has this man, distant in time and space from England, become its national saint?

Further into the medieval period, the answer lies with King Edward III (1327–77), the great military ruler of the fourteenth century and instigator of the Hundred Years' War with France. Partly to antagonise his French counterparts, and partly to provide a new rallying point around an ancient soldier renowned for his faith and devotion, Edward chose George to be the new patron saint of England. This act disregarded many other candidates from the Anglo-Saxon period and beyond. The most obvious is St Alban, but St Cuthbert has also frequently been proposed as a more suitable national saint. Even Edward's grandson, Richard II, seemed to favour older, native saints above George. In Richard's personal altarpiece, the Wilton Diptych, George's influence is reduced to a small flag. Instead, the English saints Edmund the Martyr and Edward the Confessor accompany the youthful King Richard.

Many patron saints are not natives of the countries they represent. For example, Scotland has St Andrew, companion of Christ and brother of St Peter. However, there are some saints that, particularly in the Celtic areas of Britain, connect nations with their distant past – especially the 'dark age' from the fourth to sixth century. Patrick, Maughold, Ninian and David are all figures cloaked in myth and legend, but they continue to be celebrated down the centuries in Ireland, the Isle of Man, western Scotland and Wales as significant, home-grown saints. True, of these only David seems to have stayed in the place of his birth, but all four were products of the early Celtic Church, and represent the founding moments when these nations embraced Christianity.

The Wilton Diptych is one of the finest medieval paintings to survive. Made between 1395–9 for the King of England Richard II, it could have been painted in England or France. The king is shown kneeling before the Virgin Mary and an army of angels, all of whom wear his personal emblem of the white hart. It was used for the private prayers of the King and shows an intimate relationship between the monarch and the Queen of Heaven.

Ninian: Patron Saint of Western Scotland

One place in particular provides a very real and tangible connection with this age. Whithorn lays claim to being one of the oldest continuously occupied villages in Scotland, and is known as the crucible of Christianity in this part of the world. Nestled at the edge of the Machars peninsula in western Scotland, it is an especially picturesque and significant location from which to explore the Celtic patron saints. The isle of Whithorn today is the stuff of postcards, with its harbour front a collection of bright, regular houses nestled together, peering over the sea wall and out towards Ireland and the Isle of Man. From the white tower, known as the Cairn, which has been a mariner's landmark for nearly two centuries, you can see the open expanse of the Irish Sea, while to the east is the undulating coastline of Kirkcudbright. The crags of rocks seem to collide with one another beneath, in emulation of the waves, while in spring wild flowers cover the banks and swallows whistle overhead. Across the water it is possible to make out the Isle of Man, which is just eighteen miles from Whithorn, while the Lake District rolls away to the south.

The sea was the motorway of the early medieval period, and even today it is quicker to approach Whithorn by water than by road. Its location on the edge of three nations, with the ocean just a short boat ride away, made it strategically important. Now the community is made up of just a few hundred people, but it is still frequented by pilgrims and tourists. The village of Whithorn is a short journey from the edge of the sea.

Ptolemy first mentioned Whithorn in his work *The Geography*, which around AD 140 recorded all the known parts of the Roman Empire.[3] His map has the realm of the Novantae, which included Whithorn, positioned facing north. It testifies to the great age and significance of this site.

The evidence of the first Christian settlers in this area unfolds as you pass beneath a large archway known as the Pend. Through here, away from the main road, you are faced with nearly two millennia of history. The area behind the Pend takes you past the nineteenth-century parish church, and then to the ruins of the twelfth-century priory. The importance of this site as a bishopric and a flourishing monastery is clear from the scale of the Romanesque buildings that remain. These would have catered for the flow of later medieval pilgrims visiting the reputed tomb of Scotland's first saint, Ninian, founder of Scotland's first Christian building, the Candida Casa, meaning the 'white house'. It got this name because of the white-wash plaster that covered its exterior walls, but it also connected the site more symbolically with ideas of purity and salvation.

Christianity was certainly established in Whithorn by around AD 450, as archaeological finds from the area testify. A tomb monument for a man and a four-year-old girl opens with the statement

The Latinus Stone from Whithorn was carved around AD 450 and is Scotland's oldest Christian monument. There are traces of a Chi-Rho symbol at the top of the stone that may be the 'sign' referred to in the inscription, which states: 'We praise you, the Lord! Latinus, descendant of Barravados, aged 35, and his daughter, aged 4, made a sign here.'

in Latin: 'We praise thee Lord' – a rare survival.[4] This means that Christians were setting up monuments in this part of Scotland at a time when the Romans were abandoning the British Isles, and pagan Angles, Saxons and Jutes were taking control of areas just south of Hadrian's Wall.

The retreat of the Roman garrisons that had defended the borders with the Picts was completed by AD 410. While this spelt political, economic and social upheaval to the south, in the north it appears to have brought fewer calamities. The weakened defences of the Romano-Britons in England and along the Welsh borders meant that they were vulnerable to attacks by Irish Scotti and Picts. There were no longer Roman soldiers to defend them, and their rich villas and wealthy farms were prime targets for Celtic raiders. The Irish managed to take land in Cornwall and Wales, as well as cart off slaves, which could be employed in their homelands or sold on for profit.

In the north, the Picts crossed over the old defences of Hadrian's Wall and seized slaves, property and possessions far beyond the borders. This was a perilous time for the Romano-Britons, but they did manage to regroup, and a further development began to turn the tide in the constant state of war: the Irish and the Picts became Christian. It was gradual at first, but once the rulers of these kingdoms had converted they conducted fewer raids and took fewer slaves. Hostilities between the various tribes outside and on the edges of Britain never fully abated, but the intensity of the years following the retreat of the Roman army dissipated, and certain British rulers were able to create powerful and stable settlements. The area around Whithorn was one of these, and at its heart was a saint. Ninian was a Romano-British Christian, a missionary, a stranger in a new land, a farmer, a preacher and a teacher. Or, at least, that is what we have been led to believe.

Who is the Real Ninian?

Saint Ninian is remembered as a fourth-century British Christian, who travelled up into western Scotland and may have arrived in

Whithorn before the retreat of the Roman army as early as AD 397. It is most likely he came from south of Hadrian's Wall, and he is credited with establishing Christianity in Scotland for the first time. What little we do know about St Ninian is derived from Bede's *Ecclesiastical History*:

> *The southern Picts, who dwell on this side of those*
> *mountains, had long before, as is reported, forsaken the*
> *errors of idolatry, and embraced the truth, by the preaching*
> *of Ninnias, a most reverend bishop and holy man of the*
> *British nation, who had been regularly instructed at Rome,*
> *in the faith and mysteries of the truth; whose episcopal see,*
> *named after St Martin the bishop, and famous for a stately*
> *church (wherein he and many other saints rest in the body),*
> *is still in existence among the English nation. The place*
> *belongs to the province of the Bernicians, and is generally*
> *called the White House, because he there built a church of*
> *stone, which was not usual among the Britons.*[5]

Bede's account draws attention to the fact that Ninian had founded the Candida Casa long before Columba arrived in Iona, with his particular (and in Bede's eyes, unorthodox) form of Celtic Christianity. Ninian, in contrast, is described as being 'instructed at Rome', emphasising that this was an orthodox, Roman form of Christianity that arrived with his mission. This question of orthodox versus unorthodox will gain greater resonance when the Irish and Roman missions of the sixth century come into focus, but in this case it is clear that Bede is using Ninian as leverage: an example to Irish Christians that one of their missionaries did bring with him a Roman form of Christianity.

The Candida Casa provides a lesson in tempering the symbolic hyperbole found throughout saints' written lives with the physical reality of archaeological excavations. The potency of the Latin name ascribed to this place – 'the shining white house' – associates this location and its saint with purity, radiating out from the pagan landscape. As both a monastery and a bishopric, it shone with the light of Christ's teaching. Furthermore, Bede's emphasis on the stone buildings Ninian established, with their permanence on the land-scape and echoes of the grandeur of Rome, presents the Candida Casa as a paragon of Roman missionary work. However, the archaeological remains from Whithorn suggest that the earliest buildings at the site included a modest rectangular cabin, painted white, ringed by wooden round houses.[6] The use of round houses recalls the homes found throughout Celtic territories, and it's clear that the first monastery at Whithorn was small-scale and func-tional; more of a farmstead than a major ecclesiastical site.

Ninian and his fellow monks would have worked the land to prepare food for the community, which probably included men, women and children. The Latinus Stone, with its reference to a four-year-old daughter, suggests that this wasn't one of the closed monasteries of later years. The small church could not have accommodated many, so while its very existence may be testa-ment to the presence of Christianity in fifth-century Scotland, its scale suggests that the early missionary work was modest. Ninian would have lived like his fellow Celtic settlers, huddled around the hearth in a timber round house, and sharing the labours and hard-ships of the seasons.

Ninian is still regarded as 'Apostle to the Southern Picts', and while he may have been replaced by Andrew throughout Scotland, in the area around Dumfries and Galloway he is held as a patron saint. Yet it is Bede alone who directly connects a saint called Ninian with Whithorn and the Candida Casa. We know nothing more about him: we have no physical remains for Ninian and have no evidence from the site at Whithorn to confirm he was there. Instead, it is possible that the site of the Candida Casa has been mistakenly merged with that of a later Irish saint – Finnian of Moville. This character will loom large in his role as tutor to St Columba, but in relation to the Candida Casa it seems that Finnian may have studied there once it was up and running as a monastery. As we saw with Brigid, the distinctions between real living individuals and residual echoes connected to specific sites or locations could be confused. At Whithorn we have one place – an early Christian settlement – yet two blurred names: Ninian and Finnian.

Records suggest that Finnian of Moville was at Whithorn. He returned from the monastery there to Ireland before AD 540 with a very precious manuscript: a copy of Jerome's Vulgate. This was extremely valuable, since Father of the Church and pioneering biblical scholar Jerome had created a translation of the Bible from the original Hebrew into Latin. This meant that not only were the various mistranslated Greek copies of the biblical books edited into a version more faithful to the original texts, but those in the West who didn't read Greek could consult the Bible more readily.

With his valuable biblical text and a wealth of knowledge gleaned from the monastic community at Whithorn, Finnian went to Ireland and founded his own monastery at Movilla in County Down. If you travel across the Irish Sea, Movilla is relatively near to Whithorn, and the influence of the bishop of this monastery in Ireland may have extended to the Candida Casa. He was a powerful person who moved across great distances, affecting learning and politics throughout his lifetime, and may well be the true historical individual behind the name of St Ninian. This could be a case of mistaken identity.

The combination of the Candida Casa, Ninian and Finnian of Moville may have occurred due to a simple typographical error.[7] The name Finnian would have been written Uinniau in the vernacular British, and the confusion with Ninian may be down to the common scribal error of mistaking an initial 'u' with 'n'. Certainly, the name 'Uinniau' is found in place and personal names around south-west Scotland. So it is possible that the hagiographic tradition of the otherwise unattested St Ninian was conflated with St Finnian of Moville, whose presence is felt far more in the dedications around Whithorn. The combination of the Druidic goddess Brigid with a Christian saint of this name indicates how individuals may have slipped through the cracks of texts in subsequent retellings of older hagiographical accounts. This acts as a caution in our reading of all hagiographical texts. While we may pillage them for historical data on real individuals, they were literary creations, and the characters within could reveal varying degrees of fact and fiction.

That the Christianisation of this region of Pictish Scotland was successful is corroborated around the year AD 432, by that famous

Irish saint and missionary St Patrick (whose similarly fluid identity will be discussed). One of the primary pieces of evidence recording St Patrick's words, ideas and emotions is a letter written to the people just north of Whithorn, in which he refers to them as 'apostate Picts'. Throughout his letter Patrick chastises the Christian Picts for not following a true Christian path – they have deviated from the example set to them by Ninian. The saint's work at the Candida Casa and around this region of Scotland was to have a lasting legacy, and the village where he chose to establish his monastery has remained relevant and fascinating ever since. Be he Ninian or Finnian, the saint who created this potent early Christian community brought his mission to the pagan Picts, and he will be remembered as the first evangelist of Scotland.

Patrick or Palladius?

From western Scotland it is a short leap both culturally and geographically to Ireland. However, while Patrick is arguably one of the best-known saints in the British Isles, like Ninian his world is one where the lines between fantasy and fact are repeatedly blurred. When studying the medieval period, the further back in time you go, the murkier the picture gets. Certain areas and individuals come into sharp relief thanks to a chance survival of a particularly clear text – for example, Bede's accounts of Northumbria. But, otherwise, the wealth of material we have for, say, the eleventh century, is overwhelming in comparison to the fragments we have for the fifth. So St Patrick appears 'through a glass darkly' (1 Corinthians 13:12).

Patrick is celebrated the world over, wherever Irish people have moved and settled, although he is equally popular with those boasting little or no connection with Ireland, because of the great excitement surrounding his feast day on 17 March. Now notorious for the imbibing of pints of Guinness, this tradition actually stems from the fact that St Patrick's Day was an opportunity for the harsh restrictions of Lent to be relieved for one day so people could feast and drink alcohol. In fact, Guinness developed a campaign that stated 'Everyone's Irish on March 17th', which is not only clever marketing, but also indicates how deeply engrained saints are within national identity.

Other traditional aspects of Patrick's feast day include 'wearing of the green' and the display of shamrocks. According to legendary accounts, the saint explained the three parts of the trinity using its leaf, although this could again be an echo of older Druidic practices which split a single god or goddess into triplicate form. The echoes of nature gods and goddesses are also felt in Patrick's association with the colour green. Every year, the Chicago River is turned green on his feast day in order to reflect the Emerald Isle and its patron saint. But even this famous date and these seemingly ancient traditions are only tentatively linked to a real, living, breathing individual. In fact, as with Alban, Brigid and Ninian, the real Patrick is incredibly hard to access.

It is impossible to say with certainty where or when Patrick was born. In terms of his dates, the traditional view is that he arrived in Ireland in AD 432 and died in AD 461, making him one of the earliest missionaries to bring Christianity to Ireland. However, recent work has pushed his dates back to the end of the century. This would have wider implications, since this would question his place as the country's first saint and evangelist. He couldn't have written his two famous texts, *Declaration* and *Letter to the Soldiers of Coroticus*, earlier than the beginning of the fifth century (because he quotes part of Jerome's Vulgate translations of the Bible, which were only circulated after AD 384) or any later than the end of the fifth century (as he suggests the Franks are still pagan at the time of his writing, and they converted around AD 500),[8] but these are the only dates of which we can be sure. This leaves a huge historical sweep of over a hundred years to explore, and the question of exactly when Patrick lived, wrote and died has obsessed scholars across the centuries.

One Celtic scholar, Charles Plummer, even claimed that Patrick never existed at all. But a more convincing argument has been put forward that hagiographical texts have blended two different individuals into the one figure of Patrick.[9] According to this theory, the Patrick who wrote the two famous texts should be considered as distinct and different from the bishop Patrick (also referred to as Palladius), who brought Christianity to the Irish first and was a Gaulish bishop, sent by Pope Celestine to convert the pagan Irish to Christianity in the wake of the Pelagian heresy.[10] It is highly likely that, just as the legends surrounding St Brigid seem to have blended a real woman with another figure, the goddess Brigid, so the Patrick still celebrated today is a hybrid of two individuals: one who wrote beautiful and revealing texts about his experiences, and another who was the first bishop of the Irish.

That there was a friendship between the two patron saints of Ireland – Patrick and Brigid – is suggested in the ninth-century *Book of Armagh*, which stated that the two pillars of the Irish people 'had but one heart and one mind'. Yet there appear to be distinct differences between these two saints. While Brigid emerged from an ancient, home-grown tradition of pagan Druidic beliefs and practices, Patrick represented a world of Roman Christianity, translated over from Roman Britain and clear in its links with a more Continental set of ideas. This book will focus on Patrick the younger, rather than Patrick the elder (Palladius), and presume that he was active slightly later in the fifth century, with the annals suggesting a date as late as AD 492–3 for his death. This is the St Patrick whose words have lasted over the ages in his personally and intimately written texts, and who is charged with establishing the archbishopric at Armagh. It is he who legend remembers, and the time in which he lived was a fascinating one, when the distance between Celtic Irish, Christian Britons and the rest of Christendom was being stretched.

As far as his origins are concerned, it is established fact that Patrick was not Irish. However, in terms of determining exactly where he originated, suggestions range from Wales and Cornwall to Scotland. There is some evidence to suggest that he came from the Scottish site of Dumbarton Rock in western Scotland. This was the capital of the British kingdom of Strathclyde, and was reputedly governed by a chieftain named Coroticus. Dumbarton Rock is a significant location, since it was here that Welsh Britons had set up an independent kingdom and powerbase along the Clyde. That the settlers here in western Scotland spoke a form of Welsh attests to the fluidity of identity in the early medieval period, and it was probably at Dumbarton Rock that the famous Welsh poem, *The Gododdin*, was written down. There is a church dedicated to St Patrick on the Rock.

Other suggestions for where Patrick originated include areas of Christian settlement along Hadrian's Wall. The site of Birdoswald has been suggested, since Patrick gives the name of his birthplace as 'Banna Venta Berniae'. As this site was also known as Banna, the name could be reconstructed as 'bend in the tribal pass'. This is conjecture, and all that is known for certain is that Patrick was of Romano-British stock, referring to himself as 'civites', a citizen of the Empire, despite the fact that he was writing some hundred or so years after Roman ties with Britain had been cut.

This was a time when the financial and political security felt by those previously connected to Rome was eradicated. Villas were starting to crumble, aqueducts were falling into disrepair, skills like glass- and wine-making were slipping away, and previously impressive cities were being abandoned to the elements. A way of life was dying; this was a volatile time, with a power vacuum waiting to be filled. Saint Patrick inhabited a world where legendary figures like King Arthur were the vestigial wielders of influence, and a time of relatively civilised security was replaced by uncertainty. The collapse of the dictatorial control of the Roman Empire left the native British people struggling to regroup.

Patrick tells us how these changes affected his life in two letters that have fortunately survived down the millennium and a half since he wrote them. In this respect, Patrick becomes the first British saint with a voice, since he straddles the divide between prehistory and history by writing down his own accounts.[11] Unlike other writers of his time, his work is not purely focused on issues of Christian doctrine; his letters are extremely personal, and provide details of his life and times. They are very readable, even for a modern audience, and their accessible nature has made him feel more tangible than many of his contemporary saints. This could explain his great popularity as patron saint of Ireland, in that we can still get a sense of how he lived, what he valued and the feelings he experienced.

Patrick and Slavery

Patrick's *Declaration* in particular provides nuggets of information about his life that become increasingly useful when considered alongside other evidence from late Roman Britain. For example, it states that his father was a deacon, and his grandfather a priest, so he was brought up in a Christian environment. His family were landowning aristocracy, who farmed the surrounding area and owed loyalty to the Roman system under which they had profited.[12] As a young boy Patrick would have been educated, and taught to read and write in Latin. He would have lived a relatively privileged life, with his needs taken care of by slaves and his land farmed by serfs.

However, by the fourth century most of the Romano-British population appears to have been only minimally Romanised. The majority still lived in Iron Age-style houses and used perfectly effective pre-Roman farming techniques – like Ninian and his community in Whithorn. Patrick and his family probably owned a similar sort of a rural farm-holding, and they almost certainly spoke Celtic dialects alongside Latin. Yet Patrick's aristocratic family were just as much Roman-Britons as were the few per cent that lived in villas or towns, and from early in the third century they were all legally Roman citizens. They didn't live in the highly ordered grid system of a city like Verulamium; instead, they were masters of a farming community – a form of landed gentry. But disaster struck his household when Irish pirates ransacked his property and took the young Patrick into slavery just shy of his sixteenth birthday.

There were good reasons for the Irish to invade wealthy and industrially advanced areas of Britain after the decline of the Roman military defences in the early fifth century. Not only were there good supplies of slaves, which could be sold on for profit, but also there were natural resources and new industrial advances that the raiders could benefit from. It is very likely that, when the Irish raiders attacked the farms where Patrick was seized, they would have witnessed ploughing techniques and soil cultivation with iron spades and tools, which would have been valuable on their own lands. Indeed, they probably seized ploughmen and their tools, along with other commodities from the Roman farms, such as the young noble boy Patrick.[13] It seems no accident that the young Patrick was put to work in agriculture, given responsibility for herding sheep and ensuring a good return on their wool.

Gildas, possibly writing in Gloucestershire, or elsewhere along the Welsh borders, recorded the predatory nature of the fifth- and sixth-century Irish raiders, describing them as insects emerging into the sun:

> *From curroughs in which they had been carried across the valley of the sea, there eagerly emerged foul crowds of Scotti [Irish] and Picts, like dark hoards of maggots from the narrowest cracks of recesses when the sun is overhead and its rays grow warm.*[14]

The slave trade was an active and real threat across Roman Britain in the fifth century. But, while Patrick understood the hardships of slavery from the inside and condemned the murder of Christian slaves, he did not stand against it. To him, slavery was an essential component of life, and something that he had perceived from both sides: as slave and patron. He didn't want to change the status quo, since the concept of a world without slavery would have been entirely foreign to him. He rallied against the mistreatment of slaves, but he was also a man of his time and did not want to radically reshape attitudes towards slavery.

In his other famous letter, Patrick criticises Christian soldiers under Coroticus's command, as they had stolen some of his converts and sold them to the Picts as slaves. The appeal to Coroticus to return his slaves has a personal element to it, since Patrick himself had suffered a similar fate at the hands of Celtic raiders. He spent six years in Ireland, no doubt suffering deeply, both from physically punishing work and the social frustration at having gone from being a wealthy Romano-Briton to an abused commodity. In his letter he uses the power he later acquired by rising through the Church to find justice for those who suffered a similar fate to him.

It was while working as a shepherd slave in Ireland that Patrick discovered a burning passion for Christianity, and in his own letter he describes in the most vivid terms the motivation for entering into life as a missionary:

> When I had arrived in Ireland and was looking after flocks the whole time, I prayed frequently each day. And more and more, the love of God and the fear of him grew in me, and my faith was increased and my spirit enlivened. So much so that I prayed up to a hundred times in the day and almost as often at night. I even remained in the wood and on the mountain to pray. And – come hail, rain or snow – I was up before dawn to pray ... I now understand this, that the Spirit was fervent in me.[15]

After turning twenty-one, and having lived his early adult years as a slave in Ireland, Patrick says in his *Declaration* that he escaped and returned to Britain. This was an unusual event, as few slaves would be successful in such an enterprise, while fewer still would gain safe passage across the sea back to their homeland. Patrick writes with passion about the hunger he experienced, and the arduous journey of hundreds of miles he undertook to get back to his family. He would have travelled over sea in a *curach*, bashed by the oceanic waves and fearing for his life. He would have then travelled on foot along lawless, dangerous and neglected tracks, constantly using basic navigation techniques to wend his way back to his childhood home. This journey shows the willpower and strength of character the young Patrick must have possessed.

Having been welcomed back with great surprise and adulation by his family, Patrick was, remarkably, unable to settle back into his home. Perhaps the pirate raids had changed the complexion of his property, and he may have lost members of his family and friends through the six intervening years. Whatever his reasons, Patrick was soon restless to pursue his new-found religious fervour and follow his father and grandfather's example by training as a priest. He then made the staggering decision to leave his home and return to Ireland as a missionary. That he was prepared to go back along this long and difficult journey is a sign of the extreme approach to his missionary work. Rather than a life of comfort with those who loved him, he chose hardship, ridicule and numerous brushes with death.

Patrick: Missionary and Outcast

In true missionary spirit, Patrick seemed unable to resist returning to convert the people who had held him as a slave. This may seem like a foolish decision, but it chimes with the missionary zeal that was to grow up in Ireland particularly, whereby pagans should be appealed to, even if they were terrifying and hostile, because otherwise their souls were condemned to hell. Patrick himself wrote, 'the one and only purpose I had in going back to that people from whom I had earlier escaped was the Gospels and the promises of God.'[16]

It is important to remember that the mind of Patrick was very different from those of modern-day Christians, in that he saw the end of days as being on the horizon. His world was one full of the threat of real demons and an apocalypse that would see humanity divided between the damned and saved for all eternity. He wanted to save people by converting them to Christianity while he had the chance. This is something that is hard to grasp from our modern perspective, but this was a true evangelical missionary fervour that burnt inside him, and in many of the other missionary saints of the early medieval period.

Patrick re-entered a hostile and unpredictable nation. Ireland in the early Christian period was made up of at least 120 chiefdoms, usually described as petty kingdoms, typically having about 700 warriors each. Patrick was faced with the challenge of both travelling safely between these kingdoms and calling people together. The bell that Patrick may have used as he wandered across the countryside in search of potential converts is venerated in a much later bell-shrine.[17] The interior bell may not be contemporary with Patrick, as it has been dated to the eighth to ninth centuries, while the exterior reliquary is eleventh century. Nevertheless, it has been celebrated as one of Ireland's most significant relics for over a millennium. The grandeur of the casing and its distinctly Viking style testify to the fact that it was treated with respect even by later, very different, settlers of Ireland. There are about a dozen surviving Celtic bell-shrines, which suggests that this sort of contact relic (rather than corporeal relics including parts of a saint's body) were highly prized within the Irish Church. The bell, crozier and book are symbolic of the Celtic saint's struggle through the wilderness to bring the word of God to those seeking salvation.

Patrick did not choose an easy path for himself. He was certainly rebuked, with hostility, by the native Irish Celts, and he endured criticism from other churchmen. The *Declaration* is actually written in defence of claims made against him by fellow Christians and Irish rulers. He opens the letter: 'I am Patrick – a sinner – the most unsophisticated and unworthy among all the faithful of God. Indeed, to many I am the most despised.' The accusations made against Patrick include fraud, for he states that he will return the money that wealthy women have given him and accept no payment for performing rites like baptism. It certainly casts him in a different light, but the accusation of manipulating women to commandeer their wealth for the Church is one that had been levelled against other churchmen, including St Jerome.

From the very earliest days of the Church, women were appealed to for financial support. In the Roman world wealthy women could conduct business transactions and lend money. Many of the earliest house churches, like that of Santa Pudenziana in Rome, take their names from the women who bequeathed the buildings to the Church. Individuals like Pudenziana and her sister Prassede were the benefactors of these earlier *Tituli*, which later grew into larger basilical churches. In the early centuries of Christianity, house churches were modest buildings containing a place for baptism, education and receiving the Eucharist. Widows in particular could inherit property and choose to leave this to the Church after their death.

Appealing to women for funds was not unheard of, but the fact that this is levelled against Patrick in the fifth century tells us two things: firstly, he was in need of funds to boost his missionary work in terms of converting the pagan Irish; and, secondly, that he resorted to any means possible, including sweet-talking Irish noblewomen, to secure much-needed income, protection and support. Patrick was a man alone without a lord in the wilderness, and this was a perilous situation in the early medieval period. He writes that he had to bribe the Irish kings constantly to ensure his safety. Yet he then encouraged the women in their households to become Christians, or even nuns. The removal of noblewomen from the secular sphere into the religious would have angered male rulers, since women were valuable cogs in the political machine. By becoming nuns, wealthy women could not secure bloodlines or expedient marriages. Patrick was wedging himself at the heart of Irish politics, and this would make him few friends.

There is another crime that is alluded to in the letter, which he related to a friend and which ultimately cost him his bishopric earlier in his career. While we don't know what that crime was, it must have been severe to have such repercussions many years after the event. Patrick writes:

> The pretence of that attack against me was that, after thirty years, they found out about a confession I had made in the years even before I was a deacon. At that time, because I was so troubled in my spirit, I revealed to my best friend something I had done one day in my youth – not even a day, but in an hour – because I was not yet then strong in my faith. I was, maybe, fifteen years old and didn't believe in the Living God.[18]

The two sins that most fit this description are idolatry (Patrick had rejected the Christian faith of his parents in his youth) or murder, since both acts could take an hour, yet require a lifetime of penance. These are serious crimes, and they indicate that Patrick was a complex and problematic character. While he was remarkably willing to return to a people who had subjugated and punished him, in order to spread Christianity there, to other churchmen he was a sinner, an uneducated man who had not learnt his Latin or his theology thoroughly, a political game player with no clear protection or overlord, and someone many wished to see punished.

Patrick as Bishop

As far as setting up a successful ecclesiastical system across Ireland was concerned, it must have been clear to Patrick from the start that the Roman method of Church organisation, centred on dioceses and cities, was not going to be effective in Ireland. The Roman Empire had never reached Ireland, and so it had none of its roads, cities and administrative infrastructure. Instead, Ireland was a looser form of society, with petty kings surrounded by the family groups. The fraternal relationship between an abbot and his monks seemed to fit more comfortably within this familiar setting, and so as Christianity gained a footing in Ireland through the sixth century, monasteries became more popular than dioceses and bishops.

The Ireland into which Patrick stepped was not yet fully Christian. In the fifth century some early missionaries had success exposing the Irish rulers to Christian ideas, so we find the elder Patrick (Palladius) and others making good headway in terms of converting prominent members of Celtic tribes. Although boasting little Christian conclaves from the fifth century, the predominant religious group in Ireland at the time that Patrick was preaching was the Druids. Unlike Brigid, who emerged from, and melded with, older Druidic traditions, Patrick seems to have been unpopular with the Druid leaders. Murchiú's seventh-century *Life of St Patrick* records a poem supposedly related by Druids in response to the saint. Although it was probably invented by the later writer, it presents possible insights into how Christian missionaries were perceived by the established religious leaders of pagan Ireland:

> *Across the sea will come Adze-head, crazed in the head, his cloak with hole for the head, his stick bent in the head. He will chant impieties from a table in the front of his house; all his people will answer: 'so be it, so be it.'*[19]

Here the Druids seem to cast Patrick as a mentally unstable foreign eccentric, and his followers recite their basic, sheep-like reaction as a sign that they too are 'crazed in the head'.

Patrick was unpopular with the Druids because he was directly assuming their role within society as religious guides to both the people and the royal houses. He was also upsetting the natural balance within royal households, encouraging women in particular to put aside their responsibility of bearing children and securing marriages, and instead embrace a life of chastity. Murchiú records how tensions between the Druids, the High King of Ireland and Patrick came to a head on Easter, at the symbolic location of Tara.

Long held as a potent site, the Hill of Tara was the powerbase for the high kings of Ireland, and it boasts an extensive Iron Age enclosure and the Stone of Destiny, Lia Fáil, at which the kings were crowned up to AD 500. The legendary semi-divine group the Tuatha Dé Danann, which included the goddess Brigid among its ranks, was said to have brought the stone to Ireland. In a telling account, which may be founded on grains of fact, Murchiú states that on Easter night the king and his Druid leaders were celebrating the Celtic festival of fire on the hill, during which they extinguished their flames and would not light them again until dawn. Patrick and his followers gathered at a nearby hill and lit Easter fires that illuminated the night sky. This was an act punishable by death, so Patrick was doing something extremely provocative. Although the hagiographical text dresses the event up in biblical references and symbolism, this was an act of incitement, designed to get a response from the king. Patrick, like Alban, was a political radical who was not afraid to challenge those in power.

Murchiú's account does stretch the limits of reality. In a dramatic passage, he goes on to relate how the king, Loíguire, was furious and took his nine chariots to meet with Patrick. The Druid leaders instructed the king to remain outside, for then he was less likely to be tricked by the Christian saint's acts. Patrick went out to meet the king and his followers, provocatively singing a Psalm which undermined Loíguire's ceremonial arrival: 'Some put their trust in chariots and some in horses; but we will walk in the name of the Lord our God.'[20] The personality that emerges from Murchiú's *Life* is wilful, militaristic, scheming and inflammatory.

Patrick was forced to defend his actions in a magical contest against the Druid leaders. Enflamed by one of the Druids' words against Christianity, Murchiú writes that Patrick cast a spell which raised the magician up in the air and smashed his skull on a rock. While this is largely fiction, the idea that Patrick's hagiographical text could record him murdering one of the most important advisers to the king, in his royal presence, on such a sacred site and during a sacred festival, seems remarkable.

In the following commotion, Patrick was said to have made darkness fall over the heathens, who were then slaughtered so that only the king, queen and two of his followers survived. The queen then begged for Patrick's mercy and the royal family departed, humiliated and grieving. This story was transmitted as a sign that the forceful Patrick, filled with the power of the Christian God, could defeat any enemy, particularly the pagan Druidic bedrock of pre-Christian Ireland. But it strikes the modern reader as a startling and hard-hitting way to spread a religious message. Patrick appears unforgiving and brutal towards the Druids in this account, despite the fact that he uses many of their magical actions against them. The legend of Patrick banishing snakes from Ireland may, in fact, be referring to the fact that he banished Druids.

Patrick's own letter to the soldiers of Coroticus contains a passage stating that 'No murderer can be with Christ', which casts doubt on the account of him murdering a Druid. Nevertheless, both his own letters and later legends that grew up around him suggest that Patrick was a man with many sides, capable of great and terrible acts. This fact was clearly appreciated by Christian scribes after his death. In the *Book of Armagh*, a ninth-century manuscript held in Trinity College, Dublin, a copy of his *Declaration* survives, but the sections relating to the more questionable acts he performed have been deliberately excluded. It is fortunate that six other copies survive across Ireland, France and England, with which comparison can be made. But the oldest copy now in Dublin indicates that attempts were made to clean up Patrick's image. As with other saints covered by this book, Patrick was neither black nor white, good nor bad, but lived in the real world of politics, power and passion.

The Isle of Man and Wales

Patrick is credited with extending the reach of Christianity far throughout Ireland and the surrounding Isles, and here too later texts record that he employed a rather merciless set of techniques. The conversion of the Isle of Man to Christianity in the fifth century is also thought to be due to his influence. The founding saint of Man, St Maughold, was converted after an encounter with Patrick. The legend states that Maughold was an Irish prince and part of a pirate gang. On meeting Patrick, he attempted to test his sanctity, particularly the suggestion that he could raise people from the dead. Maughold placed a living man in a shroud and asked Patrick to revive him from death. Patrick blessed the body, and when they opened it they saw that the man had died – an interesting insight into the games that a saint could play. In effect, he murdered the man to prove a point!

The legend continues that Maughold was so upset by what he'd done that he appealed to Patrick, who revived the dead man in the manner of a magician, firmly rebuked the pirates and cast Maughold away on a *curach* with no oars, by which he landed on the coast of Man.[21] Both saints come out of this encounter with a tarnished image. Maughold provoked a saint and through his foolish behaviour had one of his friends killed, while Patrick supposedly murdered someone to prove a point and then used magic to revive him.

Maughold is a particularly interesting example of an early saint who struggled to balance his virtues and vices. A later poem describes some of his failings:

> *If his sins we could fish up,*
> *Before he was bishop;*
> *He led his poor wife,*
> *It is said, a sad life,*
> *Would cheat her and beat her,*

And often ill-treat her;
Nay, threaten to kick her,
When he was in liquor,
Though now a saint, yet he
Was once of banditti.[21]

Maughold, like St Patrick who influenced him, is remembered as a complex character subject to human failings. That a saint could leave behind their sins, receive forgiveness and go on to perform good acts, features in a number of the surviving early hagiographical texts regarding conversion in the fifth and sixth centuries.

Saint David, the patron saint of Wales, also emerged from this conflicted time. He was born some time around AD 500 and died around AD 590, which is a long life at any point in history. He was renowned as a teacher, bishop and founder of churches and monasteries, mostly within the confines of Wales. It is interesting that the Celtic fringes chose saints that looked back to their earliest Christian days. David is a good example, since the texts written about him indicate he was not particularly renowned for miracles or asceticism. Instead, he seems to have been a practical leader of the Church, a bishop at the time of the Pelagian heresy.[22] His best-known miracle is said to have taken place when he was preaching against Pelagianism in the middle of a large crowd at the Synod of Brefi: the village of Llanddewi Brefi commemorates the ground where David stood, which reputedly rose up to form a small hill. One writer notes that you can scarcely 'conceive of any miracle more superfluous' in that part of Wales than the creation of a new hill.[23]

He was Bishop (probably not Archbishop) of Menevia, the Roman port in Pembrokeshire, later known as St David's, which was at the time the chief point of departure for Ireland. This is most of what's known with any certainty about the patron saint of Wales. His life was recorded some 500 years after his death, by Rhygyfarch, a son of the then bishop of St David's. Clearly, the hagiographical text is biased, firstly because it gives a partisan account designed to prop up the episcopate of St David's and support its claim of independence from the Archbishop of

Canterbury. Wales wanted devolution from England in the eleventh century too. And secondly, because so many centuries had passed between David's life and his hagiographer's. It would be like writing a biography of Henry VIII now without the benefit of documentary sources.

Saint David gets wrapped up in fascinating but farcical situations by other later authors too, all of whom have their own agendas. In one source, the chronicles of Geoffrey of Monmouth, David is described as King Arthur's uncle, while elsewhere it states that thirty years before his birth, an angel delivered a prophesy of him to St Patrick. Attempts have been made to connect these early British and Celtic saints over the centuries, and while their lives tell differing stories, they do present an image of fifth-century Britain moving gradually and haltingly towards Christianity. From Wales and Cornwall to Scotland and then over to Ireland, Christian missions did continue to spread the Gospel and spread their own influence and authority, occasionally with the backing of the Pope, and otherwise with their own guts and charisma to guide them.

The fifth and sixth centuries were difficult times to be a religious figure, since throughout the British Isles older traditions were being supplanted by Christian ideas, institutions and influential individuals. Patrick, Maughold and David all lived in a pagan Celtic world before they emerged as Christian saints. They had grown up within violent, complicated, conflicted environments, where slavery, barbarism, war and bloodshed were part of life. As they moved into a new ideology and embraced a Christian worldview that would alter society from the ground up, they would inevitably meet with resistance. It is hardly surprising that their legends retain glimpses of this world, and understanding their part as players in it allows us clearer insight into this transitional time.

The early saints of England, Ireland, Wales, Scotland and the Isle of Man are all shrouded in the mists of the darkest parts of medieval history in terms of documentary evidence – the fourth to the sixth centuries. On the basis of what can be distilled from later texts written about them, each saint had a different reason for being recognised as a founding father or patron saint. Patrick faced many struggles, in terms of being taken into slavery and battling opposition on many fronts. Yet his legacy remains in the deeply personal texts he wrote, which reveal a man battling against the odds to take his new religion to the very people who had oppressed him. He comes across as a victim, constantly having to defend himself and make excuses, but he was clearly determined enough to persevere, and if it wasn't he who was the very first to preach Christianity to the Irish, then he is still remembered as the first to have widespread success with his conversion.

The process of converting and preaching is also recorded in the founding legends of Maughold and David. In the case of the Isle of Man, the real hero of the story is Patrick, for he is credited with spreading the Christian message to the island. However, the reformed criminal and outlaw Maughold experienced extreme guilt and undertook penance, so becoming a treasured saint in Man. David is even harder to pin down, especially since Wales was rich in Christians from the fourth century onwards. However, he has been remembered as patron saint due to his role in cleansing Britain of the stain of heresy, and through his apparently orthodox stance. As the next wave of missionary activity emerged in the late sixth century, this time with a papally sanctioned enterprise, the Welsh no doubt needed a rallying figure to present them internationally as virtuous and orthodox Christians that wished to keep in line with Roman practices. David was a good rallying point, and a home-grown bishop at that, so he remains Wales's patron saint.

It has been essential to establish the emergence of sanctity, first in Roman Britain and then in Ireland, before arriving at the Anglo-Saxons. History is not a set of defined periods, sitting distinct from one another, but rather a constant flux, where changes take place gradually and are influenced by many varying factors. To leap straight into a study of Anglo-Saxon saints without first understanding the Roman period in which Christianity set down roots in Britain – and then the Celtic Church, which was to have such a profound effect on English saints – would be to begin the story far too late.

In terms of the next saint, our gaze moves towards England and the Anglo-Saxons. Though pagan in the fifth and sixth centuries, they were converted through the combined efforts of Roman and

Celtic missionaries. The year AD 597 was pivotal. A group of fearful
Roman missionaries was sent across Europe to Kent, while the
Irish saint Columba died, having established a monastery on Iona,
right on the edge of the Anglo-Saxon world. Two very different
types of sanctity emerged, and both were to impact upon the later
Anglo-Saxon saints. However, if Anglo-Saxon Christians could
have chosen a patron saint for themselves, it is clear whom they
would have picked. Like George, he was not a native of England,
but he was celebrated as the saviour of the English and the man
responsible for converting the pagan Anglo-Saxons. He was a
Roman and a pope: Gregory the Great.

Chapter Four
Gregory: A Great Mission

'He therefore again asked, what was the name
of that nation? And was answered, that they
were called Angles. "Right," said he, "for they
have an Angelic face, and it becomes such to be
co-heirs with the Angels in heaven. What is the
name," proceeded he, "of the province from
which they are brought?" It was replied, that
the natives of that province were called Deiri.
"Truly are they De ira," said he, "withdrawn
from wrath, and called to the mercy of Christ.
How is the king of that province called?" They
told him his name was Ælla: and he, alluding
to the name said, "Hallelujah, the praise of God
the Creator must be sung in those parts."'

Bede, *History of the English Church and People.*[1]

This famous anecdote records the moment when Pope Gregory, inspired by the sight of pagan Anglo-Saxon slave boys in the Roman forum, decided to send a mission to convert the nation to Christianity. Clearly a lover of puns, Gregory was motivated to send a group of Continental Christians to the very edges of the known world in order to save these 'Angels/Angles'. During his sixty-four years Gregory 'the Great' certainly earned his epithet. He was seen both by his contemporaries and every generation since as a light in the Dark Ages. A prolific writer, he is renowned as one of the four great Latin Fathers of the Western Church, alongside Augustine, Ambrose and Jerome. The writings of these four men have influenced Christian theology in the Western World more than any others. He reformed the Church liturgy, rebuilt the papacy after years of famine and hardship had all but destroyed Rome, and was the first pope from a monastic background. Even protestant reformers like John Calvin acknowledged his virtues, perceiving him as the last good pope.[2]

But to the English he was particularly significant. In the eyes of the first Anglo-Saxon converts, it was he who brought their souls to salvation – something we might find difficult to grasp today. As far as the early converts were concerned, Gregory was offering the pagan Anglo-Saxons a chance to sign up for the opportunity of a lifetime and beyond. They were guaranteed a place in paradise for all eternity – a pretty exciting prospect! His mission was to have varying degrees of success over the next few decades, but the fact that he sent his fellow monk and evangelist Augustine to the Isle of Thanet in AD 597 would ultimately transform the religious complexion of England.

This one man changed English history, and he was acknowledged a saint immediately after his death, especially among those

Anglo-Saxons filled with evangelical enthusiasm through his efforts. The 'saviour of English souls', he is the first saint covered by this book that we can access with any degree of certainty. We know where he lived, what he thought, what he valued and how he operated. There is one place in England where his efforts were most effectively realised, and it remains at the beating heart of the English Church today: Canterbury.

The cities of England are founded on layers of history, each of which has been replaced by subsequent expressions of taste, transformation and power, leaving many strata of lost worlds under basements and in sewerage systems. In locations where little development has taken place over the centuries, it's often easier to sense the past in a tangible way. But in the bustling cities of London, Southampton, York or Oxford, it can be hard to access the layers of history between the reams of Starbucks coffee shops and high-street stores. However, these places all resound with the footsteps of thousands of long-dead inhabitants, and reward the intrepid explorer. Within the thriving contemporary metropolis of London, for example, Roman ruins and medieval priories sit virtually hidden behind tower blocks, on the edge of busy road junctions. The evidence is still there, but it takes effort to find it.

Canterbury veritably teems with history, from beyond the medieval past right up to the present. There are few locations in England whose story has been told so thoroughly and fascinatingly across the ages. One of the central poems at the heart of English culture, Geoffrey Chaucer's *The Canterbury Tales*, emphasises the importance of this place in drawing people towards it over the centuries. Great dramas have occurred here; most notably the death of the Archbishop Thomas Becket on the sacred ground of the Cathedral. Canterbury is the powerbase of the Archbishop today, and to the many who have come before him, and the city has played a central role in the religious spirit of a nation. But despite its magnificent cathedral and monumental gatehouses, its origins are remarkably humble. The story of the conversion of the Anglo-Saxons to Christianity begins with a small, brick-built church on the edge of the old Canterbury to Richborough road, alongside the modern buildings of the university. Almost hidden from view, the

Church of St Martin is extremely humble in appearance, and at first sight seems an unlikely place for the emergence of Christianity in England.

St Martin's Church may well be designated a World Heritage Site, but unlike Fountains Abbey or Blenheim Palace, it commands little in the way of awe and magnificence. It is a simple church that could barely accommodate a hundred people, which has been rebuilt over the years so it now appears like a patchwork quilt of bricks from different ages. But at the chancel end some interesting features indicate why this church is so important. Small red Roman bricks, held together with pink mortar, have been incorporated into the fabric, revealing that this building has a history stretching back beyond the coming of the Angles, Saxons and Jutes to the Romano-British past.

There is a round-headed doorway in the south wall of the chancel, and a similar arch above the windows in the west wall of the nave, both of which are now blocked up yet hint at the Roman roots of this building. The original bricks in the wall are laid in horizontal lines between bands of stone blocks, so act as 'string courses'. It isn't clear whether the original Roman building was a church, or if it served some other function, perhaps as a mauso-leum. But it was certainly in use as a church by the AD 590s, and this makes it the oldest church in continuous use anywhere in the English-speaking world. Bede records that it served the Frankish princess Bertha, wife of Kent's powerful king, Aethelberht:

> There was on the east side of the city a church dedicated to the honour of St Martin, built whilst the Romans were still in the island, wherein the queen, who, as has been said before, was a Christian, used to pray.[3]

Bertha has been canonised a saint for her part in the conversion of the English. She married King Aethelberht in a politically expedi-ent union, perhaps as early as AD 567 (when her parents were alive), or more probably by about AD 580. A condition of this marriage between a Christian and a pagan was that the Frankish princess was allowed to bring a bishop with her, and to be given a suitable

The Luidhard medalet was found near St Martin's Church in Canterbury around 1844. It is a small coin or medal that has been turned into a necklace through the addition of a gold loop. It has a bust wearing a diadem on one side, and an exotic cross with two arms on the other.

church building in which to hear Mass. The bishop who came with her was called Luidhard, and a fortunate piece of evidence survives to support the claim that he was preaching the Christian faith among the pagan Anglo-Saxons more than a decade before Augustine's mission in AD 597.

The Luidhard medalet, reportedly discovered in the early nineteenth century near the graveyard at St Martin's, is in the form of a coin with a mount attached to enable it to be worn as a pendant. It was found along with seven other items, now known collectively as the Canterbury-St Martin's hoard. The items were probably strung together on the necklace of a sixth-century woman, and among the other coins were an Italian tremissis (equivalent to one third of a solidus), two Frankish tremissis, and a solidus. This was a valuable collection of booty, despite the fact that the Anglo-Saxons were still a barter society in the sixth century, so didn't use the coins as money. But the Luidhard medalet is particularly important, since it is the oldest surviving coin minted in Anglo-Saxon England.[4]

The medalet displays the bust of a man wearing a robe with a diadem on his head. On the other side is a Patriarchal cross, which has two arms, the topmost one representing the inscription that was nailed above Christ, proclaiming him King of the Jews. Both sides display exotic imagery, which would have been largely unfamiliar to pagan Anglo-Saxon metalworkers. It is the inscription, however, that reveals the embryonic nature of this first minted English coin. It is the abbreviated form of 'Leudardus Episcopus', which means 'Bishop Luidhard', and it's believed that the medalet was created to honour the arrival of Bertha and her bishop to Canterbury. However, the words appear on the coin in reverse.

There may be an explanation for this. The Anglo-Saxon goldsmith charged with creating the coin would have been looking at a foreign example from which he could copy the text and images. When creating the mould for the medal he copied the letters over verbatim, but the gold was then poured into the mould to create a reflected version. Because the smith was almost certainly illiterate, he would not have understood his mistake, and so this medal survives to give us a glimpse of Anglo-Saxon England on the edge of the literate Christian world. This was a world poised between pagan and Christian, and the driving force towards change was Gregory.

Gregory and His Mission

The quote at the beginning of this chapter comes from Bede's account of the moment Gregory felt motivated to send a Christian mission to the pagan Anglo-Saxons. That this event ever actually happened is dubious. Gregory was not ignorant of the Anglo-Saxons, and would certainly have already known of the pagan race inhabiting a previous domain of the Roman Empire: Britannia. But he would also have known that this non-Christian outpost on the edge of the world was ripe for conversion. The arrival of Bertha and her Frankish bishop Luidhard in Canterbury a decade or two earlier would not have gone unnoticed by the papacy.

The profiles of the Anglo-Saxon kingdoms were rising on the Christian continent, and their rulers were increasingly putting feelers out towards the Christian world.[5] They were compelled, as later the Vikings would be, to draw themselves closer to the networks of trade, power and political allegiances this world offered. But in addition to these links being forged between increasingly powerful Anglo-Saxon kings and Christians in Europe, Gregory would also have been aware that the pagan Germanic tribes were coming under the influence of Christianity from a different direction to Rome. On the coast of Dál Riata, from his powerbase on the island of Iona, a fervent missionary was beginning to influence the royal houses of Anglo-Saxon England.

Saint Columba and his Celtic form of Christianity posed a threat to the Pope. If the pagans were to be converted, they were to be converted to the Roman way. Pope Gregory envisaged a Roman Empire reunited as a Christian Roman Empire, with the founding fathers Romulus and Remus replaced by saints Peter and Paul. The timings were essential, for if his mission did not succeed then the island could become a heretical outpost, disconnected from Rome. Gregory was sending a missionary army to conduct an ideological conquest as significant as the coming of the Romans or the Normans.

Although not an Anglo-Saxon saint, Pope Gregory the Great had a hugely important role to play in transforming the religious and social complexion of England, and establishing the nature of sanctity throughout the nation from the sixth century onwards. He certainly deserves his epithet of 'Great', given the situation he inherited when he became pope in AD 590. Rome was in the most dire state. Despite its ancient heritage and the idea of imperial power it still exercised in the minds of rulers across Europe and beyond, the city itself had been stripped of most of its influence and population by the end of the sixth century. The imperial court had moved to Constantinople on Constantine's instructions, and the majority of the ruling families in Rome were drawn there. The influence of Gothic occupiers in Italy following the migration period, and the sack of Rome by the Visigoths in AD 410, and later by Ostrogoths in AD 546, meant that there was little wealth left in the city.

The neglect of the aqueduct system and the deliberate cutting of water supplies by the Goths had led to flooding in the areas outside the city, creating an infested swamp. The population had dropped from 800,000 in AD 400 to just 30,000 by AD 550, and the Pope at this time was impoverished, having to beg for clothing.[6] It is no wonder that Gregory did not want the position of pope. However, his aristocratic family were one of the few that had remained in service of Church and city. His great-grandfather was Pope Felix III, so there was an expectation that he would go into the Church. Gregory had intended a life of monastic seclusion, although his early adulthood was spent as Prefect, one of the highest secular positions in the city.

A number of his family had gone into the monastic life, and it seems Gregory grew tired of politics around AD 575, so he turned his family holdings between the Palatine and Caelian Hills into a monastery and retired there. In the next five years he lived an extreme life of prayer, fasting and meditating, writing his famous work *Dialogues*, which in particular stressed the virtues of the recently deceased St Benedict of Nursia, author of the Benedictine

Rule. The monastic ideals set out in this document were to have wide-reaching effects across the Christian world, and particularly in Anglo-Saxon England.

Gregory was a brilliant mind at a time when the Church most needed one, and so he could not simply retreat into monastic seclusion, but was instead ordained as deacon against his wishes. He was relocated to Constantinople, where his conservative streak shone through; he recreated his own monastery of St Andrew's in Rome at the Roman embassy in Constantinople. Despite spending seven years in the East, he refused to learn Greek, and firmly identified himself as Roman. It was the dramatic events of AD 589 that saw Gregory finally elevated to pope. The Tiber flooded, dragging infested water through the churches of Rome and destroying their winter supplies. Plague followed, and carried off Pope Pelagius, so Gregory was elected by the people to lead them through the most dismal of times. Far from the glorious, bejewelled, all-powerful figures that later generations of popes would cut, Gregory was head of a beleaguered, small church in a rotten and run-down city, with little in the way of wealth and power.

He needed an action plan, something that would set the Eternal City of Rome back on a firm footing and bring much-needed income and prestige back to the papacy. He was a pragmatist and a realist, and he relished order in the Roman manner. He was also hard-headed and brutal at times. A monk from his monastery confessed on his deathbed to stealing some coins, so Gregory ordered for him to die alone and then be thrown on the rubbish pile.[7] It seems he did this to ensure that the monk's ignominious death acted as penance for his sins, but it looks like a particularly harsh treatment of a fellow monk and brother.

Early on in his papacy he sought a solution to Rome's current predicament – to return the city to the great heights of its imperial past. Against the ever-burgeoning power of the Eastern Church, he now wanted to recreate the Western Roman Empire, but instead it would be a Holy Roman Empire. All roads would once again lead to Rome, and this would be achieved not by a marching army of soldiers, but with a marching army of missionaries.[8]

Gregory and Augustine

When Gregory set his mind to the Anglo-Saxon mission, he had to find a willing and pliable individual to take the long, dangerous and arduous journey across Europe to the point where the known world ended. Within Rome, Tacitus' accounts of Germanic warriors, their bodies painted black so they could stealthily destroy their enemies, would have filled any potential missionary with dread. Traversing Italy, the Alps, Gaul and then crossing the Channel towards the unknown threat of a pagan warrior king would have been an unpleasant prospect for many settled within the relative comfort of a Roman monastery. Add to that the promise of a northern climate, cold, dank and uninviting to a Mediterranean Christian, and the idea of Gregory's mission must not have seemed attractive. The lucky man chosen to head this most unpleasant of missions was a Sicilian monk: Augustine.

He is celebrated across England in the dedications of churches, schools and parish halls. His is one of the names most closely associated with English Christianity, and if students learn any dates from the early medieval period, one of the first they encounter is AD 597 – the date Augustine arrived on the Isle of Thanet to bring Roman Christianity to the Anglo-Saxons. Fortunately, alongside many later hagiographical texts and fanciful legends that grew up around his name, there is also a good deal of primary evidence to reveal information about the man himself, and both the time and place in which he preached to the English. He was already a right-hand man to the Pope, as prior of the monastery of St Andrew on the Caelian Hill, where Gregory himself was abbot. With Augustine at the head of a band of monks, sent by their Pope and abbot, this was an evangelical mission with its heart rooted in monastic ideals.

Augustine seems to have dragged his heels from the off. But Gregory coordinated his highly disciplined Roman monks and they embarked, relatively unprepared, for England. It took two years for Augustine and his missionaries to finally reach Kent. This is an inexplicably long time to traverse from Rome to England, and from Bede's records of the mission it is clear that Augustine turned back along the way. He states that they were:

on their journey, seized with a sudden fear, and began to think of returning home, rather than proceed to a barbarous, fierce, and unbelieving nation, to whose very language they were strangers; and this they unanimously agreed was the safest course. In short, they went back.[9]

Dogged in his determination to continue with the mission, Gregory made Augustine return to the monks, and exhorted them all to continue to England. The Pope sent letters with him addressed to bishops and the royal houses of Frankish Gaul, requesting support for the missionaries. The Franks finally seemed to answer the call, and provided safe haven and interpreters to see the missionaries on their way. Augustine was made abbot of the group, and had the promise of an archbishopric dangled before him, something many early churchmen would have embraced gratefully. But he was clearly worried by the work he was undertaking. The consolation Gregory provides has a distinctly condescending tone, as he encouraged the monks: 'Inasmuch as, though I cannot labour with you, I shall partake in the joy of the reward, because I am willing to labour.'[10]

Augustine's journey to England tells us much about the man. He was clearly inexperienced and anxious with regards to conducting papal business along the route through Frankish territories. So Gregory sent him equipped with documents that would assure those throughout Gaul that he was acting on behalf of the papacy. His correspondence with the Pope, fortunately preserved in the archives of early medieval Canterbury and, more fortunately still, consulted and documented by Bede, shows that he was also insecure in imparting the wisdom of the Church to those in need of papal guidance. He constantly deferred to the Pope, whose strong guiding hand is clear in the tone of his letters. This was Gregory's mission, and Augustine was his mouthpiece.

Augustine landed with his missionaries on the Isle of Thanet, and then set about persuading the king to allow him to spread his Christian mission throughout the kingdom of Kent. The fact that he came with Frankish interpreters, and with the support of bishops and royalty from the queen's family in Gaul, may have helped ease his passage into the Kentish kingdom.[11] At first Aethelberht was suspicious of Augustine, instructing him to meet with his representatives in the open air so he could not perform any magic tricks. The Roman missionaries must have seemed distinctly exotic and unusual to the Anglo-Saxons, and the objects they brought with them were similarly strange. They brought the symbol of the cross, whose meaning was shrouded in mystery to the majority of pagan Anglo-Saxons. They brought relics, which were also bound up with ideas of magic and miracles, and they brought books – small, box-like objects, filled with indecipherable symbols, which promised eternal life. The idea that Augustine needed a stone church in which to perform his sacred rituals must also have been unusual to the Anglo-Saxons, whose dwellings, palaces and temples were constructed in wood.

Aethelberht gave them access to the ancient city of Canterbury. The name of the city comes from the Old English 'Cantwareburh', or 'stronghold of the Kentish people', but the Jutish timber buildings were established on the ruined remains of an older settlement, which the British called Durouernon and the Romans renamed Durovernum Cantiacorum. When settlers from the Danish region of Jutland came across the North Sea and arrived on the coast of Kent, at first they avoided moving within the walls of the older Roman town. It is an interesting phenomenon that the timber-dwelling Anglo-Saxons avoided the older stone buildings of the Romans. It would have been expedient to move inside the defensive areas designated by Roman walls, and the stones could have been used to provide decent protection from the elements. Yet across England, Anglo-Saxon villages grew up away from earlier Romano-British settlements.

An Old English poem, written down in the eleventh century but probably composed centuries earlier, hints at why the Anglo-Saxons may have avoided old Roman ruins:

Wondrous is this stone-wall, wrecked by fate
the city-buildings crumble; the works of the giants decay.
Roofs have caved in, towers collapsed,
barred gates are broken, hoar frost clings to mortar,

houses are gapping, tottering and fallen,
undermined by age. The earth's embrace,
its fierce grip, holds the mighty craftsmen;
they are perished and gone. A hundred generations
have passed away since.

'The Ruin', from *The Exeter Book*, lines 1–10.[12]

This poem describes the Roman ruins as 'the labour of giants', and suggests that the Angles, Saxons and Jutes felt the stone structures they encountered in Romano-British cities were somehow supernatural. The settlers had come from Scandinavian and Germanic territories that the Romans had not conquered, and where traditional methods of building revolved around wood, not stone. But this poem, and the evidence from Canterbury, suggests that the memory of Rome was never fully erased. There was a presence of both the Roman Empire and the Christianity it had brought in its wake throughout the land. Augustine had this firmly in mind as he met with the native British Christians, and he expanded the Church of St Martin alongside the ancient Roman walls.

Anglo-Saxon England at the Time of Conversion

To understand what Augustine encountered when he began his missionary work with the Anglo-Saxons, it is essential to understand more about the unique situation England was in by the sixth century. No longer a story of the Romano-British or Celts, the Anglo-Saxons take centre stage, and theirs is a world at first entirely lacking in Christian saints. Yet, as the lives of Alban, Brigid, Patrick and David suggest, there was clearly a historical echo of Christianity throughout the British Isles that stretched back to the third century. After the Romans withdrew their armies from Britannia, their most northern frontier, to defend territories closer to the core of the Empire from barbarian attacks, the complexion of Britain changed permanently. The native British tribes, descended from Celtic settlers of the Iron Age, moved their strongholds to the western edges of the British Isles, while what we know as England today was populated by incoming Germanic tribes: the Angles, Saxons and Jutes.

England in the late sixth century, when Gregory sent over his mission, had undergone radical changes with the arrival of a new and influential ruling elite. As the conquest by the Normans brought with it the use of French by the upper classes, so the *Adventus Saxonum* ushered in the new language – Old English. This meant a dramatic change from the Celtic tongues that had previously been spoken in this area. The people in England literally began to speak a different language, and this was the one that would be preserved down the centuries, rather than the native mother tongue that had been established for over a thousand years. Not only were the Romano-British and Anglo-Saxons linguistically separate, they had different social structures, artistic tastes and religious beliefs too.

Their religion also revolved around a pantheon of gods and goddesses, and prized sacred sites on the landscape, like rivers, woods and hills. However, their culture was founded on heroic values, and their divinities often displayed military attributes. Indeed, the ultimate goal for a Germanic warrior was to be received into Valhalla after death, where he could feast and fight for eternity. The primary god of the pantheon was Odinn, known as Woden in England. There may have been substantial differences between Scandinavian and English interpretations of the god, but in the Old Norse myths he embodies a number of powerful characteristics, primarily associated with battle, poetry and wisdom. In England he is also cited as a founding father, or high king, by a number of the ruling dynasties.[13] He is portrayed on the early seventh-century Finglesham buckle, found in Kent. The naked figure has been identified as Woden, due to the two spears he holds, and the hook-beaked birds on his head, which may be an abbreviated version of his two ravens, Huginn and Muninn. The figure's head is teardrop shaped, to perhaps suggest Woden's ability to metamorphose.

The pre-Christian Germanic religious belief system is hard to access, particularly since the spiritual beliefs were not committed to writing. Although they were proto-literate in relation to the

Christian Roman-Britons, they did have a written script – runes – that was used from about the first century AD. The three main runic alphabets were the Elder Futhark (around AD 150–800), the Anglo-Saxon futhorc (AD 400–1100) and the Younger Futhark (AD 800–1100). The angular form of the symbols is due to the fact that they were designed to be carved into stone or wood. The name 'rune' comes from the Germanic word 'rūn', which means 'secret/whisper', and the symbols served a different function to the Latin alphabet.

The component letters in the Latin script have to be combined unit by unit to create words. So the letters 'T', 'A' and 'R' are composed in specific orders to give words with different meanings in each case: 'A-R-T', 'T-A-R', 'R-A-T'. In the runic alphabet the specific units can be used in the same way, so certain symbols can be combined to spell out words. However, each symbol also has a word connected to it, and beneath this are further layers of meaning. So they can stand as letters, as words or as cyphers to another set of associated ideas. An Old English rune poem survives which gives the meaning of each letter and some of the sayings connected with them. For example, the rune ᛈ means Oak:

The oak fattens the flesh of pigs for the children of men.
Often it traverses the gannet's bath,
and the ocean proves whether the oak keeps faith
in honourable fashion.[14]

This poem delves into the separate associations that the oak tree could carry: it provides nourishment; it is the main component for building ships, which in turn protects mankind against the hostile ocean. There is not a single set of associations, but a web of connected ideas. This propensity for riddling is something that seems to define the early medieval Germanic people, and visual riddles can be discerned in artefacts that survive from this time.[15] One of the finest riddling pieces comes from a collection which dates to within a couple of decades of Gregory's mission, and was discovered just a few hours' sailing up the coast from the Isle of Thanet,[16] in East Anglia: the great gold buckle from the Sutton Hoo ship burial.

The great gold buckle from Sutton Hoo is one of the finest finds from the burial. It is actually a hollow box, which opens on a hinge, and the mechanism is still in perfect condition despite being buried in the earth for around 1,400 years. It weighs 400 grams and the surface decoration is picked out with niello – a mixture of copper, silver and lead which allows the outline of the decoration to be picked out in black.

Writhing across the surface of this gold buckle are thirteen separate birds and beasts. There are serpents interlacing on the tongue, in the main boss and across the centre. Two hook-beaked birds sit on the shoulders of the buckle, while five quadrupeds circle around the sides. This object encapsulates many features of Anglo-Saxon art: it is not figurative, but zoomorphic, with animals forming the main component of the decoration. It plays on surface texture and chiaroscuro, the contrast between light and dark. It is symmetrical and centres on perfectly balanced, intricate interlacing patterns.

This is art that requires a keen eye and an understanding of visual play in order to unpick it. Furthermore, it is art that revels in the animal world, rather than the human, and senses order in chaos. This object and others like it reflect the tastes, interests and, possibly, personalities of those who commissioned and wore them. Gregory and his missionaries – Christians born and raised in bustling European cities, exposed to an entirely different aesthetic and world view – would have to adjust to the uniqueness of Anglo-Saxon society and culture.

The finds that continue to appear from this period rarely depart from the basic tastes outlined above. When the Staffordshire hoard was discovered in 2009 by detectorist Terry Herbert, some 3,500 separate pieces were found.[17] They are all military in character, and while the weapons themselves (swords, shields, helmets, chain mail etc.) are not included, the personalised fittings have been hacked off and collected together, perhaps as a physical manifestation of a particularly successful war band's victories. The discovery was heralded with trepidation by some scholars, in that it could have rewritten what was known about Anglo-Saxon artistic taste. However, the designs used across the many thousand pieces were remarkably conservative.

The artefacts feature zoomorphic interlace, and there is a predilection for gold and garnet cloisonné throughout. This discovery testifies to a shared aesthetic that stretched across centuries, and was bound up with the very identity of the Anglo-Saxons. Given that neither the gold nor garnet that Anglo-Saxons favoured were found in sufficient quantities in England, these materials must have been imported from as far afield as Sri Lanka.[18] This suggests a symbolic connection perhaps with the style of objects that had evolved nearer the original homelands of the Germanic people many centuries earlier. By making and wearing this sort of jewellery, the Anglo-Saxons were harking back to a bygone age, in a way that Scottish kilts do today. These tastes continue throughout the finds from Sutton Hoo, and the fact that they were expressed with such exuberance in this East Anglian burial suggests that the mission of Gregory would make the pagan Anglo-Saxons of this region even more entrenched. It can be seen as a reaction against the alien, exotic and unsettling group of Romans that had worked their way into Kent.

The Sutton Hoo ship burial is one of the greatest single collections of treasure found in this country. It is like an English version of Tutankhamen's Tomb, complete with all the items that one of the most high-status individuals in the country required for an active and real existence in the afterlife. The way in which the ship was found is almost as dramatic as the objects themselves. It was discovered among a set of burial mounds in East Anglia on the eve of the Second World War by the remarkably insightful local archaeologist Basil Brown, on the instructions of the prosaically named landowner Mrs Edith Pretty. Alluring tales of ghosts wandering into the mound and divination rods detecting activity at the exact location of the burial have surrounded the dig with further allure, but the hoard speaks for itself in terms of its beauty and significance.

The burial can be dated to between AD 610 and AD 635 due to the collection of gold Frankish coins placed together within a purse.[19] This means that it was deposited shortly after Gregory the Great's mission to Kent, along the opposite coast, near Woodbridge in East Anglia. The person memorialised in the burial would have lived through the arrival of the missionaries from Rome, and as a member of the Anglo-Saxon elite, would have had to respond to the changes this new relationship with the Christian Continent ushered in.

While the pouch containing the coins, which was presumably make from leather, has deteriorated, the lid with its complex patterns and images of conflict between humans, birds and beasts has survived. Although the coins from Sutton Hoo can't be narrowed down to a specific year, they were minted within a relatively limited time period. The other fascinating thing about these coins is that they form a very clear collection. Each coin has been selected from a different mint across Frankish Gaul.

Even with the resources we have today, numismatists can find it difficult to track down a specific coin and complete a collection. But for such a definite selection process to have been introduced to this set of coins in the early seventh century indicates that this was not simply gold bullion, but rather a carefully contrived and symbolically loaded diplomatic gift.

Further still, the fact that the coins have been rounded up to the number 42 through the inclusion of three blanks and two ingots suggests that there may be an association here with the payment made for passage to the afterlife. The payment of Charon's Obul, a coin placed within a burial to pay the ferryman to take the deceased across the river from the land of the living to the land of the dead, was a practice going back to ancient Rome and Greece.[20] The Sutton Hoo purse could be a particularly elaborate form of Charon's Obul, with forty coins to pay the ferrymen, and two ingots to pay the steersmen. So the collection has significance symbolically, but it also indicates that the individual interred in the ship burial had strong political links with Christian Frankish Gaul. The Anglo-Saxons were putting feelers out to the Continent, and Gregory the Great wanted to ensure that their exposure to Christian ideas and the hierarchical organisation of the Church was as orthodox as possible.

The argument over who is buried at Sutton Hoo will never fully abate, but scholars are being more assertive in the connections they draw between the ship burial and the King of East Anglia who died around AD 625, Raedwald. The argument that it's Raedwald who is buried at Sutton Hoo is borne out by examining the wide range of objects interred, as well as the form of the burial itself. Ship burial is attested to among the royal burial grounds of the Scandinavian kings, for example at Vendel in Sweden. Connected to East Anglia across the sea, and possibly through ancestry, the Swedish links with Sutton Hoo are strong. The shield and helmet both seem to have been Swedish-made heirlooms that were like regalia in terms of their significance within the burial goods. In later genealogies, Raedwald's dynasty links back to the Wuffingas of Sweden, so the presence of such items within the goods, as well as the form of burial inside a 27-metre long ship, suggests that the individual and his family were declaring affiliation with pagan royal families across the North Sea.

Other items buried with the deceased, however, indicate wide-reaching connections across Europe and with Christians. Three hanging bowls were placed within the central burial chamber. These elusive objects are often found in Anglo-Saxon graves, although their exact use remains difficult to discern. In terms of their decoration, they display features most commonly found in Irish metalwork. The largest example from Sutton Hoo has a small three-dimensional bronze fish that would have sat in the centre. The fish was on a loose socket and would move about if water were poured in. For it to be visible it is most likely that a clear fluid was held in the bowl. The most persuasive explanation is that sacred water, perhaps from a spiritual well or river, could be kept in these for ritual purposes. Their presence in the Sutton Hoo ship burial testifies to contacts between the pagan Germanic Anglo-Saxons and the Christian Irish.

Among the objects discovered at Sutton Hoo, a few in particular testify to the arrival of Gregory the Great and his mission from the Christian Continent. The burial contained a range of bowls, including a bronze Coptic bowl, the largest surviving silver Byzantine dish in the Western world and a stack of ten silver bowls.[21] The style and decoration of all these items is very different to the rest of the objects in the ship burial. Bronze and silver rather than gold and garnet, they feature life-like animals such as hares and bears, floriated designs, a female bust and cross-shaped motifs.

Nestled beneath the stack of silver cruciform bowls, and placed one upon the other, are perhaps the most suggestive pieces in the burial – two silver spoons. Their arms are inscribed in Greek with the words 'Saulos' and 'Paulos'. These names connect the spoons with the accounts from Acts of the Apostles of St Paul's conversion on the road to Damascus [Acts 9:1–19]. After the Roman soldier Saul saw a divine revelation and chose to embrace Christianity, he changed his name to Paul. This suggests that the spoons may have been baptismal gifts, for a convert who has accepted Christianity.

This implies a further connection between the individual commemorated at Sutton Hoo and the East Anglian king, Raedwald. Bede records the importance of this ruler within the national politics of Anglo-Saxon England in the sixth and early seventh centuries. He was bound to the King of Kent, Aethelberht (husband of Bertha and recipient of the Gregorian mission), through a complicated system of overlordship. The term 'bretwalda' was employed to refer to one king of the Anglo-Saxon kingdoms who possessed greater power and influence than the others. This is a slippery term, but the bretwaldship could shift from one kingdom and ruler to another. Great things were at stake for the pagan king of East Anglia, and during his life he found himself abutted by the Kentish kingdom, complete with its Christian princess, Frankish bishop and Continental affiliations. At one point, it seems, Raedwald had to appeal for protection to Kent, and the condition by which he secured support was his acceptance of Christianity, with Aethelberht most probably his baptismal sponsor:[22]

> *Raedwald had long before been admitted to the sacrament of the Christian faith in Kent, but in vain; for on his return home, he was seduced by his wife and certain perverse teachers, and turned back from the sincerity of the faith; and thus his latter state was worse than the former; so that, like the ancient Samaritans, he seemed at the same time to serve Christ and the gods whom he had served before; and in the same temple he had an altar to sacrifice to Christ, and another small one to offer victims to devils.*

Bede, *Ecclesiastical History of the English People.*[23]

This description fits almost too comfortably with the finds from Sutton Hoo. Here was deposited all a pagan warrior king would need for his journey to Valhalla, including food, clothing, weapons and his regalia, complete with gold and garnet fittings. His Swedish helm and shield, along with enigmatic items such as fittings for a possible wand, a ceremonial whetstone and a standard, chime with an impression of the deceased as the most influential of Anglo-Saxon pagan rulers. His interment in a massive ship beneath a burial mound that would rise up against the East Anglian coast was a permanent reminder to all who sailed into the kingdom of its powerful heirs – an extreme expression of a pagan ruler's potency at a moment when their world was potentially poised on the brink of collapse.

What Bede's quote and the other finds from the burial emphasise is that the Christian world – its power and its politics – was at the door of this Anglo-Saxon pagan overlord. The hanging bowls indicate that the British-Christian world was never fully redundant within Anglo-Saxon England and should not be underestimated, while the baptismal spoons, silver bowls and Frankish coins suggest that the deceased was connected economically, politically and possibly (in a nominal way) religiously with the Christian Continent. The Sutton Hoo ship burial presents a view of the Anglo-Saxon world at a moment of great change. This change would be accelerated through the powerful personality of Pope Gregory and his charge, St Augustine, who decided in 597 that it was time to convert the pagans on the edge of the known world.

Consolodating the Mission

Augustine and his missionaries faced a tough job in converting the pagan Anglo-Saxons. The exuberant expression of individuality, power and tribal pride expressed in the Sutton Hoo ship burial was just one response to the threat of change posed by these unusual men dressed in monastic habits, wielding books and crosses. Once Augustine had secured the support of King Aethelberht, and was given safe haven in Canterbury, he then had another challenge to deal with: the native British Christians. Suppressed, but not eradicated, there were still practising Christians throughout England, and they sought the guidance of this most remarkable of visitors: a papal legate.

Augustine's tense relationship with the native British Christians is clear from the tantalising example Bede cites, in which he sought advice on how to deal with the little-known cult of a native saint: Sixtus. Almost nothing survives about this saint apart from a reference to him in a letter from Augustine to Gregory. This reference occurs as one in a long line of questions the nervous missionary has for the Pope. In this case, Augustine wants to know if he should allow the continuation of practice at the site of St Sixtus's cult. Gregory rather condescendingly writes that:

> *Things are not to be loved for the sake of places, but places*
> *for the sake of good things. Choose, therefore, from every*
> *church those things that are pious, religious, and upright,*
> *and when you have, as it were, made them up into one body,*
> *let the minds of the English be accustomed thereto.*
> Gregory the Great's letter to St Augustine, from Bede's
> *Ecclesiastical History of the English People.*[24]

The Pope's next act is more derogatory, for rather than seek to understand the origins of the British saint's cult, or the foundations for his veneration, he instead sends over relics of a similarly named saint, Pope Sixtus II, from the catacombs in Rome, to replace the native relics. This should speak volumes about how sanctity was seen as less concerned with a specific individual than with the spiritual potency of a particular place, relic or memory. Sixtus may have existed in Britain, and he may have been significant to those Christians that had preserved stories of his life and death. But to the papacy he was another local saint who could be superseded by a papally sanctioned alternative. The Pope and his missionary treated the resident Romano-British Christians with a disdain that stemmed from a distrust of their potentially outdated and disconnected understanding of orthodox Christian belief. This was to be their modus operandi throughout the conversion period.

Augustine and his missionaries did meet with representatives from the British Church at a place known from then on as Augustine's Oak, on the borders of the Wiccii and West Saxons. Although the exact location has been lost, it was probably between Gloucestershire and Somerset.[25] According to Bede, Augustine rebuked the British Christians for not seeking to convert the pagan Anglo-Saxons themselves, and for the fact that they kept Easter at the wrong time. The question of dating Easter obsessed later Anglo-Saxon Christians like Bede to the point where he wrote a definitive work on how it should be properly calculated. True, the British Church did use a different dating system to establish the movable feast of Easter, but there was more at play in this meeting between British and Roman Christians. It was about establishing orthodoxy and stamping out possible heretical practices.

In a fascinating episode that reveals a good deal about British Christian practices and the personality of Augustine, the decision of the British bishops rested on their consultation with a local wise man or hermit. They had sought his advice on whether to bend their views to the Roman missionaries, and were told that, if Augustine rose to meet them when they reconvened their meeting, then he was honouring them and they should follow his guidance. However, Augustine did not get up, preferring to stay seated in the presence of bishops. This single act of apparent arrogance set the Christian mission back by many decades, and may have coloured relations between native and Continental Christians long-term. This says much about both Augustine and the Gregorian mission.

In their interaction with the British Christians they acted like the Roman invaders of centuries before, entering what they saw as a barbarian nation and imposing their more civilised and correct ideas upon the natives.

The rather anxious and lengthy letter Augustine wrote to Gregory, seeking guidance, also highlights the complex situation the missionary found himself in with regards to both the tribal rulers and Romano-British Christians.[26] He directs a number of pertinent questions to the Pope that had arisen as part of his attempts to persuade the Anglo-Saxon rulers away from their pagan beliefs and towards Christian ones. They include asking whether two brothers can marry two sisters they are not related to, and how long after birth a woman must wait before her husband can have carnal knowledge of her again. These questions give a tangible link with the concerns of the Anglo-Saxon ruling class, whom Augustine was seeking to convert.[27] It is possible to imagine the men of the court asking such questions about marrying sisters, and Augustine promising to write to Rome to ensure he gets an entirely correct response.

However, these statements also hint at the continued Christian presence and a set of British priests and bishops clinging to Old Testament guidance on such matters. They may have sought the support of a papal legate to endorse their established (by this point, outmoded) approach. At times in his letters Gregory has to admonish the missionary and tell him to use his own judgement. Augustine was determined to run all parts of his programme past his superior, and in these letters the Pope is firmly in control, while the English saint is his puppet.

Gregory continues to support Augustine in the first years of his mission, instructing the Bishop of Arles to help the new Archbishop of the English keep a stern approach and a strong hand in his conversion. In AD 601 he sends more men and resources to Canterbury, including the missionaries Mellitus, Justus, Paulinus and Rufinianus:

> *and by them all things in general that were necessary for the worship and service of the church, viz., sacred vessels and vestments for the altars, also ornaments for the churches,*

and vestments for the priests and clerks, as likewise relics of
the holy apostles and martyrs; besides many books.[28]

There may be a rare survival of one of these books, sent by Pope Gregory to Augustine. Now known as the St Augustine Gospels it is still used to swear in new Archbishops, and has even been venerated by the present pope, Pope Francis. It is a small and unassuming volume, a sixth-century manuscript, made around Naples, perhaps specifically for the purposes of the Gregorian mission. It contains just the Gospels, and its decoration, content and visual material all provide a fortunate link with Gregory the Great himself.

It is Italianate in style, as is clear from the arrangement of the Evangelist and his setting within an architectural structure, complete with marbled columns and Corinthian capitals. The Evangelist Luke has been treated with a degree of naturalism, with shading used to give his skin a lifelike hue, and gradations in colour indicating the folds in his robes. All around him, in both the space between the columns and on the facing page, are small images presenting episodes from the Gospels, including the Last Supper, where the Apostles and Christ are shown around a semi-circular table in the manner of late-antique portraits of philosophers feasting. The way in which the scenes have been broken up and set sequentially to unfold a narrative is similar to how biblical stories were treated on late-antique sarcophagi. The mid-fourth-century sarcophagus of Junius Bassus, for example, has precisely this 'comic-book' treatment of events, from Adam and Eve to Daniel in the lions' den. The St Augustine Gospels, however, includes only stories relating to the life of Christ, and in this respect it presents the basic narratives at the heart of Christianity.

It is very possible that this manuscript was designed as a teaching aid for converting the Anglo-Saxon pagans. Gregory the Great was a firm believer in the power of images at a time when iconoclasm was sweeping away depictions of God, Christ, Mary and the saints in the Eastern Church. He was of the opinion that non-literate people needed educating in the stories underlying Christianity, and images could be the means of teaching those who

The St Augustine Gospels, Cambridge, Corpus Christi College, Lib. MS. 286, was made in the sixth century around Naples. This is the oldest surviving Latin illustrated gospel book and is still used to swear in new Archbishops of Canterbury.

could not read for themselves. In this respect, it is partly down to Gregory that Christianity remains a religion with a lasting commitment to representing the divine in art. This stands in opposition to Islam and Judaism, which took the message at the heart of iconoclasm – 'thou shalt set up no false idols' – as a premise for excising depictions of holy people from their art.

Tyranical or Tolerant?

As far as converting the pagans of Britain was concerned, Gregory appears in equal measure as the suppressive tyrant and the conciliatory convertor. As with the other saints covered by the book, Gregory is not clear-cut, but displays a complex mix of characteristics. A famous passage from Bede records a letter Gregory wrote to Bishop Mellitus, one of the missionaries that followed Augustine in AD 601, encouraging him to take a moderate approach to conversion:

> The temples of the idols in that nation ought not to be destroyed; but let the idols that are in them be destroyed; let holy water be made and sprinkled in the said temples, let altars be erected, and relics placed. For if those temples are well built, it is requisite that they be converted from the worship of devils to the service of the true God; that the nation, seeing that their temples are not destroyed, may remove error from their hearts, and knowing and adoring the true God, may the more familiarly resort to the places to which they have been accustomed.
>
> Bede, *Ecclesiastical History of the English People.*[29]

This seems remarkably tolerant in terms of gradually bringing the native population round to an understanding and appreciation of Christianity. Indeed, it is incongruous when considered against the backdrop of forced conversion that was used by later Western Christian rulers like Charlemagne, who slaughtered many thousands of pagan Saxons to bring them round to his religious and political views.

Gregory appreciated the difference between giving advice on the most expedient way to win over converts to his representatives on the ground versus firing up the fervour of secular rulers. In a letter to King Aethelberht, the pope contradicts explicitly his seemingly tolerant advice to Mellitus, encouraging the king to be forceful in the conversion of his people, and win fame and reputation through his suppression of the pagan religion. He states that Aethelberht should 'suppress the worship of idols; overthrow the structures of the temples; edify the manners of your subjects by much cleanness of life, exhorting, terrifying, soothing, correcting, and giving examples of good works.' Gregory utilised all these efforts in his missionary work – terrifying and soothing in equal measures.[30]

Both Gregory and Augustine drove a form of Christianity into the pagan kingdoms of Anglo-Saxon England that was founded on Benedictine monasticism, Roman administrative structures and papal dogma. This was in sharp contrast to the Christianity that had been established for many centuries throughout Britain, and the efforts of the Roman missionaries would have a lasting effect on the next wave of saintly activity that emerged within Anglo-Saxon England. However, the British Church was not going to silently submit to the changes wrought by the papal mission without fighting for what made their form of Christianity unique and enduring. Entering the ring to challenge Gregory for the salvation of pagan Anglo-Saxon souls was a formidable opponent: Saint Columba of Iona.

Chapter Five
Columba: Sanctity Across the Sea

'On a certain day in that same summer in
which he passed to the Lord, the saint
(Columba) went in a chariot to visit some of
the brethren, who were engaged in some heavy
work in the western part of the Iouan island
(Hy, now Iona). After speaking to them some
words of comfort and encouragement, the saint
stood upon the higher ground, and uttered the
following prophecy: "My dear children, I know
that from this day you shall never see my face
again anywhere in this field." Seeing the
brethren filled with sorrow upon hearing these
words, the saint tried to comfort them as best
he could; and, raising both his holy hands, he
blessed the whole of this our island, saying:
"From this very moment poisonous reptiles
shall in no way be able to hurt men or cattle in
this island, so long as the inhabitants shall
continue to observe the commandments of
Christ."'

Adomnán's *Life of St Columba*.[1]

Columba is the first Celtic saint whose life was well recorded, and of whom we can develop a rounded picture. He was a man with one foot in the unpredictable world of Irish tribal politics, and another in the harsh ascetic existence of Celtic monastic life. While many early evangelists set up Celtic monasteries on the edges of the Anglo-Saxon world, his organisation on the Isle of Iona was to exert more influence than almost any other. A sinner and a saint, Columba had blood on his hands and a passion for missionary work in his heart. An active man in a changing world, his impact on Anglo-Saxon Christianity has long been remembered, and nowhere more so than on the island where he lived and died.

Columba's rather esoteric blessing for the island of Iona at the top of this chapter may explain, firstly, why this tiny site on the edge of the Inner Hebrides has no poisonous reptiles and, secondly, why it has remained 'blessed' for centuries. The Isle of Iona has recently celebrated an important milestone – in May 2013 it was the 1,450th anniversary of Columba's arrival.[2] Still known today as the 'Holy Isle of Iona', it remains hard to access, and the journey ever-westward across Scotland can feel like a form of modern-day pilgrimage. Leaving behind the urban noise of Glasgow, the trip towards the Inner Hebrides winds past mountains sprinkled with ice, lochs embraced by the vales surrounding them and harsh ravines alternating with rolling hillsides. It is inexpressibly dramatic, and Iona is tantalisingly out of reach, with all manner of single-track roads, highland cattle and ferry timetables to navigate before you set foot on the tiny island itself. If travelling in winter, the journey becomes even more stunning and treacherous, and once you begin the ferry ride towards the neighbouring Isle of Mull you are at the mercy of the elements.

This part of the British Isles is unique – almost Scandinavian in appearance, especially in the winter months. The distances between villages are lengthy, with the landscape in between a combination of large stretches of water, soaring mountains and dense forests. It is such a sharp contrast with the motorways, sprawling cities and bustling commuters further south that Iona itself feels eternal, as if it exists outside of the modern world. Here, life continues as it always has, with a profound link between the natural world and the stoic people who exist alongside it. The shift from day to night brings with it complete darkness, and the sound of sea birds stills as nature sleeps. The modern-day monastery stands as testament to the lasting spiritual potency this location has encapsulated.

Iona has been described as a place where mankind can get a glimpse of the divine. It is one of Scotland's smallest inhabited islands, at just 1 mile wide by 3.5 miles long, and is home to a population of around 170 people. However, it regularly welcomes pilgrims keen to travel to this tiny yet significant place. The people come to follow in the footsteps of a much earlier traveller to the site: St Columba. A hugely powerful and influential individual both in Ireland and Scotland, Columba is one of the most complex and ambiguous saints covered in this book. Described as tall and powerfully built, he delivered many prophetic predictions and performed many miracles. His greatest legacy was to found a monastery on Iona, which became a powerhouse of Celtic Christianity and exerted a strong influence on the northern Anglo-Saxon kingdoms at the same time as Roman Christianity was making inroads to the south.

As a place, Iona seems to capture the essence of Celtic Christianity. Remote and removed from the world, the island served as the Irish monks' version of the African deserts, and here they could shut themselves off from temptations to undertake spiritual battle. The suggestion of remoteness, however, belies the fact that Iona, Columba and his monastery remained firmly linked with the ruling dynasty of the Dál Riata kingdom. This small island became a burial place of kings, and its apparent isolation today is not a true reflection of the influential and vibrant place it was during Columba's lifetime. An alternative to the apparent affluence, bureaucracy and immorality that has over time become associated with the papacy, Celtic spirituality has been viewed as a simple, pious, nature-loving version of Christianity. But this is to misrepresent both the Roman and the Irish Churches in the early medieval period. As a saint, too, Columba has been perceived as the epitome of Celtic sanctity. Yet Columba was no less motivated by power, politics and prosperity than his papal counterparts, and the divide between the two worlds was perhaps less clear than first impressions suggest.

Dove or Fox?

There is a political dimension to many of Columba's acts, and while numerous tales of his modesty and meekness counterpoint them, the saint who emerges from the pages of hagiography is a major player on a turbulent stage. In order to secure land to build a monastery on Iona, Columba could not simply pull his *curach* up the pebbled beach and lay claim to the island. It is highly probable that he visited his relative, King Conall, at his hill-fort Dunadd, to appeal for land to build a monastery on.[3] Dunadd is about seventy miles from Iona, and was a stronghold (possibly the capital) of the Dál Riata kingdom. Formerly an island surrounded by boggy marsh, at the top of its craggy rocks sat an Iron Age fort. It was later used as the base for the kings of Dál Riata. A symbolically potent footprint was carved into the rock overlooking the kingdom, which was used in inauguration ceremonies for the new kings, who would place their foot here to be wed to the land.[4]

While the dates and origins of the other early saints covered in this volume have been frustratingly hard to pin down, the character of Columba comes into relatively sharp relief by comparison. His ancestry is recorded, and even the names of his parents have been preserved down the centuries. Saint Columba was born on 7 December AD 521 to Fedhlimidh and Eithne of the Uí Néill clan in Gartan (Donegal). His father was of royal descent, great grandson of the fifth-century high king of Ireland – a semi-legendary character called Niall of the Nine Hostages. This meant that Columba was directly linked to the throne, and could even have been king of the powerful Uí Néills had he not chosen to join the fledgling Christian Church.

Columba was probably born a pagan, although the hagiographical texts written about him skirt over this fact, recounting instead a miraculous dream his mother had while pregnant that she was carrying 'a prophet of God', who will be the 'leader of innumerable souls to the heavenly country'. Before taking the name of Columba, the saint had a different and rather unexpected name – Crimthann. This meant 'fox' in Gaelic, and provides a sharp contrast with the divinely symbolic 'Columba', which means 'dove' in Latin. The choice of name was probably not due to the young child being associated with foxy cunning or deceit, but rather because it was popular among the ruling families of Ireland. Nevertheless, that this individual was both 'fox' and 'dove' in his lifetime seems apt, given his complex mix of characteristics.

The reasons for choosing the name Columba after his entry into the Church was significant too. The word carries layers of Christian symbolism, connected with the Holy Spirit and the Gospels:

> There was a man ... who received the same name as the prophet Jonah. For although sounding differently in the three different languages, yet what is pronounced iona in Hebrew, and what Greek calls peristera, and what in the Latin language is named columba, means one and the same thing. So good and great a name is believed not to have been put upon the man of God without divine dispensation. [5]

The symbolism of names in early medieval societies should not be underestimated. In a world without comprehensive maps or defined geographical boundaries, and with minimal literacy, an individual's identity was structured around family and ancestral ties. The memorising of genealogies was important in terms of securing rights to land and marital links, particularly to ensure close relatives didn't marry. Reciting family names and ties is a practice that continues in Iceland and also in some parts of Scotland, where there are still some people who can recite their ancestry back many generations through a practice known in Gaelic as *sloinneadh*.[6]

When he decided to tie himself to the Celtic Church, Columba selected a new name carefully. The name 'Columba' was chosen deliberately at a time when the Irish knew they were standing in opposition to the Roman Church on matters like the dating of Easter.[7] By taking such a symbolic name and associating himself with the dove of the Holy Spirit, Columba was emphasising the purity of his form of Christianity, and the symbol of a white dove became indelibly linked to the Irish Church. In this respect, it acted like a logo of sorts, reclaimed from Roman usages where it was commonly part of a baptismal or Trinitarian scene. Columba and his followers connected the symbol of the dove instead with the 'Dove of the Church' Columba, who spread the Gospels and Holy Spirit through missionary work. This was clever and deliberate propaganda.

Much of what we know about Columba survives in one text: a seventh-century *Life* written by a later abbot of Iona, Adomnán. He was elevated to the sainthood himself, which presents a predicament to those seeking to use his text on Columba as a source of factual information. Adomnán was a man who understood how to write hagiography and how to craft an individual, both on the page and in life, into the perfect saint. He was one of the finest writers of his time, and would today be a bestselling author. Adomnán was directly related to Columba, both through blood and the abbacy of Iona, and he wrote his *Life* about a hundred years after the earlier saint's death. We should treat Adomnán's account with caution. Not only does it seek to glorify a long-dead relative, it has an agenda connected with his own abbacy of Columba's foundation at Iona.

As was the case with many hagiographers, the work Adomnán wrote tells us as much about the author as it does about the subject. He collected information from the brothers of the monastery at Iona and crafted this data into a text that met his own ends. His primary motive in writing Columba's *Life* was to present the founding father of the monastery as a paragon of sanctity, and his site at Iona as the rightful motherhouse of all the satellite foundations around it. As abbot of Iona, glorifying Columba served both

Adomnán and his community, so the text is steeped in his own interests and concerns.

The *Life of St Columba* is a dense text that is concerned with affirming the reputation of early Irish saints and the Celtic Christianity they promulgated. There are certainly interesting facts and details recorded in Adomnán's work, but his treatment of Columba is selective and edifying. The very structure of the *Life*, arranged in three parts to reflect the trinity, is copied over from the example of Gregory the Great's account of the *Life of St Benedict*. There are also similarities in style, subject matter and structure with other well-known hagiographical texts, including those of the lives of St Martin, St Anthony and St Germanus. It is an interesting aspect of medieval texts that, while this sort of plagiarism would be criticised by modern readers, to the monks who read and copied Adomnán's work, the verbal echoes with other texts was commendable.[8] Copying meant something very different in the early medieval period, where originality for the sake of it was not prized, and tradition was of greater importance. As an accomplished writer of hagiography, however, Adomnán crafted a text that, while traditional and derivative in parts, still holds readers today with it wealth of incidental drama and personal touches.

Scotland and the Picts

In one famous story Adomnán records how Columba met with the Loch Ness Monster.[9] This has proved to be an enduring legend, with many today still searching the depths of the lake to find Nessie. But the Irish saint didn't need to search, as the monster appeared before him. It seems the saint may have lured the beast to him using human bait. Columba discovered a community of Picts on the banks of Loch Ness burying the body of a man who had been mauled to death by the monster. While the people present may well have been terrified at the thought of entering the water after such an event, Columba instructed one of them to take the plunge and swim over to him.

On doing so, the man is indeed attacked again by the monster, but the saint manages to save him at the last moment: 'Then the blessed man ... commanded the ferocious monster, saying, "Thou shalt go no further, nor touch the man; go back with all speed." Then at the voice of the saint, the monster was terrified.'[10] The conclusion of this encounter is that, firstly, the cult of Nessie was born, and secondly, 'even the barbarous heathens [the Picts], who were present, were forced by the greatness of this miracle, which they themselves had seen, to magnify the God of the Christians.' It is also possible to conclude that Columba could be ruthless when necessary, and that in the eyes of his followers he had the power to control nature itself.

This story illustrates an important point, however – that Columba was instrumental in encouraging Christianity amongst the Picts. The Picts themselves are a seemingly lost people, attested to in early records like Bede's, but by the turn of the first millennium absorbed into Alba, a nation composed of Irish Gaels or Scotti (settled on the west coast), and Picts. Despite Henry of Huntingdon stating in 1140 that the Picts 'seem to be a fable we find mentioned in old writings', there is evidence that they were a separate nation, with strongholds to the east of Scotland.[11]

The Picts (named 'the painted people', because of their tattoos, by the Romans they harangued along their borders) are now largely lost to the sands of time. Their land and identities have been subsumed beneath the waves of Scotti who originally settled the west of Scotland, having travelled over from Ireland. The Scotti descended from a petty kingdom in Country Antrim, Northern Ireland – Dál Riata. It overlooked the many isles along the coast of western Scotland, and from AD 400 they began to set up Irish outposts in County Argyll. The Irish had reputedly joined forces with the Picts as early as AD 297 to attack the Romans at Hadrian's Wall, and they would continue to fight with, and against, one another until the two tribes were united into a single kingdom, perhaps under Cináed mac Ailp'n in AD 844. The Scotti would eventually give their Gaelic language and name to the whole of the nation now known as Scotland.[12]

The Picts do, however, survive in the archaeological records due to their magnificent 'brochs'. Mousa Broch, on a now uninhabited

A Pictish carved stone known as the Hilton of Cadboll Stone, now in the National Museum of Scotland, Edinburgh. It was carved around AD 800, and originally stood near the village of Hilton of Cadboll, in Ross and Cromarty, northern Scotland.

island off the Shetlands, is thought to be as much as 2,000 years old. This and the other hundreds of brochs across Scotland, the Orkneys and Shetlands feature some of the most sophisticated dry-stoned architecture anywhere in the world. Evidence for the Picts has been unearthed at the recently excavated Christian settlement at Portmahomack,[13] and they also left behind them an array of enigmatic stone carvings.

Pictish symbol stones tantalise early medieval scholars in the same way that Egyptian hieroglyphs frustrated Egyptologists before the Rosetta Stone allowed them to be deciphered. While many studies have been done to suggest possible ways of interpreting them, their full meaning remains out of reach. What they do reveal, however, is a society with a sophisticated artistic culture, capable of carving intricate designs in stone and coordinating an artistic medium across hundreds of miles and some three centuries. The majority can be dated to between the sixth and ninth centuries. The earliest display a collection of indecipherable Pictish symbols, while later ones resemble standing cross stele found throughout Britain and the Continent, where they act as gravestones or markers.

With the earliest stones, however, the land of the Picts at the time of Columba comes into greater focus. They could be memorials to individuals, or land markers, designating the edge of territories. The symbols that recur most often have been connected with defining a person or tribe. In this respect they could also be imagined to have adorned timber housing, personal objects (small bone domestic items, and two pieces of jewellery display similar carvings) or clothing. The legacy of tartan defining Scottish clans may be a residual element of this tribal differentiation.

The symbols could also have been used as tattoos. They appear across the length and breadth of Pictish Scotland, which suggests that they must have been widely understood. The fact that many symbols appear in pairs has been interpreted as a means of recording personal names in a society that otherwise didn't write down its history and genealogies.

From the thirty or so symbols that have been isolated, three main categories appear regularly. There are geometric ideograms, which have been given names like the Z-rod or double-disc;

everyday objects, like tongs or mirrors; and animals, including salmon, eagles and wolves, which are native to Scotland.[14] There is also a specific, indefinable creature, with a long snout and strange curling limbs, which resembles a dolphin and has become known as the 'Pictish beast'. Suggestions that it is a sea monster have added fuel to the myth of Nessie and other beasts believed to inhabit the many lochs of Scotland.

Certain symbols, like the comb and mirror, may be signifiers of high status and femininity, while examples like the bull symbol, which appears on six separate stones from Burghead fort, may indicate that it was connected directly with a specific place. Scientific studies have been undertaken to determine whether the stones act as a form of written language, but the results have been inconclusive.[15] Nevertheless, the combination of recognisable objects and animals with abstract symbols suggests that the Picts employed a sophisticated artistic language across different mediums. With so little left from which to reconstruct them, the hundreds of carved stones peppering the Scottish landscape frustrate those in search of long-dead ancestors, and remind us that Columba encountered a formidable, ancient society when he came to preach Christianity in the sixth century.

Columba is one of the three main saints credited with bringing Christianity to the Picts, the others being St Ninian and St Kentigern (also known as Mungo). Ninian's contribution and influence with regards to Whithorn has been discussed. Kentigern is bound up with the area around Glasgow, and only established in a twelfth-century *Life*, which includes such strange details as the rape of his mother and the resuscitation of a robin killed by his classmates at school. Columba's life is perhaps better documented, but it is still full of some inexplicable details. His training before establishing the monastery at Iona seems to have taken place first at Finnian's monastery at Movilla. This is the Finnian who had travelled to Whithorn and studied there, returning to Ireland with a Vulgate copy of the psalter. From Movilla, Columba then went on to study at the influential monastic school at Clonard.

This was an exceptional place of learning, supposedly established by a different Finnian, to make matters confusing, where many of the evangelical Irish missionaries who would go on to spread Celtic Christianity across Europe were trained. The school encouraged a strict and austere approach to monasticism, perhaps influenced by its founder's recorded visits abroad to St Martin's monastery in Tours, and to sites in Ireland like Skellig Michael and Brigid's monastery at Kildare. Clonard was clearly an influential and vibrant monastery, with suggestions that as many as 3,000 students trained there. Columba was one of these students. After leaving Clonard, Columba set up a number of important monasteries, including Derry, Durrow and Kells. However, in AD 563 he was exiled from Donegall after a dispute over a manuscript.[16] The manuscript in question was a Vulgate psalter belonging to the first Finnian, of Moville and Whithorn fame, which Columba copied. The copy may have survived to be known today as the Cathach of St Columba, and its origins are bound up in the earliest recorded instance of copyright infringement.

Columba and Manuscript Art

Columba had apparently been given permission to consult the precious manuscript, copied from Jerome's Vulgate version of the Psalms, but Finnian protested when he then took a copy of the borrowed manuscript for use in his own monasteries in order to reproduce it further. The seeds of hostility lay in Columba's breach of copyright – this was an ancient version of a modern problem. Saint Columba was involved in litigation because he made an illegal copy of the borrowed psalter. This act enraged Finnian and those loyal to him, and bubbled up into full-scale hostilities between clans.

The Battle of Cúl Dreimhne, also known as the Battle of the Book, took place in the small kingdom of Cairbre Drom Cliabh in north-west Ireland between AD 555 and AD 561. King Diarmait mac Cerbaill, High King of Tara and the Uí Néill, was forced to pass judgement on the issue of whether Columba had illegally copied Finnian's psalter, and concluded: 'to every cow its calf, and to every book its copy'. This enraged Columba, who called upon his relatives, also of the Uí Néill clan, and war ensued, which resulted in many thousands of deaths. In this instance Columba was not the monastic scholar, tirelessly studying at Clonard and setting up new monasteries. Instead he was wrapped up with an Irish war band, a violent army, engaged in battle with a rival clan. His illegal copy of the manuscript meant that many Irish men died in battle. He had blood on his hands.

The issue of the Cathach of St Columba may, however, be a later excuse for the battle. Its roots may, in fact, lie in more deep-rooted hostilities between the clans and their attitudes to Christianity. Diarmait ruled as a pagan king and rallied against the Church and saints like Columba. He was also accused of being responsible for the death of Prince Curnan of Connacht. Columba is again drawn into this controversy, since he was giving sanctuary to the prince when Diarmait's men came and slaughtered him. It was the saint's close involvement with these big political events that led to his exile in AD 563. He was too inflammatory, too political and too provocative to remain a part of the religious and political sphere of mainland Ireland. Along with twelve companions, he was sent out into a wicker *curach* covered with hides to his fellow kinsmen across the water in western Scotland.

It has long been thought that the manuscript enshrined in bejewelled reliquary casing known as the Cathach of Columba is the manuscript at the heart of the dispute between Columba and Finnian. The surviving Cathach is a Vulgate copy. A version of the Psalms according to Jerome's Vulgate version would have been extremely valuable and novel in Ireland at the time, and this was no doubt why Columba created his illegal copy. The controversy surrounding the Cathach of Columba certainly emphasises the significance of manuscripts to early Christians, and the value that could be attached to them.

The words 'book' and 'manuscript' are often used interchangeably. However, there are very important distinctions between the two, which can be lost in translation. Our modern notions of a book centre on a printed volume, on paper, which is an accessible and affordable way of digesting and disseminating knowledge. A manuscript is different in almost every respect. Manuscripts were made by hand (the Latin 'manus'), and were written onto the skins of animals: calf for vellum, sheep or goat for parchment. Each part of the process of creating a manuscript was complex and labour-intensive. The vellum had to be prepared, scraped and stretched for months, and the inks would require different techniques to prepare, with some, like orpiment, potentially deadly if handled incorrectly.[17]

The act of writing was uncomfortable, with the elements playing an important role in terms of suitable lighting, moisture and warmth for the scribe, who would be bent over their writing desk and seeking comfort wherever possible. Unlike a cheap paperback on the shelf, which we often take for granted, the people involved in manuscript production were aware of the value of their materials. In an Old English riddle from the *Exeter Book* a fascinating account of the creation of a manuscript survives, which draws attention to the many living elements that went into making a work that could provide 'salvation':

> An enemy ended my life, deprived me
> Of my physical strength; then he dipped me
> In water and drew me out again,
> And put me in the sun where I soon shed
> All my hair. After that, the knife's sharp edge
> Bit into me and all my blemishes were scraped away;
> Fingers folded me and the bird's feather
> Often moved over my brown surface,
> Sprinkling meaningful marks; it swallowed more wood-dye
> [part of the stream] and again travelled over me
> leaving black tracks. Then a man bound me,
> he stretched skin over me and adorned me
> with gold; thus I am enriched by the wondrous work
> of smiths, wound about with shining metal.
> Now my clasp and my red dye
> And these glorious adornments bring fame far and wide
> To the Protector of Men.[18]

Far from being an object intended for wide distribution and the sharing of information with many, manuscripts were expensive high-status symbols. Some of the finest illustrated manuscripts of the medieval period were the equivalent of a Rolls-Royce car by modern standards, and they reflected the tastes and interests of their patrons. Access to manuscripts was restricted to those who were literate (which was predominantly members of the Church and some prominent secular individuals) and could physically get to the manuscript, or get the manuscript to them. Information did not move instantaneously, like it does now, and the writers of the early medieval period often had to travel long distances to purchase or access manuscripts.

Columba's copy of the Psalter would have been invaluable to scribes in his monasteries, and would have been used as an exemplar for many further texts. It is testament to how sacred the manuscripts associated with saints became that the Cathach has been enshrined like a relic. More focused on contact than corporal relics, the Irish Church encased the bells, staffs and books used by their early saints in the same way that bodily parts would be adorned and preserved elsewhere in the Church. Columba's connection with manuscripts, however, extends beyond the Cathach. The scribal output of the monasteries he founded should also be considered, for some of the most famous objects produced during the so-called Dark Ages originated at them.

The Book of Kells is the most complete and esoteric expression of Celtic monastic art to survive from the medieval period. Possibly created at Columba's monastery of Iona, it was preserved at his other foundation of Kells, although it was created some 200 years after the saint's death. In contrast, the Book of Durrow is a very early survival, and was also connected with a Columban foundation.[19] Having founded his primary monastery at Derry in AD 546, from there sprang a chain of daughter houses in Ireland, among which Durrow would become particularly prominent. The Book of Durrow is now known as the earliest surviving Insular manuscript. It anticipates the remarkable developments of the Lindisfarne Gospels and the Book of Kells in its deviation from Continental exemplars. While the St Augustine Gospels focused on realistic portraits of the Evangelists, Italianate settings and instructional

The Book of Durrow, Trinity College, Dublin MS. A. 4. 5., is the oldest complete illuminated Insular Gospel book. It contains a number of full-page illuminations, including carpet pages, evangelist portraits and initials before each Gospel.

narrative scenes, the Book of Durrow abandons these in favour of a distinct and unique form of illumination.

It was made around AD 650, so over half a century after Columba's death, most probably either at Durrow, Lindisfarne or Iona. The influence of Celtic ideas and imagery pervades the manuscript, tying it closely to the Columban mission. The Book of Durrow has been enveloped in scholarly controversy, with academics pitched in two camps: one that sees the manuscript as the product of an Irish scriptorium; and another that claims it as an Anglo-Saxon creation. The nationalistic nature of these debates has cast a long and dark shadow on the study of this manuscript, but its importance lies in the fact that it is the earliest, the benchmark from which later works of international renown emerged.

The manuscript contains the four Gospels according to Jerome's Vulgate. An Irish innovation in manuscript art, however, appears in the form of four carpet pages that introduce each Gospel. Possibly derived from similar Coptic examples, in the Book of Durrow these are all full-page and combine a variety of artistic motifs, including Celtic knotwork and whorls and spirals, more commonly found on Celtic metalwork.

Such carpet pages are a notable contribution to manuscript art from the Insular world, the earliest surviving example being found in a seventh-century manuscript made at Columba's namesake and countryman Columbanus's monastery of Bobbio in Italy. Called 'carpet pages' because of their resemblance to Islamic prayer carpets, these pages come before the Gospels and are devoid of figural imagery. Instead, abstract shapes and geometric designs cover all the vellum, in a form of 'horror vacui' that was common to Anglo-Saxon jewellery, whereby no part of the surface was left undecorated. The decoration in the Book of Durrow does, at times, resemble Anglo-Saxon metalwork, for example in the image of the Evangelist Matthew, where the red and gold of his cloak mirrors the cloisonné work found famously on the Sutton Hoo shoulder clasp. The worlds of Ireland, Scotland, and Anglo-Saxon England are drawn together decoratively to create a work of art that is unique to the British Isles of the seventh century.

Another Irish innovation, which ties the Book of Durrow to Columba, can be seen in the use of a large, decorated initial in the Cathach of Columba (perhaps penned by Columba himself) to designate the beginning of a new section of the text. The following letters then reduce in size gradually, in the manner of a piece of music according to diminuendo – the sound becoming gradually quieter. This technique is expanded in the Book of Durrow into an intricate and highly illuminated letter that fills a good deal of the page. Diminuendo becomes a defining characteristic of Insular manuscripts, reaching its zenith in the Book of Kells, where one initial covers the entire page.

Columba's legacy lives on in the manuscripts associated with him and his monastic foundations. In the Cathach and the Book of Durrow it is possible to witness the innovative and unique characteristics of the Celtic Church in visual rendering. While adhering closely to orthodox Vulgate copies of the text, the decorative elements break away from tradition, and resort instead to native motifs, some of which date back to the pre-Christian past of the Celtic lands. Columba trod a fine line during his lifetime, proudly flying the flag of the Irish Church in new lands and creating a legacy that would influence many of his followers and successors.

From the information that remains about him (and there is a good deal when considered alongside other individuals alive in the sixth century), it seems that Columba was a driven and wilful saint, who took on Picts, Druids, rival Christians and the Loch Ness Monster in the course of his missionary work. Although a native of Ireland, and supposedly heir to the crown of the high kings of Tara had he wished it, Columba is best known for his work among the pagans of the Scottish Highlands and the famous monastery he established at Iona. He was a hardened traveller, who reached the Inner Hebrides as a result of being exiled through feud and battle. With eleven of his companions, symbolically recalling Christ and his Apostles, Columba crossed the sea between Ireland and the Hebrides in a simple *curach*, but his willingness to take on the waves, brave the elements and claim the small island as his own have all ensured that his memory has been preserved down the centuries.

Columba's Legacy

Columba has been called the Apostle of Scotland, and certainly his foundation of a monastery on the edges of Scotland was to have wide implications, particularly with regards to the mission to convert the pagan Anglo-Saxons of Northumbria. However, his life can appear contradictory at times, and his foundation of a monastery at Iona seems to have been as much down to chance as to a burning desire to convert the northern part of Britain. He is a complex character, subsumed in the realpolitik of his time and able to manipulate the benefits of a monastic foundation to his own ends. Strong, persuasive, well-connected and, at times, forceful, the legacy of Columba was as much down to his hard-headedness as to his piety and sanctity.

But Columba was not the only Celtic missionary circling the pagan Anglo-Saxon kingdoms and travelling across rough terrains in search of new places to spread the Christian message and set up monasteries.[20] He is remembered as one of the Twelve Apostles of Ireland – the number twelve was replicated when each of these Apostles travelled out from Ireland, as each ensured they took eleven of their own companions with them to reach this sacred number. The Twelve Apostles of Ireland all studied under the elder Finnian of Clonard, and each went throughout Ireland and further afield, establishing a vast network of monasteries that prized the Celtic ascetic way of life and encouraged biblical scholarship. A further Irish missionary, and one who shared Columba's name, also deserves mention since he appears as an early bridge between the worlds of Rome and Ireland.

Born around AD 543, Columbanus was a couple of decades younger than Columba and the other Apostles of Ireland, but like them he embraced the almost foolhardy desire to evangelise far and wide. Like his fellow Irish monks, he braved the sea on dangerous missions to convert wherever his *curach* landed. Many died on these journeys or were killed by hostile natives when they finally found land. Columbanus, however, was a different character from the abbot of Iona with which he shares a name. Columbanus is also named after the 'dove', but his has been given a Latinised ending to distinguish between the two Irish men. His missionary zeal was equivalent to that of Columba, and he founded monasteries across Europe, as far south as Bobbio in Italy.

When, at the age of forty, he was finally given permission by his abbot (later known as St Comgall) to leave his monastery at Bangor, he first went over to France. A testament to his ability to make influential connections, Columbanus managed to gain the favour of King Gontram of Burgundy, and was given land within an abandoned Roman fortress to build a monastery. Here, he reused old Roman stone from the ruined site to build his new Celtic monastery in the heart of the Frankish kingdom – a brave move for an Irish monk far from his homeland. He then founded Luxeuil Abbey in France, and encouraged the use of penitentials as a means of providing a legal code to bind Christians to reparations.[21]

Penitentials acted as a spiritual equivalent to secular law codes. If a man was wronged in life he would expect repayment in terms of compensation or revenge. If someone sinned, the one they wronged was God himself, and so Celtic Christianity encouraged the use of penitentials, which were manuals designating the specific type of penance a Christian must perform if he or she had sinned. Columbanus took the use of penitentials with him across Europe. This made him unpopular with some foreign rulers, since the imparting of punishment and justice was the preserve of secular decision makers.

He was born in AD 543, which was the same year in which Benedict (author of the famous monastic Rule) died, and just three years after the birth of Gregory. These are converging timelines, which indicate how the life and work of one saint could directly affect those working at the same time. Forty was mature in the early medieval period, which would have made travelling physically exhausting and potentially dangerous. Columbanus took a bold step in heading out to Gaul, and was clearly inspired by missionary fervour and a desire to establish Irish monastic traditions more firmly on the Continent. He may have also found inspiration in the example of his fellow Irish monk Columba, who had already established his monastery in Iona as Columbanus worked his way across the Continental nations.

His actions were perhaps further fuelled by the emergence of a new papacy under Gregory the Great. This new pope, so close in age to Columbanus himself, was attempting to redraw the Christian landscape, positioning the Roman papacy firmly at its centre. Ireland had long been on the outskirts of Christendom, yet the missionary activity of Columbanus and his followers was a means of spreading influence and creating a strong presence of Celtic practices on the Continent. While Columba seems to exemplify the Celtic Church establishing monasteries in opposition to the Roman mission, Columbanus's actions on the Continent suggest that the picture was far more blurred. There were few clear-cut divisions between the two parties, Roman and Irish.

Through the figure of Columbanus it is possible to perceive a middle ground between the two apparently opposed factions of the Irish and Roman Church. The situation was never cut and dry, with Columba and the Irish pitched on one side, and Augustine and the Romans on the other. In fact, many individuals worked tirelessly through the sixth century and into the seventh to draw the many strands of the Church together. However, within Anglo-Saxon England the camps regrouped, with certain individuals pitching their flags to one or other banner. The souls of the pagan Anglo-Saxons would be battled over for nearly a hundred years, and what resulted was a fascinating hybrid that would produce some of the most famous artworks, organisations and individuals of the medieval period. One saint would come to exemplify this eclectic and exciting time: Cuthbert of Lindisfarne.

Chapter Six
Cuthbert: Bishop or Hermit?

'*Know and remember, that, if of two evils you are compelled to choose one, I would rather that you should take up my bones, and leave these places, to reside wherever God may send you, than consent in any way to the wickedness of schismatics, and so place a yoke upon your necks. Study diligently, and carefully observe the Catholic rules of the Fathers, and practise with zeal those institutes of the monastic life, which it has pleased God to deliver to you through my ministry. For I know, that, although during my life some have despised me, yet after my death you will see what sort of man I was, and that my doctrine was by no means worthy of contempt.*'

Bede, *Prose Life of St Cuthbert*.[1]

There's something eerie about the way Bede, apparently quoting Cuthbert himself, prophesied the movement of the saint's bones. Cuthbert's body did in fact have to leave the place of its burial – Lindisfarne. Following the fateful Viking attacks of AD 793 the monks were repeatedly subjected to raids, until they finally abandoned their monastery and began carrying Cuthbert's coffin and the Lindisfarne Gospels across the north of England for over a hundred years. The monks finally settled at Durham in AD 995, where Cuthbert's body still lies. He represented so much to so many, and was the most popular English saint until Becket usurped him in the twelfth century.

An Anglo-Saxon nobleman, Celtic monk, hermit and bishop, he seems a mass of contradictions. Yet it was the multifaceted nature of this saint that made him so popular, as well as his association with some of the finest surviving Anglo-Saxon artworks. His life was recorded twice (in verse and prose) by the greatest writer of the time, his relics were lavished with care and attention, and his cult was preserved despite the destruction of its original site. Cuthbert's name is one of the most potent to pass down the centuries, and he continues to be celebrated and venerated today, particularly on the island where he was abbot and bishop.

The Holy Island of Lindisfarne is special. It is a tidal island, joined to the mainland by a sandy causeway just twice a day, and otherwise set adrift in the North Sea as the tide rises. It is also a remarkable natural habitat, populated with rare flora and fauna. There are over 300 species of birds recorded on Lindisfarne, and among the dunes and quicksand, wild flowers and insects flourish. It is special from a historical perspective due to the Celtic monastery founded here around AD 635.

The landscape of Lindisfarne made it the perfect place for Irish missionaries to found a flagship community within the borders of Anglo-Saxon England. A causeway miraculously appears at low tide, connecting the outcrop of land to the Northumbrian coastline like an umbilical cord. The only way to reach the island was by carefully traversing the mud-plains. The safest route is today marked out by wooden piles set at regular distances to avoid dangerous areas of quicksand; nevertheless, the causeway has always been deadly, and one car a month has to be rescued after getting caught in the rapidly rising waters.

The trip from the mainland to Lindisfarne depends on the elements, and away from busy cities and motorways you tune in to the regular patterns of nature, like the rising and falling of the tides. Once on the island, swirling waters engulf the only access road, and the next opportunity to return to the mainland won't occur for some five or six hours. The inhabitants of the island nestle together in the area around the site of the original monastery, now exuding a faded grandeur due to the crumbling ruins of the later Norman monastic complex. The rest of the island, however, is a nature reserve where the wonders of creation swirl over your heads, unfold beneath your feet and stretch before your eyes. The movement of the waters punctuates the passage of time, and it is possible to imagine the rounds of monastic prayers accompanying the eternal motions of the natural world.

The connections between Iona and Lindisfarne are obvious. While today the island perched on the western coast of Scotland seems more remote than the tidal isle off the coast of Northumberland, the history and impact of the two are twinned together. The islands are almost identical in size and population, with Lindisfarne measuring 1.5 miles long and 3 miles wide, and boasting a population of just 180 people. There is a direct connection between them, since the first monastery established in Northumbria, on Lindisfarne, had as its founder Aidan, a monk from Iona. Little is known of his life before he left Iona to found a monastery on land granted to him by the Northumbrian king Oswald. In pursuing his missionary work in a potentially hostile pagan environment, Aidan was continuing the work of Iona's founder, Columba. However, the isle of Lindisfarne and, even more so, the tiny isle of Inner Farne, a few miles further down the coast, still resonate with the legacy of the later saint and bishop Cuthbert.

When Cuthbert sought retreat from the world of Church politics, he would head to Inner Farne, and it was here that he introduced the first recorded bird-protection law in AD 676, to look after the eider ducks, which have since been named after him 'Cuddy ducks'. He discovered that people were stealing the birds' eggs from the island, so as bishop he issued a law to protect them. Birds were important to Cuthbert, and a number of his miracles revolve around them. This is hardly surprising given that the cliffs surrounding Inner Farne in particular teem with nesting birds in spring. Puffin burrows pepper the ground, and angry terns can swoop down at passers-by if fearing that their chicks are under threat. The isle of Lindisfarne, its birds, beasts and vistas, continues to inspire artists, musicians and tourists alike, just as it inspired its most famous saintly resident.

Cuthbert's Life and Times

Cuthbert lived during a pivotal time in Anglo-Saxon history. Born a Northumbrian nobleman and raised in the Celtic monastery of Melrose, his life reaches across the many religious and historical strands of seventh-century Britain. He was born a few years after the end of King Edwin of Northumbria's reign, and his life coincides with the zenith of that kingdom's power throughout Anglo-Saxon England, referred to as Northumbria's Golden Age.[2] Cuthbert sits firmly at its centre, and continues to fascinate down the centuries with his delicate balancing act of power and piety, humility and honour.[3] To understand Cuthbert and the legacy of Lindisfarne, however, it is essential first to consider what happened to Gregory's Roman mission when it came north, and the resistance it met from the Celtic Church, with its stronghold on Iona.

When Augustine arrived with his mission to Kent in AD 597, the kingdom of Northumbria was undergoing a period of transition. Kent was dominant among the Anglo-Saxon kingdoms, with King

Aethelberht acting as 'bretwalda' or overlord of the other kingdoms. How this manifested exactly is difficult to determine, but it seems other kings, such as Raedwald of East Anglia, sought to pacify him with gestures like nominally accepting his new religion of Christianity. The other kings may also have owed taxes or been required to provide troops in times of need. In contrast to Kent, Northumbria was a kingdom divided by rival clans. It gets its name from being composed of the regions north of the Humber, and its furthest borders reached towards southern Scotland. It was composed of two major kingdoms – Deira (from the Humber to the Tees) and Bernicia (land north of the Tees) – but as its luck began to change it would grow to include the neighbouring fiefdoms of Elmet and Gododdin.

Despite the fact that the main kingdoms of Deira and Bernicia were nominally unified around AD 604 by King Aethelfrith, conflict between the two is a feature of most of the seventh century. The situation was similar to that some AD 600 years later, when the houses of York and Lancaster placed different representatives on the throne during the Wars of the Roses. King Raedwald of East Anglia, and Sutton Hoo fame, stirred the pot of intrigue to the far north of his kingdom. Around AD 616 he defeated Aethelfrith and installed his rival, the King of Deira, Edwin, in his place. Edwin had been under Raedwald's protection while in exile from Northumbria, and it is tempting to imagine him staying in the court of East Anglia, resplendent with stunning pagan treasures like those found at Sutton Hoo.

The links between Edwin, Raedwald and Aethelberht were to have the most profound effect on the spread of Roman Christianity to the north, for Edwin was willing to accept the new religion in return for greater links with the powerful southern kingdoms. Edwin was married to Aethelburg, the Christian daughter of Aethelberht and Bertha of Kent. It was a condition of her marriage that Edwin convert to Christianity. The moment the Northumbrian court agreed to accept Christianity is recounted by Bede in one of the most poetic accounts to survive from the early medieval period. Spoken by an anonymous counsellor to the king, the soul is likened to a sparrow flying through the hall:

*The present life of man, O king, seems to me, in comparison
with that time which is unknown to us, like to the swift flight
of a sparrow through the room wherein you sit at supper in
winter amid your officers and ministers, with a good fire in
the midst whilst the storms of rain and snow prevail abroad;
the sparrow, I say, flying in at one door and immediately out
another, whilst he is within is safe from the wintry storm but
after a short space of fair weather he immediately vanishes
out of your sight into the dark winter from which he has
emerged. So this life of man appears for a short space but of
what went before or what is to follow we are ignorant. If,
therefore, this new doctrine contains something more certain,
it seems justly to deserve to be followed.*[4]

While the real discussion from Edwin's court remains forever out
of reach, there is archaeological evidence for the court itself, and
possibly the hall through which the sparrow so prosaically flies.
The archaeologist Brian Hope-Taylor was responsible for excavat-
ing the remains of an Anglo-Saxon royal settlement at a remote
site called Yeavering, in Northumberland.[5] Following references in
Bede to 'Ad Gefrin', a royal 'vill' close to the River Glen, he specu-
lated that an administrative complex could be located further
inland from the traditional seat of power at Bamburgh. This site,
he believed, was designed to exercise greater control over the
native British population, who were more established in this
central area of Northumbria.

After examining an aerial photograph taken by an RAF pilot on
a particularly dry day in 1949, Hope-Taylor determined that there
was a sequence of timber buildings close to Yeavering Bell, which
itself had a history of Iron Age settlement. At Yeavering he
discovered a fascinating survival – a ringed enclosure of huge
dimensions. It was probably deployed to secure livestock, which
the king and his retinue would use for food during their stay at the
royal hall. Anglo-Saxon England in the early seventh century was
not using coinage, so payments tended to be made in cattle,
equivalent to hides of leather. From this emerged the Tribal Hidage
– the assessment of the income of land on the basis of how many

hides of leather would be paid.[6] There is also overlap in the runic alphabet that was used by Anglo-Saxons. The 'f' rune can be interpreted to mean both 'wealth' and 'cattle', again emphasising the link between the two.

The complex at Yeavering offers many other insights into the court of King Edwin, primarily the enormous timber hall, which recalls description of Heorot in *Beowulf*. It is tempting to think of Cuthbert, a young member of the Northumbrian aristocracy, sitting upon the benches within a hall like that at Yeavering, watching the mead cup pass from hand to hand and listening to the accounts of heroic warriors while safe from the storm outside. Alongside the hall, Hope-Taylor unearthed an unusual building in the form of a wedge-shaped amphitheatre. Built of wood, with a raised stage at the base and seating for some 300 people on tiered levels, it has been called the 'cuneus'. It is unique in Britain, and Bede suggests a tantalising solution as to its use. It revolves around Paulinus – Augustine's emissary to the north.

Paulinus was sent by Pope Gregory in a second mission of AD 601 to support the work done by Augustine in Kent. He went north as a result of the marriage between Aethelburg of Kent and Edwin of Northumbria. The bishop accompanied the Kentish princess to the court at Yeavering, and began negotiations with the king about converting to Christianity:

> So great was then the fervour of the faith, as is reported, and the desire of the washing of salvation among the nation of the Northumbrians, that Paulinus at a certain time coming with the king and queen to the royal country-seat, which is called Adgefrin, stayed there with them thirty-six days, fully occupied in catechising and baptizing; during which days, from morning till night, he did nothing else but instruct the people resorting from all villages and places, in Christ's saving word; and when instructed, he washed them with the water of absolution in the river Glen, which is close by.[7]

The 'cuneus' at Yeavering may well be the remains of the site where Paulinus preached Christianity to the Anglo-Saxon people.

The proximity of the River Glen to the Yeavering site may further support the idea that this was where the first northern Christians were baptised. Paulinus's mission highlights the political nature of many early conversions. It is significant, however, that the conversion to Christianity was very much a 'top-down' process, whereby kings, queens and nobles were appealed to first, and then the message was more widely disseminated. Edwin received baptism first in AD 627, at the timber church at York, and only once the king was Christian would the message filter down to the lower strata of the population. Gregory, Augustine, Paulinus and Bede all stress that it was the decision of kings that mattered. The conversion was not about the gradual transference of religious belief among the general population, but rather a political and economic decision resting in the hands of a few.

Upon Edwin's death in battle, his kingdom was divided, with Eanfrith succeeding him in Bernicia. Ultimately, he was replaced as king of Northumbria by the Bernician line, which had retreated into Scottish and Irish territories, where they had accepted Christianity at the hands of Celtic tutors. Edwin's Bernician nephew (and Eanfrith's brother) Oswald brought a different form of Christianity to the north, one that was flourishing across the borders with Scotland. Oswald won a famous victory at the Battle of Heavenfield, and immediately afterwards erected a wooden cross as a celebration of his triumph. More significantly, perhaps, Adomnán records that before the battle he had appealed in prayer for the help of St Columba. Oswald was nailing his colours to the mast. He was for the Irish Church, unlike his Deiran predecessor Edwin.

According to Bede, Oswald ruled as 'bretwalda', and during his reign Northumbria reached the height of its power and influence.[8] Bede is very complimentary of him, and presents Oswald as the ultimate saintly king. He was responsible for granting land to St Aidan, upon which he built the monastery of Lindisfarne. In an intimate story, while Oswald and Aidan were feasting at Easter, the king was apparently moved to gift a silver plate full of food to the poor, and then ordered that the plate itself would be broken up and handed out. This led Aidan to grab hold of and bless the king's hand, saying 'may this hand never perish'. That his hand was subsequently enshrined and treated as a great relic was thanks not just to Oswald's reputation as a great warrior and king, but to its being blessed by the holy Aidan.

Oswald was killed in battle against the pagan king of Mercia, Penda, in AD 642.[9] He was dismembered, with his head and limbs stuck on spikes. His cult grew in popularity over the years after his death, possibly with the support of Irish saints like Aidan, though reports of miracles associated with his relics spread quickly among the population, indicating that his appeal was widespread. The head of St Oswald, decapitated by his captors during his martyrdom, is particularly interesting since it presented a problem to those Christians supporting his cult. To venerate the decapitated head of a king or hero was a pagan Celtic practice so, while his hand was blessed by a Christian bishop, his head was associated with questionable pre-Christian rituals.

Nevertheless, many different heads of St Oswald are reported, as far afield as Luxemburg, Switzerland, Germany and the Netherlands. Bede reports that his head was quietly taken by his successor in Bernicia, Oswui, to Lindisfarne, where the monks surreptitiously dealt with it. The most accepted resting place for Oswald's head now is in Durham where, after centuries of wandering across the northern landscape in search of a final resting place, the Lindisfarne monks carried it inside a wooden coffin alongside the bones of another important Northumbrian saint – Cuthbert.

Cuthbert: Converting Hearts and Minds

Poster boy of the Anglo-Saxon Church in the north, Cuthbert's cult was finely engineered both by Bede (who wrote two official hagiographies of him) and the monks of Lindisfarne. At a time when the Irish Church was positioning itself against pagan Anglo-Saxon, Celtic and Roman Christian ideas, Cuthbert was crafted as a paradigm for all that was good in the Insular tradition. The real Cuthbert is difficult to reconstruct, and appears a mass of contradictions – warrior, nobleman, bishop, hermit, politician. Yet the way his cult was contrived after his death provides a fascinating insight into the power of art and literature within the early Church, and the important role these media had as propaganda tools.

Like many of the Anglo-Saxons who converted to Christianity within the first decades of its arrival, Cuthbert was a character that had to play many parts on the political and religious stage. When he chose to leave behind the life of a warrior nobleman for the Celtic monastery of Melrose, he became an important and influential member of the fledgling Church. Under Oswald, the Northumbrian royal family had tied themselves firmly to the Celtic Christian cause, and their enthusiastic support for, and sponsorship of, the early Church was a means by which they asserted themselves over other kingdoms. Following the example of Aethelberht, whose acceptance of Christianity had ensured his position of 'bretwalda' within Anglo-Saxon England, Oswald – and Edwin before him – supported the Church, particularly in terms of land grants. This meant that battles against Penda and other pagan kingdoms carried a sacred element; the Northumbrians didn't simply battle for more territory, influence or wealth, as they could argue that theirs was a holy war.

It is onto this turbulent stage that Cuthbert steps. He had grown up steeped in the pagan traditions of his ancestors, and spent a good deal of his life immersed in the power and politics of the nobility. His interest in the Church was probably a result of the 'top-down' nature of conversion. As a wealthy aristocrat he was able to rise to the rank of Bishop of Lindisfarne, and he took up his strategic position directly opposite the royal palace of Bamburgh. Throughout his life he was both an engaged bishop and a monastic hermit, taking himself away to Inner Farne, where he built a cell that cut off the world, with just a view of the sky. He would have survived on the eggs and flesh of sea birds, and with the elements pounding the sides of this exposed crag in the sea, a hermit's existence must have been harsh for Cuthbert.

Although he post-dates Cuthbert slightly, Guthlac (AD 673–714) provides a useful parallel to Cuthbert, in that he too seemed to straddle two worlds. He was also an Anglo-Saxon nobleman, and he became a hermit, embracing the hostile surroundings of the Fens. Yet, between these extremes, he remained a politically and religiously active individual. As Cuthbert was Bishop of Lindisfarne and in close contact with the Northumbrian royal family, so Guthlac gave refuge to Aethelbald, the future king of Mercia. The irony of hermit life for many was that, although they retreated from human company for spiritual isolation, this made them increasingly desirable in terms of providing counsel and advice. So hermits, like anchorites, were often visited, and they retained influence in the worldly concerns they sought to escape.

Two Old English poems about Guthlac survive, indicating that he was a suitable topic for celebration not just in the traditional Latin hagiographical texts, but also in the vernacular poetic tradition more usually concerned with heroes and battles. Guthlac certainly had military roots, since he is recorded as having served in the army of the Mercian king before becoming a monk at the double monastery (containing both monks and nuns) of Repton. His life throws into sharp relief the medieval concept of the three estates, since he went from being a knight or warrior, fighting to defend the people of this world from their enemies, to being a monk and then hermit, doing battle with supernatural enemies in order to protect souls both here and in the hereafter.

Cuthbert, like Guthlac, remained a close adviser to the royal family throughout his life, even meeting with ambassadors while apparently being an isolated hermit on Inner Farne. He played the role of seer or prophet at times in terms of advising the king. In AD 685 Cuthbert descended into a seer's mist and foretold the death of King Oswui.[10] He warned the king not to go to battle, and later when walking with the queen he was struck with a vision that the king had been killed. These visions are explained as miracles, but they also served as prophetic visions, the like of which Druidic high priests and seers were subject to as part of their responsibilities towards their rulers and followers. Cuthbert was a man with one foot in the pagan past, and another in the Christian future.

The conversion to Christianity was a slow process, and saints like Cuthbert had to navigate a rocky track to direct people away from their previous beliefs and towards the new ones. We get an idea of how potent the transformation from pagan to Christian was, and how early ecclesiastics like Paulinus sought to control it on a symbolic level, when we examine a specific account from his missionary work in the north. A text known as the *Anonymous Life of Saint Gregory*, written around AD 713 by a monk of Whitby, shows that Paulinus didn't always heed Gregory the Great's guidance that the conversion of the Anglo-Saxons was to be gradual. Instead, it seems that the pagan beliefs of the Anglo-Saxons were often crushed, and at times annihilated from the landscape. The author described how Paulinus ordered a youth to shoot down a crow from a tree as proof to 'those who were still bound ... to heathenism' that divine matters couldn't be understood through birds.

Paulinus's actions reveal that birds like the crow had pagan connections with divinity, and symbolised matters of life and death to some members of early seventh-century Northumbrian society. The raven was the symbolic bird of the Germanic pagan god Odinn, and Paulinus's act of shooting the black bird was a deliberate attempt to suppress the older belief systems. It is demonstrative of how the Roman mission at times treated the native pagan beliefs they encountered. Paulinus was a powerful man, with powerful backing, tied to a powerful king. He had some success in the north, but the conversion of Anglo-Saxon England was by no means complete a full generation after Augustine arrived in Kent.

Cuthbert has a similar run-in with birds. While he was on Inner Farne he communed with the local birds.[11] He was visited by two ravens, whom he had to reprimand for destroying a hay roof on one of his buildings. The ravens flew away, but returned, begging for forgiveness, with 'half a piece of swine's lard', which they offered to the saint as reparation.[12] When Bede came to rewrite the story of the ravens he added a speech in which Cuthbert himself angrily rebuked the birds, and he described their retreat in scathing terms, saying they 'flew dismally away'. Furthermore, he included a moralising sentence at the end of the chapter, in which he stated that this miracle was significant, for it showed how, 'even the proudest bird hastened to atone for the wrong that it had done to a man of God, by means of prayers, lamentations and gifts.'[13] Paulinus, Cuthbert and Bede all understood the power of symbols. Today, a Christian might wear a cross around their neck to symbolise their beliefs. To a Germanic pagan the symbol of the raven carried similar potency. Challenging the pagan religion through rebranding their symbols was one way that Cuthbert sought to win over hearts and minds. But Cuthbert and his cult also harnessed the power of art to their cause.

The Power of Art

Cuthbert survives in our modern imagination so much more vividly than many other Anglo-Saxon saints because his life was thoroughly recorded by Bede, and his cult was preserved in a number of objects and texts that have survived to the present day. This enables a fuller picture of him to emerge, although the majority of textual references and material evidence related to Cuthbert had been carefully contrived posthumously. The 'Lives' written by Bede, the Lindisfarne Gospels and the items placed within his coffin during the various translations his body underwent, all say as much about the people writing and creating, generations after the saint's death, as they do about Cuthbert himself.

The earliest surviving objects associated with the saint do, however, provide insights into the sort of man he may have been.[14] Beginning with the pectoral cross, this small piece of jewellery indicates that Cuthbert was both a member of the Anglo-Saxon aristocracy and a newly converted Christian. It was not discovered until Cuthbert's body had been reinterred, when it was found wrapped in his shroud. This suggests that he was originally buried wearing it, which is unusual, since the majority of early medieval Christian burials tended to lack grave goods.

The style of this object recalls the pagan Anglo-Saxon past, and the many brooches, buckles and adornments included in their furnished burials for the deceased to take onwards into the afterlife. The most lavish Anglo-Saxon pagan burial is Sutton Hoo, but almost all were buried with something, be it a knife, spear (for adolescent boys and men) or simple brooches. Cuthbert's cross is clearly high status, as it is made of gold. What's more, it resorts to the familiar technique of gold and garnet cloisonné, which is so richly attested

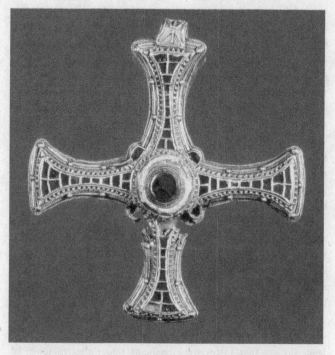

Cuthbert's pectoral cross was found buried around the neck of the saint, within his coffin. It is made of gold and garnet cloisonné and was clearly well-worn. One of the arms had almost broken off and a plate was soldered onto the back to repair it. While the style is Germanic, the shape and the inclusion of a tiny Chi-Rho symbol on the loop at the top suggest it is a Christian object.

to among the warrior class from the wealth of similar items found in the Staffordshire hoard. Nevertheless, it is clearly ecclesiastical, as suggested by the equal-armed cross shape and numerical symbolism that seems to permeate it. At its centre, the five jewels could be interpreted as the wounds of Christ, while the twelve cloisonné garnets in each of the four arms may recall the Apostles and the Evangelists.[15]

Cuthbert's cross testifies to the symbolic transformation that high-status jewellery was undergoing in the early seventh century. From around the time Augustine's mission arrived in Kent, jewellery in graves across the south in particular begins to change from the long-established zoomorphic interlacing metalwork characterised most exquisitely by the Sutton Hoo belt buckle. Instead, the shape of the cross begins to be articulated, first in the quartering of disc brooches, which featured four bosses surrounded by decorative spaces suggesting a cross, and then by equal-armed crosses like the stunning seventh-century survival from Wilton, Norfolk. Gold and garnet arms radiate from a gold Byzantine coin, suggesting that the owner was displaying their exotic international connections. The fact that this coin has been positioned upside down, with the cross on Calvary pointing upwards, has led to speculation that the makers of this piece were illiterate and had little experience with coinage. However, this recalls the watches of nurses, in that if it is worn around the neck on a chain, the cross will be viewed the right way up by the wearer. It was an object of personal devotion.

These objects, along with the appearance of exotic gems like amethyst and amber, as seen in the stunning Desborough necklace, suggest that tastes were changing under the influence of increased contact with the Christian Continent. They also indicate that Anglo-Saxon jewellers were having to work with a different set of symbols to suit the new religious leanings of their patrons. Cuthbert's cross is a hybrid reaction to the broader cultural and religious changes, for while the techniques and materials used to make it accord with a far older tradition of Germanic metalworking, the shape of the cross suggests it was part of the new style of jewellery arriving with the Roman Church.

The other object known to date from around the time of Cuthbert's death is, of course, his coffin. The oldest piece of

The Wilton Cross, now in the British Museum, was found in Norfolk. In the centre is a solidus from the reign of Emperor Heraclius, who reigned from AD 610–41. It has been set upside down so that the viewer can see the image of the cross while wearing it.

decorated wooden carving to survive from Anglo-Saxon England, it too contains layers of symbolism that hint at the role Cuthbert played in this formative period of Anglo-Saxon history. The four sides and lid of the coffin are all incised with carved figures, each of which testifies to a different aspect of the seventh-century Church in Northumbria. On the front is one of the oldest iconic representations of the Virgin Mary and Christ child to survive outside of Rome. It recalls Byzantine images in the way both Mary and Christ stare out directly at the viewer.

Along one side are the twelve apostles, the most orthodox expression of the Roman Church, with Peter, the first pope, distinguished by the two keys in his hand.[16] On the other side, however, is a sequence of archangels. The veneration of angels was common in the Celtic Church, but was a source of consternation for the Roman Church. Angels were seen as intermediaries between God and mankind, a role reserved for the saints and martyrs among Orthodox Christians in the seventh century. But Irish literature testifies to the popularity of angels, many of whom were named and venerated individually.

Depicting a sequence of angels in this manner indicates the influence of the Celtic monastery most closely associated with Cuthbert, Lindisfarne. Its stance on issues like the dating of Easter, the monastic tonsure and the veneration of angels were defining characteristics of the practices at this site and its satellite monasteries. By including this combination of images on Cuthbert's coffin, the artists that created it have made a clear statement about the uniqueness of the Celtic Church: it can conform with orthodox ideas and practices, but at the same time has its own roots, traditions and traits.

One last aspect of the coffin is worth noting as yet more evidence for the transitional period in which Cuthbert lived and died, and the conciliatory role he played. On the lid is a depiction of Christ in Majesty, surrounded by the symbols of the Four Evangelists – man for Matthew, lion for Mark, calf for Luke and eagle for John. Their form is characteristic of Insular manuscript art, where the beasts are shown full-length, with books and haloes. However, something interesting has occurred with the labels next to each of the creatures. While the name of Luke is inscribed very clearly in Latin as 'Lucas', the names of the other three are given in runes. It seems highly unlikely that, while carving the lid of this most important of ecclesiastical coffins, the craftsman would accidentally switch scripts. Instead, it may be that this is a deliberate attempt to reflect the changing world Cuthbert inhabited.

He straddled both the secular and the spiritual, the Germanic and the Continental, the pagan and the Christian. By switching scripts the creators of the coffin are appealing to the old order and the new, and both confer a degree of protection upon the saint interred within. The whole coffin can be seen as a form of eternal prayer surrounding Cuthbert's remains. It appeals to Christ, Mary, the saints and the angels, in both the language of the Church and of the Anglo-Saxon people. It brings different worlds together to make something harmonious, in the same way that Cuthbert himself did during his lifetime.

Cuthbert: the Lindisfarne and Stonyhurst Gospels

There is another famous object that will forever be tied to the name of St Cuthbert: the Lindisfarne Gospels.[17] Although it was produced a generation after the saint died, around the year AD 700, it was designed as a cult object to venerate the monastery of Lindisfarne and its most famous bishop. At the end of the manuscript stands a colophon, added in the tenth century by Aldred, the scribe responsible for the interlinear Old English gloss. It states that the writing and illumination were the work of one man, Eadfrith. This is a feat in itself, but it seems that Eadfrith balanced his immense scribal workload with the responsibilities of being Bishop of Lindisfarne. Following the example of Cuthbert in his devotion to prayer and isolation as a hermit on Inner Farne, Eadfrith's dedication to producing the Gospels would have been an act of extreme devotion, occupying a great deal of his time.

The process of making the Gospels would have been laborious and exhausting. Bending over curling vellum while balancing inkwells and quills, and searching for light either outside, with a

The Lindisfarne Gospels, London, British Library Cotton MS Nero D.IV, is recognised internationally as one of the finest illuminated manuscripts in the world. The work of one man – Eadfrith, Bishop of Lindisfarne – it is beautifully decorated throughout. The full-page illuminations include carpet pages, which combine Celtic and Anglo-Saxon motifs seamlessly.

Imago Leonis

OAGI
HA
R

US
CUS

portable writing desk, or inside dimly lit, smoke-filled timber halls would have required dedication and skill. The manuscript Eadfrith produced is stunning and inspired. He was driven both by a desire to create a cult object that would draw the admiration of pilgrims, and to express artistically the importance of his see at Lindisfarne to the uniquely insular character of northern English Christianity. He employed a series of original designs and carefully chosen motifs to decorate the gospels.

The carpet pages that occur before each gospel reflect those in the earlier Book of Durrow, but the decoration is more meticulous and expressive. Mark's Gospel opens with a geometric design, where an equal-armed cross can be discerned amidst the blue and red circular and linear patterns. The margins are composed of knots, while each of the four squares towards the corners contain a circular motif complete with spirals. These designs are drawn from a Celtic context, with the circular sections in particular recalling enamel panels from hanging bowls. In the centre is a very different design, however. Yellow, red and blue alternate in a series of stepped diamonds, and bring to mind the gold, garnet and glass cloisonné work on Anglo-Saxon jewellery like the Sutton Hoo shoulder clasp. Furthermore, the propensity for zoomorphic interlace witnessed in Germanic metalwork is echoed in the sections around the cross, where decorative, abstracted birds overlap and twine around one another. This page draws together artistic influences and ideas from the Celtic and the Anglo-Saxon worlds. It pays homage to the harmony that can be developed between two seemingly opposed visual traditions.

Each carpet page is followed by a decorative set of initials, which takes the idea of diminuendo presented in the Cathach of Columba and creates a stunning blend of text and image. The decoration draws the mind of the reader from contemplation and meditation on the non-figural carpet pages, through to the divinely inspired words of the Gospel itself.[18] There is also an Evangelist portrait before every Gospel, depicting the author at work writing or reciting (in the case of John) their accounts. These are copied from Continental exemplars, but the style is very different.

The figures are not shown as life-like or realistic. Instead, they are abstracted, so the faces are reduced to simple shapes for the features, and the drapery becomes a series of alternating bands of colour. The treatment of the Evangelists is not down to Eadfrith being 'bad' at painting people. Rather, it should be seen as a deliberate attempt to avoid depicting sacred figures too realistically, perhaps due to iconoclastic attitudes abroad. By the seventh century both Judaism and Islam had predominantly chosen to avoid representing holy figures realistically for fear of producing false idols. Eadfrith follows Pope Gregory's earlier guidance that images can help educate Christians, but he couches his figures within abstraction, the like of which anticipates the work of Picasso and Matisse. It is innovative art from an innovative place, and a benchmark of the Northumbrian Golden Age.

Yet while the Lindisfarne Gospels presents an impression of Cuthbert as a bridge between worlds, and the perfect manifestation of all that is good and worthy from both the Celtic and the Anglo-Saxon traditions, it is primarily propaganda. After his death, the cult of Cuthbert was strengthened and developed by the monastery of Lindisfarne. Laying claim to a saint was an excellent means of securing widespread admiration for their establishment, as well as a constant stream of revenue and pilgrims. The relics were important, so the monks cared for his coffin and all it contained, with one tenth-century member of the community reputedly combing Cuthbert's hair frequently. But the other trappings of a seventh-century saint's cult seem to have included a deluxe manuscript, as with Columba and the Cathach.

The Lindisfarne Gospels provided Eadfrith, as Bishop of Lindisfarne, with an opportunity to develop a sustained PR campaign for his monastery as it went into the eighth century. Within the vellum pages of this manuscript he created a visual style that presented Lindisfarne as an inclusive and avant-garde establishment, where all that was unique about the Church in Northumbria could be celebrated. This may indeed reflect how Cuthbert himself was perceived, but the Lindisfarne Gospels do not represent him directly. Instead, they reveal how the inheritors of his community wanted him to be seen.

In contrast, however, the small volume known as the Stonyhurst Gospel appears more intimately bound with Cuthbert himself. By turning the pages of fine vellum in this tiny pocket book it may be possible to peer over the shoulder of the saint as he read. The Victorian biblical scholar Christopher Wordsworth felt it was finer than the Lindisfarne Gospels, 'surpassing in delicate simplicity of neatness every manuscript that I have ever seen'.[19] It has the oldest preserved original leather binding in the West, and its remarkable condition is due to the care with which it was kept while among Cuthbert's treasures at Durham Cathedral. It was wrapped inside three additional leather satchels and kept within a box for four centuries.

It is a simple, relatively unadorned copy of John's Gospel, and in its simplicity it recalls the monastic ideal spread by the Celtic Church of wandering across the landscape with staff, bell and book, prepared to preach. Its size and apparent modesty betray the fact that, despite it being a useful pocket book, it is still a beautifully made, high-status object. The leather casing also recalls the decoration of the Lindisfarne Gospels in the way it draws together Celtic, Anglo-Saxon and Continental motifs. On the front, raised floriated scrolls sit inside a margin of knotwork, while on the back the patterns familiar from cloisonné work create a geometric incised pattern. This object, alongside the pectoral cross, coffin and Lindisfarne Gospels, tells a similar story: Cuthbert was a rallying point for the fledgling Church in Anglo-Saxon Northumbria, and a syphon for all that was good about its mixed cultural heritage.

The importance of Cuthbert and the artefacts associated with him has been recognised recently by the journey that the Lindisfarne Gospels took to Durham in 2013. Exhibited alongside the Stonyhurst Gospel, saved for the nation just a year earlier, the British Library's most precious medieval manuscript spent three months close to the bones and relics of the saint they celebrate. Yet the true character and personality of Cuthbert have become clouded behind a screen of posthumous veneration. After his death, a deliberate set of cult objects were made to bolster his reputation and ensure a constant stream of veneration and income for the monastery of Lindisfarne. Whoever Cuthbert really was remains difficult to grasp, for in the hands of sophisticated writers, artists and spin doctors he became the perfect vehicle for sustained and energetic symbolic manipulation. A bridge between worlds, he was a saint who was moulded and crafted through the texts and artworks that came to be associated with him. But his importance at a critical moment in the evolution of the Anglo-Saxon Church cannot be underestimated. During his lifetime change was becoming the norm, and a cultural revolution was taking place. We see this most clearly in the life of one of Anglo-Saxon England's most important female saints, Hilda of Whitby.

Chapter Seven
Hilda: Princess of a Powerhouse

> 'Rage fires the fiend, who formerly Eve betrayed,
> While shouting angels hail the glorious maid.
> See wedded to her God, what joy remains,
> In earth, or heaven, see with her God she reigns!
> Behold the spouse, the festal torches shine,
> He comes! Behold what joyful gifts are thine!
> Thou a new song on the sweet harp shalt sing,
> A hymn of praise to thy celestial King.'

Bede's hymn in praise of the Holy Virgin Aethelthryth.[1]

Hilda continues to captivate across the centuries. It seems hard to believe that, at a time when women were supposed to be the powerless pawns of men, she could achieve such great things. A princess for half her life, and abbess at one of the most important double monasteries in the nation for the other half, she remains celebrated as a woman who stood out in a man's world. She was influential among the highest strata of both the Church and the State, was surrounded by the most learned people of the time and commanded land, men and women as abbess of Whitby. While the ruins that sit on the outcrop on the Yorkshire coast post-date her by some 400 years, her name still resonates across this symbolic landscape.

At Whitby the spirit of Gothic, old and new, seeps out of the very cracks in the pavement of this extraordinary coastal town. The echoes of Bram Stoker's *Dracula*, in which the arrival of the fearful vampire upon the coast is set against dramatic cliffs and Norman ruins, can still be felt. In this town it feels like the centuries elide. Its coat of arms, bearing three ammonites, and the jet jewellery in shop windows, made from the compressed remains of monkey-puzzle trees, attest to its ancient geological significance. The skeletal remains of the ruined abbey stand in high relief on the East Cliff, while grand Georgian homes gaze down on humble fishing cottages along the seafront. The shipping legacy of the town is now reduced to a series of colourful fishing boats in the harbour. But at the end of the eighteenth century Whitby was the biggest ship-builder after London and Newcastle. Victorian trade and industry made the town prosperous, and its most important civic buildings stand testament to past glories. The sea washes in and out of the estuary like lifeblood.

Yet it is the haunting ruins of the monastery, high on the cliff, that constantly draw the eye. Surrounded by tall grass that ebbs and flows in the wind, the damaged stones and once-great vaulted arches seem to grow out of their surroundings. They sit on top of a much earlier monastic site: Streoneshalh. The name continues to baffle scholars; it may refer to a Roman settlement on the site, or to an earlier founder, Streona.[2] This site became increasingly significant in the Anglo-Saxon period because the land along the East Cliff was given by King Oswui of Northumbria to a noblewoman named Hilda. Here she founded a double monastery, containing both monks and nuns, and presided over them as abbess. She is one of the most important female figures of the early medieval period, and is still venerated widely as a saint. Yet, like Cuthbert, a fellow Northumbrian noble and convert, her life charts one of the most dramatic periods in English history in terms of religious transformation.

Hilda: One Life – Two Halves

Born around AD 614, Hilda was the daughter of Hereric, King Edwin's nephew. She was part of the Deiran royal family and a princess. After her father was murdered while in exile at the British court in Elmet (roughly modern-day West Yorkshire), she was taken in by Edwin and brought up within the pagan royal court. It was the king who gave protection to Hilda and her widowed mother, and in return she would have to accompany the court around the royal sites and palaces. Other widowed queens and noblewomen, as well as exiles and hostages, would have joined them: seventh-century English kingship was a cousinhood.[3] As with Cuthbert, it is tempting to imagine Hilda within the timbered hall at Yeavering, serving the warriors, passing round the mead cup, and listening to the local people appealing to their king for help or justice.

Most of what we know about Hilda's life is drawn from Bede's *Ecclesiastical History*, and in this text Bede reveals some details about the secular life she lived before becoming a nun and abbess. He records details about her family, and that she was brought up in

Bamburgh Castle on the Northumbrian coast, directly opposite Lindisfarne.[4] The original royal stronghold sat on an outcrop of volcanic rock, which allowed a natural vantage point some 150 feet above sea level. Its strategic position made it the perfect choice for an Anglo-Saxon fortress. Finds like the six-band pattern-welded Bamburgh sword, rediscovered in Brian Hope-Taylor's garage in 2001, attest to the military significance of the location. A part of the Bamburgh site shows evidence for metalworking, which suggests that weapons and jewellery could have been forged within this royal stronghold.

Furthermore, parts of a stone throne were discovered at the site, which may have been the seat of power of the Northumbrian kings. Here, Edwin could have given gifts to his loyal followers, securing the military service of thegns who lived alongside him and protected his family. Hilda would have been exposed to this warrior elite; she would have seen them train and listened to their tales of battle. Indeed, her very name carries connotations of the Anglo-Saxon warrior world, since it comes from the Old English word for battle: 'hild'. The first half of her life would have been spent performing the duties of a princess, seeing to the needs of the royal household and probably some skilled labour like embroidery and weaving.

Hilda was among the first in the north to convert to Christianity, as she joined King Edwin in a rapidly constructed timber church close to present-day York Minster for his baptism on Easter Sunday, AD 627. She was only thirteen at the time, and it is difficult to know whether her conversion was obligatory or done through choice. She would have heard Paulinus preaching to the court, and seen the great pressure the Roman missionaries were exerting on Edwin and his supporters. Whether she agreed with the ideas introduced by Paulinus or if she simply had to follow the king's example will never be known. But she would have seen first-hand the important role that women could play within a Christian court.

Edwin's wife, Queen Aethelburg, was the daughter of the first English king to convert to Christianity – Aethelberht of Kent. He too had probably accepted Christianity under pressure from his wife. Bertha played a salient role in encouraging her husband first to welcome in the missionaries from Rome, and then to convert to the new religion. Hilda would have seen the daughter of this union between Anglo-Saxon king and Christian Frankish princess work her own skills upon her Northumbrian king. She would no doubt have been struck by the changes that women could make with Christianity as the new religious framework for the kingdom. And the monasteries offered a new set of options to Anglo-Saxon noblewomen.

It might seem like becoming a nun would run counter to the intentions of many royal or noble families. A woman's role was to remain loyal to her family and lord, make good marriages to secure dowries and political affiliations, and bear children. By becoming nuns, all of these roles would be curtailed. However, convents and monasteries presented noblewomen with tantalising opportunities. Firstly, in a time when divorce was incredibly rare, a king or lord could dispose of a barren or unwanted spouse by leaving her to a convent. This would suit both parties, since early convents were often places of luxury. The woman involved would no longer have to remain in an unsatisfactory union, or bend to her husband's desire for matrimonial dues, which always insisted upon the wife being servant to her husband. Rape and abuse were often part of medieval marriage, as the woman was her husband's possession, to do with as he wished.

Secondly, the founding of convents, with an aristocratic woman at the head, could be politically and financially expedient for noble families. Monastic lands would be granted to the woman, thus staying within the control of a particular landowning family. Produce from this land, and taxes too, could be utilised by the owners, and the woman would preside over the nuns within as abbess. Women were useful for securing marriages, but not for securing land, as the family's wealth would pass into the hands of her husband. However, founding convents allowed for more land to remain in the possession of a family, even if they had daughters rather than sons. Instead of losing power and wealth through dowries, founding convents meant the terrain, its productivity and its loyalty could be secured. Finally, becoming a nun offered women many personal benefits. There was the chance to become educated, to have the respect of her fellows, the security of often-luxurious convent settings, and to have freedom from the male-dominated, misogynistic confines of court life.

However, for half of her life Hilda was subject to the secular responsibilities of Anglo-Saxon noblewomen. After Penda killed Edwin in battle in AD 633, Paulinus took his Christian queen and her female entourage to safety to her family's court in Kent. It is most likely that Hilda went with her. The women of the court needed protection, so it fell to Aethelburg's brother, King Eadbald of Kent, to protect them. Eadbald is an intriguing character. Despite the fact that both his father, Aethelberht, and mother, Bertha, were Christian, he was a pagan.

He rejected the Church when he ascended to the throne on his father's death because he wanted to marry his father's second wife. Marrying his stepmother was illegal within Christian law, so Eadbald returned the kingdom of Kent to the pagan religion. Religious change to secure a marriage is something that Henry VIII would so famously do with Anne Boleyn, but Eadbald did it some 800 years earlier. The sons of Edwin and Aethelburg were sent away from England to King Dagobert in Francia, since male heirs were significant pawns in the game and had to be protected until they were old and strong enough to reclaim their lands. But the women were in an equally dangerous position.

Rather than end up remarried by her brother in a politically expedient union, Queen Aethelburg took the decision to found one of the first Benedictine monasteries in England, at Lyminge, where she ruled as abbess over a double community of monks and nuns. Finds from close to the modern-day church at Lyminge suggest that Aethelburg's monastic church was made from reused Roman stone.[5] Remains of a large-scale timber hall, akin to that at Yeavering, have been discovered next to the monastic site. This, along with rich pagan burials and finds of Frankish glass, suggests that Aethelburg built her church next to a royal palace complex, with the secular palace forming the basis for a later Anglo-Saxon monastery. Here the queen had the safety and security to live out the end of her life, and her example must have made a striking impact on Hilda. She could continue to live in the luxury and security she had known in great royal halls, yet could govern a double

monastery too, thus preventing the need for a potentially dangerous remarriage.

Hilda at Whitby

After thirty-three years of life in the court (a symbolic number, for
that was the age at which Jesus died), involved in the political and
social machinations of the Anglo-Saxon royal families, Hilda chose
a monastic life. She had intended to follow her sister Hereswith,
who had gone to the Frankish monastery of Chelles after her
husband, the King of East Anglia, had died. Instead, Hilda went to
Aidan of Lindisfarne, and began training at a small monastery
somewhere along the banks of the River Wear. She was brought up
firmly within the Celtic tradition, and Aidan then made her abbess
of an existing monastery at Hartlepool. Hilda managed to secure
the support of Edwin's Bernician successor, King Oswui. First he
gave his daughter, Aelfflaed, into her care at Hartlepool, and then
he gave her land at Whitby to establish a double monastery.[6] This
is yet further evidence for the 'top-down' nature of Anglo-Saxon
conversion, for those with connections to the court could garner
the land and resources needed to establish monasteries.

In the manner of Queen Aethelburg before her, Hilda set up a
double monastery on the outcrop of land overlooking the sea at
Whitby. Oswui gave her ten hides (enough to support ten households) in thanks for his victory over the pagan king Penda. Here,
men and women would live in separate dormitories, but would
come together to hear mass at the church. The women would be
involved in similar crafts to those that occupied noblewomen,
namely spinning, sewing and weaving, but they would also have
the opportunity to read and write. Styli have been found at Whitby
that were used to scratch letters into wax tablets, and elaborate
book fittings also attest to the fact that manuscripts passed through
the hands of the monks and nuns.

The men would be involved in other skills, like metalworking
and possibly glass making, as there was some evidence at the site
to suggest that this ancient Roman practice was being reintroduced

at Whitby. The monastery was designed in the Celtic manner, with two or three sharing a wooden hut, and the men separated from the women. Yet finds from the site point to it being a wealthy monastery. Hairpins and pieces of Anglian glass suggest that the nobility who followed Hilda into the monastic life did not sacrifice all their luxuries.

There are finds from Whitby that give a sense both of the courtly nature of the institution she established and the transitional world this saint inhabited. The bone comb discovered in a rubbish pit on the site of Streoneshalh is interesting because it is clearly a high-status object, used to keep its owner looking respectable, and possibly given as a gift.[7] Yet it is also of interest because it is covered in runes.[8] Just as the inscriptions on Cuthbert's coffin shifted between Latin and Old English, so does the Whitby comb. It has a pious plea for God's help, *deus meus, god aluwaldo, helpæ Cy* ... – 'my God, almighty God, help Cy ...'. The Latin turns to the vernacular at the second cry to 'God'.

The grant of land from the king, the royal background of Hild herself, and the noble men and women who would have joined her fledgling monastery were all tied to the court of Northumbria. This site would become significant through its connection with royalty, and it was where Oswui, his wife, daughter and many other nobles would be buried.[9] Oswui would play an important role not only in Hilda's life, but also in the life of the Anglo-Saxon Church, due to his part in the proceedings of the famous Synod of Whitby. Oswui's life was an interesting one, since he seems to have straddled many worlds.

During his relatively long life and reign, he was married to three princesses, each from a different part of the British Isles. His first wife, Eanflaed, was the daughter of Oswui's predecessor and rival in Northumbria, King Edwin. Upon his return to Bernicia as king he married the daughter of his father's killer, as a means of unifying the Northumbrians houses. However, his second wife was the Irish princess Fin, and his third the British princess Rieinmellt. This shows not only what a culturally diverse place seventh-century Britain was, but that the Anglo-Saxon rulers consciously sought out closer links with the British, Irish and Picts. There has been a traditional tendency to separate the Germanic people from the Celtic, but the degrees of intermarriage and interaction evinced by an important individual like Oswui make these distinctions less clear-cut.

Also of significance in terms of his upbringing were the years spent as a Christian brought up under Irish tuition. Oswui and Oswald were Christian, and both were educated within the Irish tradition under the influence of St Aidan of Lindisfarne. This meant that a dynastic rivalry had emerged between the Deirans and Bernicians in the early seventh century. Edwin was from Deira and backed Paulinus and the Roman mission. Oswald was from Bernicia and backed Aidan and the Irish mission. Oswui would have to position himself carefully in relation to these parties and, fuelled by the power play of influential representatives of the newly established Roman Church like Bishop Wilfrid, the situation was to come to a head in AD 664.

The Synod of Whitby

Oswui decided to hold this important synod at Hilda's monastery of Whitby. She was a powerful personality, who acted as a royal adviser and saw to the spiritual guidance of those under her watch. Furthermore, like Cuthbert she could be seen as a bridge between different groups. She had grown up in the court of Edwin, was baptised by Paulinus and yet trained under the guidance of Aidan of Lindisfarne. Tensions between the two parties of the Irish and Roman Church were culminating. Now that Gregory's mission had been largely successful and a generation of Anglo-Saxon Christians were emerging, a decision on the Celtic practices had to be made.

Whitby was the perfect place to host such an important synod. Hilda would have coordinated the travel and lodgings of bishops and Church representatives from across the country and abroad. The food and accommodation required for such an event would have put great pressure on Hilda's monastery, yet she would have been celebrated as the abbess able to accommodate the good and the great of the Church. She also would have played the role of peace-weaver, keeping tensions at bay between representatives of the different parties. Hilda must have been diplomatic and capable to steer so many opinionated men through the proceedings of the synod.

The impact of the Synod of Whitby may have been overstretched due to the huge emphasis Bede placed on it in his *Ecclesiastical History*.[10] He was interested in the correct calculation of Easter, writing a whole tract on *The Reckoning of Time*, and his main concern through his theological, scientific and historical texts was to stress the unity of the English Church. Yet, however much Bede may have overemphasised it, the Synod of Whitby was a pivotal moment for the Irish Church in England, and would determine the fate of monastic communities at sites like Lindisfarne and Iona. The debate at the heart of the Synod of Whitby revolved around two seemingly simple matters: the dating of Easter and the shape of the monk's tonsure. These may not seem the most exciting or significant issues, but the implications of the synod ran far deeper.

The conversion of the Anglo-Saxons to Christianity was a relatively slow process. While certain royal houses and their entourages were encouraged by missionaries from Ireland or Rome to convert, others resisted. In some kingdoms, like Northumbria, the kings shifted allegiance, beginning Christian then returning to paganism. The large and powerful kingdom of Mercia under its king Penda resisted Christianity until AD 655, and the last pagan king, Arwald of the Isle of Wight, died in AD 686. The Synod of Whitby was held at a time when pockets of Christian power had become entrenched throughout England, and the Archbishop of Canterbury, Theodore, was making attempts to bring the various branches of the Church together. In some parts of Anglo-Saxon England it seems that individual churchmen and women were instructing specific royal households in a similar way to Druidic seers; their approach was parochial rather than coordinated. The Roman Church wanted this to stop.

There were deeper political reasons for the synod too, particularly in Northumbria, where the shift in power between the houses of Bernicia and Deira had meant that different approaches had developed in different establishments. Under Edwin and Paulinus, the Roman method of calculating Easter had spread throughout monastic foundations and the royal family. Yet with Oswald's sponsorship of Aidan at Lindisfarne, alternative practices were observed elsewhere. Tensions reached a head when Aidan died and Oswui, King of Northumbria, was celebrating Easter on a different day to his queen and her followers. The date of Christ's resurrection from death is the central event in the Christian calendar, so to miscalculate it was tantamount to heresy.

The problem revolves around the fact that the Irish Church had not followed changes in the way Easter was calculated in Rome. For much of the fourth, fifth and sixth centuries they had worked out Easter in relation to the dating of the Jewish Passover, but the First Council of Nicea in AD 325 decreed against this, and so different approaches were developed. By the time of the Synod of Whitby most monastic establishments in mainland Ireland had already decided to adapt their way to the Roman method, but Iona and its sister houses stood firm. As a result, the Synod of Whitby was really a battle between the Ionan and Roman approaches.

This extended to the issue of the monastic tonsure. Why should a hairstyle cause such controversy and outrage? This again runs deeper than may first appear. The Irish monks had developed a tonsure that was shaved at the front and grew long at the back. This had emerged over time, becoming traditional by the seventh century. Along with their staff, book and bell, this tonsure was a way of identifying an Irish monk. In contrast, the Petrine tonsure, which rings around the head with the centre portion shaved bare, was associated with Peter himself. It was a sign of conformity with the Church of Rome, while the Irish tonsure was an outward sign of difference. The Irish monks looked different to those elsewhere on the Continent, and this difference could border on threatening when the individuals concerned had the ears of some of the most important people in the land. By AD 664 there was less tolerance for religious regionalism, and the Roman party wanted to bring a greater uniformity to the Church across all of Anglo-Saxon England.

The two main representatives at the synod were men: Colman of Lindisfarne and Wilfrid of Hexham. Both were politically active, educated, noteworthy leaders within the Anglo-Saxon Church. Nevertheless, Wilfrid emerged as the dominant voice, presenting sound reasons for the widespread acceptance of Roman practice. Colman based his argument on the fact that Lindisfarne and Iona had a tradition going back to that saintly individual Columba, 'the dove of the Church', which they were going to hold to. Wilfrid said, however, that Peter was Christ's 'rock' (his name, Petrus, means stone or rock) upon which he built his church, and his successors as pope were the ultimate authority on all matters.

Oswui, in the manner of a Roman Emperor at the gladiatorial games, gave the proverbial 'thumbs down' to Colman and the Ionan party. The Celtic Church had been full of variety, and individual churchmen or missionaries would establish monasteries that were adapted to the local surroundings or took on board the needs of the local people and aristocratic families. The main outcome of the Synod of Whitby was to squeeze the uniqueness out of the early Christian outposts across the British Isles. Coupled with an increased use of the Benedictine Rule, with its rigour and regulation, the Church in England became a more structured place.

The Synod of Whitby was about power and control.[11] The Ionan Church had to step back, and as a result Bishop Colman of Lindisfarne quit his seat, eventually returning to Ireland. Lindisfarne continued as a monastery and bishopric, however, realigning itself with Roman practices and rallying behind a new abbot and bishop – Cuthbert – who would remove some of the stigma the Synod of Whitby had left behind. Hilda also had to change her ways. Her monastery at Whitby had followed the Ionan practice of dating Easter, so her organisation had to develop. But it remained a powerhouse of authority; so much so that, immediately after the synod, a new art form began to emerge around Whitby.

Whitby, Art and Poetry

One result of the Synod of Whitby was the emergence of free-standing stone high crosses. The legacy of this development can still be felt in market squares across the British Isles, and indeed, the world, where memorial crosses act as focal points for the town. At first they were roughly hewn crosses, not much taller than a tombstone. But there was an explosion of taller, more elaborate versions, particularly across the north of England. The links with Whitby are symbolic: the Roman Church triumphed at the synod, and the papacy – based on Petrus/Peter, the 'rock' upon which Christ built his Church – had to imprint its presence on the landscape. What better than a large piece of stone, breaking up the hills and fields, guiding the eye and providing a highly visible meeting point? That the stone was a permanent fixture on the landscape, not subject to weathering as wood and timber were, also reinforced the message that the Roman Church was here to stay. The more elaborate versions, like the Ruthwell Cross, appear in the eighth century, but the idea seems to have originated in and around Hilda's monastery at Whitby.[12]

Hilda has been remembered as a patron of the arts through her support of the Old English poet Caedmon. Bede records how Caedmon tended to the animals on the estate at Streoneshalh. He was wary of being in the hall when the revelry began, as he feared he would have to join in the courtly song that rang around the mead benches. It is worth remembering that Bede is recording monks in this act of feasting, singing and passing around the harp, which again suggests that Hilda's abbey at Whitby resembled a secular hall. Caedmon felt he could compose and sing nothing. Yet when he slept he was visited by 'someone' who encouraged him to sing 'the beginning of created things'. The only part of his poetic output to survive is the so-called 'Caedmon's Hymn':

Now [we] must honour the guardian of heaven,
the might of the architect, and his purpose,
the work of the father of glory
as he, the eternal lord, established the beginning of wonders;
he first created for the children of men
heaven as a roof, the holy creator
Then the guardian of mankind,
the eternal lord, afterwards appointed the middle earth,
the lands for men, the Lord almighty.[13]

This poem – the oldest Old English poem to survive in manuscript form – occurs only in Bede's *Ecclesiastical History*. Yet it attests to an early oral poetic tradition that flourished in Anglo-Saxon halls, and which adapted to the new subject matter of Christianity in the seventh century. According to Bede, Hilda encouraged Caedmon, and he became a monk at Whitby. Indeed, many important individuals passed through her monastery, including five future Anglo-Saxon bishops, one of whom was Wilfrid himself. It is surprising to think that a woman could wield such power and influence in the seventh century. Hilda was a transitional figure, poised at a transitional moment. The role of women would change as the Church increasingly controlled, monitored and suppressed their influence, but Hilda represents a high point for early medieval Christian women. She was not alone, either.

Aethelthryth: Queen, Mother and Nun

Hilda was not the only Anglo-Saxon woman to found important monastic institutions and be declared a saint upon her death. In the century after the Roman mission of AD 597, women within Anglo-Saxon England were systematically raised to the status of abbess, and ultimately saint.[14] The family tree of King Anna of East Anglia is particularly interesting. All four of his daughters were declared saints. Despite the fact that the memory of Hilda seems to have come down through the centuries more clearly, it's been suggested that Anna's daughter Aethelthryth was the most popular of the female Anglo-Saxons saints, with more vernacular texts written about her than any other.[15]

Aethelthryth was a contemporary of Hilda, born around AD 636 and died in AD 679, and her life was tied to that of the Northumbrian noblewoman's, particularly as Hilda's sister Hereswith had married her uncle. She was of royal birth, and her father, Anna, was a fascinating character. He was a member of the Wuffingas dynasty – that warrior clan who had settled in the area around East Anglia after travelling from Sweden, and whose legacy appears to be commemorated in the array of finds from Sutton Hoo. Yet, while his ancestors were pagan, Anna was celebrated as a pious Christian. It seems that the East Anglians had to do whatever the rulers of the other kingdoms did, but with even greater results. So Anna, nephew of Raedwald (who is possibly the ruler commemorated in the Sutton Hoo ship burial), embraced Christianity with such aplomb that all of his children were declared saints.

Aethelthryth was a valuable commodity as daughter to the king of East Anglia. Her worth lay in her ability to secure allegiances through marriage and provide rulers with heirs. In the warrior culture of the Anglo-Saxons, marriage was akin to the relationship between a lord and his retainer; a man and wife were not equal, but rather a wife owed her husband undivided loyalty until death.[16] According to Bede, Aethelthryth desired a religious life early on, and chose virginity despite being married twice. Through her two marriages she secured a number of benefits, including political allegiances and dowry payments. Her first husband was Tondberct, prince of the South Gyrwe (the area around the Fens, which included Ely), while her second was Ecgfrith of Northumbria.

However, she proved to be a problematic wife in both instances, refusing to provide her husbands with the opportunity to consummate their marriage and thereby sire an heir. This is explained by the fact that she had taken a vow of chastity before being wed, but there is another, political, way to read this. It is possible that she was unable to bear children, and the suggestion of extreme piety and virginity meant that she would not simply be cast aside by her husband, but would be provided for in terms of becoming a nun.[17]

When her first husband died, having apparently respected her vow of chastity, he left her the area around Ely as a mourning gift, and here she established a monastery. According to Bede, she had imagined this would signal her retirement from the world of courtly politics, but her family weren't done exploiting her worth yet; they married her a second time, to Ecgfrith, King of Deira from AD 664. Again, Aethelthryth requested that her husband respect her virginity, but this proved hard for Ecgfrith, who needed a legitimate heir to his unstable kingdom. They remained married for ten years, but when he ascended to the throne as king of all Northumbria he became more demanding of his wife. It was the intervention of Wilfrid, one of the most powerful churchmen of his time, which seems to have finally determined the outcome of Aethelthryth and Ecgfrith's marriage. He encouraged her to remain chaste, and she eventually left court for a monastic life.

The ideals of purity and devotion that underlie the story of Aethelthryth made her extremely popular, and Bede and Wilfrid promoted her cult. However, the reality of her situation was more complex. Bede himself questioned Wilfrid as to whether she really had been a virgin, for twelve years of marriage to a king was a long time. It may be possible, through the story of Aethelthryth, to glimpse some of the private difficulties faced by rulers. Kings wanted fertile wives who could do their bidding and provide heirs.

Ecgfrith and Aethelthryth may have found themselves in a barren union, where one or other of them could not provide children – Ecgfrith did in fact take a second wife, and she was also unable to provide an heir. As divorce laws were strict, with adultery the only legitimate reason to put a wife aside, Aethelthryth joining a convent must have been the next best option. Whether she went willingly or was coerced into making way for another queen, Aethelthryth's story was given a spin doctor's treatment in the hands of Bede, and she became a saint whose body was incorrupt after death, and who resembled the early Continental virgin saints and martyrs.

Aethelthryth wasn't the only one of Anna's daughters to walk the fine line between the secular and spiritual. Her sister Seaxburh married the King of Kent before taking over from Aethelthryth as abbess of Ely. As queen she gave birth to two sons, who both ruled as king, and to two daughters, who were both declared saints. Indeed, Seaxburh became an exemplar for ruling women, as once she retired from public life (having been a daughter, wife and mother of kings, and ruled as regent for her young son), she was able to become an abbess of a monastery and then be declared a saint.[18]

The response of King Anna and his family to the rise of Christianity was to embrace it with enthusiasm and draw as much benefit from the new rituals of the Church as was possible. The effect of accepting Christianity in this early wave would have been to create a further divide between this kingdom and its neighbour – the kingdom of Mercia, run by the ruthless pagan king Penda. Anna understood the benefits of Christianity in its earliest manifestation among the Anglo-Saxons in terms of empowering royal women through the establishment of monasteries. While it is tempting to see the acts of Aethelthryth and her sister Seaxburh, abbesses of Ely, as inspired by new-found devotion to the Christian faith, it is perhaps more accurate to see the establishment of monasteries and the placing of royal princesses at their head as a form of land-grabbing.

Anglo-Saxon princesses could rise in prominence through marriage in the pre-Christian period, but they were rarely able to possess land and power in their own right. The first generation of Christians, however, seemed to find a new opportunity by assigning their daughters land upon which they could establish monasteries. This enabled them to retain or even take possession of tracts of land that could be farmed and controlled under the guidance of the loyal royal or noble family. The Church was owed its taxes and share of the produce, but the ties to the local ruling dynasty meant that these areas would remain loyal and the lands would not have to leave them to pass into the hands of an opposing neighbour. Daughters had previously been a source of consternation to kings, but they could now be virgins, abbesses and saints.

Issues surrounding marriage and divorce concerned Anglo-Saxon royalty and nobility from the arrival of the Christian missionaries, and they pressed Augustine and Gregory for guidance on these matters as soon as the Roman party arrived in Kent. While the position of women within Anglo-Saxon society was affected by the early monasteries, in that it provided another option, the realities of entering a religious community were dictated by male Church leaders, many of whom had fixed views on women as descendants of Eve, the first sinner. Within the Church, women were not equal, although for a short while in the seventh century and into the eighth they carved out new niches for themselves that gave them greater power than they would come to have in the following centuries. Yet powerful male saints were far more prominent in the Anglo-Saxon period, and none more so than the fearless, powerful and uncompromising Bishop Wilfrid.

Chapter Eight
Wilfrid: God's Nobleman

> '*And then we should all strive*
> *that we might go there*
> *to the eternal*
> *blessedness*
> *that is a belonging life*
> *in the love of the Lord,*
> *joy in the heavens.*'
>
> The Seafarer.[1]

Wilfrid was difficult during his life, and he continues to prove difficult after his death. He was the first Anglo-Saxon saint to truly appreciate and exploit the political, cultural and spiritual connections that the conversion brought with it. Born to wealthy noble parents, he was destined for a life of privilege, but the Church allowed him to soar to the heights of power, whereby he had the ear of the Pope and sway over kings and queens. He stood firm for what the Gregorian mission endorsed, often in opposition to Irish Churchmen whom he had grown up and trained with. But his dogmatic stance gave him security on the Continent, and he became a well-travelled, cosmopolitan European. Even into his old age he continued to fight his corner, constantly seeking greater power and influence. He enraged and enchanted people during his lifetime, and his legacy in the north of England survives today in the two abbeys he founded at Ripon and Hexham.

Deep within Hexham Abbey there is a place where you can stand completely inside a true, authentic Anglo-Saxon space. Down steep, irregular steps beneath the solid stone floor of the Romanesque abbey church lies a dark, unsettling crypt hewn out of the earth and supported by ancient Roman stones. Originally, the space would have been plastered and decorated, with relics and lamps placed in niches. But now the walls are bare, displaying the grooves on the surface of the stones made by the chisels of Roman masons who first carved them nearly two millennia ago. The crypt was designed to underpin the lavish church building of one of Anglo-Saxon England's first home-grown saints: Wilfrid. His ambitious building projects at Hexham and nearby Ripon were celebrated at the time as 'the finest buildings north of the Alps'.[2] But inside the cramped and dimly lit crypts at Hexham the hyperbole seems irrelevant. This powerfully evocative place offers a unique insight into the fascinating Wilfrid and the nature of the very earliest Anglo-Saxon saints.

Hexham lies twenty-five miles to the west of Newcastle, in the county of Northumberland. It is a ruddy yet picturesque town, which has seen the passage of history played out on its streets. At the heart of the town springs the crenellated, darkened stone of the church spire. It is a modest-sized building, which displays its age and historical significance through the variety of Anglo-Saxon carved stones arranged around the walls either side of the nave inside. At the east end of the church, behind the altar screen, sits a potent reminder of the powerful man who was the first bishop at Hexham.

Wilfrid's episcopal throne, known as the frith stool, is in more or less the same place it has occupied since he became abbot of Hexham on receiving a land donation from Queen Aethelthryth in AD 674. The frith stool remained a place of sanctuary for those in danger or accused, right up to the reign of Henry VIII. It acts as a potent reminder of what made Wilfrid unique: his power rivalled that of the Anglo-Saxon kings; his support of the Roman Church took inspiration from Gaul, the papacy and the Romano-British past (the throne was probably made from reused Roman stone pillaged from the nearby site of Corbridge); and, finally, he and the Roman Church he represented were to leave a lasting impression, a permanent imprint, on the Church in England.

The uneven, roughly hewn passages in Wilfrid's crypt at Hexham also carry deep symbolism. True, the architectural naivety of the reused Roman stone may indicate that the building was made at a time when worked stone was difficult to access. Wilfrid had to import masons from Gaul to build his churches, as there were no native Anglo-Saxons trained to work with stone. However, by reusing stones from the nearby ruins along Hadrian's Wall, the echoes of the Roman-Christian past in England would be recalled.

The church buildings of Wilfrid and his contemporaries were the first substantial structures built in stone for some 300 years. By tying the new church buildings at Hexham and Ripon with the power and legacy of the Roman Empire, Wilfrid was declaring his edifices permanent fixtures on the landscape, designed to withstand time

Wilfrid's frith stool is in the east end, within the choir, of the church at Hexham. It is most probably carved from reused Roman stone, and has been worn smooth by centuries of use.

and the elements as part of a new religious climate. This was cutting-edge architecture that would have made a massive impression on the rest of the population, who continued the age-long tradition of building in timber. If a building like the Pompidou Centre made an impact in 1970s Paris, then it is hard to imagine the sort of effect Wilfrid's stone basilicas would have had in seventh-century England. This was unfamiliar, otherworldly design, inspired by far-off lands with which the majority of Anglo-Saxons were unfamiliar. Wilfrid wanted his stone churches, his crypts and his own position within Anglo-Saxon society to be noticed.

The crypts recall other structures too, like the ring crypt around St Peter's tomb at the Vatican, and the dimensions have been shown to mirror those of Christ's tomb.[3] The ways in which the passages twist and turn, surprising visitors with areas of light and darkness, and unsettling the feet with irregular steps, brings to mind the catacombs of Rome. These underground chambers and passages were the burial places of the earliest saints and martyrs, and were visited by pilgrims to Rome, like Wilfrid himself. He undertook the first recorded pilgrimage of an Englishman to the papacy around AD 653. During this, and later visits, he would have wound his way beneath the city in search of relics of earlier saints. Recreating this experience in the north of England would enable pilgrims to fulfil a miniature version of a journey through Rome's most sacred spaces, and to come into contact with saints that would connect them to both the papacy and the blessed in heaven.

Wilfrid brought relics back from Rome and had them displayed in his crypts. The niches carved into the walls may have contained reliquaries or lamps designed to illuminate the treasures within. There are certainly records to suggest that saints' relics were displayed in lavish containers. For example, Cuthbert's hair, taken from him during his elevation in AD 698, was kept in a casket described as a 'theca reliquiarum' – a reliquary vessel.[4] Wilfrid was also reported as owning a reliquary, a 'chrismarium', filled with relics that Queen Eormenburg wore as ornaments.[5] Relics were big business, and a materially minded man like Wilfrid wanted to invest in a finer collection than any of his contemporaries.

A Complex Character: a Transitional Time

Wilfrid is one of the most complicated saints of the Anglo-Saxon period, probably because of the complexity of the time in which he lived. He, more than most saints, embodies the compromising pull between spiritual and secular matters. He was a born fighter, a provocative diplomat, headstrong, wilful, powerful, wealthy and controversial. Far from being a pious monk or victim martyr, Wilfrid fought a hard battle to forcibly instil the Roman Church into Anglo-Saxon England. He lived a long life, but much of it was spent in exile, traversing the roads between his foundations in England and the papacy.

He reflects a time when the pagan Anglo-Saxon nobility were embracing Christianity and all it offered. Born a pagan nobleman, and most probably related to the aristocratic families of the Northumbrian region of Deira, his upbringing was firmly rooted in the warrior society of the period. He provides a perfect point of connection with the power and politics of seventh-century Anglo-Saxon England, but because of his ceaseless wanderings, his training at the Celtic monastery of Lindisfarne and in Canterbury, Gaul and Rome, his life also opens a window onto the Celtic West and the rest of Christian Europe.

He crossed vast distances in his lifetime, sometimes with an entourage of over a hundred people, moving between the monasteries he had founded in northern England, the Midlands and Sussex, and across the Continent, to Italy. Travel was laborious, difficult and dangerous, but Wilfrid serves as a reminder that many people could traverse great distances in the early medieval period. Far from living and dying within a few miles of where they were born, Wilfrid and his contemporaries embraced travel with a passion.

During his forty-six years as Bishop, he spent more than half – twenty-six years – in exile due to his constant disagreements with rulers and nobles. He was not afraid to court controversy, and he made many powerful friends and enemies over his long life. One particular friend and patron was Queen Eanflaed, wife of Oswui of Northumbria. She did much to develop his education and early career, personally writing to her cousin, the King of Kent, for

Wilfrid to be accepted into the monastery at Canterbury. She was something of a patron to him, endorsing his application to study at one of the best schools in the country. But she wasn't his only high-profile supporter. He would receive the land and monks for his monastery at Ripon directly from Alhfrith, heir to the Northumbrian throne, and the land for Hexham abbey from a later queen of Northumbria, Aethelthryth. He gained the support of powerful Gaulish bishops and even the Pope. But he made influential enemies as easily as he made friends.

His life is recorded in two main sources: one, a piece of commissioned hagiography by his follower, Stephen of Ripon; another, the writings of Bede. Wilfrid was still alive during Bede's early years, and the two reputedly met. In fact, Bede had the opportunity to question the then bishop, and the subject he chose was a controversial one. He asked Wilfrid whether Queen Aethelthryth had indeed been a virgin; a serious topic that had ultimately led to Wilfrid losing his bishopric.[6] It seems Bede was not afraid to probe the powerful bishop on some uncomfortable topics.

Wilfrid should have been an entirely fitting rallying point for Bede, as the paragon of Roman Christianity, trained under Continental bishops in Gaul and Rome. He reflected many aspects of the Church in Anglo-Saxon England that Bede supported, especially regarding the dating of Easter and the introduction of the Benedictine Rule. However, when compared with the lavish compliments he bestows upon Cuthbert, Wilfrid is handled with greater reticence. Bede does present him as the major representative of the Roman party of the Synod of Whitby in AD 664, and celebrates the fact that he took a strong orthodox line, despite having close connections with the Celtic Church. Yet Bede is often as telling in what he doesn't say as what he does. His treatment of Wilfrid may not be openly hostile, but it lacks warmth and is distinctly subdued in comparison with his celebration of other Anglo-Saxon Christians.

Wilfrid's *Life* was written down as an official hagiographical text by one of his followers, Stephen of Ripon, as part of a concerted effort to have him declared a saint after his death. The text was accompanied by other investments in art, particularly the creation of an empurpled gospel book. This manuscript is now lost, but its rich appearance is described by Stephen:

> For he had ordered, for the good of his soul, the four gospels to be written out in letters of purest gold on purpled parchment and illuminated. He also ordered jewellers to construct for the books a case all made of purest gold and set with most precious gems; all these things and others besides are preserved in our church until these times as a witness to his blessed memory.[7]

The Cathach of Columba highlighted the important connection between specific manuscripts and saints. But the respective manuscripts associated with Columba and Wilfrid were markedly different. The Cathach reflects the Celtic Church in terms of its decoration, and the way in which it was venerated by being encased like a relic. Wilfrid's, although lost, conforms with descriptions of Continental books of the highest status. To stain vellum purple and write purely in gold was the most costly and ostentatious way of displaying power.[8] The colour purple has imperial associations, so by creating an empurpled manuscript Wilfrid's scriptorium was developing an object that would display his power during life, and act as a rallying point for his cult after his death.

That the manuscript has been lost is to be expected, since such a lavish religious book was likely to have been targeted by Reformers and destroyed. Sadly, now it can only be imagined from the very briefest description in Wilfrid's *Life*. A similar empurpled Anglo-Saxon manuscript may, however, survive in the Stockholm Codex Aureus, now in the National Library of Sweden. It is a mid-eighth-century Anglo-Saxon manuscript, probably originally written in Canterbury. Every other double page is empurpled, and the manuscript gets its name 'Aureus' from the fact that many of the pages are written in gold. It was such a valued object that, when it was looted by Viking raiders in the ninth century, the Ealdorman of Surrey paid a huge ransom to get it back. Like many millionaires today, Wilfrid understood the importance of patronising the finest and most impressive art. He was a man with expensive taste, and the cult manuscript he had designed to commemorate him after death would have been an incredibly exclusive and rare object.

Wilfrid and the Franks Casket

There is another high-status object, however, that may have been made at one of Wilfrid's monasteries during his lifetime and does survive. We can gain a clearer understanding of the complex environment Wilfrid inhabited by examining one fortunate survival: the Franks Casket.

Made in Northumbria around the year AD 700, so towards the end of Wilfrid's lifetime, it is a whalebone casket.[9] Its many sides are carved with low-relief figures and runes, and form a complex sequence of images that have to be interpreted alongside one another. Its linked meanings work over each side, rather like an early medieval Rubik's Cube. The handwriting and Old English dialect of the inscriptions on the casket suggest that it could have been made in one of Wilfrid's ecclesiastical organisations at Hexham or Ripon.[10] Indeed, the scope of historical, religious and

mythical scenes, combined with the level of literacy displayed, indicates that it could only have emerged from the minds and hands of well-read northern monks.

It is a very rare survival. The Franks Casket is one of those powerful objects that seems poised at a transitional moment in history. It looks back to the pagan Germanic past, and projects forward to the Christian world of the Continent. It encompasses a mass of information about the time in which it was made and the individual with which it is most closely associated. This is important when considering how eclectic the subject matter is, as pagan gods jostle with Roman kings. It seems to undermine our modern conceptions of what was acceptable within this climate of extreme Christian fervour. Yet it can help us understand what Wilfrid's objectives were, particularly in terms of reinforcing the fledgling Church in Anglo-Saxon England and modifying the pre-Christian beliefs of his nation.

For many years it had served as a sewing box for a family in Auzon. How it came to France is unknown, but its presence there supports the theory that it changed hands as a diplomatic gift. It eventually found its way to an antiques shop in France, where the ever-vigilant eye of the British Museum Keeper, Sir Augustus Wollaston Franks, recognised its worth and brought it back to England. Its size means it cannot have contained any large objects, but the metal lock (now lost – melted down to make a ring during the French Revolution) and detailed carvings on almost every surface suggest that it was designed to hold something precious, and to be seen by powerful, informed, influential viewers. It possibly contained relics or, most plausibly, diplomatic documents, designed to relate information about the newly converted, globally minded Anglo-Saxons in the north of England.

In a similar manner to the reuse of Roman stones in the creation of Wilfrid's crypts at Hexham, the format of the Franks Casket recycles an earlier form. The object itself has clear parallels in the Christian world. Late Antique examples like the fourth-century Brescia Casket clearly use the sides to present images and iconography connected with Christianity and the imperial past, all executed in the highest status of mediums – ivory. This is not the case with the Franks Casket – in fact, it is an utterly unique object and has no known parallels. Entering via the lock, the front immediately transports the viewer to a different world, as runes run along the sides.

The Franks Casket displays some of the longest and earliest stretches of runic text to survive in the West. The multi-layered ways in which runes functioned made them the perfect mode of expression for an object, and an audience, imbued with a passion for riddling. Indeed, it opens with a riddle:

> *The fish beat up the sea(s) on to the mountainous cliff*
> *The king of terror became sad when he swam onto the grit.*
> *Whale's bone.*[11]

This short riddle provides its own answer – the casket is made of 'whale's bone' – but the intention is to challenge the viewer regarding the origins of the object and its earlier life as part of the 'king of terror' – a whale. It recreates the dramatic moment when a whale was beached on the sands, its bones ultimately reincarnated as a casket. Once again the imaginative world of the Anglo-Saxons comes starkly into view, as here the casket employs prosopopoeia (a rhetorical device where objects speak for themselves) to give this inanimate artefact a voice. This is something we encounter repeatedly in Old English riddles, where manuscripts, weaponry and creatures challenge the reader to 'say what I am'.

This desire to give a voice to supposedly inanimate objects suggests a different way of engaging with the world – a world in which nature was powerful and vocal, populated with spirits and sounds outside the realm of man. Rivers, glens, woods and mounds all contained the potential to act as meeting points between the worldly and the otherworldly. In the pagan spiritual framework, gods could metamorphose into animals, and stones could tell their ancient stories. This was a mindset not easily put aside, and the legacy of this tradition lived on for many centuries.

With the riddle on the front of the Franks Casket answered, the images present the next challenge. On the front, two very distinct scenes are paired alongside one another. On the right are three

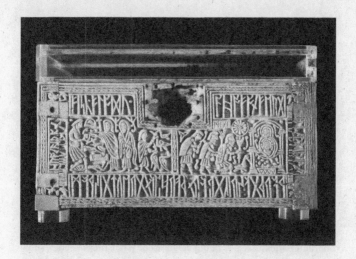

men dressed as soldiers, approaching a woman and child enveloped one inside the other within an enclosure.[12] Other strange symbols include a sunburst, a bird and a range of objects held by the men. Four runes float above the figures, helping to decipher just this scene alone. They read MAGI, which means this must represent the account of the three wise men visiting Jesus after his birth. But there are no other depictions from across the Christian world that mirror this portrayal of the event. It is utterly unique.

To the right, a bearded man with one bent leg presents a woman with a cup. Another figure lies beneath him, and in front is an array of tools.[13] Further along, another woman holds a purse, while another character appears to be plucking birds. Already a visual link has been established with the other scene, as a bird seems to have escaped from one and run through to the next. But the connections apparently stop there. This scene depicts the pagan Germanic legend of Weland the Smith, in which he was kept hostage by King Niðhad, and hamstrung to stop him escaping. To exact his revenge, he lured first the king's son, whom he beheaded before fashioning a goblet from his skull. Then the king's daughter visited him, during which he drugged, raped and impregnated her. The skill with which this myth is reduced to small set pieces suggests that this story was well known, needing only the basic details.

What might Christian figures like Wilfrid have made of this juxtaposition of such opposing images? The two scenes come from very different cultural contexts and seem to celebrate very different things: on the one hand, the importance of revenge, in this case on a king; and on the other, the birth and acknowledgement by kings of a peace-loving, child king-of-kings. Yet, there are parallels between the two that require some mental acrobatics to unravel. Weland was said to have escaped on a flying machine made from bird feathers (presumably those being plucked to the right). His ascension was later employed on Viking sculptures as a pagan equivalent to the ascension of Christ into heaven. Both main figures are shown in a heroic guise, and it is surely their super-human characteristics that are being celebrated. What these scenes show us is that the Christian world Wilfrid lived in was part of a transition from a previous worldview that still consumed contemporary minds. This object means we must question whether the pious and righteously Christian presentation of Wilfrid accords with the real world he inhabited.

These two scenes and the surrounding riddle are sufficient to illustrate the many problems the Franks Casket poses, and the complex transitional period that gave rise to its creation. The other sides present an equally problematic sequence of images, with unique versions of the wolf suckling Romulus and Remus (shown prostrate and adult),[14] and Titus's sacking of the temple in Jerusalem during the Jewish-Roman wars of AD 70. These episodes from Roman and Jewish history are testament to the far-reaching and cosmopolitan place that eight-century Northumbria was, and work with the front in terms of reinforcing questions of divine and human rulers.

What's more, the Titus scene includes an incredible bit of linguistic play – at the top-right of the scene the inscription switches from runic to Latin script. This is not an accident, as it's impossible to think of a skilled carver not realising he has changed language and script halfway through a sentence. Instead, it appears to be a deliberate comment on the changes of the time, shown symbolically through this shift from Old English to the language of the new Church.

The last side, which is separate from the others and held in the Bargello Museum in Florence, is in many ways the most enigmatic. Its runes are encoded, with some symbols standing in for letters and some for words, which means they are extremely difficult to interpret clearly. Despite defying convincing interpretation, the images suggest that it represents ideas of a warrior's journey after death, complete with the trappings of the hall – goblet, horse and weaponry. The right-hand side of the casket and the lid, which appears to show an episode from the legend of Egil, seem firmly rooted in the pre-Christian, Germanic pagan tradition. The combination of images reflects the turbulent time in which it was made.

The flying bird that goes around the casket and across the bottom of the right-hand scene is an important motif. It is perhaps symbolic of the soul's flight from life to death, something Bede explores in his famous account of a sparrow flying through a hall. Wilfrid inhabited the complex, transitional world of the Franks

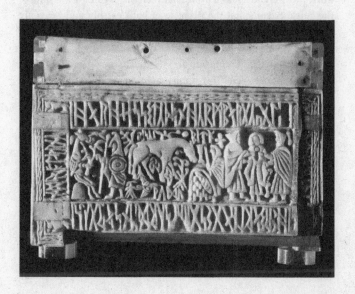

Casket. Examining the casket as a multi-faceted object, and exploring the historical, cultural and religious context in which it was made, all help to shed light on the imaginative world of early eighth-century Northumbria – the world of Wilfrid. It certainly puts more traditional approaches towards this pious Christian against a much more ambiguous backdrop, and enables a different set of insights into this saintly man and his monastic community.

Powerful Friends and Enemies

Through his elaborate stone buildings, lavish manuscripts and high-status luxury objects, Wilfrid was surrounding himself in the aura of *Romanitas* (Roman-ness).[15] He gains further potency by harnessing the trappings of the Anglo-Saxon warrior culture in which he was brought up; for example, tying his monastery of Hexham to the saint-king Oswald. Rather than endorsing the cult of King Edwin (connected to him through the Deiran nobility), Wilfrid instead developed the idea of the Bernician Oswald as holy warrior. He could act as a bridge between the pagan warrior elite of the Anglo-Saxons and the promise of both earthly and heavenly rewards offered by the Church. At Hexham, sponsoring the cult of Oswald was a canny move, since it took a cult figure popular with the people of Northumbria and dressed him in the finery of Wilfrid's elaborate Romanised Christianity. Wilfrid worked hard at his public image, but his strength of character and bullishness meant he struggled to keep the most influential people in Anglo-Saxon England onside. This is nowhere more true than in his relationship with Archbishop Theodore.

Theodore was the eighth Archbishop of Canterbury, who inherited the legacy of Augustine before him in terms of enforcing the presence of Rome in Anglo-Saxon England. He was from Tarsus, a Greek-speaking area within Byzantium, and along with his native tongue he could speak Latin and Syrian. He most probably trained at the School of Antioch, and later in Constantinople, where he learnt astrology, medicine, rhetoric and law. He was a highly educated man from a turbulent world; following wars between the

Byzantines, Muslims and Persians, he eventually travelled to Rome, where he joined a monastery and embraced the teachings of the Western Church. It was from the peace of his Roman monastery that he was plucked by Pope Vitalian in AD 667, and sent to fill the vacant see of Canterbury.

He had been volunteered for the position by his friend, the North African Hadrian, who was settled in a monastery near Naples. He had been offered the Archbishopric of Canterbury himself twice, but put Theodore forward instead as he felt he was too old to take the post. The Pope sent Theodore on the condition that Hadrian accompanied him, since he had been to Gaul before and knew the journey. Together, these new leaders of the Anglo-Saxon Church made a formidable, worldly, experienced and exotic team. Hadrian was made abbot of the monastery of Saints Peter and Paul in Canterbury, and together with Theodore he developed a school at the monastery, which drew the new and enthusiastic Christian Anglo-Saxon minds of the seventh century.

From the manuscripts connected with the school of Theodore and Hadrian it is possible to glean nuggets of insight into long-dead readers through the annotations and emendations they made as they read. Glosses and commentaries on medieval manuscripts are equivalent to notes in the margins of our own books. They provide a very real connection with the person who was sitting in front of and interacting with that manuscript centuries earlier – what they were thinking as they read, how their mind could make connections and ask questions of the text. When you see a glossed manuscript, you get close to reading over the shoulder of an Anglo-Saxon. In these early manuscripts it's possible to see the minds of the northern Germanic students struggling to comprehend biblical references by contextualising them. Not only were Theodore and Hadrian themselves exotic, but the world of the Bible and the Middle East that they exposed their first-generation Christian Anglo-Saxons to was full of esoteric and alien terms, ideas and settings. This can be seen throughout the commentaries from their school in Canterbury, where students grappled with unfamiliar concepts, like the ways of determining weights, measures and coinage referenced in the Bible:

> *'The last farthing [V.26]: the last thought'. A farthing*
> *(quadrans) has two mites. There are twelve mites in one*
> *tremiss. In one solidus there are three tremissis. An argeneus*
> *and a solidus are the same thing. There are thirty-six mites*
> *in one solidus; there are twenty siliquae in one penny.*[16]

The work of Theodore and Hadrian in Canterbury cannot be underestimated. In the churches of the city it is clear to see that the example of Rome was never far from their minds. The major basilical church, which was to become the burial place of Anglo-Saxon monarchs, was dedicated to the two major patron saints of Rome – Peter and Paul.[17] The foundations they laid in terms of educating the enthusiastic new converts in many practically expedient areas of Christian scholarship meant that the Anglo-Saxon conversion was founded upon the firmest and most intellectually vigorous bedrock. Bede, writing sixty years later, states that they soon 'attracted a crowd of students into whose minds they daily poured the streams of wholesome learning'. Bede also states that some of their students who survived to his own day were as fluent in Greek and Latin as in their native language.[18]

Theodore was responsible for making Wilfrid bishop of the enlarged diocese of Northumbria, which heralded the start of nine years of power and autonomy within the north. Wilfrid lived an ostentatious lifestyle, possibly because of his noble upbringing, and this reinforces for us that modern-day distinctions between the spiritual life and the secular were largely redundant in the Anglo-Saxon period. He spent nine years delegating his episcopal duties, spending more time founding monasteries, building extremely grand churches and improving the liturgy. The region he governed was enormous, and after these years of extravagance Theodore wanted to reduce Wilfrid's power by carving the bishopric of Northumbria into smaller areas.

Theodore and Wilfrid locked horns over the size of the diocese. The Archbishop took advantage of a conflict with the then king of Northumbria, Ecgfrith, to oust Wilfrid from court and implement his changes. Wilfrid was expelled from York and went to Pope Agatho in Rome, who found in his favour. However, when he returned to Northumbria the king went against the papal decision, imprisoning then exiling Wilfrid – a sign of how difficult a character he was. It would have taken great determination on the part of King Ecgfrith to rule against the Pope, but that was the level of animosity between he and Wilfrid.

In exile in Sussex, Wilfrid converted the pagan inhabitants to Christianity. He achieved great things, working tirelessly in often dangerous and hostile circumstances. He was eventually reconciled with Theodore, who then advised the new King of Northumbria, Aldfrith, to allow him to return to his native kingdom. That he could both court and lose the backing of the most influential individuals in Christendom is a defining feature of Wilfrid. He founded a number of monasteries throughout the Anglo-Saxon kingdoms. This meant he was equivalent to a powerful secular landowner, as the monasteries channelled great wealth and made him an important, influential and rich member of Anglo-Saxon society.

His power could be seen to rival that of the various kings of the English kingdoms, but his came with the additional benefits of being national and international, with the backing of powerful allies in Gaul and Rome. Wilfrid made strong links with the Continent, and modelled his style of monastery upon examples he'd seen throughout Europe. He claimed to have introduced the Benedictine Rule into England, perhaps as a way of showing his allegiance to the Roman Church. He was aware of the stain of heresy the British wore within the Church, right back to the time of Pelagius, and therefore tried to be more Roman than the Romans. But he simply could not get along with the major decision-makers of the Anglo-Saxon kingdoms.

He died in AD 709–10, and soon after he was venerated as a saint. There was a concerted effort made on the part of his supporters to sanctify him. This involved the production of 'cult objects' and the commissioning of Stephen of Ripon to write his hagiography. Stephen's account is highly partisan, focusing in particular on his machinations within Northumbria. It may have been written as a defence of his reputation in this kingdom, where both his power and infamy were at their height. Stephen knew how to craft a hagiographical text, and Wilfrid's *Life* puts the saint firmly at the centre as its hero. Individuals who opposed him, like Theodore, deliver heartfelt apologies to the wronged Wilfrid, and punishment comes the way of those who offended him. He performs a number of astonishing miracles, such as raising a boy from death, and his relics continue to perform great feats posthumously.

Stephen casts Wilfrid as an Old Testament prophet. The parallels with figures like Joseph and Moses are apt, since they were similarly cast away and went into exile. The suggestion is that Wilfrid's controversial behaviour can be excused by the idea that he is a prophetic figure. Like Solomon, at Hexham he dedicated a temple to the Lord, and there are New Testament parallels too. He is like Andrew, his favourite saint, a fisher of souls. It is well-written hagiography, but it distils the character of Wilfrid behind a veneer of tropes and truisms. Wilfrid and his community managed to ensure all the parts of his cult were in place just a few years after his death. Powerful and influential to the end, Wilfrid, it seems, was able to call the shots even from the grave.

Benedict Biscop and Ceolfrith

On his way from Rome to Canterbury, Theodore was accompanied by an Anglo-Saxon nobleman-turned-monk named Biscop Baducing. He was born around AD 629, a time when the majority of Anglo-Saxon rulers were reacting to the arrival of Christianity, and bloody battles were fought by the British king Cadwallon and the pagan ruler Penda of Mercia. A few years older than his friend Wilfrid, Biscop travelled to the Continent with him when he was twenty-five and the younger man just twenty-one years old. Wilfrid stayed in Gaul, but Biscop continued on to Rome, where, like so many young men over the centuries, he was seduced by the art and architecture of the ancient city. Both men were from the Northumbrian royal household, and they embraced the new exotic world that Christianity opened up to them. They were entranced by what they saw on the Continent, and both developed an expensive taste for relics, manuscripts and art. Yet while Wilfrid sought to rise up through the ranks of the Church and have the ears of the most influential people in Anglo-Saxon England, Biscop was more interested in the potential of founding monasteries.

While in Rome and Gaul he visited a number of different types of monasteries, spending two years at the island monastery of Lérins, off the French Riviera. Here, he went from being an enthusiastic Christian convert to taking monastic vows, and it was at this point that he chose the name Benedict, after the author of the famous monastic rule. His time at Lérins allowed him to develop his own ideas as to what sort of monastery he wanted to found in England.[19] He had seen the Benedictine Rule in action, alongside the more varied rules in place throughout Gaulish communities. When he returned to England after his second trip to Rome, with Archbishop Theodore as his companion, he was given the chance to implement what he'd learnt as abbot of SS Peter and Paul in Canterbury.

Biscop was extremely fortunate to secure such an important post, particularly at a time when the Church in England was about to be reinvigorated under the guidance of Theodore. He was essentially holding the role of abbot until Hadrian arrived to take up the post, but it was a high-profile position for a Northumbrian monk fresh from his novitiate. Soon after retiring from Canterbury, Biscop was granted land to build a monastery by King Ecgfrith of Northumbria in AD 674. Ecgfrith clearly saw the potential in his northern kingdom of nurturing a homegrown talent who had been trained abroad and had the ear of the new Archbishop of Canterbury. Like Northumbrian saints before him, Biscop had led an active life within the court before founding a monastery. He had served as a warrior thegn under King Oswui, and was popular with the Northumbrian nobility. Yet, while Cuthbert, Hilda and Wilfrid had all been trained in the Celtic tradition, Biscop looked to Rome on all matters.

After appealing to Rome for books, relics, masons and personnel for his new monastery, Biscop was given the added support from Pope Agatho of a papal bill exempting Wearmouth from any external control. This was pure power and autonomy for the monastery, which meant it was the papacy, not the royal house of Northumbria, to which it owed allegiance. Greatly impressed by

Biscop and his model monastery, it was only a matter of a few years before, in AD 682, the king granted more land to Biscop to found a second monastery at Jarrow. Despite being seven miles apart, the two monasteries were known as one: Wearmouth–Jarrow. In keeping with Biscop's devotion to Rome, the churches were dedicated to Peter and Paul respectively. In their very construction they recalled the stone edifices Biscop had encountered on his travels, and stood in sharp contrast with the Columban foundations that had edged across Northumbria throughout the seventh century.

The buildings at Wearmouth were designed from the beginning as startlingly new. Not content with utilising the native architectural styles or materials, Biscop followed Wilfrid's example and appealed for masons from the Continent. The buildings that resulted were groundbreaking. Not only were they built in stone and plastered so they would have shone on the Anglo-Saxon landscape, but the monks' dormitory was also stone and benefitted from glazed windows. This might seem like a small development from our modern perspective, but windows would transform medieval life previously. If an individual wanted light inside a building they had the option of opening shutters or doors and letting in the elements, or lighting fires or candles and coping with smoke-filled interiors. Glass windows meant that the harsh wind, rain or snow could be kept outside while precious light could be let in. The monks' lodgings at Biscop's monasteries would have been the finest available in the Anglo-Saxon period, and the buildings would have appeared as avant-garde and unfamiliar as the Gherkin in London.[20]

It was not only the stone buildings and glass windows that would have appeared new to the Northumbrian people. Biscop also brought back from Rome vestments and vessels, relics and a sequence of paintings that he had displayed within the church. These featured images of the Virgin and the Apostles at the east end, figures from the Gospels along the south and visions from St John's Revelations on the north wall. In accordance with Gregory the Great's instructions on the value of images for guiding the illiterate towards knowledge, these paintings were apparently included by Biscop because 'even if ignorant of letters, they might be able to contemplate, in what direction so ever they looked, the ever gracious countenance of Christ and his saints'.[21] Biscop understood the power of art, and was an avid patron and collector.

The other great addition to Biscop's monasteries was a large collection of books. He was a wealthy man, who inherited a great deal of disposable income, and he used this to secure some of the most important books in Rome. It is highly likely that he purchased a set of manuscripts known as the *Novem Codices* – a complete Vulgate version of the Bible, which was a very rare possession at this time – written by the great biblical scholar Cassiodorus in the sixth century. Cassiodorus's library at Vivarium was renowned, but was disbanded in the seventh century.

Biscop made a monk named Ceolfrith abbot to Jarrow. The anonymous *Life of St Ceolfrith* states that he joined a group of Benedictine monks led by Wilfrid, possibly the foundations for the monastery at Ripon.[22] He also spent time training under St Botolph, 'a man of remarkable life and learning'. While the monks and abbots of Northumbria feel three-dimensional and complex because there are sources left documenting their lives in some detail, fewer such records exist of the East Anglian Church. Botolph was clearly an influential early churchman, but he survives in fragmentary references and later legends. The hints at characters like Botolph in Northumbrian records acts as a reminder of the many saints who have been lost to time, with only their names remaining as testament to their importance.

Ceolfrith took with him to Jarrow just twenty monks, and also given into his care was a young boy who had been dedicated to the monastery by his parents at the age of seven, named Bede. Still set above the chancel arch is the dedicatory stone, which records the grant of land from the king and the appointment of Ceolfrith as Abbot of Jarrow in AD 684. He introduced Biscop's ideals at this new site, and was as much a bibliophile and scholar as the monastery's founder. Ceolfrith was dedicated to pursuing learning at Jarrow, doubling the size of the monastic libraries and embarking on a huge publishing campaign, the impact of which is still felt today. Every time a copy of the Vulgate Bible is produced for print, it is still based on a manuscript painstakingly produced under Ceolfrith's guidance. Despite only being decoded in the 1880s, and spending most of its 1,400-year life in an Italian library, the famous Codex Amiatinus was in fact produced in the monastery of Wearmouth–Jarrow, just outside Newcastle, under the guidance of Abbot Ceolfrith.

The Codex Amiatinus

The Codex Amiatinus is an enormous manuscript, made of over 1,000 calf skins. As an early scholar on the text so prosaically put it, the manuscript weighs the same as a Great Dane.[23] Each page is poster-sized, and the ability to hold the numerous folios together in a single binding was cutting-edge technology of its time. While it is an illuminated manuscript, boasting three large-scale full-page illustrations, it is very distinct in style from Insular manuscripts like the Lindisfarne Gospels and the Book of Durrow. Instead, the images seem to have been copied faithfully from Late Antique originals, possibly even a frontispiece from the *Novem Codices* of Cassiodorus that Biscop brought back on his travels. The appearance and sheer intellectual achievement of the Codex Amiatinus – the whole Bible in the Vulgate version – meant that its resting place in the Biblioteca Medicea Laurenziana in Florence went unquestioned. Surely only Italian minds could have produced such a remarkable manuscript: the first complete pandect copy of the Vulgate Bible.

However, an insightful palaeographer named Giovanni Battista de Rossi discovered that the dedicatory page at the front of the manuscript had been tampered with. As the manuscript stands today, it states that the Codex Amiatinus was dedicated by Peter of the Langobards, who were a ruling tribe in Italy in the seventh century. This chimed with the illuminations to secure an Italian origin for this spectacular tome. But de Rossi found an identical inscription recorded in the *Anonymous Lives of the Abbots of Wearmouth and Jarrow,* and in that version the line that now reads 'Peter of the Langobards' read 'Abbot Ceolfrith'. Within this account there was also a description of the remarkable copies of

The Codex Amiatinus is the oldest surviving single-volume copy of the Vulgate Bible in the world. It was made, along with two other copies, at the monastery of Wearmouth–Jarrow, and Bede the Venerable had a hand in correcting and editing the text. The style of the full-page illuminations is distinctly Italianate, with the figures painted naturalistically.

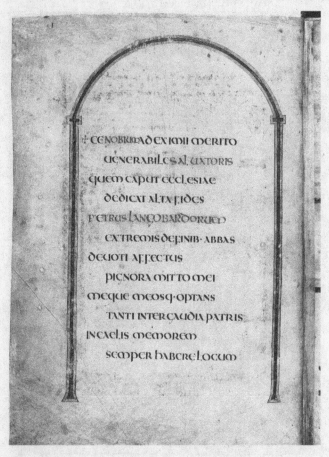

+ CENOBRICAD EX IMII MERITO
UENERABILES AL UXTORIS
QUEM CAPUT ECCLESIAE
DEDICAT ALTA FIDES
PETRUS LANGOBARDORUM
EXTREMIS DEFINIB· ABBAS
DEUOTI AFFECTUS
PICNORA MITTO MEI
MEQUE MEOSQ·OPTANS
TANTI INTERCAUDIA PATRIS
INCAELIS MEMOREM
SEMPER HABERE LOCUM

This is an example of both medieval plagiarism and graffiti. The fifth line down in this dedication page has been erased using a knife, and the name Peter of the Langobards has been inserted. The ink is slightly browner at this point, indicating the change that has taken place.

the Bible that Ceolfrith ordered to be made at his monasteries of Wearmouth–Jarrow, one of which he took as a gift to Rome.

Suddenly, this most significant of biblical manuscripts was no longer a product of Italy, but instead was produced by first-generation Christian converts at the edges of the known world. While Lindisfarne invested in a Gospel book that reconciled Anglo-Saxon, Irish and Roman imagery, and Wilfrid developed an empurpled manuscript written in gold, Biscop and Ceolfrith's monasteries produced an astounding piece of scholarship. The funds and investment in learning required to get the greatest minds and scribes of the age together in a scriptorium alongside accurate versions of the Vulgate Bible, not to mention the sheer resources in terms of calf skin, ink and time, all attest to the scale of this project. What is remarkable, however, is that Ceolfrith's monasteries didn't produce just one, but three complete Bible manuscripts. The one that survives was taken as a gift to Rome by Ceolfrith, who died on his way there, thus ensuring the manuscript's stay in Italy. But one copy remained at Wearmouth, while another was kept at Jarrow. In a remarkable twist of fate, fragments of one of the lost manuscripts were later found reused as covers for the correspondence of Sir Francis Willoughby's clerks in the late sixteenth century.[24]

Ceolfrith is best remembered for his role in the Codex Amiatinus project and for keeping alive the monastery of Jarrow when it was decimated by plague in AD 686. Just he and Bede, who was fourteen at the time, were able to sing the monastic hours, so preserving them for posterity. From what survives about Ceolfrith it seems that he was a driven and intelligent man, who sought out a particularly orthodox and strict form of monastic life, and relished the opportunities that scribal activity and scholarship could provide. His predecessor, Benedict Biscop, also appears to have been a rounded individual from the written sources of his life that have been preserved. He is easier to grasp than his friend and contemporary Wilfrid. Less of a political game-player, Biscop was interested in creating an intellectual powerhouse at his impressive new monasteries. He was a bibliophile, a seasoned traveller, an art connoisseur and a patron of learning, developing a creative hub that was like the Silicon Valley of its time. In the right place at the right time, and able to make strong interpersonal bonds with those he encountered, Biscop was in many ways the opposite of Wilfrid. His legacy was the twin foundations at Wearmouth–Jarrow, and the brilliant scholar who was given unparalleled resources and opportunities in his remarkable foundations: Bede the Venerable.

Chapter Nine
Bede: Writing History; Writing Sanctity

> 'That Son was victory-fast in that great
> venture, with might and good-speed, when he
> with many, vast host of souls, came to God's
> kingdom, One-Wielder Almighty: bliss to the
> angels and all the saints – those who in
> heaven dwelt long in glory – when their
> Wielder came, Almighty God, where his
> homeland was.'

The Dream of the Rood.[1]

Bede literally wrote the history books. As one of the only Anglo-Saxon voices to have remained strong and clear across the millennia, what Bede does or doesn't say has become canonical. He was recognised as supremely gifted in his own lifetime, particularly in terms of his prodigious literary outpourings. And after his death his popularity continued. Multiple copies of his books were requested across Europe, so much so that his monastery at Wearmouth–Jarrow couldn't keep up with the demand. He was the bestselling author of his time, and possessed one of the most respected intellects of the Anglo-Saxon period. Although he seems to have avoided direct involvement with the political intrigues of seventh- to eighth-century Northumbria, staying firmly within the walls of his monastery, he would play a more subtle and persuasive role with quill and vellum. Bede was the spin doctor of his time, and through his words he manipulated Anglo-Saxon England.

While he has never been fully canonised, and bears the title 'Venerable' more often than 'Saint', he has been remembered and treasured the world over. His significance to the English is unparalleled. He wrote the first history of the English people, and every historical text that has followed has based its information about Anglo-Saxon England upon his words. A game player at a turbulent time, he was able to harness the power of words in such a way as adviser to kings and bishops that he affected the period in which he lived. Not only that, he continues to condition how we view the Anglo-Saxon period today. He was someone who understood that history is written by the victors. In fact, by writing so much he became one of history's greatest victors, able still to alter perceptions and challenge expectations 1,300 years after his living voice was silenced. The best way to get close to Bede is to follow in his footsteps and soak up the atmosphere of the site where he spent his whole life.

The monastery at Jarrow is now reduced to the outlines of stone buildings, rolling down towards the river on the edge of a humble parish church. Walking through fragmentary doorways out from the monastic complex, the approach to the church is overhung with trees, whose leaves dapple light into dancing patterns on the path up to the entrance. The simple exterior of St Paul's Church belies the fact that it preserves the remains of one of the oldest stone buildings to survive from Anglo-Saxon England. Moving down the nave, under the later Norman tower, you enter a space that still resembles the chancel where Bede and Ceolfrith kept the monastery of Wearmouth–Jarrow alive. The stones of this building have resounded with monastic song for well over a millennium, and the modest pieces of seventh-century glass set high in the walls act as a reminder that this was a place of ancient luxury and pre-eminence, as well as national importance.

A short walk from the Church of St Paul's, the busy estuary of the Tyne bristles with colossal cargo ships. Colourful haulage cranes punctuate the horizon, and the bonnets of reams of new cars, parked along the riverbank ready for export, glint in the sunlight as you gaze down from the incongruous setting of a reconstructed Anglo-Saxon town within the confines of the 'Bede's World' Museum. Here, archaeologists have created replicas of halls, *grubenhaus* and even the 'cuneus' from Edwin's palace complex at Yeavering. Alongside farm animals bred to resemble most closely their Anglo-Saxon ancestors, the buildings evoke the atmosphere of eighth-century Northumbria with great clarity. Past and present collide and, standing on a ridge next to a reconstruction of a stone high cross, the busy waterway recalls more recent history like the Jarrow March against unemployment in 1936. A dramatic place in both medieval and modern history, Jarrow remains full of contrasts and ancient echoes.

Bede is eternally etched on this landscape. His significance in terms of documenting the Anglo-Saxon period cannot be over-emphasised, and the fact that his voice has resonated throughout this study on saints testifies that he is almost solely responsible for making the Dark Ages feel slightly less dark. Holed up in his glazed, plastered dormitory, or in his well-equipped scriptorium, Bede would have been well aware of the changes taking place around him. As he dipped his feathered quill into a pot of iron gall ink and wrote on animal skins in Latin about a Middle Eastern world hundreds of miles away from his own homeland, the alien nature of his environment and occupation must have been apparent. This may explain why he was so reluctant to leave his monastery; he travelled out only twice to nearby Lindisfarne, and never further afield to powerfully symbolic sites like Rome or Jerusalem. It may also explain the distinctly hostile stance he took towards the pagan past of his people, and the clever ways he engineered future views in his lifetime.

The double monastery of Wearmouth–Jarrow was advanced even in terms of monasteries on the Christian continent. Bede's own background must have meant this new Roman outpost on the banks of the river Tyne was thrillingly new to him. Born around AD 672, he seems to have come from a wealthy family due to the fact that he was given to a rich monastery by his parents – something that was the preserve of the nobility at this point. His name, which was rare at the time, appears on a king list from Lindsey, also suggesting that he was of noble stock. This would fit with other saintly figures from this period, like the founder of his monastery, Benedict Biscop. Bede's early life would have involved exposure to the world of the Anglo-Saxon hall, with its poetry, warrior elite and pagan traditions.

Bede had one foot in the pagan past and one in the Christian present. Yet, from the age of seven, he was part of the early vanguard of Christians, brought up with promises of an eternal afterlife, the power of the written word and an idea of an autonomous yet forgiving God. Emotionally and imaginatively, he was not tied to his native people (many of whom still adhered to earlier pre-Christian traditions, ideas and attitudes), but instead linked himself to Continental Europe, and particularly to the Roman papacy.[2] His very name seems to be derived from the Old English word for prayer – *bed* – which may suggest that from his earliest upbringing he was destined for a life of monastic sanctity.

Despite his great contributions to the fledgling Church in England, no major cult grew up around him after his death, and he was apparently content to remain a simple monk throughout the many decades of his life, rather than rise to the heights of abbot or bishop. Yet he was considered, during his lifetime and down to the present day, to have been a most saintly man. What's more, his contributions to our understanding of Anglo-Saxon England are second to none, and his life provides a compelling lens on the imaginative world of his time – one of the most significant transformations of Britain. The north of England, where he lived and died, changed from a Germanic warrior elite – a population centred on villages with wooden halls, subsistence agriculture, a belief-system rooted in the natural environment and a pantheon of pagan gods – to honouring a new powerhouse, the Church, with stone monasteries implanted on the horizon, a new set of prized objects, including books and relics, and a world view centred on a perfect afterlife achieved through piety and purity. This was spiritual revolution.

Bede: Mouthpiece of the Conversion

The circumstances surrounding Bede and his fellow early Christians' conversion were complex, involving large-scale changes within the imaginative and physical world of Anglo-Saxon England. Bede has become the eternal mouthpiece for this transitional period. Proclaimed the 'Father of English History', he was a cautious and deliberate writer of the history he wanted preserved. He is best known for his famous text, *The Ecclesiastical History of the English People*.[3] The bedrock of most studies of early Anglo-Saxon England, this text also contains almost all we know about the man Bede, in an autobiography. This short account of his life gives a telling insight into how he wished to be remembered for posterity:

> *I was born in the territory of the said monastery*
> *[Wearmouth and Jarrow], and at the age of seven I was, by*
> *the care of my relations, given to the most reverend Abbot*

Benedict, and afterwards to Ceolfrid, to be educated. From
that time I have spent the whole of my life within that
monastery, devoting all my pains to the study of the
Scriptures, and amid the observance of monastic discipline
and the daily charge of singing in the Church, it has been
ever my delight to learn or teach or write.[4]

His legacy has resonated through many different fields. To theologians, he was an erudite biblical scholar, Doctor of the Church, and author of the first full-length tracts on the Temple and the Tabernacle. For historians, he was responsible for the seminal text on the Anglo-Saxon period. For cosmologists, his scientific treatise gave rise to our modern dating system. To textual scholars, he had a significant impact on biblical and patristic literature through his influence on manuscripts like the Codex Amiatinus. To archaeologists, he has provided details that have enabled them to locate such important sites as Yeavering. To art historians, his work provides a symbolic and imaginative framework to examine artefacts from the period.

Alongside his autobiographical account, there was also a later story that grew up around Bede and helped reinforce his piety. It recounts how, nearly blind in his old age, he was fooled by some students that he was preaching to a full church. He was in fact talking to an array of stones. He finished his sermon, and to the surprise of those poking fun at the rambling, blind old man, a choir of angels chanted 'Amen, very venerable Bede'. This account has many obvious inconsistencies, and was surely designed to secure his status as 'most venerable'. However, it reinforces the idea that Bede and his followers were conscious to control his public image and create a cultural context that fitted with the deeply religious work to which he dedicated himself. His reputation is one of the man with near blindness dedicated to pursuing the spread of the Christian message.

Other texts support the singularly significant role Bede played in firming up the new Church in England. The *Anonymous Life of Abbot Ceolfrith* describes how, after the plague of AD 686, only Bede and Ceolfrith kept the monastery alive in terms of singing the offices.[5] As a result Bede is partly responsible for preserving Wearmouth–Jarrow. His role in its earlier troubles no doubt earned him a special place within the monastery and in the eyes of Ceolfrith. This explains the strong relationship that emerged between the two men, as revealed in a telling emotional account by Bede of the abbot's departure and death. In accounting for the long break he had taken between writing books three and four of his *Commentary of Samuel*, he states:

> *Having completed the third book … I thought that I would rest a while, and, after recovering in that way my delight in study and writing, proceed to take in hand the fourth. But that rest, if sudden anguish of mind can be called rest, has turned out much longer than I had intended owing to the sudden change of circumstances brought about by the departure of my beloved most revered abbot; who, after long devotion to the care of his monastery, suddenly determined to go to Rome, and to breathe his last breath amid the localities sanctified by the bodies of the blessed apostles and martyrs of Christ, thus causing no little consternation to those committed to his charge, the greater because it was unexpected.*[6]

The tone of this extract, and its emphasis on the suddenness of Ceolfrith's departure, attest to a strong bond between Bede and the abbot, and also provide a uniquely human glimpse into the personal sufferings and emotional frailty of the dedicated scholar.

Yet, despite displaying moments of humanity and vulnerability in his works, Bede's public image as a stoic, driven, focused scholar has survived the test of time, and he has continued to be perceived as a cornerstone of a strong and self-assured early Anglo-Saxon Church. In a time when the previous generation had been orally literate, but did not widely employ writing, he had the historical foresight to see that his version of the period could become canonical, shaping not just his own time, but how that time would come to be perceived elsewhere in the literate world and in the future.

His texts were so influential that the monastery of Wearmouth–Jarrow was akin to a famous publishing house, creating multiple copies of their bestselling author's work. He records having written about sixty texts and, remarkably for this period, copies of almost all of them survive, standing as testament to his popularity. He was a master of rhetoric, and seems to have manipulated his material to suit his ends – the glorification of the Church and papacy, and the erasure of heresy and paganism from his nation. He was greatly concerned that the newly emerging eighth-century English Church should not be associated with heretical practices (such as the Pelagian heresy which dogged Britain in the fifth century) or paganism, which Gregory the Great sought to excise.

His work is almost too thorough in removing the saintly Christian figures and Church events from a context that would connect them with non-orthodox or pre-Christian connections – the very world outside his monastery's doors. Unlike objects like the Franks Casket, which weave past and present belief systems together, Bede was a master of propaganda, who consistently applied a filter on all pagan beliefs and practices throughout his works. At times, however, he let the occasional detail slip through which paints a different picture of both him and the period in which he wrote. This is certainly the case with regards to his story of the poet Caedmon, which he alone records in detail.

In order to set up the miraculous gift that Caedmon receives directly from God, he has to contrast it with the shepherd's life prior to his revelation. As a result, he gives an account of a pagan Anglo-Saxon hall: its feasting, recitation of heroic poetry and celebration of 'comitatus'. Furthermore, after condemning the songs of the hall as 'lying or idle', he then records (possibly creates) the so-called 'Caedmon's Hymn'. This poem – apparently the oldest Old English poem to survive in manuscript form – occurs only in Bede's *Ecclesiastical History*. While it is clear that it preserves a poetic tradition and set of techniques stretching back beyond Bede, it is intriguing that it is only he who records it, and it is possible that he adapted an existing poem himself.

Purely the fact that it is recorded in the vernacular suggests that Bede had an understanding and, indeed, an appreciation of pre-Christian poetic traditions.[7] In describing his Latin translation of the text he states 'it is impossible to make a literal translation, no matter how well written, of poetry into another language without losing some of the beauty and dignity'. So, in the account of Caedmon, Bede gives us a glimpse into the world around him; a world where the life of the hall was central, poetry was alliterative and enigmatic, and where the 'guardian of mankind' is shifting from heroic war-leader to a plethora of Christian saints, martyrs and godheads.

Bede gives us some of the few remaining insights into pagan Anglo-Saxon religion. Indeed, it is in his work that a clue to the worship of Odinn (Woden in Old English) is given, for he records how a local priest converted to Christianity and turned his back on his temple to Woden, deconsecrating it by casting a spear into its midst. The connection between Woden and spears is clear from other objects like the Finglesham buckle, but this is the only surviving textual evidence of this pagan ritual. Bede has acted as a reticent mouthpiece for this world.

Bede and the Raven

While he gives us these tantalising glimpses, Bede was also, like a true spin doctor, able to do subtle things to influence his readers. This is clear in his treatment of one of the most potent symbols of the pagan Germanic religion – the raven, which was the sacred bird of Woden. This bird seems to have acted as a shorthand reference to Woden in the same way that a crucifix could denote a wearer as Christian. For example, a seventh-century gold and garnet pendant, found in Faversham, shows a triple spiral of ravens and would have been worn round the neck as a pendant. As Paulinus ordered the shooting down of a crow, Bede did something similar in terms of redefining the symbol of the raven. It has had a profound effect on Christian attitudes to this bird, right down to the present day. Indeed, we still tend to think of ravens as birds associated with death and evil, in contrast to their purer Christian siblings, doves. The clues to Bede's intentions lie in the famous Codex Amiatinus.[8]

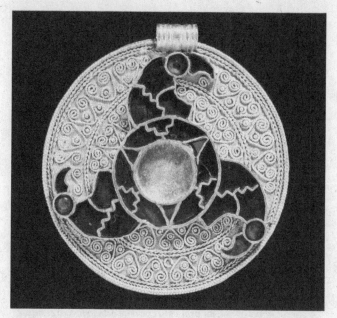

This gold and garnet pendant would have been strung together with others on a necklace. Fine gold filigree work gives texture to the background, while a triskele of three ravens radiates out from the centre. The eyes of the birds are picked out as cabochon gems, while the rest of the garnets are cloisonné.

Abbot Ceolfrith took this colossal manuscript with him as he departed for Rome from Wearmouth–Jarrow. He intended for it to be a present to the papacy from a devoutly orthodox scriptorium on the edges of the Christian world, and Bede seems to have been employed to ensure this gift was absolutely scrupulous throughout. Bede's handwriting appears at crucial moments throughout the book, editing parts of the biblical text with the skill of an accomplished theologian and scholar.[9] Manuscript additions and excisions can provide tantalising links with the minds of many centuries ago, and in the case of the Codex Amiatinus, Bede's scribblings were of particular significance. This manuscript has continued to be copied verbatim as the earliest and best Vulgate text up to the present day. This means that his additions have made their way into the canonical text of the Bible. Bede didn't just write history; he had a hand in rewriting the Bible.

How does this affect the raven? Well, there is one addition of particular significance: a small 'non' added into the Genesis account of Noah's ark. It sounds like a minor point, but it has transformed the way the raven has been perceived by Christians. There were two main versions of the Bible that early Christians used – the Vulgate and the Old Latin.[10] One was translated by Jerome from the original Hebrew, while the other relied on Greek translations. They diverge at points, and one such place is in Genesis 8:7:

> VULGATE: *(Noe ... dimisit corvum) qui egrediebatur et revertebatur donec siccarentur aquae super terram.*

> (Noah ... sent forth the raven) who was going out and **was returning** until the waters over the earth dried up.

> OLD LATIN: *(Noe ... emisit corvum) ut videret utrum cessasset aqua et exiens **non est reversus** donec siccaret aqua a terra.*

> (Noah sent out the raven) in order that it might see whether the water had ceased and departing, it **did not return** until the waters over the earth had dried up.

It is clear that, in the Vulgate version, the raven went back and forth, unlike the Old Latin, where it simply failed to return. What happened with the Codex Amiatinus, however, is very revealing. Despite the fact that it was intended to be the definite Vulgate version of the Bible, Bede has added a small 'non' before 'revertebatur'. It flies in the face of the Vulgate translation, but instead creates a negative action for the raven – he goes away and does *not* come back.

This little addition could be more loaded than at first appears. By making the raven a bird that did not return to the ark and help Noah, Bede has given it a new symbolic life. To so consciously and cleverly redefine this bird's role in the Genesis story allowed Bede to cast a dark light on it, and align it with a new, negative set of connections.[11] Bede was doing something deliberate to rework the imaginative world of the Anglo-Saxons, and he built on this in his patristic texts, where he casts the raven in ever more dark and dismal ways – it symbolised the heretic, those who betrayed their baptism, and those who would not achieve salvation.

Despite the fact that he was effectively rewriting the Bible to his own ends, Bede was playing a clever marketing game in taking a symbol of central importance to the pre-Christian world of Anglo-Saxon England and realigning its meaning. This casts his work in a different light and gives the impression that he was deliberately seeking to erase the pagan world of his people from the record. With this sort of intellectual religious cleansing in mind, Bede appears a very different character to the one painted by him and his followers. He wanted to be remembered as a saintly scholar, toiling away in a well-established monastery, with his mind and heart focused firmly on the papacy. He appears here, however, as a clever manipulator of the written text for his own religion's ends.

Bede's Changing World: the Ruthwell Cross

Bede's monastery was an oasis on the landscape, built in stone, boasting glazed windows and a thriving scriptorium. But it was that – an oasis. The surrounding environment was a far more complex and evolving place than even Bede's dense and detailed writings seem to allow. He is largely responsible for creating this oasis, raising the profile of his unusual monastic environment and giving it a greater presence in the historical record than it perhaps enjoyed at the time. That is the power of the written word, and Bede knew it. He could create his own version of reality and pass it down through the centuries. He was a profound wordsmith, manipulator of facts and supreme weaver of new symbolic and imaginative worlds.

There is a particularly enigmatic object that now stands within a church in Dumfries, almost directly parallel with Wearmouth–Jarrow, on the western coast of the country, which highlights the way disparate worlds could be drawn together by eighth-century

Northumbrian monks. Despite the fact that the object was made on the other side of the kingdom, the intellectual sophistication it displays recalls the work of Bede and the Wearmouth–Jarrow monks. The Ruthwell Cross is an eighth-century Anglo-Saxon high cross, now reconstructed from fragments discovered around the church site.[12] Parts of the original are still missing, including the crossbeam, but it has been carefully reconstructed so that it now stands 5.5 metres high in a sunken section of Ruthwell Church.

The Ruthwell Cross is, of course, made of stone.[13] The medium is directly associated with the Church, given Christ's statements regarding Peter as his cornerstone and the apostles as pillars. What's more, the papacy continued the artistic and architectural heritage of the Roman Empire, and as a result continued to build in stone, which in turn created statements of permanence and power on the landscape.

But it is important to note that what we see today in terms of the bare stone is merely the skeleton of the original piece. These crosses would have been plastered and painted, sometimes inlaid with gemstones or glass to add to the luxurious appearance. They were colourful and, some might say, garish objects. Using colour for highlights would, however, have made the imagery on the crosses much clearer to interpret. For example, a scene showing Cain and Abel could be coloured with red paint to emphasise that Cain had struck his brother. The bright colours would also have made them even more noticeable on the landscape, and enhanced their role as educational tools for spreading Christian imagery and narratives to the populace.

The Irish examples of high crosses are much better preserved than their English counterparts, as far fewer were systematically destroyed in the Reformation. Indeed, the ring-headed stone crosses of Ireland are so familiar that it has been traditional to think of them as emerging out of a Celtic context. It seems, however, that the Irish crosses evolved out of the earlier experiments in Anglo-Saxon England following the Synod of Whitby. The ring head that has become so closely tied with Celtic Christianity was an Irish development, designed to stop the cross arms collapsing. Earlier Anglo-Saxon examples were weak at the point where the heavy stone arms met the narrowing crosshead. By adding the ring, Irish sculptors were able to prop up the arms more effectively. So, rather than having great symbolic resonance, the ring head was designed as a technological development, intended to preserve the integrity of the cross head.

The arrival of Christianity within Anglo-Saxon England instigated new kinds of iconographically and stylistically complex art. From its inception, Christianity was founded upon the written word and stories from the Bible – Christ is even described as 'the Word' in John's Gospel. Therefore, the newly converted Anglo-Saxons had to learn many new skills in order to become Christians. They had to learn Latin, the language of the Church; they had to learn to write and produce books; and they had to learn to build in stone. After the Synod of Whitby there was an explosion of artistic creativity, especially in the monasteries of the north, where there was a form of Northumbrian renaissance. One of its most exceptional products is the Ruthwell Cross.

The history of this cross is complex. It has been destroyed and buried – and then pieced back together in the nineteenth century.[14] It consciously and cleverly combines the styles and runes of the pre-Christian artistic tradition with biblical inscriptions and figural imagery that were in tune with art being produced on the Christian Continent. The scenes on the Ruthwell Cross are both uniquely Anglo-Saxon and completely orthodox in their adherence to Christian iconography. Like the Franks Casket and Cuthbert's coffin, it needs to be thought of as a three-dimensional object in the round, with each of the sides interacting with one another.

To understand the cross, it is essential to imagine it within its original setting. The cross was most likely designed to stand at the head of the nave in an Anglo-Saxon church, perhaps in the place where later rood screens stood.[15] Were it positioned as such, then the east and west sides would face different audiences. To the west the cross would be visible to the congregation, while to the east the monastic and priestly men conducting the ceremony at the altar would be the intended audience.

The difference in the intended audience becomes clearer by examining the subject matter of the two sides.[16] The face that would have been visible to the monks and priest contains two mysterious scenes. The first shows Christ, haloed, standing on two beasts which cross their front paws in adoration beneath his feet. And above this scene is an image of John the Baptist holding and pointing to a lamb. So what is the relevance of these scenes? The image of Christ seems to combine a passage from Psalm 90:13, where Christ treads on the asp and basilisk, lion and dragon, with the Canticle of Habakkuk, where the beasts of the desert bow down to him. This is a unique image within Christian art, but it coincides with the introduction in Rome of the Canticle of Habakkuk as part of the liturgy. The monks that gazed on this image could see it as a memo from the papacy, keeping them up to date with the latest liturgical developments.

And the scene of John the Baptist with the Lamb of God? The Ruthwell Cross is thought to date to the second half of the eighth century, when the papacy introduced the Agnus Dei – Lamb of God – chant to the liturgy, and images of the lamb proliferated throughout Christian Europe. Together, these two scenes indicate that the monks of Ruthwell wanted to remain orthodox in terms of creating Christian imagery that accorded with papal laws and canons. They show that the monks at the edge of the world were in tune with developments taking place at the Christian heart. The fact that these scenes faced the monks indicate that this sense of orthodox Christianity was important to them. Only the literate and educated monks could interpret such esoteric symbolism and understand the Latin inscriptions that run around each panel. At the base is a final image that has great monastic resonance: Paul and Anthony breaking bread. This refers to the account of the two desert fathers coming together for the Eucharist. It was a central premise of monasticism that monks came together to be alone, and this image at the foot of the Ruthwell Cross exemplified this ideal. These were not frequently depicted scenes, and only monks could make sense of them.

On the other face, in contrast, are scenes and inscriptions taken from the Gospels. At the base is an image of the Annunciation, with Mary greeted by the Angel Gabriel, while above Christ heals the blind man and has his feet washed by

Mary Magdalene. Below the cross head, Mary and Martha come together. If this face of the cross is imagined as facing towards a lay population of recently converted Anglo-Saxons then their relevance becomes clearer. Rather than complex and esoteric images loaded with theological significance, this face shows scenes that would have been relevant to the people. They are important stories at the heart of the Gospels, and scenes that introduce the fundamental principles of Christianity. Christ performs miracles, forgives a sinner and is shown as being born human through his handmaid Mary.

These scenes humanise Christ and make Christianity relevant to the viewers. They too can benefit from miraculous cures, eternal forgiveness and the love of an empathetic God who took human form. What's more, while the east face shows scenes of relevance to a monastic audience, the west face features women in all the scenes, and focuses on central human concerns like childbirth. The makers of the Ruthwell Cross were able to conceive of the viewers looking upon their work, and crafted their imagery to carry the most potent messages. This is incredibly sophisticated art, and the visual imagery is accompanied by inscriptions, as text and image weave together.[17]

Yet there are two more sides to this three-dimensional object, and the artists have not wasted the opportunity to make use of them. Facing south and north, the thin sides of the cross present a very different set of images. Instead of figural scenes separated by inscribed borders, these sides feature interlacing vine scrolls inhabited by birds and beasts who feed on the fruits of the vine. Not only do these sides reveal once again the Anglo-Saxon propensity for featuring animals and birds in their art, but they also show an attempt to understand a basic Christian premise by making use of native motifs. The idea of Christ as the True Vine, who nourishes and protects his followers, has been depicted here, with the vine actually surrounding and feeding the faithful, represented as birds and beasts. Just as the imagery seems drawn from a native context, so the text presents a surprise. Instead of Latin, the inscription that runs up and down both sides is in Old English and presented in runes. In fact, this is the longest-surviving piece of runic text from Anglo-Saxon England.

The runes are an extract from a longer poem, preserved in a later eleventh-century manuscript and known as *The Dream of the Rood*. This is part of the section included on the cross:

Then the young warrior, Almighty God, mounted the
Cross, in the sight of many.
I held the King, Heaven's lord, I dared not bow.
They mocked us together. I was wet with blood
Christ was on the Cross.
But there quickly came from afar, many to the Prince.
I was sorely smitten with sorrow
wounded with shafts. Limb-weary they laid him down.
They stood at his head. They looked on him there.[18]

This is a truly unique version of the Crucifixion, written from the point of view of the Cross and casting Christ not as a victim, but as a hero in the guise of a Germanic warrior. The use of prosopopoeia allows the Cross to speak for itself, and to take on Christ's suffering so that he is able to die a valiant death. This aspect of the Ruthwell Cross is intimately connected with the literary tradition of the Anglo-Saxon people. By combining this runic poem with interlacing animals, the artists of the Ruthwell Cross are making a powerful statement about the cultural identity of Anglo-Saxon Christians: they are orthodox and accord with the practices and teachings of the papacy; but they are also proud of their heritage, and see a role for their pre-Christian tradition in the service of the new Church. Furthermore, they are aware that they are poised between two worlds – that of their pagan Germanic past, and of the Christian future.

These complex high crosses, full of interlace, geometric panels and runic inscriptions, became regular statements on the landscape of the new Church's power. Examples like the Bewcastle Cross carry over all these features verbatim, and indicate how much energy the Anglo-Saxons invested in their new art form. While Bede cannot be connected directly with these advertising billboards that the Church was erecting across the landscape, he would have endorsed their efforts in presenting Christian ideas to the populace to guide them away from the ignorance of their pagan ways. He used the written word to bend the minds of the English people towards a new world view, while the high crosses used visual messages in accordance with Gregory the Great's instructions. But the intentions were the same: to bring an ideological change throughout the English populace, not just to those members of society targeted by the initial missions.

Bede is a central character within the world of Anglo-Saxon saints, and his connections with the other individuals covered by this volume are profound and telling. He shared a death day with St Augustine of Canterbury; he had met Wilfrid and Hilda; he trained under Biscop and Ceolfrith; and his body was taken from Jarrow to lie in the same grave as St Cuthbert in Durham. His works provide essential evidence for all aspects of life in Anglo-Saxon times, and have coloured many interpretations of the period. It remains of vital importance, therefore, to understand him and his motives clearly, for he has become the conduit through which so much of our understanding of Anglo-Saxon England flows. It is thanks to a later Northumbrian saint, however, that his importance was recognised and his legacy preserved. He was supported by Alcuin of York, who distributed his works across the Continent.

Alcuin

In the year that Bede died, AD 735, a new Northumbrian scholar saint entered the stage. Alcuin was probably born near York, where he subsequently received his education. Like Bede, he was dedicated to the church as a young child, and grew up within the family of clergy that served the cathedral. Also like Bede, Gregory's mission to the English loomed heavy in his thoughts, and he owed his loyalty to the See of St Peter's in Rome.[19] He never lost his connection with his home town, and some touching correspondence with his old brothers of York survives, testifying to the nostalgic affection he held for this place throughout his life. Growing up within a bustling urban environment such as the city of York coloured his perceptions of the role of the Church. To him, Christians had to take the knowledge and guidance from civilised centres of learning out to the people. The heart of the Church lay within cities, not on hostile outcrops of rock or disconnected islands, and widespread urban renewal was a necessary part of spreading its messages.

While growing up in York, Alcuin would have witnessed the great impact that trade had in terms of strengthening and empowering the Church. As the major port along the River Ouse brought greater links with the Continent, it also brought the possibility of enriching the cathedral and monastery. When the church Wilfrid originally built in York burnt down in AD 741, there came an opportunity to rebuild the cathedral in a grand manner. Alcuin helped to design the new building of Hagia Sophia (Holy Wisdom), which he described as having glazed windows and thirty altars. No remains have been found of it, but in its description it sounds extremely lavish. It may have been round like the chapel in Aachen, the consummate architectural achievement of Alcuin's later patron, Charlemagne, and it's tempting to see similarities between the two. The site in York may have anticipated later Carolingian innovations, and Alcuin may have been instrumental in this.[20]

Northumbria had changed in the generation since Bede was writing so that, in Alcuin's lifetime, it was firmly Christian, and the intrigues of the Church were no longer centred on converting pagans, but rather on the distribution of episcopal power. There had been much controversy over who would hold the bishop's 'pallium' in the north. Lindisfarne had clung onto theirs with zeal. While the tension between the episcopal sees of Lindisfarne, Hexham and York had previously been an enduring problem, Alcuin witnessed the ascension of his home town to archiepiscopal see, rivalled in power only by Canterbury. He wrote a long and rhetorically sophisticated poem about the church, monastery and library at York. It can be read as an advert for the Church in York against the counter-claims of Hexham and Lindisfarne. Cuthbert's role is played down, and virtually no mention is made of the Irish party. It's pure rhetoric and a piece of clever propaganda, founded on the work of Bede, and, like Bede, what he leaves out is as interesting as what he emphasises. The idea of 'Holy Wisdom' seems to lie at the core of much of Alcuin's work – he believes learning and teaching can save.

Alcuin witnessed a particularly successful relationship between Church and State that was fostered around York from the AD 730s to the AD 750s. The Archbishop – and Alcuin's primary supporter – was Ecgberht, whose brother, Eadberht, was the King of Northumbria. Ecgberht had been a pupil of Bede, and under the joint governance of these brothers the region grew in power and reach. The school at York became highly influential, and introduced a form of university education by specialising in the seven liberal arts: grammar, logic, rhetoric, arithmetic, geometry, music and astronomy. This was the education system developed by the Greeks, and creating a monastic school focused on such classical concerns allowed Alcuin to endorse and disseminate the work of Bede, who in his textual scholarship was the most important precursor to the Carolingian Renaissance.[21] But he was also anticipating the wider changes that the renaissance would bring in terms of preserving and spreading the wisdom of the classical age.

Alcuin and the Carolingian Renaissance

Although Alcuin was a Northumbrian, raised in and around York, the majority of his working life was spent abroad.[22] Like Wilfrid, Biscop and the Anglo-Saxon missionaries Willibrord and Boniface, who had taken Christian missions to the Continent, Alcuin travelled extensively, and made close bonds particularly with the Frankish Church. Alcuin was dedicated to both learning from and influencing the places he travelled to. He was effectively headhunted by the self-styled Holy Roman Emperor, Charlemagne, Ruler of the Carolingian Empire, and became a driving force behind his new approach to Christian learning and the arts.[23] As a religious adviser to the Carolingian regime, Alcuin had the unenviable job of balancing the moral ambiguities of Charlemagne's military career with his investment in scholarship and Christian education. It took a strong personality to forge such a lasting career within one of the most radical courts of its time, and yet Alcuin managed it.

The efforts of the Carolingian court were deliberate and politically motivated. During the seventh century, the previous powerful royal house, the Merovingians, was eroded by war and a sequence of *rois fainéants* (do-nothing kings) for whom power was exercised by their chief officer, the mayor of the palace. Charlemagne was descended from this line of 'mayors', so there is a sense in which his campaign to transform Western Europe may have been based on a desire to stress the legitimacy of his reign and that of his family. Creating a holier-than-holy imperial rule, concerned with crafting the perfect vision of a Christian emperor, was the method Charlemagne and Alcuin employed to whitewash the ruler's legitimacy.

The greatest asset to the Carolingian family was the support of the papacy. While Charlemagne's father, Pepin, was ruling the Frankish lands, the then pope, Zachary, decreed that he should be made a 'true king', despite the fact he had no legal claim to the throne. In turn, Pepin provided the weakened Vatican state with military support against the Lombards, and secured many major cities for the papacy. This gave the Carolingians legitimacy and a greater cause, since they were presented as holy leaders protecting the Church and spreading the Christian mission. It was in the name of evangelising that Charlemagne conducted one of his most bloody and controversial campaigns in Saxony, in the north-west corner of modern Germany.

Charlemagne was almost continually at war during his long reign, and while his battles against the Moors, Muslims and Lombards were bitter, one particular attack against the pagan Saxons was incredibly brutal. In AD 782 he imposed a law that all Saxons should convert to Christianity on pain of death. In response a campaign was led against him, but Charlemagne retaliated by ordering the death of 4,500 Saxon prisoners. Known as the Massacre of Verden, this was mass genocide, and provides a startling contrast to the guise of sacred Christian ruler that Alcuin and his fellow scholars had to present.

Alcuin was responsible for a good deal of the public façade of the imperial court. In some of his texts he appears to be akin to a modern-day spin doctor, who was supposed to control how the events of Charlemagne's reign were perceived. His letters reveal that he was often homesick, confused about his goals and concerned by the almost fascistic manner in which the emperor sought to control every aspect of courtly and ecclesiastic creativity.[24] Alcuin even reproached Charlemagne over his attempts to force people to convert, stating that belief can only emerge through free will. He had some success, for a few years later Charlemagne abolished the death penalty for paganism.

At Charlemagne's court in Aachen, Alcuin became central to the intellectual pursuits of the scholars the emperor had drawn together. They worked to preserve ancient texts, making copies of pagan Greek and Roman literature within Christian scriptoriums. We get an insight into Alcuin as a young boy from an account he told to one of his students, Sigwulf. It tells how, when asleep beside a peasant boy, Alcuin had a nightmare that he was reproached for enjoying Vergil more than the Psalms. When he woke up he found that the peasant boy had slept through the Divine Office, and Alcuin had to protect him by singing the Psalms to ward off the devil. This shows that he had a complicated relationship with classical learning. Yet had Alcuin and those around him at Aachen not taken this potentially controversial decision to record the wisdom of non-Christians, most of the classical texts available today would have been lost. We would not have our collections of ancient texts were it not for these brave monastic scholars.

There is no doubt that under Charlemagne's rule Christian art made radical strides. Carolingian manuscript illumination was decidedly classical in style, with figures represented in a natural manner, and drapery emphasised. For example, the Lorsch Gospels cover was made between AD 778 and AD 820, during the reign of Charlemagne. The cover panels are made of ivory, so very precious, and the imagery recalls Late Antique carvings in the naturalistic way the figures are represented. Those involved in the Carolingian Renaissance were not content simply to copy the texts of antiquity; they looked to the classical tradition for artistic inspiration too. Having amassed territories equivalent to the Western Roman Empire, the Carolingian Court were aware that they needed an artistic tradition to reflect their power. In contrast to the Byzantine

Empire, which was gripped by iconoclasm in the late eighth century, the Carolingians defiantly clung to figural art, developing it to include more elaborate and realistically rendered figures for the purposes of creating narrative and devotional works.

The effects of the Carolingian Renaissance were felt close to Alcuin's home of York, for a number of 'Apostle shafts' (high crosses with images of the Apostles up the front and back) appeared around the year AD 800 which bore the hallmarks of the art emerging from the powerful court of Charlemagne, Holy Roman Emperor.[25] The Easby Cross, from near Richmond in North Yorkshire, shows the influence of the more naturalistic treatment of human figures and the elaborate drapery commonly found in Carolingian manuscripts. The heads of the Apostles, clustered together to prop up the shaft in a symbolic rendering of their role as pillars of the Church, display variety, and each has delicately carved hair and facial features. A similar cross shaft from nearby Otley, West Yorkshire, also shows the Apostles framed within architectural arches. The Anglo-Saxons were keen to maintain their native style too, however, as down the narrow shafts and along the back, animal interlace, knotwork and geometric designs balance the figurative images.

Alcuin stands as testament to the multicultural and international reach of the Christian Church in the early medieval period. It is tempting to think of this time like the Victorians did, as nasty, brutish and short, where people lived and died within a few miles of their shabby huts. But there are numerous exceptions to this picture. One who seems to embody the more modern notion of international business and travel is Alcuin. The Church was a binding force across continents, and the bureaucracy of supporting such an omnipresent institution meant that churchmen would travel vast distances. It is important to think of Alcuin in context. While cosmopolitan and worldly, he was born and raised in Anglo-Saxon England. The view of Christianity he had developed growing up in York left an imprint on him – that their faith had papal support and had developed strictly along orthodox lines. Charlemagne sought to propel both Church and State forward together into the ninth century, and with Alcuin's support he was able to achieve incredible success. A remarkable achievement for an Anglo-Saxon saint.

The cross shaft at Otley, Yorkshire, is now in fragments, but it would have had busts of the apostles stretching up the sides. Each apostle is shown within an architectural frame, and they are given naturalistic details like finely carved hair and individual features.

However, the many successes of the late eighth and early ninth century in terms of developing the Church and its representatives received a damaging blow in AD 793. The event is recorded by Alcuin in a letter he sent to Aethelred, King of Northumbria:

> We and our fathers have now lived in this fair land for nearly 350 years, and never before has such an atrocity been seen in Britain as we have now suffered at the hands of a pagan people ... The Church of St Cuthbert is spattered with the blood of the priests of God, stripped of all its furnishings, exposed to the plunderings of pagans – a place more sacred than any in Britain.[26]

Vikings attacked the monastery at Lindisfarne, seizing treasure and massacring many monks. A haunting survival from the time shows

Viking raiders, carved in stone, wielding axes and swords. This event marked the start of the Viking Age, and many more attacks on Anglo-Saxon monasteries were to follow. Times were changing, and the saints that had developed over the previous 200 years were no longer safe within their enriched monasteries to be preoccupied with Christian learning and prop up the royal households. The next wave of saints was very different, and their attempts to hold back the flood of pagans from across the North Sea are somewhat ironic, since this was the very direction from which the earlier Angles, Saxons and Jutes had travelled just 350 years earlier. It would take a new kind of saint, a royal saint, to stem this flood.

Chapter Ten
Alfred: Rise and Fall of the Royal Saints

> '*Never before has such terror appeared in
> Britain as we have now suffered from a pagan
> race ... The heathens poured out the blood of
> saints around the altar, and trampled on the
> bodies of saints in the temple of God, like dung
> in the streets.*'

Alcuin's 'Letter to Higbald'.[1]

The Great Heathen Army, as the Anglo-Saxons so explicitly named it, would have succeeded in bringing about a complete conquest of Britain in the late ninth century had it not been for the efforts of one man. A saintly king if ever there was one, Alfred the Great almost single-handedly changed the fortunes of the Anglo-Saxons, halting the Viking incursions south and rebuilding a fragile Church and State. He was an intelligent, determined and insightful ruler, who understood that national identity had to be forged through art, literature and religion, as much as through battles. A successful military leader and a patron of the Church, Alfred, like Constantine and Gregory before him, truly deserves the title 'Great'.

Nevertheless, Alfred halted, rather than ended, the progress of the Scandinavian troops. Over half of the country remained governed by pagan settlers from across the seas during his reign. The decline of Anglo-Saxon saints had begun, and now the complexion of sanctity was changing. From the ninth to the eleventh century, saintliness was becoming the concern of royalty, and the divide between secular and spiritual worlds was increasingly blurred. The idea that a king could now be both a divine ruler during his life and a sacred intercessor after his death strengthened their positions and imbued them with great power. It was a process that royalty actively encouraged, and Alfred himself promoted the cult of royal saints by elevating his rival Edmund, the King of East Anglia from AD 855 to AD 869, to the sainthood. Known as Edmund the Martyr, he was a rallying point for a nation threatened by conquest. Yet now the greatest testament to this largely forgotten English saint remains the town named after him: Bury St Edmunds.

Surrounded on both sides by the East Anglian Heights, Bury St Edmunds lies nestled in an area of lower ground. The modern town is extremely picturesque, with the remains of the extravagant gate-house and the now-ruined monastic complex framing the large market square. The ivy-clad Georgian grandeur of the Angel hotel, which Charles Dickens described in *The Pickwick Papers*, over-looks a Norman tower, the remains of a medieval hospital and an array of boutique shops and quaint cafes. Passing through the magnificent gates, the sorry remains of the once-great monastery act as a reminder of the destruction wrought by Thomas Cromwell's Visitors during the Dissolution. Very little remains of the monastery's medieval grandeur, and less still of the Anglo-Saxon cult centre that predated it. Yet echoes of the past resonate everywhere, and Bury St Edmunds wears its former glories like a faded veil.

The reason this town gained such wealth, power and influence during the medieval period was largely down to the man after whom the town is named. Edmund's tomb is long since destroyed and his memory largely lost to the sands of time, so only his name remains significant. Despite the wealth of native saints like Cuthbert, Wilfrid and Hilda, the patron saint of England for some centuries was none of these well-known and documented individuals. Instead, Edmund, this barely recorded East Anglian king, was chosen. Almost nothing is known about him, and his hagiographies, written some time after his death, take almost every detail from the lives of other saints like Sebastian, Mary of Egypt and Denis.[2] What little we do know of his life comes from the writings of Dunstan, Abbot of Glastonbury, the tenth-century saint. It is significant that Dunstan chose to record his cult, as he was bound up with promoting the work of a later Anglo-Saxon king, Edgar. Yet, despite very little evidence for the saint himself, two things seem to have secured his legacy as one of the premier saints of England: the fact that he was a king *and* a martyr.

Edmund lived through a particularly violent and turbulent time. He had to defend his kingdom of East Anglia against Vikings that were attacking along the coast and increasingly moving inland to engage the Anglo-Saxons in battle. What had started out as fortuitous raiding missions on poorly defended yet wealthy sites like Lindisfarne had escalated through the ninth century into a more coordinated assault, with Viking armies set on seizing land and influence in England. The Great Heathen Army was led by the Danish king Ragnar Lodbrok, and made up of warriors from across Scandinavia. Their intention was no longer to raid and depart, but to conquer and settle.

In East Anglia they destroyed virtually all the major church and monastic sites. Monks, manuscripts and material wealth were eradicated in their path.[3] The exact circumstances of Edmund's death are unclear, but later legends report that he was captured in battle, beaten, tied to a tree then shot through with arrows. He was finally beheaded. Images of the martyred king pierced with arrow shafts recall those of St Sebastian, one of the most popular saints of the medieval period. Edmund was martyred not at the hands of pagan Romans (like Alban and Sebastian), but at the hands of pagan Vikings. The Vikings may have brought chaos, destruction and bloodshed, but to the Christian Anglo-Saxons' pious minds they also brought the opportunity of eternal communion with the saints through martyrdom. The chance of dying a martyr's death was born again.

Edmund, Alfred and the Viking Threat

Alfred, King of Wessex, had been an opponent of Edmund and his royal house of East Anglia. Tribal identities ran deep in England, and the kings of East Anglia and Wessex were fiercely protective of their own lands and rights. However, they were bound together in their animosity towards the Danes. Alongside the other Anglo-Saxon rulers, of Mercia and Northumbria, Alfred and Edmund were desperate to keep the Vikings from conquering their lands.

After Edmund's death, Alfred had his rival king declared a saint. The motivations for declaring him a royal saint were manifold. Firstly, this would set a precedent for canonising kings, particularly those who had fought against the Danes like Alfred himself. Secondly, Alfred was attempting to unify the Anglo-Saxon kingdoms under his leadership. Bringing a member of the royal house of East Anglia into his protection would serve to unite the people of that region behind him. Thirdly, Alfred could control the way in which Edmund's cult developed. He could pump investment into the town now known as Bury St Edmunds, and benefit from the monastic establishment and stream of pilgrims that would then be drawn to the site. In many ways, it was sensible town development and heritage management.

Alfred was canny to promote a cult to Edmund at Bury, given its strategic location. The town was on the edge of the area established by the Danelaw (the region of Danish-conquered lands running roughly from London to Chester), and placing a thriving cult centre at this position would give him a Christian stronghold on the border of his kingdom. The cult of St Edmund would go on to gain great exposure among the Danish settlers north of Alfred's borders. By the tenth century Edmund was celebrated by the very people who had killed him. They made a commemorative coin with the words 'O St Edmund the king!' inscribed on it.[4] This is remarkable. The Viking hoard discovered at Cuerdale included 1,800 examples of these St Edmund pennies, indicating that they were in wide circulation. His reputation is bound up with the town of Bury, whose coat of arms is a pair of crossed arrows with a crown, in honour of his martyrdom.

His cult continued to fascinate kings and rulers on both sides of the Danelaw. Churches dedicated to him are found throughout the north of England, and as far afield as Iceland. English kings continued to visit the shrine and bequeath tracts of lands to the abbey in memory of this royal saintly martyr. This enabled Bury St Edmunds to become one of the wealthiest institutions in the country. At the time of the Dissolution, the monastery was a morally corrupt and vastly wealthy organisation. Edmund was possibly the last independent East Anglian king, so he became a focal point for latent resentment towards their loss of autonomy, and a rallying point for the kingdom.

This could be extended, however, to provide a tangible link between Anglo-Saxons and Danes. On both sides of the virtual border defining the Danelaw, the idea of a divine sacrificial king was resonant. This was something the Vikings could relate to, since the heroic death of a king in battle resonated with their pagan Germanic beliefs in bravery and honour. The fact that Edmund's relics were also connected with fertility and the protection of his kingdom fuelled these pre-Christian associations even more.

Attempts have been made to reinstate Edmund as the patron saint of England. Sadly, the place of his burial is almost invisible now and his body long gone, yet his reputation as the primary English martyr king lives on.

Alfred the Great

Alfred is still considered a saint by some Catholics, but he was never canonised. Indeed, the efforts of Henry VI to have him recognised as an Anglo-Saxon saint-king were unsuccessful, although he did receive the more secular epithet reserved for only the most exceptional leaders: 'the Great'. This means that he is celebrated by the Anglican Church as a 'Christian hero', alongside the formidable characters of Constantine (the first Christian emperor) and Charlemagne (the first Holy Roman Emperor).

Alfred was primarily a ruler and a military leader, yet he was also a patron of the Church and a deeply pious man who understood the importance of sacred art and literature.[5] He epitomises a development that was taking place more broadly across England from the ninth through to the eleventh centuries. Kings, queens and members of the royal family had been declared saints in the earlier centuries, but moving through the Viking incursions towards the Norman Conquest this process of canonising royalty gathered momentum. Alfred has to make an appearance within this book since it is largely down to him that any distinct kingdom of the Anglo-Saxons survived at all beyond the ninth century. Furthermore, his approach to Christian learning and education had a profound effect on future generations of scholars and monks, particularly in terms of providing access to sacred material in the vernacular; in Old English rather than Latin.

Like Constantine, Charlemagne and a number of the saints covered in this volume, Alfred had an official version of his life written. His biographer, Asser, was hand-picked to ensure that his account would be written in the correct hagiographical style, and would emphasise only those points that would present Alfred in a favourable light. Looking to Charlemagne, who predated him by some fifty years, it's easy to see how these texts can clean up a ruler's image. Charlemagne's biographer, Einheard, was so verbose in his praise of his Holy Roman Emperor that even horrific events are presented through a rose-tinted lens. From the example of Charlemagne, the celebrated military and Christian ruler before him, Alfred realised that a good biographer was essential to kings, bishops and saints alike.[6]

The most famous story attached to Alfred the Great, however, was not recorded by Asser, and was concerned with burning loaves. It was recorded in a piece of hagiography, the *Life of St Neot*, written by an anonymous monk over a century after Alfred's death, and describes a scene that almost certainly never happened.[7] According to the monk, Alfred was wandering dejectedly through the Somerset Levels, having been pushed back by Viking assaults to the Isle of Athelney with just a handful of loyal Anglo-Saxon followers. The story goes that Alfred was taken in by a swineherd and his wife, and asked to watch that the bread baking in the oven didn't burn. Consumed with contemplating how to defeat the Viking armies, he let them burn and then humbly took the rebukes of the angry wife.

This is almost entirely rhetoric and fancy – a sign of Alfred's humility as king, in that he was happy to take insults from one of his lowliest subjects. But it also acts as a metaphor for what was happening within his kingdom. Wessex, along with all the other Anglo-Saxon kingdoms, had been raided, attacked and overrun on Alfred's watch. He needed to look within himself and find the fiery resolve to defeat the Vikings. What it shows us is that this anonymous monk, writing long after the life of the subject he describes, was a creative individual, penning not historical fact, but entertaining fiction.[8]

Yet enough additional material survives from Alfred's reign to allow greater insight into him and his time. The objects that have made their way down the historical record may similarly distort our view of him, since only those that support his image as a pious and reforming saviour of England have remained in the public domain. For example, the coins struck to commemorate his successful reconquest of London around AD 886 were sophisticated propaganda, with Alfred depicted as an emperor, and trace letters used to create the word 'London'.[9]

Yet later archaeological finds do seem to bear out aspects of the more fantastical legends surrounding him. His peace treaty with Guthrum, drawn up after his decisive victory against the Viking forces at the Battle of Edington in AD 878, indicates that he was reluctant to engage continually in armed combat with the Vikings, opting instead for legislative agreements modelled on Continental examples and rooted in Christian terminology. Guthrum was forced to convert to Christianity and take Alfred as his godfather – a hugely symbolic role in early conversions.

Then there are the finds associated with Alfred's building of burhs (fortified defences) to strengthen the position of the Anglo-Saxons against Viking attacks. The effort and cost required to bring about the sort of national town development that archaeology bears witness to over the few decades of Alfred's reign is astonishing, particularly given that the king was also having to fund a standing army and an almost unbroken series of expensive battles. He introduced taxes to pay for the armies and development of burhs. Hyperbole and legend aside, Alfred must have been a formidable person. He was capable as a military leader, able to defeat the Vikings at what was their forte – pitched battle. He was also historically minded, with a sense of the importance of legacy. Furthermore, he was educated and literate, writing some of the only pieces of text to be penned by an English king before the fifteenth century.

Alfred had a two-pronged approach to saving his kingdom of Wessex. On the one hand he had to deal with the immediate threat: the Viking attacks. In response to this he piled money and personnel into building fortified burhs and developing the army so that the Anglo-Saxons could beat the Vikings at their own game. But, in Alfred's eyes, the Viking attacks were a just punishment sent to the Anglo-Saxons because they had been sinfully letting their Christian morality and learning slide away. So once he'd dealt with the result, he turned his attentions to the cause. He invested half his annual revenue in projects that would be 'pleasing to God'.[10]

Alfred wanted to invest in education, for he realised that both the Church and State needed young people who could read Latin and knew essential texts. He himself was well educated as a boy, in both Latin and the vernacular. His biographer, Asser, records how he won a collection of Old English poetry from his mother for being able to remember and recite a set of poems. We get the fullest insight into his plans for reforming the education system of Anglo-Saxon England from a remarkable survival: his own preface to a translation of Gregory the Great's 'Pastoral Care'. The first point of significance with this text is that it is a translation from Latin into Old English. Alfred stands at the fore of a long line of Anglo-Saxons who saw the expediency of providing vernacular translations of essential texts.

There are Old English glosses in a number of biblical manuscripts, including the Lindisfarne Gospels. While it would take until the Great Bible of Henry VIII of 1535 for a translation of the Bible into English to be recognised by the Church, the Anglo-Saxons had long felt it expedient to gloss or translate biblical texts into the vernacular to aid scriptural learning. They were avant-garde in their approach to using the native spoken tongue of their people to communicate spiritual matters, with one Anglo-Saxon scholar, Aelfric of Evesham, crafting his sermons and theological works in Old English. Alfred shared this approach.

He instigated a programme of translating those books which were 'most needful to know' (niedbeðearfosta), stating that the process of translating sacred texts into the vernacular was something frequently done by Christians:

> When I considered all this, I remembered also how I saw, before it had all been ravaged and burned, how the churches throughout the whole of England stood filled with treasures and books; and there were also a great multitude of God's servants, but they had very little benefit from those books, for they could not understand anything of them, because they were not written in their own language ... Therefore it seems better to me, if you think so, for us also to translate some books which are most needful for all men to know into that language which we all can understand.

Alfred's Preface to his translation of Gregory the Great's 'Pastoral Care'.[11]

The Bible itself was translated from Hebrew into Greek, and then into Latin, and Alfred cites this almost as a defence for why he will be translating works into Old English – a spoken tongue, not the formal language of the Church. His preface also gives fascinating glimpses into the state of the English nation by his reign. He describes the frequent Danish raids in terms of how they affected both Christian learning and the very buildings that had for centuries fostered and educated Christians. This world feels tangible in the light of manuscripts like the Codex Amiatinus and Lindisfarne Gospels, or the remains of Wilfrid's crypts at Hexham and Ripon. It acts as a reminder as to why so little has survived, and that what little does remain indicates a much fuller and richer tapestry of lost art and architecture.

Alfred tries to right the neglect of both the learning of the Church and its artistic legacy. It seems to have had wide-reaching implications, for one part of this campaign has left a surprisingly clear presence in the archaeological and codicological record. Not only does Alfred's translation of Gregory's 'Pastoral Care' survive in a later copy, but in it he describes the manufacturing of a specific object that was to travel with his translations: an aestel.

The text records that these aestels were worth 'fifty mancuses', which meant they were very valuable (about the equivalent of a month's wages for a skilled craftsman), and that 'no man take the aestel from the book, or the book from the minster'.[12] The nature of these aestels has been widely discussed, but a treasure in the Ashmolean Museum, Oxford, now housed just a few hundred yards from the surviving text of Alfred's translation in the Bodleian Library, may hold the clue. It is known as the Alfred Jewel, and appears to be some sort of handle. It may be similar to the 'yad' used by Jewish readers of the Torah to prevent them from touching the vellum and it being rendered ritually impure. It seems most likely to be a pointer, designed to make following the sacred text clearer and easier.

Around the edge of the Alfred Jewel, picked out in gold letters, are the words in Old English *Aelfred mec heht gewyrcan*, 'Alfred ordered me to be made'. In the centre a regal figure, picked out in enamel and holding foliate sceptres, stares out at the viewer. The

The Alfred Jewel is one of the treasures of the Ashmolean Museum in Oxford. Gold fittings enclose a teardrop-shaped piece of rock crystal placed above cloisonné enamel. The figure within stares out at the viewer, holding two foliate fronds. The socket of the jewel is decorated with filigree and depicts the head of a boar.

body of the Jewel is made of rock crystal, which was prized for its beauty, clarity and symbolism. Glass produced during the early medieval period was rarely completely clear or free from blemishes, so rock crystal was the alternative for providing a transparent surface. What's more, it was incredibly hard to work on, requiring great skill to apply corrosives to the surface, as it was too tough to carve. Like porphyry, which was preserved for use in imperial burials during the Roman Empire, the difficultly of working the material was part of its value.

The figure at the centre of the Alfred Jewel could be seen to represent sight, one of the five senses. Yet, separated from the other four senses, it carries further layers of symbolism. Here it suggests not just vision, but insight – the form of Holy Wisdom that was celebrated by Alcuin and prized as a great Christian virtue.[13] That this aestel was designed to be distributed along with Alfred's translations of those texts 'most needful to know' suggests that the two objects together were intended to impart such wisdom.

The success of Alfred's education campaign is attested to through the survival of six other aestels, discovered throughout England. The use of rock crystal in the Warminster Jewel, and the similarities in style between the Minster Lovell and Alfred Jewel, indicate that the king's programme was rolled out across the nation in an organised and effective manner. As a result, Alfred became significant not just for his successful military campaigns against the Vikings and his extensive building campaigns, but also for the support he gave to the floundering Anglo-Saxon Church. Without this king and the foresight he displayed in terms of planning for the future well-being of the Church, the next few centuries of Anglo-Saxon history would have turned out very differently.

Anglo-Saxon Royal Saints

In Bede's time, Anglo-Saxon England was already remarkable for the number of royal saints it venerated. These were not necessarily formalised by the papacy, as the process of canonisation had yet to be firmly established, but instead were revered within local

The Fuller Brooch was made in the late ninth century. It depicts the five senses, with the states of creation (man, animals, flora, elements) in the edges. Neillo has been added to the silver to give definition to the decoration. It was a large brooch full of esoteric imagery that would have been easily interpreted by educated Christians during the reign of Alfred the Great.

communities and by the regional church.[14] Research on the role of saint-kings elsewhere in Europe suggests that when political power and the position of the royal family were weak, the Church could support the Crown by creating a saint-king.[15] Alfred's reign was characterised by great change and many military successes. However, his position was always tentative, and could at any point have been overturned by either Viking incursions or internal strife.

The increasing encroachment of the Viking world into Anglo-Saxon England would come to define the tenth and eleventh centuries. The changes that were taking place on a social and political level were also represented in artistic developments, as tastes on either side of the Danelaw absorbed and assimilated one another. For example, the remarkable Fuller Brooch takes the imagery of sight from the Alfred Jewel and surrounds it with the other senses. The personification of taste has his hand in his mouth, smell has an arrow moving towards his nose, touch strokes his own hand and hearing raises a hand to his ear. In its style, scale and decoration, the Fuller Brooch resembles Viking brooches, and the fact that objects like it begin to appear south of the Danelaw suggests that there was a cultural symbiosis between the apparently distinct groups of Anglo-Saxons and Danes.[16]

The importance of Anglo-Saxon royal saints, standing firm in the face of pagan Viking incursions, would continue to be emphasised after Alfred. Indeed, many of his ancestors drew upon his example and continued to fund Church projects, art and literature. His son and successor, Edward the Elder (c. AD 874–924), continued his father's military campaigns, managing to take back East Anglia, the East Midlands and Mercia. These were great achievements, since just a few decades earlier the Danish conquests had absorbed nearly all of England. He carried over the title styled by his father, 'King of the Anglo-Saxons', and continued to define himself, his court and his people as distinct and different from those settled across the northern stretches of the country.

Edward and his siblings had been educated at the court school that Alfred had fashioned after Charlemagne's example. Here, he had drawn together great Christian minds from across the British Isles and Europe, in order to educate his children so they could become wise Christian rulers. Alfred clearly knew what he was doing, because his son Edward had great success. By the end of his reign he had been acknowledged as 'father and lord' by the Danes, Welsh and Scots. What's more, his building programme at Winchester, which culminated in the royal cult centre of the New Minster, shows he continued to invest in both the Church and the saints. He had his father buried in the Minster, making it an important pilgrimage site and the heart of the newly empowered Kingdom of Wessex. Positioning his father's burial within this complex indicates that it was intended as a cult centre for royal saints.

King Edgar and Saint Edith

Alfred's successors continued to invest in the Church, but it was his great-grandson Edgar (AD 943–975) who was to exploit the cult of royal saints most successfully.[17] He wore his family connections with honour and was a formidable Anglo-Saxon king, insomuch as he addressed the major problems affecting his court, Church and people. Like his predecessors, Edgar was singularly skilled in utilising the Church to his own ends. Learning from the example of his relatives, Edgar also engineered his reputation through manuscripts and art.

The image of Edgar that survives from the frontispiece of the New Minster Charter provides a revealing insight into how the man was perceived, and how he wished to manage his image as king. He is shown beneath a mandorla of Christ, raising up that very book, the Charter, and surrounded by angels, Mary and St Peter.[18] Yet the image is revealing in terms of how Edgar saw his position of king. Mary and Peter are smaller than him in the composition. Furthermore, through creating links between the hands of the king, the wings of the angels and the mandorla around Christ, the artists of this manuscript have made the visual suggestion that Edgar is God's rightful representative on earth. It is powerful propaganda, and would continue to inspire rulers like Cnut, who saw in this image the potential to craft the divine right of kings to rule.

Edgar found more ingenious ways to raise his status, coordinating a spectacular coronation ceremony, during which six kings of Britain, the King of Scotland and the King of Strathclyde paid their allegiance to him. This still forms the basis of the modern coronation service, and Edgar also introduced the tradition of the king being crowned alongside his queen. He was a difficult ruler, subject to human failings, particularly with regards to women. In AD 963 he killed a love rival, and in an act of passion he carried off Wilfrida, a nun from Wilton Abbey, and forced her to become his mistress. He was made to do penance for this indiscretion for seven years by not wearing his crown and fasting twice a week. It is telling that, after a year, Wilfrida escaped from him and went back to Wilton Abbey

This image forms the frontispiece of the New Minster Charter, created during King Edgar's reign and endowing the monastic complex at Winchester with land and power. The illumination is elaborate, with foliate margins that are characteristic of the Winchester School. King Edgar occupies the central place, and is larger in scale than Christ, Mary or John.

when she had the opportunity. The result of this illicit affair between king and nun was a young daughter, Edith, and she acts as a useful lens through which to focus on the rise of royal saints during the tenth century.[19]

Alongside creating potent propaganda and crafting state drama like the coronation, Edgar also found an ingenious way to connect himself and his royal family to God: his relatives would be elevated to saints. This was most clear through the royal women, who over the generations had secured ties between noble families and sponsored saints' cults.[20] When Wilfrida returned to Wilton as abbess, she had her daughter educated within the abbey and brought up as a nun. Edgar continued to support his ex-mistress and daughter through continual and large land grants to Wilton Abbey, which empowered it. The location of Wilton was important, due to its proximity to Salisbury in the heart of Wessex. It became a strategic place, close to a royal palace, and a powerful home to the Wessex royal family. The elevation of Edith from illegitimate princess to saint was of primary importance in securing the future prosperity of this royally endowed abbey.

Edith's mother seems to have engineered the cult of her daughter early on, no doubt supported in her efforts by King Edgar, who would have realised the significance of having his daughter declared a saint. The reasons for her sanctity remain vague. She was renowned for being beautiful and learned,[21] and she was rebuked for wearing fine golden gowns during her lifetime, so was hardly a humble nun; few significant miracles were recorded either during her life or after her death. Her cult seems to have been cleverly engineered, and the styling of this saint was not lost on contemporaries of the time. For example, William of Malmesbury records how Cnut was unconvinced of the legitimacy of her sanctity:

> [Cnut] was at Wilton one Pentecost, when, with his customary bloody-mindedness, he burst into a frightful peal of laughter against the virgin herself [St Edith]: he would never believe that the daughter of King Edgar was a saint, seeing that the king had surrendered himself to his vices and was a complete slave to his lusts, while he ruled his subjects more like a tyrant.[22]

Athelwold, Dunstan and Oswald

Edgar found a further way to bolster his reign. He surrounded himself with powerful, loyal and radical churchmen. The three main supporters of the king were Athelwold, Bishop of Winchester from AD 963 to AD 984, Dunstan, Archbishop of Canterbury from AD 960 to AD 978, and Oswald, Archbishop of York from AD 972 to AD 992. These three commanded the major roles within the English Church and were able to prop up Edgar's reign. He, in turn, supported them with the extensive monastic reform they rolled out across the country. Church and State scratched one another's backs, and all three of these supporters of Edgar were also declared saints upon their deaths.

The character of Athelwold is one of the most impressive and influential of the later Anglo-Saxon period.[23] He was born to noble parents in Winchester around AD 904; a time when the monasteries of England were at their lowest ebb following the Viking attacks of the previous century. His early adulthood was spent serving in the court of King Athelstan, and he developed a firm appreciation for the workings of state government. The king, however, perceived that Athelwold would be of greater use within the Church, and encouraged him to become a priest. After training in Winchester, he moved to Glastonbury where he studied grammar, rhetoric and patristics under the abbot, Dunstan.

It has been traditional to see Dunstan as the primary force behind the changes that took place within the tenth-century Anglo-Saxon Church, although his role is constantly balanced by that of the more forthright and power-hungry Athelwold.[24] An image, possibly even a self-portrait, of Dunstan survives in a class book he developed for his students at Glastonbury. Here, Dunstan is depicted prostrate at the feet of Christ. He is humbled and wears a monastic gown, but the fact that he is included at all is a telling sign that he wished his legacy, and his image, to be remembered.

The monastery of Glastonbury, under his careful guidance, was a shining example of how successful such establishments could be if governed effectively. Indeed, later legends associated with Glastonbury, such the stories of Avalon, Arthur and the Holy Grail, may have been instigated by Dunstan himself in an attempt to imbue his monastery with antiquity and significance.[25] Under Dunstan's leadership, Glastonbury was propelled to first rank among England's great abbeys.

Athelwold's time at Glastonbury was formative, not only in providing him with the skills he would later employ to propel the Anglo-Saxon Church forward, but also because of the relationship he would come to develop with Dunstan. These two men, together with Oswald of Worcester, would bring about a radical resurgence in the fortunes of the Anglo-Saxon Church, and return it to some of the glories it had experienced in the seventh century. They would achieve this, largely, by tying themselves to the monastic reforms that were sweeping across Europe at the time and introducing the Benedictine Rule, sometimes with force, throughout English religious sites.

Athelwold had wanted to travel to the Continent to see the effects of the Benedictine Reform that was gathering momentum throughout European monasteries.[26] But his family and the king had other plans for him. Instead, on his mother's suggestion, he was given the run-down and empty monastic lands at Abingdon as a project.[27] He was granted licence to flatten what was previously there and create a brand new Benedictine monastery for the tenth century. It was a ground-up project, staffed by monks who were already exposed to the ideas of Dunstan and Athelwold through their time at Glastonbury. Athelwold was the sole translator of the Rule into Old English, an act that meant he could introduce it to monasteries even quicker and more effectively. Novices, who may have struggled with the Latin text, were left in no doubt of what they had to do with the text translated into the vernacular. This translation of essential texts into Old English continued the tradition established by King Alfred of giving people religious texts in their own language.

As Abbot of Abingdon, Athelwold became a hugely influential churchman. The young Prince Edgar was educated there, so he was teacher to the king. He also educated two of the later Anglo-Saxon period's greatest writers, Aelfric and Wulfstan. We can access the man through some of the texts he had a hand in. For example, he and Dunstan both displayed an interest in the work of Aldhelm, a sixth- to seventh-century Anglo-Saxon writer, whose texts had great impact throughout the period. Athelwold's hand has glossed a manuscript of his *De Virginitate*, a text that extols the merits of virginity and commemorates a great number of male and female saints.[28]

The two surviving lives of Athelwold were written by two of his students, Alcuin and Wulfstan. This indicates the power of institutions in terms of their ability to craft the cults of their saints for the benefit of their community. Investing time and energy into penning not one, but two hagiographical accounts of Athelwold's life would be paid back in bequests and dedications if he was later recognised as a saint. After remodelling Abingdon and making it a vibrant hub for the Benedictine Revival, Athelwold was elevated to Bishop of Winchester in AD 963, and responsibility for King Edgar's grand remodelling of the country's capital city was placed in his hands.

The monastic complex at Winchester was in need of substantial redevelopment. Not only had various buildings been erected haphazardly so that the monastic song from one group clashed with that of the church nearby, the personnel responsible for running the site were no longer monks, but priests. Athelwold called together an armed force and had the priests forcibly removed. This was revolutionary, and displays the strong arm that Athelwold would continue to wield throughout his life. He replaced the priests with monks, trained by him at Abingdon, and then began to demolish the existing buildings at the centre of the city.

The scale of development in the area at this time was almost unprecedented, and it saw the building of a royal palace complex, complete with administrative departments, alongside a huge new Benedictine monastery and a lavish new cathedral church. The outline of this enormous ecclesiastical building still survives, although admittedly now appears dwarfed by the Gothic cathedral next to it. At the time it was one of the largest buildings in the country, and the overall impression of these immense stone buildings, all going up within years of one another, would have been of a vibrant, exciting and powerful focal point for Church and State.

The driving force behind the development of Winchester, the Benedictine Reform, spread rapidly as Athelwold established new communities at Peterborough, Ely and Thorney, to name a few. Athelwold, however, was not content simply with enforcing strict adherence to the Benedictine Rule. He devised a new version of it, complete with supplements: the *Regularis Concordia* (known as 'the Monastic Agreement of the Monks and Nuns of the English Nation'), which impressed even stronger rule on the monks.[29] Athelwold saw obedience as the underlying virtue of the Benedictine Reform, and an account survives which illustrates this brutally. In the process of instructing a particularly virtuous monk, Athelwold ordered him to put his hand in a boiling cauldron of water to get him a morsel of food. The monk did it, and Athelwold's response was that he had learnt a lesson in obedience. He was harsh with both malefactors and the obedient.

The new agreement, *Regularis Concordia*, was passed at a meeting of England's monastic leaders in AD 970 coordinated by King Edgar himself. It is preserved in a later copy, which shows a particularly telling image at the front. King Edgar, Athelwold and Dunstan are tied together by a copy of the Rule, while a humble monk from Winchester is bound up in it below. As well as such visually striking imagery, the manuscript opens with an extensive tract in praise of the king. It made the king the protector of the monks, and the queen protector of the nuns. The links between Church and State were now being set down formally. It also contains specific procedures for the election of bishops that differed from Continental practice, and which led to a predominantly monastic episcopacy. Athelwold was empowering himself, his fellow monks and the king.

Athelwold was a ruthless reformer, who sought to reduce – almost to annihilate – the power of the clergy, replacing it instead with an ordered and controlled monastic elite. The monasteries certainly flourished under his hard hand, and places like Winchester were vastly remodelled, with religious buildings tied into royal and administrative ones. It is important not to underestimate the importance of the Rule of Benedict in terms of its impact on the Anglo-Saxons.[30] It provided a yardstick by which the religious change of the time could be measured and controlled, and also supplied a doctrinal and liturgical framework for the Church which tied it to its Roman past and gave structure to the monastic organisations across the country. It enabled Athelwold to micro-manage the routine, education and productivity of his army of

This manuscript illumination, from the *Regularis Concordia* (a rule for the monks of Winchester in the light of the Benedictine Reform), is one of the most potent expressions of the ties linking Church and State in the tenth century. King Edgar is surrounded by Athelwold and Dunstan, and tied together by the Rule, while a monk is enclosed by it beneath.

monks. Monasteries were big business, powerhouses of education, legislation, finance, industry and religious guidance. They were the multinationals of their day, and keeping them in check with a set of rules was essential to the success of Church and State.

The Winchester School

The Benedictine Reform of the tenth century, propelled by the triumvirate of Anglo-Saxon saints, had far-reaching effects. There was immense investment into the Church, which in turn led to ecclesiastical leaders taking on the responsibilities of landowners. They established new buildings across their lands, including parish churches and cathedrals. These were furnished with vestments, artworks and books – all of which were necessary for the smooth running of the community.[31] Dunstan himself had been an illuminator and bell-maker, so he had a firm understanding of the importance of the arts in service of the Church.

Manuscript art had all but perished in the years of the Viking attacks. Monks were too concerned with surviving raids, rebuilding damage and seeing to the needs of their community to be involved in producing lavish illuminated manuscripts. However, with the reforms of Athelwold, Dunstan and Oswald, fine manuscripts again started to emerge. In fact, over a relatively short period of time a school of illumination was to develop, centred on the scriptorium at Winchester, which would produce some of the most beautiful works of art of the early medieval period.

The wealth and influence of the Church at this time was great, and this is evinced by the work of the southern scriptoria. They launched a concerted effort to standardise written English (something that wouldn't happen completely until the dawn of the *Oxford English Dictionary* in the nineteenth century) and archive vernacular literature. This indicates how far the Church had come from the times of Bede, as by this stage there is almost a nostalgic attitude towards stories like *Beowulf* that hark back to a distant national past.

One manuscript in particular chimes with the lavishness and power of the tenth-century saints: *The Benedictional of St Athelwold*.

This image from *The Benedictional of St Athelwold*, London, British Library Additional MS. 49598, shows St Aethelthryth, who was the patron saint of Athelwold's monastery at Ely. The style is distinctive to the south of England in the tenth century. Known as the Winchester School of illumination, the borders are lavish, drapery is exuberant, and a good deal of gold is employed throughout.

It was made by the monk Godeman at the direct instruction of Athelwold, to be the latter's own personal prayer book. It is beautifully decorated throughout, with twenty-eight full-page miniatures. In its style it shows the influence of Carolingian art, but its figures have even more drama through the almost excessive use of drapery and floriated decoration. The figures seem to burst out of the constraints of the borders, giving each image vibrancy. The use of gold and bright inks throughout also stress that this was an extremely high-status object; one more worthy of a monarch than a monk.

The Benedictional of St Athelwold is particularly important in terms of both its content and its artistry. It contains the blessings pronounced by a bishop throughout the ecclesiastical calendar. The inscription records the role Athelwold played in its production. He was clearly an involved patron:

> *A bishop, the great Athelwold, whom the Lord had made patron of Winchester, ordered a certain monk subject to him to write the present book … He commanded also to be made in this book many frames well adorned and filled with various figures decorated with many beautiful colours and with gold.*[32]

Many of the subjects depicted relate to aspects of Athelwold's programme of reform. For example, Aethelthryth, who was commemorated at the abbey she founded in Ely, is depicted in a full-page illumination. This is most probably because of the involvement Athelwold had in rebuilding the abbey there. Swithun too, whose bones were ceremonially re-laid in the New Minster at Winchester, is presented in an elaborate miniature. It is a stunning achievement of the Winchester School that, after centuries of destruction, the Anglo-Saxon art of illumination could re-emerge with such sophisticated results.

A Different Kind of Sanctity

The royal saints of the ninth and tenth centuries were very different to the Anglo-Saxon saints of the previous centuries. Required to be both effective rulers and pious Christians, Alfred and Edgar found that their worldly concerns often stood in opposition to more saintly behaviour. The saints covered in this chapter testify to the transformation of sanctity that took place in the wake of the Viking attacks. This was a time of turmoil politically, and from Edgar's death in AD 975 every succession to the throne was contested. In the following century conquests by the Danes (twice) and Normans would herald the end of Anglo-Saxon England. Sanctity was attached to certain royal individuals in an attempt to bolster rival claims to the throne. But the Golden Age of Anglo-Saxon saints had passed. The three prominent saints – Athelwold, Dunstan and Oswald – indicate that there was a final flourish, but with the death of King Edgar the decline of Anglo-Saxon saints was secured.

There was a strong backlash against the monasteries established under the Benedictine Reform after the death of King Edgar. The situation was further steeped in controversy due to the issue of succession after his death. It became a power play between his first and second wives, leading to the murder of one king and the election of a potentially illegitimate ruler to the throne. The incredible amount of power saints like Athelwold, Dunstan and Oswald had acquired under Edgar, and the monopolising influence of their hungry monasteries, angered the nobility. The new foundations had eaten into the landscape and into the wealth of the nation with the land taken from noblemen and women to fund the rapid expansion of the king's new spiritual army.

Edgar had not left any clear instructions on how he was to be succeeded when he died. He had a son from his first marriage, Edward, but when Edgar took his second wife, Aelfthryth, his claim to his father's throne was declared illegitimate in a charter. A second son, Aethelred, was born the legitimate child of the queen, and she believed he should be made king with her acting as regent.[33] Nevertheless, with the backing of Oswald and Dunstan, the first son, Edward was proclaimed king in AD 975. This indicates the level of political control these monastic saints had reached by the end of Edgar's reign. No sooner had Edward taken the throne than his rule was plunged into strife. A rift between the leading noble families almost resulted in civil war, and amid the chaos many took the opportunity to grab back land from the newly established Benedictine monasteries. The revival was at an end, and in its place warfare and disharmony raged.

Edward's reign was short, for in AD 978 he was murdered while at Corfe Castle. It is possible that the wronged queen, Aelfthryth, had a part in these events, but soon after a cult seems to have grown up around him. His half-brother, Aethelred was made king, becoming known as Aethelred the Unready, and, perhaps wary of the part he and his mother were perceived to have played in Edward's death, he honoured his half-brother with a ceremonial reburial. The fact that a murdered king was proclaimed a saint shows the ends to which sanctity was being manipulated by the tenth century. Individuals who may not have displayed any saintly virtues during their lives were held as rallying points for various factions, and their relics were exhibited as a means of securing wealth and prestige.

The tides were turning for Anglo-Saxon England. Aethelred's kingdom became increasingly disunited, and Danish raiders took advantage of the instability.[34] From AD 991, Aethelred began to pay increasingly large sums in Danegeld to hold the Danes back from his borders. There were moments of calm between the Danish attacks, but as far as saints and the Church were concerned, this was a dark time. The nation was plunged into thirty years of uncertainty and violence. Wulfstan, who was Archbishop of York from 1002 to 1023, felt that the murder of the saint-king Edward could explain the sufferings that the nation was experiencing. Wulfstan refers to his martyrdom in his famous *Sermo Lupi ad Anglos* ('Sermon of the Wolf to the English'):

> *And a very great betrayal of a lord it is also in the world, that a man betray his lord to death, or drive him living from the land, and both have come to pass in this land: Edward was betrayed, and then killed, and after that burned ...*[35]

Wulfstan was part of Aethelred the Unready's government and played a large part in politics, both religious and secular. He was a state-builder, administrator, politician, theologian, liturgist and patron of the arts, a man who affected the shape of his nation. He laid down the legislative infrastructure of England at a time of conflicting cultures, each with its own legal framework. Wulfstan also managed in some ways to complete the Benedictine Reform begun by Dunstan. The idea that the Benedictine monasteries could ride the changing tides of first Viking, then Norman conquerors shows an investment on the part of churchmen to preserve some form of Anglo-Saxon identity after cataclysmic secular change.

However, his words give a powerful impression of the state of English politics around 1016. Having suffered decades of Viking raids because of their sins, which included the death of their anointed king, Edward the Martyr, the English were finally conquered by the Vikings. Cnut, King of Denmark, became King of England, and 200 years of Viking incursions reached their culmination.

Wulfstan's sermon to the people, delivered in their own language, Old English, laments the collapse of Anglo-Saxon society and sanctity:

> For there are in this nation great disloyalties for matters of the Church and the State, and also there are in the land many who betray their lords in various ways: and the greatest of all betrayals of a lord one can think of is that a man betrays the soul of his lord. And a very great betrayal of a lord it is also in the world, that a man betray his lord to death, or drive him living from the land, and both have come to pass in this land: Edward was betrayed, and then killed, and after that burned; and Aethelred was driven out of his land.[36]

Edward the Confessor: the End of Anglo-Saxon Sanctity

There is arguably one more notable Anglo-Saxon saint: Edward the Confessor.

That Edward was declared a saint after his death was not unusual. He came from a long line of Anglo-Saxon royal saints. As William of Malmesbury so aptly observed:

This section from the Bayeux Tapestry shows Edward the Confessor to the right. He is enthroned, but he is not shown frontally and powerful; he is instead slumped to the left. Behind his back, literally, Harold is shown as dynamic and thrusting, involved in the noble pursuit of hunting.

> *It is not necessary to name any of the common people but only the male and female members of the royal stock, most of them innocently murdered, who have been consecrated martyrs not by human conjecture but by divine acknowledgment.*[37]

It seems that the Anglo-Saxons were far more inclined to venerate their secular leaders as saints than in other parts of Christendom, perhaps because of the sacred role played by kings in the pre-Christian Anglo-Saxon world, when kings were the protectors of their people in not only a physical (often military) sense, but also in a spiritual one. Edward, however, was not a strong military ruler, no matter how saintly he may have been. His death was the nail in the coffin for Anglo-Saxon England.

Upon his death the king, who had seemed so pious in his life-time, was proclaimed a saint and buried at the heart of Westminster Abbey. Subsequent burials of kings and queens radiate out from his tomb in acknowledgement of his role as England's primary royal

saint. However, the Anglo-Saxon period had, in truth, ended decades before the traditional date of 1066.[38] The England that William the Conqueror invaded had been altered substantially over the preceding century, particularly through constant interaction – both military and peaceful – with Scandinavians. Examining the complexion of England's ruling families in the run-up to 1066, only Leofric of the three major noble households (those of Leofric's own, Mercia, Siward of Northumbria and Godwin of Wessex) had an English line of descent traceable to the previous Anglo-Saxon king.

The increasingly tense relationship between saintly and temporal power embodied by so many of the Anglo-Saxon saints reaches its zenith in the hugely significant figure of Edward the Confessor.[39] He was singularly unfit to rule, and anticipates individuals like Henry VI in the way he allowed his piety to undermine the stability of the nation. Presented as saintly in compensation for his ineptitude, surviving sources emphasise his failings. For example, in the Bayeux Tapestry he is not depicted as energetic or dynamic. Indeed, he is pious and divinely inspired, but he is not a vigorous and capable leader like William. His increasing lethargy and ineffectiveness is emphasised in an image on the tapestry, where a frail Edward slumps in a seat while Harold is busy betraying him in Normandy.

Edward the Confessor acts as an excellent counter for Alfred the Great, as both had grown up under the threat of Danish invasion. However, while Alfred sought to create solid images of power, investing in the Church and funding cults of saints, Edward was undermined by powerful noblemen, and his piety was all that remained worthy of celebration. The fact that the last of the Anglo-Saxon saints was the king who effectively allowed the full-scale invasion and occupation of England by a new and destructive force – the Normans – is singularly apt. It indicates how so much of this nation's history can be told through the lives of its saints.

The arrival of the Normans in 1066 had a profound effect on the saints of Anglo-Saxon England. As the country went from independent nation to a vassal state of a larger Continental empire, so the morale of native Anglo-Saxons sank. They were deprived of land and influence, with both secular and ecclesiastical positions filled predominantly by Normans. But within the Anglo-Saxon monasteries the Norman abbots were pursuing a subtler means of undermining native pride and identity. At Abingdon the feasts of Athelwold and Edward were banned, while the Abbot of Malmesbury simply threw out the relics of English saints.[40] The Archbishop of Canterbury, Lanfranc, seems to have fuelled scepticism among his Norman priests, bishops and abbots with regards to Anglo-Saxon saints by investigating the validity of the miracles attributed to St Aelfheah. He was thus sowing seeds of doubt throughout the Church, and undermining the cults that had over time put down roots throughout the nation. This was a psychological conquest whereby the Normans manipulated the very emotional and sacred focal points of the English. Saints had played a long and important role in helping the nation define itself, and the death of the saints went hand in hand with the death of Anglo-Saxon England.

Chapter Eleven
A Journey with the Saints

> *'All it takes to make a man a saint is grace.*
> *Anyone who doubts this knows neither what*
> *makes a saint nor a man.'*
>
> Blaise Pascal, *Pensées*, VII, 508

As the country changed, so did its saints. The earliest, Alban, emerged from a time of persecution, when being Christian was punishable by death and martyrdom was the highest form of devotion. With the collapse of the Roman Empire sanctity became the preserve of other parts of the British Isles, as England was populated by pagans from across the sea. In Ireland, Scotland, Wales and throughout the isles, saints were emerging from the pagan Celtic past and embracing a harsh monastic way of life. This was spread by fervent missionaries, and through the sixth century began to exert influence on the highest strata of Anglo-Saxon society, particularly along the northern borders.

To the south, across that small stretch of water – the English Channel – that has proved to be a barrier and a conduit over the millennia, a papal mission brought with it a new kind of saint. Along with relics, manuscripts and personnel, Gregory the Great's mission would clash with the contrasting Celtic Church, and only home-grown saints like Cuthbert could bridge the divide. The Golden Age of Northumbria has loomed heavy in this book, because Bede's texts and remarkable survivals from the time allow the saints of seventh- and eighth-century Northumbria, more than most, to come into sharp relief. The life and times of Wilfrid, Benedict Biscop and Hilda can be reconstructed from a range of evidence, and individual artworks like the Franks Casket, Ruthwell Cross and Lindisfarne Gospels bring them and their environments into sharp relief.

There is a notable shift towards royal saints as the political situation in England changed. The threat of Viking raids that began at the end of the eighth century culminated in sustained invasion by the Great Heathen Army in the ninth, and would challenge Anglo-Saxon rulers like never before. Ironically, the Angles, Saxons and Jutes were similar in many ways to the Vikings who came to Britain in the ninth and tenth centuries. The major change, however, was that by embracing Christianity so completely, the Anglo-Saxons had distanced themselves from their pagan Germanic roots.

Kings like Alfred and Edgar understood the power of saints within the psyche of the English and created cults to suit their own ends. Edgar's own illegitimate daughter was crafted into a saint for no apparent reason other than her connection to the king, while the three men who propped up his reign – Athelwold, Oswald and Dunstan – were also commemorated as saints. Ultimately, however, even with a saint on the throne as king it was impossible to stem the inevitable flux of change. The Normans, recognising the influence of Anglo-Saxon saints, supressed their cults. The time of Anglo-Saxon saints was relatively short-lived, but it has had a lasting effect on this nation and its relationship with its past.

To understand the saints is to shed light on those individuals who were celebrated in their time. What they were celebrated for – their virtues and achievements – holds a mirror to the communities around them. As we have our celebrities, notorious characters, national treasures and high achievers, so did the Anglo-Saxons. As our representatives reflect aspects of our society, so did the saints during the early medieval period. And their notoriety has meant that their names have been remembered down the centuries. The individuals covered here range from revolutionary martyrs to bibliophiles, princesses to goddesses, hermits to spin doctors. There are no cut-and-dry answers as to what makes a saint. Yet their diversity is, for me, what makes them so fascinating.

Each saint covered in this book tells a different story about the British Isles from the fourth to the eleventh century. And this shouldn't come as a surprise. If a cross-section of the British public today was sampled, and their lives, interests and achievements were documented, the variety would be staggering. To lump 'saints' together as somehow interchangeable and interconnected is misleading. They should be studied as individuals, and each one holds up a different lens to their lives and times.

Yet they are bound together through the hagiographical texts that record their actions and through the powerhouse of the Church, which has perceived unity and harmony among its representatives on earth. They are reduced to names, with feast days attached, and their stories chime with similar miracles and pronouncements, built upon the foundations of earlier biblical and theological texts. Yet, stripped from this setting, they were real, living, breathing people, who walked on the same land we can still visit, and touched some of the same objects we can still see today. More work needs to be done to add flesh to the one-dimensional impressions we have now of these seminal, important people. Yet the Anglo-Saxon saints represent the colours and shades of humanity across the ages. Examining their lives and stories outside of the official hagiography doesn't diminish their relevance; it makes them more relevant, since they become a syphon for the cultural, social and intellectual developments taking place around them.

By looking at saints this work has not sought to cast judgement on the people who have been celebrated in a previous age. Some of them behaved questionably at times, and can appear far from our modern notions of saintly. Yet this study has attempted to understand them and appreciate how they allow a reflection of wider concerns and ideas of which they formed a part. The word 'saint' is not necessarily wrapped up in ideas of faith or belief. Instead, it can provide another means of defining an individual's role within society and the impact they had on the people around them. Terms like bishop, king, knight, monk, wife, princess or saint in the medieval people are modes of definition akin to doctor, teacher, aristocrat, stay-at-home mum or entrepreneur today.

There are repeating themes throughout this book, particularly the complex lines between religious and secular, spiritual and worldly. Each saint traversed these lines differently, and the ways in which they respond to the problems of balancing concerns for this world with those of the next reveal much about who they were.

This period was one of transition. The developments that took place between the fourth and eleventh centuries, and the individual saints who led these changes, would leave a lasting echo on the collective consciousness of nations.

This book has also shown, however, that the British Isles as we know it has a diverse and complex history. There is no history of the English, Irish, Welsh or Scots, but rather a merging web where different races intermarry, coexist and integrate. The fact that the main racial group at the heart of this study are immigrants – Angles, Saxons and Jutes who left their homeland in search of a better place to live – should carry resonance in our modern ethnically diverse nation. Our notions of identity are firmly imprinted with concepts of countries, geographical boundaries and religious affiliations, yet the early medieval period can be instructive in terms of eroding the importance of these distinctions.

As the example of the saints should highlight that intermarriage and integration have bound humanity together across space, so too should it demonstrate that we are bound together across time. History tends to box up names, events and ideologies, keeping one time and place separate from another, and suggesting that evolution continues on a micro level from generation to generation. There are obvious differences between Britain now and over a thousand years ago, particularly in terms of science and technology. However, spiritually, emotionally and imaginatively, the saints of the Anglo-Saxon period were not a separate breed of humanity. We can understand the issues that concerned them, and the day-to-day challenges that would have beset them. As historical figures they don't need dressing up in alien garb and parading as a curiosity. They are not the subject of a condescending anthropological study. Instead, they reflect us as we are now, just at a distance through time. Their diversity reflects our own, and each is unique as we are ourselves.

Writing this book has meant straddling different worlds. Those that hold to the saints for spiritual security and guidance may find that this study strips them of their dignity and grandeur. This is not intentional, but it is somewhat inevitable once they are returned to their real earthly environments. Yet I have found that taking the individuals out of the painted icons, out from the pages of formulaic hagiography and the repeated cycles of liturgies, makes them all the more impressive. They were declared saints for a reason – because they profoundly influenced the people around them and the spirit of their time. To those that treasure the saints, this means that, as they continue to wield power in heaven, connecting the divine with the human, so too did they wield power on earth.

At times this has been an uneasy path to tread, manoeuvring through fragmented information, across disciplinary boundaries, over wide geographical areas and many centuries. But this journey with the saints has been a hugely illuminating one, and I look forward to many more developments in our understanding of these misrepresented and misunderstood characters. A quote by the wonderfully insightful nineteenth-century French novelist Honoré de Balzac seems a fitting place to draw this study on saints to a close:

> *What a splendid book one could put together by narrating the life and adventures of a word. The events for which a word was used have undoubtedly left various imprints on it; depending on place it has awakened different notions; but does it not become grander still when considered in its trinity of soul, body, and movement.*[1]

The word 'saint' has been on a journey, and it continues to travel onwards. This work is just one attempt to trace the adventures the word went through. Those individuals who gained the epitaph 'saint' form a rich, diverse and complex canvas. Taking saints as the lens, many other insights into their lives and times can come into focus. But whether I can answer Pascal's quote at the very start of this book is still uncertain. I am not sure I will ever know what makes a 'man' or a 'saint', since both these words carry infinite shades of possibility and impenetrable layers of complexity. Nevertheless, the journey remains inspiring.

Acknowledgements

I publish this well aware that my own understanding of the topic is still evolving, and will continue to grow and change. So will the work of others in this field, the debt to so many of which I acknowledge and extend my gratitude. A number of recent publications in particular have been formative in shaping my ideas about Anglo-Saxon saints. The spectacular tome by Robert Bartlett, *Why Can the Dead Do Such Great Things?*, has proved seminal to positioning the saints covered in this volume on a pan-European platform. Sarah Foot's volume *Monastic Life in Anglo-Saxon England, c.600–900*, John Blair's *The Church in Anglo-Saxon Society* and Malcolm Lambert's *Christians and Pagans: The Conversion of Britain from Alban to Bede* have rarely been far from my side, and I've returned to them repeatedly in the writing of this book. I acknowledge that my work sits firmly in their shadows.

This book has been given a new angle, however, through my work for the BBC. Academic study can lead scholars into ever-narrowing avenues, and research can become more concerned with minutiae than with creating broad vistas. I have learnt as both a lecturer and a broadcaster that the people you relate your ideas to enjoy the details, but they need to know the larger narratives too. The ability to tell a good story was something the Anglo-Saxons prized, and I feel my teaching and television work is a small contribution to spreading narratives to more people than might read my PhD thesis.

I need to thank many people who made this book possible, supported me and were patient with me. The remarkable Department for Continuing Education in Oxford, whose remit of broadening access to knowledge is so close to my heart. Cathy Oakes, Angus Hawkins, Sandie Byrne, Kristine MacMichael, you all have my love and respect. As do my students, past and present, in Oxford, Warwick, Winchester, York, Duke and UNC. You have inspired me, and continue to broaden my knowledge year after year. To those at the V&A, especially Sally Dormer. My colleagues and friends at the Centre for Medieval Studies and Department of History of Art in York, including Mary Garrison, Jane Hawkes, Anthony Geraghty, Jason Edwards, Matthew Townend, Sarah Rees Jones and Elizabeth Tyler. Friends who have offered support and advice, particularly Sally Mapstone, Heather O'Donaghue and Sarah Foot. The staff and curators at the Bodleian and Sackler libraries, the Ashmolean and the British Museum. Those who made this book a reality, Rosemary Scoular, Aoife Rice, Ed Faulkner, Elen Jones, Steve Burdett, Jason Wolfe and Harriet Beadnell. Jamie Simpson, Nick Tanner, Paul Tilzey and the brilliant team at OFTV. The communities of Oxford and Woodstock that have supported me day in, day out. My wonderful family, Babi, Papa, Sheila, Mundo, Tom, Carole, Effie, Dodo, Nana Boo, Ciabia and, most importantly, Dan, Kuba and Kama. This is dedicated to you.

Endnotes

Introduction

1. Anne Klinck, *The Old English Elegies: A Critical Edition and Genre Study* (Montreal, 1992), 'The Wanderer', lines 107–110.
2. Thomas Hobbes, *Leviathan*, ed. Tom Griffith (London, 2014), p. 97.
3. Bede, *Historia ecclesiastica gentis Anglorum*, eds. and trans. Betram Colgrave and R. A. B. Mynors, *Bede's Ecclesiastical History of the English People*. Oxford, 1969. Hereafter *HE*,1, xiv.
4. Donald A. White, 'Changing Views of the *Adventus Saxonum* in Nineteenth and Twentieth Century English Scholarship', *Journal of the History of Ideas*, Vol. 32, No. 4 (1971), pp. 585–94.
5. Bede, *HE*, I, xv.
6. Toby F. Martin, *The Cruciform Brooch and Anglo-Saxon England* (Woodbridge, 2015).
7. Gale R. Owen-Crocker, *Dress in Anglo-Saxon England* (revised edition, 2010), pp. 35–103.
8. Barbara Yorke, *The Conversion of Britain: 600–800* (Harlow, 2006), p. 81.
9. T. M Charles-Edwards, *Wales and the Britons: 350–1064* (Oxford, 2013), p. 227.
10. M. Filppula, J. Klemola, H. Paulasto and H. Pitkanen, *English and Celtic in Contact* (Routledge, 2008), p. 1.
11. George Henderson, *Vision and Image in Early Christian England* (Cambridge, 1999), pp. 19–53.
12. M. K. Lawson, *Cnut: The Danes in England in the Early Eleventh Century* (London and New York, 2nd edn. 1995), p. 222.
13. Robert Bartlett, *Why Can The Dead Do Such Great Things?* (Princeton, 2013), p. 3.
14. This requirement has recently been waived twice, with the waiting time for Mother Teresa reduced to three years, and the beatification of Pope John Paul II declared on the elevation of his successor, Benedict XVI.
15. Yorke (2006), p. 11.
16. Bartlett (2013), p. 3.
17. Susan J Ridyard, *The Royal Saints of Anglo-Saxon England: A Study of West Saxon and East Anglian Cult* (Cambridge,1988), p. 5.
18. P. Aries, trans. P. Ranum, *Western Attitudes towards Death: from the Middle Ages to the Present* (London, 1974), p. 16.

19. Sister Glory G. Thompson, *Discerning Perspective* (Victoria, 2010), p. 121.
20. Allen J. Frantzen, *Food, Eating and Identity in Early Medieval England* (Woodbridge, 2014).

1. Alban: Dying for Faith

1. Bede, *HE*, I, vii.
2. Thomas F. Matthews, *The Clash of the Gods: A Reinterpretation of Christian Early Art* (Princeton, 1995).
3. Bede, *HE*, I, vii.
4. Lerner, Ralph, 'The *Jihād* of St Alban.' *The Review of Politics*. Vol. 64:1 Winter, 2002. pp. 5–26.
5. Malcolm Lambert, *Christians and Pagans: The Conversion of Britain from Alban to Bede* (New Haven and London, 2010), p. 7.
6. David Petts, *Christianity in Roman Britain* (Stroud, 2003), p. 34.
7. Rebecca Harden Weaver, *Divine Grace and Human Agency: Study of the Saint Pelagian Controversy* (Mercer, 1996).
8. I. N. Wood, 'The End of Roman Britain: Continental Evidence and Parallels', *in* M. Lapidge and D. N. Dumville (ed.), *Gildas: New Approaches* (Woodbridge, 1984), pp. 1–25, at pp. 12–14.
9. Rosalind Niblett, *Verulamium: The Roman City of St Albans* (Stroud, 2001).
10. Joan Liversidge, 'Wall Paintings from Verulamium', in *The British Museum Quarterly* (Spring, 1971), pp. 87–93.
11. Martin Biddle and Birthe Kjolby, 'The origins of St Albans Abbey: Romano-British cemetery and Anglo-Saxon monastery', in ed. M. Henig, *Alban and St Albans. Roman and Medieval Art and Archaeology* (Leeds, 2001), pp. 45–77.
12. Simon Webb, *In Search of Saint Alban* (Langley Press, 2010).
13. Barry Cunliffe, *The Ancient Celts* (Oxford and New York, 1997), p. 184.
14. Elizabeth Rees, *Celtic Saints in Their Landscape* (Stroud, 2001/2011).
15. John G. Gager, *Curse Tablets and Binding Spells from the Ancient World* (OUP, 1999), p. 195.
16. D. G. Kousoulas, *The First Christian Emperor: The Life and Times of Constantine the Great* (Routledge, 2nd edn. 2003), pp. 143–61.
17. Dominic Perring, 'Gnosticism' in early Fourth-Century Britain: The Frampton Mosaics Reconsidered, in *Britannia*, Vol. 34 (2003), pp. 97–127.

2. Brigid: Rebirth of a Goddess

1. Rutilius Namatianus, *De Reditu Suo*. The Latin text and English translation by J. Wight Duff and Arnold M. Duff, *Minor Latin Poets* (Loeb Classical Library, 1922) Volume II, p. 805.

2. Edward Bourke, Alan R. Hayden and Ann Lynch, *Skellig Michael, Co. Kerry: The Monastery and South Peak. Archaeological strati-graphic report: excavations 1986–2010* (Dublin, 2011).

3. Walter Horn, Jenny White Marshall, and Grellan D. Rourke, *The Forgotten Hermitage of Skellig Michael* (Berkeley, 1990).

4. H. Waddell, *The Desert Fathers* (London, reprinted 1998), pp. 30–44.

5. A. M. Allchin, *Pennant Melangell; Place of Pilgrimage* (Pennant Melangell, 1994).

6. M. A. Green, *Celtic Art: Reading the Message* (London, 1996), p. 135.

7. Prosper, *Contra Collatorem*, c. 21, ed. Migne, PL li 271, quoted from T. M. Charles-Edwards, *Wales and the Britons, 350–1064*, p. 227.

8. Philip Freeman, *The World of Saint Patrick* (OUP, 2014), p. 95.

9. Conrad Bladey, *Brigid of the Gael: A Complete Collection of Primary Resources* (Hutman, 2000).

10. Gerald of Wales, *The History and Topography of Ireland* ed. John J. O'Meara (Penguin, 1982), Book II, chapter xxxviii.

11. Brian Wright, *Brigid: Goddess, Druidess and Saint* (Stroud, 2009).

12. *De ratione temporum* 15. (*The reckoning of time*, tr. Faith Wallis, Liverpool University Press 1988), pp. 53–54.

13. Brian Wright, *Brigid: Goddess, Druidess and Saint* (Stroud, 2009), p. 21.

14. J.T. Koch, *Celtic Culture: A Historical Encyclopedia* (Aberystwyth, 2006), Vol. I, pp. 312–13.

15. Dio Chrysostom, 'The Forty-ninth Discourse: A Refusal of the Office of Archon Delivered before the Council', *Discourses* (Loeb Classical Library, 1949), p. 301.

3. Patrick: From Slave to Patron

1. Jacobus de Voragine, *The Golden Legend: Readings on the Saints*, trans. William Granger Ryan (Princeton, reprint 2012), pp. 238-41.

2. *Today* programme poll for Radio 4, October 2014, see http://www.bbc.co.uk/radio4/today/reports/archive/features/results_stgeorge.shtml.

3. Ptolemy, *Ptolemy's 'Geography': An Annotated Translation of the Theoretical Chapters*, trans. J. Lennart Berggren and Alexander Jones (Princeton, 2000).

4. Daphne Brooke, *Wild Men and Holy Places: St Ninian, Whithorn and the Medieval Realm of Galloway* (Edinburgh, 1994/98), p. 9.

5. Bede, *HE*, III, iv.

6. Peter Hill and Tony Graham, *Whithorn and St. Ninian: The Excavations of a Monastic Town, 1984–91* (Sutton, 1997).

7. Thomas Owen, 'The Real St Ninian', in *Innes Review*, 52: 1 (2001), pp. 1–28.

8. K. R. Dark, 'The *Floruit* of St Patrick: Common and Less Common

Ground', in ed. David N. Dumville, *St Patrick A.D. 493–1993* (Woodbridge, 1993), pp. 13–19.

9. Brendan Lehane, *Early Celtic Christianity* (London, 2005), p. 45.

10. Ian Wood, 'Germanus, Alban and Auxerre', *Bulletin du centre d'études médiévales d'Auxerre BUCEMA*, 13 (2009), pp. 123–29.

11. Thomas O'Laughlin, *Saint Patrick: The Man and his Works* (Oxford, 2014), p. 4.

12. Philip Freeman, *St Patrick of Ireland* (New York, 2004), p. 2.

13. G. Frank Mitchell, 'Introduction' in *Treasures of early Irish art, 1500 B.C. to 1500 A.D: From the collections of the National Museum of Ireland, Royal Irish Academy Trinity College, Dublin* (Metropolitan Museum of Art, 1977), pp.10–17, esp. p.13.

14. Gildas, *The Ruin of Britain and other works*, Latin and trans. M. Winterbottom, *History from the Sources* 7, (Old Woking 1978), book 1, chapter 19.

15. Quoted from Philip Freeman, *St Patrick of Ireland* (New York, 2004), 'Confession', hereafter Patrick, 'Confessions', chapter 20.

16. Patrick, 'Confession', chapter 56.

17. J. Romilly Allen, *Celtic Art in Pagan and Christian Times* (California, 1993), p. 206.

18. Patrick, 'Confession', chapter 35.

19. Murchiú, *St. Patrick: His writings and Muirchu's life*, ed. A. B. E. Hood (London: Phillimore, 1978), chapter 10.

20. Murchiú, *Life*, chaper 17.

21. For the legends of Man, see W. Harrison (ed.), *Mona Miscellany: A Selection of Proverbs, Sayings, Ballads, Customs, Superstitions and Legends Peculiar to the Isle of Man* (Douglas, 1869), pp. 220–23.

22. J. Wyn Evans and Jonathan M. Wooding (eds.), *St David of Wales: Cult, Church and Nation* (Woodbridge, 2007).

23. John Davies, *A History of Wales* (London: Penguin, 1993/2007), p. 74.

4. Gregory: A Great Mission

1. Bede, *HE*, II, i.

2. L. K. Little, 'Calvin's Appreciation of Gregory the Great', *Harvard Theological Review* 56 (1963), pp. 145–57.

3. Bede, *HE*, I, xxvi.

4. Martin Werner, 'The Luidhard Medalet', in *Anglo-Saxon England*, Vol. 20 (Cambridge, 1991), pp. 27–41.

5. See D. P. Kirby, *The Earliest English Kings* (London, 1992), pp. 31–3.

6. Eamon Duffy, *Saints and Sinners: A History of the Popes* (Yale, revised 4th edn. 2014), pp. 59–60.

7. Carole E. Straw, *Gregory the Great: Perfection in Imperfection* (Berkley, 1988), p. 47.

8. Eric John, *Reassessing Anglo-Saxon England* (Manchester, 1996), pp. 28–30.

9. Bede, *HE,* I, xxiii.
10. *Ibid.*
11. Nicholas Brooks, *The Early History of the Church of Canterbury: Christ Church from 597 to 1066* (London, 1984), p. 6.
12. Translation from Kevin Crossley-Holland, *The Anglo-Saxon World* (Oxford, reissued 2009), p. 59.
13. Richard Marsden, *The Cambridge Old English Reader* (Cambridge, 1995), p. 204.
14. Frederick George Jones, *The Old English Rune Poem, an Edition - Primary Source Edition* (Nabu Press, 2014), lines 80–83.
15. Leslie Webster, *Anglo-Saxon Art* (London, 2012), pp. 34–36.
16. Edwin and Joyce Gifford, 'And What of the Ship?' *Saxon*, No. 19 (1997), p. 2.
17. Kevin Leahy and Roger Bland, *The Staffordshire Hoard* (London, 2014).
18. Kevin Leahy, *Anglo-Saxon Crafts* (Stroud, 2010), p. 160.
19. Gareth Williams, *Treasures from Sutton Hoo* (London, 2011).
20. Gareth Williams, 'The Circulation and Function of Coinage in Conversion-Period England', in *Coinage and History in the North Sea World,* c. *AD 500–1250* (Brill, 2006), pp. 147–79.
21. M.D.J. Bintley, 'The Byzantine Silver Bowls in the Sutton Hoo Ship Burial and Tree-Worship in Anglo-Saxon England', *Papers from the Institute of Archaeology*, Vol. 21 (2011), pp. 34-45.
22. Steven Plunkett, *Suffolk in Anglo-Saxon Times* (Stroud, 2005), p. 72.
23. Bede, *HE*, II.15.
24. Bede, *HE,* I, xxvi.
25. John P. Blair, *The Church in Anglo-Saxon Society* (Oxford, 2005), p. 29.
26. Bede, *HE,* I, xxvii.
27. Ian Wood, 'The Mission of Augustine of Canterbury to the English', *Speculum* Vol. 69:1 (1994), pp. 1–17.
28. Bede, *HE,* I, xxix.
29. Bede, *HE,* I, 30.
30. R. A. Markus, 'Gregory the Great and a Papal Missionary Strategy', *Studies in Church History 6: The Mission of the Church and the Propagation of the Faith* (Cambridge, 1970), pp. 29–38.

5. Columba: Sanctity Across the Sea

1. Adomnán, *Vita S. Columbae*. Ed. and trans. A. O. Anderson and M. O. Anderson, *Adomnán's Life of Columba*. Oxford, 1961, second edition 1991, hereafter *VC,* Book II, chapter xxix.
2. Rosalind K. Marshall, *Columba's Iona: A New History* (Dingwall, 2013), introduction.
3. Alan Lane and Ewan Campbell, *Dunadd: An early Dalriadic capital* (Oxbow Books, Oxford, 2000).
4. I. Zaczek, *Ireland: land of the Celts* (London, 2000), pp. 95–6.

5. Adomnán, *VC*, preface, pp. 2–5.
6. Ian W.G. Forbes, *The Last of the Druids: The Mystery of the Pictish Symbol Stone* (Stroud, 2012), p. 6.
7. Jennifer O'Reilly, 'Reading the Scriptures in the Life of Columba.' Ed. Cormac Bourke, *Studies in the Cult of Saint Columba* (Dublin, 1997), pp. 80–106.
8. Tim Clarkson, *Columba* (Edinburgh, 2012), p. 10.
9. Adomnán, *VC,* Book II, xxviii.
10. *Ibid.*
11. Alex Woolf, *From Pictland to Alba, 789–1070.* The New Edinburgh History of Scotland: Volume 2 (Edinburgh, 2007), pp. 87–122.
12. Dean R. Snow, 'Scotland's Irish Origins', in *Archaeology,* Vol. 54, No. 4 (July/August, 2001).
13. Martin Carver, *Portmahomack: Monastery of the Picts* (Edinburgh, 2008).
14. W. A. Cummins, *Decoding the Pictish Symbols* (Stroud, 2009).
15. Rob Lee, Philip Jonathan and Pauline Ziman, 'Pictish symbols revealed as a written language through application of Shannon entropy', *Proceedings of the Royal Society A: Mathematical, Physical and Engineering Science* (2010).
16. Tim Clarkson, *Columba* (Edinburgh, 2012), chapter 2.
17. Richard Gameson, 'The Material Fabric of Early British Books', in *The Cambridge History of the Book in Britain: Volume 1 c. 400–1100* (Cambridge, 2011), pp. 13–94.
18. Kevin Crossley-Holland, *The Anglo-Saxon World: An Anthology* (Oxford, 2009), p. 241.
19. George Henderson, *From Durrow to Kells: The Insular Gospel-books 650–800* (London, 1987), pp. 19–57.
20. Michael Richter, *Medieval Ireland (New Gill History of Ireland 1): The Enduring Tradition – Ireland from the Coming of Christianity to the Reformation* (Dublin, 2005).
21. Tomas O Fiaich, *Columbanus in His Own Words* (Dublin, reprint 2012), p. 71.

6. Cuthbert: Bishop or Hermit?

1. Bede, *Vita Cuthberti.* Ed. B. Colgrave. *Two Lives of Saint Cuthbert: A Life by an Anonymous Monk of Lindisfarne and Bede's Prose Life* (Cambridge, 1940), chapter 39.
2. James Campbell, 'Elements in the Background to the Life of St Cuthbert and His Early Cult' in eds. Gerald Bonner, David Rollason and Clare Stancliffe, *St Cuthbert, His Cult and His Community to AD 1200* (Woodbridge, 1989), pp. 1–19.
3. Jane Hawkes and Susan Mills, *Northumbria's Golden Age* (Sutton, 1999).
4. Bede, *HE,* II, xiii.
5. Brian Hope Taylor, *Yeavering: An Anglo-British Centre of Early Northumbria* (London, 1977, reprinted 2010).

6. Alan Thacker, 'England in the Seventh-century', in ed. Paul Fouracre, *The New Cambridge Medieval History, Volume 1: c.500– 700* (Cambridge, 2005), pp. 462–95, esp. p. 477.

7. Bede, *HE*, II, xiv.

8. S. Fanning, 'Bede, *Imperium*, and the Bretwaldas.' *Speculum* 66 (1991), pp. 1–26.

9. Alan Thacker, '*Membra Disjecta*: The Division of the Body and the Diffusion of the Cult', in eds. Claire Stancliffe and Eric Cambridge, *Oswald: Northumbrian King to European Saint* (Stamford, 1995), pp. 87–127.

10. James Campbell, 'Elements in the Background to the Life of St Cuthbert and his Early Cult', in eds. G. Bonner, D. Rollason and C. Stancliffe, *St Cuthbert, His Cult and Community to A.D. 1200* (Woodbridge, 1989, reprinted 1995), pp. 3–20.

11. Christian Aggeler, 'The Eccentric Hermit-Bishop: Bede, Cuthbert, and Farne Island,' *Essays in Medieval Studies* 16 (1999), pp. 17–25.

12. B. Colgrave, *Vita Cuthberti*, III.iii, *Two Lives of Saint Cuthbert: A Life by an Anonymous Monk of Lindisfarne and Bede's Prose Life* (Cambridge, 1940), pp. 102–3.

13. Bede, xx, *VC*, pp. 225–6.

14. C. F. Battiscombe, *The Relics of Saint Cuthbert* (Oxford, 1956).

15. Gale R. Owen-Crocker, 'Image Making: Portraits of Anglo-Saxon Church Leaders', in ed. Alexander R. Rumble, *Leaders of the Anglo-Saxon Church: From Bede to Stigand* (Boydell, 2012), pp. 109–29.

16. John Higgitt, 'The Iconography of St Peter in Anglo-Saxon England and St Cuthbert's Coffin', in eds. G. Bonner, D. Rollason and C. Stancliffe, *St Cuthbert, His Cult and Community to A.D. 1200* (Woodbridge, reprinted 1995), pp. 267–86.

17. Michelle Brown, *The Lindisfarne Gospels: Society, Spirituality and the Scribe* (London, 2003).

18. Michelle Brown, 'The Book as Sacred Space', in eds. P. North and J. North, *Sacred Space: House of God, Gate of Heaven* (Bloomsbury, 2007), pp. 43–64.

19. C. F. Battiscombe, *The Relics of Saint Cuthbert* (Oxford, 1956), p. 358.

7. Hilda: Princess of a Powerhouse

1. Bede, *HE*, IV, 22.

2. N. J. Higham, *(Re-)Reading Bede: The Ecclesiastical History in context* (Abingdon, 2006), p. 46.

3. James Campbell, 'Archipelagic thoughts: comparing early medieval polities in Britain and Ireland', in: Baxter, Stephen, Catherine E. Karkov, Janet L. Nelson, and David Pelteret (eds), *Early medieval studies in memory of Patrick Wormald*, Studies in Early Medieval Britain (Aldershot: Ashgate, 2009), pp. 47–64, esp. p. 61.

4. See Graeme Leslie Young and Paul Anthony Gething, *Bamburgh*

Castle: The Archaeology of the Fortress of Bamburgh, AD. 500 to AD. 1500 (Bamburgh Research Project, 2003).

5. G. Thomas, 'Bishopstone and Lyminge', in *British Archaeology* (July/August, 2011), pp. 42–48.

6. Robin Daniels, 'The Anglo-Saxon Monastery at Hartlepool, England', in eds. J. Hawkes and S. Mills, *Northumbria's Golden Age* (Stroud, 1999), pp. 105–12.

7. R. I. Page, *An Introduction to English Runes* (Woodbridge, second edition 1999), p. 164.

8. A. Bammesburger, 'A Note on the Whitby Comb Runic Inscription', *Notes and Queries* 57:3 (2010), pp. 292–5.

9. Bede, *HE*, III, 24.

10. Bede, *HE*, III, xxv.

11. Benedicta Ward, *A True Easter: The Synod of Whitby AD 664* (Fairacres Press, 2007).

12. Jane Hawkes, 'Statements in Stone: Anglo-Saxon Sculpture, Whitby and the Christianisation of the North', in C. Karkov (ed.), *Anglo-Saxon Archaeology: Basic Readings* (N.Y. Garland Press, 1999), pp. 403–21.

13. Bede, *HE*, IV, xxiv.

14. Christine Fell, *Women in Anglo-Saxon England* (1984).

15. Jocelyn Wogan-Browne, 'Rerouting the Dower: The Anglo-Norman Life of St. Audrey by Marie (of Chatteris?)', in *Power of the Weak: Studies on Medieval Women*, ed. Jennifer Carpenter and Sally-Beth Maclean (Champaign: University of Illinois Press, 1995), pp. 27–56.

16. Stephanie Hollis, *Anglo-Saxon Women and the Church* (Woodbridge, 1992), p. 49.

17. See John Black, '"Nutrix pia"': The Flowering of the Cult of St AEthelthryth in Anglo-Saxon England', in ed. Paul E. Szarmach, *Writing Women Saints in Anglo-Saxon England* (Toronto, 2013), pp. 167–90.

18. Barbara Yorke, *Nunneries and the Anglo-Saxon Royal Houses* (London, 2003), p. 154.

8. Wilfrid: God's Nobleman

1. Anne Klinck, *The Old English Elegies: A Critical Edition and Genre Study* (Montreal, 1992), 'The Seafarer', lines 119–22.

2. Eddius Stephanus, *The Life of Bishop Wilfrid by Eddius Stephanus*, ed. B. Colgrave (Cambridge, 1985), hereafter Eddius, *Life*, chapter xxii, p. 47.

3. Richard N. Bailey, 'St Wilfrid, Ripon and Hexham', in *Studies in Insular Art and Archaeology* (Oxford Ohio, 1991), pp. 3–25.

4. Bede, *HE*, IV. 32.

5. David Rollason, *Saints and Relics in Anglo-Saxon England* (Oxford, 1989), p. 28.

6. D. P. Kirby, 'Bede, Eddius Stephanus and *The Life of Wilfrid*', in *The English Historical Review*, vol. 98, No. 386 (1983), pp. 101–14.

7. Eddius, *Life,* chapter xvii, p. 37.
8. Michelle Brown, *'In the Beginning was the Word': Books and Faith in the Age of Bede* (Jarrow, 2000).
9. Amy L. Vandersall, 'The Date and Provenance of the Franks Casket', *Gesta* 11, 2 (1972), pp. 9–26.
10. Ian N. Wood, 'Ripon, Francia and the Franks Casket in the Early Middle Ages', *Northern History*, 26 (1990), pp. 1–19.
11. Carole Hough and John Corbett, *Beginning Old English* (Palgrave, 2013), p. 106.
12. P. W. Souers, 'The Magi on the Franks Casket', *Harvard Studies and Notes in Philology and Literature* 19 (1937), pp. 249–54.
13. P. W. Souers, 'The Weyland Scene on the Franks Casket'. *Speculum* 18.1 (1943), pp. 104–11.
14. Carol L. Neuman de Vegvar, 'The Travelling Twins: Romulus and Remus in Anglo-Saxon England'. Ch. 21 in Jane Hawkes and Susan Mills, eds., *Northumbria's Golden Age* (Stroud,1999), pp. 256–67.
15. Jane Hawkes, 'Anglo-Saxon Romanitas: the transmission and use of early Christian art in Anglo-Saxon England', in (ed.) P. Horden, *Freedom of Movement in the Middle Ages.* Harlaxton Medieval Studies, vol. 15 (Donnington, 2007), pp. 19–36.
16. Bernhard Bischoff and Michael Lapidge, *Biblical Commentaries from the Canterbury School of Theodore and Hadrian* (Cambridge, 1995), p. 397.
17. David Rollason, *Saints and Relics in Anglo-Saxon England* (Oxford, 1989).
18. See M. Lapidge, 'The School of Theodore and Hadrian', in *Anglo-Saxon England* Vol. 15 (1986), pp. 45–72.
19. Eric Fletcher, *Benedict Biscop* (Jarrow, 1981).
20. Sam Turner and Sarah Semple, *Wearmouth and Jarrow: Northumbrian Monasteries in an Historic Landscape* (Hertfordshire, 2013).
21. Paul Meyvaert, 'Bede and the Church Paintings at Wearmouth–Jarrow', in *Anglo-Saxon England,* vol. 8 (1979), pp. 63–77.
22. C. Plummer, *Historia abbatum auctore anonymo: Venerabilis Baedae: Opera historica.* 2 vols. (Oxford, 1896), Vol. 1, pp. 388–404.
23. R. L. S. Bruce-Mitford, *The Art of the Codex Amiatinus* (Jarrow, 1967).
24. Richard Marsden, *The Text of the Old Testament in Anglo-Saxon England* (Cambridge, 1995), p. 98.

9. Bede: Writing History; Writing Sanctity

1. *The Dream of the Rood*, ed. Michael Swanton (Manchester, 1970), lines 150–55.
2. Nicholas Brooks, 'From British to English Christianity: Deconstructing Bede's Interpretation of the Conversion', in eds. Nicholas Howe and Catherine Karkov, *Conversion and Colonization in Anglo-Saxon England* (Tempe, 2006), pp. 1–30.

3. Joanna Story, 'After Bede: Continuing the *Ecclesiastical History*', in eds. S. Baxter, C. Karkov, J. Nelson and D. Pelteret, *Early Medieval Studies in Memory of Patrick Wormald* (Farnham, 2009), pp. 165–85.

4. Bede, *HE*, V, xxiv.

5. C. Plummer, *Historia abbatum auctore anonymo: Venerabilis Baedae: Opera historica*. 2 vols. (Oxford, 1896) Vol. 1, pp. 388–404.

6. Bede, *In Samuelem prophetam allegoria expositio*. Ed. D. Hurst. CCSL 119 (Turnhout, 1962), pp. 1–272.

7. Jeff Opland, *Anglo-Saxon Oral Poetry: A Study of the Traditions* (New Haven and London, 1980).

8. C. V. Franklin, 'Bilingual Philology in Bede's Exegesis', in ed. R. F. Gyug, *Medieval Cultures in Context* (New York, 2003), pp. 3–18.

9. Richard Marsden, '*Manus Bedae:* Bede's contributions to Ceolfrith's Bibles', in *Anglo-Saxon England,* Vol. 27, pp. 65–85.

10. Philip Burton, *The Old Latin Gospels: A Study of the Texts and Language* (Oxford, 2000), pp. 5–11, especially p. 6.

11. Milton McC.Gatch, 'Noah's Raven in Genesis A and Illustrated Old English Hexateuch'. *Gesta* 14.2 (1975), pp. 3–15.

12. D. MacLean, 'The Date of the Ruthwell Cross', in ed. B. Cassidy, *The Ruthwell Cross: Papers from the Colloquium Sponsored by the Index of Christian Art, Princeton University, 8 December 1989*. (Princeton, 1992), pp. 49–70.

13. É. Ó Carragáin, *Ritual and the Rood: Liturgical Images and the Old English Poems of the Dream of the Rood* (Toronto, 2005).

14. Bredan Cassidy, *The Ruthwell Cross: Papers from the Colloquium Sponsored by the Index of Christian Art* (Princeton, 1992).

15. See Éamonn Ó Carragáin, *Ritual and the Rood: Liturgical Images and the Old English Poems of the Dream of the Rood Tradition* (Toronto, 2005).

16. Paul Meyvaert, 'A New Perspective on the Ruthwell Cross: *Ecclesia* and *Vita Monastica*', in ed. B. Cassidy, *The Ruthwell Cross: Papers from the Colloquium Sponsored by the Index of Christian Art*. (Princeton, 1992), pp. 95–166.

17. Jane Hawkes, 'Anglo-Saxon Sculpture: Questions of Context'. Eds. J. Hawkes and S. Mills, *Northumbria's Golden Age* (Stroud, 1999), pp. 204–15.

18. *The Dream of the Rood*, ed. Michael Swanton (Manchester, 1970), taken from lines 35–65.

19. Douglas Dales, *Alcuin, His Life and Legacy* (Cambridge, 2012), p. 15.

20. Christopher E. Norton, 'The Anglo-Saxon cathedral at York and the topography of the Anglian city', in *Journal of the British Archaeological Association*, Vol. 151 (1998), pp. 1–42.

21. Paul Meyvaert, 'Bede the Scholar', in G. I. Bonner, *Famulus Christi: Essays in Commemoration of the Thirteenth Centenary of the Birth of Bede* (London, 1976), p. 48.

22. D. A. Bullough, *Alcuin – Achievement and Reputation* (Brill, 2004).

23. M. Garrison, J. Nelson and D. Tweddle, *Alcuin and Charlemagne: The Golden Age of York* (York, 2001).

24. Mary Garrison, 'The Social World of Alcuin: Nicknames at York and at the Carolingian Court', in eds. L. A. R. J. Houwen and A. A. MacDonald, *Alcuin of York: Scholar at the Carolingian Court*. Germania Latina 3 (Groningen, 1998), pp. 59–79.
25. J. Lang, 'The Apostles in Anglo-Saxon Sculpture in the Age of Alcuin'. *Early Medieval Europe* 8 (1999), pp. 271–82.
26. Dorothy Whitelock, *English Historical Documents, 500–1042* (London, reissued 1996), document 193, p. 899.

10. Alfred: Rise and Fall of the Royal Saints

1. Dorothy Whitelock, *English Historical Documents, 500–1042* (London, reissued 1996), document 194, p. 901.
2. Susan J. Ridyard, *The Royal Saints of Anglo-Saxon England: A Study of West Saxon and East Anglian Cults* (Cambridge, first published 1988), p. 61.
3. Barbara Yorke, *Wessex in the Early Middle Ages* (New York, 1995), p. 109.
4. Mark Taylor, *Edmund: The Untold Story of the Martyr-King and his Kingdom* (Fordaro, 2013), p. 2.
5. Richard Abels, *Alfred the Great: War, Kingship and Culture in Anglo-Saxon England* (Longman, 1998).
6. Asser 'Life of King Alfred', in eds. Keynes, Simon; Lapidge, Michael, *Alfred the Great: Asser's Life of King Alfred & Other Contemporary Sources* (Penguin Classics, 1983), pp. 67–112.
7. Justin Pollard, *Alfred the Great: The Man who made England* (London, 2005).
8. David Horspool, *Why Alfred Burned the Cakes* (London, 2006).
9. S. D. Keynes, 'King Alfred and the Mercians', in *Kings, Currency and Alliances* (Woodbridge, Boydell Press, 1998), pp. 1–46.
10. See eds. Janet Backhouse, D. H. Turner and Leslie Webster, *The Golden Age of Anglo-Saxon Art* (London, 1984), p. 11.
11. Kevin Crossley-Holland, *The Anglo-Saxon World: An Anthology* (Oxford, 2009), pp. 219–20.
12. D. A. Hinton, *The Alfred Jewel: and Other Late Anglo-Saxon Decorated Metalwork* (Oxford, 2008).
13. E. Bakka, 'The Alfred Jewel and Sight'. *Antiquaries Journal* 46 (1966), pp. 277–82.
14. Susan J. Ridyard, *The Royal Saints of Anglo-Saxon England: A Study of West Saxon and East Anglian Cults* (Cambridge, 1988, reprinted 2008).
15. See Ridyard, p. 5.
16. Leslie Webster, *Anglo-Saxon Art* (London, 2012), p. 154.
17. Donald Scragg, *Edgar, King of the English, 959–975: New Interpretations* (Woodbridge, 2008).
18. Catherine Karkov, 'The frontispiece to the New Minster Charter and the King's Two Bodies', in D. Scragg (ed.) *Edgar King of the English 959–975*, (Woodbridge, 2008), pp. 224–41.

19. C. Karkov, 'Pictured in the Heart: the Ediths and the Church at Wilton', in V. Blanton; H. Scheck (eds.) *(Inter)Texts: Studies in Early Insular Culture Presented to Paul E Szarmach* (Tempe, 2008), pp. 273–85.

20. Yorke, Barbara, 'The Women in Edgar's Life', in ed. D. G. Scragg, *Edgar, King of the English, 959–975: New Interpretations* (Woodbridge, 2008), p. 144.

21. Catherine Karkov, 'Pictured in the Heart: the Ediths and the Church at Wilton', in (eds.) V. Blanton and H. Scheck *(Inter)Texts: Studies in Early Insular Culture Presented to Paul E Szarmach*. Tempe, 2008), pp. 273–85.

22. William of Malmesbury, *The Deeds of the Bishops of England (Gesta Pontificum Anglorum)*, trans. D. Preest (Woodbridge, 2002), ch. 87, p. 127.

23. Barbara Yorke, *Bishop Athelwold* (Woodbridge, 1997).

24. Douglas Dales, *Dunstan: Saint and Statesman* (Cambridge, 1988/2013).

25. Michael Wood, *In Search of the Dark Ages* (London, reprinted 2005), p. 39.

26. Julia Barrow, *The Ideology of the Tenth-Century English Benedictine 'Reform'*, in Patricia Skinner (ed.), *Challenging the Boundaries of Medieval History: The Legacy of Timothy Reuter* (Brepols, 2009), pp. 141–54.

27. Barbara Yorke, *Bishop Aethelwold* (Woodbridge, 1997), p. 2.

28. Mechthild Gretsch, *The Intellectual Foundations of the English Benedictine Reform*, Cambridge Studies in Anglo-Saxon England 25 (Cambridge, 1999).

29. Michael Lapidge, John Blair, Simon Keynes and Donald Scragg, *The Blackwell Encyclopaedia of Anglo-Saxon England* (Oxford, 2001), p. 389.

30. James G. Clark, *The Benedictines in the Middle Ages* (Woodbridge, 2011).

31. Simon Keynes, 'Introduction', in eds. Janet Backhouse, D. H. Turner and Leslie Webster, *The Golden Age of Anglo-Saxon Art* (Bloomington, 1984), p. 15.

32. R. Deshman, *The Benedictional of Athelwold* (Princeton, 1995).

33. Ann Williams, *Æthelred the Unready: The Ill-Counselled King* (London, 2003), p. 88.

34. Katharin Mack, 'Changing Thegns: Cnut's Conquest and the English Aristocracy', *Albion* 16:4 (Winter 1984), pp. 375–87.

35. Wulfstan, *Sermo Lupi Ad Anglos,* ed. Dorothy Whitelock (London, 3rd ed. 1963).

36. *Ibid.*

37. Quoted from S. Ridyard, *The Royal Saints of Anglo-Saxon England: A Study of West Saxon and East Anglian Cults* (Cambridge, first published 1988), p. 2.

38. Robin Fleming, *Kings & Lords in Conquest England*, Cambridge Studies in Medieval Life and Thought: Fourth Series, volume 15 (Cambridge, 1991).

39. Peter Rex, *King & Saint: The Life of Edward the Confessor* (Stroud, 2008).

40. S. Ridyard, *The Royal Saints of Anglo-Saxon England: A Study of West Saxon and East Anglian Cults* (Cambridge, first published 1988), p. 6.

11. A Journey with the Saints

1. Louise Lambert, *Honoré de Balzac: Oeuvres Complètes de M. de Balzac. La Comédie Humaine*, vol. 16.2 (Paris, 1846), p. 111. Quoted from Frank (1988), p. 91. Frank, R., '"Interdisciplinarity": The First Half Century'. Eds. Eric G. Stanley and Terry F. Hoad, *Words: For Robert Burchfield's Sixty-Fifth Birthday. (*Cambridge, 1988). pp. 91–101.

Picture Credits

Bibliography

Primary Sources

Adomnán, *De locis sanctis*. Ed. D. Meehan. Dublin, 1958.

Adomnán, *Vita S. Columbae*. Ed. and trans. A. O. Anderson and M. O. Anderson, *Adomnán's Life of Columba*. Oxford, 1961, second edition 1991.

Alcuin, *Interrogationes et responsiones in Genesin. PL* 100. 515–565.

Aldhelm, *De laudibus uirginitatis*. Ed. R. Ehwald. CCSL 124A. Turnhout, 2001.

Asser 'Life of King Alfred', in eds. Keynes, Simon; Lapidge, Michael, *Alfred the Great: Asser's Life of King Alfred & Other Contemporary Sources* (Penguin Classics, 1983), pp. 67–112.

Bede, *Baedae Venerabilis: Opera historica*. Ed. C. Plummer. Oxford, 1896.

Bede, *Bede: On the Tabernacle*. Ed. A. G. Holder. Translated Texts for Historians 18. Liverpool, 1994.

Bede, *Bede: On the Temple*. Ed. S. Connolly. Translated Texts for Historians 21. Liverpool, 1995.

Bede, *In Samuelem prophetam allegoria expositio*. Ed. D. Hurst. CCSL 119. Turnhout, 1962. pp. 1–272.

Bede, *De temporum rationes*. Ed. C. W. Jones. CCSL 123B. Turnhout, 1977.

Bede, *Historia ecclesiastica gentis Anglorum*. Eds. and trans. Bertram Colgrave and R. A. B. Mynors, *Bede's Ecclesiastical History of the English People*. Oxford, 1969.

Bede, *Lives of the Abbots of Wearmouth and Jarrow*. Ed. D. H. Farmer, *The Age of Bede*. London, 1998.

Bede, *Vita BB. Abbatum Benedicti, Ceolfridi, Eosterwini, Sigfridi et Hwaetberti*. Ed. C. Plummer, *Baedae Venerabilis: Opera historica*. Oxford, 1896. Vol. 1. pp. 364–87.

Bede, *Vita Cuthberti*. Ed. B. Colgrave. *Two Lives of Saint Cuthbert: A Life by an Anonymous Monk of Lindisfarne and Bede's Prose Life*. Cambridge, 1940. pp. 61–140.

Bradley, S. A. J., *Anglo-Saxon Poetry*. London, reprinted 1995.

Colgrave, B., *Two Lives of Saint Cuthbert: A Life by an Anonymous Monk of Lindisfarne and Bede's Prose Life*. Cambridge, 1940.

Colgrave, B., *The Earliest Life of Gregory the Great by an Anonymous Monk of Whitby*. Kansas, 1968.

Colgrave, B., *The Life of Bishop Wilfrid by Eddius Stephanus*. Cambridge, 1985.

313

Crossley-Holland, Kevin, *The Anglo-Saxon World: An Anthology*. Oxford, reprinted 2009.

Gerald of Wales, *The History and Topography of Ireland*. Ed. John J. O'Meara. Penguin, 1982.

Gildas, *The Ruin of Britain and other works*, Latin and trans. M. Winterbottom, *History from the Sources 7*. Old Woking 1978.

Gregory, *Epistola lxii ad Ioannem Episcopum*. Ed. D. Norberg, *Registrum epistularum libri I-VIII*. CCSL 140. Turnhout, 1982.

Hobbes, Thomas *Leviathan*, ed. Tom Griffith. London, 2014.

Jacobus de Voragine, *The Golden Legend: Readings on the Saints*, trans. William Granger Ryan. Princeton, reprint 2012.

Jerome, *Vita S. Pauli. PL* 23. pp. 17–28.

Klaeber, F., *Beowulf*. London, 1922.

Klinck, Anne, *The Old English Elegies: A Critical Edition and Genre Study*. Montreal, 1992.

Lapidge, M., and Herren, M., *Aldhelm; The Prose Works*. Cambridge, 1979.

Larrington, C., *The Poetic Edda*. Oxford, 1999.

Murchiú, *St. Patrick: His writings and Muirchu's life,* trans. A.B.E. Hood. London: Phillimore, 1978.

Plummer, C., *Historia abbatum auctore anonymo: Venerabilis Baedae: Opera historica*. 2 vols. Oxford, 1896. Vol. 1. pp. 388–404.

Ptolemy, *Ptolemy's 'Geography': An Annotated Translation of the Theoretical Chapters*, trans. J. Lennart Berggren and Alexander Jones (Princeton, 2000).

Soanes, C., and Stevenson, A., *The Oxford English Dictionary. Oxford Reference Online*. Oxford, 2005.

St Patrick, *The Confession of St. Patrick Translated from the Original Latin with an Introduction and Notes*, trans. Thomas Olden. Eremitical Press, 2010.

Swanton, M., *The Dream of the Rood*. Manchester, 1970.

Webb, J. F., and Farmer, D. H., *The Age of Bede*. Harmondsworth, 1983.

Weber, R., Fischer, B., Gribomont, J., Sparks, H.F.D. and Thiele, W., *Biblia Sacra iuxta Vulgatam Versionem*, 4th edn. Stuttgart, 1994.

Whitelock, Dorothy, *English Historical Documents,* 500–1042 (London, reissued 1996).

William of Malmesbury, *The Deeds of the Bishops of England (Gesta Pontificum Anglorum)*, trans. D. Preest. Woodbridge, 2002.

Wulfstan, *Sermo Lupi Ad Anglos,* ed. Dorothy Whitelock (London, 3rd ed.1963).

Secondary Sources

Abels, Richard *Alfred the Great: War, Kingship and Culture in Anglo-Saxon England*. Longman, 1998.

Abou-El-Haj, Barbara, *The Medieval Cult of Saints: Formations and Transformations*. Cambridge, 1994.

Aggeler, C., 'The Eccentric Hermit-Bishop: Bede, Cuthbert, and Farne Island.' *Essays in Medieval Studies* 16 (1999). pp. 17–25.

Alexander, Dominic, *Saints and Animals in the Middle Ages*. Woodbridge, 2008.

Allchin, A. M., *Pennant Melangell; Place of Pilgrimage*. Pennant Melangell, 1994.

Allen, J. R., and Anderson, J., *The Early Christian Monuments of Scotland*. Society of Antiquaries of Scotland. Vol. 2. Edinburgh, 1903, reprinted 1993.

Ameisenowa, Z., 'Animal-Headed Gods, Evangelists, Saints, and Righteous Men.' *Journal of the Warburg and Courtauld Institutes* 12 (1949). pp. 21–45.

Antonsson, Haki, and Ildar H. Garipzanov (eds.), *Saints and Their Lives on the Periphery: Veneration of Saints in Scandinavia and Eastern Europe (c.1000–1200)*. Turnholt, 2010.

Ash, Mearinell, and Dauvit Broun, 'The Adoption of St Andrew as Patron Saint of Scotland', in ed. John Higgitt, *Medieval Art and Architecture in the Diocese of St Andrews*. BAR, 1994. pp. 16–24.

Atherton, M., *Celts and Christians: New Approaches to the Religious Traditions of Britain and Ireland*. Cardiff, 2002.

Bachrach, David S., *Religion and the Conduct of War, c.300–1215*. Woodbridge, 2003.

Backhouse, Janet, Turner, D.H. and Webster, Leslie (eds.), *The Golden Age of Anglo-Saxon Art*. Bloomington, 1984.

Backhouse, J., *The Lindisfarne Gospels*. London, 1981.

Bailey, R., *England's Earliest Sculptors*. Toronto, 1996.

Bailey, R., 'St Wilfrid, Ripon and Hexham,' in *Studies in Insular Art and Archaeology*. Oxford Ohio, 1991. pp. 3–25.

Bakka, E., 'The Alfred Jewel and Sight.' *Antiquaries Journal* 46 (1966). pp. 277–82.

Bammesburger, A., 'A Note on the Whitby Comb Runic Inscription', *Notes and Queries* 57:3 (2010). pp. 292–5.

Barrow, Julia, *The Ideology of the Tenth-Century English Benedictine 'Reform'*, in Patricia Skinner (ed.), *Challenging the Boundaries of Medieval History: The Legacy of Timothy Reuter*. Brepols, 2009. pp. 141–54.

Bartlett, Robert, *'Why Can The Dead Do Such Great Things?'* Princeton and Oxford, 2013.

Bartlett, Robert, *The Making of Europe: Conquest, Colonization and Cultural Change 950–1350*. Harmondsway and Princeton, 1993.

Battiscombe, C. F. (ed.), *The Relics of Saint Cuthbert*. Oxford, 1956.

Baxter, S., Karkov, C., Nelson J. and Pelteret, D., *Early Medieval Studies in Memory of Patrick Wormald*. Farnham, 2009.

Becker, A., *Franks Casket: zu den Bildern und Inschriften des Runenkastchens von Auson*. Regensburg, 1973.

Bengtson, Jonathan, "St. George and the Formation of English Nationalism," *Journal of Medieval and Early Modern Studies* 27 (1997). pp. 317–40.

Biddle, Martin and Kjolby, Birthe, 'The origins of St Albans Abbey: Romano-British cemetery and Anglo-Saxon monastery', in ed. M. Henig, *Alban and St Albans. Roman and Medieval Art and Archaeology*, Leeds, 2001. pp. 45–77.

Biddle, Martin (ed.), *Winchester in the Early Middle Ages*. Oxford, 1976.

Birch, Debra, *Pilgrimage to Rome in the Middle Ages*. Woodbridge, 1998.

Bischoff, Bernhard and Lapidge, Michael, *Biblical Commentaries from the Canterbury School of Theodore and Hadrian*. Cambridge, 1995.

Black, John, ' *"Nutrix pia"*: The Flowering of the Cult of St AEthelthryth in Anglo-Saxon England'. Ed. Paul E. Szarmach, *Writing Women Saints in Anglo-Saxon England*. Toronto, 2013. pp. 167–90.

Bladey, Conrad, *Brigid of the Gael: A Complete Collection of Primary Resources*. Hutman, 2000.

Blair, J. and Sharpe, R., *Pastoral Care Before the Parish*. Leicester, 1992.

Blair, John, *The Church in Anglo-Saxon Society*. Oxford, 2005.

Blair, John, "A Saint for Every Minster? Local Cults in Anglo-Saxon England," in (eds.) Thacker and Sharpe, *Local Saints and Local Churches*. Oxford, 1992. pp. 455–94.

Bonner, G. I., 'Ireland and Rome: the Double Inheritance of Christian Northumbria.' Eds. Margot W. King and Wesley M. Stevens, *Saints, Scholars and Heroes: Studies in Medieval Culture in Honour of Charles W. Jones*, Vol. 1. Collegeville, 1979. pp. 101–17.

Bonner, G. I., *Famulus Christi: Essays in Commemoration of the Thirteenth Centenary of the Birth of Bede*. London, 1976.

Bonner, G. I., 'The Christian Life in the Thought of the Venerable Bede.' *Durham University Journal* 63 (1970). pp. 37–55.

Bonner, G., Rollason, D., and Stancliffe, C., *St Cuthbert, His Cult and His Community to 1200*. Woodbridge, 1989.

Borst, Arno, 'Patron Saints in Medieval Society,' in *Medieval Worlds: Barbarians, Heretics and Artists in the Middle Ages*. Cambridge, 1991. pp. 125–44.

Bourke, Cormac (ed.), *Studies in the Cult of Saint Columba*. Dublin, 1997.

Bourke, Edward, Hayden, Alan R., and Lynch, Ann, *Skellig Michael, Co. Kerry: The Monastery and South Peak. Archaeological stratigraphic report: excavations 1986–2010*. Dublin, 2011.

Bray, Dorothy Ann, *A List of Motifs in the Lives of Early Irish Saints*. Helsinki, 1992.

Brooks, Nicholas, 'From British to English Christianity: Deconstructing Bede's Interpretation of the Conversion', in eds. Nicholas Howe and Catherine Karkov, *Conversion and Colonization in Anglo-Saxon England*. Tempe, 2006. pp. 1–30.

Broun, Dauvit, and Thomas Owen Clancy (eds.), *Spes Scotorum: Hope of Scots. Saint Columba, Iona and Scotland*. Edinburgh, 1999.

Brooks, Nicholas, *Early History of the Church of Canterbury: Christ Church from 597 to 1066*. Leicester, 1996.

Brown, Peter, *The Cult of Saints: Its rise and function in Latin Christianity*. Chicago, 1981.

Brown, G. H., *Bede the Educator*. Jarrow, 1996.

Brown, Michelle, *'In the Beginning was the Word': Books and Faith in the Age of Bede*. Jarrow, 2000.

Brown, Michelle, 'The Book as Sacred Space'. Eds. P. North and J. North, *Sacred Space: House of God, Gate of Heaven*. Bloomsbury, 2007.

Brown, M., *The Lindisfarne Gospels: Society, Spirituality and the Scribe*. London, 2003.

Bruce-Mitford, R. L. S., *The Art of the Codex Amiatinus*. Jarrow, 1967.

Burton, Philip *The Old Latin Gospels: A Study of the Texts and Language*. Oxford, 2000. pp. 5–11.

Bullough, D. A., *Alcuin - Achievement and Reputation*. Brill, 2004.

Campbell, James, 'Archipelagic thoughts: comparing early medieval polities in Britain and Ireland', in: Baxter, Stephen, Catherine E. Karkov, Janet L. Nelson, and David Pelteret (eds), *Early medieval studies in memory of Patrick Wormald*, Studies in Early Medieval Britain. Aldershot: Ashgate, 2009. pp. 47–64.

Campbell, James, *Essays in Anglo-Saxon History*. London, 1986.

Campbell, James, 'Elements in the Background to the Life of St Cuthbert and his Early Cult'. Eds. G. Bonner, D. Rollason and C. Stancliffe, *St Cuthbert, His Cult and Community to A.D. 1200*. Woodbridge, 1989, reprinted 1995. pp. 3–20.

Caroli, Martina, 'Bringing Saints to Cities and Monasteries: 'Translationes' in the Making of a Sacred Geography (9th–10th centuries)', in ed. G. P. Brogliolo et al. *Towns and Their Territories between Late Antiquity and the Early Middle Ages*. Leiden, 2000. pp. 259–74.

Carruthers, M., *The Book of Memory: A Study of Memory in Medieval Culture*. Cambridge, 1990.

Cartwright, Jane, *Celtic Hagiography and Saints' Cults*. Cardiff, 2003.

Carver, Martin, Sanmark, Alex and Semple, Sarah, *Signals of Belief: Anglo-Saxon Paganism Revisited*, Oxbow, 2010.

Carver, Martin, *Portmahomack: Monastery of the Picts*. Edinburgh, 2008.

Cassidy, B., and Howlett, D., 'Some Eighteenth-Century Drawings of the Ruthwell Cross.' *Antiquaries Journal* 72 (1992). pp. 102–17.

Cassidy, B., *The Ruthwell Cross: Papers from the Colloquium Sponsored by the Index of Christian Art*. Princeton, 1992.

Chadwick, Nora K., *The Age of the Saints in the Early Celtic Church*. Oxford, 1961.

Chapman, J., 'The Codex Amiatinus and Cassiodorus.' *Revue Bénédictine* 38 (1926). pp. 139–50.

Charles-Edward, T. M., *Early Christian Ireland*. Cambridge, 2000.

Charles-Edwards, T. M, *Wales and the Britons: 350-1064*, Oxford, 2013.

Chazelle, C., 'Ceolfrid's Gift to St. Peter: The First Quire of the Codex Amiatinus and the Evidence of its Roman Destination.' *Early Medieval Europe* 12 (2003). pp. 129–57.

Clark, David and Perkins, Nicholas, *Anglo-Saxon Culture and the Modern Imagination,* Boydell and Brewer, 2010.

Clark, James G., *The Benedictines in the Middle Ages*. Woodbridge, 2011.

Clark, E. G., 'The Right Side of the Franks Casket.' *Publications of the Modern Language Association of America* 45.2 (1930). pp. 339–53.

Clarke, J. R., and Hinton, D. A., *The Alfred and Minster Lovell Jewels*. Oxford, 1984.

Clarkson, Tim, *Columba*. Edinburgh, 2012.

Clemoes, Peter, *The Cult of St Oswald on the Continent*. Jarrow, 1984.

Corsano, K., 'The First Quire of the Codex Amiatinus and the *Institutiones* of Cassiodorus.' *Scriptorium* 41 (1987). pp. 3–34.

Cramp, R., 'A Reconsideration of the Monastic Site at Whitby.' Eds. John Higgitt and R. Michael Spearman, *The Age of Migrating Ideas*. Edinburgh, 1993. pp. 64–73.

Cramp, R., 'Monastic sites.' Ed. D. M. Wilson, *The Archaeology of Anglo-Saxon England*. Cambridge, 1976. pp. 201–52.

Crépin, A., 'Bede and the Vernacular.' Ed. Gerald Bonner, *Famulus Christi: Essays in Commemoration of the Thirteenth Centenary of the Birth of Bede*. London, 1976. pp. 170–92.

Cronyn, J. M. and Horie, C. V., *St Cuthbert's Coffin: The History, Technology and Conservation*. Durham, 1985.

Cubitt, Catherine, 'Sites and Sanctity: Revisiting the Cult of Murdered and Martyred Anglo-Saxon Royal Saints', *Early Medieval Europe* 9, 2000. pp. 53–83.

Cummins, W. A., *Decoding the Pictish Symbols*. Stroud, 2009.

Dal Santo, Matthew, *Debating the Saints' Cults in the Age of Gregory the Great*. Oxford, 2012.

Dales, D., *Light to the Isles: a Study of Missionary Theology in Celtic and Early Anglo-Saxon Britain*. Cambridge, 1997.

Dales, Douglas, *Dunstan: Saint and Statesman*. Cambridge, 1988/2013.

Deshman, R., *The Benedictional of Athelwold*. Princeton, 1995.

Duffy, Eamon, *The Stripping of the Altars: Traditional Religion in England, c.1400–1580*. New Haven, 1992.

Eddius Stephanus, *The Life of Bishop Wilfrid by Eddius Stephanus*, trans. Bertram Colgrave. Cambridge, 1927, reprinted 1985.

Edmonds, Fiona, "Personal Names and the Cult of Patrick in Eleventh-century Strathclyde and Northumbria," in ed. Steve Boardman, *Saints' Cults in the Celtic World*. Woodbridge, 2009. pp. 42–65.

Evans, A. C., *The Sutton Hoo Ship Burial*. London, 1986, reprinted 2000.

Fanning, S., 'Bede, *Imperium*, and the Bretwaldas.' *Speculum* 66 (1991). pp. 1–26.

Farmer, David Hugh, *The Oxford Dictionary of Saints*. 5th Edition. Oxford, 2003.

Farr, C. A., 'The Shape of Learning at Wearmouth–Jarrow: The Diagram pages in the Codex Amiatinus.' Eds. Jane Hawkes and Susan Mills, *Northumbria's Golden Age*. Stroud, 1999. pp. 336–345.

Farr, C. A., *The Book of Kells: its Function and Audience*. London, 1997.

Farrell, R. T., and Neumann de Vegvar, C., *Sutton Hoo: Fifty Years After*. Ohio, 1992.

Fell, Christine, *Women in Anglo-Saxon England*. Oxford, 1984.

Filppula, M., Klemola, J., Paulasto, H., and Pitkanen, H., *English and Celtic in Contact*, Routledge, 2008.

Fleming, Robin, *Kings & Lords in Conquest England*, Cambridge Studies in Medieval Life and Thought: Fourth Series, volume 15. Cambridge, 1991.

Foot, Sarah, *Athelstan: First King of England*. Yale, 2010.

Foot, Sarah, *Monastic Life in Anglo-Saxon England c.600–900*. Cambridge, 2009.

Foot, Sarah, 'Anglo-Saxon Minsters: A Review of Terminology', in eds. J. Blair and R. Sharpe, *Pastoral Care Before the Parish*. Leicester, 1992, pp. 212–25.

Forbes, Ian W.G., *The Last of the Druids: The Mystery of the Pictish Symbol Stone*. Stroud, 2012.

Foster, S. M. and Cross, M., *Able Minds and Practised Hands: Scotland's Early Medieval Sculpture in the 21st Century*. Leeds, 2005.

Frank, R., ' 'Interdisciplinarity': The First Half Century.' Eds. Eric G. Stanley and Terry F. Hoad, *Words: For Robert Burchfield's Sixty-Fifth Birthday*. Cambridge, 1988. pp. 91–101.

Franklin, C. V., 'Bilingual Philology in Bede's Exegesis.' Ed. R. F. Gyug, *Medieval Cultures in Context*. New York, 2003. pp. 3–18.

Frantzen, Allen J., *Food, Eating and Identity in Early Medieval England*. Woodbridge, 2014.

Gager, John G., *Curse Tablets and Binding Spells from the Ancient World*. OUP, 1999.

Gameson, R., 'The Material Fabric of Early British Books', in *The Cambridge History of the Book in Britain: Volume 1 c. 400–1100*. Cambridge, 2011. pp. 13–94.

Gameson, R., *St Augustine and the Conversion of England*. Stroud, 1999.

Gameson, R., 'The Earliest Books of Christian Kent.' *St Augustine and the Conversion of England*. Stroud, 1999. pp. 313–73.

Garrison, M., '*Praesagum nomen tibi*: The Significance of Name-Wordplay in Alcuin's letters to Arn.' Eds. M. Niederkorn-Bruck and A. Scharer, *Erzbischof Arn von Salzburg 784/85-821*. Vienna 2004. pp. 107–27.

Garrison, M., 'The Franks as the New Israel: Education for an Identity from Pippin to Charlemagne.' Eds. Y. Hen and M. Innes, *The Uses of the Past in Early Medieval Europe*. Cambridge, 2000. pp. 114–61.

Garrison, M., 'The Social World of Alcuin: Nicknames at York and at the Carolingian Court.' Eds. L. A. R. J. Houwen and A. A. MacDonald, *Alcuin of York: Scholar at the Carolingian Court*. Germania Latina 3. Groningen 1998. pp. 59–79.

Garrison, M., Nelson, J., and Tweddle, D., *Alcuin and Charlemagne: The Golden Age of York*. York, 2001.

Geary, Patrick, *Furta sacra: Theft of Relics in the Central Middle Ages*. 2nd edition. Princeton, 1990.

Geddes, Jane, *The St Albans Psalter*. London, 2005.

Goffart, Walter, *The Narrators of Barbarian History (A.D. 550–800): Jordanes, Gregory of Tours, Bede, and Paul the Deacon*. Princeton, 1988.

Good, Jonathan, *The Cult of St. George in Medieval England*. Woodbridge, 2009.

Goodich, Michael, *Lives and Miracles of the Saints: Studies in Medieval Latin Hagiography*. Aldershot, 2004.

Goodich, Michael, *Miracles and Wonders: The Development of the Concept of Miracle, 1150–1350*. Aldershot, 2004.

Green, M. A., *Celtic Art: Reading the Message*. London, 1996.

Gretsch, Mechthild, *Aelfric and the Cult of Saints in Late Anglo-Saxon England*. Cambridge, 2005.

Griffiths, M., 'Convention and Originality in the Old English "Beasts of Battle" Typescene.' *Anglo-Saxon England* 22 (1993). pp. 179–99.

Halsall, Guy, *Worlds of Arthur: Facts and Fictions of the Dark Ages*, OUP, 2013.

Hammond, G., 'English Translations of the Bible.' Eds. Robert Alter and Frank Kermode, *The Literary Guide to the Bible*. London, 1989. pp. 647–68.

Harbison, Peter, *The High Crosses of Ireland: An Iconographical and Photographic Survey*. Bonn, 1992.

Harden Weaver, Rebecca, *Divine Grace and Human Agency: Study of the Saint Pelagian Controversy*. Mercer, 1996.

Hartley, E., Hawkes, J., Henig, M., and Mee, F., *Constantine the Great: York's Roman Emperor*. York, 2006.

Hawkes, Jane, *Stones of the North: Sculpture in Northumbria in the 'Age of Bede'*. Leeds, 2013.

Hawkes, J., '*Iuxta morem Romanorum*: Stone and Sculpture in the Style of Rome.' Eds. G. Hardin Brown and C. Karkov, *Anglo-Saxon Styles*. New York, 2003. pp. 69–100.

Hawkes, J., *The Sandbach Crosses: Sign and Significance in Anglo-Saxon Sculpture*. Dublin, 2002.

Hawkes, J., 'The Age of the Church in Ninth-Century Anglo-Saxon England: The Case of the Masham Column.' *Hortus Artium Medievalium* 8 (2002). pp. 337–48.

Hawkes, J., 'Statements in Stone: Anglo-Saxon Sculpture, Whitby and the Christianisation of the North.' Ed. C. Karkov, *Reader in Anglo-Saxon Archaeology*. New York, 1999. pp. 403–21.

Hawkes, J., 'Anglo-Saxon Sculpture: Questions of Context.' Eds. J. Hawkes and S. Mills, *Northumbria's Golden Age*. Stroud, 1999. pp. 204–15.

Hawkes, J., 'Symbolic Lives: The Visual Evidence.' Ed. J. Hines, *The Anglo-Saxons from the Migration Period to the Eighth Century: An Ethnographic Perspective*. Woodbridge, 1997. pp. 311–44.

Hawkes, Jane and Mills, Susan, *Northumbria's Golden Age*. Sutton, 1999.

Henig, M., *Alban and St Albans. Roman and Medieval Art and Archaeology*, Leeds, 2001.

Henderson, G. and Henderson, I., *Art of the Picts: Sculpture and Metalwork in Early Medieval Scotland*. New York, 2004.

Henderson, G., *Vision and Image in Early Christian England*. Cambridge, 1999.

Henderson, G., *From Durrow to Kells: the Insular Gospel-books, 650–800*. London, 1987.

Henderson, I., *The Picts*. London, 1967.

Herbert, M., *Iona, Kells and Derry: the History and Hagiography of the Monastic Familia of Columba*. Oxford, 1988.

Heslop, T. A., 'Art and the Man: Archbishop Wulfstan and the York Gospelbook'. Ed. M. Townend, *Wulfstan, Archbishop of York*. Brepols, 2002. pp. 279–3

Higham, N. J. *(Re-)Reading Bede: The Ecclesiastical History in context*. Abingdon, 2006.

Higham, Nicholas J., 'Bede and the Early English Church', in Alexander

R. Rumble, *Leaders of the Anglo-Saxon Church: From Bede to Stigand*. Boydell, 2012. pp. 25–40.

Higham, Nicholas and Ryan, Martin, *The Anglo-Saxon World*, Yale 2013.

Higham, Nicholas, *The Convert Kings: Power and Religious Affiliation in Early Anglo-Saxon England*. Manchester University Press, 1997.

Higgitt, John, 'The Iconography of St Peter in Anglo-Saxon England and St Cuthbert's Coffin'. Eds. G. Bonner, D. Rollason and C. Stancliffe, *St Cuthbert, His Cult and Community to A.D. 1200*. Woodbridge, reprinted 1995. pp. 267–86.

Higgitt, J., and Spearman, R. M., *The Age of Migrating Ideas*. Edinburgh, 1993.

Hill, Joyce, *Bede and the Benedictine Reform*. Jarrow, 1998.

Hill, Peter, and Graham, Tony, *Whithorn and St. Ninian: The Excavations of a Monastic Town, 1984–91*. Sutton, 1997.

Hill, T. D., 'The Cross as Symbolic Body: An Anglo-Latin Liturgical Analogue to The Dream of the Rood.' *Neophilologus* 77.2 (1993). pp. 297–301.

Hines, J., *The Anglo-Saxons from the Migration Period to the Eighth Century: An Ethnographic Perspective*. Woodbridge, 1997.

Hinton, D. A., *The Alfred Jewel: and Other Late Anglo-Saxon Decorated Metalwork*, Oxford, 2008.

Hollis, Stephanie, *Anglo-Saxon Women and the Church*. Woodbridge, 1992.

Hope-Taylor, B., *Yeavering: An Anglo-British Centre of Early Northumbria*. London, 1977, reprinted 2010.

Horspool, David *Why Alfred Burned the Cakes*. London, 2006.

Houwen, L. A. J. R. and MacDonald, A. A., *Alcuin of York: Scholar at the Carolingian Court*. Groningen, 1998.

Howorth, H., *Augustine the Missionary*. London, 1913.

Gretsch, Mechthild, *The Intellectual Foundations of the English Benedictine Reform* Cambridge Studies in Anglo-Saxon England 25. Cambridge, 1999.

James, E., 'Bede and the Tonsure Question.' *Peritia* 3 (1984). pp. 85–93.

Jones, C.W., 'Bede's Place in Medieval Schools.' Ed. G. Bonner, *Famulus Christi*. London, 1976. pp. 261–86.

Kamesar, A., *Jerome, Greek Scholarship, and the Hebrew Bible*. Oxford, 1993.

Karkov, C., *Reader in Anglo-Saxon Archaeology*. New York, 1999.

Karkov, C., "The frontispiece to the New Minster Charter and the King's Two Bodies", in Scragg D (eds.) *Edgar King of the English 959-975*. Woodbridge: Woodbridge, 2008. pp. 224–41.

Karkov, C., 'Pictured in the Heart: the Ediths and the Church at Wilton', In: Blanton V; Scheck H (eds.) *(Inter)Texts: Studies in Early Insular Culture Presented to Paul E Szarmach*. Tempe, 2008. pp. 273–85.

Kelly, J. F., 'The Letter of Columbanus to Gregory the Great.' *Gregorio Magno e il Suo Tempo*, Studia Ephemeridis Augustinianum 33. Rome, 1991.

Kendrick, T. D., *Anglo-Saxon Art to A.D. 900*. London and New York, 1972.

Kendrick, T. D., Brown, T. J., Bruce-Mitford, R. L. S., Roosen-Kunge, H.,

Ross, A. S. C., Stanley, E. G., and Werner, A. E. A., *Evangeliorum Quattuor Codex Lindisfarnensis.* 2 Vols. New York, 1960.

Keynes, Simon, 'Introduction', in eds. Janet Backhouse, D.H. Turner and Leslie Webster, *The Golden Age of Anglo-Saxon Art.* Bloomington, 1984. pp. 11–16.

Keynes, S. D., 'King Alfred and the Mercians' in *Kings, currency and alliances.* Woodbridge, Boydell Press, 1998, pp. 1–46.

Kirby, D. P., 'Bede, Eddius Stephanus and *The Life of Wilfrid*', in *The English Historical Review*, vol. 98, No. 386 (1983). pp. 101–14.

Kirby, D. P., *St Wilfrid at Hexham.* Newcastle, 1974.

Kirby, D. P., 'Bede's Native Sources for the *Historia Ecclesiastica.*' *Proceedings of the John Rylands Library* 48 (1966). pp. 341–71.

Knowles, Dom David, *The Monastic Order in England: A History of its Development from the times of St Dunstan to the Fourth Lateran Council 940–1216.*

Korhammer, P. M., 'The Origin of the Bosworth Psalter', *Anglo-Saxon England.* Vol 2, December, 1973. pp. 173–87.

Koudounaris, Paul, *Heavenly Bodies Cult Treasures and Spectacular Saints from the Catacombs.* Thames & Hudson, 2013.

Kousoulas, D. G., *The First Christian Emperor: The Life and Times of Constantine the Great.* Routledge, 2nd edn. 2003.

Lambert, Louise, *Honoré de Balzac: Oeuvres Complètes de M. de Balzac. La Comédie Humaine*, vol. 16.2. Paris, 1846.

Lambert, Malcolm, *Christians and Pagans: The Conversion of Britain from Alban to Bede,* New Haven and London, 2010.

Lang, J., *Corpus of Anglo-Saxon Stone Sculpture: Volume VI Northern Yorkshire.* Oxford, 2001.

Lang, J., 'The Apostles in Anglo-Saxon Sculpture in the Age of Alcuin.' *Early Medieval Europe* 8 (1999). pp. 271–82.

Lapidge, Michael, Blair, John, Keynes, Simon and Scragg, Donald *The Blackwell Encyclopaedia of Anglo-Saxon England.* Oxford, 2001.

Lapidge, M., 'Aldhelm's Latin Poetry and Old English Verse.' *Comparative Literature* 31 (1979). pp. 209–23.

Lapidge, M. and Dumville, D. N., *Gildas: New Approaches.* Woodbridge, 1984.

Lapidge, M., 'Surviving Booklists from Anglo-Saxon England.' Eds. M. Lapidge and H. Gneuss, *Learning and Literature in Anglo-Saxon England: Studies Presented to Peter Clemoes on the Occasion of his Sixty-fifth Birthday.* Cambridge, 1985. pp. 33–90.

Lapidge, Malcolm, 'The School of Theodore and Hadrian', in *Anglo-Saxon England* Vol. 15 (1986). pp. 45–72.

Lapidge, M., *Bede the Poet.* Jarrow, 1993.

Leahy, Kevin, *Anglo-Saxon Crafts.* Stroud, 2010.

Leahy, Kevin and Bland, Roger, *The Staffordshire Hoard.* London, 2014.

Lee, Rob, Jonathan, Philip and Ziman, Pauline, 'Pictish symbols revealed as a written language through application of Shannon entropy', *Proceedings of the Royal Society A: Mathematical, Physical and Engineering Science* (2010).

Lehane, Brendan, *Early Celtic Christianity.* London, reprinted 2005.

Lerner, Ralph, 'The *Jihād* of St Alban.' *The Review of Politics.* Vol. 64:1 Winter, 2002. pp. 5–26.

Levison, W., *England and the Continent in the Eighth Century: The Ford Lectures Delivered in the University of Oxford in the Hilary Term 1943.* Oxford, 1946, reprinted 1998.

Leyser, Henrietta, *Medieval Women: A Social History of Women in England 450-1500.* London, 1995.

Little, L. K., 'Calvin's Appreciation of Gregory the Great', *Harvard Theological Review* 56 (1963). pp. 145–57.

Losack, Marcus, *Rediscovering Saint Patrick.* Columba Press, Blackrock, 2013.

Low, M., 'The Natural World in Early Irish Christianity: An Ecological Footnote.' Ed. Mark Atherton, *Celts and Christians: New Approaches to the Religious Traditions of Britain and Ireland.* Cardiff, 2002. pp. 169–191.

Lubac, H. De, *Medieval Exegesis: Volume 1, The Four Senses of Scripture.* Michigan and Edinburgh, 1998.

Luiselli Fadda, A. M., and Ó. Carragáin, É., *Le Isole Britanniche e Roma in Età Romanobarbarica.* Rome, 1998.

Mack, Katharin, 'Changing Thegns: Cnut's Conquest and the English Aristocracy', *Albion* 16:4, (Winter 1984). pp. 375–87.

Mackey, J. P., 'Introduction: Is there a Celtic Christianity?' *An Introduction to Celtic Christianity.* Edinburgh, 1989. pp. 1–21.

MacLean, D., 'The Date of the Ruthwell Cross.' Ed. B. Cassidy, *The Ruthwell Cross: Papers from the Colloquium Sponsored by the Index of Christian Art, Princeton University, 8 December 1989.* Princeton, 1992. pp. 49–70.

Markus, R., *Bede and the Tradition of Ecclesiastical Historiography.* Jarrow, 1975.

Marsden, R., *The Text of the Old Testament in Anglo-Saxon England.* Cambridge, 1995.

Marsden, R., 'The Gospels of St Augustine.' Ed. R. Gameson, *St Augustine and the Conversion of England.* Stroud, 1999. pp. 285–312.

Marsden, R., *'Manus Bedae*: Bede's Contribution to Ceolfrith's Bibles.' *Anglo-Saxon England,* 27 (1998). pp. 65–85.

Marsden, Richard, *The Text of the Old Testament in Anglo-Saxon England.* Cambridge, 1995.

Martin, Toby F., *The Cruciform Brooch and Anglo-Saxon England.* Woodbridge, 2015.

Martyn, J. R. C., *The Letters of Gregory the Great.* Vol. 2. Toronto, 2004.

Matthews, T. F., *The Clash of the Gods: A Reinterpretation of Christian Early Art.* Princeton, 1995.

Mayr-Harting, H., *The Coming of Christianity to Anglo-Saxon England.* 3rd edition. Pennsylvania, 1991.

McC.Gatch, M., 'Noah's Raven in Genesis A and Illustrated Old English Hexateuch.' *Gesta* 14.2 (1975). pp. 3–15.

McNamara, J., 'Bede's Role in Circulating Legend in the Historia Ecclesiastica.' *Anglo-Saxon Studies in Archaeology and History* 9 (1994). pp. 61–9.

Meaney, A. L., 'Bede and Anglo-Saxon Paganism.' *Parergon* 3 (1985). pp. 1–29.

Meehan, B., *The Book of Kells: an Illustrated Introduction to the Manuscript in Trinity College, Dublin.* New York, 1994.

Meer, F. van der, *Early Christian Art.* London, 1969.

Meyer, K., *Iconography of Pictish Sculpture.* Unpublished PhD thesis, University of York, 2005.

Meyvaert, P., 'The Date of Bede's *In Ezram* and his Image of Ezra in the Codex Amiatinus.' *Speculum* 80.4 (2005). pp. 1087–133.

Meyvaert, P., 'Bede, Cassiodorus and the Codex Amiatinus.' *Speculum* 71 (1996). pp. 827–83.

Meyvaert, P., 'A New Perspective on the Ruthwell Cross: *Ecclesia* and *Vita Monastica*.' Ed. B. Cassidy, *The Ruthwell Cross: Papers from the Colloquium Sponsored by the Index of Christian Art.* Princeton, 1992. pp. 95–166.

Meyvaert, P., *Bede and Gregory the Great.* Jarrow, 1964.

Michelli, P., 'What's in the Cupboard? Ezra and Matthew Reconsidered.' Ed. J. Hawkes and S. Mills, *Northumbria's Golden Age.* Stroud, 1999. pp. 345–58.

Miller, T., *The Old English Version of Bede's Ecclesiastical History of the English People*, Early English Text Society 95. London, 1890. pp. 134–6.

Mitchell, B., 'Life in Heroic Society and the Impact of Christianity.' *An Invitation to Old English and Anglo-Saxon England.* Oxford, 1995. pp. 193–244.

Nees, L., 'A Fifth-Century Book Cover and the Origin of the Four Evangelist Symbols Page of the Book of Durrow.' *Gesta* 17.1 (1978). pp. 3–8.

Nelson, J. L., 'Charlemagne.' Eds. Mary Garrison, Janet L. Nelson and Dominic Tweddle, *Alcuin and Charlemagne: The Golden Age of York.* York, 2001. pp. 15–23.

Nelson, M., 'The Rhetoric of the Exeter Book Riddles.' *Speculum* 49.3 (1974). pp. 421–40.

Neuman de Vegvar, Carol L., 'The Travelling Twins: Romulus and Remus in Anglo-Saxon England,' in Jane Hawkes and Susan Mills, eds., *Northumbria's Golden Age.* Stroud,1999. pp. 256–67.

Neville, J., *Representations of the Natural World in Old English Poetry.* Cambridge Studies in Anglo-Saxon England 27. Cambridge, 1999.

Niblett, Rosalind, *Verulamium: The Roman City of St Albans.* Stroud, 2001.

Nicolai, V. F., Bisconti, F., and Mazzoleni, D., *The Christian Catacombs of Rome: History, Decoration, Inscriptions.* Regensburg, 2nd edn. 2002.

Niles, J. D., 'The Myth of the Anglo-Saxon Oral Poet.' *Western Folklore* 62:1&2 (2003). pp. 7–61.

Nordhagen, P. J., *The Codex Amiatinus and the Byzantine Element in the Northumbiran Renaissance.* Jarrow, 1977.

North, P. and North, J., *Sacred Space: House of God, Gate of Heaven.* Bloomsbury, 2007.

Norton, Christopher E. 'The Anglo-Saxon cathedral at York and the topography of the Anglian city', in *Journal of the British Archaeological Association*, Vol. 151 (1998). pp. 1–42.

Norton, Elizabeth, *Elfrida: England's first crowned queen*, Amberley, 2009, 2013.

O'Brien O'Keefe, Katherine, *Stealing Obedience: Narratives of Agency and Identity in Later Anglo-Saxon England.* Toronto, 2012.

Ó Carragáin, É., *Ritual and the Rood: Liturgical Images and the Old English Poem of the Dream of the Rood.* Toronto, 2005.

Ó Carragáin, É., 'The Necessary Distance: *Imitatio Romae* and the Ruthwell Cross.' Eds. J. Hawkes and S. Mills, *Northumbria's Golden Age.* Stroud, 1999. pp. 191–203.

Ó Carragáin, É., *The City of Rome and the World of Bede.* Jarrow, 1994.

Ó Carragáin, É., 'The Meeting of St. Paul and St. Anthony: Visual and Literary Uses of an Eucharistic Motif.' Eds. G. MacNiocaill and P. Wallace, *Keimelia: Studies in Archaeology and History in Honour of Tom Delaney.* Galway, 1988. pp. 1–58.

Ó Carragáin, É., 'Christ Over the Beasts and the *Agnus Dei*: Two Multivalent Panels on the Ruthwell and Bewcastle Crosses.' Ed. P. E. Szarmach, *Sources of Anglo-Saxon Culture.* Kalamazoo, 1986. pp. 377–403.

Ó Carragáin, É., 'Liturgical Innovations associated with Pope Sergius and the Iconography of the Ruthwell and Bewcastle Crosses.' Ed. Robert T. Farrell, in *Bede and Anglo-Saxon England: Papers in Honour of the 1300th Anniversary of the Birth of Bede, Given at Cornell University in 1973 and 1974.* British Archaeological Report, Brit. Ser. 46. Oxford, 1978. pp. 96–117.

O Fiaich, Tomas *Columbanus in his own words.* Dublin, reprint 2012.

O'Mahony, F., *The Book of Kells.* Aldershot, 1994.

O'Reilly, J., 'Islands and Idols at the Ends of the Earth: Exegesis and Conversion in Bede's *Historia Ecclesiastica*.' Eds. Stéphane Lebecq, Michel Perrin and Olivier Szerwiniack, *Bède le Vénérable: entre tradition et postérité.* Lille, 2005. pp. 119–45.

O'Reilly, J., 'The Library of Scripture: Views from Vivarium and Wearmouth–Jarrow.' Ed. P. Binski and W. Noel, *New Offerings, Ancient Treasures: Studies in Medieval Art for George Henderson.* Stroud, 2001. pp. 1–39.

O'Reilly, J., 'Patristic and Insular Traditions of the Evangelists: Exegesis and Iconography.' Ed. Luiselli Fadda, A. M., and Ó. Carragáin, É., *Le Isole Britanniche e Roma in Etá Romanobarbarica.* Rome, 1998. pp. 49–94.

O'Reilly, J., 'Reading the Scriptures in the Life of Columba.' Ed. Cormac Bourke, *Studies in the Cult of Saint Columba.* Dublin, 1997. pp. 80–106.

O'Reilly, J., 'Introduction.' Ed. Sean Connolly, *Bede: On the Temple.* Liverpool, 1995. pp. xvii–lv.

O'Reilly, J., 'Exegesis and the Book of Kells: The Lucan Genealogy.' Ed. Felicity O'Mahoney, *The Book of Kells: Proceedings of a Conference at Trinity College, Dublin, 6–9 September 1992.* Aldershot, 1994. pp. 344–97.

Ohlgren, T. H., *Insular and Anglo-Saxon Illuminated Manuscripts: An Iconographic Catalogue c. A.D. 625 to 1100.* New York and London, 1986.

Oldfather W. A., *Studies in the Text Tradition of St Jerome's Vitae Patrum.* Urbana, 1943.

Opland, J., *Anglo-Saxon Oral Poetry: A Study of the Traditions.* New Haven and London, 1980.

Orchard, A., 'Latin and the Vernacular Languages: The Creation of a Bilingual Textual Culture.' Ed. Thomas Charles-Edwards, *After Rome.* Oxford, 2003. pp. 191–219.

Orton, F., 'Northumbrian Sculpture (the Ruthwell and Bewcastle Monuments): Questions of Difference.' Eds. Jane Hawkes and Susan Mills, *Northumbria's Golden Age.* Stroud, 1999. pp. 216–26.

Owen-Crocker, Gale R., 'Image Making: Portraits of Anglo-Saxon Church Leaders', in ed. Alexander R. Rumble, *Leaders of the Anglo-Saxon Church: From Bede to Stigand.* Woodbridge, 2012. pp. 109–29.

Owen-Crocker, Gale R. *Dress in Anglo-Saxon England.* Revised edition, Woodbridge, 2010. pp. 35–103.

Page, R. I. *An Introduction to English Runes.* Woodbridge, second edition, 1999.

Parkes, M. B., *The Scriptorium of Wearmouth–Jarrow.* Jarrow, 1982.

Pollard, Justin, *Alfred the Great: The Man who made England.* London, 2005.

Ramsay, Nigel, Sparks, Margaret, and Tatton-Brown, Tim, *St Dunstan: His Life, Times and Cult.* Woodbridge, 1992.

Reece, R., *The Coinage of Roman Britain.* Stroud, 2002.

Rex, Peter, *King & Saint: The Life of Edward the Confessor* (Stroud, 2008).

Richie, G., *The Royal Commission on the Ancient and Historical Monuments of Scotland: Argyll Volume 5 – Islay, Jura, Colonsay and Oronsay.* Edinburgh, 1985.

Richter, Michael, *Medieval Ireland (New Gill History of Ireland 1): The Enduring Tradition – Ireland from the Coming of Christianity to the Reformation.* Dublin, 2005.

Ridyard, Susan J., *The Royal Saints of Anglo-Saxon England: A Study of West Saxon and East Anglian Cults.* Cambridge, first published 1988.

Rollason, David, *Saints and Relics in Anglo-Saxon England*, Wiley-Blackwell, 1989.

Romilly Allen, J., *Celtic Art in Pagan and Christian Times.* California, 1993.

Rooth, A. B., *The Raven and the Carcass: An Investigation of a Motif in the Deluge Myth in Europe, Asia and North America.* Helsinki, 1962.

Rumble, Alexander R., 'Introduction: Church Leadership and the Anglo-Saxons', in Alexander R. Rumble, *Leaders of the Anglo-Saxon Church: From Bede to Stigand.* Boydell, 2012. pp. 1–24.

Rumble, Alexander R., *Leaders of the Anglo-Saxon Church: From Bede to Stigand.* Boydell, 2012.

Ryan, J., *Irish Monasticism; Origins and Early Development.* Shannon, 1972.

Saxl, F., 'The Ruthwell Cross.' *Journal of the Warburg and Courtauld Institute* 6, (1943). pp. 1–19.

Scragg, D. G., *Edgar, King of the English, 959–975: New Interpretations*. Woodbridge, 2008.

Sears, E., and Thomas, T. K., *Reading Medieval Images: The Art Historian and the Object*. Michigan, 2002.

Selzer, J. L., '*The Wanderer* and the Meditative Tradition.' *Studies in Philology* 80.3 (1983). pp. 227–37.

Shippey, T. A., *Old English Verse*. London, 1972.

Shippey, T. A., 'Wisdom and Experience: The Old English "Elegies".' *Old English Verse*. London, 1972. pp.53–79.

Shepherd, Ian A. G & Ralston, Ian B. M, *Early Grampian: A Guide to the Archaeology*. Aberdeen, 1979.

Slator, R. L., *The Iconography of the Weland Myth on Pre-Conquest Northumbrian Carvings*. Unpublished M.A. thesis, York, 1996.

Smit, J. W., *Studies on the Language and Style of Columba the Younger (Columbanus)*. Amsterdam, 1971.

Smithers, G. V., 'The Meaning of *The Seafarer* and *The Wanderer*.' *Medium Aevum* 26 (1957). pp. 135–53.

Smithers, G. V., 'The Meaning of *The Seafarer* and *The Wanderer* (continued).' *Medium Aevum* 28 (1959). pp. 1–22.

Snow, Dean R., 'Scotland's Irish Origins', in *Archaeology*, Vol. 54, No. 4 (July/August, 2001).

Souers, P. W., 'The Weyland Scene on the Franks Casket.' *Speculum* 18.1 (1943). pp. 104–11.

Souers, P. W., 'The Magi on the Franks Casket.' *Harvard Studies and Notes in Philology and Literature* 19 (1937). pp. 249–54.

Speake, G., *Anglo-Saxon Animal Art and its Germanic Background*, Oxford, 1980.

Spearman R. M., and Higgitt, J., *The Age of Migrating Ideas: Early Medieval Art in Northern Britain and Ireland*. Edinburgh and Stroud, 1993.

Stancliffe, C., *Bede, Wilfrid, and the Irish*. Jarrow, 2004.

Stork, N. P., *Through a Gloss Darkly: Aldhelm's Riddles in the British Library, MS Royal 12.C.xxiii*. Toronto, 1990.

Story, Joanna, 'After Bede: Continuing the *Ecclesiastical History*'. Eds. S. Baxter, C. Karkov, J. Nelson and D. Pelteret, *Early Medieval Studies in Memory of Patrick Wormald*. Farnham, 2009. pp. 165–85.

Szarmach, Paul E., *Writing Women Saints in Anglo-Saxon England*. Toronto, 2013.

Thacker, A., 'Memorializing Gregory the Great: The Origin and Transmission of a Papal Cult in the Seventh and Early Eighth Centuries.' *Early Medieval Europe*, 7.1, (1998). pp. 59–84.

Thompson, Sister Glory G., *Discerning Perspective*. Victoria, 2010.

Toswell, M. J., 'Bede's Sparrow and the Psalter in Anglo-Saxon England.' *American Notes and Queries* 13.1 (Winter, 2000). pp. 7–12.

Toynbee, J. M. C., *Animals in Roman Life and Art*. London, 1973.

Toynbee, J. M. C., and Perkins, J. W., *The Shrine of St Peter and the Vatican Excavations*. London, 1956.

Thacker, Alan, 'England in the Seventh-century', in ed. Paul Fouracre, *The New Cambridge Medieval History, Volume 1: c.500–700.* Cambridge, 2005.

Thomas, G., 'Bishopstone and Lyminge', in *British Archaeology* (July/August, 2011). pp. 42–8.

Turner, Sam and Semple, Sarah, *Wearmouth and Jarrow: Northumbrian Monasteries in an Historic Landscape.* Hertfordshire, 2013.

Vandersall, A. L., 'The Date and Provenance of the Franks Casket.' *Gesta* 11.2 (1972). pp. 9–26.

Veelenturf, K., 'Irish High Crosses and Continental Art: Shades of Iconographical Ambiguity.' Ed. C. Hourihane, *From Ireland Coming: Irish Art from the Early Christian to the Late Gothic Period and its European Context.* Princeton, 2001. pp. 83–101.

Waddell, H., *The Desert Fathers.* London, 1936, reprinted 1998.

Walker, F. C., 'Fresh Light on the Franks Casket.' *Washington University Studies* 11 (1915). pp. 165–76.

Ward, B,. *Bede and the Psalter.* Jarrow, 1991.

Ward, B., *A True Easter: The Synod of Whitby AD 664.* Fairacres Press, 2007.

Webb, Simon, *In Search of Saint Alban,* Langley Press, 2010.

Webster, L., 'The Iconographic Programme of the Franks Casket.' Ed. Hawkes, J., and Mills, S., *Northumbria's Golden Age.* Stroud, 1999. pp. 227–247.

Webster, L., and Backhouse, J., *The Making of England: Anglo-Saxon Art and Culture A.D. 600–900.* London, 1991.

Webster, L., 'Stylistic aspects of the Franks Casket.' Ed. Robert T. Farrell, *The Vikings.* London and Chichester, 1982. pp. 20–32.

Webster, Leslie, *Anglo-Saxon Art: A New History*, British Museum Press, 2012.

Werner, M., 'The Luidhard Medallet.' *Anglo-Saxon England* 20 (1991). pp. 27–41.

Werner, M., 'The Four Evangelist Symbols Page in the Book of Durrow,' *Gesta* 8 (1969). pp. 3–17.

West Haddan, A., and Stubbs, W., *Councils and Ecclesiastical Documents Relating to Great Britain and Ireland*, Vol.III. Oxford, 1964.

White, Donald A. "Changing Views of the *Adventus Saxonum* in Nineteenth and Twentieth Century English Scholarship." *Journal of the History of Ideas* 32: 4 (1971). pp. 585–94.

Whitelock, D., 'The Old English Bede.' *The Proceedings of the British Academy* 48 (1962). pp. 57–90.

Wilcox, J., ' "Tell me what I am:" the Old English Riddles.' Eds. David F. Johnson and Elaine Treharne, *Readings in Medieval Texts: Interpreting Old and Middle English Literature.* Oxford, 2005. pp. 46–59.

Williams, Ann, *Æthelred the Unready: The Ill-Counselled King.* London, 2003.

Williams, Gareth, 'The Circulation and Function of Coinage in Conversion-Period England,' in *Coinage and History in the North Sea World,* c. AD 500–1250. Brill, 2006. pp. 147–79.

Williamson, C., *The Old English Riddles of the Exeter Book.* Chapel Hill, 1977.

Wilson, D. M., *Anglo-Saxon Art: from the Seventh Century to the Norman Conquest*. London, 1984.

Winterbottom, Michael, and Lapidge, Michael, *The Early Lives of St Dunstan*. Oxford, 2011.

Wogan-Browne, Jocelyn, 'Rerouting the Dower: The Anglo-Norman Life of St. Audrey by Marie (of Chatteris?)', in *Power of the Weak: Studies on Medieval Women*, ed. Jennifer Carpenter and Sally-Beth Maclean. Champaign: University of Illinois Press, 1995. pp. 27–56.

Wood, I. N., 'Ripon, Francia and the Franks Casket in the Early Middle Ages.' *Northern History* 26 (1990). pp. 1–19.

Wormald, F., *The Miniatures in the Gospel of St Augustine, Corpus Christi College MS 286*. Cambridge, 1954.

Wormald, P., 'Bede, *Beowulf* and the Conversion of the Anglo-Saxon Aristocracy.' Ed. R. T. Farrell, *Bede and Anglo-Saxon England: Papers in Honour of the 1300th Anniversary of the Birth of Bede*, British Archaeological Report, Brit. Ser. 46. London, 1978. pp. 32–95.

Wood, I. N., 'The End of Roman Britain: Continental Evidence and Parallels', in Eds. M. Lapidge and D. N. Dumville, *Gildas: New Approaches*. Woodbridge, 1984. pp. 1–25.

Wood, Michael, *In Search of the Dark Ages*. London, reprinted 2005.

Woolf, Alex, *From Pictland to Alba, 789-1070*. The New Edinburgh History of Scotland: Volume 2. Edinburgh, 2007.

Wright, Brian, *Brigid: Goddess, Druidess and Saint*. Stroud, 2009.

Yorke, Barbara, 'The Women in Edgar's Life', in ed. D. G. Scragg, *Edgar, King of the English, 959-975: New Interpretations*. Woodbridge, 2008. pp. 143–57.

Yorke, Barbara, *The Conversion of Britain: 600-800*, Longman, 2006.

Yorke, Barbara, *Nunneries and the Anglo-Saxon Royal Houses*. London, 2003.

Yorke, Barbara, *Bishop Athelwold*. Woodbridge, 1997.

Young, Graeme Leslie and Gething, Paul Anthony, *Bamburgh Castle: The Archaeology of the Fortress of Bamburgh, AD 500 to AD 1500*. Bamburgh Research Project, 2003.

Index

Entries in *italics* indicate *photographs or illustrations.*